Thy Path Begins

"I am merely a novice, and sometimes a fool, and am only now learning to wear the cloak of my destiny."

Magic is a lark to Donemere Saunders, something her feline familiar Sylvester believes she will never take seriously enough in order to meet her destiny. But as Donnie reluctantly embraces the mantle of power that has been thrust upon her, she realizes that she can do wondrous things for others with her gift and she begins to understand why she has been given it. But there comes the day when her adventures turn heartbreakingly real and Donnie must find her place in her family's rich magical history to become the witch she was always meant to be.

This is a work of fiction. Names, characters, songs, businesses, places, events and incidents are either the products of the author's imagination or used in a fictitious manner. Any resemblance to actual persons, living or dead, or actual events is purely coincidental.

Donemere's Music, Thy Path Begins. Copyright © 2016 by Cheryl A. Gross. All rights reserved. Printed in the United States of America.

First U.S. Printed Edition: November 2016.

Cover photo by Ms. Gross.

CAG Publishing, 2016
ISBN: 978-0-9978411-1-4
Ebook ISBN: 978-0-9978411-0-7

Acknowledgements: My everlasting thanks to those who were brave enough to read this story in its first incarnation and to kindly give me their invaluable input. These wonderful personages include LisaKay and John Krizan, Cynthia and Norvin Green, Maura O'Neill and Bob Shelby, Ina Wilms, Belinda Frost, Arlene Gross and J'té Argent (to whom a special thanks is owed for confirming that Donnie's circle spell was sufficiently reverent toward modern witchcraft). And to all others who read it and lent their support in other ways, I also give my sincerest thanks, even to those who did not particularly like the tale.

You all had a hand in shaping at least one character's journey.

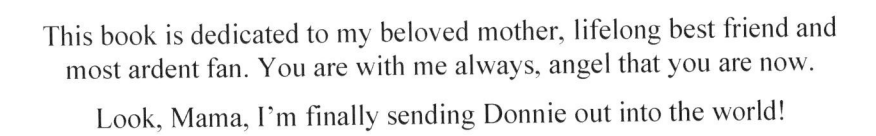

This book is dedicated to my beloved mother, lifelong best friend and most ardent fan. You are with me always, angel that you are now.

Look, Mama, I'm finally sending Donnie out into the world!

And to Rex, my real-life Wonder Dog: Thank you for teaching me so much about life and love.

Cast of Main Characters

Donemere (Donnie) Saunders is brought to an ancient land by Catie, an eccentric ancestor, because Catie failed to meet her destiny. This destiny is now passed to Donnie, who understands what it will mean for her and does not like her fast-approaching future one bit.

Rex the Wonder Dog is Donnie's German Shepherd Dog. He is her heart and her love, a piece of home that keeps her sane.

Tanygrisiau yr Eglwys Wen is Donnie's dour familiar, who she immediately renames **Sylvester**. Occasionally, he allows her to see how impressed he is with her magical abilities.

The boombox provides clues to what Donnie should do next in the form of songs and their lyrics. While it will listen to her requests and sometimes her remonstrances, she cannot touch it with her magic, nor can anyone else.

Otis the horse and **Diana** the cow are Donnie's best friends at the Codlebærn valley. Otis loves blues music and Diana has a penchant for romance novels.

The chickens on the Codlebærn farm are Donnie's affectionate prognosticators for expected visitors.

Brindle is the leader of the six magical trees Donnie uses to expand her house. He is also used for the stirrups on her cotton saddle, so he is able to travel with Donnie on her adventures.

Parry, another house tree, is in love with Brindle.

Carly, the youngest of the house trees, is great friends with Rex and oftentimes plays word games with him in the bathroom.

Fine Fellow is a curious, very talkative house tree who loves nothing more than to learn. Brindle is the only one who can reliably get him to shut up.

Mournful Jack is a very quiet house tree and seldom speaks. He is apparently quite depressed, as evidenced by the forlorn sough he emits whenever he converses with anyone.

Sophie is the oldest of the house trees and has known Brindle for thousands of years. She is tired, always very tired.

Mecholætera, who Donnie renames **Mickey T**, is a venerable Noctule bat who is good friends with Sylvester. He loves to play board games with his friends at the farm.

Mynydd Uchaf, King of the Free Wolves, who Donnie renames **Warren**, is usually the first to reprimand Donnie whenever she is being unhelpful.

Falwaïn, Prince of Faen Eárna, is a widower who has been traveling the northern lands in search of adventure and death. Instead he finds Catie, who gives him her amulet and begs him to take it to Donemere at the Codlebærn farm.

Don **Diego**, known in Medregai as the Black Rider, has also been stolen away from his world, but by whom is a mystery. One thing he does know, he was rescued from certain death by Valledai…or was he?

Cyllwyn Mérd, is an old willow tree who gives his life, and his life essence, to Donnie when she requests it.

Ungôl is a Badûran Vírat who Donnie mischievously renames **Uncle** after he unceremoniously grabs her off her comfy saddle and drags her through several miles of filthy marsh water to his den.

Valledai is an evil sorcerer who wants to exact his revenge on his enemies of old in Medregai. Donnie renames him **Valley Guy**. He is successful in shattering Donnie's heart, but has he also broken her resolve?

Table of Contents

Prologue 1

Chapter 1 Do You Believe in Magic? 5

Chapter 2 This Home Is Yours 33

Chapter 3 She's Gone 54

Chapter 4 Comin' Straight for You 80

Chapter 5 The Werewolf Way 103

Chapter 6 Forever Love 125

Chapter 7 Won't You Come In? 141

Chapter 8 Take a Little Trip with Me 168

Chapter 9 Find My Girl 190

Chapter 10 Look What's Goin' Down 201

Chapter 11 Soul's Solace 225

Chapter 12 Lone Tree Requiem 258

Chapter 13 Love Prayer 283

Chapter 14 Stay and Talk with Me a While 317

Chapter 15 Little Mysteries 345

Chapter 16 We're All Guilty of Something 374

Chapter 17 Magic Carpet 404

Epilogue I 426

Epilogue II 430

Prologue

In the office at the back of the Drake Manor sat its current owner, Mr. Franklin Vale, deeply ensconced in what had recently become his favorite armchair; a red Corinthian leather wingback to be precise. All other residents of the cavernous domicile were in their beds, soundly asleep.

Behind Franklin's chair stood a diminutive young woman, most bizarrely and colorfully dressed. She had blended herself into the shadows there with a lazily set cloaking charm the moment she'd arrived through her magical portal a few minutes earlier. Her small face was obscured by the wide-brimmed, ridiculously ostentatious hat that was skewed jauntily atop her head, its red feathers swaying with her every movement as she bent over Franklin's shoulder, reading with avid interest the open book in his hands. Periodically, she waggled her left hand to turn the enchanted pages of the book. Unnoticed by her, a small, vermillion feather fluttered to the man's shirtfront after one of her more vigorous wags.

Franklin was slumped down in the chair, his head nestled snugly against the right wing of smooth leather. Although the antique reading lamp to his right shone brightly onto the book's pages, his eyes were closed and his mouth opened wide. He was snoring loudly. He'd nearly finished reading the book, had only the last couple of chapters to go, in fact, when his tired eyelids had drooped a few minutes before midnight and he'd fallen fast asleep in the quiet of the night.

The sole evidence of the little witch's presence was the feather, which had seemed to pop out of nowhere above Franklin's head before drifting lazily to its white silken perch. For a while the room was silent; the only movement was of pages turning seemingly by themselves upon Franklin's lap. This was because, of course, to the nonmagical eye, the single being in the room appeared to be the sleeping man.

But there was another magical entity hovering a few feet above the polished wooden floor, who had positioned himself in the opposite corner of the room from the chair. More shadow than creature of substance, this necromantic spirit, after much difficulty, finally achieved a somewhat clouded view of the little witch through her sight charm as she leaned over the back of the red chair.

Catie is a fool, he thought to himself contemptuously. She must know that he, Valledai, as he had decided to call himself in this incarnation, had traveled with her once again and that he was here now, in this very room; yet she clearly was unconcerned by his presence. His soul burned with envy. Exhausted and weak though she was from controlling her portion of the Magic of the Nine, the little witch still had more than enough power left to defeat him as he was now. They both knew this. But not for long, not after tonight.

Valledai glided through the air so that he was now in front of the man, this Franklin Vale, whom Catie had been so determined to visit tonight. In fact, this late-night errand of hers looked to be quite fortuitous for Valledai, for the sleeping man possessed powerful Witch-magic within him; Witch-magic that had never even been accessed by its vacuous owner. For the next few moments, Valledai focused his attention solely on Franklin, exerting his black will onto the man's mind. He delved into Franklin's dreams and searched his soul for what would entice him the most.

Valledai felt only disdain at the ease with which he filled Franklin's mind with visions of exactly the kinds of successes the greedy film director desired and could achieve if he were to join himself with Valledai. All he need do is let Valledai possess his triune; for only a short while, he hastily assured Franklin when the dolt put up a token resistance, obviously wanting to be convinced. With Valledai's solemn promise of brevity crowding his mind, Franklin eagerly offered his triune to Valledai unconditionally.

The strange little witch, Catie, continued to read, skipping ahead several pages excitedly here and there. Her occasional, distracted low murmurs and exclamations of "Ah, so it 'az got ta be her, 'azit?", "Ooh, 'e'z got ta be there as well, eh? Well then, luv, ye shall 'ave ta get 'im too!", and "Me merry saints! I wouldna like to meet 'im, not fer every bit o' magic that be asmolderin' 'neath the soil! Ta! Ye gods can keep it all t'yerselves, izzwat I say!" only slightly disturbed Valledai's concentration from his task.

He reached further and further into Franklin's heart, mind and soul, welcoming their release into his own triune. Not too quickly though; he did not want the man dying while the little witch was still here in the room. Surely even Catie would notice that, and she must not yet know his true purpose in following and remaining with her tonight. But once he had this witch-man's extensive powers absorbed within himself, Valledai was certain he'd be strong enough to take Catie's magic. His mind raced in anticipation of his plans.

But, no, he must content himself to wait a while longer. He needed Catie to get back through the portal, return him to his world. From there, it would take him no more than two days to weave this man's powers into his own, to settle into their depths and discover their limitations.

Once he had them mastered, he could begin his campaign of revenge on his enemies of old. Valledai imagined the upstart king kneeling at his feet, broken and begging for mercy for himself and his people. A mercy Valledai felt no compunction to bestow.

And after that? Valledai felt his heart lift with pleasure. After that, he would take Catie's powers and her "pretty trinket," as she called it. Once he possessed the portal and her knowledge of it, along with her unparalleled powers, combined with those of this witch-man and the other witches before him, then he, Valledai, would change time forever. The future would be his to do with as he pleased. And this time, no one would thwart him.

He had been promised this.

Catie straightened and moved away from Franklin's chair, exclaiming softly, "Catie girl, ye must be on yer way, fer ye canna reed the whole thing naow. 'Tis enuff ta know the bloodline shall be safe in 'er 'ands. Ware it ends is up ta Donnie ta deevine. Ye 'ave seen what ye must do and when ta do it," she proclaimed, adding with satisfaction, "and ye shall play yer part well in this *cynllun drwg*." She lifted a large, blood-red pendant from her breast and began the incantation to open the portal, the words of which, no matter how hard Valledai tried, he could not hear, could not understand.

Knowing he would have but a few seconds, he readied himself, for he would have to seize the remainder of Franklin's triune and quickly follow her through the portal before it closed. It mattered naught to him that this witch-man would die in the process; his only concern was that he reach his objective before the portal closed. His timing must be perfect.

As soon as the portal was called forth, Valledai's triune responded in the now-familiar manner; his heartbeat quickened so that it moved in time with the rhythm of the amulet's magic and his soul felt its snakes' heads calling their song of desire to him.

None of the occupants of the room noticed that the pages of the book in Franklin's hands suddenly cleared, or that the book, disturbed by the mysterious erasure of its contents, slid silently to the floor near the sleeping man's feet. Nor did they note that other books, still nestled into the bookshelf near the chair, quivered faintly.

When Catie stepped toward the portal doorway, Valledai set upon Franklin once more, poised to devour the last of the witch-man's triune.

What was this? He could not reach one small fragment of Franklin's triune! He needed all of the triune, else none of the man's fantastical powers would remain within himself and this he could not let happen!

Nor was there time to unlock the hidden chamber in the man's mind because the portal was soon to close.

Franklin Vale would have to come back with him, Valledai realized, even though this meant his plans must needs change. If, by some strange circumstance, Catie saw Franklin before he, Valledai, had managed to take possession of the man's entire triune, she would certainly recognize the witch-man's countenance, and she would not take kindly to Franklin's arrival in their world. Who knows what she would do then? Catie was a fool, yes, but even in her current state she was still powerful, and she was always unpredictable. She might even call upon the Magic of the Nine once more.

Valledai's shadowy figure shimmered with fear at the thought for he had no desire to face them again, especially as himself. He trusted the goddesses' warning that they would destroy him when next they met. For now they let him live, believing him still to be ensnared in his concrete prison. But if they discovered the true identity of this creature they knew only as Valledai, he would taste their wrath for the final time.

There was nothing else to do; this man must accompany him. At any rate, perhaps it *was* time he sought a corporeal form for himself, and Franklin Vale's body would be as good as any.

Chapter 1
Do You Believe in Magic?

Donemere Saunders was uncomfortable and something was biting her leg. She pulled her knee up and slapped her ankle where the bug had been using her as a pin cushion the moment before. The bed rustled and crackled when she moved. This made her open her eyes with a surprised frown. She sat up and stared at the grey woolen blanket covering her. Where had that come from?

Donnie glanced around, scanning the room curiously, her right eyebrow slowly raising higher and higher. What was she doing in the spare room? No, wait a minute, while the mantle over the fireplace did look like the one in the guest bedroom of her rented cottage, nothing else about the room was familiar to her.

What was going on?

She sat there staring at the gloomy room with growing bewilderment and rubbed her eyes hard. Darn it, everything looked the same, so this couldn't be a dream. But this certainly wasn't her cottage; why, just look at that window! She'd seldom seen anything quite like it except in a cathedral.

Her disbelieving gaze traveled the room again, taking in the shabby furnishings, the dirty, almost indecently bright-colored clothing tossed about willy-nilly, and the varied manner of woodland debris that covered the floorboards. Where was she? And for heaven's sake, how could this have happened? How could she have drifted off to sleep in a perfectly comfortable house one night, only to awaken the next morning in an entirely different one? One that didn't look half so comfortable! This just didn't make sense.

Feeling a rising tide of urgency within her breast, Donnie slipped her feet out from under the covers and to the floor, then she almost ran to the door and grabbed the wooden door handle. The door opened with a creak and she stuck her head out it carefully, calling softly, "Hello?...Anyone here?...Helloooo?"

A large black and white cat, lying on a bare wooden table in the middle of a spacious, raftered room, lifted his head off his paws and responded with a long series of sharp, staccato meows.

Donnie moved farther into the room and gave the cat a tentative smile. "Hey there, sweetie, whatcha doin'? Don't suppose you know where we are, do you?" Slowly, she walked over to the table and reached toward the cat, noticing that he wore a silver chain with some sort of charm or pendant around his neck. "Who are you, I wonder? Hmm? What's your name, little guy? Let me just see what your tag says there—"

The cat stood up and hissed at her, again letting out an angry series of needle-like meows, his ears plastered back to his head throughout this entire tirade.

Donnie's hands flew back as she reassured the cat, "Okay, okay, you don't want me to touch you, I get it. I won't, I promise!" All the while regarding him warily, she added under her breath, "Sheesh, I was just tryin' to be friendly." Backing away carefully, she inspected her new surroundings. Once more she felt an unsettling, vague sense of familiarity for this room. But upon second thought, no, she didn't know this one either, not really.

She turned toward the cat, studying him pensively for several seconds before enquiring, "Where's your owner, kitty? And whyever did they bring me here? Well, golly, how did they bring me here? For that matter, where is here?" She laughed nervously and added, "It seems I've got all the questions, but who's got the answers?"

The cat settled into a sitting position with his tail curled around his front paws and stared at her. He meowed once, a razor-sharp blast of pure displeasure.

Donnie dipped her head in acknowledgement of the cat's attitude and said, "My, that was helpful. I can see you're not much of a morning cat, are you? So," she breathed, "are you crotchety because I woke you up or just crotchety in general? Sorry, but I don't really know much about the ways of cats; I'm more of a dog person, myself." She waited as though for another response, but none came. The cat merely stared at her stonily.

Donnie decided to check outside, so she went over to the front door and wrenched it open. There was a little wooden stoop set before it, roughly built and wobbly, but she gamely stepped onto that and looked around her. The brambles in the front yard stretched out a hundred feet or so and there the ground dropped into a valley. She looked up and saw that the top of the ridge above her was lined with forest. It reminded her uncannily of where her rented cottage was situated.

With a sweeping gaze, she stared around her in ever-deepening confusion. She groaned in anguish, looked back at the cat, and whined, "Why do all the cottages here have to look so damned similar? I can't believe only yesterday I thought that was charming! The thing is, I may not have seen this one before, but then again, it could be any one of twenty I've driven by since I've been in Wales."

The cat did not reply.

The only other building in sight was to her left and it appeared to house some stables and a hayloft. An old-fashioned stone well was placed about halfway between the house and the stables. Beside it were some large apple trees, heavy with fruit, and underneath the farthest of these trees stood a wooden bench.

It struck Donnie suddenly that there were no cars in sight. For that matter, she couldn't even see any tire tracks, only what looked like horse and cart tracks. But wait a second, everybody had cars nowadays, or some sort of automotive. Where in blazes was she?

"Yoo-hoo! Hello?...Is anyone here?...Hellooooo?...Anyone?" she yelled desperately. Waiting a minute or two for an answer that never came, she finally jumped back into the house, her bare feet freezing from the frosty morning air.

Telling herself, "First things first, Donnie, my girl, let's get some heat in here," she began to build a fire in the large fireplace of the main room. She placed some kindling and wood shavings into a pile and struck one of the long wooden matches stored in an iron pot on the hearth. The fire lit easily and she soon stacked a couple of bigger pieces of kindling upon it. She stood up and held first one foot, then the other, near the warmth of the spreading flames. As the fire intensified, she placed two logs in its midst and watched them begin to burn, still warming her feet and hands alternately. Once her appendages were no longer frozen, she sighed and sank down onto a chair at the crudely built table to think.

Okay, what had happened to her? Had she somehow been drugged and carted away by some villainous home invader while she was sleeping? The wine she'd had last night, had that been laced with narcotics? If so, she certainly didn't feel like she'd been under the influence of any drug. She didn't even have cotton mouth from the wine. Perhaps the elusive intruder had gassed her while she slept or had stolen into the house in the middle of the night and injected her with something? She thought about this and began checking herself carefully for any telltale signs of either of these furtive methods of attack. Her breathing was good, she felt no other side effects that might imply an inhalation of a noxious substance, nor could she see any needle marks on her skin anywhere, which pretty much ruled out those two possibilities.

Next she wondered if she'd somehow wandered here in her sleep. But that wasn't very likely as she had never been one to sleepwalk. Besides, her feet would be a mess of cuts from the rough, dried grass and brambles outside, wouldn't they? No, she hadn't sleepwalked here. Not that she could imagine even a halfway decent reason why anyone would *want* to sleepwalk their way to this hovel. It was dirty and crowded with all sorts of junk, including books and papers left carelessly lying everywhere; bundle after bundle of dried or drying, overpoweringly pungent vegetation hanging from the rafters; stacks of dirty metal dishes; more, even dirtier, yet mostly garish Victorian-style clothing lying or hanging on almost all flat *and* vertical surfaces; and row upon row of cast-iron pots lined up neatly against the wall. These were stacked shoulder-high with thickly padded cloths carefully lain between them.

Strange furnishings for a kidnapper's den, Donnie reflected absently.

Well, if she had indeed been kidnapped, how was that monumental feat accomplished? How was she snatched out of her cozy, warm bed and brought to this little hole in the wall, all without being made aware of that rather singular act? And for that matter, why? Why her? She was just a journalist—nobody special. While she was good at her job and had investigated more than one business and governmental scandal in her time, she was pretty sure she hadn't made the kind of enemies who would go to the extremes of stealing her away from all of civilization just to obtain a little retribution, for heaven's sake!

Thoughtfully, she posited the question to herself if whether, perhaps, her predicament had been engineered by someone close to her. Maybe her mother had something to do with this? Yeah, that must be it—why, the only reason she was even in Wales in the first place was because of her mother's insistence that she take at least a six-month sabbatical from her job at the *SFTimes* to finish writing her book.

Lorraine maintained that while Donnie's study of the Junction Uprising was nearly finished, it had basically consumed her daughter's life for well over two years now, and even Donnie's stories for the newspaper had begun to suffer. They just weren't up to her usual dynamic sparkle anymore.

And she'd been right to give her daughter grief about that. Donnie had been burning the candle at both ends for some time and it had become quite wearing, even to Donnie's editor at the *SFTimes*, who'd gotten fed up with trying to fix the mistakes that seemed to dog Donnie since late last year. Which was around the time she'd really started working at a fantastically frenetic pace on her investigation of the uprising and had let so many other things fall to the wayside. Donnie, as Lorraine must've known she would, had heeded her mother's advice to concentrate on the Junction Uprising project alone, even agreeing to go to her mother's home country of Wales while she worked on the final editing stages of the book.

Could kidnapping Donnie be her mother's way of ensuring her eldest daughter got some peace and quiet? But that would be ridiculous. Not even Lorraine (who was known for her sometimes elaborate pranks) would go to those extremes, especially since she was well aware how important the book was to Donnie. Besides, her mother would be much more likely to arrange exquisite and impeccably clean accommodations for her daughter, not a filthy pig sty like this place. No, her mother would never send anyone here.

Well then, perhaps her kidnapping did have something to do with her work at the *SFTimes*? What stories had she worked on during the past year or two that could warrant a response such as this?

Regrettably, nothing extraordinary came to mind, no matter how deep she delved into her memory.

As the long minutes passed, a succession of emotions overtook her, naturally beginning with disbelief and denial. Maybe she really was still asleep and dreaming? No, she told herself sternly, she wasn't dreaming; no dream was this detailed. Which meant that she truly was here in this dismal little cottage.

Okay then, maybe she was delusional? Again, not very likely as her family had a long, dull history of being clinically sane. They were sometimes known for unpredictable antics, surely, but were they delusional? Not so much, really.

Still…her mother did have that rather insistent penchant for wearing outlandish hats. "Could it have been a sign, a plea for help, and I missed it?" Donnie muttered under her breath.

And, of course, there was always Dad's Aunt Bella Moira. Aunt Bea had dressed and looked exactly the same since Donnie had been seven, when her aunt had come to visit the family for the first time that Donnie could remember. Donnie had stared wide-eyed at her, looking from her aunt to the TV, where the real "Aunt Bee" had just happened to be holding court over Ferdinand and Farley. As Donnie recalled, this had ticked *her* Aunt Bea off to no end when she'd noticed it, and Donnie had, for the first time ever, witnessed her great-aunt's disconcerting ability to swear a mean blue-streak at the drop of a hat, leaving Donnie with one of the most vivid memories of her early childhood.

But no, there was nothing really that strange about Aunt Bea. After all, didn't every over-eighty inhabitant of Florida habitually drive their particular land ark into the nearest available culvert? Well, except for Aunt Bea, now that her driver's license had finally been revoked after the fourth incident in as many years.

Donnie impatiently dismissed the possibility of an obscure mental condition, latent either in herself or her family, and got up to pace the room and think. She focused on who she thought could've, or would've, engineered her current predicament. After a few moments, she felt a burgeoning sense of giddy elation within her which bordered sharply on hysteria. She became absolutely convinced that a group of her friends had gotten together to play a hoax on her. The whole thing was probably spearheaded by her best friend, Liz, and Donnie's younger sister, Emily.

Somehow they'd managed to bring Donnie here without her being aware of it and had probably hidden cameras all around the derelict cottage to record her every move. Donnie swung around the room somewhat manically, laughing reflexively and trying not to show her relief because she didn't want her friends to know just how badly they'd scared her.

"Ha ha, very funny, guys!" she exclaimed heartily, going on to add, "Okay, Liz and Emmy, and whoever else you got to help you, you've had your little joke, so come on and get me; the party's over. This isn't really all that funny, you know."

She stood still and glanced around the room with a hopeful expression hanging on her face, waiting silently for several moments until, biting her lip apprehensively now, she finally implored, "Seriously, guys, this isn't funny. Come and get me, I wanna get outta here!"

But nobody came. After five minutes of sitting stalwartly in one of the two roughly hewn chairs placed around the table, with the cat staring at her as though she were a loon, Donnie got up again and began searching the cottage high and low for signs of a camera or other recording devices. During this investigation, which included forays into the darkest corners of the darkest cupboards, she noticed that there were no appliances of any kind, no internet or telephone hookups, no running water, don't even mention electricity, and, just her luck, no bathroom. And her with a bladder the size of a pea!

She decided that if this was a prank, it wasn't going to be funny to her for a long, long, *long* time. In the end, she found no signs whatsoever of recording equipment, even after carefully scrutinizing every inch of the stone walls and each of the knotholes in the timbers of the doors and low ceilings in both rooms of the desolate little house.

When every bit of the place had been thoroughly inspected, Donnie stood in the middle of the main room and deliberated a moment, pulling on her lip distractedly. Maybe she should search the stables, a voice inside her head suggested. Yeah, that was probably her best bet— although it was mighty cold and wet out there, another little voice reminded her, and here's her with no shoes.

Oh, but wait a minute, while inspecting the cottage, she'd found a pair of leather buckled boots she could wear outside, the first little voice retorted. Admittedly, they were rather odd-looking, being both very pointed and very fluorescent green, neither a style nor color she would normally be caught dead wearing. And okay, yes, they were probably a little too small for her, but they were much better than slogging barefoot through the cold, wet mud that covered the yard between the buildings and ending up with frostbitten toes, weren't they? And so what if they clashed horribly with her pale blue pajamas? She really couldn't afford to be picky about wardrobe at a time like this, could she?

Donnie rolled her eyes at the silent war being waged in her head between her innate common sense and an obviously overdeveloped sense of fashion. Resolutely, she donned the offending boots and trudged out to the other building. Alas, she found no evidence of recording equipment in either the stables or in the workshop she discovered existed at the back of the building. All she found of interest in the workshop, besides a gigantic forge and its related tools and another twenty or so iron cauldrons, were several barrels of what appeared to be table salt and a chalk-drawn circular shape in the center of the room that was mostly covered by the barrels.

As for the stables...well, admittedly, her search of them was perhaps somewhat cursory because of the various farm animals living there, namely the chickens. Donnie was a city girl, born and bred, and had never been around live chickens before in her life. Maybe it was because they reminded her of Blackburn's classic horror movie, *The Day of the Birds*, that Donnie found she had a distinct aversion to them. Dead, plucked ones were fine, especially on the grill. But these just gave her the willies, with their ominous clucking and pecking as they advanced upon her, following closely in her footsteps while she explored the building.

After almost half an hour of searching the stables and workshop without gaining any real enlightenment, Donnie gave up and returned dejectedly to the house, secure in the knowledge that no way was this a hoax perpetrated by her friends because they couldn't do anything without recording it in some fashion.

When she reentered the house, she noticed that the fire was burning low, so she stacked some more logs onto it, and in just a couple of minutes it was roaring brightly once again. She was cold, wet and very disheartened from her fruitless search of the premises. Pulling one of the chairs closer to the fireplace, Donnie sank down upon it, pulled off the muddy boots, and stretched her bare feet toward the fire. Only then did she close her eyes and let the tears fall. As testament to the panic that had been slowly welling up inside her for the last hour or so, she began imagining all sorts of improbable, wild explanations for her predicament, including slave traders, local sexual predators and even political terrorists. All of these she rejected after logic kicked in, especially considering that no one in the area even knew all that much about her because she'd kept pretty much to herself for the last six weeks, focusing mostly on her work.

Although, come to think of it, there was that handsome stranger with the gorgeous, long blonde locks she'd spotted several times over the last three weeks in the village shops and on the moors, always walking just far enough away so she couldn't get a really good look at him. Wait a minute—had he been following her? After all, she'd seen him on almost all of her local walks lately. ("Bloody unlikely, innit? And aren't you just the paranoid little freak?" was how Donnie dismissed this conjecture aloud). What *was* likely was that he was merely one of her neighbors, a completely innocent bystander. She really should not read more into his appearances than was healthy, regardless of her current situation. Even though her current situation was totally inexplicable and immensely frightening and more than a little creepy and…

"I needn't take that any further, need I?" she asked desperately of the cat, as if he'd been able to read her thoughts and now knew exactly what she was referring to.

The cat stared at her and let out another long burst of short, sharp meows, hesitating for a couple moments before adding a very loud one, as though to punctuate his unfavorable opinion of her hysterical ramblings of the morning.

And so, Donnie forced herself to really and truly calm down this time so she could think rationally. She straightened in her chair, sniffled and sighed a couple of times, then shook her head decisively. "Nope, none of that's gonna help," she remonstrated herself. "For Fortin's sake, woman, think; what the hell is going on here? And what are you going to do?" Taking some deep breaths and staring intently at the fire for a few moments, the answer to her dilemma suddenly came to her. It really was quite simple: someone from the ubiquitous Roamers would soon turn up and then she'd know exactly where she was. Easy peasy.

But the hours turned into days with no sign of other humans in or around the vicinity of the small farm. Whoever her captors were, if they indeed existed, they were definitely making themselves scarce. And at the end of the sixth day, she was brutally forced to give up even that double-edged hope.

A few hours after she arose that first day, she decided her best course was to be proactive about her situation and had therefore saddled the horse in the stables, obviously much against his wishes. When she'd approached him with the bridle, he'd shied away from her and whinnied nervously, but Donnie had persevered and soon had him both bridled and saddled. She had a plan; she was going to ride him out to search for signs of civilization. Grateful that her mother had insisted she take riding lessons since she was five, Donnie was right at home with the horse.

But the cow was another story. Donnie wasn't even sure if it was the milking kind or not. It just stood there when she'd first come upon it and looked at her with its sad, liquidy eyes. "Are cows always as big as you or are you on steroids?" she'd asked it, nervously stepping away when it seemed to understand the gist of what she'd said and stomped its feet angrily at her.

For the next few days, each dawn saw Donnie riding the horse away from the cottage, starting out the first day on a slightly southwest course. She had hurriedly scratched a notice with a remnant of charcoal upon a piece of thick parchment that read: "If you come here while I'm gone, don't leave! I'll be back in just a few hours. Really, I will!" She'd signed her name to it and affixed it firmly to the front door with a small knife, then hauled herself onto the horse and off they went to begin their search. She turned her steed east at around noon and, after traveling another mile or so, they headed back toward the valley, all the while moving progressively counterclockwise. Logic dictated that if, by chance, she was anywhere near her rented cottage, then the closest village was due south, with another town, extraordinarily similar to the first in many respects, less than three miles beyond that to the east.

She and the horse luncheoned picnic-style on these daily jaunts. Donnie ate the cheese and fruit she packed for herself, and the horse would get the carrots she shoved in the voluminous pockets of the grey woolen cloak she donned each morning that she'd found balled up in a corner of the bedroom and now kept hanging by the front door. Whoever had brought her here had thoughtfully left the little farm well-provisioned for both her and the livestock, so, thankfully, food and drink, or lack thereof, would not present a problem anytime soon. Her dietary needs would be met just jake for the duration of her (with any luck) temporary visit; as long as she didn't die first of lead poisoning from the hand-pounded pewter plates and cups she'd found strewn around the room, with more stacked somewhat haphazardly on a makeshift shelf in the pantry. This "pantry" was really no more than a crowded little closet that was approximately four feet square, situated in the far corner of the cottage's main room. She'd searched high and low again, but unfortunately these were the only dinnerware she could find besides an odd assortment of wickedly sharp knives and a few large metal and wooden spoons.

To her relief though, she'd come upon a stock of fresh vegetables and dried meats and fruits in the underground larder, which was actually more of a cellar than a true larder, as it also contained seeds and bulbs for a variety of plants and herbs. The cellar was accessed by lifting the trapdoor in the wooden floor of the pantry, as she'd discovered by tripping over its smoothly worn handle when she'd searched the cottage on her first day looking for signs of a hidden camera.

Off this large, beamed, cool and somewhat dank room was a smaller one carved out of the thick, moist earth beneath the house much less carefully than the cellar had been and which was apparently used as a buttery, where bottles of ale were stored along with casks of something called *metheglin*. Donnie hadn't the nerve to open any of these casks for she had no idea what metheglin was, although the word was scrawled across the fronts of all barrels, along with a differing series of obscure abbreviations for each. She had tried some of the ale, a little hesitantly at first, and had decided it was certainly potable. She also decided that it would be an acquired taste, one she was not going to be here long enough to acquire herself.

Oh, and she mustn't forget the vast collection of cast-iron cauldrons. There were easily fifty of them in the house, most of which were stacked neatly along the back wall of the cottage's main room. Donnie found three more in the pantry and, of course, there was the very large pot sitting on the hearth that had apparently seen much use, judging from the numerous scratches on its outer rim. And that was not even counting those she'd found in the stables. Each cauldron appeared to be uniquely and skillfully cast, ranging in size from not much larger than a soup bowl to being big enough for a very large man to take a bath in. And every one of them had different, intricate and sometimes delicate designs cast into their curved sides, handles or feet. They struck her as being really rather quaint.

While she and the horse were out searching the relentless moors for neighboring farms, Donnie began to sense within her a mounting, yet still shadowy and vague familiarity for the countryside, especially the area around the cottage and its valley. Since the moors all looked very similar to one another anyway, perhaps because they were so oddly bereft of human habitation, she firmly thrust the idea away immediately each time it intruded into her head, telling herself it was a useless train of thought. She needed to find something more concrete that would tell her exactly where she was.

Disappointingly, though she looked constantly for it, Donnie found absolutely no signs of other people anywhere, only a couple of worn paths whose few, clearly defined footprints appeared to be equine in nature; probably made by the very horse she was riding now. Even the thin, deep wheel ruts that traversed the little valley surrounding the cottage, forming two trails which split off to travel north and east, appeared to mostly (although she was certainly no expert at this sort of thing) match the little cart she'd found parked to the right of the stables. Adding to the eeriness of her situation was the unnerving scarcity of wildlife, as if the entire animal world (other than the farm's inhabitants) had decided collectively to avoid her. Only occasionally would she hear the chattering and calls of the forest denizens to each other in the distance, all of which would end abruptly as soon as she drew near.

Try as she might to quell her disturbing suspicions, they grew with each passing day until Donnie finally had to admit that there truly was something familiar about the tiny, crowded cottage and its immediate surroundings. Yet, she just couldn't put her finger on what it was exactly that made her so sure she was not really a stranger to these parts. She was reasonably certain she'd never seen these little buildings before, nor the cobbled stone well positioned strategically between them. And the countryside all around was much wilder than what she'd seen in Wales, or in any of the other British Isles she'd visited to-date. Nonetheless, the worrisome feeling grew.

On the morning of the sixth day, she decided to follow one of the established paths made long ago by the farm's cart instead of, yet again, forging her own way though the dense undergrowth within the forest that surrounded the valley. She chose the trail heading east, in the direction of a mountain range she'd seen the day before, far off in the distance, while on her daily recon trip. Because of the somewhat unnecessarily winding route the trail led at its beginnings, it took almost an hour for the ambling, but nonetheless amiable horse to get close enough for the mountain range to come properly into view, and even then the nearest mountains could only be seen from the summits of those moors not covered with either trees or mist. Whenever Donnie and the horse rounded each successive, bare hilltop, the mountains would again come into view, looming larger and showing greater detail than on the previous glimpses of them.

As they approached closer and closer, Donnie could see that the dense fog blanketing the lower regions between the moors also held a goodly portion of the mountain range in its grip. But the sun was already working hard at banishing the highest reaches of suspended precipitate, driving the thick mist ever-downward. By the time the horse scaled the last moor and emerged into clear air once more, the mountains were still somewhat silhouetted against the late-morning, rising sun. Actually, Donnie and the horse crested this particular moor right as the sun rose above the tip of the closest and biggest of the mountains and bright, glorious light began cascading down its western face.

Upon this beautiful sight, Donnie slumped in the saddle and stared at the mountain with increasing horror as the horse shambled down the descending slope of the moor toward a wide lake, where he stopped and began taking long, unbidden draughts of its cooling waters. Here, the mist had almost totally dissipated, with just wisps of it still hovering over the lake's waters. Only half aware of her actions, Donnie slipped from the horse to fall to her knees in a fluid, though certainly not graceful movement, completely mesmerized by what, to all accounts, appeared to be a perfectly tranquil scene set before her. She then proceeded to groan and curse in a manner that would have made her Aunt Bea proud, while the horse blithely ignored her outburst and continued to drink deeply of the lake water.

Bewilderment, fear, disbelief and abandonment, along with their prerequisite onslaught of tears, eventually overtook her and peace, of a sort, was restored to the land—that is, once her entire repertoire of expletives was thoroughly exhausted. She raised her head after several minutes and wiped her cheeks with trembling fingers, whispering, "This can't be true. It's not possible. It's just not possible."

Nevertheless, there it was—the unmistakable outline of Treyfal, showing quite clearly against the deep blue of the morning sky. Although, and this was the cause of Donnie's grief, the huge peak rose a little higher and was noticeably craggier in relief than it had been when she'd hiked here to picnic at *Llyn y Cawr* for the first time two weeks earlier. She knew it was Treyfal for there was the mammoth, jutting stone ledge on the southwestern face of the peak that had been popularized by thousands of hikers, many of whom were surprisingly *not* card-carrying members of the Roamers' hiking association. Only now it was a whole outcropping of rock slabs. But the two rounded boulders serving as a counterweight to hold down the top slab on one end so the other end could suspend freely over the sharp peak on which it balanced, still reminded her of cartoon mouse ears etched against a backdrop of blue. There was no denying that the placement and unique topography of the ledge were identical to the one she'd watched two hikers skitter around on that day at Treyfal, especially since she was viewing the mountain from almost exactly the same spot on the western edge of the lake.

She let her eyes scan the area, noting other impossibly coincidental landmarks. To the east of the lake was a long, high escarpment running for at least a mile to the south but which, northward, stopped abruptly at the foot of Treyfal. Set into the sheer face of its foreland wall was the enormous entrance to a cave that, according to the guidebook Donnie had purchased when she'd first arrived in this part of Wales, had at some time most likely reached all the way into Treyfal itself through a large tunnel at its rear. The book also informed its readers that off this main tunnel were two satellite passageways branching in different directions deeper into the mountain range beyond. "An interesting and breathtakingly lovely haven for the hardy, avid spelunker" was how the book had described the cave and its appurtenant tunnels. Seeing the dark outline of the cave's entrance once again, Donnie noted its perfectly sculpted keystone shape with a shudder.

Next came the same, though larger, neat pile of huge boulders, each rock nearly half the size of a golf cart, that sat to the left of the cave and made her think of great mounds of mashed potatoes with a gravy dip in the middle of each. Only now, the cave entrance was flanked by two such fastidiously stacked piles. She remembered wondering that day at Treyfal whatever could account for the smooth, uniform erosion that had occurred on each and every one of the boulders, even those on the bottom of the pile.

And finally there was the hillock ("Such a grand word for such a little hill," she'd deadpanned the first time she'd seen it) to the northwest of Treyfal's base that still looked to her as though it had been shoved into its place unexpectedly, much like a poor excuse for a third breast hunched forlornly between two exquisite ones. It was squeezed between the soaring Treyfal and the next mountain over, whose Welsh name Donnie couldn't ever hope to be able to pronounce properly. That slightly smaller mountain's name, *Angel Uchel Dialgar*, meant something like "High Avenging Angel," or so the guidebook had informed her. Donnie had wanted to know if there was a name for the hillock. If one existed, it hadn't been given in the guidebook.

Ever so slowly—little by little, because she wasn't going to rush into this—she allowed herself to more fully comprehend her nebulous recognition over the past week of the myriad similarities in the countryside. It basically looked much the same as when she'd come to Wales a little more than six weeks ago. Once she'd settled into the cottage, whenever she wasn't working on her book, she'd fallen into the habit of taking long walks or drives, sometimes two or three a day, to clear her head and help herself focus. So she'd gotten to know the general area around the rented cottage quite well, and realized now that there were far too many likenesses between it and the area surrounding the strange, smaller cottage she currently inhabited than could possibly be explained by pure happenstance. But this countryside here was also different in so, so many ways. The moors were steeper and sharper, less weather-beaten and rolling. Some of the same pathways were there, only no cairns or signposts adorned their routes.

The forests she'd seen over the last six days were thickly overgrown and rambling, unlike the well-tended small copses she'd passed on her daily walks back in her own—Donnie stopped herself from completing that thought, not yet able to face its stark ramifications. She glanced about her again and remembered that a forest should be here now, all around this very spot, except for right in front of the lake. She winced, recalling that on her previous visit most of its trees had been huge and obviously quite ancient. It was called the *Fforest yr Anfodlonr*, which the guidebook told her translated (rather whimsically, she thought) to "Forest of the Unwilling."

She stared up at the hillside behind her, noticing with alarm that the big crater on the western face of the moor was also missing. Yet, a mere two weeks ago, there'd been a huge dip cut right out of the moor. Whoa, that was a lot of dirt to move, so how could it be filled in now, with tall, dried grass carpeting the soil? And what's the deal with an entire forest missing? How was that possible?

For a few, desperate moments more, she stubbornly ignored the voice in her head that insisted she knew darned well how it was possible. Deep down, she'd known all along, the obdurate voice continued to chide her, and no amount of denial was going to change the situation, so wasn't it time to face facts?

Donnie steeled herself for what was to come. She reflected on the last few days and, for the first time, allowed herself to deliberately and consciously register the other things that were absent from the countryside which definitely should have been there—all the man-made things like electrical and telephone wires; or the countless, beautiful little stone houses she'd admired so much; or the winding cobblestone and asphalt roads. Tremulously, Donnie admitted to herself that she'd seen no parking lots or cars here. As a matter of fact, there were no cars anywhere, nor had she spied any traces of such modern contraptions during any of her jaunts this past week.

Uh-oh, here it came, plodding relentlessly toward her, the ugly reality she'd avoided long enough. Her conscious mind opened up and let the truth bludgeon its way through her flimsy defenses.

"Face it, girlie," she commanded herself aloud, "this is no joke, no dream, certainly no terrorist plot. You are in the right place, all right, but it's the wrong time!"

Wait, could she be mistaken again? Could she? But...oh jeez, there was the cottage! She now conceded why it seemed so weirdly familiar—that was because it comprised the main entryway, parlor and guest bedroom from the cottage she'd rented in her time! The large front room of the cottage here had obviously, at some point in history, been partitioned into two rooms and several other rooms had been added by the time Donnie rented it later.

No-no, she had to be wrong again! Donnie stared at Treyfal or whatever this mountain was. There could exist two mountains in the world that looked really, really similar, couldn't there? With almost identical surroundings? Surely that was at least possible, wasn't it?

Besides, she reminded herself, frantically attempting to inject sense into the situation, if she was indeed in another time, then who could've sent her here? No one she knew or had ever heard of had that ability. What she was thinking was absurd—time travel was an impossibility! Okay, okay, even supposing it wasn't, for the umpteenth time Donnie asked herself, why do this to her, of all people? And whyever was she sent to this specific time period—just what was she supposed to do here? A modern woman such as herself had absolutely no business being thrust into the Middle Ages, as Donnie suspected had been done to her.

She sat there with the same questions looping continuously in her mind for some time. Through tear-filled eyes, she stared blankly at first the lake (*Who did this to me?*), the cave (*What am I supposed to do here?*), then up to the mountain (*Why me?*), then back again, hoping one of the landmarks would change and she'd be wrong again. Donnie repeated this circle countless times, fully conscious that her behavior was ridiculous, but unable to stop herself from doing it anyway. Her wide and generous mouth, usually lifted into a joyous, wry or sometimes mischievous grin, now had the pronounced downward curve of what her father deemed her "serious pout." She was desperately unhappy and frightened. While usually up for an adventure, this was a bit much even for her.

She was only vaguely aware that the sun had moved significantly in the sky when the horse began nudging her insistently, his tongue reaching into her pockets, finding and eating every one of the carrots she'd brought with her that day. He finally succeeded in knocking Donnie right over, which broke her out of her trance-like state and into semi-consciousness. She climbed up onto him clumsily and he turned homeward, increasing his normal lumbering pace to a brisk walk on the return trip in his haste to receive his oats and hay. They made it back to the small farm in a little over two hours. Mechanically, Donnie fed him and the cow and the chickens. By the time she was finished with the chores, it was nearly dark as the days were becoming shorter, heralding the approaching winter.

She entered the cold house in a massively depressed haze and stood helplessly in the middle of the main room, hating the fact that she now felt as though she recognized every stone, every floorboard, every beam in it. Knowing there was really only one way to prove her theories, she reluctantly made herself check the last stone on the far side under the fireplace mantle in the bedroom. She felt around its top edge and her faltering fingers found the small latch there. A foot-long section of the ornately carved wooden mantle swung open, revealing a secret hiding place for important papers and other valuables. At least that's what the land-agent, a very proper and dignified Mr. Humphrey Lambert of Lambert, Lambert and Feldsbury in London, had informed her was its purpose, his pink, kindly face and white tufts of hair and sideburns peeping out at the world from beneath his utterly dignified and spotless, oh-so Englishly dapper bowler.

Donnie had emailed her housing requirements to the agency several weeks earlier, again at her mother's urging. As agreed upon in their ensuing correspondence, Mr. Lambert appeared at Donnie's hotel three days after her arrival in London. He had then driven her all the way to Wales to view the cottage with her before she took occupancy of it. The little niche had been the last feature of the cottage he'd shown her that day.

Horrified by the recess now, Donnie backed up to the bed and sank down upon it slowly, unable to tear her eyes away from the small black cavity less than ten feet away from her. It was as though the little rectangular opening was a physical representation of the metaphorical yawning chasm that lay before her. She stared at it until the sun's light was almost gone, then got up quickly and slammed its door shut, vowing never to open it again.

She curled up on the bed, feeling utterly defeated, where she remained until late the next day. At that point, the animals made an unholy ruckus, squawking, mooing and kicking their hooves repeatedly on the outside of the cottage. "How'd they get out of their stalls?" Donnie murmured listlessly, positive she'd closed the gates to each the night before. She finally had to crawl out of bed and feed them just to get some peace and quiet so she could return to her morose, all-consuming misery and suffering.

The next few days were spent in pretty much the same routine; she would lie in bed until what she judged to be noon, by which time the animals would once again make their demands known. Donnie had no sense of what was real and what was nightmare. After feeding the livestock, she too ate only once a day, and then just barely enough to survive. Whenever she managed to stay out of bed for any length of time, she lit the numerous candles she'd found in the pantry, hoping to banish her fears with the brightest light she could amass, no matter the time of day. In the evenings, she'd sit at the table in the main room, aimlessly reading one of the huge leather-bound tomes (it didn't matter which one) retrieved from the shelves in the corner or staring at the wall (again, it didn't matter which one), trying desperately to keep her mind blank. It served her no good to think because that just brought on palpitations. Mostly, she would crawl into bed, always curling into the fetal position, and alternate between sleeping and crying, crying and sleeping. She didn't know how she was ever going to be able to grasp the enormity of her situation. She was completely alone, with nothing from her world other than herself and her increasingly pungent pajamas to comfort her.

Nonetheless, as the days wore on, Donnie could feel her brain relentlessly adjusting to her predicament, just as normal, healthy brains are wont to do, with a growing part of her eventually coming to grips with the fact that her life as she knew it was indeed well and truly over, and one day soon she'd have to get on with life here, such as it was going to be. But this too she was not going to rush; she was by no means ready to admit that she'd even partially accepted this abrupt and cruel turn her life had taken. A large part of her stubbornly refused to believe that she'd never experience another rock and roll concert, or sit down with the Sunday *SFTimes* and have an all-day read, or argue politics and religion with complete strangers at the local coffee and bagel shop—gawd, never to have another banana blueberry smoothie? No more tapas? No World Series? No Super Bowl? What kind of life was that going to be?

Then she would inevitably begin thinking about her family and friends and how much she missed them and how she'd never get to see them again, never get to talk to them again because whoever or whatever had brought her here had obviously abandoned her to the horrible fate of becoming a complete recluse in a time that was not her own—it was invariably at this point that the bawling thing would take over again and she'd be reduced to a sniveling heap for hours.

By the end of this most miserable period, Donnie was thoroughly exhausted and more than a little ill. It was, by her best reckoning, her tenth day here. She would've bet her entire life savings that she probably looked the worst she ever had in all her forty-three years. Thankfully, she didn't have a mirror handy, so she was not subjected to that, sure to be, oh-so pretty picture. But at her age, no matter how well preserved one is, this kind of behavior was certain to make you look just terrible, so betting her life savings would not have put it at risk.

Ah, that was better. Her indomitable sense of humor had, at long last, returned.

The cat, who obviously belonged with the house, didn't bother to disguise his growing disgust with her. She was grateful that, from her first day here, he would somehow find his way out of the cottage in the morning and would only come back to it in the evening. Just after sundown each day, he would jump onto the outer window sill of whichever room she was in and either bat at the pane, making it rattle annoyingly, or caterwaul at the top of his lungs until Donnie would get up, unbolt the door and let him in. He'd then spend the entire evening stalking around her, mewling accusingly in the now-familiar short bursts of staccato meows, driving her nuts with his incessant vocalizations.

No matter how hard she tried to make friends with him, he would simply and inevitably hiss or meow sharply at her if she ventured within four feet of him, usually for no apparent reason other than the fact that she existed. He still clearly did not want her to touch him. Donnie gave up trying to make amends with him for whatever unknown and inadvertent slight she had done him and studiously ignored him thereafter.

But he always did a very curious thing whenever she was in the outer room with him. Every so often he would run to the crudely built bookshelf in the corner and jump to the third shelf. His curious behavior did not end there. He would then push a book to the floor. It was always the same book. Donnie finally left it lying on the floor because she got tired of replacing it on its shelf. So the cat took up the habit of sliding it across the floorboards toward her. Each time Donnie found the book close by, she kicked it back across the room, telling herself that she was not behaving like a spoiled child—no way, not her. And since the cat staunchly refused to give her the time of day, so to speak, Donnie spitefully took a few of the other books off the shelves and feigned perusing them.

While she did not technically read these books, except for the one and that only in parts, for her mind was far too frazzled to concentrate on anything for longer than five minutes at a stretch, she left these books lying open upon any and all available flat surfaces in close proximity to her for a hurried pickup whenever the cat made another of his increasingly fractious demands, just to let him know that she was *not* going to read the book he kept pushing at her, again reassuring herself that she was not being at all immature toward the dour feline.

And so, on Donnie's tenth and eminently fateful evening here, after she'd gained the much-needed return of her humor, the cat became even more insistent than ever and slid the book across the floor until it was at Donnie's feet. He then sat on the book and stared up at her, daring her to kick it, and him, across the room this time.

Donnie let out an exasperated snort and exclaimed, "All right, you obnoxious puss, you win; I'll read your blasted book!" As though he understood her words perfectly, he stepped off the volume and leapt lightly onto the table. Donnie reached down to pick up the book, untied the leather strings binding it, and set it before her on the table, open to the first page. A thick, silvery metal bookmark, about seven or eight inches long and an inch and a half wide, fell onto the rough wooden boards of the tabletop. This bookmark was curved into a shape reminiscent of a foreshortened "S" and was inscribed with what looked to her untrained eyes to be runes of some sort. It apparently had, at one time, borne a kind of slanted, rectangular jewel with rounded corners set into its one end, but if so, the gem must've fallen out because it was nowhere to be seen now. She tucked the bookmark into the leather binding, drew two candles closer, and turned her attention to what was written in the book.

She realized after reading a few handwritten sentences that it was a journal of sorts. The other books, while also handwritten, but each in quite beautiful and distinctive scripts (and not the childish scrawl exhibited in the cat's book), had pertained in one way or another to historic adventures in some rather strange lands, or so Donnie had gleaned from what little reading she did do of the one and the skimming she'd done in the others. Granted, she hadn't recognized any of the names of the central characters or even the places in the verbose and oddly familiar intrigues that played out over the one book's pages, but since it was so dryly written, she figured it was a safe bet that it was mainly non-fiction, albeit with some rather heavy-duty exaggerations on the storyteller's part.

The cat's book, though, was different. It was randomly textbookish, giving somewhat deranged instructions on which plants to eat, which to never ever touch under any circumstances, and which to use for medicinal purposes; how to tend or dress animals, depending on whether they were for farm use or were game; how to preserve food with salt; and, oddly enough, it also provided various practical instructions on working with metals and woods and on refining salt brine to make table salt. Mingled within these jumbled directives were the personal ramblings of an obviously lonely woman who appeared to be quite convinced that she was a time-traveling witch.

She gave her name as Caterin of the Codlebærn and called herself "Caat" or "Caatee luf." It took Donnie a minute to decipher Caterin's writing code. Apparently, if you doubled up the vowels it gave you a long sound and all single vowels were short. There seemed to be no organized system for consonants though.

Reading the book was not an easy task. Nonetheless, Donnie valiantly plowed through the puerile writing until she came almost to the end. Well, if truth be told, she mostly leafed through the book because the inventive spelling was giving her a headache. But a quick glance over the final three pages revealed her own name and what might be the reason she was here. She even exclaimed aloud, "Aha! At last!"

The cat immediately leaped onto the open book and meowed a loud, frustrated, "What?"

Donnie glared back at him, retorting, "I suppose you want me to read it to you, is that it? Will that finally make you happy? Will it make you stop griping at me every time you're within ten feet of me? Will it?"

He climbed off the book and sat down to gaze steadily at her with his green eyes, clearly promising nothing. He curled his white-tipped black tail tightly around his white feet, a pose which exposed most of his white belly to her. Now that she'd gotten this close to him, Donnie realized that he was a really beautiful cat, with luxuriant, thick black fur on his back, while his underside was pure snowy white. The bottom half of his face was also white. He still wore around his neck the thin silver chain she'd noticed the first time she'd seen him. She could see now that it was a small, tilted, sort of parallelogram-looking locket which slid easily upon the chain. This locket gleamed radiantly against his breast and was inscribed in delicate lettering of some sort. She could only think that it was apparently the medieval equivalent of an ID tag.

"Hmm, you remind me of someone, you know that?" she told the cat.

He meowed arrogantly at her.

Donnie shrugged and began reading one of the final passages slowly, stumbling several times over the phonetics. " 'Well Caatee luf yee av dun it naow, avint yee just, and wot aa mess yee maad wit yee nowt gooen ta bee arrowend ta cleenn it up, Nuttin for it, yee av ta fiind wun ov yer ahff spriggs an brink er bakk ta saav thu werlld'."

The next entry read: " 'I fowend wun fahr dowen thu liin miind yee bott sheez thu oonlee wun wot kumms in kleer liik, Naow Caat yee av ta giff Dahnnee'—That's me, I presume," Donnie added, looking up at the cat to make her point before resuming, "—'giff Dahnnee thu powers wich shud bilon ta ahll beetwikks uss, bot nun o them will reelee miind az thaa wudint noo it iff thaa wuz born wiffowt em'."

Feeling a bit chary, Donnie skipped down a page or so, then continued with the final entry. " 'Tahniit it must bee. Mii Donnie'—Hey, she spelled my name correctly this time! Oh, okay, okay, I'm reading already!" Donnie exclaimed, waving a hand at the impatient cat, who had just growled at her. "Er, where was I? Oh, yeah—'Mii Donnie will bee az feersum aa witch az effer thar woz, wunst shee udderz thu furst werdz wich ahll wee Codlebærn musst saa ter kumm intu owr powerz, Tanee will allp her, eez aa reell guud kat'—Aha, so that's your name, eh?"

Donnie looked up once more at the cat and cocked her head to the side. "Tanny?"

The cat replied by yowling sharply at her and placing an imperious paw on the book.

Donnie stuck her tongue out at him, then shook her head ruefully, asking the room at large, "Can you believe I'm being bullied by a cat?" She returned her attention to the book and continued reading the line, "— 'aa reell guud kat'." She couldn't help herself; she let out a snicker of disbelief when she repeated that part. " 'Naow ahllz eez got ta duu is maak her saa ahmii see'."

It seemed as though the whole world began to rock and shake after Donnie finished speaking and she immediately surged to her feet, moving instinctively toward the front door. A particularly large jolt halted her progress at two steps and her response to this, as she stumbled back toward the table while the floor of the cottage heaved up at her, was a horrified, "Omigod, did I just make myself a witch? Nah, no way—" And then the air around her went funny, kind of dead-like. At first, she thought she'd gone deaf, but suddenly a visible and vibrant, cobalt-hued shock wave, originating within her, expanded around her, hung there for a moment encasing her entire body, then shot outwardly with a muffled percussive burst that returned hearing to her ears. As this wave passed through the furniture, walls, ceiling and floor, it made them shimmer and blaze with light. Even the cat was subjected to this electric phenomenon.

Paralyzed in astonishment, Donnie helplessly watched this shock wave clear the room and, from what she could see through the window, apparently continue on outside the walls of the house. Her eyes widened further as every single thing within and without the shabby little cottage began to glow with this brilliant blue luminescence, not the least of which was her own body.

As a matter of fact, the entire valley shone with it, and almost instantly this power wave rose to the surface outside the valley and again spread outward, looking from above as though it were consuming the very Earth and all things upon it as it raced over the landscape and rose up toward the heavens until it reached the outer atmosphere. The entire planet was engulfed by it in mere seconds. But Donnie knew none of that, of course.

This intense cobalt radiance should have been blinding at its apex, yet somehow Donnie could see perfectly well through the effulgent glare to plainly make out the pages of the scattered books riffling; dust bunnies tumbling to the corners of the room; the small, cast iron cauldron she used for making her teas swaying precariously on the spit above the roaring fire; even the cat's fur flattening against his body. He smiled smugly and began to preen his ruffled coat as the magnificent light faded at last and fell to the ground like a curtain. The whole thing probably lasted around ten seconds.

"Wow, that was so Hollywood!" Donnie whispered in awe when it was done and she had plopped down heavily into the chair she had vacated seconds before. Just then, a series of loud thuds could be heard outside. It sounded to her like the heavens were pitching huge boulders around the front and side of the cottage, sending shock tremors through the timbered floor of the structure once more. She jumped to her feet again and shouted, "What the hell was that?"

What happened next caused her to faint. When she returned to consciousness several seconds later, the cat's face was hanging over the corner of the table, looking down upon her. Stupefied, Donnie cried up at him, "I didn't really hear you talk, did I, kitty? No-no, that would be crazy and, no matter the evidence to the contrary, I am not crazy!" She swallowed hard and cringed, running her hands over her face. "At least, I'm pretty sure I'm not crazy. But I suppose that's what every nut case says, isn't it?" She looked straight up at the ceiling from where she lay and groaned, "I knew I should've been more worried about Mom and her hats. And poor Aunt Bea! Oh, dubious DNAs, not from both sides of the family!"

The cat, ignoring this increasingly ambiguous tirade, replied haughtily, "I said, 'tis the cacophony of thy trappings falling to earth. Their presence was insisted upon by thee, as thou shouldst verily recall!" he remonstrated her.

Donnie sat up abruptly and hit her head on the table, nearly knocking herself unconscious again. She screeched in pain, which sent the cat flying from her. Pressing her hand onto the top of her head, she carefully raised herself back into the chair, wincing at the lightning bolt pains mere breathing sent ricocheting through her skull.

She rubbed the knot on her head gingerly and looked at the cat in desperation. "Stop that, will you? Everybody knows cats can't talk, and even if they could, they'd never, ever sound like someone from a medieval play. Who says *thee* and *thy* anymore, let alone *thou*? Or *cacophony* and *trappings*, for that matter? Now, if you were a dragon or a drunken lord or a damsel in high dudgeon, I could maybe go with the antiquated elocution, but a house cat? Nope, no way! So there, that's settled; you will stop talking like that! Better yet, you will stop talking altogether, if you please. Oh, hold on, I get it now, this means I must be dreaming—yeah-yeah, no-no, now wait, don't interrupt me. No, seriously, wait! This really is all a dream, see? And, may I interject at this point, a dang nasty one!"

The cat, after trying to get a word in edgewise, settled back onto the table in front of Donnie, his tail curled tightly around his feet. He appeared ready to let her rant.

And so she did. "Oh, crazed kittens," Donnie crowed with sudden relief, "Why, I'll bet I haven't even left San Francisco for Wales yet! I was probably in some streetcar or city bus accident, because, you know," she informed the cat pedantically, "they happen all the time! And so, wait for it, here it comes…what's really happening is, I'm lying in some hospital bed right now, probably in a coma, havin' one whale of a dream! I'll bet you anything I'll wake up in a moment and when I'm recovered from my injuries I'll return to my oh-so comfortable, real house in my beloved San Fran! And then I'll go to work every day, my sister and I will visit our parents for dinner on Wednesdays, and I'll have lunch with my best friend on Saturdays, just like I always do. And I will forget all about ever wanting to take a trip to Wales, or anywhere else for that matter, and my life will be mine, forever!"

She added a triumphant yell of anticipation to this, declaring loudly, "Silly strumpets of the world unite! I'm gettin' the heck outta here—I'm goin' home! Do you hear me, cruel world? I've figured out what's really going on here, and by this time tomorrow, I'll be awake and everything will be right as rain; no talking cats, no drafty cottages, no having to go potty out in the middle of the friggin' woods anymore! I'll have—why, I'll have civilization again! A real kitchen with electricity and…and indoor plumbing and…oh, and my Heavenly Sleeper mattress! Omigod, my car! I love my car, have I told you that yet, kitty? Why, I have never loved that car more than I do at this very moment! Hoo-boy, will everybody crack up when they hear about this dream! My friends are really gonna think I'm as wacky as—well, as they're always kidding me I am. And you know what, kitty-kitty? I may even agree with them this time!" She looked at him eagerly, obviously expecting him to agree with her.

But the cat merely shook his head before opining in his rich, pompous voice, "Of all Catie's progeny, why must she have been able to call out only to thee? There had to have been plenty of others betwixt you who are not complete imbeciles. Any number of them would have been eminently more suitable than thou!"

Donnie turned a bright red at this insult. "Well, I can't help that I was the only one to hear her call, whenever, whatever that was!" she snapped back at him. "But believe you me, if I'd known this was going to be the result, I would've let my answering machine get it! And no more thee, thou or thy; I mean it!" Her expression suddenly changed to one of disbelief. "Oh, jeepers," she cried in frustration, "I can't believe I'm actually trading barbs with a cat! Heeeyyy, hold the phone," she was suddenly wary again, "did I hear you say something about me insisting that Catie send some things along with me? Well now, that's quite a stretch, don't ya think, since I've never even met her? Where is she, by the way? Off flying her broomstick somewhere, yanking more innocent people out of their perfectly comfortable centuries and stealing them away to this backwater hell-hole? You must know what happened to her, so spill it like the nice little puddy tat she swears you are in her journal."

The cat sniffed the air as if it had suddenly turned rancid. "*You* are not amusing. Though I must say you are stupid, foolish, lazy, thoughtless and cowardly."

"Oh, yeah?" Donnie looked shocked and then blustered angrily, "Oh, yeah? Well...I liked you a whole lot better when I only thought you were bitchin' at me all the time. Now it seems I'm doomed to knowing exactly what it is you're bitching at me about! And how dare you call me those horrible things?" she huffed in outrage. "You don't even know me! Okay, maybe I haven't been at my best since coming here, but I think I deserve some leeway due to mitigating circumstances."

The cat eyed her superiorly and sniffed sharply again. "Humph!" he said. "A Codlebærn you may be, but clearly the bloodline has been severely diluted throughout the centuries!"

Donnie's jaw dropped and her eyes widened. She glared at the cat, counting to ten under her breath before replying sweetly, "Hey, did anyone ever tell you that you look just like the cartoon cat Sylvester? I have a great idea—now that I'm a witch, I'll conjure you up a talking mouse sidekick named Lucy, then I'll work out some comedy routines for us all—you know, where I'm your owner and you constantly try to outwit the oh-so smarter mouse, but fail hilariously each and every time, with increasingly violent results for *you*."

She leaned forward, warming to her subject, and still keeping her tone sugared. "And once we've got our skits honed to perfection, we'll hook up the horse to the cart and become traveling minstrels...or troubadours...or whatever they're called around here! Anyway, I'll bet we take every town we visit by storm. And trust me, I know it'll work because audiences around the globe fall all over themselves for really brutal comedy, no matter the century. It'll be an absolute riot and I guarantee we'll end up becoming unbelievably rich and famous!"

She sat back and her face took on a mock-pained expression while she deadpanned, "Either that or we'll get burned at the stake. Which, come to think about it, would put a bit of a damper on the whole shebang, wouldn't it? Oh, well, you mull it over for a while and let me know what you think you can contribute." She bent forward and glared once more at the cat. "After all, I gather this is a partnership and having you as my familiar is part and parcel of the package deal, right?"

The cat leapt off the table, stalked to the window and jumped up onto its sill. He sat down stiffly with his back to Donnie, immutable.

Donnie mugged at the cat's back. By golly, it felt good to get back at that annoying feline! But her triumph over the caustic cat was short lived. For the next few minutes, Donnie sat silently at the table, holding her head in her hands, and simply tried to digest what had just occurred. Was she truly a witch now? Was that possible? Well, something otherworldly had certainly happened to her, that much was clear. One doesn't become a Dr. Pennywell on a normal day, does one?

She let the cat sulk for a while, then eventually inquired of him, "Hey, Sylvester? Seriously this time, where's Catie now?"

The cat shot her a sullen glance over his back before deigning to reply to the window. "My name is Tanygrisiau yr Eglwys Wen," he said, "and I do not know where Catie has gone. Were that she was here, she might provide the explanations you have cried aloud for so insistently and so pathetically over the past fortnight."

Donnie scowled at him. "It has not been a fortnight; not yet!" she retorted. "And I'll thank you not to exaggerate that part…but I guess I can give you the other bit," she admitted grudgingly. She sighed heavily, sagged back in her chair and pointedly ignored the cat's previous protest over his new name to bemoan, "Why did she do this to me, Sylvester? And without even asking me if I was okay with it!"

Other than the glance he'd given her a few moments ago, the cat had continued to sit with his backside facing Donnie. He now turned completely around and stared at her in consternation. "She most definitely did ask you that the night she brought you here!"

Thunderstruck, Donnie considered this for a few moments, about to protest until an elusive image of a young woman dressed in bright yellow taffeta floated to the surface of her mind, chasing around in her memory and refusing to stand still. It was sort of a half-memory of a dream she'd had the night before her arrival here, and in it the odd little woman had asked her some decidedly curious questions. Now eyeing the cat with incredulity, Donnie almost shouted at him, "You mean that was Catie in my dream that night?"

" 'Twas no dream!" he informed her impatiently. "I will grant that you were in a dream state when she asked you what was, really, an altogether simple inquiry. Which you then answered exhaustively. She brought everything you requested, although we both felt it excessive and we truly could not see what good most of it would do you here. But you were insistent and time was running too short to quibble. Why did you answer her queries at all if you did not wish to come?"

Donnie stared at him, shaking her head disbelievingly. "Because I thought they were hypothetical, of course! I mean, who would think something like that was real? A bizarrely dressed young woman appears out of nowhere in the middle of a perfectly good dream and croaks, 'Dearie, if I sent ye back to ancient times to become the most powerful witch that ever was, what would ye want to be bringin' with ye? From yer world, I mean.' Now I ask you, what kind of a question is that, if not hypothetical?" she demanded angrily of the cat.

"You could have told her no!" he argued.

Donnie huffed. "I tell you I thought it was a dream! I had no idea—let me stress that—*no* idea she was real, or that she was serious." Tears were welling up in Donnie's eyes now. "I didn't know she meant it for keeps. How was I supposed to know she meant it for keeps?" she wailed, her voice breaking with emotion.

The cat watched silently as Donnie stood from the chair and began collecting the scattered books. She carried them to the bookshelf and put each away, her movements exaggeratedly deliberate and precise. When finished, she announced in a small, tight voice, "I'm going to bed. I've had enough for one day. No, scratch that and make it one lifetime." She then slipped quietly into the bedroom.

That night Donnie had one of the worst dreams she'd ever experienced in her life. More nightmare than simple dream, it was a vivid, haunting and unsettling thing, with her being chased by all manner of monsters. She ended up flying down several stone passageways blindly and into a cave where she found herself entirely alone. The cave was lit with an eerie, flickering light and was filled was a huge roar of sound, like that of water rushing over a dam during a great flood, which occluded all other noises. She felt trapped and immobilized by her fears there, utterly helpless and unable to free herself.

She awoke from this dream in the early morning, just before sunrise, and, with her cheeks wet from her tears, cried out softly, "No one even knows I'm here, do they? Oh, someone, please help me!" Depression assaulted her senses, leaving her heart heavy and her eyes streaming until the grey of dawn approached, when she determinedly steeled herself to meet the day. Only then did she reach up to wipe away her tears and see a blueish energy flit from her fingertips to her face. It *was* true then. Last night really had happened.

Sitting up suddenly, Donnie experienced a strangely exhilarating epiphany because she realized this also meant that her belongings must be waiting for her out in the yard. For the life of her, she couldn't remember what all she'd told Catie she'd need, but she distinctly recalled asking for her clothes. Oh, and her pooch! She'd specifically asked for him, she now recollected with glee. Someone from her world, she thought to herself longingly. He was her baby, the closest she'd probably ever come to having a child. And, jeez Louise, had she missed him terribly since leaving California. Missed his snout either in her hand or coming up from behind to goose her—well, okay, she hadn't missed the last part all that much, she decided.

She got up and tiptoed to the outer room, moving across it quickly to the front door with the green boots in her hand. She unbolted and opened the door slowly, hoping not to waken the cat because she didn't think she could face him right now. She slipped outside and pulled the door to behind her, leaving it slightly ajar. Turning, she gaped with joy. Her belongings had indeed arrived! The first thing she noticed was that all eighteen bookshelves seemed to have made it through safely. And her books were there too—hallelujah, hallelujah, hallelujah, she'd brought all her books!

There were also several very large black trunks strewn all about the overgrown front and side yards. Two trunks, standing side by side, had broken locks and their lids were flung wide open. She could see clothing spilling out from the depths of one. Yes! They were her own clothes, or at least some that looked very much like it.

Slipping into the green boots, Donnie ran over to these two trunks. She cooed with delight when she looked in the other open trunk and found her mother's (still serviceable) old boombox and headphones, her own digital music player (she'd had it forever) and its charging station and speakers, and her extensive CD collection, along with her CD organizer racks. For years, she'd made an art form of recording her own rock, folk and blues compilations from her and her father's extensive digital music collections. Randomly, she chose a CD marked with an "H" for "Happy" and popped it into the player. "Do You Believe in Magic?" by David Dean Smith began wafting from the speakers.

"Wow, good pick!" Donnie exclaimed, somewhat bemused at the unexpected appropriateness of song. It was a classic her father had played for her over and over when she was a little girl. She now danced happily to the other open trunk, singing along with the much beloved melody.

She picked up a set of clean sweats and underclothes fortuitously laying on top of the other clothing, still humming along with the song. Then she almost skipped over to the well, where she filled the well's water bucket and proceeded to peel off the, by now, putrid pajamas she'd been living in for far too long, deciding she would throw them in the fire as soon as she went back inside. Ha, let the bedbugs crackle in the flames!

She dipped her hand into the bucket's freezing contents with a yelp and, grabbing the rough bar of lye soap from the rim of the well, scrubbed her body until it was squeaky clean.

When Donnie was finished with her bath, she shivered, suddenly realizing that she had no towel. She really wished she had one of her big, fluffy yellow towels because she was definitely getting chilled. Instantly, a towel of that exact description materialized into her wet hands. She nearly dropped it in surprise.

With an absurd pang of triumph, she chuckled and crowed out to her new world, "Hey, I've just performed my first magic act!" She continued washing herself and, once she'd dried off, she dressed in the fresh, clean clothes she'd gotten from the trunk. She pulled up some fresh water with the bucket, plunged her head into its depths, lathered and rinsed her hair a couple of times, and wrapped the towel tightly around her head when she was done. Then she went hunting for sneakers and the dog.

Chapter 2
This Home Is Yours

The trunks were a treasure trove to Donnie. She dug into each one eagerly, flinging clothing, bedding, pots and pans, tools and other implements aloft, laughing with delight at each rediscovered possession. And, to her great surprise, everything she unpacked floated gently from its trunk to the ground in an orderly manner as soon as she tugged on them and sent them flying. Judging from the condition of the cottage when she'd first arrived, she would not have thought Catie capable of such careful systemization.

In the third trunk she opened, Donnie found Rex the Wonder Dog, her huge, long-haired German Shepherd Dog. He bounded out as soon as the trunk lid lifted, and then raced around his mama, wriggling and crouching in play stance every time she caught him in a happy embrace. His silky-soft, red, black and tan coat gleamed and sparkled in the morning sunlight. Then, as was his habit, he came up behind Donnie, stuck his head between her knees and sat down, looking up at her with his expressive brown eyes. Quivering, he suddenly said in a youthful voice, much to their mutual astonishment, "Where are we, Mama?"

He growled once and whipped around wildly (nearly knocking Donnie over), looking for whoever it was who'd spoken. No one there. He began sniffing every inch of the surrounding ten-foot area, all the while repeating, "Who said that? Now, who said *that*? Hey, who just said *that*?"

In a few more moments, Rex mumbled happily, "Oh, I do believe it's me that's speaking! Why, yes, it is me! I can talk now! Hey, Mama," he shouted, "I can talk! D'ya hear me? Listen, I can talk just like you can!" He proceeded to run pell-mell around the yard trying out his voice, assuming different accents and timbres (she clearly had watched too much TV in his presence), having a merry old time discovering the wonder of speech.

Donnie stared at him glassy-eyed throughout these antics, her heart sinking. It wasn't bad enough to have a talking cat, now she also had a talking slash yodeling dog? Shaking her head slowly, she reached inside Rex's trunk and pulled out his bed, food bin and dishes, medicines and other sundries, plus his chews and toys. She looked at the pile they made and realized that she'd have to figure out what she was going to feed him once the dog food ran out, which was likely to be soon.

She vowed he would not have free run of the chickens. Even though they made the hair rise on the back of her neck, especially at feeding time when they all advanced on her at once, clucking and pecking ominously, making her want to dump the corn in a pile and run like hell, they were now under her protection, and she felt duty-bound to ensure their survival. Resignedly, she expelled a long, heavy breath and moved on to the next trunk.

In one, Donnie came upon the stylish white marble bathroom sink and matching toilet that she'd paid a month's salary for two years ago. When she'd pulled those out, she saw a corner of the huge shower stall that she'd paid another month's salary for. She drew it out too, although how it fit in the trunk in the first place, she had no idea. But there it was, and what good it would do her here, even she had to admit she didn't know. She also found her soaps, creams, lotions and makeup—in fact, all her bathroom and cosmetic paraphernalia.

In the next trunk was the beautiful Georgian mirror she'd inherited from her grandmother. Miraculously, it was intact. Donnie reached inside again and found the matching desk. "Wow, this is so Dusty Bobbins!" she shouted with glee to the cat, who, by this time had slipped through the open door and was watching her and the dog somewhat anxiously.

"What, pray tell, are dusty baw bins?" Sylvester asked, perfunctorily polite.

"Pray tell?" Donnie repeated under her breath, once again taken aback by the cat's antiquated allocution. She said to him, "Well, firstly, it's Bobbins, not baw bins; Bob-ins, get it? As to what she is..." Doubtful as to how to explain that peculiar children's literary character, Donnie chewed her lip a moment, then suddenly brightened, exclaiming, "Why, she's only the best teacher that ever lived! And, hey, guess what—she's magical too! Although, I really don't think she's a witch, just a magical teacher with a crazy, morphing whiteboard."

Still considerably unenlightened, the cat decided not to pursue this line of conversation. When he'd asked his one question, the dog had noticed his presence and was now approaching him with great interest, letting out a high-pitched play whine. Sylvester haughtily rebuffed this fresh arrival with, "Do not think it, for if you come any closer, I shall turn you into a toad."

The dog sat down abruptly, a few feet away from the cat, and cocked his head in surprise, his black eyebrows knitted together and his big tan paws set primly on the ground. He deliberated on this new development for a bit, then inquired curiously (echoing Donnie's own train of thought), "Can you really do that?"

Sylvester gravely nodded his head. Rex scampered away quick as rabbit.

At first, Donnie was astounded that she'd brought along her kitchen appliances. She nearly said so to the cat, but a sudden feeling of expectancy came over her and stilled her lips. It was followed by the surprisingly crystal-clear memory of her insistence the night Catie came to collect her that everything Donnie owned must be brought along. It had been essential that Catie bring it all—for what reason, Donnie could not fathom. But she now remembered how adamant she'd been when Catie had questioned her a second time about it.

Why hadn't she remembered all of this sooner? It was almost as though there were some sort of shroud on her memory, a veil that seemed to be lifting in part, at least. Yet, even now, there was no explanation whatsoever within her memory as to *why* she'd insisted all her belongings must be brought.

Well, okay then, so everything had to be here with her, for whatever reason. Donnie decided just to accept this for now because it felt right to her. Hopefully, before long, she'd figure out the answer to this and several other mysteries swirling around in her head.

But she still didn't know what she should do with her kitchen appliances. Storage maybe? Without electricity, it's not like she could use them for their original purpose, so what good would they do her here? Finding the sink gave Donnie inspiration; she hoped her book on plumbing was still on the Fix-It-Yourself bookshelf. After all, what's the point of being magical if you can't plumb a bathroom and a proper kitchen with it?

In yet another trunk she found her desktop computer and its assorted peripherals, her TV and stereo, her DVD player, her extensive movie collection, and her laptop and its wireless speakers. The presence of the laptop told her that Catie must also have included in the trunks the belongings Donnie had taken with her to Wales. Donnie shook her head sadly, relegating her electronics to "storage" for the time being.

Her huge cedar wardrobe and bench with built-in drawers were in the final trunk. She stuffed all her clothing inside the wardrobe and all the shoes and boots into the bench, deciding she'd write a spell on them there and then. She canted:

"Fill this cedar with all the things,
Any girl can wear from day to day.
Whatever her heart's desire,
When opening the door she'll only have to think or say,
I want to wear my blank today!"

She wasn't sure how this spell thingy worked, but she hoped it was understood about that "blank" part.

She looked inside the trunk again and continued to take out more of her bedroom furniture until the trunk appeared empty. Donnie reached into its blackness one more time anyway. Her hand found something solid, smooth and long. She tugged hard on it and out flew the king-sized bronze bed she'd sent all the way to New York for last year. The box springs came out next. She dug around inside the trunk again, but found nothing more in it. She closed the lid and locked it, preparing it to be stored in the hayloft above the stables.

"Rats, when I said I wanted my bed, I should've made it clear that meant the whole thing!" she grumbled, gazing forlornly at the bed frame. "I'm really gonna miss my Heavenly Sleeper. I don't suppose any of my books have a section on making mattresses. That would probably be asking too much!"

Sylvester, who had remained silent for some time, responded to this complaint. "Catie could not bring the mattress because a young woman had just fallen asleep on it. She could not very well have taken that from the girl also."

Donnie stared at him, her mouth agape. "You mean all this stuff really was ripped from my house in San Francisco that night and not just duplicated? Ha!" she crowed. "What a hoot! I wonder how Julia's gonna explain my empty house to Liz? And to the cops, because you know Liz will call them! Oh, m'gosh, the bathroom—how on earth is she going to account for that? Aw, now that's just priceless!"

She thought about her friend Liz warmly. Her greatest pal ever was small, barely five foot in her stockinged feet, and a perfect sized one. Her long, silky, burgundy-colored hair, admittedly not a hair color found in nature, was her pride and joy. Donnie had known her since they'd worked together at the *SFTimes* seven years before. Although Liz had left the paper for a corporate training job long ago, their friendship had developed fast and remained solid all these years later.

Julia was Liz's younger sister by about sixteen years. Once she'd heard Donnie was going to Wales for several months' sabbatical to finish her book, Julia had begun a relentless, campaigned attack on her sister. She complained incessantly to Liz of how tired she was of living in the crowded little apartment she shared with two other girls near the college campus and really needed, had to have a break from it or she'd just kill herself. There was simply no way she'd be able to write her master's thesis there, what with all the partying and general mayhem always going on, and Liz did want her to get her master's, didn't she?

It was only when Liz had reluctantly agreed that Julia's situation was indeed intolerable and asked how she could fix it that Julia had finally coughed up what she was really after. She wanted Donnie to let her housesit.

Donnie obviously didn't like Julia all that much, but since Liz was the one who'd asked, she hadn't been able to refuse the arrangement. Plus, it was cheaper than hiring a professional house and dog sitter. Under penalty of having to get a deliberately bad cut and color job and live with it for six weeks, Liz had agreed to check the house at least twice a week to make sure Julia didn't destroy anything in it. Otherwise, no deal. Liz had sworn solemnly on a stack of fashion magazines that she would take care of the place and watch over Julia and Rex like a hawk.

Donnie could just imagine Julia spluttering on the phone to Liz, "They took everything but the mattress I was sleeping on!" Liz would've been ready to kill her, Donnie thought cheerfully. Then she immediately sobered. Liz also would've tried to get in touch with Donnie in Wales.

She realized that her family and friends would be very worried about her disappearance and she now swung around toward the cat. "My family!" she cried. "Oh, jeez, Sylvester, my mom will be beside herself once she finds out I'm not in Wales anymore. Is there any way I can get a message to her and tell her I'm okay?" she demanded frantically.

Sylvester looked up from his morning bath, licked his chops, and said calmly, "She knows already." Noting Donnie's surprise at this revelation, he went on to explain, "You must understand, your coming here is part of your family lore. Catie told me this the night she brought you here. She said the volumes containing the tales of your adventures have been passed from generation to generation. Your mother grew up knowing full well that her eldest daughter would be sent to ancient times to save the family bloodline. Why do you think she named you Donemere, a most uncommon name for your time?" The cat studied Donnie's still-startled face for a second more, then asked incredulously, "Your mother truly never gave you any hint of this?"

"No, she didn't!" Donnie exclaimed once she could find her voice. "But that certainly explains why my parents cursed me with such a weird name, yet gave my sister the nice, normal name of Emily. I always wondered where *Donemere* had come from, but Mom would never say. It also explains why she insisted I come to Wales—oh, felonious families! That means my own mother sent me to my doom! But no, she wouldn't do that if things end badly, so they must turn out okay, right?" She suddenly processed the other news the cat had imparted to her and, again stunned, enquired, "What did you mean when you said I was sent here to save the family bloodline?"

Sylvester gazed at her steadily and silently, clearly sizing her up and, just as clearly, gauging her as falling far short of the expected requirements. He said dourly, "One day I shall be allowed to tell you this and much more with it, Donemere. That day is not today. There is much you must do, much you must learn. Do well with all I shall teach you and it will not be long before I may impart to you what must be done to save the Codlebærn bloodline. For now, believe that your family is in peace. Worries such as this must not distract you."

Donnie eyed him back doubtfully. "That's easy for you to say, O' Master Cat. Not so easy for me to do, though," she informed him. "Well...I suppose if you won't tell me now, you won't tell me. But don't expect me to drop the subject; I'll bug you every day until you do tell me. I'm just giving you fair warning. Hey, you say my mother knew all my life that I'd disappear one day? How weird is that? I wonder what she's going to tell everyone."

The cat spoke kindly to Donnie for the very first time in their brief acquaintance. "Catie said your mother was one in a million. She visited her before taking you away, so she could inform her that it was time for you to go. When Catie returned to your house, she told me that your mother was quite gracious throughout their visit. She will think of a suitable tale for all."

Donnie thought of her mother tenderly and her eyes filled with tears, which she brushed away immediately. No sense in starting that behavior again. What she needed right now was activity. Okay, what she really needed was to go home, but until she could figure out a way to do that, she was determined to make this place seem like home. And since her belongings had arrived, it was time to get busy.

Her most pressing problem was how to fit everything into the cottage. Even though its main room was quite large, it was, nonetheless, far too small for all of her furniture. She decided there and then that she'd just have to add a room or two. "How hard can it be?" she muttered wryly. "It's not like I don't already know the floor plan. Although, I really hope my DIY section's somehow improved because I don't think I have anything to fit this bill."

She considered what to use for materials. She had no clue how to cut stone from a quarry, but she did know how to fell trees; well, in theory anyway. Besides, the house she'd rented in Wales was mostly a wooden structure. And so, using magic, she could easily build the necessary rooms herself, right? She figured she could use Catie's instructions on woodworking to help her and she would just have to pray that she could actually trust the information the book contained.

She went back into the house and began reading the most relevant sections of Catie's journal. Most of the tools Donnie needed, she herself owned. Those tools she didn't have, she found amongst Catie's in the workshop at the back of the stables. Thankfully, Donnie's parents believed in teaching their daughters to be independent and, even better, handy with tools. She wished she could use her electric saw to shape the boards, but, for the present, her power tools were useless to her. Eventually, she would attempt to build an electric generator—but then again, no, she didn't intend on being here that long, now did she, she scolded herself severely, if not convincingly.

She decided to add a bathroom and a larger room at the back of the cottage for her office, which would also house her bookshelves. It took a little while for Donnie to realize that she truly was modeling her construction plans after the rambling cottage she'd been renting the past few months, although she was still a number of rooms short. She guessed they must've been added at another time. "Who knows, maybe even by me!" she grinned cheerfully.

A little while later, she rode the horse down the small rise the farm was situated on and up the hill to the top of the valley, where the forest began. There she walked around and started choosing which trees she would cut down. Sylvester and Rex came along with her; the dog to explore and the cat apparently to stare at her with curiosity. For the longest time, he neither said anything nor moved from the horse's rump, where he sat almost statue-like with his tail curled tightly around his feet.

Donnie had brought along a hand saw and, once she had two appropriately sized trees chosen, she untied the implement from the pack on the horse's back. Sylvester turned to watch her, unblinking, following her every move with his green eyes until finally he spoke, his tone forbidding. "You are not intending to fell a tree, surely?" he inquired.

"Well, yeah, how else can I build some extra rooms?" Donnie replied, absentmindedly pacing around while she worked out the directions in which she wanted the trees to fall.

"You might try asking the trees first."

Donnie took a few more steps before comprehending exactly what the cat had said, then she stopped in her tracks and twisted back to look at him. "*Ask* a tree if I can cut it down? Well, that's an angle I would not have thought of," she deadpanned. "Um, what happens if I don't ask it? Is it going to do something nasty to me?"

"Most assuredly."

"Ah, these are magical trees then," she said knowingly, bobbing her head.

"Naturally," Sylvester assured her. "This area resonates with magic. Therefore, its inhabitants are, by and large, almost all magical. Most magical creatures must live on magical lands."

"Why?"

"These days, they tend to distress nonmagical beings."

"I can see that. So, *pray tell*, just how far does this particular magical land extend?" Donnie asked with a devilish gleam in her eye.

The cat ignored her mockery and answered smugly, "Outside the valley, it runs for precisely twenty-four miles in every direction."

Donnie pursed her lips. "Let me guess, that's why there're no other humans living within twenty-five miles of here, right? Isn't that what you said earlier when you gave me that unbelievably long-winded lecture about my clothing?"

"You are correct."

"Okay, so why don't humans live closer to us? I seriously doubt they're aware the land is magical, so what's to keep them from settling here? Is there something in the water?" When Sylvester merely stared at Donnie for several seconds without speaking, she added, "You know, makes it taste bad or something like that."

The cat, still sitting on the horse's back with his tail wrapped tightly around his feet, blinked and intensified his stare, obviously perplexed. "I am unaware what water, bad tasting or otherwise, could possibly have to do with it," he finally intoned.

"Okay," Donnie sighed dramatically, just barely managing to stop herself from rolling her eyes heavenward, "instead of me guessing, how about you just tell me why no other humans live in these magical lands."

The cat looked at her as if she were a particularly dense specimen of her kind. "They are not magical creatures, of course," he said, clearly believing he was stating the obvious.

Donnie put the saw down carefully, leaned back on her hips, and crossed her arms in front of her. "Oh, I see, it's kind of a vicious circle then, innit? I mean, you can't be magical if you don't live in some part of the magical lands, but you can't live in any part of the magical lands if you're not magical. Well...I guess that'll certainly cut down on urban sprawl." She put a finger to her lip thoughtfully and tapped it, arching her right eyebrow as she enquired, "Does this mean that if I leave the area, my magic won't work?"

"No, your powers are permanent."

"Oh, goody," she drawled. "What happens if a nonmagical human does come onto the magical lands?"

"They become magical to some degree," the cat said, then admitted uncomfortably, "Mostly, they go mad from it."

"Why?" Donnie asked suspiciously.

"Because they fear magic so. Therefore, it weighs heavily upon their sanity."

She gave the cat a long look before pointing out, "I wonder what that says about me? Or haven't I been here long enough to tell whether I've gone mad yet?"

Again, Sylvester ignored her. "Catie always swore to the villagers that if only they would not fear the power in the land, but rather simply accept its existence, it would be far less harmful to them. Regardless, its effects would wear off within a day of their exiting the magical lands, and, since they needed Catie's salt, they ventured here whenever necessary."

"Ah, so it's fair to assume that nobody believed her about magic's effects, izzat right?" Donnie eyed Sylvester sardonically and quipped, "Imagine that, medieval villagers who don't trust the local witch; who'd have thunk it possible? Oh, by the way, where did Catie get all the salt? She didn't really refine it herself, did she, like she says in her journal?"

Rex called out to Donnie just then, running up to her at full speed and shouting excitedly, "Hey, Mama, the trees talk too! C'mere, c'mere, you gotta come talk to 'em! They're really nice and they're just dyin' to meet ya! Come on!" He grabbed the bottom of Donnie's shirt with his mouth and tugged.

As she was being led away, Sylvester called out to Donnie to remember to ask the trees before cutting them down. She waved a hand to indicate her agreement, then, under her breath, questioned who was crazier, her or him? Him for even suggesting such a silly thing, or her because she actually was going to try talking a bunch of magical trees into "letting" her cut them down.

Rex finally let go of her after being swatted lightly on the nose several times and ran on ahead. He stopped a few feet away from a small stand of very large, mostly ancient oak trees, and sat down, his ears perked straight up. As soon as she came within earshot, Donnie heard him telling about all the strange things that had been happening lately to him and his mama.

She decided this was a wonderful approach to take, and so she sat down nearby to listen to her dog's tale. She supplemented Rex's story whenever necessary, mainly where he didn't know the details. They chatted with the trees for nearly fifteen minutes, with Rex embellishing his part in the story only a little—for him, that is. He seemed to have picked up Donnie's habit of effusive hyperbole now that he could talk.

Many of the trees all around them displayed suitable interest in Rex's chronicle of woe, actually nodding their branches and emitting sympathetic tut-tuts in response to his emotional recounting of his ordeal. And they very kindly asked questions in all the right places in order to keep the conversation rolling along rather nicely, their rumbling voices emanating from deep within their trunks.

Finally, Rex's overly dramatic narrative came to an end, allowing Donnie to broach the subject she'd come about. Her dog had explained how their belongings were just sitting there, completely unprotected from the elements—"They're strewn *all* over the yard, can you believe it?"—and how he was just beside himself with worry as to how they were ever going to fit everything into that little bitty cottage, especially with winter coming on so soon. It's just terrible the way he was expected to—

Donnie interrupted him in the middle of his plaints to venture as cheerfully as she could, "Don't suppose you'd like to help us out with that situation, would you?"

A gnarled old apple tree, situated off to her right, piped up suddenly to ask, "How can we be of assistance to you, Donemere of the Codlebærn?"

"Well," she began delicately, her face registering surprise at the name she was apparently to be called here, "see, where we come from, wood is one of the best building materials around. It's strong, solid, lasts a long, long time, all that. And so, I was wondering if I could, er, well, if any of you would, um, if a few of you wouldn't mind, say...allowing me to use you for the floor, walls and roof of some new rooms on the cottage? Er, obviously it would mean I'd have to cut you down...well, I imagine you know what I'm saying." She stopped there, realizing that she had probably said quite enough.

The trees grew quiet for some while, during which time Rex stared at his mama reproachfully. She shrugged diffidently in return, mouthing to him, "Sylvester said I had to ask them that!"

Bryn Ddu (who Donnie immediately rechristened Brindle upon hearing his real name), a particularly large oak, finally spoke up and said, "I am more than twenty-one thousand years old and have spent many ages of my life moving all around the magical lands, but now that they have diminished so greatly, a tree cannot travel as before. I, like my brethren, have been forced to root myself permanently and, while I have accepted my fate, it has become wearisome to stand in only one place, knowing I shall die and be of little use to anyone. I find now I am yearning for change." He hesitated for a moment more before adding decisively, "You may use me for your magical house, Donemere of the Codlebærn."

Other trees chimed in that they too wished to experience a different future from what they had envisioned until now. A future which would not leave them rooted to one spot simply to wither and die, to become nothing more than a mute, worthless monument to their rich, vibrant history.

"Why are the magical lands shrinking? I don't understand." Donnie asked Brindle, after thanking the trees profusely.

The mighty oak responded slowly. "There was a great battle some years past between men and the powers of darkness," he said. "Men prevailed, but, in doing so, many fair magical creatures were forced to make the exodus to Canavar. 'Tis the age of men now, and our time is coming to a close. You and your friend here are the most powerful magical creatures we have met in a very long time. Few remain who can hear our voices, and most of the trees outside your realm no longer even have theirs. This place is one of the few strongholds of magic left."

"But there are others?" By now, Donnie was standing in front of the old oak. She reached out a sympathetic hand to caress its bark.

Brindle soughed deeply. "There are but a few, and they are spread too far apart for a tree to move between without becoming rooted. We must stay here, next to the Codlebærn farm, or we too shall lose our voices."

"Then you will keep your voices when you become part of my magical house, as you call it." Donnie made this a statement of fact, then was nonplussed by the small wave of blue light that unexpectedly rushed outward from her body.

Accepting the trees' cries of gratitude, she pointed out, "After all, if I'm the most powerful witch ever, as Sylvester assures me I am, I should at least be able to offer you that comfort, wouldn't you think?" She then outlined her plan to them. They, in turn, gave her instructions on just where to cut.

She remembered reading in Catie's journal that whenever she needed wood, the little witch would use a spell that would soften any tree for a day, letting her cut through it like churned butter. Keeping this thought in her head and willing it to be so, Donnie canted:

"To make the day a good one,
Tree and bark are not so much,
To cut by hand and shape to touch,
With which to build a house, as such.
The day shall indeed be a good one,
When loving hands make the house a wood one."

The trees who had volunteered shimmered with a bright blue light. In a quiet voice, Brindle told her they were ready.

Donnie went to get the saw, while Rex cavorted amongst the trees. They seemed to like his presence, even his somewhat nonsensical chatter. She smiled broadly at her pup. Although he might not be the brightest bulb in the package, he had more personality than any other dog she'd ever known. And a vocabulary that seemed to grow exponentially with each passing hour.

"Say, Sylvester, thanks for the tip about the trees," she said as she approached him and the horse. "A bunch of them agreed to be part of the new rooms. Too many in fact. I may have to build more rooms than I planned, since they all want to be used."

"Yes, like most of us, the trees have a keen desire to feel useful. Catie endeavored to befriend them on several occasions. Unfortunately, though she could sense the souls of all magical trees on her lands, she attained real discourse with only the strongest weald spirits, for her strengths lay in other directions."

"Oh? And what directions would those be?"

"Well, for one, her powers of prophecy were unerring whenever she put them to use. For another, she became a mistress of time travel. Regrettably, it has been her undoing."

"What do you mean, her *undoing*? How's she undone? What's happened to her?" Donnie asked in rapid succession, her curiosity greatly aroused.

But Rex came bounding up to them just then, calling excitedly, "Hey, Mama, guess what I found! A whole nest of those little black and white thingies that kinda look like Sylvester and kinda don't. Whaddya call them? Oh, that's right, skunks! Remember when I chased that one on the mountain when I was little?" He sat down and cocked his head inquiringly, his nose scrunched up and a painful look on his features. "And you yelled at me for a real long time and smashed those itty bitty tomatoes all over me when we got home—'member?"

Donnie vividly recalled the incident. It had happened in late spring, a few weeks after she'd adopted the dog as a puppy of seven months' age. They'd gone for a lengthy, evening hike in the headlands, where the overzealous dog had flushed out a grandfatherly skunk. The ride home had been unforgettable, even with all the windows down. The vehicles behind and around her car had given them a wide berth for the entire two hours they spent sitting in Saturday night traffic waiting to traverse the City.

Once they'd gotten home, Donnie found she had nothing, not even tomato juice, with which to de-skunk the dog, and it was far too late to go to the pet supply store. Unfortunately, the only tomatoes she had in the house were cherry tomatoes, so she'd mashed those all over Rex's head, where he'd been sprayed directly by the skunk. When this hadn't seem to work too well, she'd tried vinegar. Neither were successful in ridding him of the skunk smell, but after putting them both through all that trauma, she'd found she had a dog *and* a house that smelled like a skunky salad. It was impossible to tell, by that point, who was the more miserable.

"And you smell like that again, don't you, my love?" Donnie observed with amusement, noting that oh-so distinct perfume in the air around her dog.

"Well, sure! It's not a very good smell, though, is it? It kinda makes my eyes water," he said, his nose somehow scrunching up even more than it already was. "Three or four of the skunks almost sprayed me, but only one of 'em actually got me, and that was mostly on my tail. I'm teaching 'em how to play keep-away and, boy, are we havin' fun! I'm actin' the part of the ball. Then they all hide behind trees and jump out when I race by, sprayin' for all they're worth! They're real quick on the draw, but I run way too fast for 'em!" Rex declared proudly.

"Yeah, okay," Donnie said with a shudder, deciding it was best for Rex to make friends his own way without interference from her. "But later today you're getting a good scrubbing, little mister! And you can tell your newfound friends that if you guys ever do this again, I will hunt them down and bring them back to the house. I will then de-skunk them with a bath exactly like the one you're going to get! And I will do that every time they skunk you in the future."

"Um, but Mama," the dog protested, "I don't think you can de-skunk a skunk that way, can you?"

"No, but I'm guessing that if they have to feel your pain just once, they'll never spray you again. I want you to promise me that after today, you will not play the object to be kept away, because if you do..." Donnie shook her finger at the dog and let her words trail off.

Rex grinned, pearly white teeth gleaming brightly amidst his grey-black muzzle, and agreed, "Okay, okay. Can I go back now? We haven't finished our game!"

Donnie shrugged, as if to actually say, *I don't care what you do today.*

Rex stood, his tail wagging furiously, and shouted, "I love you, Mama!" And with that, the dog was off, darting back into the forest.

Donnie smiled after him, very glad her full store of de-skunking cleanser had arrived with his trunk.

When she turned around to continue her conversation with Sylvester, she found he was gone. She spied him running up the hillside and toward the house. Well, well, it seemed the cat was developing quite a repertoire of avoidance mechanisms, wasn't he? She'd have to work on that aspect of his personality, see if she could trick him into giving away at least part of the ghost.

Donnie picked up the saw and headed back to the forest. Before an hour's time was through, she had felled the six trees who had volunteered themselves, cut them into the proper lengths where they lay, and was soon engaged in sawing them into planks. It was hard going, even though the spell worked beautifully and allowed her blade to slash through the wood quite easily. She found that whenever she touched the trees with her hands, their wood became much lighter, allowing her to manipulate them with ease. Shaping the timber into planks and boards was, by far, the most difficult part. But a simple string, attached to both ends of a log, sufficed as a guide to make a straight cut.

In another hour or two, all that remained of the trees were six massive piles of planks and smaller boards, and one large jumble of small tree limbs, twigs and leaves. Brindle advised Donnie to leave the tangled mass where it was, as many forest creatures would come round later to take what they needed to fortify their nests and dens. Within a few weeks, he assured her, the debris would be cleared and many homes would be much warmer and drier this winter. It was the way of the weald, he said, for trees to provide shelter for their neighbors by shedding a portion of their limbs every year. He then remarked dryly that, in this regard, it looked to be a particularly bountiful year for the animal nations.

Donnie acknowledged this with a bemused nod. She'd never thought of it like that whenever she'd seen tree limbs carpeting the forest floor. She considered this to be a very nice way indeed for trees to behave, and she told him so in a warm voice. He was silent for a time, and when he respectfully reminded her, " 'Tis the way of the weald," she could tell that he had been quite puzzled by her encomium.

She nodded again, more thoughtfully this time, then looked around her, studying the thick flush of vegetation that ran along the rim of the valley. She sensed numerous eyes staring back at her, each of them avidly curious, although none held either fear or malice in their depths. The woodland inhabitants seemed simply to accept her presence now and, she realized (greatly startled by this revelation), they could actually feel her soul, the same as she could theirs.

How funny; she no longer felt as though she'd just been abandoned here in this strange land. Oddly comforted by this discovery, Donnie smiled to herself and returned her attention to the task at hand. Her next obstacle would be to find a way to get the lumber nearer the house. She eyed the horse dubiously, deciding he would not thank her if she hitched him up to the wagon and made him pull that massive load down the hill and up the rise to the house, especially since she could only touch a few of the thick, heavy planks at one time, so most of them would remain their normal weight. No, the horse would certainly rebel if she tried that. And she wouldn't blame him one bit.

She called out loudly to her familiar, "Hey, Sylvester, you there? I'm done shaping all the trees into planks and I was wondering if I should just sort of float them back to the house? Oh, heavens, I just thought of something: do I need a wand to do that kind of magic? Sylvester?"

The cat lifted his head above the tall grass so that he could now be seen. He was about halfway up the hill below the house, where he'd gotten quite involved in chasing noseeums. "I must admit," he began slowly, "I am astounded that you have finished shaping all planks so quickly. That I had not expected. No, I had not expected that at all." He paused thoughtfully and stared at her across the distance between them for a few moments. "You should make an attempt at using your levitation skills," he finally instructed her, "so do that first. If you fail, there are other methods you may use, but they are more difficult and, at present, I am not prepared to have you try them. Yes-yes, I believe levitation will serve your purposes and will be one of the easier tasks for you to master. I will watch you from here to see how well you take to your powers without direction. As to your inquiry regarding a wand, 'tis my understanding that all wands seek out their master or mistress by themselves. You must wait for yours to find you. Until then, you will learn to wield your magic without one.

"Tomorrow," here, the cat paused for effect, "we begin your magic lessons in earnest." With this foreboding announcement, he disappeared back into the grass, presumably to critique her form.

Donnie wondered nervously how she was supposed to begin. Up 'til now, she'd only said a couple of spells and materialized one thing, and that only by accident. Nothing all that grand, certainly not on the scale of levitating hundreds and hundreds of huge planks across the valley, hundreds of feet away. She thought about some of the TV shows and movies she'd seen in the past that were about witchcraft. How did the witches in them usually do it? Was she supposed to write a spell for it, or was there a particular motion she was required to use?

In the end, she tried the most straightforward method she could think of. She flung her arm wide while she concentrated hard on one of the planks, visualizing it floating up into the air and down the hill, to the back yard. It, and several of its nearest companions, instantly shot high into the air, then zoomed at a downward angle to somewhere behind the house. Donnie heard them crash to the ground with loud bangs and groans of bewilderment.

"I am so sorry!" she shouted across the valley, then sheepishly looked down at the remaining pile of lumber from that particular tree to add, "I am such an idiot! I honestly didn't mean to do that to you and I am very, very sorry."

After this reprimand to herself, she straightened her shoulders and stood tall. *It's also one heck of a start*, she encouraged herself silently and tried again. This time, she neither concentrated nor flung her arm quite so hard. The planks floated gently down toward the farm and stacked themselves neatly into one big pile of raw wood. In no time at all, she had every one of the planks and boards moved to the back yard. A hardly noticeable small wave of blue shot out from her midriff, right when she looked up at the sky, totally thrilled with her efforts so far. She marveled at how electric the heavens seemed to be today, then gathered up her equipment and scrambled clumsily onto the big horse. He shuffled down the hill and up to the farm. It was lunchtime.

Donnie took the lead rope off her steed and left him grazing in the front yard. She stepped up onto the little wooden stoop and then, the front door (which up to this point had behaved just as any door should) suddenly swung open on its own. Taken aback, Donnie hurried into the house, desperately hoping the darned thing wouldn't close behind her. It did not. After watching the door for a minute or so, and it doing nothing in the meantime, she turned toward the pantry, wondering what other surprises were in store for her now that she was magical. Not feeling particularly overjoyed at that prospect, she had what had become her usual midday repast of bread and cheese, eating quickly so that she could continue her home improvement project, her mood lightening again with the replenishment of fuel for her body.

When she was finished with her meal, she moved hesitantly toward the front door. She was relieved to find the thing behaved itself, although she practically darted past it to escape to the outside, admonishing herself with a murmured "Scaredy-cat," as soon as her feet touched the wooden stoop.

Once outside, she picked her way through her belongings to the trunk that held her music. She randomly chose another CD and popped it into the player. As soon as the first strains of "Flash to Dash" by Wooden Nickel emanated from the stereo, she went looking for her toolboxes. She searched in her largest for her compartmentalized nail box and took out a 20d nail, setting it on the wide ledge of the toolbox. By golly, she was going to try her hand at replicating them! After a moment's thought, Donnie canted:

"Take this one and find two,
Take those two and make them four,
Take those four and birth a score,

Take that score and times it four,
Take those four score and render four more."

Before long, she had hundreds of nails. Then she replicated a few hundred 60d nails just in case she needed them. She put on her tool belt and filled the front pockets with nails. Digging farther into the toolbox drawer, she withdrew a six-inch long, one-inch diameter bolt, the only one left of those she'd bought to reinforce certain portions of her house in San Francisco in case of earthquakes. Bolts like this would be perfect to attach the addition to the existing stonework of the house. While drilling them into the stone was not going to be easy, she felt she could manage it. Especially if she concentrated really, really hard on them.

She laid the bolt on her palm, this time deciding to try something different: she simply asked politely for two hundred replicates. She got them instantly. They, of course, all materialized in a great mass right above her hand. This thick cloud of glinting aluminum fell to the ground the moment it appeared. Numerous errant bolts bounded up around her feet, making her hop madly and shout, "Ow, ow, ow, ow, ow! Talk about steel stilettos, you empty-headed, moronic, foolhardy—" She went on to include more of her most colorful epithets while she soundly berated herself. When she was finally finished with her hissy fit and the pain in her shins had subsided, she got down on her haunches to collect the bolts, shoving a bunch of them into her tool belt, with the remainder getting crammed into the toolbox drawer.

Now fully equipped with nails and bolts, Donnie grabbed the portable toolbox with her right hand and the boombox with her left, then trudged to the back of the house. The Hawks' "Lovin' Tonight" came on. She noticed that the animals had followed her to the back yard; was it her imagination or were they actually groovin' to the music? Even Sylvester appeared mesmerized. Hiding a grin, Donnie got to work on building the new rooms.

Using levitation, she laid down two narrow boards running parallel to each other, about ten feet apart. Again using levitation, she placed some wider planks across their lengths, on top of the two bottom boards. She walked around and nudged the planks with her foot to make sure they were positioned evenly along the two-by-fours. When she was satisfied that it was all square, she reached into a pocket of the tool belt and pulled out a handful of 20d nails. She made them float about six inches above her hand, grinning with pleasure at the sight. Man, she was really getting the hang of this magic stuff pretty easily!

She flung her arm toward the planks. The nails hit the wooden surface awkwardly, then rolled and flipped around, scattering all over the yard. Donnie hung her head, shoulders slumped dejectedly. So much for getting the hang of magic on her first try. She shook herself and straightened her shoulders. Holding out her hand again, she willed the errant nails to float up and come to rest gently upon her palm.

She barely managed to move in time to keep from getting pierced by several of the sharp projectiles that sailed toward her. Donnie's whole body drooped as she stared dismally at the one nail she'd managed to actually catch. "You are making your point beautifully, you know," she complained to it.

Abruptly, the boombox stopped playing the Stone Chairs' "Locomotive Roar," cutting off the last few notes of the hard-driving song. It skipped into the smooth ballad "This Home Is Yours" by Ferris, Thompson and Jacksbridge. Donnie looked over at the thing and cocked her head to the side with a quizzical brow. "Now, those are two songs I wouldn't think I'd ever put back-to-back on a CD. Wonder what I was smokin' that day?" But the song was perfectly timed. She *had* been thinking about giving up her home improvement dreams because it was turning out to be much harder than she would've thought, even with magic. Listening to the song now, though, reminded her of just how wonderful it is to have the kind of home you really want.

Yep, the home improvement plan was here to stay, she decided, gritting her teeth and trying harder to control the magic in her fingertips. She concentrated on floating only one nail to her hand. When it hit her palm, it had the head turned toward her skin so, while it stung, it did no real damage. She tried again and again, finally finding just the right balance of will and concentration. Next, she tried two nails, and was once again successful in not maiming herself permanently. She increased the number of nails she was manipulating until she'd gotten up to sixteen. Then she began practicing making them drive themselves into one of the extra boards.

Learning how to drive the nails into a board at the same time only took Donnie about five minutes to master. She also practiced removing them. Whenever a nail became too bent, she'd float up another to replace it in the four rows of nails hovering above her hand. When she felt she was ready, she again floated all sixteen nails above her hand. She repeated her movements of before, flinging her arm toward the carefully assembled planks on the ground.

This time, the nails shot straight into the two layers of wood, one row at the top and another at the bottom, with each nail drilled in exactly where she'd imagined they should go. She was positively giddy with excitement. She could do this! She really could build her house, all by herself, just using her ingenuity and this gift of magic that had been bestowed upon her, she told herself, her heart swelling with pride.

Unnoticed by all because the surrounding area still glowed with a bluish cast from the induction of her magic the night before, another faint, pale blue wave of power pulsed outwardly from her midsection at practically the same moment as when she raised a fist and shouted, "Woo-hoo!"

Donnie continued flinging nails into the wood until all the planks were nailed securely to the frame and she had a solid section of flooring. Levitating this square into place, she quickly built the necessary bracing for underneath it. She then attached the flooring to the masonry of the house with several of the bolts. She'd been absolutely right; when she concentrated hard enough, the bolts seemed to almost melt through the wood and into the stone wall. She repeated this process for the remainder of the flooring and for each outer and inner wall, and also for installing the rafters and the rest of the roofing framework. Within a couple of hours, she'd built three rooms that were securely attached to the existing stone structure.

She began to build the roofs. This took her another hour, mostly due to making sure her measurements were accurate. When she had the roofs finished, she stepped back and admired her handiwork. They looked nice and solid, their peaks perfectly formed. Obviously, she'd have to cover them with thatch before winter set in, presupposing she could figure out what thatch actually was and where to get it. She'd also have to come up with a water-proofing resin for the wood. But she had a little time yet for all that; it shouldn't be needed for at least a month or more.

The smallest room, attached to her bedroom, would become the bathroom; the second her office and library, with its inner doorway opening into the kitchen and an outer door opening to a porch she had yet to build; and the third room she just might use as a workshop since Catie's was rather cramped, what with the mammoth forge and all those barrels of salt and assorted cauldrons stored in it. This last room Donnie had built on the other side of the house and was quite the largest of the three new rooms.

But it was now time for creating the inner doorways into the existing part of the little stone cottage. She started small, willing just one stone to dematerialize at first. It shimmered, went transparent, then re-solidified. Grunting at the effort, she tried again several times, to no avail.

Sylvester eventually took pity on his new pupil and offered this bit of advice, "You must have a destination in mind for the stone."

That's what I forgot with the bolts, was to say where I wanted them to materialize! Donnie thought to herself, glancing round and mumbling self-consciously, "Oh, thanks; that makes sense." Trying again, she dematerialized the stone to the field above the back yard. Instantly, it disappeared from the wall. Once more, the air all around glowed momentarily with a hint of cerulean, an occurrence which, although Donnie noticed this time, she also studiously ignored. She methodically dematerialized stone after stone until rough rectangles were opened for both the office and workshop doors.

Eyeing the opening that led into the office, she dematerialized one-half of an offset stone. Again, though it was plodding work, she painstakingly worked through the offset stones, shaving off just what was needed to make the opening smooth enough to hang a door frame around. She repeated this same process for the inside doorway to the workshop and for the doorway from her bedroom into the bathroom.

After that she built and attached the door frames, along with the frames for the big window in each of the two larger rooms and the smaller one for the bathroom. All this in one day, and she still had well over half the lumber left for more building projects. She might even add on those other rooms and make the cottage's floorplan the same as it was in 2025!

"Just look at that," she purred, gazing at her handiwork proudly. "When I get back home, I'll bet I can carve out a fine little niche for myself in the home improvement blogosphere!"

The cat stared at her as if he thought her a loon after she made this unfathomable remark. Since this had early on become his choice expression to present to her, he now had it perfected. So much so, that Donnie, upon noticing it, shrugged her shoulders and conceded, "Well, okay, maybe that's not the best utilization of my new skills."

She set to work constructing the covered porch that would run around the entire back of the house. While she was working on the one step up to the deck, "In September" came on. Bad Blood was one of her favorite groups and her voice rose in unison with the recording. Out of the corner of her eye, she saw that the animals were definitely grooving now. She herself took some time out from throwing nails to dance up and down the unfinished step and onto the porch.

A song later came "Wasting the Day." The horse soon began swinging his head in time with the bluesy music. And then he shivered in ecstasy, his snowy white coat rippling in the late afternoon sunshine. When the song ended, he immediately swung his head around to look at Donnie, whinnied loudly to get her attention, and gave her one of the biggest smiles she'd ever seen in her life. "Might you repeat that melody, please? If that is possible?" he asked.

What, did every animal around here talk? An astonished Donnie replied, "Um, sure," and walked over to the boombox to hit the *Back* button, cutting off the next song a few bars in. Otis Waters' classic rendition began again. Donnie also obligingly cranked up the volume. The horse proceeded to sing the full chorus and much of the words in the verses, which was very amusing for Donnie.

She told herself not to stare at the animals, but that was impossible. The cow was swinging her head in time with the beat and the horse was stepping forward and backward or side to side as the music moved him. As Waters' famous whistling faded, both animals begged Donnie to repeat the song yet again. She shook her head and said, "Nope, that's it. While I love that tune dearly, I have absolutely no desire to hear it three times in a row. Besides, if you like that one so much, you're really gonna love this next one."

Little Davy Ray's "Cold Heart" had come on and, as she'd predicted, the animals went wild. Donnie noticed out of the corner of her eye that even Sylvester's head was bobbing and his body twitching in time with the guitar riffs. She hid a wide grin and finished nailing the last of the facing onto the long step. The next song was the Harringtons' version of "Heard It on the Street." It finally had everybody dancing in the back yard, even the chickens.

Rex came back just as Donnie was attaching the door hinges and hanging the doors. He said he'd only been caught two more times by the skunks and wasn't that pretty good? His mama finished what she was doing *very* quickly, then pointed her finger toward the front yard, keeping her other hand over her mouth and nose. She followed her aromatic pooch over to the well, filled the bucket with water and drenched him with it, filling the bucket again with fresh water immediately. She doused Rex three times with the de-skunking solution and finally pronounced him fit to be around without needing a gas mask. By now, it was nearly dinnertime and Donnie had to get a move on. She still had to transfer her possessions into the new rooms.

Chapter 3
She's Gone

Donnie moved her belongings into the house that evening while there was still just enough light to see what she was doing, sending all manner of things floating through the outer doors in great batches into their assigned rooms, where they seemed almost to settle into place by themselves. Anything breakable she carried in manually if it was light enough or levitated in by itself, not trusting her control over her magic to float more than one fragile article at a time.

All the while, the cat watched her closely, providing an increasing number of superfluous instructions and dire warnings, already beginning his campaign to drive her nuts with his unrelenting pedagogy. But whenever Donnie was out of earshot, to himself he muttered a string of peevish cavils, beginning with, "Why did she demand that all of this nonsense be brought with her? Most of these monstrosities cannot possibly have any real purpose!" then, "How can she be acquiring these Gordian skills so readily? Catie complained once that it had taken her nearly an entire new moon to learn the art of levitation properly, and yet this foolhardy novice is mastering it on her first day of magic? I would believe that to be impossible but for the fact that I have witnessed it with my own eyes!" followed by, "Considering the amount of power she is wielding, one would expect Donemere to encounter even more difficulty than other witches of lesser *ilca* have when first entering the realm of Wiccecræft—and yet she is not. Each thaumaturgical skill she has attempted, while commanded most errantly to be sure, on the whole has been controlled and accomplished resourcefully, with uncommon dexterity for a Yfel Witch. A mere initiate, she is!" he snorted. "Can it be that Donemere truly is the only Codlebærn fit for her intended destiny? Is it possible that she will become Fægre by the time that destiny calls to her, which assuredly it must before another year passes? If so, then I perceive that she will be most difficult to instruct in the skills of her craft, for they will present no challenge to her. Given her recalcitrant temperament, married with her considerable aptitude, she means only to provide certain vexation for me, that much I can see. I see also that I must reconsider my intended approach to her lessons!" and then, " 'Tis fortunate Donemere does not yet possess a wand to focus her power even more efficiently than she is doing currently, without that most sacred of magical aids. I dare not even contemplate the consequences of what might happen then. Bah!" he spat. "The gods have not set me an easy task with this witch!"

Finally, after having watched his new charge float well over half of her strange and bewildering belongings into the house with practically no missteps in her magic (discounting the wobbliness of her early efforts, resulting in more than a few, frantic near-misses), the cat turned to the heavens and demanded to know, "As if Catie herself has not caused sufficient anxiety for me these long centuries, what manner of *dewines problemau* have I been burdened with this time? I tell you, Gwydion, I do not need this labor! I foresee an arduous path ahead of me, one riddled with unwonted hindrances, most of which shall undoubtedly be raised by Donemere herself!"

Donnie filled the back of the office with her bookshelves, the books still neatly organized in each one, and cleared some space for Catie's tomes by stacking her own books and magazines from two shelves onto materials of other shelves. Miraculously, she managed to cram all of Catie's books onto the two open shelves by also stacking them on top of each other. Twelve of Donnie's eighteen bookshelves were arranged in three rows, back-to-back, with the remaining six lined up against three of the walls in the room in sets of two. She left gaps for the only window and also for the fireplace she planned to build on the east wall using the masonry instructions she'd found in Catie's journal when she'd searched through it again. She would build the fireplace as soon as she'd plumbed the bathroom, which lay directly on the other side of the wall, then she'd duct some of the fire's heat into the bathroom.

The glass for her new windows she materialized from a place Catie recommended in her journal. Catie wrote that there were legions of window panes there, all stored in row upon row in this one particular room. Catie herself had gotten the cathedral-like panes for the main room and the bedroom from there. The journal's description of this window repository was detailed enough for Donnie to visualize it in order to take the glass she needed and actually included a spell to do so. She was thrilled that she could materialize something by description only, albeit using someone else's directions and spell instead of her own, which Sylvester informed her is not how you're supposed to work magic. Magic is an individual experience and every witch must make his or her own way with it, he reproached.

And although each of the windows was beautiful, delicately formed into incredibly detailed images with hundreds of pieces of multi-colored leaded glass, Donnie had to admit that she was rather embarrassed they were stolen goods. She hadn't set out to become a thief, though. After charming her bookshelves to always make it easy for her to find a specific book or books on a particular subject she was researching just by walking up to one of the shelves and thinking about what she wanted so that it would appear in front of her, she'd found a book on blowing glass. She hadn't even realized that she owned a book which detailed the process, but there it was nevertheless. Unfortunately, according to the book, blowing glass demanded long experience and real skill. Reluctantly, she felt she had no choice but to follow Catie's journal instructions to the letter.

The three panes Donnie had snatched were based solely upon their dimensions, so imagine her surprise when they also turned out to be strikingly beautiful. How could she feel bad once she saw them? Besides, it wasn't likely the original owner of the glass would find their way here, was it? She finally managed to convince herself that it was a petty crime at most and thereafter serenely admired the colorful panes firmly ensconced in their new sills with the light of the rising moon filtering through their artistically intricate flora and fauna images. She couldn't help but wonder what had happened to them by the year 2025 because the windows then were just plain old, clear, double-paned glass. The house was warmer with those, sure, but not nearly so interesting.

Donnie hung the moss-colored sheers that had originally been in her family room in the City in front of the window in the new office. Her Georgian desk and mirror also went into this room, as did the olive-colored, sateen-covered sofa, recliner and armchair, and the walnut coffee and side tables. She decided to go ahead and set up the walnut entertainment center and computer desk, complete with their associated electronics, not knowing what else to do with them. Her small art glass and crystal collections she spread around the room on various surfaces. Her paintings and other artwork she'd save to decorate the remaining rooms of the house.

When she'd finished in the office, Donnie stepped back to the doorway and surveyed the overall effect. The room was delightfully rustic; peaceful, yet still inviting curiosity and learning.

She artfully managed to fit all of her bedroom furniture into the bedroom. It didn't leave much room to walk around, just three or four feet or so all around the bed. Other than the bed frame and the wardrobe, the furniture was heavy wicker, painted in a light moss color with white accents, giving the room the illusion of space. She placed her thick, white chenille bedspread on the bed over her moss-green down comforter with a satisfied grin.

There hadn't been much she could do about the straw mattress, other than cover it with her worst sheets and lay another white down comforter on top of that. She realized that she would literally have to "make" the bed on a daily basis to stave off bedbugs. Her experience with them, from day one here, had brought home to her what truly nasty little creatures they could be.

As a final touch to the room, she placed a large, soft, white woven-yarn rug on the floor beside the bed.

Donnie moved Catie's kitchen furniture to the workroom at the back of the stables, along with the rest of the little witch's roughly hewn bedroom and sitting room furniture. Some of Catie's personal belongings Donnie stored in her office and workshop since Sylvester wouldn't let her pack them away in the hayloft above the stables, which was accessed by Catie's workshop via a narrow staircase. Catie's complete and prolific set of thirty-two journals, many of which had been strewn haphazardly around the old workshop at the back of the stables, also went onto the bookshelves in Donnie's office, stacked in front of other books. And when she came upon Catie's small silver hairbrush and mirror set, with oddly familiar, finely raised glyphs of some sort and whorling designs in both gold and silver upon their backs, even Donnie murmured, "Can't part with those, if you'll pardon the pun." She wrapped these in a black velvet cloth bag and placed them carefully in the cupboard in her office.

Again, not knowing what else to do with them, she moved her kitchen appliances into the main room, even though there was no electricity for the fridge, the convection microwave oven and the dishwasher, or gas for the stove. While she hadn't intended to do this, she realized that she was already beginning to formulate in her mind a rather vague plan to one day provide power or fuel as needed for each.

She furnished the makeshift kitchen area, centered around the fireplace and complete with knotty pine cabinets high and low from her kitchen in San Francisco, with her matching breakfast table and its six chairs. Her white-washed oak formal dining set and its two matching oak hutches and sideboard containing all her dishes and cookware also went into this spacious room. The hutches and sideboard she placed as close to the kitchen area as possible, leaving space only for the door to her office, while the dining table and its ten chairs sat just a few feet away from both the front door and the door to Donnie's workshop, in the opposite corner from the pantry.

After she finished moving and rearranging things in the kitchen, she started on her workroom. This room was somewhat narrow and very long. She decided it would be perfect for storing her tools and other junk that had been kept in her garage in San Francisco, in addition to a few, odd pieces of furniture from around the house. To the left of the inside workroom door was her long, butcher-block worktable. She hung some pegboard above that and put most of her tools up there on pegs. Beside the worktable, right behind the door that led to the rest of the house, were her power tools and two tool cabinets. She made sure that everything here was neat and orderly, so all tools could be found easily when sought. On the other side of the worktable, in the corner there, she planned to build another fireplace. For the time being though, she left the corner mostly bare, placing just the stand for her second, smaller TV and its associated electronics.

Across the room from the worktable she put the low, knotty-pine coffee table and its matching side tables that had come from her sitting room. Between these were her two wingback red Corinthian leather chairs. The matching leather couch, like her bed mattress, also appeared to be missing. Donnie hadn't realized that this morning when she'd unpacked her trunks, so she asked Sylvester about it now.

It was at this point that the boombox displayed its puzzling behavior again. Earlier, Donnie had set it on the floor next to the TV stand and, as soon as she inquired about the couch, the boombox suddenly cut to the middle of the Phantoms' ethereal "She's Gone." Donnie turned her head to stare down at the boombox, as she had earlier in the afternoon, her head cocked to one side and a deep frown knitting her brow. The volume suddenly increased when the song hit the chorus and spoke of the woman no longer being where she should be. Donnie listened to the song a few moments, somewhat bewildered by it, then decided her best course would be to ignore the whole thing and put the boombox's increasingly peculiar actions down to either a skipping CD or a waning battery.

Sylvester sat on the worktable watching the play of emotions on his new pupil's face silently. He finally replied that another female had been sleeping on the couch at Donnie's home and, like the girl on the mattress, Catie hadn't wanted to disturb her. From the description he gave of the woman, Donnie knew it must have been Liz, which meant Julia hadn't had to do much explaining about Donnie's missing things. What the two of them must have thought about the sudden disappearance of her furnishings, she couldn't even venture a guess.

After the darkly mysterious song ended, Lester Carlysle's "Stand Still" began emanating from the speakers, with the boombox gliding smoothly through the song as if nothing aberrant had occurred only a minute before. Shrugging uneasily, Donnie turned back toward the outside door of the workshop and resumed moving her furniture, boxes and other assorted oddball possessions into the workroom, carefully levitating the various pieces into place simultaneously or in long chains. She was determined to not let anything keep her from finishing tonight.

Beyond her workshop's sitting and work spaces, she hung the red velvet curtains from her former formal dining room, which, like most of her things, had arrived at the cottage fully assembled and intact. The curtains turned out to be an attractive method of separating the front of the room from the storage area behind, although, when closed, they did cut the light from the large window at the back of the room. Behind the curtains, she ringed the room with the chrome shelving that had come from her garage. Stored neatly upon the shelves were all her sports equipment, those tools that she couldn't give a home to in the front, and the assorted junk she'd accumulated over the years and kept in the back of the garage both in boxes and just lying loose. It somehow made it so much more homey to have it all packed back there.

Next, Donnie moved the bathroom fixtures into the new bathroom, levitating everything in except the shower stall. This, she soon found, wouldn't fit through the doorways of the house, which meant she'd have to materialize it into the room. She hadn't dematerialized anything nearly so large yet and she wasn't sure if the mechanics of sending it elsewhere would be different. Well, she was about to find out. Figuring an empty room would be safest, she once again floated everything else in it to the middle of the kitchen, then went back outside to where the shower stall stood.

Following Sylvester's uninvited instructions, she placed her hands on the cold marble and concentrated on dematerializing the entire stall from the front yard and rematerializing it into the empty bathroom. It shimmered for a few moments and slowly disappeared beneath her fingers. Donnie looked toward the porch where Sylvester was sitting and observed nervously, "It certainly went somewhere, didn't it?" She went back inside, the cat at her heels, and found the shower stall sitting in the middle of the bathroom, right where everything else had been a few minutes before. She would definitely have to work on her placement of things when she rematerialized them, which, she could see, was the most difficult part of materialization. Sending things was easy; making sure they arrived in the correct place was not. But it would come to her, Sylvester said, especially as she seemed to be learning magic uncommonly quick. Almost as though she were born to it, he added pensively.

Donnie stopped still, her face frozen with surprise. Her expression then sobered to a sort of enigmatic watchfulness. After a few moments' silent consideration, her eyes cleared. She told herself firmly to stick to the here and now, and to get her stuff inside. Until she had some real answers to her situation, she should refrain from obsessing over every casual remark the cat made, or at least she should *try* to keep obsessing about them. She forced her mind to focus back onto what she was doing and levitated the shower into a corner. Once it was safely tucked away, she floated her other bathroom stuff to the room again. She would arrange it all properly later, she decided.

When she had the remainder of her belongings moved into the house and had levitated the trunks to the hayloft, she built a fire in both the kitchen and bedroom fireplaces to stave off the nightly cold. Since she'd already used all the wood she'd brought inside the night before, she had to go out to the stables to replenish her stock from the huge stacks of it the elusive Catie had left for her there. It sure was a whole lot easier getting several pieces of the dry, split wood into the house tonight than it had been the day before.

That night, Donnie ate dinner on her best china, mostly because she felt she deserved her best china on this of all nights, and left the dirty dishes in the sink. Sleepily, she stumbled her way into the fire-lit bedroom, intending to fall onto the bed as soon as possible and pass out. She was thoroughly exhausted from both her mistrials and her successes of the day, and more than a little bemused at how perfectly her furnishings fit into each of the rooms, as if they'd been bought specifically for this house and its expanded floor plan.

Once she had the fire banked for the night, she changed into some clean pajamas, kissed Rex goodnight, and plopped down onto the side of the bed. Feeble fortunes, it sure felt good to get off her feet! She glanced at her watch as she removed it from her wrist and saw that its lighted dial read 2:38 am. No wonder she was so wiped out!

The boombox was sitting on the night table nearest to her, which was strange since she couldn't remember putting it there. She removed the CD she'd been playing earlier from its carriage and, seeing its jewel case sitting on top of the boombox, put the disk away. That was when she looked at the list of songs she'd created for the case. "She's Gone" was nowhere among the song titles.

Donnie drew back in surprise and dropped the jewel case onto the night table. It was the correct jewel case because it matched all the other songs and their order. Apprehensively, she picked up the CD case again, holding it at arm's length, and took it into her workroom, where she placed it on a shelf in the back of the room by the light of a candle she'd brought with her. She hoped she'd sleep more soundly with the screwy thing as far away from her as she could get it. She thought about destroying it, but decided she wanted to keep an eye on it in case it was haunted or possessed.

Feeling ridiculous, she whispered defensively to herself, "Well, it could be possessed. Anything's possible here, it seems," before padding nervously back to the bedroom.

Sleep came slowly and fitfully that night. Her dreams were wild and filled with numerous chase scenes from several of her favorite action movies, with Donnie herself acting as the heroine of each. The final dream of the night was again of the cave, but in this dream, she was herself. And this time, the dream seemed much more real.

She awoke from it abruptly, feeling savagely hunted by some unseen, malevolent force. Edgily, she rolled over and let her eyes close again, her thoughts racing. She forced her mind to still, to concentrate hard so that she could recall as much as possible about the dream. She'd been running, almost flying, down this gigantic tunnel carved through what looked to be solid rock, a tunnel which led to the same cave she'd dreamt of last night. Tonight, she'd been chased into the cave by an unbelievably large and fantastical creature whose body she couldn't remember seeing, except for its eyes, as it pursued her down the wide passage all the way to the cave. Whatever that thing was, its enormous eyes, each more than three feet wide, had been both fierce and minacious, a deep, angry orange in color, with a rim of brilliant yellow around their irises…and the pupils had been funny, they had dilated funny somehow…and there were flames reflected in their depths; violent, red-hot fingers of fire that she was sure would have engulfed her if she hadn't flown like a bat out of hell into the cave, where the dream ended.

She shivered, opened her eyes slowly, and stared at the moonlight streaming in through the window. The dream creature and its eyes, in addition to frightening her, had also left her with a lingering sadness, as though she'd done something terrible to the creature, something to warrant being chased by it. Donnie felt the pain and anger in its heart once more and knew it was all directed deliberately upon her. But why, she wondered, why was it angry with *her*? What had she done to cause it such pain, so much hurt that it wanted only to destroy her, to burn her to ashes?

After racking her brain for a few more minutes, she finally had to admit that she just couldn't remember that part of the dream. Perhaps she would dream it again and maybe then she'd know what she'd done to make the creature hate her so. Setting her mind toward sleep, only half-hoping to experience the dream again so she could recall its beginnings, she dozed intermittently over the next two hours until the dawn's groping fingers of light brightened the room.

When she arose from bed that morning and had received her good morning kiss from the dog, the boombox again exhibited its alarming behavior of the day before by coming to life on its own and playing "Blue Silk" by the Garthal Brothers, a song Donnie loved. When she realized that there was no CD in the boombox, she got dressed in record time and almost ran out of the room, closing the door firmly behind her and Rex.

Donnie sat for a long time at breakfast staring into space, fighting to keep her mind on an even keel. She purposely ignored the little blue bolts of magical power that kept escaping from her agitated fingertips and the strange feel of her bones and skin now, as though a billion tiny pinpricks were constantly being applied to them from some unseen force, making them alternately hot, then cold with amazing amounts of energy. She desperately did not want to think about the permanency of her situation, nor of how lonely she was going to be here with no one to remind her of what it meant simply to be human, instead of being yet another magical creature amongst many. She tried hard to convince herself that she should look upon this magic thing positively and just focus on all the good she could do with it, eventually bolstering her flagging spirits by reminding herself that she had too many things to do and some new talents to discover.

Now that the house was enlarged and her belongings safely stored within it, the next major task she set for herself was to rig together a plumbing system of copper pipes, complete with septic tank. This project she began her second morning of magic. The instructions in Catie's journals had included not only methods of handling metals and minerals, but also how best to mine them, and over the next several weeks, Donnie became proficient at materializing the raw materials she needed, refining them according to Catie's journals, and then molding them into the desired shapes in her workshop, materializing the molten metal directly from Catie's forge into the molds Donnie created.

Throughout most of these initial days, Donnie succeeded in keeping her conscious mind mostly fastened on what she was doing, always moving forward with her quest to make her living quarters as modern as possible. Her subconscious, though, was an entirely different matter. The disturbing, violent nightmares continued to possess her nights for weeks, especially the dream of being chased into the cave by the creature with the flaming, orange eyes—although sometimes she was chased there by several creatures just as large, but with piercing yellow eyes instead of the incendiary orange ones. Even nearly a month later, these haunting visions were still leaving her unrested and jittery when she awoke. She figured that they must be her subconscious's way of working out her anxieties regarding her new life and the changes wrought in her body chemistry by the fantastical magic which had, within a few days of invoking her power, infiltrated every nerve, every sinew, every bone, until she truly felt as though her body were no longer her own. Nevertheless, she was determined to persevere, resolutely shoving these underlying fears back down whenever they reared up to confront her during the daylight hours.

But no matter how hard she concentrated in the grey morning light, Donnie still could not recall the beginning of that one particular, terrifying dream. She always came awake as soon as she entered the cave and could never remember anything before the part where she was being chased down the tunnel toward the cavern. And each time she had the dream, she awoke feeling ever more bereft and melancholy toward the creature, completely unable to determine what it could possibly represent in her psyche.

To her daily magic lessons with Sylvester, she took a scientific approach, trying to work out the physics of each new skill as he suggested them, or as she herself thought them up. She had the feeling that the cat was amazed at her ingenuity (not that he ever let on about it, if he indeed was impressed), but he nevertheless constantly complained that Donnie was wasting precious time with this ludicrous modernization project of hers. She blithely ignored the cat's reproaches (and his accompanying belittlements) and plowed ahead with her plumbing plans.

She became quite adept at mixing manual labor with magic and purposely gave herself increasingly difficult tests of multitasking with her magic. Nothing was ever too heavy or too bulky to lift because she simply levitated or materialized things where she needed them. For instance, she didn't have to do any real digging with a shovel; rather, she levitated the shovel and set it into a pattern of digging. And dig it did; furiously, much faster than she would ever have been able to dig under her own physical power. And while the shovel was doing its thing in a corner of the back yard, and copper ore for the pipes was being refined and smelted in the forge in Catie's workshop, Donnie was in her own workshop measuring and fitting together the copper pipes she made. Strangely driven to achieve complete mastery over her powers, Donnie constantly strained her ability to set unsupervised magical tasks for various and unseen implements until she had this skill perfected.

Finally, it came time to actually lay the piping for the water and septic systems. Not telling the cat why she needed to know it, she explained to Sylvester that she wanted to be able to displace earth from a few feet down and replace it with something else, without having the earth around the hollow she'd created sink back in before she could fill the space. But, to do this, she'd have to see what she was doing. So how, she asked, would she go about performing a psychical magical act such as that?

Sylvester replied that she should begin by casting her mind into the Earth. At first Donnie couldn't understand what he wanted her to do and continued to question him until he finally yelled caustically at her to stop thinking of the world as existing only above the surface, but to listen to the planet, hear its rhythms and its echoes. Doing this would tell her what was occurring around and below her and would give her mind a clearer picture of what she wanted to see. He ordered her to sit on the ground, with her palms flat upon it, and listen to what was going on below. What he did not confess for some long while was that this was a skill which Catie had learned on her own and he therefore only knew of it what few remarks she'd made about what happened when she did it and what he'd noticed when he'd seen her perform it; hence his increasingly ill-tempered frustrations with Donnie's queries.

But since Donnie didn't know this at the time, she rolled her eyes at his captious remonstrations and sighed, then plopped down heavily on the ground in order to attempt what the cat had told her to do. Eventually, she was able to filter out the sounds of the wind in the trees, the birds as they sang, and the insects buzzing on the plants in the yard until all was silent and she could focus only on what was happening beneath her. She heard the rhythm of the Earth first, its almost mechanical chug-chug-chug, chug-chug, chug-chug-chug. Donnie concentrated on its cadence for a while, fancifully deciding that it reminded her of a heartbeat and not, as she had first thought, of some machine. And, finally, she let herself hear the Earth's echoes, as millions of noises bounced off tree roots, rocks and living beings.

Who knew it would be such a busy place? Or so darned confusing! At first, she became totally disoriented each time she listened, even though she realized that she was only hearing what was going on in a very localized vicinity directly below her.

Feeling somewhat braver after almost an hour of focusing on these myriad Earth sounds, Donnie began to practice moving small clods of dirt up through the topsoil to the grass above. She carefully and very slowly, so as not to harm them, moved up some beetles and worms she heard scratching around until they and their immediate surroundings were on the surface, and she then watched with fascination as they scrabbled back into the darkness of their underground world. She did this to several things, both organic and inorganic, so she could learn to recognize and identify the sounds they made and the exact tone emitted when other sounds bounced off them. That way she'd know just what she was listening to on future attempts at casting her mind into the ground. It also helped her to visualize what was actually going on down there and, after a long day of repeating this over and over, Donnie was able to let her mind float down confidently a little more than thirty feet into the Earth to "see" the world below her.

Then she practiced dematerializing cubic yards of earth from deep in the ground and dumping just the dirt onto the grass above, leaving all insect and animal life behind in the hollow created because she felt it was kinder than brutally subjecting them to the light of day. Besides, what if she miscalculated and rematerialized two living beings into the very same space when she put the dirt back below ground? Did she have the right to mess with nature like that? She didn't think so.

While she was practicing the art of dematerializing any amount of dirt she set her mind to, Donnie also set her magic to maintaining the shape of the hollow she'd just created below ground so that it didn't cave in. This she did with walls of magic, letting the energy slip from her fingertips and down into the ground, shaping its field to the exact dimensions she needed to hold the hole's form. She maintained this hollow shape steadily for hours on end, filling it with things, moving them in and out, sometimes having a pipe materialize into it at the same moment she dematerialized a mixing bowl out of it. And all the while, of course, she herself was at work in her workshop making copper pipes, joints and fittings. This constant stream of multitasking went a long way toward helping her compartmentalize her mind and her powers effortlessly.

Some days later, when she felt comfortable enough with these skills, she again knelt down on the ground outside the house and, in accordance with Sylvester's instructions, placed her hands palms-down on the cold, moist earth. She concentrated on using her mind's eye to see the best routes for the pipes to the well and those to the septic tank. Once she had decided those, Donnie dematerialized the earth that needed to be removed to make room for the piping, simultaneously setting up the properly configured energy barrier to hold the shapes of the hollows. She then materialized the pipes into the newly formed tunnels, fitting them together tightly as she materialized one length of pipe after the other. From that point, it took her less than three days to actually set up the entire water and septic systems.

One of her own books provided the recipe for mixing concrete, and after carefully building a mold for the septic tank, she poured the concrete into it. The mold was built out of planks Catie had stored in the corner of her workshop, which Sylvester strenuously asserted came from nonmagical trees. The inside of the mold Donnie covered with a thick layer of resin from some of the magical trees that rimmed the valley, having asked them nicely for it, 'natch. When the concrete was finally set, Donnie broke away the mold and levitated the tank to the huge pit the shovel had taken nearly eight days to dig, even though it had shoveled continuously all day and all night long—it was, after all, a rather small shovel.

The longest part of the process had been the curing of the concrete. Donnie managed to speed it up significantly by increasing the temperature and lowering the humidity around the tank, encasing it within a protective bubble of her magical energy that she made quasi-resistant to cold temperatures and water vapor. But the bubble was too large and took too much of her power to make it truly impermeable. And even though she managed to keep this protective covering somewhat active while she slept, it still took nearly three weeks before the concrete was sufficiently cured and she was confident of its integrity enough to lower it into the ground, hook up the pipes to it, then bury it with packed dirt.

Throughout these weeks, Donnie incessantly asked the cat (sometimes ten or more times a day—he kept a running tally, beginning anew each morning) just where was she exactly; why was she sent here; who had really done this to her, because it couldn't possibly have been accomplished by Catie alone, could it; and oh, by the way, what year was it?

Sylvester either looked at her with a set expression on his face, completely ignoring her questions, or, when he did deign to reply, answered something to the effect of, "On this, the fifth occasion today that you have enquired, Donemere, I again refuse to impart any such knowledge to you." Only once did he add, "What I can tell you is, the date here is the same as it is in your world. Catie was always quite insistent about that being the way time constancy works."

Donnie would usually turn from him with a frustrated snort and continue her modernization activities, which, in their own unique way, completely frustrated the cat. The sewage system she was currently building was unseemly for a student witch, or any witch, for that matter (who would do that sort of thing indoors?), nor did it come anywhere near to what he was trying to instruct her on in the lessons he had so carefully planned for her. And although even he was forced to admit now and then that Donemere learned to wield her magic so well it flowed smoothly through her, he nonetheless felt it was not learned in the proper manner. To his conventional mind, this was quite distressing. Equally distressing was her complete disregard for his opinion on the matter.

Once she had the plumbing system set up, it was comparatively simple for Donnie to actually install the bathroom fixtures. She hadn't yet figured out how to build a hydraulic pump for the water intake system, but she could use her magic to levitate water from the well through the pipes in the meantime. For storing water, she'd built a large cistern high above the toilet, with pipes routed from it to each fixture separately. This water was released through the faucet spigot and shower head whenever she turned either of their handles. The dirty, used water drained by gravity to the septic tank through a different set of pipes. The toilet was set up along these lines also, with two big stones stored in its tank to keep it low-flow.

In little more than five weeks of her arrival at the isolated little cottage, Donnie had a working bathroom. The day she finished it, she kept showing it off to the cat, who declared it the most revolting affront he had ever witnessed. So Donnie got out her copy of *We All Gotta Go* by LeAnne Wiggett and showed that to him. Sylvester looked at its pages with horrified amazement, succinctly voicing his concern over the future of mankind when he proffered an acerbic, "This book, much like your bathroom, is an unforgivable travesty of gentility. I would expect no less from your culture."

When the bathroom was fully plumbed, Donnie set up the same type of system for the kitchen sink. She semi-heated the stored water in the cisterns by zapping them with small lightning bolts of her magical energy, which turned out to be a wonderfully effective method of providing warm water for showers and for washing dishes.

She soon found that there was an unforeseen bonus to using the magical trees as her building materials: the rooms adjusted their size according to what was put into them. Which meant she could push any of the wooden walls back as far as she wanted, or stretch them as high as she needed. But you wouldn't know this by looking at the house from the outside. From there, the addition appeared to be the exact same size as what she'd built originally. It also meant the cisterns could hold as much water as she cared to fill them with.

Oh, and of course, the walls of the new rooms talked to her. Now, that had taken some getting used to, especially in the bathroom. Somewhat unwittingly (actually, mostly because she liked the varying patterns of wood grains), she'd used planks from all six trees in each of the new rooms or in their doors, so she had six voices to contend with at any given time of the day, except for when she was in her bedroom. There she had only the voices of the three trees she'd used in the door to the bathroom: Brindle, Carly and Parry.

Donnie learned not only how to differentiate between the trees' voices, but also their personalities. Brindle, the great oak, was the boldest of the six and quite obviously their defacto leader. His voice was low and deep, and he was very wise from having traveled the world so extensively. And luckily for her, he had a pretty decent sense of humor.

Caer Lyen, or Carly to Donnie and soon to all others too, was a young female oak of nearly five hundred years, whose voice was both youthful and boisterous. She and Rex struck up quite a fast friendship and played all sorts of word and riddle games with each other for hours in the bathroom. Neither of them would say why they chose this particular room to play in, and Donnie didn't have the heart to delve all that deeply into it, figuring their friendship was their affair, not hers.

Parenon, or Parry, was a capable, mature female oak who, if Donnie was any judge in matters of the heart, appeared to be rather deeply in love with Brindle. Donnie also suspected that Carly was their child, if such a thing were actually possible, but she had difficulty building up the courage to ask this question of either tree.

Ffen Fællieu, or Fine Fellow, a good-sized ash tree, loved nothing more than to be read to from the encyclopedia or some other instructional textbook, otherwise he'd talk your ear off in his rapid-fire, questioning manner. But he loved to learn and, if Brindle was asleep or elsewhere occupied (by what Donnie had no clue; he would sometimes simply not respond to her calls), could only be silenced by the imparting of information. As a matter of fact, Brindle appeared to be the only one who could successfully exert mastery over the oh-so curious tree and silence him with a quiet, yet steely, "That will be enough questions for now, I think."

Solffanye, or Sophie, was very, very old. She'd been by far the largest of the oak trees and, because of her interesting wood grain, Donnie had therefore used more of her boards in the house than any of the others. At last count (that Sophie could remember, anyway) just slightly over thirty-six thousand years had gone by since she had been a sapling, so she slept a great deal of the time. She was very tired, she said. Always very tired.

And finally, there was Marn Vôl, or Mournful Jack. He was an alder tree, and the majority of the planks in the rooftops were his because, of the six trees, he was the best suited to withstand the elements, as he'd informed Donnie when she'd begun building the roofs for the additions to the house. His personality was hard for Donnie to peg, really, since he was very quiet, seldom speaking and then only slightly above a whisper. One thing she did know about him was that he was apparently very depressed, as signified by his tone and by the forlorn sough he expelled after each and every response he gave whenever anyone conversed with him. Donnie ruefully acknowledged that this made his new appellation of "mournful" much more apropos than she had ever intended it to be.

Thankfully, the trees gave her privacy whenever she requested it, even Fine Fellow. They all had many stories though and could keep her company for hours, if encouraged. But they too were not allowed to tell

Donnie anything about when or where she was, as they informed her when she asked them one day. She nodded her head at this and replied quietly, "Yeah, I figured that would be the way of it."

Only after she had her modernization projects completed did she give in to Sylvester and agree to apply herself fully to his lessons. Over the ensuing months, the cat taught her various magical skills, walking her pedantically through the steps for each, such as shooting lightning bolts with unerring accuracy. For those, Donnie was to concentrate on her power, visualizing it as the electrical energy it, in fact, was. She was to then release a controlled flow of this energy, down to the exact amperage, carefully directing its path and its destination; both of which were equally important in reaching the desired target.

At first she blew up everything she shot at, which were mainly bowls of water she replicated by the dozens. After a morning of that, she finally dug out a few of Catie's cauldrons and filled them with water to practice on since they were sturdier and withstood her energy better than her ceramic mixing bowls had. She actually managed to not blow apart any of the iron pots, although a few were deformed into rather arresting shapes, which she guiltily reformed into their original condition, believing it was not her place to destroy Catie's handiwork. One of the more artistically pleasing malformed pots, though, found its way onto a shelf of the large cupboard behind the door in Donnie's office as a twisted memorial to her painstaking labors.

After she'd mastered how to minimize the energy shooting from her fingertips, she then went through just as excruciatingly laborious classes with Sylvester on maximizing her power shots, blowing up huge mounds of sifted dirt until the area around the farm looked as though it had been attacked by giant gophers. With such dedicated practice sessions as these, Donnie learned to control the exact flow of energy being discharged from her fingertips until she could get the desired effect automatically. She took away from her lessons the hard-learned fact that the key to successfully working magic was in the details.

Sylvester always kept a close eye on her, not letting her stray too far off the farm because, as he reiterated hundreds of times and in as many ways, he was afraid she would get into trouble out in the world now that she was magical. Donnie couldn't even wheedle Otis into taking her anywhere. Each time she tried, her weirdly omnipresent familiar would invariably be lurking just out of sight and would briskly interrupt these clandestine whisperings, reprimanding both her and the horse with a snappish, "Otis, you know better than to help her! And Donemere of the Codlebærn, as I have informed you on several instances now, 'tis not yet time for you to leave the valley. Once you have your powers fully under control, you may go anywhere you wish."

It hadn't taken long to find out that Sylvester was right, of course. Each of the times Donnie had ignored the cat's admonitions and tried to leave anyway, she'd gotten over the rim of the valley and through the forest, only to find herself once more looking down upon the cottage as though she were returning to it instead of trying to leave it. Just where or how she got turned around, she could never figure, no matter what she tried, whether it be making sure she walked a straight line by placing one foot carefully and directly in front of the other, or laying a string down as she went. She always came back out of the forest just a few feet away from where she'd entered it.

And on numerous occasions, she surreptitiously tried to arm herself with that one magical device (besides a wand, that is, which hers sure seemed to be taking its own sweet time in finding her, didn't it?) that all self-respecting witches must have—a flying broomstick. Unfortunately, every time even just the thought entered Donnie's head to see if she could make her own broom float, say when she was sweeping out the front room, the darned thing would immediately disappear from her hands. And then, of course, she was not able to conjure a replacement one, not even to actually *do* the sweeping. Apparently, she was well and truly stuck with her aberrant sassafras broom. The disappearing broomstick would be missing for days at a time until it would reappear sometime during the night whenever the mounting debris on the floorboards became too noticeable even for its thief's judgment. It was also the only object Donnie was not allowed to animate in any way whatsoever, which meant that sweeping out the cabin required manual labor on her part; something she never tired of grousing about, especially to the cat.

Obviously, something, or someone (she was pretty sure it was not Sylvester, no matter what he said), wasn't going to let her leave the farm until it felt she was fit for whatever duty they had planned for her. Naturally, she didn't know what this was since Sylvester would only allude to it in a vague, confusing sort of way. Donnie secretly suspected that the cat might not know the answer himself. But because of his excessively cryptic intimations on the subject (a habit of his which so seldom limited itself), Donnie couldn't help but be immensely apprehensive about her future, for she knew that she could not have been brought here for no reason, and it only made sense that the reason must be pretty immense.

And so, magic filled her waking hours for the next few months. She impatiently watched winter come and go, the snow often so deep from the frequent, violent storms that seemed to occur every day or two that, when she magically cleared a path between the house and stables wide enough for her and the animals to traverse comfortably, the snow banks were piled at least as high as her shoulders.

For several weeks in the middle of the worst of the snow season, all the animals stayed in the house with Donnie, at her insistence, because she felt it was just too cold in the stables for them. This included the chickens, who immediately took to roosting on the bookshelves in the library. After several days' residency, Donnie reluctantly gave up shooing them off the shelves and resigned herself to their noisy presence there. But she gave them a stern warning about their potty particulars, decreeing that they were never to leave any leavings inside the house because dysentery is a dreadful disease and she, for one, had no desire to experience just how dreadful it could be. Amazingly, it seemed the birds took her wishes to heart and nary a one dropped anything other than their daily egg or the occasional feather.

Donnie spent these weeks companionably with the others, growing closer and closer to all, including Sylvester, although he wouldn't have agreed that their relationship was anything but instructor and pupil. She would do well not to forget that he was no pet like Rex, as he reminded her every time she unthinkingly reached out to stroke his fur.

The evenings they were all sequestered within the cottage were mostly spent playing board games. *Kingdom* became a particular favorite of everyone, even the cat. At first this was a bit tedious for Donnie because she had to roll the dice and make all player-piece moves for everyone, as requested. However, when she became sufficiently precise with her magic (and sufficiently frustrated by how very busy she was kept when they played), she placed a charm on the game so that the dice and all pieces, cards and cash were automatically moved or doled out according to the players' telepathically relayed directions.

She was so pleased with the effectiveness of this charm that within days she had nearly the entire cottage and everything in it and around it charmed in one way or another. This bout of feverish charming finally came to an end when the others intervened one afternoon, desperately begging her to stop charming things because it was making their heads spin with the effort of remembering just what everything did or didn't do and when it would do it or not do it. Reluctantly, Donnie consolidated many of the charms, keeping only those she felt were truly necessary for peace and harmony in their lives.

Throughout the long winter, the cat scheduled four hours of indoor magic classes in the morning and another four in the afternoon or evening. The hours that were left free Donnie filled with lessons of her own or with exercising. From mid-November on, when the deepest snowfalls began, she cleared and maintained a set of long, parallel running paths that crisscrossed the valley north to south, so she could get some real cardio workout and also exercise the animals. She eventually expanded this into a whole network of paths that covered the valley.

At eleven a.m. sharp on any day that wasn't storming, Donnie looked up from her class work and announced that it was time for their constitutional and maybe a game or two of hide-and-seek. Since she would get dressed for the outdoors without even so much as asking his leave, Sylvester had no choice but to acquiesce, although he never did so gracefully, since this cut short his morning schedule by half an hour. Nevertheless, he too went along on these jaunts, informing her that, as always, he was merely keeping an eye on her.

Many a morning found them all traipsing out the door after Donnie as she prepared to race up and down her trackway. Rex dubbed her path system the "Ternate Tunnel" one day late in December after playing a word game he'd just invented with Carly, which he'd won by stumping the young tree as to the meaning of the word "ternate." He then proudly announced the new appellation for the trackway to the others, explaining that he had chosen "ternate" because the tunnel was now split into three separate sections that were connected in only a couple of places, and "tunnel" because of the height of its walls, which rose to thirty feet at the lowest point of the valley due to the staggering amounts of snow that had both fallen and drifted there. For much of the winter, as a matter of fact, even in the areas with lesser drifting (that is, the upper regions of the valley and the small, flat rise on which the farm buildings were situated), the top of Donnie's knit cap and Otis's head and neck bobbing up and down along the hillside were the only parts of the group that were visible to anyone who might have been looking down upon the cleared maze of footpaths from the edge of the valley.

The chickens too usually went along for some fresh air, flying and hopping short distances just at the rear of the little troupe. They would soon lag behind though, as their attention spans were about as long as one would think they'd be. Which meant that each time the birds accompanied Donnie and the others on these outings, they would reach the outskirts of the farm proper, then apparently would lose interest in trekking through the snow, and instead would wander around for a little while before suddenly recollecting as a group that there was a warm house and bookshelves back in the direction they'd first come. Their chaotic, feathery migration to the house was always performed quickly and *en masse*.

Diana, the cow, would only join in on the walks every so often, saying that she saw no need to subject herself to the freezing cold—unless Donnie liked having frozen milk for breakfast every morning? To which Donnie would grinningly reply something like, "Honey, you feel free to stay here and enjoy your Irine Norbert in peace!" Diana would invariably toss her head at this and retort, "Irine Norbert? Oh, mind you, she's okay, but she's basically an amateur! Callida Cardin's the queen of romance novels—now that woman could write a thrilling love story!" After bestowing upon her friends a beaming, pleased smile, the cow would sidle back up to the table and resume reading the latest passionate paperback, while the others would file out the door.

Most of the time, Donnie and Otis trotted or walked several laps on the long track until their hour was spent. Rex and Sylvester usually raced ahead together, one chasing the other round the next bend, but there they would wait for Donnie and Otis to catch up to them. Truth be told, the snow tunnels kinda creeped out both the cat and dog because they were so desolate in places and so eerily silent all over. Rex, at least, had no problem admitting this to his mama, whereas Sylvester disdainfully denied that his fur was standing on edge, irrespective of the clear evidence to the contrary.

Two or three times a week, they'd end this exercise period with a couple of games in either of the mazes Donnie created to the east and to the west of her long trackway paths. To ease the *dog's* fears, she and Otis surreptitiously kept an eye on either the dog or cat at all times, making sure they were never far away from whichever of the two were their respective charge for that particular game. Regardless of just how they spent it, everyone seemed to get what they needed from the time passed outdoors, be it fresh air, sunshine, or just plain old movement. Most mornings they came back laughing heartily with each other, feeling much invigorated and ready to eat lunch with a sharpened appetite.

Countless times throughout these months, Donnie's magical power would suddenly increase in little bursts of blue waves, but she did not at first know why. Sylvester had no explanation for it either, but he clearly was not pleased with her progress through the formal levels of Witchcraft. He spent a goodly portion of his free time denouncing the great many hours of each day she wasted on unnecessary or nonmagical activities. Donnie, as was becoming her habit more and more, blatantly ignored the cat's remonstrations and did as she wanted anyway. Her propensity for autonomy became even more pronounced once she realized that her power increases occurred whenever she mastered any new skill and sometimes even when just her acceptance of her abilities increased. To further that psychological end, she read as many books as she could about her new craft. If every witch was supposed to forge their own magical path, then she wanted to learn enough about others' experiences to be able to make informed choices about her own methodology.

Winter eventually gave way to spring and their lives became more centered around day-long outdoor activities again. Warm rains soon had the valley surrounding the cottage looking lush and verdant. It seemed everywhere Donnie looked she saw the green of budding vegetation and renewed life. Deep within her began to grow a tiny seed of contentment.

At almost exactly six months after her arrival in this strange land, she started replanting Catie's vegetable and herb garden, mostly with the seeds and bulbs from the cellar. Donnie enlarged the original garden by looking up the flowers, herbs and spices she needed for her current medicinal studies. She chose only those that would survive the climate, visualized their seedlings or bulbs from their pictures in an old gardening catalog, and called for several to come to her if they existed anywhere in this land. So far, everything she'd called for had arrived instantly.

By the end of the second day of her horticultural efforts, the garden was complete. Donnie was tired, having done some of the work manually so she could feel the moist, rich earth in her fingers and let its freshness fill her lungs. She stood and stretched her aching back, gazing up at the dark clouds rolling in from the east. It looked to be yet another severe thunderstorm heading their way and would be at the cottage in less than half an hour. She hoped her seedlings would survive the beating they were going to take tonight. With a snap of her fingers, she materialized a couple of tarps onto the new plantings to provide them what protection she could. With another snap, she sent the gardening implements she'd been using to their proper places, then turned toward the animals, most of whom were either grazing or rolling around in the grass, whichever suited them for the moment.

Okay, it was only Rex who was doing the rolling.

"Hey, guys?" Donnie called out. "If anyone wants to sleep in the stables tonight, would you mind if I get you bedded down now? I don't want to have to come back out once that storm has arrived." She pointed a finger in the tempest's direction, while at the same time she magically set afire the logs in the hearth inside the house. It would probably be a cool night too, not just a wet and windy one.

Diana and Otis took one look at the clouds and the lightning flashing within them before heading toward the stables, saying they would indeed prefer to weather the storm in their stalls. The cottage just got too close when it was this humid, they added by way of explanation. Donnie nodded, eyeing the black clouds with a touch of trepidation, then followed the horse and cow.

Rex elected to stay in the stables, telling Donnie as she passed by him, "Otis and I are gonna play *Trivia Hound* and we've both been looking forward to it all day long 'cause we're only usin' the music questions. That way it'll be real competitive."

Sylvester, on the other hand, as any smart cat would when rain is imminent, bolted from his lazy perch on the bench by the well and darted into the house.

Twenty minutes later, Donnie emerged from the stables to find the rain had already begun with a vengeance. It was pouring bucketfuls. She dashed to the cottage and jumped through the open doorway, sloughing off the heavy raindrops from her face and arms with her hands before reaching for the towel she kept near the door. It was only five o'clock but it already looked nearly night outside.

"This is going to be a really bad storm," she announced, "it came on even faster than I thought it would. And I wouldn't be surprised if it hails some later because the temperature is dropping fast. Hey, Brindle, are you guys going to be okay with this rain, do you think? Or should I have put more resin on you? Well, I guess it's too late for that anyway, innit?" She grimaced facetiously, still vigorously toweling herself off.

The tree's low voice rumbled back at her, "We shall do quite well in it, Donnie, regardless of the thinning resin. Although, I would recommend that you soon replace the roof over the kitchen and the bedroom with some of Mournful Jack's boards. I believe what is there now will weather this storm, but not many more like it, most definitely."

Parry added, "This looks to be the robin storm anyway, you know, so you should have plenty of time to repair the roofing over the coming months."

Donnie looked at the office door, from which Parry's voice had emanated, and flashed it a smile. "Parry, sweetie, I hate to remind you of this, but you've said the very same thing for the last three storms in a row now. Where I come from, we have a groundhog that's about as accurate at predicting the end of winter as your robin seems to be."

Parry soughed softly. "I suppose that is possible, although unlikely. Curiously, it is a system which has never failed until now. But then, many storms this season have been most unusual, arising so fast and furiously, and uncharacteristically from the east. Well, at least this storm should be another of those rather prodigious downpours to which you love to fall asleep. Let me see, it's been nearly two weeks since we had a storm such as this; has it not? Which means you should rest quite well tonight, Donnie."

"Oh, won't I just!" Donnie agreed heartily, grinning at the door. She glanced around the room and asked, "Do you know where Rex went, Sylvester? He ran off up the hillside after saying he was going to spend the night with Otis and Diana and still wasn't there when I left the stables."

"I have not seen him since I came into the cottage," the cat replied. "You know how he loves to play in the woods with the skunks and the deer. Even he is sensible enough to find shelter, so do not fret over him. He hates it when you do, you know."

Donnie nodded and strode toward her bedroom, intending to take a shower. "Yeah, I know he does. But I can't help it; I worry about him because that's my job. Besides, I hate not being able to—"

"Kiss him goodnight," the cat interjected sourly. "Yes, I believe we are all aware of that pointless penchant of yours, and of his for kissing *you* good morning."

Donnie stopped in the doorway of her room and stared back at the cat. "Why, I do believe Rex is right, Sylvester, and you're just jealous of our pointless penchant, as you like to call it. Y'know, anytime you want to participate, just say the word and we'll include you in it, okay?" She gave the cat a wink, which he ignored. She chortled in amusement and said, "Hey, I'm gonna jump in the shower and then fix dinner. How about a game of *Murder about Town* afterward?"

"That will be fine, Donemere," replied Sylvester, yawning indolently and sleepily deciding to stretch out in front of the roaring fire for a while longer.

Major Pine committed his murder in the Jailhouse with the pistol, with the motive being fraud, the first time they played the game, as Sylvester was the one to discover, and they were almost finished with the second game, with Miss Rose looking mighty guilty in the City Hall, when suddenly there sounded a small *thunk*! and the kitchen window flew inward.

Donnie and Sylvester both jumped in surprise. Turning, they waited to see who was looking to gain entry to the house, the turbulent wind outside blowing gusts of rain through the opening, down the stone wall, and onto the wooden floorboards below. A few moments later, something very small, very wet, and very black crawled over the sill, gasping for breath and groaning. It was the bat, Mecholætera.

Donnie chuckled and said, "Come on in, Mickey T, we're just playing a game of *Murder*. We're almost finished, if you want to play the next game with us," she offered with a cheery smile, adding sympathetically, "It sure is a nasty night out there. Probably not a lot of moths and mosquitoes flying around, which means you'll have to settle with beetles for dinner tonight, I expect."

The bat shook himself, more water droplets scattering onto the wall and floor, then he glided over to the table, his fur already beginning to show the true brown of his species. The window closed firmly behind him once he'd cleared its span. "Oh, it be juth terrible out there, Donnie. And I thwear thith window geth thmaller every time I go through it! Theemth I can never make it on the firth try becauthe my eyethight ith juth not what it uthed to be, you know?" he lisped chattily, teetering precariously on the very edge of the table.

One of Mickey T's front teeth had gone missing a year or so ago now. The elderly, garrulous bat always told everyone that he'd lost it in a battle with an eagle who'd been hunting him, but Donnie had her doubts about the veracity of that story. Mickey T had a habit of running into things at full speed because, as he'd just said, the keen eyesight of his youth had deserted him some time before. He was a close friend of Sylvester's and had become a regular visitor to the cottage.

Donnie reached over and gently cupped the bat from behind to give him a boost onto the flat surface of the table when his teetering became even more pronounced.

"Well, my friend, you are getting up there in years, you know. Most Noctules only live to about twelve or thirteen years of age and you say you're already pushing eighteen. So losing your eyesight is probably to be expected at this stage." Donnie's response was stated somewhat offhandedly because she completed her turn and came up with the answer to the game. "Okay, Sylvester, I say it was Miss Rose in City Hall with the knife because Mr. Black, our victim, had the deeds to her old homestead and he refused to return them. Eeeuuuwwww, a bit gruesome, huh? And I thought she was such a lady! Let me just check the cards. Yep, I'm right. That makes it one to one. Ready to play the tie-breaker? Whaddya say, Mickey T, wanna try your hand at making it a three-way tie?"

The bat had pushed his way unsteadily onto the board and was peering closely at the upturned cards. Donnie suspected that he'd been quite an important bat in his day and was now allowed to live his life out peacefully, resting somewhat on his laurels with the rest of the magical bat population. He was really very old and rather rickety.

When she'd looked him up in her library, she'd found that his species was called Noctule. You'd have thought she'd bestowed everlasting life upon him when she'd told him this. Mickey T's cloudy eyes had lit up and he'd beamed at her, declaring, "Aha, tho that ith who we are! I exthpected that we muth have another name inthead of juth plain old bat!

Not very colorful, the word *bat*, ith it? But Noctule...now that ith a word you can really think your teeth into. Noct...tule."

Donnie liked Mickey T enormously.

He looked up now and gave her his brightest gap-toothed grin. "That Mith Rothee ith a wily woman, ith thee not? Thee makth my fur thtand on edge. It theemth thee ith alwayth the culprit! Well, yeth then, deal me in, Donemere."

"How do Sephala and Malerop fare?" asked Sylvester, turning to his old friend, while Donnie collected the game cards and began separating them into three piles. "Is Sephala recovered yet?"

"Ah, the kidth are getting along wonderfully now that the lateth litter hath been born. Loth of mouthth to feed though, you know? And theeth oneth are a handful, believe you me! They all have thuch very tharp teeth! Juth look at what they did to my wing thith morning." The bat extended the injured appendage, pointing out the little, ragged teeth marks along its bottom edge. "They are making me crathy with their conthant crying and gibbering. I thwear they nibble away at everything ath though they never get fed anything at all! They've taken three monthth off my life already and they're only a few dayth old!"

"Oh, Sephala finally had the kids?" Donnie exclaimed excitedly, hiding a smile behind the cards she was shuffling. "You didn't tell me that, Sylvester. How many did she have, Mickey T?"

"A thouthand, I think!" the old bat joked. "They thertainly make enough noithe for that many!"

"When was this then?" Donnie snorted her laughter, unable to keep a straight face any longer. Even Sylvester chuckled broadly and shook his head at his friend's frankness.

"Three dayth ago. I came by to inform you that I am a grandfather onthe more, but I believe you were drething at the time."

Donnie finished preparing the board for the next game and said, "It's your turn, Sylvester, you go first. Well, Mickey T, be sure to give your kids my congratulations and best wishes. When the grandchildren get big enough, bring 'em on by so we can meet them. I'll turn on a big light outside and you can have a moth fest."

"Thank you, Donemere, you are tho kind to uth when almoth no one elthe ith. We batth apprethiate that greatly, believe me."

"Oh, think nothing of it, really. It's just that I know only too well what it's like to be different and feared. Apparently my own kind are so frightened of me, they refuse to venture anywhere near the cottage."

Sylvester looked up sharply at her and said, "Whatever gave you that idea?"

"Well, no one ever comes here, do they?" she pointed out dryly.

The cat said nothing to this, wishing to avoid the subject completely, and instead inquired of Mickey T, "What brings you out on a night such as this, dear friend?"

The bat started to reply and then stopped short, his mouth hanging wide. "Well, there," he sputtered, "that ith what I came about! Good heaventh, I almoth forgot—I am becoming tho thenile! We cannot play thith game, I thay! We muth rethcue the man who appearth to have fallen on your landth, Donemere. He ith athleep in a ravine north of here, no more than three leagueth away!" The bat then added somewhat anxiously, "I don't think he even knowth it'th raining becauthe he ith thleeping tho heavily. If he'th not careful, he'th going to catch a cold, ithn't he? And doethn't that alwayth thpell death for you humanth?"

Stunned at first into utter silence, once the bat finished speaking, Sylvester let out a hiss and Donnie gulped, and then they both turned to stare incredulously at each other.

"There's a man on my lands?" Donnie finally croaked.

Chapter 4
Comin' Straight for You

Donnie's eyelids fluttered a couple of times, then stilled as the first rays of the rising sun filtered through the bedroom curtains the next morning. She yawned and stretched luxuriously. The mattress beneath her was lumpy and crackled with her movements.

"Hell's hags, I'm still here," she muttered with a heartfelt sigh, letting her arms flop to the bed in a dramatic, sweeping gesture of defeat, once again beginning her morning pretty much the same way she had for months.

She lay there quietly, with sleep slowly falling away from her, and briefly contemplated turning over to slip back into oblivion. But no, that notion was doomed to failure. When had Sylvester ever allowed her to sleep past dawn? Well, other than her first ten days here, which apparently had been vacation time. If only she'd known...she would have tried to actually enjoy them.

The instant she'd awakened, the boombox had materialized on the night table beside the bed and, for the third day in a row, had begun softly playing the first strains of Mackenzie Mack's "Don't Give Up." Donnie pursed her lips and blew at the hair covering her face, only half-listening to the song as it told her to look at things in a different way. She supposed its intent was to make her feel better.

And then, in a sudden rush, her heart began to pound at the memory of Mickey T's message. Sylvester had seemed so certain last night that she and the others could now leave the valley. Just why he thought this he had refused to explain, of course, but he'd insisted that they must rescue this mysterious man who, for whatever reason, was reportedly lying face up in the mud on the moors, apparently passed out cold. They'd debated for a while whether it would actually be a rescue mission or the rousting of a drunken trespasser, with Sylvester arguing the former and her the latter. Mickey T had wisely stayed mum, leaving shortly after the argument had become heated.

At the end of their exchange, Donnie had retorted acerbically to the cat's back side, "You just don't understand human nature, Sylvester. And why should you; you're a cat! I mean, who, in their right mind, would go out—on the moors, may I remind you—in such unbelievably stormy weather like tonight's, unless their common sense was a bit, um, altered, shall we say, by something like imbibing six tankards too many of the best public-house ale? Golly, what a surprise if the guy rode his horse into a ravine and then got all banged up on the fast trip down! Dipsy drunkards, if that's actually true, what was the idiot thinking? Do I even want to know someone that stupid? Why else wouldn't our dastardly infiltrator have sought shelter before passing out? I mean really, Sylvester, just listen to that wind! I'll bet it's up to seventy, nearly eighty miles an hour now, which means it's blowing a right hurricane out there. And on top of that, I bet we're averaging more than an inch of rainfall every hour. It'll be a flooded, muddy mess wherever you go! There is no way I'm going to endanger my life, yours, or Otis's by trying to find this guy tonight. Unless perhaps there's something about our mysterious stranger that you'd like to share with me that might convince me to risk all of us for him? Well, is there?"

She had then glared at the cat pointedly, but Sylvester still had his head turned away and steadfastly refused to meet her gaze.

"Of course there isn't," Donnie growled, "because you never tell me anything about anything really important, do you? So that's it, end of argument, Sylvester. Okay? I mean it, I won't even attempt to go anywhere tonight unless you explain a few things first!"

The cat turned and scowled at her from his position on the hearth, but then angrily showed his back to her again, this time curling up into a ball and feigning sleep.

Which was when Donnie had gotten up and gone to her own bed. Around midnight, she'd pulled the covers from her head in frustration and yelled at Sylvester, who had moved to the end of her bed, that if he was so damned determined to go out and find the man, he was welcome to do that by himself, but, for the last time, there was no way she was going to abandon sanity by tripping lightly into that maelstrom howling outside, so would he *puhleeze* stop his caterwauling, go back to the kitchen, and let her get some sleep?

Donnie now turned to her right side and gave the boombox a wry smile. "You betcha I'm gonna look at things differently today, boombox. I've got a trespasser to find and I'm not gonna give up until I find him. Which should make this a very good day—a red-letter day, in fact, so feel free to be as annoyingly cheerful as you want. I promise I won't interfere with your selections for the next twenty-four hours. Girl Guide's honor."

Of late, the boombox had developed the dogged habit of displaying a decidedly optimistic bent at the onset of each day, blithely ignoring Donnie's irritated groans. Wisely though, it had finally refrained from playing the Franks' kid-friendly "A Happy Sun Rises Every Day" first thing. It had insisted on playing that as its opening number for thirty-five days straight until she'd threatened to melt the box down and make a coffee mug from it. It had then changed to Lambent's "Keep Going On" for ten days, but a judiciously placed zap from Donnie in its general direction two days ago had produced "Don't Give Up."

Donnie moved over and sat up on the side of the bed, stretching her back and yawning widely as she wondered if she truly was to be released from her forced confinement on the farm. She'd been kept here for so long with only the animals and trees for company, she was beginning to believe that the rest of her days might well be spent confined to the valley. Was that phase of her ordeal finally over?

And yet, with an unpleasant jolt, Donnie realized that now the time had apparently come for her to leave, a part of her was actually content to remain here, surrounded by the friends she knew and loved. What was that about, she wondered. Wasn't she ready to leave? Well…wasn't she?

For heaven's sake, she wasn't sure that she was! She slumped her shoulders and gasped in disbelief, greatly disturbed by this unwelcome discovery. Oh, now this just wouldn't do! Why didn't she want to leave?

Nervously, she rose from the bed and shuffled over to the window. She slid back the curtains to allow the dawn to light the corners of her bedroom and stared unseeingly out at the rain-soaked bucolic world that appeared through some of the more transparent pieces of colored lead glass within the window. Last night's storm had formed large pools of water throughout the yard, concentrated mostly around the well where the ground dipped a little. These puddles now glistened and danced prettily from the combination of a light breeze and the reflection of the strengthening sunlight. Asteriated drops of rain still adorned the branches of the apple trees, their star-like patterns lending an ethereal glow to the morning fog that hugged the ground.

Stifling another yawn, Donnie felt frustration well up within her. What if she were to finally get some answers to her predicament because of this uninvited visitor to her lands? What would that mean for her? Could his arrival actually signal the journey to what Sylvester kept obscurely referring to as her destiny?

But more importantly, a rather doubtful voice in her head added, are you ready to meet that destiny?

"Go away, you!" she whispered hotly, hating the fact that her strongest underlying emotion this morning was fear. "You're really not helping here, you know that?"

She groaned despondently, then stretched her arms upward and behind her, minute blue sparks arcing from her fingertips, which she felt, but ignored. Truthfully, no matter how hard she'd tried to accept her lot, to this day she was still unable to make herself completely at home with this power she constantly felt stirring within her, like a second set of bones rattling alongside her real ones. More than anything else, she wanted to know why she'd been gifted it. There had to be purpose to it, didn't there? Even she was tired of asking the same, monotonous questions over and over of Sylvester. She could only imagine how wearying they must've become to the cat. Surely then, she was more than ready to face whatever awaited her outside the valley…right?

Donnie shook her head, thoroughly disgusted with herself, and looked over at the boombox with a raised eyebrow. The song had apparently repeated while she'd been thinking, only this time it was a version that had been recorded live and it was now loudly assuring her that it only wanted her to be happy.

It must be Tuesday. The boombox only gave her two-fers on Tuesdays. Which was kind of nice because it lent Donnie's life a semblance of normalcy, knowing that today was Tuesday. But the same song twice? That was unusual. Wondering vaguely why it had repeated, she turned back toward the window and sang the last few lines of the song under her breath. "And then you'll be free," she mumbled as the song wound down, pressing her forehead against the cold glass of the window pane. "I sincerely hope so," she added when the song ended a moment later. She lifted her head to look out at the morning sun as it finally rose above the valley's edge and shone fully upon her face.

The volume on the boombox increased as Martha Kee's saucy blues classic "Comin' Straight for You" began to play and almost immediately pointed out that until now she had been held back by her own fears. Donnie noted this with a nod in the direction of the boombox and snorted her agreement with the sentiment.

Sylvester, alerted by the more audible strains of the song that Donnie was up, pushed open the door of the bedroom and began pacing impatiently back and forth across the floor. "We must hurry or we may not reach the man before he dies," the cat stated testily.

Donnie turned around, right eyebrow again arched high, this time in exasperation with the cat, and retorted, "So you're still presupposing he's at death's door, huh? Look, for all we know, he may have actually tried to kill himself by deliberately tumbling down the steepest moor he could find, unerringly choosing to do this in the middle of the worst storm of the season. And exactly where did he do this, one might be forgiven for asking. Ah, such a good question! All we know is that he's somewhere on my northern lands. And here's you, expecting me to go in search of him for hours and hours last night, on the say-so of a self-professed senile bat who one day just might succeed in hurtling himself through a wide-open window on the first try, although I sincerely doubt Mickey T's aim will ever be good enough again to manage that. It took him—let me see, what was it—oh yeah, three tries to make it *out* the window last night, didn't it?"

She crossed her arms in front of her, warming to her subject. "And beyond that, this makes, what, the third supposedly dire message he's had for us just this month? The last one was that his little bat-buddies were all crumbling to dust right before his very eyes, which even he admits are almost blind! Don't get me wrong, you know I love Mickey T dearly, but he's by no means eagle-eyed anymore, so I sure wouldn't have trusted him to show us the way to our supposed suicidal camper in the midst of a hurricane during the day, let alone at night—would you? Be honest, Sylvester, and I'll bet deep down you agree with me."

The cat looked at her uncomfortably, but offered no reply.

"Besides, leaving last night would've been just plain stupid. Don't you know that it's safest to perform rescues when there's daylight?" Donnie had begun to gather her clothes for the day from the wardrobe as she continued to rant at the cat. "Jeezum, I thought everybody knew that. You go out there at night, tripping around in the dark, and you'll end up falling down a hillside into a quarry, or worse, a bog, making yourself yet another accident victim. Then what use would you be as a hero?

"Furthermore, I'll bet the idiot—er, poor fellow, I mean, is still alive and in the pink of health when we find him, other than having a gargantuan hangover and the beginnings of a head cold. Tell you what, I'll bet you Hollow Castle right now. If he's alive, I automatically get it the next time we play *Kingdom*; if he's toast by the time we get there, Hollow Castle is yours."

Sylvester arched his back angrily and huffed in protest, "No! I will not wager on a man's life—nor should you! Now make haste, we truly must be quick about finding him!" With an aggrieved flick of his tail, the cat turned and stalked back into the kitchen.

Donnie stilled her motions and let out a fretful sigh before abruptly sweeping her nightdress over her head, thoroughly nonplussed at her own crass behavior. She pulled on the sweatpants and long-sleeved t-shirt she'd taken from the wardrobe. What was wrong with her this morning? She was being peevish and mordant, both of which weren't like her. But why? And was it fair to take her frustrations out on Sylvester?

Well, the answer to that question was easy. He often brought out the worst in Donnie, especially whenever he started in on her first thing, like he'd just done. But...then again, she had to admit that she'd gone too far and he was absolutely right to criticize her over her comments.

She hurriedly continued dressing, wondering, as was her habit when starting out her day, what was going on in her world right now with her family. In the midst of yanking her socks onto her feet, Donnie stared up at the window, her expression pained. If her calculations were correct then today was April twenty-second—her sister's birthday.

No wonder she felt off-kilter; missed holidays and family celebrations were particularly distressing for her to endure anymore. Her eyes immediately filled with bitter tears. "Hey, happy birthday, Em. I'm sorry I'm not there to tell you that in person. I—I, oh God, I miss everyone so much!" she cried softly, a large tear spilling down her cheek. She wiped it away forlornly and bit back a bunch more just like it, all threatening to well over at a moment's notice.

"No, you silly fool, this really won't do!" she reprimanded herself severely, gulping back a sob. This was crazy! She had things to do, important things, and she ought to just do them instead of letting her emotions crush her like this.

"Comin' Straight for You" had ended a couple minutes before and then, oddly enough, the boombox had played a live version of it next. With her eyes still stinging, Donnie forced herself to be present, glancing quizzically at the discombobulated boombox. Apparently, it too was out of sorts today. Shaking her head at this shared odd behavior, Donnie pulled on the pair of black rubber boots she'd gotten out of the wardrobe's matching bench. She went into the bathroom and placed her hands under the sink faucet, thinking about what she wanted for breakfast when her stomach rumbled noisily. The cold water handle turned and a small stream of clear liquid flowed down into her cupped hands. Deciding not to heat the water this morning since it would have more of a bracing effect if left alone, she splashed her face vigorously, hoping the cold shock would help get her equanimity back.

The boombox joined her in the bathroom, materializing so quickly on the long vanity that it barely missed a note between rooms. Kee's song ended and the Blonde Horses' version of "Beautiful Lady" played while Donnie washed up. When it asked loudly if she was lonely and wanted to meet someone new, Donnie gave the box a mutinous glare over the top of her towel and said, "Very funny," then hissed at it, "Go bother someone else!" She tossed her damp towel over it and, a second later, it disappeared.

"Besides, if this guy we're going to rescue actually even exists, I may not be so lonely after today," she called after it, mugging irritably at her reflection, her toothbrush hovering in the air next to her, already primed with toothpaste.

She realized that now she was being flippant, but, honestly, Mickey T often did exaggerate his claims of both real and imagined horrors. Something about his failing eyesight distorted the most normal-looking creature into a haunting monster to the bat, so it would not be surprising to discover that the "man" was, in fact, a perfectly innocent log. A little over a week ago, the elderly bat had firmly announced that he intended to take his increasing blindness in stride and had ever since stoically managed to refrain from hurling himself willy-nilly at her every time he approached the cottage, no longer screeching that a horrible demon was right behind him which Donnie must vanquish right now! Too many times, and always to his utter embarrassment, these "horrible demons" turned out to be the bat scout sent by his daughter, Sephala, to guide the old bat back to the family cave.

Parry offered a sleepy good morning when Donnie passed by the door to leave the bathroom. The others, Parry yawned, were still asleep.

Donnie stopped to lay a tender hand on the wood and nodded. "As any self-respecting tree should be, I s'pose. It is awfully early, my friend. Well, according to Sylvester we should be gone for a few hours, so let the others sleep. Who knows, perhaps you can get some sleep yourself. See you later, okay?"

Parry yawned loudly again and replied, "Yes, Donnie, I shall get some rest as soon as I wake Brindle. It's his day to keep watch."

Donnie smiled at the door, softly telling her tree friend, "I'll say goodnight then. And I'd better get a move on or Sylvester will be back in here looking for me." She hurried through the bedroom to the kitchen, where she reached into the refrigerator as soon as its door opened and got out the jug with the remainder of yesterday's milk, draining it in one long pull.

The pan on the stove suddenly jerked off the flame, sending its contents flying upward. Two semi-scrambled eggs flipped over once, then floated out of the small pan and onto a piece of bread already situated on a plate. The ketchup bottle burst from the fridge and turned on its side, its top flipped open, so that a zigzag of the homemade, sweet tomato condiment could be deposited on the eggs. Meanwhile, a fresh avocado was being sliced by a knife; four slivers of the smooth green fruit soon twirling away from the cutting board to land atop the ketchuped eggs, the rinds on each thin round of avocado peeling away into the lidded ceramic jar Donnie kept on the counter for anything that could be composted. Another slice of bread zoomed from the cutting board to top off the sandwich, and the small plate began to lift from the counter. With a flick of Donnie's finger, the plate stopped in mid-air and a plastic container slid out of one of the lower cupboards, its lid lifting momentarily to receive the sandwich that floated toward it. It sealed tightly once Donnie's breakfast was secured within, and thereafter waited patiently on the counter.

In seconds, the remaining fixings disappeared into their proper places and the dishes flew to the sink, where the pot scrubber hovered, poised to start scrubbing the pan, plate and knife as soon as Donnie either left the room or sat down to eat. This was all performed automatically by one of Donnie's charms—except, or course, for the small change she'd made in the routine this morning.

She grabbed a canteen off the shelf beside the fridge and filled it with a mixture of water and some of the berry juice she'd made Saturday from the frozen berries she'd picked back in the fall. There was only about two more cups of the juice concentrate left, which meant that, until the berry bushes around the house began bearing fruit again, she would soon have to send a call out to the world at large for others. When she'd first become magical and had charmed the containers in her fridge to never empty, she'd been astonished to learn that replicated foods lasted, at best, only one day before disintegrating or evaporating into nothingness, their flavor and nutrients slowly diminishing as the hours passed. At the end of each twenty-four hour period, they would break down totally, suddenly leaving just a small pile of greying mush in place of, say, mustard, or dried bits of orange in a bottle of OJ. The containers would then immediately refill with perfectly edible substances, which, again would last only one day. Truth be told, this escalated decomposition process freaked Donnie out so much that she now kept just the most exotic of replicated foods and mostly stuck to the vittles stored in the larder or, of course, those she called out for.

Which meant that thievery was becoming somewhat of a habit with her, although she always conferred a little charm upon her victims that gifted them an adequate windfall from other sources with which to recompense them for the missing items, sort of robbing Paul to pay Peter. Admittedly, she felt regretful about this petty larceny, but she supposed that one day she'd somehow have to pay for all of these defrayed debts personally anyway, so there was no sense in worrying about it before its time was due.

Striding over to the front door, she lifted a thick, hooded sweatshirt off a hook there, put it on and slung the canteen across her chest. She capped these movements off by placing upon her head the tall, wide-brimmed, pointed black hat that hung on another hook. It was from a sexy witch's costume she'd worn two Halloweens ago to the street party in the Castro. It was Donnie's only concession to her new life as a medieval witch. Sylvester thought the hat ridiculous, which was another good reason for her to wear it every chance she got.

Reaching inside a pocket of the dark teal sweatshirt, she found a pair of sunglasses and put them on top of her head, lifting her hat with an exaggerated flourish in order to do so. "Did Rex come home last night?" she turned to ask the cat. "Have you seen him this morning?"

Sylvester paused his morning bath to eye her dourly, the tension between them almost palpable, and replied, "No, but he may be here somewhere."

Donnie acknowledged this possibility with a low grunt and went over to the pantry. She got out a couple of white linen tablecloths and put them in a carryall bag that she slid off a shelf. As she went by the kitchen counter, the plastic container with her sandwich jumped into the carryall and the bag's zipper closed in one smooth stroke. She then hoisted the bag's strap over her shoulder. The cat coughed inquiringly at her. "For bandages, just in case this guy really is hurt," she responded curtly.

Sylvester was right behind her when she went out the door and followed her toward the stables, close on her heels the entire way. "You really should dress more in keeping with this century, especially this day of all days" he informed Donnie disdainfully. "Your strange costumes will arouse too much curiosity if seen by the villagers."

Donnie blew a raspberry in the air, rebutting his argument exasperatedly with, "You know, I do believe we go through this every time I walk out the door. But let's do it just one more time, 'kay? Okay, the nearest village is twenty-five miles away, right? Now, it seems to me that, even on a good day, we're not likely to get too many visitors because we're not exactly on the beaten path, if you know what I mean. Oh, and we can't forget the added curse of the land being magical, which, as I said last night, is apparently quite an effective deterrent to any would-be guests. After all, may I point out once again that I've been here six months and haven't even seen another human being? Nope, not a one of those phantom villagers you keep referring to has made it to my doorstep. Zip. Zero. Nada. Kinda makes one wonder exactly why that is, doesn't it?

"Furthermore," she continued sardonically, "I'm comfortable in these clothes, and at my age, that's what really counts. Besides, it's not like any of these supposed villagers, if they actually do exist—and, mind you, I'm not totally convinced they do—are really going to care what I wear, what with worrying about pestilence and death, not to mention all the other medieval woes they must face just getting out of bed every morning. That's presupposing they even have a bed to get out of, that is. You know, the more I think about it, it actually would be rather nice if this guy we're going to 'rescue' isn't dead. We can at least test my wardrobe out on him then, can't we? So, for the millionth time, will you please quit harping at me about it?"

Glancing down at the cat and noting that he was about to explode on her, Donnie suddenly halted her footsteps to shake herself, both mentally and literally, and gave a frustrated sigh. "Oh, never mind me, Sylvester. I'm sorry," she apologized. "It appears I'm a bit touchier than usual this morning. I just can't believe that I'm actually going to be allowed to leave this place and yet I'm not really sure I want to go. Imagine that! And believe you me, that revelation is driving me nuts. I mean, what am I going to find out there in the wide, wide world of sports, Sylvester? I gather it's all still a magical land to some degree, so what sorts of creatures are we likely to run into? Are most of them good and kind or horrible and menacing?...Well? Which are they?" she added urgently, after waiting a few seconds for Sylvester to reply.

The cat merely stared up at her without saying a word.

Donnie gave him a fed-up scowl and said, "I can see by your expression that you're still not going to tell me anything, are you? Don't you realize that for months I've been wondering just what it is that awaits me outside this valley? To tell you the truth, not knowing that scares the bejeezus out of me. I think that's why a part of me wants to stay home today. Better the devil you know than the devil you don't. At least here, we're all safe and—ah cripes, what am I saying? Of course I want to leave! Seriously, Sylvester, forget my paranoid rantings. I'm just being silly, I guess, what with it being my sister's—oh, hell! Look, I'll do my best not to embarrass you too badly out there in the great unknown, all right? So, c'mon, O' Master Cat, let's get Otis and find this mysterious stranger of yours. Then we'll see for ourselves if he really is at death's door, as you kept whining at me all night long," she added mock-resentfully, doing her best to assume her normal bantering manner as she proceeded to the stables.

Sylvester once again ran along right behind her and replied tartly, "I was not whining all night! Besides, how would you know? You slept like the dead for hours."

"You know I always sleep well when it rains like it did last night!" Donnie reminded him. "Heeeyyy, wait a second, I bet you did sit up all night worrying about this guy after you finally let me get some sleep, didn't you, you old softie?" She stopped at the doorway of the stables and swung around again to look down at the cat, her right eyebrow crooked high, daring him to refute the accusation.

Sylvester avoided her stare and this time darted ahead of her into the stables, calling back, "Well, at least one of us has a heart!"

"I knew it!" Donnie crowed, then proclaimed much more soberly, "You are a very predictable cat, Sylvester." She followed him inside and walked straight to the cow's stall. "Good morning, Diana, my friend."

She stroked the cow's cheek gently and gave her a light kiss on the forehead.

The Jersey cow yawned very sleepily, stretched her neck, and then began to complain about, "last night's behavior of those flighty chickens and that moronic rooster with his overactive pecker!" She swore that if he jumped on her backside one more time in the middle of the night, she was going to shove his beak up his you-know-what! Imagine, a little cock like him thinking he could satisfy a big, beautiful bovine like her. Ridiculous! "Just because a record six chicks were born yesterday, he really thinks he's somethin' special, don't he? Like I'm gonna give him some chicks too, if he tries hard enough! Well, he certainly tried hard enough last night—like to drove me nuts with all his bawking and squawking back there! Cock-a-doodle doo, nuthin'! He tries that again and, I mean it, I'll have him yodelin' out his ass!"

Both Donnie and Otis were choking with laughter by the time Diana finished her dead-on imitation of the overly amorous rooster. Wiping the tears from her eyes, Donnie finally managed to declare, "Di, you are one sex-starved cow, do you know that? And I'm right there with ya, girlfriend! Can't say as I wouldn't mind gettin' a little myself, but like you, I don't want it to be that little. As my Aunt Bea always says, *Don't ever let a man tell you size doesn't matter, sweetheart, 'cause all that's about is wishful thinkin'!*"

Diana rolled her eyes and agreed vigorously with this sentiment. "Ain't that the truth! But it sure seems to've made every male I've ever known feel better to say it—as if sayin' it makes it so! Now, am I far wrong, Otis?" Both Donnie and Diana turned to the horse, who was tossing his head and grinning from ear to ear.

"Well, I really wouldn't know, would I," he pointed out, his voice nearly strangled with laughter, "being as I don't have that particular problem myself. But, on the other hand, I *have* known some men in my time who could've sorely used a bit of equine DNA in their private parts!" Again they all laughed uproariously at this early morning badinage.

Diana had slipped gracefully into the place of Donnie's best friend Liz, with Otis a close second. While Donnie missed her old friend sorely, she wouldn't wish Liz here for the world. But Donnie was more grateful than she could express that she had Diana and Otis to console her. "Oh, you two, thanks so much for the laugh," she cried, her heart lifting with friendship, "you have no idea how much I needed it. I've been going crazy ever since I got up this morning. I can't seem to keep my mind focused on any one thing for long."

"Wow, you haven't had a bad day like this for a while. What's up?" Diana eyed her with concern.

Donnie briefly explained about Mickey T's visit last night, ending with, "The short and long of it is, according to Sylvester, apparently I get to leave the valley now. I know, I know, can you believe it? But am I thrilled about that development? Oh, no, not this little Mary, Mary, quite contrary, because I'm too darned worried about what I'm gonna find out there, if it's more than I can handle, both magically and emotionally. And now we get to the real show stopper—a few minutes ago, I woke up all fidgety and nervous and out of sorts, and realized that I don't even *want* to leave the valley, regardless of whether this man is someone important or not! Now, how weird is that?" she asked, looking suitably scandalized.

"But, sweetie, this is wonderful news!" Diana assured Donnie enthusiastically. "It's what you've really wanted for so long, deep down. I think you're right in that you're scared simply because you don't know what our world is like. Well, my friend, I for one bet dollars to doughnuts that you're going to do just fine out there! Oh, think about it, Donnie, you may finally, actually get to leave the valley!" Diana said, then laughed wryly. "And all because of a man! Wouldn't you know it? I sincerely hope for your sake, he's at least cute."

Donnie winked at the cow and said with a mischievous grin, "Me too! But I still say that five will get you ten he's some fat, old tinker who was drunk as a skunk last night and merely lost his way home, so he thought to himself, *hey, why don't I just pass out right here on the moors*—I know, I know, Sylvester, I shouldn't lay odds on his life. Okay, so we'll go with the really gory version you prefer. He's lying at the bottom of some ravine, all broken and bloodied, and we're gonna get him, bring him here, and I'm gonna patch him up—isn't that right?"

She turned to face the cat fully, her hands on her hips, and deadpanned, "Yeah, us and what army? Or should I make that, what army doctor? As if I know anything about saving someone's life who's just suffered a bad fall and probably has massive internal injuries, not to mention a bunch of external ones." Most of the sarcasm left her voice, but there was still a devilish glint in her eye. "Seriously, Sylvester, this is all pretty pointless, you know, unless what you really want me to do is put him out of his misery." She somehow managed to keep a straight face when she said this, even when the cat's face registered abject horror.

Although he could plainly hear both Diana's and Otis's poorly stifled snorts and guffaws from behind Donnie, Sylvester, at first, wasn't certain whether she was being facetious as usual, nor, quite honestly, did he fully understand just what she meant by her suggestion. But his instincts told him that it was bad, definitely very bad. He forced himself to regain his calm and replied in a withering tone, "As you well know, you must practice your craft whenever possible and this is a golden opportunity for you to work with the medicines you have prepared over the last two months. You must also remember that you are a Codlebærn and, if any Codlebærn could save him, it would be you."

"Very charmingly said, I'm sure, kind sir," Donnie curtsied to him, real surprise coloring her voice. "Since when are you my biggest fan? And don't worry, I promise not to put our mysterious stranger out of his misery, no matter how miserable the fat, old tinker turns out to be. I was only kidding anyway. I just like to rattle your cage sometimes, Sylvester, perhaps because it rattles so freely. Besides, you know as well as I do that if he's as important as you say he is, the gods will be watching over him and won't let him die before we get there."

"Of course they will not allow that to happen," the cat agreed shortly. "Nevertheless, they will not heal his wounds, only ensure his survival until we reach him—although the more time we take, the less likely he will be to recover fully. Therefore, tarry no longer, Donemere; we must be away!" And with that stern command, Sylvester jumped to the top rail of Otis's gate and onto the white stallion's back, his long cat's tail swishing crossly.

Donnie shrugged her shoulders at Diana and whispered, "Notice he'll never admit to giving me a compliment?" The cow winked at Donnie conspiratorially. Donnie left her munching some hay and strode over to Otis's stall. She reached under the rail to give him a carrot from her pocket. "So, what's shakin' with you this morning, Otis? Did you eat your breakfast yet?"

The huge, magnificent horse crunched the carrot, tossed his head affirmatively, then grumbled good naturedly, "Your charm's levitation needs some fixing, Donnie girl. Half the oats fell onto the floor instead of in the pail. But it's okay, I ate 'em anyway. Five second rule, you know." He grinned at her. "And, oh yeah, you coulda put some sugar in with 'em!"

"I thought you were watching your boyish figure!" Donnie protested with a laugh. "How are you ever going to keep that hard body of yours if you go eatin' sugar in your oats all the time?"

"That's so yesterday, young miss!" the horse replied. Both he and Diana had taken to Donnie's idiomatic speech like ducks to water, as had many of the other magical animals who regularly visited the farm. Otis now lowered his voice to a deep bass and sang, "Gimme some sugar tonight, won'tcha, baby?"

Donnie laughed again and rubbed his long, handsome face affectionately. "Sure, you old lecher, no problem."

"Okay then, enough of that!" the cat urged in a high, sing-songy voice fraught with annoyance. "We must be going—naow!"

Otis rolled his eyes and walked out of his stall as soon as Donnie opened the gate. Donnie climbed the small stepladder she used for the purpose of mounting the horse with dignity. Unbeknownst to Catie, who'd never been able to communicate that well with either the cow or horse, the old leather saddle greatly offended them both by its very existence. So Donnie had made a new saddle out of some tablecloth linens, stuffed tightly with cotton, and lots of it because she liked to be comfortable. Unfortunately, that first linen saddle hadn't lasted long and she was still in the process of making another one. All she had now was a thick horse blanket, which she threw over Otis's back. She only needed to attach the stirrups and the new saddle would be complete, but it's not like that helped her this morning. She'd already been awake all of twenty minutes and Sylvester was correct, they did need to get going, especially if they were to find this errant visitor of theirs before he broke camp and left her lands.

When Donnie and Sylvester were both aboard, Otis trotted out the door of the stables and headed north. The boombox appeared beside the well and, you guessed it, blasted out a live version of Kay-Lo Hell-O's cover of "Beautiful Lady," apparently feeling the irresistible need to complete the latter half of the repeating two-fer. The song finally faded from Donnie's hearing as they trotted away from the farm and up into the forest surrounding the valley. She was more than a little troubled by the increasingly independent behavior of the boombox, but was honestly at a loss to say why. This whole place was weird with magical things, not the least of which was Donnie herself, so why shouldn't her boombox do its utmost to fit right in?

When they came to the forest's outer edge, Donnie peered through the opening between the trees and gulped. It wasn't the valley that greeted her this time! While numerous stands of trees carpeted the hills immediately before her, beyond them lay lush, green moors stretched out for as far as she could see, resplendent with the glory of the new day. She'd almost forgotten the sight, how achingly beautiful the rugged hills could be, especially in the mornings when they were swirled with fog, the airborne, crystalline water droplets glistening dreamily around the trees and bushes in the rising sun's rays. She quietly asked Otis to stop for a moment and closed her eyes on her tears.

So Sylvester had been correct in his surmise of last night and she *was* finally freed from confinement. Donnie breathed deeply and opened her eyes, her face set resolutely. Then, with a wide, slow smile spreading across her cheeks, she declared, "Okay, Otis, I'm ready whenever you are, my friend."

Sylvester and Otis both noticed the sudden, pale blue wave of magical power that emanated from her when she gave the horse her command, but neither of them mentioned it because they knew how uncomfortable these waves made her feel. Donnie, on the other hand, was far too busy looking around her with renewed hope (and humor) to notice anything other than the countryside and how good she felt inside suddenly. Much relieved to find she was (mostly) glad to be away and that her earlier fears had subsided for the moment, her heart soon began to soar with joy.

Even the birds seemed to have caught her mood and sang melodically to her from their perches high in the trees. About a mile or so from the valley, Donnie saw one flock that particularly captivated her interest. They were small songbirds, about the size of a wren, and a good fifty or sixty of them crowded the limbs of a young elm off to her right. At first, Donnie thought they *were* wrens because of their rufous coloring and said as much to Sylvester.

The cat replied that the birds were called Sûlrím, or Wind Wings. "They once were quite common throughout the land," he explained, "but for years now they have been sighted only rarely, and never in such a large grouping. This flock took refuge some while ago on Catie's, or rather *your* lands, just as the trees and other magical creatures have done. Their name derives from their ability to—"

Donnie gasped in surprise, cutting the cat off in mid-sentence to exclaim, "Omigod, they just changed color!" It was true; in the blink of an eye, the birds' coloring changed to neon-bright apple green, then again almost immediately to a darker, richer green, making the elm's branches appear to glow unnaturally for perhaps a half-second. The effect was quite startling. Donnie stared in consternation at the still sweetly singing birds. The most amazing part of this phenomenon had been that the shift in color had been as complete as it was sudden.

Otis tossed his head toward the birds as he passed under the elm tree. "There you go, Donnie, now you know why they're called Wind Wings. Practically every time the wind shifts, they change color, and not only that, but every last one of the same flock changes color at exactly the same moment. Weird, eh? I've never figured out how they all know to do it at the same time, but they do it whenever two or more of 'em get together. Legend has it that they are the Salvation of A'Rontauk, but who or what A'Rontauk was and what part the Sûlrím played in its salvation, no one seems to know anymore."

"Well, they are certainly very dramatic, or, as the dormouse said to Frannie, that's a flea from a different family," Donnie muttered, doing her best to remain calm and force a return of her former lightheartedness. She'd wondered what sorts of creatures she would encounter in this unknown world, and now that she'd had a small taste of just how strange they could be, her nervousness threatened to rear up again. Okay, the Sûlrím appeared to be perfectly benign, but there were sure to be some not-so-benign beasts and monsters running around here too; she'd bet on it.

Then again, she reasoned with herself, what could possibly be more of a monster or beast than man himself and she'd survived thousands of encounters with them; why, she'd even been mugged a couple of times, once in San Francisco and another time in New York City. Sure, she'd walked away from those rather violent incidents a bit lighter in the pocketbook (all right, *without* her pocketbook both times) and, yeah, the one time she'd gotten a blackened eye and a badly bruised and bloodied set of knees and a painfully wrenched ankle and a—well, the point was, she'd walked away from these brushes with the worst side of humanity. And she had not let the terror she'd felt then get to her, to change her or how she lived her life. She would just have to take it on faith that she would prevail here too, no matter what or who she met.

So Donnie again looked around her with interest. The thick groves of trees soon ended and the landscape changed to open moorland, with hedges and shrubs crisscrossing the hills, and only a few hardy trees dotting the countryside here and there. They rode northward for more than half an hour at a fairly brisk walk, although the going was rough and sometimes downright tricky because of the mud from the night's storm. Donnie and Otis spent much of this time regaling each other with risqué tales from their misspent youths until Sylvester finally shouted at them, "Silence! May we not have peace on this, our first journey together of real import?"

After meekly agreeing to hush, Donnie leaned forward and joked in Otis's ear, "He just has no sense of humor about these things, does he? Well, okay, about anything. Seems I'm not the only one who needs to lighten up this morning. How about going a little faster so we can get this boondoggle over with sooner, rather than later?"

Otis nodded his head a couple of times in agreement and sped up to a slow trot whenever the path allowed. Sylvester soon tired of being bounced around in the back and leapt in front of Donnie, surreptitiously (he thought) eating the bits of sandwich Donnie (deliberately) dropped onto Otis's broad shoulders.

Another three miles or so on, the worn path took a sharp turn ahead. When Otis began to follow it to the right, something stirred inside Donnie and she suddenly blurted out, "No, go straight, Otis."

The horse stopped in surprise, uncertain what to do. Sylvester protested loudly, arguing that the moors were uncharted here, making them even more dangerous than those around the established pathways, especially after a storm like last night's. The fallen man surely would have been following the trail and, therefore, along the trail is where they would find him.

Donnie insisted, "No, I'm telling you, he's due north. I don't know how I know that, but I know it. Trust me, Otis, he's in that direction."

Otis did as she asked. Sylvester grumbled moodily about nobody ever listening to him, but he eventually gave up and looked around them quietly. While the moors here were about as steep as those surrounding the cottage, there were a lot more upturned chunks of granite, which the Earth had apparently felt inclined to oust rather forcefully from her belly. Otis picked his way around these treacherous outcroppings and the shrubs and stunted trees that sought to hide them, sometimes having to skirt an entire moor, but he nevertheless maintained his course. A blanket of silence settled over the land, with the only sounds being the thud of Otis's hooves, the rustle of the light wind as it caressed the hills, and water either dripping off the heavily laden bushes or trickling over blocks of granite to form cold, dark pools with unknown depths.

To keep her mind occupied, Donnie settled back on the horse and wondered for the umpteenth time why Sylvester was so secretive about everything. It was clear that her little kitty was keeping a great deal of information from her, but she didn't know what would be the one thing that could happen which would tip the scales in her favor and finally make him unload at least the most germane facts to her. He was also adamantly averse to imparting any helpful knowledge of the most advanced thaumaturgical or psychical spells of Witchcraft to her, especially those that might be strong enough to take her back to her time. He said (quite pedantically, every time the topic arose), because she wasn't taking her magic lessons seriously enough to suit him, he saw no cause to enlighten her on magical subjects such as this.

She supposed, to a point, that what he said was true. She certainly did not take the same grave approach to magic as he did. Which threw them into an almost continuous conflict that both appeared to thrive upon. There'd been many times when he'd pushed Donnie so hard in her lessons, she'd shouted at him in sheer vexation, "There had better be a damn good reason for all this, Sylvester, because this kind of thing just shouldn't happen to a person without a *really* damn good reason!"

Sylvester ignored these angry outbursts and calmly continued to drone on each time about the proper way to do this or that magical task. So Donnie would devise yet another impossibly outrageous scheme that was destined to drive the cat bonkers, which nearly always worked beautifully. The best thing about these crazy schemes of hers was that she usually came up with at least one new magical skill from each. Not that all of these new skills were necessarily useful, even she had to admit that. But some of them had turned out to be a whole lot of fun.

All in all, looking back on it now, Donnie would have to say that it had been an exceedingly frustrating six months for both her *and* the cat. Sighing, she realized that, deep down, she actually liked and admired this pompous little windbag sitting in front of her on Otis's shoulders. Sylvester had conviction in spades, and you gotta admire someone that dedicated to his creed. He took this magic stuff very seriously. Since she hadn't, that is until the last couple of months or so, their enforced relationship could best be described as "mostly strained."

But she truly had found the honorable side of magic through her long hours of studying its history and its principles. Of late, she could usually be found in her office, during her rare periods of spare time, poring over books on various types of Witchcraft (or Wiccecræft as Sylvester would sometimes call it, which Donnie had looked up in her library and found was the Old English way of saying the word, providing her with one of the very few clues she'd garnered about the cat's background). In the tenets of Witchcraft, she'd found a way of life and love for nature that she could respect and live by happily. She'd even begun to notice that there now resided a small core of peacefulness deep within her whenever she practiced her craft.

But Donnie was very careful with her magic. For instance, she didn't yet have the nerve to try casting a theurgical spell, which called for a protected circle. According to her research, they would be the big daddies of her powers because she would be mixing her magic with that of the gods. These were the sorts of incantations that just might prove impossible even for her to reverse. Her aversion to casting spells this way was about the only point she and the cat agreed upon. Sylvester never tired of announcing that he definitely didn't think she was ready for them either.

Underlying everything she did was the Witches' Rede, which Donnie had instinctively adopted as her own credo, recognizing its intrinsic common sense almost immediately upon reading it. It stated:

An Ye Harm None, Do What Ye Will

Doing what you want, as long as you don't harm others, when strictly adhered to, could make life somewhat convoluted. The ramifications of your actions could be endless. And then there was the Rule of Three, or Threefold Law of Return, which decreed that everything you do will come back to you at some karmic level. It ran:

> *Ever Mind The Rule Of Three*
> *Three Times Your Acts Return To Thee*
> *This Lesson Well, Thou Must Learn*
> *Thou Only Gets What Thee Dost Earn*

For a while, after learning about this lodestar, Donnie had refused to practice any magic at all. Early on, she'd been overwhelmed by the possibility of doing harm to another living creature with her magic, an abhorrent thought to her. On top of that, the fear of having this rebound on her had finally made her revolt against her craft and she'd vowed to abstain from using it. Not surprisingly, the magic in her fingertips had refused to cooperate with this decision and she'd often found that merely wishing for something would suddenly make it happen. But she had plugged on, staunchly doing her best to avoid overtly and consciously using magic.

The cat had suffered through this period for nearly a week before unloading on his errant pupil. He'd listened patiently to Donnie's passionate explanations of her developing beliefs and then had reminded her testily that avoiding doing real, deliberate harm to others with your magic is one thing, which is certainly what all Codlebærn must do or risk forfeiting their power to the next strongest of their line; but inadvertently shielding anyone from peril, regardless of its origin, went against other tenets of Wiccecræft that teach all creatures are here to live and let live. She would simply have to trust her instincts and use her powers judiciously.

But Donemere must learn never to correct the natural formula of life, he said, even if that meant she must stand by and let something die because of her magic. And when this were to happen, as it most surely would one day, then Donemere, like every other living creature, would just have to deal with the consequences. Caution, when measured, was required by any witch, but not to the point where it overshadowed living or made one deny their very nature.

Thinking about it now, Donnie could see that it was at this point that she'd begun to like the cat. Her magic lessons had continued thereafter without interruption and she had progressed from being a Yfel Witch to Déadl and from Déadl to a Madra Witch in record time. In truth, she'd been ready to welcome magic back into her life anyway; she'd had enough freezing cold sponge baths that long week without it to last a lifetime.

As though sensing that she was thinking about him, Sylvester gingerly backed up so he was nestled in the space between her legs. When he'd begun to scoot backward, she'd lifted her hands until he was comfortable, then let them come to rest in front of him. This was getting to be their habit of late, now that the weather had improved, whenever Donnie would ride Otis in the afternoons to exercise him, and was the closest she and the cat ever came to being affectionate toward each other.

A quarter of an hour later, Sylvester asked Otis to stop. Startled, Donnie realized that he must've seen something she and Otis had so far missed. Yes, there he was, there was the man, or rather, there was his horse. Otis slowly began making his way down the steep ravine where the other horse stood underneath the branches of a big oak tree that had somehow managed to gain enough purchase in between the granite rocks to grow strong and tall. The horse was a magnificent chestnut, every inch the stallion.

"Oh, what a beauty he is!" Donnie breathed, before letting out a low whistle of appreciation. Cocking her head to the side, she announced, "I think I'll call him Gallantry." The newly christened horse was standing in front of the heap that was his master, watching their approach with more than a little trepidation. As they came closer, Donnie's smile faded. Okay, she'd been wrong. The man was obviously not camping, nor did he look as though he'd passed out drunk. From what she could see of him between the horse's legs, she could tell that there was way too much mud and some rusty red stuff covering him for either of those explanations to account for his presence.

After a quick survey of the scene, she muttered thoughtfully, "This guy is no ordinary villager. Not with a horse like Gallantry." Sylvester nodded his head in agreement.

As unobtrusively as possible, Donnie tried to read the horse's thoughts, which were almost completely disjointed. "Master...hurt...pain," were the first "words" that came to Donnie's mind, reflecting the jumbled state of the horse's emotions. Then came "Stranger...battle," and "Stranger...follow...close." It insisted urgently, "Master...home."

"Gee whiz, Sylvester, Gallantry's pretty upset, isn't he?" Donnie said in a low voice. "Something about another man and a battle. And I think this guy was riding home, or the horse just really wants to go home, whichever, and the other guy must be following them. It's impossible to tell how far behind the other guy is, but it sounds like he's probably close. I can't make much more sense of Gallantry's thoughts than that."

"Neither can I" Sylvester replied. "But then, he is not a magical horse, so 'tis unlikely we would. He may also be disoriented and, therefore, confusing events."

Otis approached the prone man, stopping about twenty feet away. Donnie slid to the ground after Sylvester moved to the horse's rump, where he sat very still, his tail curled tightly around his feet. Donnie made her way slowly through the thick mud toward the unconscious man. His skittish horse watched her intently until she stood just a couple feet away from him. All the while Donnie had been sending soothing thoughts to it and it now moved aside a few steps in an obvious gesture of trust, allowing the rescuers to get a clearer view of the man.

Donnie could just barely detect the rise and fall of the man's breast, although she could plainly hear each loud, tortured breath he was taking in through his parted lips. She looked back at Sylvester apprehensively. "I think he may be in really bad shape, Sylvester. If he is, I honestly don't know if I can help him," she confessed.

"You must," was the only reply she got from her cat.

So Donnie resolutely turned toward the man once more. He was laid close to the trunk of the tree and therefore had been semi-sheltered from the worst of last night's rain. When the tree informed her he'd done his best to protect the man, Donnie nodded and said with a warm smile, "That was very kind of you."

Nonetheless, the man was still a gruesome sight, with thick smears of blood covering his armor and clothing. Much of the skin that was visible was also stained with it. As a matter of fact, there were a whole lot of smeared bloodstains positioned pretty much all over him and Donnie had never, ever, in her entire life, been a big fan of blood.

"Okay, Donnie girl, stay calm and approach this scientifically," she whispered under her breath, steeling herself. One of the man's arms lay behind him at a distinctly odd angle. The other rested across his breast. His legs looked intact, but bloodied in several places. Fresh blood was also seeping from a deep wound on his right side, which was partially hidden by his armored breastplate. Donnie knelt down to get a closer look at his injuries, gloomily deciding that her self-taught triage and other medical lessons hadn't quite prepared her for wounds of this degree, darn her luck—or, she supposed dryly, that should probably be, darn the stranger's luck, shouldn't it?

She poked and prodded the man a little while, then calmly gave her diagnosis. "He might have a broken left arm. If not, he'll probably have a sore shoulder from landing on it like that. His legs don't look broken, but he's got a bunch of shallow lacerations on them. Well, one of them is pretty deep, but it's not as bad as the cut on his right side. That one's still seeping blood. Most of the others don't actually look too bad and have already started healing. I can't tell much about the rest of him until we get him back to the house and cleaned up." She shook her head slowly and added *sotto voce*, "If he lives that long." She was more than a little worried about the long, deep wound in the man's side. That one did not look good at all.

Snapping her fingers, Donnie materialized a white linen towel from home onto her hand. She folded it small, holding it to the wound for a second, then pulled it away. A couple moments later, more blood began to seep from the cut. Thank the sunny skies above, at least it wasn't gushing. But it, and several others, would have to be packed and wrapped before they made the return trip to the cottage. She refolded the towel and pressed it to the wound again, leaving it tucked under the man's breastplate. Then she peered closely at the man's other cuts again.

"You know, these don't look like something you'd get from a fall," she observed. "I mean, they're clean lacerations, like he was sliced up with something razor sharp. Whereas, if the cuts were from him falling down into this ravine, they'd be more like torn gashes and abrasions, wouldn't ya think? So, I'd have to say the horse must be telling the truth and these injuries were made in a fight. Whoever this guy's attacker was, they used a really fine blade, like a rapier or maybe even a sword like the one over there on Gallantry, although that one looks a little too thick for these cuts." Donnie jerked her thumb in the direction of the hefty sword hilt protruding from the scabbard belted to the horse's saddle. "Not that I would know though, realistically," she added, standing to scrutinize the area around the man.

"I do not believe his fight was fought here," Sylvester offered quietly and Donnie nodded in agreement.

"No, there's no blood, other than what's on him. While I'm no Girl Guide, it doesn't look like there's been a struggle around here anyway—no obvious scuff marks or footprints in the mud other than Gallantry's. My guess is that this guy got away from the other one and rode this way. He probably passed out and fell off his horse when the pain got too bad."

"Tell me, do you finally possess penitence in your heart for refusing to search for him last night?" the cat demanded querulously.

"No, I do not!" Donnie replied, her tone just as truculent as her familiar's. "Look at how long it took us to find him in daylight with good weather. And have you noticed the wickedly sharp outcroppings of rock all around us? No, Sylvester, I stand by my decision that it would've been way too risky to try getting here last night. Half the time these particular moors wouldn't be safe to travel on during the day, let alone at night, what with all these crags of granite lying around waiting to trip you up or rip you to shreds if you're unlucky enough to be tripped up by them. I say again, there's no way in hell you'd catch me out here at night in the pouring rain and gale-force winds." By now, Donnie was arguing on auto-pilot and was gazing fixedly at the man's face; there was something familiar about it.

"I will debate with you no more. We must take him to the cottage immediately," the cat sniffed superiorly.

"Yes, that is imperative," a deep voice said from high up the hill above them. "One of the man's injuries is more severe than the others and has bled much. I was able to follow its trail to this location easily and I fear he is weakened considerably by it."

They all swung around in surprise when the voice spoke, with Gallantry neighing frantically as a huge wolf gamboled down the north side of the ravine, his gait slowing as he approached. He was tremendously and overpoweringly beautiful, with glittering blue eyes and a dark grey, nearly black, coat of fur. Donnie figured that he weighed in at just under two hundred pounds and could probably stand taller on his hind legs than her five feet, nine inches would take her.

The surprises didn't end there. When he neared them he transformed into what she could only describe as a werewolf. He reared up on the aforementioned hind legs, while his paws elongated into feet and hands with lethal-looking claws, and his facial features flattened out some, so that, in a way, he very much resembled a man, albeit one with dark fur covering almost everything except his face and neck. He kept walking stealthily toward them, his intense, hunter's eyes fixed on Donnie.

She stumbled backward about four steps. She would've gone farther, but Gallantry had moved behind her and was now in her way, his sides trembling with a terror that was echoed in Donnie's own heart. As a matter of fact, the only thing keeping her heart from exploding with fear, oddly enough, was that this newcomer looked very much like Chase Egan, the famous star of the futuristic *Wolf Hunter* movies.

Chapter 5
The Werewolf Way

Sylvester cleared his throat importantly so that attention shifted to him and then he nodded his head in a respectful, welcoming manner, greeting the fresh arrival with a calm, "You also had word of our visitor, I see."

The werewolf gave the cat an answering nod before replying, "Yes, news of him reached me this morning. I decided to come myself because I wanted to ensure that the information passed to me about him was correct and that he was not the Black Rider." The werewolf turned his vivid blue eyes back to Donnie and said crisply, "You have brought medicinal herbs with you, I expect."

Donnie, bewildered and bemused by the oh-so, matter-of-course, almost mundane manner of this exchange, stared from her cat to the werewolf mutely. It was not until the boombox appeared on the ground close to her, blaring out the last verse of Warren Lupin's kitschy "The Werewolf Way" that she even moved. Although her heart was barely recovered from its sudden shock, she managed to sing (and do a bit of a jig) along with the song.

All eyes flashed to the boombox, then to Donnie as soon as she began to sing along with it. She gamely ignored this at first, prancing and parading around simply to relieve some of her stress, but finally, under the weight of their collective stare, she belted out her last, "Ah-rrroooooohhh," with a diminishing flourish, came to a standstill, and clasped her hands in front of her. The music emanating from the boombox petered out too. Nobody said anything for a full ten seconds.

Donnie gave a faintly nervous chuckle in response to their stunned silence, suddenly feeling the need to protest half-heartedly, "How could I pass up the opportunity to sing along with that? It was Warren Lupin's greatest hit and I'll probably never get another chance to use it like that ever again in my entire lifetime. I mean, who would've thought I'd meet a real, live werewolf today? Especially one with the most beautiful blue eyes I've ever seen in my life? So, I ask again, how could I pass up that opportunity?"

She looked at the werewolf uneasily and mouthed "Sorry" to him. He continued to stare at her. Donnie wasn't sure which unnerved her more, the fact that he looked like one of her favorite movie stars, or his unwavering stare (did he never blink?), or his nakedness. Oh, had she mentioned that he was naked once he turned into a werewolf? Well, he was; very naked. Which is something a werewolf just shouldn't be, especially one who looks like Chase Egan, particularly in the light of day. At least, not in front of a woman who hasn't had sex in more than six months.

He was tall and broad, with a very human shape to him. When he'd transformed into a werewolf, his fur had receded until it was just a brush, so his musculature was quite evident. He clearly had not an ounce of fat on him. His head was covered with actual hair, shoulder length and dark, and he had a full, thick beard covering the lower part of his face. And he was blessed with some rather sharp teeth, from the little Donnie had seen of them so far. Not that she wanted to get a really close look at them, mind you. And then there were those startlingly blue eyes that seemed to just pin you with their intensity.

What a mixture of emotions this gorgeous lycanthrope churned up inside her! Between the fading terror in her knees and the rising heat of her libido, Donnie wasn't sure just how to respond to him. Who knew a real werewolf could be so darned handsome? And so terrifying at the same time? While it might be every girl's dream to see a screen star such as Egan *au natural*; sharp, wicked-looking claws and menacingly pointed teeth were probably not part of their fantasy. Not real claws and teeth, anyway.

Feeling quite a bit braver, Donnie decided that maybe she should take care of the latter problem, since the former was taking care of itself. "In answer to your question, I brought only some tablecloths for bandages," she said. "Um, here's an idea, and I hope you won't take this the wrong way, but how about you use one of them to cover yourself up with? You know, wrap it around you; er, if you wouldn't mind, that is. I'm a modern gal and all, but it's still a little unnerving to be talking to a naked werewolf. Not that talking to a fully clothed one would be any less unnerving. I mean, you're quite frightening with or without clothes, don't get me wrong."

She realized she was babbling, so she shut up and walked with just slightly unsteady legs over to Otis. She reached into the carryall and tossed a tablecloth backward, over her shoulder. "Yeah, so...okay, now that my heart's no longer jumping out of my chest, I've got a question for you—just who are you? You and Sylvester seem to be well acquainted, which, I'm assuming, means you're a friend and you're not here to kill me. May I add how grateful I am for that?" She chuckled, still somewhat nervy, and turned to face the werewolf.

His haughty, deep voice rounded on Donnie in its majesty as he wrapped the tablecloth around his waist. "My name is Mynydd Uchaf. I am of the North Wolves and I am King of the Free Wolves."

"Ri-i-ight," Donnie nodded. "You would be. King of something. Royalty, I mean. Um, Muneth, what was the rest of it? It's kind of a mouthful, innit? Can somebody explain to me why everyone around here has to have a tongue-twisting name? I mean what, you can't have a nice, easy name like Bill or Bob or Chase—aw crap, what am I saying? Everybody knows that Fantasy characters always have unintelligible names! Nimblest nomenclatures, what was I thinkin'?" she complained cynically, deliberately overdoing her already exaggerated airs, then grinned mischievously at the werewolf. "I suppose your name has some deep inner meaning, doesn't it?"

Taken aback, the werewolf answered in the affirmative, "It means *highest mountain* in Mannish, yes."

"Oh! Oh! Let me take a shot at this before you, Sylvester," Donnie cried and raised her hand in the air, as if to stop Sylvester from speaking, something he had not been about to do. "That's where you were born, right?"

"No." The Wolf King said with finality, bestowing upon her a long, penetrating stare. "We must not stray from our purpose here, Donemere," he quietly chastised her. "You must take this man back to Caterin's cottage and heal him. You are the only one who can help him now and you must do so quickly," he said with force, making it more of a command than a suggestion.

In response, Donnie's eyes shone with a downright rebellious glint as she put her hands on her hips. Behind her, she heard Sylvester clear his throat warningly, but she didn't even hesitate to throw caution to the wind. She was so very tired of the animals in this place taking the liberty of telling her what she *must* do every time she turned around, even if this one was not only a king but a huge, hulking werewolf.

"Nope, Warren, not gonna do it. Read my lips." She paused for effect, her movements animated throughout her ensuing protests. "I've endured enough crap here already. I have diligently practiced each and every one of the million or so parlor tricks Sylvester has relentlessly insisted on teaching me—twenty-four seven, might I add, and yes, that does include the wee hours of the night. Don't think I don't know you come into my bedroom when I'm fast asleep, Sylvester, and drone on all night long about how to do this and how to do that, or that you continually try to place a spell on me that will keep me from ever turning you into a toad!" She wetted her lips with her tongue and turned back to the Wolf King. "Furthermore, my new-found ferocious friend, in addition to being subjected to Sylvester's pious presence for the past six months, I've just about memorized three-quarters of Catie's journals, all thirty-two of them! Gangling gorgons, could that girl write! Actually, no she couldn't, at least not well. When I catch up with her, one of the first things I'm going to do is teach her how to spell correctly. Then I'm going to make her read her own journals. It'd serve her right. After all, why should I be the only one getting a headache from them? On top of all that, I've studied herbal and holistic treatments until I'm just a bit holistic myself, if you catch my meaning, and I've also wrung pretty much every tidbit of knowledge from my overtaxed brain regarding anything even remotely connected with the imagined world of witches, both in print and on video."

The werewolf opened his mouth to speak at this juncture, but Donnie forestalled him with an upraised hand. She took a determined, deep breath and pressed on. "So I have this to say now: I will *not* be saddled with a dying man on top of everything else. Admittedly, he's not dying right this minute, nor is he likely to from any of the wounds he currently has, but what if they become infected because of something I do and I can't save his life, especially considering that I won't have antibiotics to treat him with? Huh, what happens then? How's that going to make me feel about this place, having that on my conscience? No, I truly don't see how this is any of my business. I think I should just wrap his wounds, put him back on his blatantly terrified horse, and send them both on their merry way, because all I want to do is write a perfectly good spell that will send me home, back to my time."

Turning to study the injured man again, she grumbled, "I really thought the last one was going to work. Why didn't it, I wonder?" Swinging her head toward the cat, Donnie repeated her querulous query, "Why didn't it work, Sylvester? What did I have wrong in it?"

It was Mynydd Uchaf who answered her. "I am certain it was a fine spell, Donemere," he said placatingly. "But no spell will send you back to your time as long as Valledai is here and his dark magic continues to grow."

Donnie gawked at the Wolf King, slowly arching her right eyebrow higher and higher, then she looked over suspiciously at the cat. "You *have* been holding out on me, haven't you, you bad, bad puddy tat?"

The werewolf turned an incredulous stare toward Sylvester. "You have not yet warned her of Valledai?" he inquired reprovingly.

The cat gave an irritated snort. "You are not the one who has had to live with her these many months, so do not blame me for withholding this news until you have spent time with her! There is no telling what she would have done with this knowledge. I assure you, Mynydd Uchaf, Donemere is not yet trustworthy."

Donnie was thoroughly affronted by the cat's accusation and her expression showed it. "Oh, that's rich, Sylvester," she exclaimed, "seeing as you're the one who's just been found out in a lie. Okay, so it's only one of omission and everybody knows those aren't as bad as an out-and-out bald-faced one, I'll give you that much." She rolled her eyes and grimaced after making this concession. "But now you have the unmitigated gall to say that I'm not trustworthy? What do you think this makes you?"

"Prudent!" her cat retorted angrily. "If you applied yourself more diligently to our studies, you might be Fægre by now; but no, you insist upon—"

"Enough! She must be told immediately!" Mynydd Uchaf roared. He heaved a deep, exasperated breath before continuing, entreating the cat almost desperately with, "Tanny, she must be convinced to heal this man's wounds! It appears the message given to me this morning was correct. My sources tell me that he has played an integral part already in our campaign to defeat the dark powers threatening our land once again. You and I must now provide Donemere with counsel on battling Valledai. The time is urgent; there is word from the Mountain Wolves that the meeting between our forces draws near."

Donnie's face was now a veritable study in alarm. "Battle? Draws near?" she shrieked. "Now you want me to fight someone? What, magically or hand-to-hand combat? I'm not really good at either, just ask Sylvester! And apparently this is gonna happen in the not-too-distant future? Hey, newsflash to Sylvester," she swung around, fuming at the cat, "woulda been nice to know all this before now! Look, I'm not like you guys; I'm no barbarian. I come from a civilized world where we just don't do this kind of thing to each other!" She jabbed a thumb in the direction of the injured man.

Sylvester, having learned a great deal about her world over the last six months, eyed her flintily. "Oh, really?" he drawled. "There is no war in your time, then?"

Caught off guard, Donnie had to admit that, well, yes, there was war in her time. There were, in fact, a few wars being waged full tilt when she was yanked so unceremoniously from it.

"Is there no murder?"

Again she had to concede that there was murder and, okay, plenty of it. Horrible ones. Perpetrated by all kinds of people. Every day. All over the planet.

Sylvester's eyes gleamed with triumph, knowing full well he'd hit his mark. "And are there no other atrocities committed there? No thievery, no bribery, no betrayal...no treachery?"

"All right, you've made your point!" Donnie grouched. "We haven't come as far as we'd hoped in my century and, in actual fact, we are just as barbaric as you are here in this primitive, backwater hell. Feel better?" She put her hands on her hips and declared huffily, "Unlike some creatures, who shall remain nameless, *Sylvester*, I have no problem with being wrong every once in a while. Nonetheless, can't you understand, O' Master Cat, that, no matter what, I'd still rather be in my own barbaric time, than in yours?"

Mynydd Uchaf chuffed at her. "Really, Donemere, can you not understand that no spell will take you back to your world until you have defeated Valledai?"

She turned to study him, her mouth agape, real comprehension at last dawning on her mobile features. After several seconds with her mouth hanging wide, she finally recalled herself and said, "Let me see if I have this straight: as soon as I get rid of this guy—what'd you call him, Valley Guy? Omigod!"

The wolf, cat and even Otis stared at her in consternation. She merely shrugged her shoulders, blithely informing them, "You had to be there. In the eighties, I mean. We little girls just loved that movie! But the really shameful part is that we big girls loved it again when they remade it in 2020!" She gave them a look of studied chagrin, then, beginning to feel uncomfortable under the heat of their still stunned gazes, she hastily went back to the pertinent subject and asked brightly, "So, what you're telling me is that as soon as I get rid of this Valley Guy character for you, any spell I write to take me home will work; izzat right?"

Mynydd Uchaf nodded his head, albeit hesitantly, but it was enough for Donnie.

"Well, hallelujah! Slap a pair of emerald slippers on my feet and call me Francesca!" she crowed. "If I'd known that's all I have to do to get outta here, I would've worked a heck of a lot harder at this magic stuff." She turned and shook a stern finger at Sylvester. "Funny how a little information goes a long way toward achieving mutual goals, huh, pal?" she pointed out to the cat. "Don't you know that's one of the cardinal rules of business? Tell ya what, maybe we oughta start havin' Monday morning meetings, eight a.m. sharp, so you can catch me up on what's been happening around here. How about that, kitten, kitten, who's got the mitten?"

"Then you are willing to work hard to defeat Valledai? And you will heal this man?" the Wolf King interjected, speaking fast before the furious, spluttering cat could reply.

Donnie nodded her head a couple of times, biting her thumbnail in concentration, then bent down again to look at the injured man. "Sure thing, Warren, I'm willing to try just about anything once. Besides, it doesn't look like I have much of a choice. You've kinda got me over a barrel, you know?" She heaved a resolute sigh and gave another curt nod. "So then, to start, I should probably bandage the worst of this guy's wounds while we're here, so's to inhibit the blood loss." There, that was the proper tone to take. It made her sound as though she actually knew what she was doing. And she sorta did, when it came right down to it.

Just remember, she added to herself hastily, *it's only flesh and blood*. But, as she once again looked at all that blood, she could only pray that she was going to get through this new ordeal without fainting.

Mynydd Uchaf had frowned at her and grunted his displeasure at her new name for him, all of which Donnie ignored of course, including his low-key reminder of his real name. With a bewildered shake of his head, the Wolf King turned from eyeing her disapprovingly and became business-like once again, informing Sylvester, "I will leave you now and track back to the edge of the magical lands. If I meet this man's enemy, I will do what I can to delay or, if need be, defeat him. Once I am certain there is no other of Valledai's forces within Caterin's—forgive me—I mean Donemere's realm, then I shall return to you at the cottage." He then looked at Donnie, who had just twisted around so she could see him and Sylvester, and advised her, "Be quick, Donemere. You are running out of time." With that ambiguous warning, he dropped the tablecloth covering him and was gone, transforming back into his wolven form after he'd traveled twenty feet or so.

Donnie and Sylvester surveyed each other for some while before she broke the silence by inquiring dryly, "Running out of time? Don't suppose you'd like to tell me what he meant by that, would you? Or what he's got to do with all this? Or how he knows my name? No-o-o, I didn't think so. Okay, okay, I'm willing to do my part in this business—as long as I don't have to hurt anyone, that is," she said resolutely, then she pointed a finger at the unconscious man on the ground and added, "Anyway, I think the more pressing question right now is, how am I going to get *him* onto Otis?"

"Why do you wish to place him on Otis, if I may ask, and not his own horse?" Sylvester queried, wondering just what Donemere could be thinking now. He was always very cautious when questioning her motivations or plans because, usually, he was either embarrassed or confused by her explanations, and quite often both. He really must warn Warren—er, Mynydd Uchaf about some of her more egregious peculiarities, he thought to himself.

Donnie raised an eyebrow at the curiously pensive cat. She waited until his eyes focused on her again before replying to him. "Has it not occurred to you, my little feline friend," she said, "that if the situation did indeed happen as we posited earlier, then, as Warren also fears, this man's foe is still out here looking for him? And I'm guessing this foe of his will be a good tracker. The bad guy's always the best tracker around—next to the hero, that is. Everybody knows that, or at least it always seems that way in the adventure stories I read. Which means he'll probably manage to stay away from Warren. So, until we know more about the situation, we'll go on the presumption that ours is the good guy and the other guy is the bad guy. Therefore, if the bad guy tracks the good guy to here, which it's a sure bet he can, then it would be best if Otis and Gallantry leave in different directions, with Gallantry running away hard and us trotting just as calmly back home as when we came. Get my drift?"

The cat, parsing through what she had just said, indicated his comprehension with a nod. "Ah yes, so this bad guy, as you call him, will think that the good guy," Sylvester inclined his head toward the prone figure of the man beside Donnie, "rode off on Gallantry—er, his own horse—and that we came here merely by happenstance." The cat's voice filled with something akin to respect. "Not necessarily at the same time as the good guy, so if the bad guy tracks us back to the cottage, you can avow that we were not here at the same time as his foe and thereby know nothing of his whereabouts."

Donnie beamed at him, pleased. "Yep, you got it. Although that might not be all that believable, now that I think about it, because both sets of tracks will be too fresh. Oh, I've got it, we can just say we rousted this dude early this morning because he was trespassing and I, being a solitary-type witch, don't like trespassers. Wounds? What wounds? We didn't see any wounds, just some bloody fool who had the nerve to trespass on my lands, can you believe it?" she wisecracked. "You never know, Sylvester, the bad guy just might buy it, if I play my part well enough. Otherwise, let's hope this resident bad guy of yours doesn't want to search the farm when he comes calling, 'cause something tells me he's definitely going to visit us. I guess we'll cross that bridge when we get to it."

She stood decisively, adding, "As you're so fond of saying to me, Sylvester, we'd better get a move on." She turned toward Gallantry and gave him very specific and rigid instructions. He was to keep moving fast for the rest of the day in any direction but south, the direction of the cottage. He was to make his trail as confusing as possible, maybe run through a few towns, over hill and dale, maybe even cross a few rivers or creeks whenever he got the chance. After that, he was to come back here as quick as he could and keep an eye on the area. If the bad stranger came around, he was to tell someone, anyone—a bird, a bat, or even a butterfly—to tell Sylvester. He was to remember that name, Sylvester, because practically every living creature within twenty-five miles of the house knew Sylvester. She then remembered that the cat's name was not actually Sylvester.

"Damn, what's your real name again, Sylvester? You know, the one everybody else around here knows you by?" Donnie asked.

"Tanygrisiau yr Eglwys Wen, as I have reminded you on several occasions," the cat replied with an air of forbearance. "Before you inquire yet again, it means *below the steps of the white church*, and yes, it is where I was born. But, if you told him Sylvester, that will succeed in getting the message to me. All creatures hereabouts know what you call me and will readily recognize the name."

She eyed the cat narrowly, deadpanning, "Really? I wonder how it got around to all the creatures hereabouts? Oh, let me guess, you've been telling stories about me to the squirrels and probably the starlings again, haven't you? Shame on you, Sylvester, you know what inveterate gossips they are!"

The cat refused to meet her gaze and Donnie let the argument drop, knowing full well how much he complained about her to anyone who'd listen.

She once again directed her thoughts toward Gallantry, sending as many visualizations as possible along with her instructions. A minute later, the chestnut took off on a northeastern course, hooves pounding hard.

Quite an interesting turn of events, Donnie mused, as she looked downward and studied the unconscious man at her feet. She really was getting some answers finally. And who'd have thought it possible: she now had a man and a sort-of man in her life, all in one morning. The man, although he was covered with mud and blood (and passed out cold), appeared to be well built, tall—*Why, he might even be handsome!* she thought to herself lecherously. Well, she'd know that for sure once she got a chance to wash his face. He had shoulder-length fair hair, although it was too dirty to tell its exact color, and a long, aristocratic nose, full lips, strong chin, a high forehead and cheekbones. Jeepers, was he in need of a shave, or what? Unless he liked having a scruffy beard? Hmm, the more she looked at his face, the more he definitely reminded her of someone.

She turned her attention back to the problem of getting him onto Otis. It wasn't as though she could just lift him onto the horse's back—oh, wait a minute, why not do just that? By Jove, she was going to levitate him there! Just last week she'd begun practicing levitating living creatures and had, by this time, gotten halfway decent at it, although she'd found it to be very different from levitating inanimate objects. Live beings usually have at least a couple of appendages that must be accounted for, so Donnie had to make sure that she had just the right amount of lift for every part of the body she was trying to levitate, otherwise she'd send them spinning or tumbling end-over-end through the air. But that sort of thing hadn't happened for at least two days. Perhaps a little overconfidently, she canted:

"Lift this man, I say,
Lift him high.
To ride the pony,
He must fly,
Up in the air today."

The man's body was hurled at the sky, his back arched at what looked to be a painful degree since Donnie had mostly concentrated on lifting his torso so she could take the pressure off his left arm, which had been pinned beneath him. Luckily, the tree he lay beside spread its branches in time to save the man's skull from being cracked open by one of them. Donnie recoiled in horror, only to have the man's body begin to plummet just as quickly toward the ground, his legs and arms extended upward now.

"Stop!" she screamed, lifting out a cupped hand as if to catch the man with it.

His precipitous descent halted two feet from the rocks beneath him, his limbs dangling outward in mid-air.

"Oh-jeez-oh-man, was that close! Omigod, omigod, omigod!" she chanted helplessly, thoroughly panicked and deeply distressed by what she'd just done. "See? See, Sylvester? Do we need any more proof than *that* that I can't do this?" she cried to the cat.

Without sympathy, Sylvester berated her angrily. "He is not a boulder to be tossed around lightly, you foolish Madra Witch! You must take great care with humans!" the cat remonstrated. "You would know this if you practiced more seriously with me!"

Donnie, breathing hard and shaking, lowered her hand slowly and the man's body floated just as slowly to the ground in response. Her knees felt weak and rubbery, so she too sank to the muddy, rocky soil. "Oh! My! God! I nearly killed him! I can't believe it. No! More than that, I can't do this, I tell you! I just can't do this; it's all way too weird for me. You'll have to find some other 'aff sprig' of Catie's and have them do it. At this rate, I'm likely to kill this man before we even get him back to the house!"

Sylvester jumped to the ground and then to her lap in two bounds. He looked her squarely in the face and reminded her acidly, "You do not have a choice, if you wish to go back to your time; do you? You will do this, but you will not kill this man in the doing!"

Donnie rubbed at the tears welling up in her eyes and puffed out her cheeks, wailing, "Oh, fine!" after a few moments.

"Now try again, only use more care," Sylvester advised. "And, as I have informed you on numerous occasions, because of the depth and breadth of your power, you need not make a rhyme. You need only to will it, for it to happen." The cat left her lap and once more jumped onto Otis's back.

Donnie blew a fractious breath. "Yes, I know that. The rhyming just makes it more fun," she retorted petulantly, adding under her breath, "It also drives you crazy."

"This is not about having fun," Sylvester scolded, " 'tis about saving this man's life. Now, you must make haste in doing so!"

"You know as well as I do, Sylvester, that he's not anywhere near death at the moment, so quit exaggerating the situation just to make me feel even worse," said Donnie, staring mutinously at the cat. Then she grimaced ruefully and her shoulders slumped. "Okay, I admit that levitating a person is a lot different from lifting inanimate objects, or even you or Otis or the others, especially since you were all conscious and could help balance yourselves." She let out an anguished groan, then squared her shoulders and nodded to herself. "All right, I think I'm set now. I'm going to concentrate on levitating his arms and legs just enough, and then I'll lift the rest of him manually."

The cat looked at her with confusion, waiting to see what she would do next. Otis whinnied and said encouragingly, "You can do this, Donnie, I know you can. Remember, Diana and I both trust you to levitate us anytime you need to practice. If you can lift us, you can definitely lift this guy."

Donnie stood over the man, took a deep breath, and tried again, this time raising her cupped hands very slowly. The man's hands lifted first, then his feet. When he was bent into a u-shape, she reached down to put her arms underneath his body and straightened, lifting him chest high. Since almost all of his weight was already levitating, it took practically no effort on her part to move him this way. She carried him over to a silent, but shaking Otis and, once there, placed the man's butt on the horse's rump, his legs slightly spread-eagled above her much-amused steed. Donnie concentrated her mind on lifting the man's hands a little bit higher, though not a lot, while letting his legs down slowly. His torso rose to a sitting position and his feet slid down the sides of the horse.

Donnie realized that she was sweating. This particular task had taken a lot out of her. Not the magic part of it, but the control part, which really surprised her.

Sylvester had watched her lift the man onto Otis with outraged incredulity. Donnie was made aware of this only when the cat moved onto Otis's trembling shoulder, into her line of sight, and glared at her in mute disbelief.

"Okay, so it wasn't pretty," she admitted truculently in response to the cat's unspoken criticism. "But he's on, isn't he?"

The horse began to choke and cough with laughter, which both Donnie and Sylvester ignored.

Donnie took the extra tablecloth out of the carryall bag and picked up the discarded one from the rock where Warren had left it. With her utility knife, she ripped the latter into long strips and the former into squares. Standing on an outcropping of rock beside Otis to give herself some added height, she carefully packed the deep lacerations on the man's abdomen with rolled squares of cloth, then loosely wrapped and tied the longer pieces of cotton around his mid-section, using his armored breastplate to press the bandages in place. She continued bandaging most of the cuts in an attempt to staunch the flow of blood that was now seeping from several of them, after their clots had been disturbed by her, um, shall we say, *mishap* in levitation. She had the worst of the cuts bandaged in less than ten minutes. The others would have to wait for later. Having gotten a closer look at his wounds, Donnie was even more confident that the man would live to fight many more battles, as long as *she* didn't do anything lethal to him in the meantime.

Still concentrating on keeping the injured man upright, she gingerly climbed aboard as Sylvester jumped to the rear. Donnie reached up in the air to grab the man's hands, pulling his arms down so that they rested around her. Gripping them firmly, she told Otis to take them home quickly but carefully, the man's head lolling heavily on her shoulder.

Sylvester hopped in front of Donnie before the horse took off and sat there the entire journey, repeating several magical instructions that he'd been attempting for months to beat into her brain. Although he had no idea of this, he wasn't enjoying any more success than he had in the past. Donnie spent the entire trip home trying to take in the revelations Warren had let drop and just what they might mean for her situation. She didn't get far with that since, obviously, there was still a whole lot more the cat and his wolven friend had yet to relate. Nevertheless, she couldn't stop herself from obsessing.

By the time they reached the valley, Donnie's arms had fallen asleep from holding the man's tightly around her waist. As they exited the forest and began their descent toward the house, she realized that it was time to decide where to have their injured guest stay. Should she put him in her room, while she slept on the couch in the office?

Hmm, a man in her bed? Between her sheets? His head nestled into her pillow? She probably should, but what if he turned out to be really, really handsome?

When they crested the rise where the little farm stood, she asked Otis to go to the stables. Sylvester cleared his throat excessively, his query obvious.

"I'm going to put him in here for a while, maybe in Diana's stall, just until he's up and around," Donnie informed the cat, who then wanted to know why. "Well, the stables' doorways are a heck of a lot wider than the ones in the house, you know. If I try to get him through the house doors, he could very well end up with concussion and we can't have that, can we?" And besides, out here he wouldn't be as much of a temptation to her—not that she was going to tell the cat this.

Sylvester harrumphed disapprovingly, silently wondering what this "concussion" thing was, then he jumped lightly onto the top of the gate, hit the ground, and scampered around the back of the stables, out of sight. Donnie let go of the unconscious man's hands and sat there with him leaning on her back while she rubbed the life back into her own hands. She took an inordinate time doing this, she knew, because she wasn't looking forward to lifting the man off the horse. She did not want a repeat performance of him shooting through the air, especially since the stables had such a solid roof.

Once she felt the needles in her arms had subsided sufficiently for her to make use of those appendages again, she lifted her right leg over Otis's neck and sat on him sideways. Before slipping to the ground, she willed the injured man's hands to again rise above his head. When she was back on terra firma and the man was safely sitting upright by way of her magic, she led the horse into the stables and in front of Diana's stall.

"Hiya, Diana," Donnie blurted, anxiously attempting to hide her extreme nervousness over the coming ordeal. "I've got a roomie for you, 'kay? Please don't kick him or step on him; you'll kill him if you do. And that would be a bad thing. Believe me, a very bad thing. As a matter of fact, I think he's the hero of our story, y'see.

"Oh," she continued hurriedly, too frantic to realize what she was saying, "he's probably going to get really cold at night, so you'll have to lie next to him to keep him warm. Now, I said next to him, not on him, all right?" She caught her breath at the expression on Diana's face, and then let it expel through her parted lips. She ran to her friend and cried, "Omigod, I'm so, so sorry about that, Diana! How unbelievably bitchy of me! I didn't mean a word of it; honest I didn't! I was blathering simply because I'm a blithering idiot! Truly, I was, er, I am! Oh, look, I'm just so damned nervous over the near-certainty that I'm about to murder this man in the next few minutes, merely by attempting to get him off Otis, that I don't even know what I'm babbling right now. I mean it, you should've seen what happened when I tried to get him *on* Otis, then you'd know that's not just my usual hype. And if, by some weird happenstance, I manage to get him to the ground without maiming him for life, there will be several more opportunities coming up to drastically shorten his lifespan by any one of hundreds of methods, not the least of which is dysentery. Oh, bless my pathetic little soul, I am so not looking forward to this!"

Diana scoffed, looked the man over, then turned her glistening gaze to the wall on her right. "You needn't worry, Donnie," said the cow, her tone stiff with hurt, "you won't kill *him*. I've known a lot of men, and even from here I can see he's of the high-breed."

"Ah, well, that's good to know. But what does 'high-breed' mean?" Donnie enquired timidly, utterly stunned by her horrid treatment of her friend, which had resulted in Diana apparently not wanting even to look at Donnie now.

"It refers to someone born of the aristocracy, which means they have high blood in them, or the blood of the gods," Diana explained, still refusing to meet Donnie's eyes. "They live longer than the common folk, unless they're killed in battle, and believe you me, they're very hard to kill in battle, or so my brothers always said. They're known as the Sarn." The cow shook her head, her voice warming as she relaxed a little, and she finally glanced at Donnie. "Well, bring your patient on in. I don't mind."

Donnie gushed her relief. "Thanks," she said, a little too enthusiastically. "My apologies for asking this of you, but your stall is bigger than Otis's and, besides, you do like to lie down a lot so you really will be able to keep him warm. I suppose I could put him on my bed and I'll sleep on the couch, but—oh, really, you're sure you don't mind?" said Donnie when Diana tossed her head. "Thank you, Diana, especially after my totally moronic, stupid and unforgivable rudeness to you a minute ago."

Diana's soft brown eyes blinked back her offended tears. "It's okay, Donnie; I know you'd never mean to hurt me with anything you'd say or do because that's just not your way. But it does tell me exactly how frightened you are. I think maybe you need to take some deep breaths and center yourself, that's all, and then you'll be okay."

Donnie smiled, grateful tears blurring her vision. She hugged the cow mightily and, after taking four of the prescribed breaths, exclaimed, "You are a brick, you know that, Diana? A very, very smart brick, by the way. I can't even imagine being here without you; I'd probably be totally insane if I didn't have you to keep me grounded. Thank you for forgiving me. And you are correct, my friend, hurting you is the absolute last thing I'd ever want to do. A pox on me if I ever do that to you again!" She crossed her arms in front of her, pressing her palms to her shoulders, as she said this.

"Without justification," the cow interjected hastily. Then, when Donnie looked at her in surprise, she insisted, "Go on, say it, Donnie. Make it part of the spell."

Donnie shrugged her acquiescence and added, "Without justification." She dropped her arms to her sides and sighed—a long, long, heavy one. "That being said, I guess it's time for me to get my 'patient' off Otis. Let's pray I don't kill the poor man in the process. You ready? Here he comes."

Donnie levitated the man's feet so that he was in the now-familiar u-shape, with his butt resting on the rump of the horse, and, as before, she put her arms underneath him to carry him to the far side of the stall. Ever so gently, she let him float downward until his body rested fully on the straw-covered floor. Diana tried to suppress her giggles at the sight they presented, but soon was chortling with delight. Otis accompanied her in guffawing, once again unable to contain his own amusement.

Sylvester joined them in the stables while Diana and Otis were still razzing Donnie about her unorthodox mode of levitation. The cat jumped onto the top rail of the fence and sat near the opening to Diana's stall, clearly much aggrieved about something. Donnie, pointedly ignoring the others, sat back on her haunches and noisily blew out an exaggerated breath, turning around to look at her preoccupied familiar with resignation. "Wow, that was way harder than it should have been, Sylvester. As much as it pains me to admit this, you were right to criticize me about not practicing more diligently and I was wrong not to listen to you. Sorry about that. I guess I've been a pretty difficult student for you, huh?"

"My heart will not survive the novelty of receiving an apology from you," the cat replied sarcastically. Donnie decided to pointedly ignore this also and turned back to her patient.

About then, Warren trotted purposefully into the stables, paying no heed to the chickens' loud protests of fear when he transformed from wolf into werewolf. He stopped outside Diana's stall and leant against the wall separating it from Otis's stall, informing the assembled group, "I found no sign of the other man. You must begin your ministrations to this one immediately, Donemere. He is much weakened by the journey."

Donnie pursed her lips and nodded. "When you're right, Warren, you're right. Okay, first things first, he needs some water." While Diana and Warren traded warm greetings, Donnie magically fetched the drinking cup hanging by the well, after having it fill itself with water. Catching it deftly with her right hand, she bent over the man and dribbled some water onto his lips. They parted and she let a little of the clear, cold liquid trickle slowly over them and into his mouth. She firmly refused to notice that they were very full and sensuous lips.

On her way to round up everything she would need to treat the man's wounds, Donnie paused at the well to fill a bucket, then carefully floated that to the cottage door. Once inside the house, she dumped the water into a big cast iron cauldron and levitated the pot onto a burner of the stove, which turned on to high heat. She kept sending the bucket flying outside to fill itself and then return to dump its load into the cauldron until the pot was full. She also grabbed the teakettle and filled it with water from the kitchen tap, setting that on another burner to boil.

According to every old movie Donnie had ever watched that had even a remotely similar situation in it, she was going to need a lot of boiling water. She wasn't quite sure what for exactly, other than to bathe the injured man with, but it was probably best to have as much of it as possible on hand, in case some other need became apparent to her. And boiling it the old-fashioned way gave her time to prepare herself for the gruesome task ahead.

She'd have to make poultices for the man's deeper cuts. But the first thing she'd do is give him a sponge bath so she could see how well he cleaned up—er, how many cuts he actually had, she rebuked herself sternly. To cleanse her patient's wounds, she decided to use the Klein Liniment she'd first made a couple of months ago during her "Introduction to Herbal Medicine" phase. Donnie had studied Catie's journals carefully, comparing its notes and recipes with those she found in books by Josef Klein and Bay Gladstone, finding their ingredients and instructions for use markedly similar. While she was still no expert, Donnie had worked hard at familiarizing herself with medicinal herbs and their properties, producing various herbal remedies, tinctures, ointments, creams and liniments. Sylvester's talents did not run to medicines, so she'd been on her own for this field of study.

She walked toward the sideboard in the corner to get a mixing bowl and tripped over something unseen in the walkway between it and the table. Immediately, her dog appeared when he pulled his nose out from under the sideboard.

Exasperated, Donnie exclaimed for at least the millionth time since arriving here, "Oh, it wasn't bad enough back home when you'd do that and just think you were invisible, but now you've actually got to *be* invisible! At least I could see you sticking out from things then."

Rex, after nearly eight years of living with her, was used to her endless, and mostly harmless, ranting at him and had nothing to add but his usual disgruntled sigh. To him, this was their own very special means of communicating and he thought she'd be thoroughly disappointed if he didn't always exhibit displeasure in one form or another whenever she went off on him. Once he had accomplished his part of their routine, he rolled over onto his side and stuck his head back under the sideboard. And immediately disappeared again.

"Now that's good, just spread out and make yourself a bigger target I still can't see!" Donnie complained. "Uh-uh, I don't think so. Will you please get out of the kitchen?" She waved her foot in the dog's general direction.

Rex pulled his head out again, reappeared on the floor, and reluctantly got to his feet. "Okay, okay. Why are you in such a bad mood? Is it 'cause I wasn't here to kiss you good morning? I'm sorry 'bout that, but I got caught up playing with Harry and Kim, so when that storm came on quicker than even you'd figured, we decided to just hunker down in the caves and ride it out." He stretched sleepily, singing out an "Aaarrruuuffff" as was his habit whenever he performed this particular dog activity. He shook himself, then peered up at her curiously. "What did I ask you—oh, yeah, how come you're in such a bad mood?" he recalled hastily, noting the stern set to her chin.

"I've got a man's life to save," she retorted. "He's practically bleeding to death out in Diana's stall." Great, now she was the one who was completely distorting the man's status.

"Oh, is that all?" Rex mumbled, then began to speak in a rush as he came fully awake, his bushy tail wagging furiously, obviously unfazed by the news of the man's presence. "Hey, anytime you wanna feed me is fine with me. Sooner would be better than later. I'm pretty hungry, ya know? Yeah, I know what you're gonna say, *When are you not hungry*, huh? I can't help it, I'm a growin' boy! Ya got any of that chicken left? That'd be really good this morning, don'tcha think? I ran my tail off last night in the caves and I'm starvin'!"

Donnie rolled her eyes at him and replied, "No, I don't get meat all that often around here, so I'm keeping it for me. You can eat dog food today or go hunting in the forest. Yes, I know full well you do that and I've been meaning to talk to you about it. Please tell me that you don't eat magical creatures," she said, crossing her arms before asking forcefully, "do you?"

The dog sat down and looked up at his mama, panting loudly. No sense in lying to her, so it was probably best to not say anything. He hadn't eaten it on purpose, after all, and he'd only done it once. And afterward he'd had the most terrible indigestion, so now he always asked his prey if they were magical before even thinking about scarfing them down.

Donnie tapped an impatient toe. "Well?"

Rex grunted unhappily, his expression pained. She wasn't going to let him off the hook that easily, which meant she must be in a really bad mood today. "Not as a rule, no, Mama."

"Then make sure you keep it that way. I know that not all the animals around here are magical, so there should be plenty of them to suit your hunting needs. I mean it, Rex, stay away from the magical ones, okay?" Donnie glared steadily at her dog, making him feel totally guilty about that Silver Sparrow.

Rex licked his chops nervously before responding. "Yes, Mama...I will, Mama....whatever you say, Mama. Really, Mama, I mean it!" Would she please stop glaring at him like that? It had happened ever so long ago; in fact, he'd done it the first two weeks after he'd arrived here. He was now starting to feel the same horrible indigestion rise in him as when he'd eaten the bird. Okay, maybe he had known the sparrow was magical before he'd eaten it, but how was he to have known it would make him sick? After all, every other nonmagical sparrow he'd eaten here had made a tasty snack, really crunchy, which had sat just fine with his usually sensitive tummy. It was only later that he found out being miserably sick to the stomach for days and days was always the consequence when one magical animal ate another, at least for those who dwelt upon the magical lands.

Donnie, silently berating herself for taking her bad mood out on first Sylvester, then Diana, and now Rex, turned around and spun the top off the dog's food bin. She scooped out three cups of food and dumped them into his food dish, then poured over that some of the vitamin and mineral-fortified chicken stock that she'd concocted in order to give his food an enhanced flavor and supplemental nutrients, especially as it was nearing the end of the food's charmed cycle. In a couple of hours or so, the replicated kibble would disintegrate, but even now it would serve quite well as both filler and dental aid.

During her fervent charming phase this winter, all cupboards, bins, drawers, closets, boxes and holders of any kind had been charmed to produce an unending supply of whatever was stowed in them. She found this reduced her irritation level with this place substantially. The best part about it, though, was that it eliminated laundry days.

The dog walked over to his bowl and dipped his head into its interior. Donnie heard him crunching away as she opened the door to the sideboard and got out a mixing bowl, setting it on the kitchen table. Even though she was in a bad mood, no way was she going to apologize for putting Rex on the spot. He knew full well her attitude toward protecting magical creatures. Sure, they were a dying breed and Sylvester said they sometimes fought each other to the death, but that didn't mean Donnie thought it proper for her or her dog to help them along in their demise.

By the time Rex finished eating his meal (or rather, inhaling it) and, as usual, tried coercing his mama into playing a game of combined keep-away and fetch with one of his favorite squeaky toys (a plastic newspaper aptly entitled *The Daily Howler*), Donnie had convinced herself that taking the high road had been the right thing to do with him. And so, in response to his numerous, high-pitched, pseudo-pathetic play whines, his seductive shaking of the toy, and his best mesmerizing stare (which he'd learned from watching Sylvester hunt nonmagical birds), she met his gaze squarely for a few, long seconds, then looked pointedly at the crowded kitchen counter. Rex dropped the toy, sighed with disappointment, and ran into the bathroom to ask Carly if she would play word games with him.

Donnie shook her head at his retreating backside and let out a heavy sigh of her own. While waiting for the water to boil, she collected several jars of herbs and other medical supplies from the pantry and various cupboards, a wide assortment that left just the cutting board area clear. The water in the pot was only now beginning to heat up, so Donnie sat on the corner of the kitchen table and gazed unseeingly at the herbal paraphernalia waiting for her, reflecting on the real reason she'd delved so deeply into their healing properties. Her depression had mounted slowly after arriving here. For the first month and a half, her days had been filled with activity, but her nights had been consumed by restless worry. Once her home improvements were finished, the mantle of depression had settled closely around her shoulders.

Even Sylvester soon noticed the dark circles that had developed under her eyes and the tiredness in her lackluster movements, and so had voiced the obvious opinion that she was quite unwell and this should not be. Donemere must stop her destructive emotions, he advised her sternly. If only she would focus on doing everything just the way he told her to and accept who she was now, her mentality would return to normal. Exactly what Sylvester thought of as normal, he would never specify.

One of the things Donnie had learned early on about the cat was that he was a great one for leaving his many abstruse remarks unexplained.

Although, in his way, Sylvester had been absolutely correct. Pretending her life here was only temporary and somehow not real had been destructive for Donnie and she had finally realized that she had to stop the slow meltdown she was spiraling toward. She needed to deal with the anxiety and fears that roiled only slightly below the surface, determine the ramifications of what had been done to her, and somehow make her peace with it all. Possibly then she could do something about her predicament.

First things first, she'd read up on methods of dealing with acute depression and had put these into practice. She'd bolstered her campaign against her condition greatly by taking to meditating for ten to fifteen minutes whenever a panic attack would come, sometimes six or seven times a day, breaking from her lessons without so much as a by-your-leave to the cat (to his intense annoyance) to retreat to her bedroom. But this diligence showed real promise almost immediately and within a couple of weeks Donnie had whittled these attacks down to only one or two per day, so that her meditation sessions became more scheduled, usually saved for the evenings. She'd also started paying closer attention to her diet and was careful to include the proper amounts of what she called "happy foods" such as milk, chickpeas, dates, peanuts, sunflower and pumpkins seeds, all manner of greens and other vegetables, and lots of fruit, carefully herbing and spicing the latter groups until her taste buds were adroit at differentiating even minute traces of a spice or an herb.

It was also at this time that she began studying herbal remedies for her condition. One thing led to another and before Donnie realized it she was knee-deep in herbal remedies for all sorts of maladies. Her efforts had met with success from their beginning and she'd steadily advanced to the point where most mornings her mood was one of wry watchfulness instead of total despair. The nightmares too had subsided finally and she'd been able to enjoy a full night's rest for months now.

That was also when she'd devised her exercise regimen. Every day, weather permitting, she continued going for runs around the valley. Once the snow had melted, in the coolness of the early evenings, she completed at least half an hour of resistance and weight training, having set up her old weights and other workout equipment on the back porch outside her workshop. The endorphin high from all this exercise would usually carry her through the rest of the evening without one single attack of panic. And this past month, she'd added yoga to her routine to expand her flexibility and range of motion.

At first, Sylvester had, quite incessantly, made it clear that he thought her twenty-first century methodology for combating "depression" was nuts. But, since it continually improved her disposition, his complaints about its time consumption lessened with each passing week.

Perhaps most importantly, Donnie had allowed herself to get closer to her craft, reading avidly of its history and its traditions. It had come as a surprise when she realized that what Sylvester had said was true: she *had* been resisting it instead of embracing it. Therefore, the last couple of months she'd set herself the task of working especially hard to hone her skills. This too had met with unqualified success, actually even earning real praise on one occasion from Sylvester for her efforts at transmogrification. But, in her heart of hearts, she knew there was still a reticence within her toward this amazing power she carried in her fingertips. And this reticence, as she was discovering now, was due primarily to her fear of the future. According to Catie and Sylvester, she was the most powerful witch that ever was, but what exactly did that mean for her? While she'd avoided giving that particular subject much consideration until now, it appeared the time had come for her to study it in detail.

The water in the teakettle and the pot were hissing and bubbling merrily, bringing Donnie back to the present. She took from each of the herb containers the correct amounts of their contents that she needed for the poultices. She'd chosen goldenseal root, myrrh gum, shepherd's purse and plantain leaves, along with the flowers of yarrow and St. John's Wort as her mix. Heaping all the foliage into a pile, she deftly lacerated the leaves and flowers with her herb knife. When finished with this task, she deposited the herb powders and striated foliage into the mixing bowl, then poured a little of the piping hot water over them, letting them soak for just a little while, only until they were thoroughly wetted. After that, she unrolled some gauze and began to make the poultices. She also brewed herself some jasmine tea from the kettle water.

She was fully cognizant that, by making the poultices manually, she was again postponing the task ahead of her. She couldn't help this though, since the very real possibility of making the man worse by her ministrations shook her to the core. It's one thing to read books about doing this sort of thing, but applying that knowledge practically was entirely different. What if she messed up and he really did die on her? She'd never be able to forgive herself that.

Nonetheless, as Sylvester had pointed out, she had no choice but to do her best at healing the man, so she would just have to believe that her efforts to familiarize herself with incantations, herbal medicines and all the other "parlor tricks" (as she insisted on calling them because it irritated Sylvester to no end) hadn't been wasted and she'd actually learned her craft reasonably well.

She straightened her shoulders with assumed resolve, her hands working busily on the poultices, and mumbled to herself, "This man's life may depend on it. So, hag's bags, Donnie, don't screw up."

Chapter 6
Forever Love

The poultices were finished far too soon for Donnie's liking. She even griped, "Rats, aren't there any more to make?" after she'd wrapped up the last one, not at all sure she was ready to go back to the stables. Then again, what else did she have planned for the day? A little gardening, her daily workout, some studying and practicing, driving the cat nuts in one way or another—you know, the usual stuff. So saving a man's life would at least break the routine.

Steeling her resolve, she got out the Klein Liniment, setting it beside the bowl containing the poultices. After taking out her ceramic washbasin and another large, glass mixing bowl from the sideboard, then filling the latter with boiling water, she materialized her supplies to the stables.

Now, materializing things was one of the hardest skills for her to understand. It wasn't exactly like using *Star Voyager*'s bioport, she reasoned, where you knew that matter was converted to energy, then reconstituted into matter at the destination point. Whenever she dematerialized something with magic, she couldn't help but wonder just where it went before it reappeared. Short of materializing herself into the place where all dematerialized things go, wherever that was (which she was not about to try), Donnie eventually learned to trust that things would simply be there, fully intact, wherever she sent them. But once she also realized the extent of the dangers of materialization with magic, she'd been unable to deliberately and knowingly transport any living being anywhere with this method—heck, not even a worm or beetle anymore.

This was just one of the many contentious issues between her and Sylvester. Basically, the cat called her a pansy over it and Donnie let him because, basically, he was right. She remembered only too well those episodes of *Star Voyager* where the bioport screwed up and left a steaming pile of matter in place of a healthy human being.

After filling the bucket with boiled water from the cauldron, she went outside, levitating the bucket beside her as she walked toward the stables, just to practice not spilling so much as a drop. Part-way there, she reached over to the boombox where it was sitting on the ledge of the well and turned it on. Mackenzie Mack's "Lifestyle" CD materialized within its depths and started playing. She thought this was fine music for the task at hand, nice and soothing. Maybe it would help quieten her frazzled nerves.

Warren, transforming into his werewolf form again when Donnie entered the stables, stepped backward into Otis's stall as she went by him and remained there in the shadows. He and Sylvester were quietly discussing recent attacks of some sort that had apparently been committed on bear families in the area.

Donnie passed by Diana and knelt once more beside the injured man. Diana backed up to give her more room and watched over her friend's shoulder. Donnie poured boiling water into the washbasin, then snapped her fingers. A stack of small white linen towels appeared on her palm. These she set beside the bucket and bowls. She snapped again and a pair of long scissors materialized in her hand. As gently as possible, Donnie cut off the temporary bandages she'd wrapped around the man's wounds earlier and began to undress him. Off came what remained of his weaponry and their sheaths. Off came his armored breastplate. His boots gave her more than a little difficulty. She had to cut away his tunic, his linen undershirt and then his pants. These were all mostly in tatters anyway.

From behind her, Warren paused in his conversation with the cat and murmured something about saving and mending the clothing. Donnie was about to answer when she heard Sylvester say in a clear, low whisper, "She has a charmed wardrobe to take care of that. 'Tis truly one of her better spells, I think. All she does is ask for any article of attire, open the door, and there it is, freshly laundered and in perfect condition. It holds all of her garments, all that she will ever need. And the matching chest holds her footwear. It will be a simple thing for her to modify the spell to provide fresh clothing for this man. Now, tell me, my friend, what do you know of this curious situation concerning the *aderyn* nations?"

Wait a minute, was that pride she'd heard in Sylvester's voice? And just what was going on with the birds, she wondered. Donnie tried, but couldn't hear Warren's reply to the cat's question.

She turned her attention back to the injured man. Dipping one of the towels into the hot water in the washbasin, she began cleaning the mud and blood from his face and hair. His shoulder-length hair turned out to be dark-blond in color. It was thick and healthy, as was his beard, and shot with strands of silver. Again, Donnie refused to notice how incredibly handsome he was, now that she could get a good look at him. She couldn't shake the feeling that she knew him from somewhere. But where? Since she'd only seen him unconscious, with facial muscles relaxed and eyes closed, she couldn't yet tell. Perhaps once he was up and about it would come to her.

Rex came racing through the stables into Diana's stall, skidded to a halt, and exclaimed with surprise, "Hey, you weren't kidding, there really is a man here!"

Donnie took the time to face him and ask, crooking her right eyebrow at her dog, "Why would I kid about having a wounded man in our stables?"

Rex, assuming a nonplussed demeanor, sat back on his haunches and shrugged his shoulders. He leaned his head to one side, deadpanning, "I dunno. Why?" Then he grinned at Donnie. He liked to amuse her and, right now, she really looked like she could use some levity.

She didn't disappoint him, as usual. She gave a full, throaty laugh and said in a warm voice, "I love you, you big, goofy pup. Thanks for lightening the moment for me. Tell you what, do me a favor and go talk to the forest animals, will ya? Or this guy's horse, if you find him. He's a tall chestnut named Gallantry. Oh, he's not magical, so you'll have to contact him telepathically. And be careful not to get lost, 'cause the moors all kinda look the same and they seem to go on forever! I want you to keep an eye and ear out for the guy who did this mess," Donnie jerked a thumb in her patient's direction, "or for a message for Sylvester *about* the guy who did this mess. If you see or hear anything regarding him, or for that matter, regarding anyone approaching the house, come tell me immediately, okay?"

The shepherd was silent a moment, nodding and looking thoughtfully at the man. "Okay, Mama, but you don't need to worry about me, I can find my way almost anywhere," he said reassuringly. "Besides, you've got your hands full with this guy. Those cuts he's got look like they'd really hurt, huh? Something tells me something important's happening. Is this guy part of that?"

" 'Tis almost certain, yes," Warren answered and, for the first time, Rex noticed his presence.

The dog whirled around to face this intruder and his hackles raised. He'd wondered what that smell was, the one that was not quite right for a man. He began to growl and then bray, throwing in some barking just for fun. The wolf in Warren responded in kind as he backed away from the stalls, with Rex advancing after him. Rex again brayed loudly when Warren changed from werewolf to wolf. Having reached the open front section of the stables by now, the dog and wolf circled each other warily, sniffing first the air and then each other.

Donnie turned her back on this tableau with resignation, knowing there was absolutely nothing she could do about it, and resumed bathing her patient. She changed towels, refreshing the water in the basin at the same time, and moved her attentions to the unconscious man's body. Try as she might to stymie her reaction, she soon realized that her internal temperature was rising fast as she surveyed his beefy chest and broad shoulders, his thickly muscled arms, his washboard abs and narrow hips, his well-toned thighs and calves—"Oh, my gawd! I'm channeling Callida Cardin!" she hissed at herself in horror. She realized with a start that no one had spoken for some time, although the sounds of a scuffle could be heard behind her. She glanced round, but all she could see was Sylvester's backside since he was watching the dog and wolf. She looked to her right at the giggling Diana and whispered, "Well, he is really cute, you know!" Donnie winked at her friend before gazing down once again at the man. Yes, he was rather handsome. He also had an earthy, manly smell to him that was not yet unpleasant, but would get there soon if he wasn't washed.

The cow, no longer giggling, was now eyeing Donnie doubtfully. "Him? You like him? Give me a two-thousand-pound stud bull any day of the week over this or any other man!" she opined.

Pointedly, Donnie looked around them, raising an eyebrow as her gaze came back to rest on her friend, and inquired, "Just how many two-thousand-pound stud bulls have you, um, *had*?"

"Only one," Diana practically purred in remembrance. "They're in rather short supply around here, as you've noticed." She tossed her head as if she had a full head of hair, like when she'd been a young girl, before she was magically turned into a cow. "It was magnificent! I never felt anything even close to it with a man. He filled me with his—"

Donnie raised her hands in protest and interjected, "Whoa! It's okay, I get it! I do! Let's not go into that right now, okay? Maybe later you can tell me all about it." In reality, as much as she loved her friend, Donnie honestly didn't think she'd ever be ready for that discussion.

About this time, Rex and Warren separated, the wolf apparently having won the upper hand. Warren murmured something that sounded like, "There, are you satisfied? That is how it is done!" to Rex, who gave his thanks breathlessly and ran outside. Warren calmly went back to his previous place, transforming again into werewolf, and then he and Sylvester resumed their whispered discussion as if there had been no interruption at all.

Donnie once more returned her attention to her doctoring. She squared her shoulders and muttered to herself under her breath, "Okay, Donnie, you can do this. You've washed off most of the dirt and blood; now it's simply a matter of cleaning the wounds themselves. They're just some little ol' cuts, barely scratches; nothing to get het up about.

Remember, people have been doing this for thousands of years. And if they could do it, so can you, my dear."

Added to her own encouraging words was Diana's murmured, "That's right, sweetheart, you just keep all that in mind and you'll do just fine."

Pouring some of the liniment into the mixing bowl she'd filled with hot water, Donnie swirled a fresh towel in it and began washing the blood away from the man's wounds, scrubbing where she dared.

"He's not exactly small," she observed quietly, "not for a man anyway." She reckoned he was at least six and a half feet tall and around one hundred and ninety to two hundred pounds. Trim yet very muscular. Did she mention that he was, if truth be told, downright gorgeous? Her heart sank. How was she supposed to maintain her equanimity with him around? "I'm just a slave to love," she mumbled to herself, noisily sloshing the towel in the bowl of liniment solution.

Diana, who still stood just behind Donnie, was the only one who heard her last words. The cow pulled back her lips in a smile and whispered in Donnie's ear, "Aren't we all?"

With a chuckle, Donnie nodded. "Yes, I suppose so. Tell me, don't you ever miss being human?" she asked curiously, sitting back on her heels for a moment to push her hair from her face with the back of her hand. She silently thanked the heavens above that she didn't have to worry about any of the modern blood diseases because the man's blood was getting all over her clothes and her skin. The stables were filled with the metallic odor of it, in fact. Donnie swallowed the bile that rose in her throat at the thought of the word "blood" because there was just so damn much of it right in front of her and all around her; even her hands were totally stained with its redness. She herself was looking a little green about the gills, although none of the others seemed to notice anything amiss with her.

"Not really," replied Diana, matter-of-factly. "Remember, I was a slave girl. The life of a slave is neither to be envied nor yearned for."

Donnie nodded her head in agreement and said, "Well, sure, that's a given. But haven't you ever thought of being human again now? I mean, you know you wouldn't be a slave to anyone here, right? You'd just be a girl, footloose and fancy free. We can always get another cow, if you're worried about that. Not a magical one though. I don't think I could handle another talking animal at present. So, what do you think? How about I see what I can do to reverse the cow spell?" Because she was wringing the excess liniment mixture from the cloth again, she missed Warren's sharp intake of breath behind her.

Shooting a quick glance at the werewolf, Sylvester interjected in a subdued tone, "Diana, if anyone could do it, it would be Donemere. Though I must warn you, I do not believe that even she can reverse that type of spell."

Donnie shrugged. "Maybe, maybe not. I can but do my best and try. So, what do you say, my friend? Shall we give it a whirl?"

Diana looked at her with something very near to panic and replied, "I don't know. I have no frame of reference for that. I've never been free to just be a girl."

"Well, think about it," Donnie urged her friend earnestly. "Seriously, if you want me to, I can look for a way to do it. There're some clues in Catie's journals about at least modifying a permanent transmogrifying spell cast by someone else."

The cow stared at her for a long moment and then spoke haltingly, "I—I will...certainly...think about it." She looked confused and pensive, and clearly did not wish to discuss the subject further right now.

So Donnie let it drop and finished washing the front side of the man. Most of the numerous cuts on him were indeed superficial. But the one on his right side and another on his left leg looked rather nasty and were now seeping blood freely. Both of these lacerations were partially covered by his, well, to put it plainly, by his underwear.

"Nothing for it, they're going to have to come off too," she announced. It was with mixed feelings that she took the scissors and began to make two slits up the legs of the man's medieval undershorts and through the drawstring at the waist.

Sylvester, glancing over Donnie's shoulder from where he sat on the gate, saw enough to realize what was happening and gave a loud, sharp cough. "Pardon me, but what exactly are you doing, Donemere?" he asked.

She jumped guiltily at his harsh tone, hesitating in her scissoring. "Washing him, of course!" she retorted. "His wounds all have to be cleaned, don't you know that? They can get infected and then I really wouldn't be able to save him. As I've told you before, with wounds of any kind it's very important to kill the bacteria."

The cat was silent for a few moments, wondering once again just what this bacteria was and why it needed to be *killed*. It apparently was not a creature in the usual sense, so he was not sure how something that, technically, was not even alive, could therefore be killed. As he had the other times this particular subject had arisen, he decided against asking Donemere for a deeper explanation because he ran the risk of not understanding that either.

Perhaps he should not have left Donemere so much to her own devices whilst she studied herbal remedies? When she had expressed an interest in them, he had been forced to admit that he would be unable to provide any guidance whatsoever on that particular subject. He had wondered at the time if that was possibly a mistake on his part and he wondered this very same thing now. Moving restlessly on the rail, the cat finally settled down upon it with his tail wrapped tightly around his feet, the little locket he always wore on the silver chain around his neck glinting on his breast. He had thought of a question he could ask.

"But why are you removing his underclothing?" he inquired suspiciously.

"Well, these cuts run pretty far beneath them," Donnie replied defensively, "and since I'll need to see them to treat them, it'll be easier if he's not wearing anything. Besides, I'll have to bathe him all over eventually anyway. Oh, don't worry, kitty, kitty, I promise not to take his virtue, at least not while he's unconscious!" she vowed solemnly, then grinned at her familiar with a mischievous sparkle in her eye.

Okay, here was the big moment, she had to do it. She removed the cloth and, astonishment winning out over decorum, whistled a long, low catcall. Her voice filled with ribald awe and her eyes now gleamed lustily as she pronounced the man "very, *very* pretty, all over!" She swung to her right, beaming widely at the cow. "And you thought he was just a puny little human, didn't you, Diana? Silly girl! How about now, huh, whaddya think of him now? I dare you to produce any stud bull of your choice for comparison with our mysterious stranger here. Why, he's hung better than any—"

"No, no, no!" shouted Sylvester, while Warren gasped an outraged, "What?"

Donnie turned around in time to catch their matching appalled expressions. Warren's quickly changed to one of anger, which he directed toward the cat. "In what have you been instructing her all this time, Tanny?"

The cat turned to him and spat indignantly, "In what have *I* been instructing *her*?" He turned back to glare at Donnie, roaring, "I never schooled her in any such thing as that!"

Donnie and Diana were both laughing so hard at this, tears were forming in their eyes. Otis was also snorting his amusement from his stall.

When she could speak again, Donnie protested, "For Permissive Pete's sake, you guys, relax! I was only making a simple observation. Haven't you ever heard of the sexual revolution of the sixties? Okay, maybe not," she conceded, chuckling humorously. "Well, see, nowadays, women are allowed to admire a man's body. Honestly, it's no big deal, you know. Besides, I already promised not to take his virtue from him while he's like this. Now, as soon as he regains consciousness, all bets are off and he's fair game, got it?" she said, looking serious. "But until he's out of the woods, all I'll do is nurse him back to health, like any good little heroine would."

Donnie was having a hard time avoiding looking at her patient, all of him, especially the nether regions. Twice now, in the same day, her libido had been aroused by the sight of a naked man, but this time it was skyrocketing. And that wide, silly grin was once again plastered on her face because it just refused to be banished. "Oh, my, it's been a long time," she noted happily. "I'd almost forgotten what it was like to feel this way, my friends. Kind of rejuvenates the soul, if you know what I mean."

"Get on with it, will you?" Sylvester bit out between clenched teeth, thoroughly shocked at Donnie's behavior. "Time is wasting and I simply cannot watch you devour this man with your eyes any longer. I will await you in the cottage." The cat's own eyes narrowed as he ordered ominously, "Do *try* to accomplish more good than harm with your ministrations, Donemere!" And with that parting shot, he was gone.

Warren, on the other hand, had regained his composure and spoke with his usual reserve. "Sylvester is correct; you must make haste, Donemere of the Codlebærn. When you are finished here, come to the cottage. We have much to impart." With a short nod to both Donnie and Diana, and then to Otis, he too strode out of the stables.

Donnie turned to Diana and said sardonically, "Don't s'pose it would do any good to tell him my name is Donemere Saunders, huh?"

Diana's first response was to laugh outright and then to shake her head negatively, adding a, "No!" for good measure.

"I didn't think so," agreed Donnie, continuing her patient's bath. When she had his front side clean, she slowly levitated him a couple of feet above the floor and put a clean sheet underneath him. Leaving him to float in mid-air, she gently turned him over so she could clean his back. There were virtually no cuts here, just dried blood.

The boombox materialized beside Donnie and began playing Mackenzie Mack's "Forever Love." Donnie hummed along with it.

The man wore a thick, silver-looking chain around his neck, on which hung a massive pendant that had slid around to his back. Donnie shifted the pendant to get a proper look at it and laid it upon the man's shoulder. It gleamed red and silver against his skin. The pendant was comprised of an immense garnet-colored stone held within an ornate setting, with nine serpent heads snaked across the stone to keep it in place. At first glance, she'd thought the setting was made from silver, but upon closer inspection she could tell that it was not. It was of a metal composition she'd never seen before. It had veins of bright and dark colors running through its quick-silvery depths, along with glowing, miniscule multi-colored flakes of a substance unfamiliar to her that were embedded within the metal. The colors of the veins and flakes appeared to change with the shifting light as Donnie moved the pendant this way and that with her fingers. The metal itself was sparkling and warm, as though it had just this minute been polished. She noted that the metal in the chain was also of the same curious composition as the setting.

She turned the pendant over to inspect the smooth, rounded backing. The glare from the refractive metal danced across her face, its myriad colors flitting over her features. Only faintly detectable at first glance, she saw that an inscription ran across the oval backing. She squinted, trying hard to read the letters, but to no avail. They were too small and blurry for her to see clearly. Donnie realized wryly that she was going to need reading glasses soon. Oh, great joy, she loved getting old. She hefted the pendant in her hand a few times. It was inordinately heavy and looked extremely valuable to her. She took the chain off her patient and stashed the necklace in the far corner of the stall, under some hay. It could remain there safely until he was well enough to retrieve it.

She resumed washing the man as the song went into its last verse. Donnie murmured to the box, "He's my forever love, is that right, boombox? Well, I guess that remains to be seen...or are you just trying to tell me that he's immortal?"

She suddenly sat back and stared off into space, her expression one of shock. *Oh, good God, no—does this mean I'm immortal?* she wondered to herself, greatly disturbed by this very much unwanted possibility.

She shook her head and blinked several times, completely unnerved by her musings. Which was really stupid of her, she chastised herself a moment later. More information was needed before she could safely start forming conclusions about her situation and where this was all headed, so it would be best to wait until she'd talked to Warren and Sylvester before letting herself freak out over what were only guesses right now, right? Right. And after that, then she could freak out quite properly, she promised her pounding heart. Donnie quashed her misgivings as best she could and resumed the man's sponge bath, first going over him with hot water, then with the Klein solution.

Once the man's backside was relatively clean, Donnie turned him over again and let him sink slowly onto the sheet, using another sheet to cover his legs since chill air was beginning to seep into the stables. She dematerialized the basin and bowl to the back yard and dumped the filthy water each contained, brought them back, rinsed them, then refilled the bowl with fresh hot water. This time, she washed the man's wounds with a very strong solution of liniment, carefully and thoroughly wiping away any remaining vestiges of dirt and blood.

On her first pass over him, she'd noticed the man bore several scars from previous wounds, some of which were long cuts like the fresh ones she was tending, while others appeared to be old puncture wounds. The two most serious scars of the latter type were on the man's right side: one in his chest, under his arm, and the other in his abdomen. They looked as though they'd probably been life-threatening and must've taken months to heal. The new cuts were mostly on that side too, other than the severe one on his left leg and the wounds that ran across his midsection. Donnie looked twice at the fresh, deep cuts on the man's abdomen; was it just her or did they deliberately cross and was one of them a downward arrow? "Nah, can't be. Has to be a coincidence," she rebuked her overactive imagination.

She packed the deepest of the cuts with poultices and wrapped them all firmly with fresh bandages from the carryall bag, gently levitating the man's body again so she could reach all the way around him. Fortunately, most of the cuts were no longer bleeding. But, once more, Donnie felt rather faint while she worked on the worst of them. Surely the average person wasn't meant to see this far inside someone else's body, were they? She'd have to check her medical books again to see if she should suture any of the man's cuts. Ugh, wouldn't that be a thrill to experience?

She thought viciously of that quaint little euphemistic phrase always used in books: *She nursed him back to health.* "They never mention how gory and bloody this is, do they?" she exclaimed heatedly, to no one in particular. "Oh, no, they make it sound so noble and so, so...so refined! Such a suitable profession for any young miss!" she mocked in a high falsetto. "Ha! When I write a book about this weird adventure, I'm going to tell the truth! Nursing horrific wounds is not noble and most definitely it is *not* refined! It's messy and disgusting and gross and, well...horrific! And more than a little overwhelming, so don't ever let anyone tell you it's not!" she wailed, nearly hysterical by now.

"Are you talking to me, sweetie?" Diana asked with concern, calmly munching on some hay behind Donnie.

The cow's soothing voice was like a bucket of ice water poured on Donnie's inner fire. She took a deep breath and answered her friend quietly, "Nope, just blowin' off steam. Beats passin' out, letting him slam to the floor, probably planting my face smack in the middle of one of these bloody deep cuts! Eeeuuuwwww, now that's really disgusting,

Donemere Huntley Saunders!" she reprimanded herself, pushing back another errant strand of her hair. She turned to look at the cow and sighed. "Oh, hell, Diana, pay me no mind, it's just that I've only now realized that I'm the hired gun sent in to do all the dirty work in this sordid little tale. And I'm not sure I like it. What's more, I don't think there's a damn thing I can do to get out of it."

Diana studied Donnie, sympathy in her brown eyes, and then nuzzled her friend's shoulder. "Yeah, I think you're right about that, from what I know of the situation. Otis and I wanted to tell you, but Sylvester said we were magically bound not to discuss it, even amongst ourselves, in case you overheard us."

"Magically bound?" asked Donnie curiously.

"Yeah, he said that we all had a binding spell placed on us to keep our mouths shut, even him."

Donnie looked skeptical. "Sylvester said that?"

"Well, okay, I'm paraphrasing; you know how Sylvester is." Diana rolled her eyes heavenward. "At first, he went on and on about how it was his responsibility to ensure that you were brought along in your magic lessons at a pace that was comfortable to you, but which would still make you well-enough prepared when the time came for you to battle some Valledai character. Then he continued to go on and on about us not messing up his timetable. And when he was finally finished with that load of...rhetoric, shall we call it, he reluctantly conceded that we'd all been magically bound anyway, himself included, so that none of us could talk to you about what was really going on here even if we wanted to, until you were advanced enough to handle it."

The cow nodded her head vigorously before continuing. "That part was definitely true. Otis and I tried to answer your questions a few times, but whenever we opened our mouths to do so, all that would come out is a *moo* from me and a *neigh* from him. Yeah, that's what that was all about whenever we did that—we really weren't just having you on, I swear. Oh, it was utterly exasperating! And afterward, we weren't able to speak in words for a couple of hours. Each time we tried to tell you what was truly going on, the length of time we'd revert to animal sounds grew longer. So we gave it up because we didn't want to lose the ability to speak to you. I'm sorry I couldn't tell you all that before, but I'm glad I can now."

Donnie's brow was puzzled. "Who bound us?"

"Sylvester didn't know. He didn't think it was Catie, though, because she's not strong enough. Now, don't get me wrong, Catie's pretty powerful, but she can't hold a candle to you," Diana explained. "Besides,

Sylvester seemed positive that it wasn't her. If he does know who did it, he hasn't told us. Right, Otis?"

From his stall, where he'd been listening to this exchange, the horse replied softly, "No, he hasn't. And Donnie? I want to apologize too for not letting you know what you were in for. I've felt so guilty that we didn't try harder to inform you somehow, maybe written it in the snow after you taught us to read and write, or something like that, you know?"

Donnie leaned over to kiss Diana's cheek and turned to smile at Otis, tears in her eyes. Her voice was thick with emotion when she reassured them, "Hey, don't worry about it. What would I do if I didn't have you to talk to—spend hours and hours every day listening to Sylvester deliver one long-winded speech after another? Oh, what am I saying? That's what I've had to do anyway!" Everyone laughed shakily at this. "Let me tell you something, my dears, my days here would have been a whole lot less fun if I didn't have you two as my friends and cohorts, helping me however you could to annoy the heck out of Sylvester! Besides, if he says that you were magically bound, then no matter what you'd tried, you would've failed. Well, you might have succeeded in turning yourselves into nonmagical animals; but that couldn't really be categorized as a success, could it? So, don't let's worry about it ever again."

Diana smiled wide and said warmly, "Oh, thanks for that Donnie. I was so worried that you'd be angry with us."

"Ah, now I understand why you had me add that line to my pox spell," Donnie observed knowingly. "Did you really think I'd get mad at you guys for not being able to tell me what's really going on? Pshaw, you should know me better than that!" She flashed a humorous grimace at her friend, who looked surprised.

Otis stuck his head out over his gate and around the corner of Diana's stall again, a huge smile on his face. "I kept telling her that if anyone would understand about the binding spell, it would be you."

Donnie grinned back at him and finished wrapping the last of her patient's wounds. "Well, I knew something of the sort must've been done to me, since I couldn't leave the valley. But I didn't know it was that extensive a spell for everyone else too. Considering how frustrated I was at having to stay here all this time without ever getting answers to my thousands of repeated questions, I can just imagine how exasperating it must've been for you guys to be stuck here with me and not be able to give me those answers!" She let the man float down once again to the floor, snapped her fingers to materialize a cable-knit red blanket and spread this over the sheet that covered him, tucking both tightly under his body, then got up and walked over to Otis, kissing him soundly on his nose. Otis tossed his head and whinnied softly in response.

Donnie stepped back to the rail and asked her friends, "Hey, I've been wondering about something. Do either of you know why Sylvester was so adamant that we go out and rescue this guy?" She pointed to the prone figure on the sheet. "Who is he that he warrants all this personal attention, especially from the King Wolf himself?"

Otis twisted his head quickly from side to side and shrugged his shoulders while saying, "Got no idea."

Diana stared intently at the man lying only a couple feet from her, then she too shook her head negatively. "I don't know either, but he looks kinda familiar. Maybe that's just because he's high-bred. They look very different from the common folk. Taller, more refined...and healthier. I'm sorry, honey, but I don't know anything more than that about him." She heaved a disgusted sigh and said, "Sylvester's kept us mostly in the dark too. But I will tell you this: I thought it very strange that nobody came to the farm before now."

Donnie's eyes widened. "What do you mean? I thought people hardly ever came here because the lands are magical."

It was Diana's turn to look taken aback. "Oh, no," she said firmly. "We used to have all kinds of people come whenever Catie had a fresh batch of salt ready. That was every few weeks. As you know, she's very skilled at collecting salt brine and refining it. By the way, her evaporation works are up over the hill, to the west. You can probably go see them now, if you want to, since the binding spell's been released."

Donnie acknowledged this news with a short nod. "You know, Sylvester's only told me a tiny bit about Catie and her salt refining, and darn little else about her. He mentioned the salt business a couple of times when I first got here, but then he started clamming up like Mervin Mussel whenever I questioned him about Catie, as if she's a subject I'm not supposed to study. You know how he is about anything he deems unnecessary!" There were general snorts of agreement all around at this. "So, go on, Di, tell me more about Catie's salt operation," urged Donnie.

"Well," Diana began, much relieved to be able to answer Donnie's questions, "for years Catie supplied most of the villagers and other settlers around here with all the salt they needed for curing their meats and preserving other foods. She built up quite a trade before she left. That's mostly how she got our food and her libations, and well, pretty much everything else we needed. You know, by bartering her salt."

"And her iron castings," Otis added. He then lowered his head and delicately took up a few strands of hay with his mouth.

Donnie leaned back on her hips and crossed her arms in front of her. "The cauldrons," she said. "I get it now."

Otis nodded, swallowing the hay. "Yeah, Catie's pretty famous around here for them. She's got lots of molds in her workshop that she made herself. She loved coming up with new designs for the handles and feet, and the castings themselves. You know, different thicknesses, different compositions, or grades as she called them, different markings and designs on the sides, all that kind of stuff. She's got it down to a science and used to spend days at a time in her workshop. Every one of the cauldrons she's ever cast is an original and she never makes two alike. Never. She's very adamant about that. Don't know why though. And she refused to make anything except cauldrons, even though she was asked by several of the villagers to make all sorts of things. And I'll tell you something really weird: she went crazy with her cauldron casting just before she brought you here and made dozens of 'em. That's what all those ones were when you first got here—you know, like the ones that were in the house? She made every one of 'em just before she brought you here and stacked 'em all just so. I figured maybe she did that because she knew she wouldn't be able to make more for a long while. She certainly wasn't planning on bartering anything for them, 'cause she'd already gotten us fully stocked up with supplies for the winter. The only thing she might be expected to need would've been lettuces and such, and she would've traded salt for those."

Otis took another mouthful of hay at this point, leaving Donnie to gaze at him with a slightly confused expression. "Hmm," she said, "I didn't realize that making cauldrons was such a passion for her. I just thought she—well, I thought maybe it was a Zen thing, you know? Gave her something to keep her hands busy with, but just to fill her spare time, I mean. I had no idea she took it quite so seriously."

"Oh, yes," Diana interjected forcefully, "Catie was very serious about it! I'd go so far as to say she was obsessed with it, both her cauldrons and iron making in general. The iron composition had to be perfect every time, or else she'd dump it somewhere and start all over with a new batch of the stuff, even if the bad batch was only off by the tiniest bit. How's that for anal retentiveness? Oh, and another thing that was kinda strange was that whenever anyone would barter for one of her cauldrons, Catie always insisted on teaching them how to look after it. She was obsessive about that too. She said they had to care for it just the way she told them to or else the cauldron wouldn't work right."

"Wouldn't work right? Whatever did she mean by that?" Donnie asked, consternated.

"Well, that *was* funny," Diana agreed. "I'm not really sure what she meant. But she'd start out by telling any new owner that whenever they used the cauldron, they needed to wipe it out with a dry cloth, then rub some butter into it. Okay, so far so good. But she'd add that before they even used it once, they first needed to boil this concoction of magical herbs she'd come up with, then she'd give them the herbal recipe for the cauldron size they'd chosen. They were to boil these herbs for half a day, take the water in the cauldron and pour it outside their windows and doors, or all around the house if they had enough water. She swore that would protect any home from all sorts of evil creatures. She'd even tell them to do this regularly, every three days, in fact, to ward off all evil from their house. I honestly think most people believed she was nuts, but Catie adamantly refused to trade a cauldron to anyone who didn't swear an oath on their own grave to take care of it just the way she told them to; she was that rigid about it! And they were all so scared of her and her magic that they probably still do exactly what she told them to and boil the herbs every three days even now! But, anyway, like I said before, casting iron was her obsession. Her busy work was the salt works—oh, and refining other metals that she needed for her tools and equipment so that she could make the iron and her molds. Almost everything Catie did whenever she was here at the cottage was intended to further, in one way or another, her iron making."

Fascinated, Donnie marveled at these revelations about the elusive Catie. "But where'd she get the raw materials for the iron making? You know, the iron ore and carbon, silicon, all that stuff? And the other metals too for her tools?" Donnie inquired, looking at Diana and then Otis. "And where'd she store it, 'cause there isn't any of it around here now. Nothing's mentioned about her personalized composition of iron in her journals either, other than how to work with the metals; you know, how to mine them, refine and smelt them, then cast or form them into whatever tool or pot she was making. Do you know where any of that stuff is?"

Otis twisted his head again from side to side. "Not sure," he said. "Like you, she mined the stuff herself, I guess. I think she was just gettin' into that when she brought you here. Don't know where she got the materials from before that. She didn't say anything to me about it because, remember, we couldn't really talk to her, not like we do with you. We could understand her, but like most people—until you came along, that is, and your magic made ours stronger—Catie couldn't really understand much of what we said. So, most of what we know about her is what we saw or what Sylvester would tell us. See, she could talk to him all right. I guess that's 'cause he's got more magical power than either of us has ever had, so if you ask him now, he can probably tell you. If he even knows the answer, that is."

Donnie nodded in agreement and looked at her watch. "Well, speaking of Sylvester, I'd better go find him and Warren. Perhaps kitty cat is ready to spill the beans to me about a bunch of things. I certainly hope he agrees that it's time for a good long chat, anyway. I also want to know more about this Wolf King and what the heck he has to do with things. You all seem to know him pretty well, I noticed."

"Oh, sure," Otis replied cheerfully. "He used to live here, you know, but he left a long time ago. Actually, I gather he comes and goes, sometimes staying for years and then he's gone for years. Why, it must be at least fifteen years or more now, I think, since the last time he struck out on his own, long before even Diana came here. She's only been here a year or so now, while I've been here nearly seventeen, no, eighteen years. Time flies, you know? Obviously, Mynydd Uchaf, or as you call him, Warren, still visits the valley quite often—well, except since you've been here. But I guess I ought to let him tell you his story. All in all, it's pretty sad."

Donnie looked at Otis thoughtfully, then went back into Diana's stall and stood over her patient. The man lay quietly, his breathing even, but still a bit labored. Donnie said to Diana, "Keep an eye on him, will you? I don't really want him moving much, if it can be helped. I'll be back in an hour or so to check on him."

Before leaving the stall, Donnie gathered up all the paraphernalia she'd been using to treat the man's wounds and shoved it up on the high shelf above the stall, including the unused poultices. She placed his armor and weaponry at the far side of the stall and covered them with two bales of hay, along with his tattered clothing. Then she dematerialized the blood-soaked towels and bandages, sending them into the roaring fire in the kitchen, including any soiled hay. She figured she might as well get rid of that evidence as well.

When she had all signs of her doctoring cleared away, she left the stables and visited Catie's workshop in order to collect an overly large cloak she'd found amongst Catie's things months ago before striding back to the house, determined to finally get some answers from the cat and the werewolf.

Chapter 7
Won't You Come In?

Donnie scrubbed her hands thoroughly with soap, using a brush to scrape under her fingernails, wafts of blood odor bringing bile to her throat again. "Brindle," she whispered, "where are Sylvester and this other guy, the Wolf King?"

"In your workshop, Donnie," the tree answered quietly from the cistern over her head.

"Do you know him, the Wolf King I mean?" she asked, glancing up at the wooden water tank.

"Yes," replied Brindle. "Mynydd Uchaf is highly regarded throughout the land. And, since he is a dear friend of Catie's, I too know him well. He grew up here and has always visited frequently since leaving us, even after darkness changed both his life and his appearance for the second time, as you have no doubt seen for yourself. Nevertheless, Catie always had great confidence in him. I believe that you may trust him as well, Donemere."

"I sure hope so. He doesn't look like someone I'd like to piss off," she noted, digging the brush industriously at a particularly stubborn spot of blood on her thumbnail.

"No," agreed Brindle. "I've heard rumor that he is quite ruthless when crossed. I believe it was Catie who taught him just which blood vessels of most predatory creatures to sever that will also inflict the greatest damage upon them, including humans, of course."

Donnie's eyes widened. "Oh, now that's great news!" she exclaimed. "Just who I wanted to meet today—a werewolf who kills with surgical precision. I'll certainly keep that in mind when I'm around him," she assured the tree dryly as she rinsed the soap off her hands.

Brindle hesitated before imparting the main thrust of his warning. "That might be wise, Donnie," he said, "in case he is ever breached by dark magic again. Although...I do not believe any harm could befall you unless you allowed it to happen."

Donnie raised an eyebrow at the cistern. "What do you mean?" she asked.

"On several occasions now, I have seen your magic's reaction time to some very surprising situations and I've noted with wonder that it's become instantaneous." Brindle's voice was filled with respect when he said this. "Which tells me that it would be nearly impossible for any object, magical or otherwise, to penetrate your field of self-awareness, as

I've said, unless you decided to let it through. You see, in all my years, I have neither witnessed nor heard of quicker reflexes than yours. Remember the knife that flew from Mournful Jack last month, when you were standing beneath the new shelves you built from him? It made no sound as it soared off the shelf above your head and hurled straight down, tip first, toward your neck. Yet it came no closer than six inches before you had it frozen in mid-air."

"Hey, you know, I'd almost forgotten that incident!" Donnie said, not altogether truthfully, and dried her wet hands on one of the dish towels stacked beside the sink. The scrubber floated an inch above its usual perch, poised to begin its duties on the bowls. "I still wonder how the thing came to be there. I know I put all of Catie's knives in her workshop months ago, so for the life of me I can't explain how one of them got into *my* workshop, nor how it got onto a brand new shelf I'd built just the day before. I wish you trees hadn't all been asleep at the same time the night before because I'm sure one of you would've seen something to help solve that little mystery."

Brindle, still embarrassed by the incident, reminded her stiffly, "As you know, that is why the six of us agreed that one must always be on guard now. But the time has come for that too, to change. I believe, from what Sylvester and Mynydd Uchaf have been discussing for the past half hour, it would be most prudent for there to be two of us awake at all times from this day forward. It appears the need for extreme caution is upon us."

Donnie nodded. "Yeah, I agree. Call me crazy, but I've got a feeling that there are some pretty nasty creatures roaming this land and I think every precautionary measure we can all take is a step in the right direction. I'll leave you to coordinate that with the other five, okay?"

"That would be best, yes, Donemere."

Donnie turned toward the workshop and slowly approached its closed door. She could hear Sylvester and Warren discussing her, so she waited outside the room to eavesdrop.

"—I have learned all this through many trials, I tell you, Mynydd Uchaf. I seldom ask her to explain herself. You will come to know this too," Sylvester warned his wolf friend. " 'Tis impossible to understand these explanations. Why, do you know that every morning and evening she puts this terribly pungent ointment on her knees and then sets off running? It was bad enough during the snow season when she would do that in the late morning, but now she does it twice a day! And where does she go, you might ask, since she has not been allowed to leave the valley? Nowhere! She runs in wide circles, all around the rim of the valley, and then, after a time, she comes back to the cottage. Why should anyone do that? She is not hunting or tracking; she is merely running in circles! And when she is done, she removes bags of some viscous, nearly frozen material from that monstrosity she calls *the fridge* and lays these on top of her knees. All she will say when she returns to the house is that it sucks to get old."

Donnie heard only an answering murmur from Warren.

"Well, to that she says she is getting exercise because of something called an *endorphin high*," Sylvester said, "which she swears aids in combating what she calls her *depression*. All of which is ridiculous. 'Tis a temporary case of the vapors, pure and simple." The cat sniffed disdainfully. "She also says she does it because she wants to stay in shape. She has a definite shape already and to my mind she displays it far too freely. I have lectured her time and time again about her wardro—"

Donnie suddenly breezed into the room, demanding, "Okay, who is this man in the stables and what's the deal with the binding spell?"

She took a few steps into the room and tossed the cloak in her hand toward Warren, noticing that he, in his wolf's form, was deeply ensconced in one of her red-leather chairs, while Sylvester was sitting atop the stool in front of the worktable. The cat jumped visibly at her sudden appearance, sending her a guilty look. And when Donnie entered the room, putting her within twenty feet of the wolf, as if on cue, he transformed into a werewolf. With a grateful look at Donnie, he pulled the cloak over his nakedness.

Donnie studiously ignored his transformation, which freaked her out anew each time she saw it. Would the fear ever go away, she wondered, willing her heart rate to slow down. And what exactly was his story? That had her greatly intrigued, but she knew the Wolf King would certainly not appreciate an inquisition into his life right off the bat. He would tell her in his own time and his own way, or not at all. Patience would be needed with him. The cat, on the other hand, usually responded best to a little edgy encouragement. To that end, Donnie flounced across the room and sat in the other armchair, facing her familiar. "Well? Who is he?" she asked defiantly.

"We do not know who he is." Donnie turned to look at Warren when he said this. "Nevertheless, because the binding spell has been released, we can be assured that he is someone of import."

Donnie nodded her head. "Yeah, Warren, that much I'd already figured out." She raised her chin truculently to the cat and said, "All right, Sylvester, tell me about the binding spell."

Warren also looked at Sylvester expectantly.

"Very well, Donemere," the cat susurrated grievously. " 'Tis a most extensive binding spell, to be sure. All who reside on your magical lands were put under it when Catie left. Even the occasional traveler who happened to pass nearby would have been affected by it. Only a very few creatures were allowed in and out in order to pass messages between Mynydd Uchaf and myself. A few more were granted access to the valley, but many of those are not magical."

Ah, now she understood how the Wolf King knew her name, amongst a few other oddities. "That's why I kept seeing the same magical birds and squirrels and other animals all the time, isn't it?" she asked. "They must've been stuck here in the valley with us. So, was Catie the one who placed the binding spell?"

"No," Sylvester shook his head. "I do not believe so, although she told me before she left that she was going to lay one. But the actual spell itself was too far-ranging for her to have managed, so I feel quite confident in saying that it could not have been she who cast it. I know what you will ask next, Donemere. The answer is, I do not know who else might have. Whenever I asked the gods, they repeatedly insisted it was not they. I only know that I awoke the morning after you had said the first words certain that it had been cast and that it would not be released until you were sufficiently advanced in your powers."

Donnie raised an eyebrow and observed humorously, "Catie claimed credit for it, while the gods said no too many times, eh? Well, like you, I'm not sure I'd trust either of those groups, Sylvester. So let's try this: now, I know you still don't think I'm advanced enough, certainly not to suit your standards anyway, but why were you so darned sure last night that the binding spell had finally been released?"

The cat paused to study her before finally answering, "The binding spell prevented *anyone* from entering your realm, other than the few magical animals who knew the only access point, which changed with each use. They would then lead hunts for food a few times a week. If, by ill fate, something occurred to the designated guide, a new one was automatically chosen. That animal would then lead their brethren back to the magical lands and the previous guide was no longer granted access. For a man to have penetrated the binding spell to any degree at all meant he must be of consequence. Therefore, I knew you would be allowed to leave the valley."

"Which means this spell was cast not only on us here, as you say, but also on those phantom villagers you are forever alluding to whenever you give me crap about my wardrobe, right?" Donnie asked, just to needle the cat, privately musing over what "ill fate" could have happened to cause a shift in guides.

"Er, yes." Sylvester cleared his throat uncomfortably and went on to say, "All creatures, magical and nonmagical alike, were prevented from even finding your lands unless led by one of the few scouts who were allowed access to it, and those who were granted that particular leave were not then allowed within the valley. They had to pass any messages to someone who was, and by this route, I had word of doings in the greater world. It was really quite a clever arrangement, although somewhat cumbersome, especially whenever the outer messenger was compromised by evil. Yet, even then, the originator of the message was alerted so that a new scout could be sent. All quite automatic, as I said. As to the outer perimeter of your lands, it seems that for those who passed by, they were diverted around them entirely. I can only assume that this was for the express purpose of ensuring there would be no interruptions to your lessons."

Donnie gave this some consideration before remarking mildly, "Someone sure went to a lot of trouble just to give me time and space to settle into my magic, don't ya think?"

Sylvester nodded his head and agreed solemnly. "It would appear so, yes."

Another hint of mischief flashed across her face and she inquired, "So, the binding spell is why no one ever came here to barter for Catie's salt or one of her cauldrons, right? It wasn't just because the lands are magical and the villagers are all way too scared of me to venture here?"

The cat stared disapprovingly at her. "Yes. As I have told you before, the majority of the villagers are, most likely, unaware of your existence. For all they know, Catie lives here still, so a few may soon come to visit her."

"What, they wouldn't have noticed her absence before this?" Donnie protested.

Sylvester shrugged and replied carelessly, "Why should they? Catie seldom visited them and, with the spell in effect, 'tis likely none of them ever gave her a thought. But getting back to the spell, I see Diana and Otis have already informed you of it and its effects." His tone was, once again, one of disapprobation.

"Only inasmuch as they themselves know, yes," Donnie admitted. "And obviously they gave me a little background info on Catie. You needn't worry though, kitty, nobody's stolen your thunder. I've still got simply hundreds of questions, which means you two have a lot of explaining to do." She sat back and smiled brightly, lacing her fingers together and settling her hands onto her lap. "Okay, so who's gonna give me the skinny? What the heck is going on here?"

Sylvester nervously cleared his throat again and said, "I suppose I should be the one to start. Ahem, ahem; may we possibly have a flagon of wine?" he suggested.

Donnie rolled her eyes. "You don't drink spirits, remember, kitten? Quit stalling and just give me the scoop. I am not leaving the room so you can discuss with Warren just how little to tell me."

He looked away from her, cleared his throat yet again, and spoke pedantically to the room at large. "Harrumph!" he said, signaling commencement of another "lesson." "I shall begin by giving you a small, but noteworthy sampling of the history of the Codlebærn line," he intoned gravely.

Donnie grimaced, joking, "Oh my, this isn't going to take forever is it? I've got things to do, places to go, people to meet, and I'd like to do it all before I'm old and grey. Seriously, Sylvester, I'll have to go check on our patient in an hour, so try to kept it short for now, will ya?" She materialized into her hands the cup of jasmine tea she'd brewed earlier and which she'd left sitting on the kitchen counter. As she knew only too well, whenever the cat got to orating, he could go on for a very, *very* long time.

Sylvester sent Warren a knowing look and settled down more comfortably on the stool with his tail wrapped tightly around his front paws. "Throughout the ages," he announced, "the Codlebærn witches have been the fortunate recipients of one of the most powerful bloodlines in the history of magic. Wielding this unparalleled power, they have been called upon to perform acts of eminent significance for kings and gods alike. Many daughters of the gods were born unto them, strengthening the bloodline. These daughters were renowned throughout the lands for their great beauty.

"Catie's grandmother, Morrían, was fathered by Lugh at his festival, Lughnasadh. As you will remember from our studies, Lugh is the Sun God of Prophecy. He passed his skill of foretelling the future to Morrían. She was prophet to many kings and warriors during her lifetime, and once was in service to Cuchulain, the Hound of Ulster. She foresaw his doom, yet he heeded not her warnings, nor those of others. Disheartened by her failure and devastated by his demise, she sailed over the seas to this land and built the cottage in which you now live. She bore one daughter by Arawn, God of the Dead. Arawn came to her whilst she was grieving the loss of her beloved Cuchulain, whom she had adored in secret.

"Their daughter was named Margawse, after the Mother Goddess, and was birthed in yon bedroom. She was so named because of her innate gift of seeing inside the minds of others, which allowed her to know all about them instantly, and because of her unusual ability to absorb the memories of the dying, providing them everlasting life.

"Margawse was of extraordinary beauty, even for a Codlebærn. One night, when she was little more than a girl, Gwydion, Sky God of Magic, appeared to her in the form of the white stallion. He fell under the spell of her beauty and stole her off to Moên Tádtelu, where she lay with him through the long fires of Beltane. When she returned to the cottage, many cycles of the moon later, she was heavy with child. The result of their coupling was Caterin," Sylvester proclaimed, positively preening as though this somehow reflected favorably upon himself.

"Well, providential pedigrees, isn't it nice to know that Grandpa's somebody special?" Donnie murmured, causing the cat to glare at her. Being a big girl, she resisted the overwhelming urge to stick her tongue out at him.

"As Sylvester said, this makes the most royal of bloodlines in any magical family," interjected Warren, ignoring Donnie's quip and nodding at the cat to continue.

Sylvester huffed, clearly irritated, but continued with his story. "Caterin, our Catie, became the strongest witch known to man—that is, until you were granted your powers, Donemere, and were appointed the most powerful witch of all time; unless you fail at mastering that much power, of course." The cat paused to give Donnie a level stare. This errant pupil of his had never seemed to grasp the gravity of her calling. Nor had his previous mistress, for that matter. "Catie, though exceptionally skilled in working with metals and other bountiful resources of the Earth," here he hesitated, for some reason glancing nervously at Warren before resuming, "is not the most, ah, *venerable* witch in history. She is much like you in that respect, Donemere. She did not take to staying here on the Codlebærn farm until such time as she would be summoned by king or god. Rather, she had an insatiable desire to journey to other lands. Seeking adventures, ideas and raw materials was how she described it. And, by her account, she usually found whatever she sought," he added disparagingly.

Donnie hid a smile behind the cup of tea in her hands. Catie's wanderlust didn't sound like a bad thing to her, although Donnie could certainly see how Sylvester would not agree.

"On one such journey, Catie came across a dark sorcerer. This necromancer wore a great amulet, with a fire stone in its center. Catie tricked the foul man into playing a game of shooting stones, with the amulet as the prize for the winner. She, quite naturally, won their game and demanded the amulet. Her opponent obstinately refused, accusing Catie of using magic to cheat their wager. Since they both had cheated with magic, they argued for hours, with the result that Catie finally transformed the luckless sorcerer into a tortoise. She took the amulet and went on with her journey. Later that night, once she was safely in her bed at an inn, a beam of light shot from the amulet, and there before her appeared the wavering figure of Heimdallr, the White God. Donemere, you will remember from our studies this winter that he is also the Guardian of Bifröst Bridge. Now, the ill-hearted sorcerer had apparently held the White God captive within the amulet for many years. Heimdallr begged Catie to set him free and told her the spell with which to do so. Catie agreed, but at a price she would name once he was released.

"Of course she wanted to keep the amulet and she wanted Heimdallr to tell her how to use it. He was so grateful to her, he readily agreed to her demands, though he warned that she must use it sparingly and only when truly needed. He then gave Catie the spell that would allow her to work it."

"Huh, really?" Donnie drawled, sending Sylvester a skeptical look before asking, "Just what did this amulet do?"

Sylvester hesitated in his narrative to look at Warren again, this time obviously seeking permission. Warren nodded his head and Sylvester continued. " 'Twas a portal, as Heimdallr explained to Catie, which allowed one to travel to other times and places throughout history. While Catie had sworn a solemn oath to seldom use it, a mere two days later she met a contingent of the Dark Master's highest servants on her path. She was frightened when they came after her, for there was nowhere to hide in the fields. She used the amulet and escaped to your century. She was fascinated by your world and its machines, and stayed there for three days. When she returned, the Dark Master's servants naturally had moved on in their hunt. Catie was then able to journey back to the cottage safely. But now she could not let the amulet be; she visited other times, capriciously crossing throughout history until I could no longer keep track of her. For as long as I can remember, she was possessed by the amulet and its power, and often could not leave it for more than a few days' time before she was off yet again to another time and place."

"So she really caught the travel bug this time, eh? Well, I can relate to that, I suppose. Go on, what happened next?" Donnie said encouragingly.

Sylvester thought for a moment and then replied, "No more than two years whilom, Catie became aware that whenever she traveled through the portal, a magical presence was following her. At first she thought nothing of it, until terrible events began occurring where they ought not. Senseless wars broke out suddenly between neighbors who had been at peace for centuries, evil creatures were set loose upon peoples of simple origins who had no way of either conjuring or defeating them, mysterious and devastating plagues devoured two entire kingdoms Catie visited, and several witches she befriended were murdered with no visible trace of what could have occasioned their deaths; these were the sorts of horrors that were unleashed. Catie came to realize that many of these evil incarnations were from the wrong age. She explained to me that they were too early or too late for the period of time she was visiting. She was at a loss to account for this, but did what she could to combat the summoned devilries that preyed upon these worlds."

"Well, at least she tried to do something to help," Donne noted wryly, "although I sure hope she didn't muck with what was really supposed to happen; you know, what would've happened anyway if she'd never visited that particular time." Donnie waved her hand, as if to brush away her own apprehensions. She looked from Sylvester to Warren and asked, "But why did Catie think this magical presence that was following her was responsible for all these terrible events?"

"Over the ensuing months," Sylvester answered, "Catie began to use her magical self more and more when she traveled. She practiced the old ways of magic to hide from the peoples of the times she visited instead of blending into their midst, as she had done previously. She also took to drawing herself in several times throughout the day to listen to the rhythms of the Earth. It was on one such occasion that she heard the dark power's whispers. It was calling forth yet another vile creature. Catie cast a spell to block the dark one and came home at once, finally fully aware that she brought the black shadow and its evil influence with her wherever she went. She used the amulet only once more—in order to transport you, that is—because she wanted to contain the fiendish entity here." The cat hesitated again, frowned, then went on hurriedly, "And so it came to pass during the last year, evil has once again beset our own lands. The Sire Lord, the would-be god, had been sent to oblivion years ago. In his stead rose another dark power; this creature who threatens us now, this Valledai. And he has made it known that he wants the amulet from Catie. On two occasions, she was nearly killed by those caught within his magical slavery in their attempts to steal it from her." Once more, Sylvester looked at Warren, who again signaled his approval with a nod.

Sylvester resumed the tale. "Catie eventually decided to call upon another witch to aid her. Something had happened after Valledai's first attempt at having her killed, something that she would never speak of, but which changed her opinion of him. All she would say was that she could feel his power expanding and knew that if his growth continued, as it was certain to, he would soon be far stronger than she herself would ever be. She said that she had already cast a spell which called out to all her progeny, searching for the strongest, and that you were the only one whose image had come to her, Donemere. After the second attempt on her life, she used the amulet one last time and went to your world to get you. I went with her there to keep watch. The shadow followed us, but did not show itself. I felt his presence though and I can attest to his power. It was indeed already far greater than Catie's by then, and he himself was much more substantive than a mere shadow should be. But neither Catie nor I could get a glimpse of his true self.

"We brought you, Donemere, and your belongings back almost immediately. Again the shadow followed, but when we arrived here at the cottage, it was no longer with us. Catie stayed for only a short while that night before bidding me goodbye. She instructed me to watch over you and do whatever I must to get you to read the final entry in her latest journal. Then she disappeared. I have not seen her since, but we have recently had word of her. She was observed near Moên Tádtelu, or Mount Treyfal as both you and Catie refer to it, Donemere, and was seen leaving that area little more than a full moon ago, heading northward. That is the last knowledge any here in Medregai, perhaps even Írtha, have of her."

Donnie jumped on this immediately. "Medregai? Írtha? That's where we are?"

The cat nodded, adding, "To be most precise, we are in Ga'Medregai."

"Really? Why do those names ring a bell?" cried Donnie, breaking off momentarily. "No-no, I'm wrong, they can't—but, yet they do too sound familiar! Why? Why do I feel like I should know them?" She stared at the cat, who was viewing her with incredulity.

"Do you remember so little of your first fortnight here, Donemere?" he reproached her. "You certainly picked up Catie's book regarding this land often enough before I persuaded you to read her journal instead. I would have thought the story would be seared into your mind, you read the book so often and so avidly."

Donnie gaped at him, then hastily recollected herself and closed her mouth. She called out to the library to give her the book. Nothing happened, so she rolled her eyes toward the heavens, heaving a loud sigh, then held up a finger and put her tea cup on the table. She raced from the room and returned a minute later with a thick book in her hands, in the midst of muttering absentmindedly, "Damn testy library, it could've given it to me in here, but oh no, I couldn't have a library that's that trusting! After all, it's been at least two months since any of us damaged one its kiddies."

The cat and werewolf exchanged glances with each other and then Warren went back to watching Donnie intently with his hunter's eyes, while Sylvester appeared to be perfectly content to sit silently.

Donnie sighed again, then began to flip through the book when she sat back down. After a minute or two of perusing its initial pages, she exclaimed, "Oh, yeah, now I remember this one! I wouldn't say I actually read it though, because I was kind of an emotional wreck way back then. But I do recall thinking it was a total rip-off of a Fantasy story from my time, albeit slimmer on details. You see, I really wasn't sure if it was fiction or non-fiction since the story was so fantastical, yet the writing so dry—er, scholarly, I mean. I guess I just figured that the fantastical stuff was metaphorical, not literal, but that the rest of it was basically true, so I eventually settled on non-fiction." She paused for effect, looked up from the pages of the book which she was still riffling through, and quipped impishly, "And of course, the names of people and places were changed to protect the innocent." She shot the other two a quick grin and then realized they hadn't gotten the joke. Jeepers, how she missed talking to people from her own time. Aw, hell; she missed talking to people, period!

With a resigned shrug, she said, "I'll read this more thoroughly tonight, I guess. I want to see just where it differs from the story I know. So, all right, what do *Írtha* and *Medregai* translate to exactly, in English, I mean?"

"The peoples here speak Mannish, Donemere, not English," Sylvester corrected her austerely, then dipped his head in concession to add, "though, as you know, they are remarkably similar languages." Donnie let out a small snort of amusement at the cat's reluctant admission, which he ignored. "As far as I know, Írtha translates merely into *world*. The country in which we are living is named Ga'Medregai, or, most often, it is called Medregai. Catie usually called it Midgard or its obvious alternative, Mannheim." As an afterthought, he added, "She sometimes also referred to it as Vinland the Good."

Donnie frowned with thought. "Midgard, Mannheim or Vinland the Good? Heavens, how confusing for you all. Well, it's definitely not Vinland; that was somewhere around Labrador or Newfoundland, wasn't it? It was on the North American Continent, I remember that much." She stared down at the book in her hands. When she'd skimmed through it all those months ago, it had reminded her of an uncanny, but rather inferior knockoff of *Songs of the Earth*, the first collaboration of Martin Drake and Erik Mueler that had skyrocketed them to fame, respectively, as director and author.

"Medregai is Írtha's trade center," Warren informed her. "Catie always said it was supposed to be Midgard, or the center world of Yggdrasil which, she explained, is a tree comprised of nine worlds, and she staunchly maintained that that is where she was. She said it reminded her of this Vinland place, but then she would concede, sadly, that it was not the same as that lovely land."

Donnie pursed her lips and stared at him in silence for several seconds. "She said it was supposed to be Midgard, eh? I wonder why she thought that?" she asked rhetorically, obviously not expecting an answer. "And, goodness, isn't it a funny coincidence that I once wrote a series of articles about the Norse mythologies, so I understand what Catie's referring to? But why would she word it like that? *Supposed to be Midgard?*" Donnie repeated wonderingly.

Warren, wearing a puzzled frown, asked, "Who are the Norse?"

"Oh, I'm sorry!" Donnie apologized. "I forgot that's what we call that particular culture in my century. If I remember correctly, they referred to themselves as *Norðmen* or *Noorsch*. Sylvester can explain more about them to you later, if you're really interested." She grimaced in thought. "Well, at least now I know where I am—sort of, anyway."

As was her habit, she allowed her mind to run freely while she mulled over this new development, musing aloud, "I don't suppose this Írtha could essentially *be* Mueler's land of magical enchantment, could it? It can't be his Erde though, can it? I mean, that place wasn't real...well, for that matter, silly girl, neither is the Yggdrasil of Norse mythology—after all, that's why it's called *mythology*. Sheesh. But...if all that's true, then why would this place be called Medregai, or rather Ga'Medregai, I guess, and yet, here's Catie, so determined to call it Midgard? And why did she insist that she was in Yggdrasil and not Írtha? Is it one or the other, or someplace else entirely that's maybe what the Norse based their legends upon? No, that can't be right because I don't recall any Norse stories like the one we have here, although I'm certainly no expert." Donnie tilted her head, still lost in thought.

After pausing for several perplexed seconds, she bent over the book again and scanned through more pages, muttering, "But why the heck is its history so very much like Mueler's imaginary antediluvian epic? How could he have known so much about this place? I mean, okay, here it was a book of evil magic that had to be destroyed instead of a crown because it was captivating whole communities and making them turn on each other in the nastiest ways imaginable, and there was that one nearly unstoppable spell from the book that opened up the crack between worlds and let in all those horrible creatures, but if I remember correctly, just about everything else I read was nearly identical to the *Songs of the Earth*, most especially some of the key battles in the War of Unity that occurred in both worlds. And there's the little guy...let's see, he's named Dreena here and Pully in Mueler's story—oh, how funny, he and his kind are called noakies in both versions. I seem to recall the noakies are something between a dwarf and a wood sprite and make their homes in the root systems of giant oak trees, something like that, and from what this book describes they must be a bit bigger than Mueler thought…with pale green or brown, rather thick skin and very large noses and ears, huh? Anyway, just like in Mueler's story, this Dreena was the only one who could go near the *Book of the Var* without succumbing to its evil; well, him and—oh, what's his name in this story?"

Several pages of the book in Donnie's hands flipped over and the name she sought was highlighted momentarily on the new page. "That's it, *Falwaïn*. He was the only other one who wasn't affected by the *Blackest Book of Books*, as Dreena called it, and he protected Dreena and his brothers from the wicked townspeople and the okûn, which are some kind of hybrid between the vinca and a horrible, but unnamed creature," she read from the book absently. "Their skin is such a pale yellow it's almost white, and they hate being in the sun—why do they—oh, here it is, that's because of this creature, the one that's mixed with the vinca to make an okûn. Those creatures live deep in the Earth and never leave it, at least not willingly. Not much more is known about them, though, which is really not helpful. But, consequent to these creatures' DNA, there is something about direct sunlight that blinds their bastardized progeny, the okûn, and makes their skin sizzle and drop off that other forms of light don't cause to happen, no matter how bright a light it is. Weird…" murmured Donnie, lost in the book. "What the heck are vinca? Oh, here it is; they're tall, skinny, bipedal creatures with dark grey skin, pale yellow eyes, and black manes that go to white at the tips, and they have two arms that end in claws and faces that look sort of like bats. Hmm, they even have ears like bats…and their hearing works the same way as bats' hearing does—with echolocation, I mean."

The book flipped several more of its pages and Donnie continued, "Then there was Belnesem, who was the King of Medregai, and Déagmun, who became the Meurdane, or High Wizard, after Kaledar was turned bad by the book and started working for the okûns' mysterious master, some guy named Orgos who thought of himself as either the Sire Lord or as the One True Lord, which," Donnie looked up momentarily to say in an aside, "just shrieks god-complex to me! And, of course, there were Belnesem's trusty friends, Galæron the Woodland Elf, Akanna the vinca warrioress, and Gâ'Duk the odd, but kindly troll." As real understanding began to hit her, Donnie looked up and stared first at Sylvester and then at Warren, squeaking in disbelief, "And you're telling me that the *Book of the Var* and those people and creatures I just described really did exist?"

"To my knowledge, they all continue to live," the Wolf King replied, "though I personally know but a few of those you cited. Their deeds and the *Book of the Var*, on the other hand, are well-known throughout Medregai. The book's influence was widespread and many communities throughout the land fell under its dark power."

Donnie hissed impatiently at herself, then slowly shook her head, trying to make sense of what she'd learned. "So, this world must be the real one then, right?" she asked, again rhetorically. "Or, maybe it really is Midgard, like Catie thought it should be, and the name Medregai just kinda got morphed into Midgard by the thirteenth century when good ol' Snorri Sturluson did his stuff with the Norse legends, which probably would mean that the stories about this specific time in history got lost somehow by the time Snorri came along. Oh, hell and damnation!" she cursed abruptly. "I suppose it might be possible that Medregai and Midgard are actually one and the same..." she allowed, although without conviction, adding, "but I doubt it."

And then a most dreadful thought occurred to her. "Uh-oh, if we really are in Midgard, I sure hope we're not headed for Ragnarök anytime soon. Ah, you don't happen to have lots of gods warring with each other right now, do you?" She looked from the cat to the werewolf sharply. They only blinked at her in response. " 'Cause, I don't know about you guys, but I personally do not have a death wish, and since I'm pretty sure none of us are mentioned in the *Prose Edda*, we're all doomed to die if the upcoming battle you warned me about earlier, Warren, is the Ragnarök. Very, very few survive that particular war—as in, like practically *nobody*."

Warren leaned back, his appraising werewolf stare fixed on Donnie's mobile face. "The gods are not in conflict, either with themselves or with us," he replied quietly.

"Well, that, at least, is one bright spot." Donnie studied the coffee table for a few moments with relief before murmuring, "Huh, it all just gets curiouser and curiouser. Well, go on, Sylvester—"

The boombox had appeared on the worktable behind the cat a few moments earlier and had begun playing Fariya's mystical "Oslander Floe." Sylvester now shot Donnie an exasperated glare and reproached her in mid-sentence. "This is not an appropriate time for your music, Donemere!"

"My dear feline friend," she chided, shaking her head, "have you really not noticed that the boombox has acquired a mind of its own? It plays whatever it wants, whenever it wants. It's rather like having my very own sentient digital DJ; which is a little freaky, I must admit. Even more unsettling, it doesn't seem to need batteries anymore either, so I gotta wonder what the heck it's running on."

"Do not ask!" Sylvester quickly interjected before Warren could speak. "I told you, I have come to recognize when it is best to ignore what she says."

Donnie shook her head slowly from side to side in resignation. "How can you make flan if you don't know the difference between condensed and evaporated milk?" she asked.

Warren regarded her thoughtfully, then inquired, as more of a statement really than a question, "If we do not attempt to know and understand you, how can we expect you to help us defeat Valledai; is that what you mean?"

Donnie turned to him gratefully and gushed, "Exactly! Well, actually, I think it's important that we get to know each other, don't you? I mean, I'm learning a lot about your world; the least you can do is learn some things about mine. You never know, we just might give each other ideas on how to defeat this Valley Guy of yours. Of course, it totally goes against Precept Prime, but I'm willing to take my chances on that end."

Warren gave this some consideration before agreeing with her. "Very well," he said, "we shall keep it simple. What are batteries and, er, what is *Precept Prime*?"

"Let's see, how can I explain batteries so you'll understand them?" mused Donnie, looking up at the ceiling, apparently for inspiration. "Um, let's call them portable energy. You stick them in a machine like that one," she said, pointing to the boombox, "and they give the machine the energy to work. But their energy is limited and eventually dissipates, or dies out. Without them, the machine won't work, get it? Or at least it shouldn't. Well, the boombox does work without them. What's more, the refrigerator started working by itself months ago. So did the stove, even though there's no gas line hooked up to it. I have a feeling that if I plumbed the dishwasher, it would also work. Gee, maybe I don't even have to plumb it, come to think of it. Which is all kinda bemusing when you realize that these appliances have absolutely no power or fuel supplies connected to them at all."

Warren obviously understood far less than half of all this but he continued to present a polite and interested face to Donnie, whereas the cat laid down and covered his ears with his paws.

"As for Precept Prime," Donnie continued, "well, that's from a TV show—a kind of stage play or theatre production—which is set in the future. Precept Prime says that someone from an advanced civilization shouldn't share technological devices and information with less advanced people. It might screw up their natural evolution, see? Make them too advanced, way too soon for their own good. Get it?" She could see that Warren didn't, really. "Well, it is only a TV show," she conceded.

"I, for one, look forward to learning much more about your world!" declared Warren with a gusto that stopped just short of clearly being feigned. "What you have accomplished here in the cottage with these furnishings of the future is certainly different by our standards and quite comfortable." He flashed a toothy grin at Donnie, which made her wish he hadn't because it was really very frightening.

"Yeah, okay," she gulped hastily, "getting back to your side of the story, you left out a mighty big chunk there. How did Valley Guy make it known that he wanted the amulet from Catie by nearly killing her twice for it, and what other things has he been doing around here?" she asked suspiciously, wondering what else the cat had been keeping from her.

Her questions sobered the werewolf immediately. He traded glances with the cat before turning back to Donnie to explain. "For one thing, he has changed many fair wolves into dark ones. Every member of my own pack was taken by his evil magic. Which is why I patrol these lands alone and will not rest until he is destroyed. I escaped the full impact of his power, but only with Catie's aid. For I was not born as you see me now. I am not a man-wolf; I am a wolf. Since his dark magic touched me, whenever I am in the presence of humans, I become what you see before you. Once I am away from them, I revert back to my normal state, that of wolf. It…" he paused to look at Donnie meaningfully, and then confessed, "has caused great torment for me to live like this."

"Um, yeah, I can see how life would be difficult for you. How'd it happen?" she inquired curiously.

" 'Twas in the dark of Ærra Litha, at the start of the sun blessing day itself—" Warren began, then was interrupted by Sylvester.

"If you will remember, Donemere," the cat interjected, "that is in your modern month of June. And, I am sure, you will recall from our studies that Litha, while used by the Anglo-Saxons for not only one, but two of their calendar months centered around the summer solstice, also marks that sabbat on your modern Wheel of the Year," he supplied needlessly. Since they had studied many calendars together this winter, ancient and modern alike, until they could recite their months and holidays backwards and forwards, Donnie raised a sardonic eyebrow in his direction, but otherwise kept silent.

What she really wanted to know was how the Wolf King had come to know the Anglo-Saxon name for the summer solstice? Through either Catie or Sylvester, apparently; which begged the question of just how much Witchcraft from other times had been taught to him? And for that matter, why was he taught it? Was he not, as were most of the magical animals she'd met here, merely an Ísolé, a simple practitioner of magic, one who is unable to wield more than small amounts of magical power and that then only within themselves—except under certain conditions, of course, when their magic could be augmented by others?

Warren continued now, bringing her back to the present, "Yes," he said, "it was during the summer solstice. We were returning to our den in the mountains after a successful hunt. One of my pack ran inside to check the den and called that all was clear. The others in my family went in before me, while I guarded the entrance. I was the last to enter. When I had taken only one step into the cave, a beam of red light shone upon the wall. I stopped at the entryway and tried to retreat, but a dark power drew me inside and held me fast.

"A formless figure in a hooded robe appeared in the midst of my stilled pack. It threw back its hood to show that it was really no more than a cloud of dark mist under the cloak, yet it spoke some words of power in a low voice that seemed to resound from the depths of the earth itself, and then it flung a staff toward the wall of the cave. The staff did not touch the wall, but began to move over my family, making its way round the cave. It went from wolf to wolf, floating above each for a time, then it spun rapidly, passing through the paralyzed wolf below. The staff moved to each of us, young and old, in turn. Once it left a wolf, they were transformed into man-wolves.

"It took my entire family, all of them, until it came to me. I fought desperately to retreat just those few steps out of the den, but I could not because his power held me firm. I felt his grip on my mind and body and knew him to be called Valledai. To my deepening dismay and horror this Valledai was forcing me to become a servant of evil once again and I was powerless against his dark magic." Warren bowed his head at this and shivered with the memory of his plunge into the darkest regions of his soul.

After a moment, he took a deep breath, raised his head, and recalled with wonder, "It was just as the staff began to spin through me that I felt another power, a fair one. It was Catie's. I could actually feel her magic warring against his and the air within and without the cave suddenly grew wild and tumultuous. I could hear its roars all around me—why, even the ground shook with it. Then suddenly, several massive black creatures with wormlike bodies, fat and reeking of the earth, tunneled out of the walls and floor of the cave and crawled toward me. Valledai must have called them forth, for they obeyed his bidding. They were terrible creatures. Their ringed mouths were rimmed with great sharp teeth, which they bared ever they moved closer between the still forms of what had been my family only minutes before.

"That was when Catie herself appeared beside me. She stepped in front of me, her body glowing white, and raised her hands. She spoke to those she called her sisters and a blinding white light shot from her bosom and from both sides of me, enveloping me in its glow. The dark creatures around me recoiled and began to retreat. Catie stood there, pushing her fair magic out at them, driving them back farther and farther. Then she shouted for me to run, which broke me free from my trance. I turned and caught a glimpse of eight," here Warren hesitated, clearly searching for just the right word, "*fantastical* female figures standing behind me. I did not know them or from whence they came.

"Catie again commanded me to leave and so I ran as I had never run before, reaching her lands in what seemed moments although I knew it must have taken hours. I did not stop until I reached the cottage. The door was open and inside I found Catie, exhausted and weakened, bleeding profusely from her nose, mouth and ears. Even her eyelids oozed blood from the strain of conjuring and trying to control her part of the Magic of the Nine, as I heard her refer to it when I approached the cottage, although to whom she spoke I never knew because she was alone when I entered the house. At that moment, I immediately transformed into a man-wolf."

The Wolf King looked directly at Donnie, but he was not seeing her, she knew. From the shadows in his eyes, she could tell that deep within, the events he was relaying held him imprisoned painfully within the past. "I believed then that Catie had not arrived at the cave in time to save me," he murmured sadly. "I felt an all-consuming desire course through my body to taste human flesh and wanted nothing more than to eviscerate my dear friend. I leapt at her and would have torn out her heart, but ere I could reach her, I felt the same fair magic that had shone in the cave. And there, between us, now stood those same eight women blocking my path to Catie. Their power held me still as they whispered in a language that was strangely familiar, but which I myself do not speak. They encircled me and passed their hands over my body until I felt the darkness leave me. I fell to the ground and knew nothing more until morning.

"Catie had also recovered well enough by then to move around the cottage. Both of us were quite weak and ill for many days afterward. Although I pressed her often during the time we had together thereafter, Catie refused to speak further of the eight women or the Magic of the Nine. She would only beg my forgiveness for being unable to save my family. Her magic was not strong enough, she cried. Over the following three—no, nearly four moon cycles she regained her strength and we provided counsel to each other. We soon discovered that many more dark deeds had been accomplished by Valledai and his armies than either of us knew separately."

Warren stopped to regroup his thoughts. When ready, he continued slowly. "A few days after the incident in the cave," he said, "Catie called out to other magical creatures, those who were still under the influence of their own magic and not Valledai's. We met in this cottage a fortnight later on the eve of the new moon, under the concealment the black night provided. Each of the fair creatures who came had bitter tales of their own to tell, of losing family and friends to Valledai's dark magic and his savage hordes of roving warriors. We agreed as one that someone with much stronger magic than Catie's was needed if we were to defeat Valledai and his vast legions. But who that was to be was stuff of legend, or so we believed."

Donnie raised an appraising eyebrow and repeated, "Stuff of legend, you say?"

"Yes," the Wolf King assured her guilelessly. "At this juncture, Catie left us to be alone in her workshop. What she did there, none of us knows. She returned to the gathering an hour later and explained her plan of bringing one of her progeny here. She also told us of the amulet and that she feared it was through her that Valledai came to be in our world. There were those in our alliance who wanted to leave and take their chances on the Sarn King of Medregai and his men, but Catie averred that her plan could not fail. She held that there was no longer anyone left in this world who could hope to challenge Valledai and the armies he leads. Even combined our magical powers would soon not be enough. I remember her telling us, '*Massive and overwhelming fair magic is the one tool that can defeat this lunatic and his black earth-eaters, for their power will only continue to grow. I have foreseen this,*' she exhorted the council, for the strange beings aiding Valledai had greatly shaken her confidence in her ability to face him again.

"She went on to argue that with her descendent here, that being you, Donemere, and that once you had accepted your powers, Valledai would know a force far more powerful than his existed in this world. He and his allies would do nothing more for a time but wait and watch the new power. She hoped this would give you the opportunity to embrace your magic and become wise enough in your powers to defeat him in battle. The need for that time is come," Warren announced, peering intensely at Donnie.

She, completely spellbound by this time by Warren's mesmerizing account, was caught off-guard by his last statement. A few beats went by until, realizing that he was expecting a reply from her, Donnie blurted out, "Why, what's happening now?" She raised her teacup to her lips to cover her nervousness and added, "I mean, I haven't noticed any dark shadows, er, pun intended there folks, ah, following me around or anything like that. Valley Guy still seems to be lying pretty low, doesn't he?" She took a sip of her tea and wondered just what the heck she was supposed to do in this looming battle!

Warren gave her a level stare. "As far as we could tell, for the first few months after you were brought here, Valledai did nothing because of your presence. But, recently, with the new moon of Hrethmonath, he has openly resumed amassing an army of dark magical creatures. He has the fair creatures he has turned to his will, and there were also many dark creatures left over from the great battle between the forces of the Sire Lord and the Free Peoples of Medregai. Most of the Sire Lord's fiends have migrated to the mountains just north and east of here, desiring to be close to your realm, where magic still resides even though it was meant to have died out by now. Valledai has taken command of these creatures and is laboring without restraint to increase their numbers many times over. His domain extends throughout the Brumal Mountains, all the way to their eastern edge, where his legions are gathering in his mountain keep at Moên Gjendeben. His influence is felt as far north as Marn Dím, home to most of the Mountain Folk. He has filled their hearts with darkness once more and their hatred for the Free Peoples of Medregai grows, overshadowing the great steps we've taken toward an alliance.

"Since the night Valledai stole my pack, the remainder of my people, the North Wolves, have taken to the ground to ensure our survival as a free race. Though we have suffered great losses at the hands of Valledai's armies, we have managed to gain knowledge of their intentions. They are planning to march on Marn Dím in less than a fortnight and, once that is taken, as it is sure to be, they will make their way south to meet with the main thrust of Valledai's forces, which shall undoubtedly come from Moên Gjendeben."

Here, Warren's tone deepened and filled with great anger. "They will ride over all in their path, burning a wide swathe through the countryside, killing every fair magical animal, every free man and their families, their livestock—in fact, all living creatures, until they reach the lands of the west, where the Sarn King makes his home. They will destroy the world of men and, in the process, they will attempt to bend all magic to their dark will, if they are able. This farm lies directly in the path Valledai's forces must take from Gjendeben." The Wolf King looked intently into Donnie's eyes once more and warned, "Donemere, do not underestimate your foe, for he means to conquer all of this world and, with the aid of the amulet, rule time itself."

Donnie blinked and returned his stare. "Okay, Warren, that's...really frightening," she said in a small, thin voice that was strangled with apprehension. "I guess we can't just bury our heads in the sand and let them go by unhindered, can we?" she grimaced, biting her lip. She released a heavy, slow breath and with it exclaimed, "Hoo! Not exactly gonna be a cakewalk, is this?" She looked at the other two and gulped down the huge lump that had formed in her throat. Things were getting worse and worse, not only for her, but for Medregai as well, it seemed. Just how was she going to stop an entire army of dark magical creatures, plus their apparently quite powerful leader and his wormy buddies? She shuddered and then shut down the fearful part of her thoughts.

A good start, logic dictated, would be to gather as much information as possible about Valley Guy and how he did things. She nodded to herself before saying to the others, "All right, I'm beginning to understand the situation—not that I like it, mind you. Being an intrepid heroine has never been one of my goals." She knew that her voice had come out sounding high and tight from stress, so she again paused to collect herself and cleared her throat. "Putting all that aside for the moment, I need to learn more about this Valley Guy of yours. How did Catie even know that he wanted the amulet or that he was the shadow following her through the portal each time she traveled?"

It was Sylvester who answered this time. "She recognized Valledai's triune when she rescued Mynydd Uchaf, from the cave. That is how she came to know the shadow's name. As to your first question, Valledai sent a man to steal it," the cat announced with asperity, adding disapprovingly, "Catie has always had a weakness for comely men. This one was beautiful...*and deadly.*"

Warren grimaced ruefully at Sylvester's dramatic comment and explained, "It occurred during the waning moon of Haligmonath, at least three fortnights after our council of magical animals. I was called away from the cottage and was traveling north to my people. They were under orders to learn what they could of Valledai's plans and I had received word that a certain pack had news of grave import to relay."

The Wolf King shook his head slowly, in amazement. "When I eventually tracked them down, they knew nothing of this supposed message. I saw then that I had been duped, drawn away from the cottage by ruse, so I raced back as quickly as I could. Early the next morning I returned to the cottage to find this man standing over Catie's body, sword drawn and bloodied. He had run her through with it and made his mark upon her shoulder."

Sylvester snorted angrily. "He had arrived at the cottage the afternoon before," the cat spat, "under the pretense of running from Valledai. He wore a black mask, which he removed when he dismounted his horse. His beauty overwhelmed poor Catie and she foolishly invited him into the cottage. He stayed the night with her there. I do not know what was said or done because she would not allow me access to the house," here the cat's voice was brimming with reproach. "I spent those long hours waiting in the stables with Diana and Otis, praying that Catie would be safe with this stranger. At the dawn, I heard her cry of agony. Fortunately, Mynydd Uchaf came back to the cottage at that same moment. He threw his wolf's body at the door and it opened. We both ran inside and found Catie and this stranger as Mynydd Uchaf has described. In the stranger's hand was the amulet. Mynydd Uchaf was on him in one bound, but the stranger was quicker. He had already turned and swung his rapier." Sylvester looked at the werewolf, who took up the narration once again.

"I stopped just out of his reach, before he could cut my throat. I lunged downward at him, tearing the amulet from his hand, ripping it to the floor. Tanny raced to where it landed, picked it up with his teeth, and shot out of the room. The man shouted in frustration and followed Tanny outside." Warren turned briefly toward Sylvester and, with a look, encouraged the cat to continue.

At that moment, Fariya's "Follow Me Home" ended and the Hoogles' "Long Way Round" began as Sylvester took his cue.

The cat explained, "I jumped to the roof as soon as I was past the doorway and flattened myself upon it. The Black Rider never thought to look for me up there. He gave a sweeping glance round the outside of the cottage, then ran to the stables. He quickly searched both it and Catie's workshop, came back out, jumped onto his horse and was gone. When I was sure he was no longer within sight, I leapt to the ground and ran back inside the cottage." He glanced at both Donnie and Warren before confessing, "I am not one to imagine fanciful things, but I would swear that when I hid on the roof with the amulet, the nine snakes securing its blood-red stone came alive. I am certain I felt the beat of my—"

"Bless my bells, the amulet!" cried Donnie. She jumped up from her chair and sped out of the room before anyone could stop her. She was back a few minutes later, carrying something in her right hand. Going over to the candelabra on the workbench, near where the cat sat, she held up the glittering object. It was the necklace she'd found around the injured man's neck. The light of the candles reflected off it, casting a deep red glow onto the ceiling.

"Is this the amulet Catie had?" Donnie asked Sylvester, spreading the necklace across her palms.

He leaned forward to study the article in question. "I believe so. Why, yes...yes, look at the serpent heads; they are one and the same! This is most certainly Catie's amulet. Donemere, how long have you had it?" the cat demanded, suddenly suspicious of her.

"Oh, don't get your shorts in a bunch, Sylvester," she retorted. "I wasn't holding out on you. This was on the man we found today; he wore it underneath his clothing. You didn't see it earlier because it had slid around to the back of his neck. When I turned him over to clean his backside, I saw it, took it off him and put it in a corner of Diana's stall to keep it safe for him. It finally penetrated my brain when you said something about the serpent heads that the two might be one and the same, so I ran out and got it," she informed him, not adding that the trip to the stables had afforded her the opportunity to stop at the well and splash some cold water on her neck so she could take a much needed break from all the revelations being dropped on her and allow her to regain her failing equilibrium a little. "That's exactly how long I've had it, okay?" she snapped, making a face at the cat. "But, more to the point, how did that guy out there end up with it?"

"He must have stolen it from Catie," Sylvester said gravely. "I think we should face the probability that what Mynydd Uchaf was told of him is erroneous and that he is, in fact, in league with Valledai."

"No, I don't believe it," Donnie countered, mindful of the song the boombox had played about the man when she was wrapping his wounds. It had been so perfectly timed, as had other songs the boombox had played at certain key points in today's events, that she just couldn't believe it was all coincidental. Thinking back, she realized that the boombox had been exhibiting this trait more and more often of late, not just today, almost as though it wanted to convey not only encouragement to Donnie, but maybe even information at times. Goodness gracious, it seemed she'd been right about it earlier; it had, in its own way, become a sentient entity. But she doubted that she could convince either her familiar or the Wolf King of this, so she added, "Don't ask me why, but I'm sure he's not. I guess it's just a feeling I have about him. He's on our side, I know it."

Sylvester and Warren exchanged looks, then Warren advised Donnie, "You must test him when he awakens. 'Tis the only way we can make certain his intentions."

She turned toward the werewolf, who by now had joined her and Sylvester at the worktable, and reluctantly nodded her head in agreement. "Yeah, I suppose you're right, if we think it's truly necessary once he wakes up and we find out who he is and how he got the amulet. We can cross that bridge when we get to it. So, getting back to the amulet, what's it say on the back, Sylvester, in the inscription?"

"What inscription?" Sylvester queried, clearly surprised.

"This one here on the back." Donnie turned the amulet over and pointed to the inscription.

The cat studied the smooth surface of the pendant's backing for a few moments, peering closely at it, then shook his head slowly. He looked up at Donnie as if he thought she were nuts. "I see no inscription, Donemere."

"It's right there, in those small, blurry letters!" she protested.

"I repeat, I see no letters etched anywhere upon it," the cat staunchly asserted.

Donnie scowled at him. "Enough fun and games, Sylvester."

"I am not jesting with you, Donemere! I truly do not see marks of any kind upon it!"

"They're right there! Please tell me you see them, Warren!" Donnie pleaded.

Warren leaned forward and studied the back of the amulet where Donnie was pointing. The Wolf King met her look and hesitated, finally shaking his head. "I see no marks either. Are you certain they are there?"

"Of course they're there!" she cried. "Go on, touch them, see if you can at least feel them." Donnie was staring at the other two somewhat desperately. Was she, in fact, imagining the engraving?

Warren ran a sharp-nailed fingertip over the surface of the amulet's backing. When he did so, he gasped with surprise and said, "I do feel something there, yet I still cannot see what it is!"

Donnie breathed a sigh of relief. "Oh, thank the heavens above!" she said. "I really feared I was going crazy there for a minute."

Sylvester ran his paw over the amulet too, at once feeling the roughness of the lettering. He raised his head sharply to look at the other two. "What could this mean? A cloaking charm of some sort?"

Warren shook his head, completely baffled. "I do not know."

"Neither do I," chimed Donnie, moving her shoulders agitatedly. She turned and went back to her chair, plopping down heavily into its depths. "We might as well worry about the amulet later, I guess. Right now, I want to hear what happened to Catie after she got stabbed by the Black Rider," she prompted, carefully examining the amulet in her hands, looking for any signs that the snake heads were moveable. She fingered them, trying to push them around; but no, their forms were solid and stationary.

Warren had rejoined her, again sitting in the other armchair before resuming his tale. "Catie awakened when I picked her up after the Black Rider ran out of the cottage. She told me to drag her bed into the main room so that her presence would keep me in my man-wolf form. When I had done that, she gave me instructions on which herbs to mix for poultices. The puncture wound the Black Rider had given her was in her left shoulder, just above his mark. She told me how to position the poultices and how to bandage her other wounds in such a manner that they would heal properly. His sword must have had an evil potion on it because for nine days Catie fought a raging fever. That broke upon the tenth day, and from there she improved daily."

An enlightened Donnie nodded. "Now I understand why it took her so long to recover after the incident in the cavern where you were changed into a werewolf," she said. "It sounds as though Catie had probably just gotten her full strength back from that night when, only maybe a couple of fortnights later, the Black Rider shows up and attacks her. Is that about right? Okay then, let me ask you another question, Warren. Do you remember if, when you wanted to kill Catie the night of Litha, did you also want the amulet so you could take it back to your new supposed master, this Valley Guy character?"

Marcus Randry and the Hoogles' version of "Won't You Come In?" began to emanate softly from the speakers of the boombox. It occurred to Donnie that the boombox was no longer playing the same song twice, nor was it playing live versions of any of its songs. Apparently its discombobulation was now fully bobulated, as was her own—she suddenly felt sharp and eminently alive, thankfully. Her confidence in her abilities was on the rise once again. She looked at the box for a moment more, then refocused her attention on Warren.

The Wolf King had bowed his head in shame. "Yes," he replied. "Catie asked that same question of me when she recovered from the fever. She was certain *that* had been the first attempt at stealing the amulet from her."

Donnie studied Warren with renewed interest. She couldn't help but notice that whenever he spoke of Catie, his voice softened. He didn't have the classical look of the fictional werewolves from her time. Sure, he had wicked-looking nails and more than a few razor-sharp teeth, but other than this, and being rather hirsute, he could easily pass for a man. Well, for an intensely blue-eyed Chase Egan anyway.

Warren went on, speaking louder now, so as to be heard over the increasing volume of the boombox where Marcus Randry was telling the world to let whoever was at the door come in. "From then on, Catie trusted no one. She confessed to me that she had lain with the man, but that he had put her under a spell to do so."

"Yeah, right, a witch who needs to be under a spell to have sex with a handsome man? Ha! That's a new one," Donnie remarked dryly.

Warren stiffened, defending his friend with a simple, "I believed her." Donnie could see that he had done no such thing, but, hey, he seemed to be in love with Catie. What else could he do but play along with her deception?

"Okay," said Donnie, nodding her head, "sorry I doubted her morals. Promise I won't do it again. Hey, Sylvester, how does this thing work?" She gestured toward the amulet now lying on the arm of her chair.

Sylvester shrugged diffidently. "Alas, I do not know," he confessed. "When we ventured through it to retrieve you, Catie said something I could not understand, but which took us to your time. She said something similar when we were finished and that brought us back here. Regretfully, she seems to be the only one who knows how to work it."

"Which explains why she wanted to disappear." Donnie looked at Warren, asking, "Do you really not know where she is?"

Warren met her gaze steadily and declared, "No, I do not. Though she may be imprisoned by Valledai. As Sylvester said, she has been neither seen nor heard from in a month. But my people, along with other creatures of the forest and mountain, are still trying to glean as much as we can about Valledai's forces and his plans. It is rumored that he holds someone captive, but who and where they are is still unknown."

The other two grew silent and watched Donnie as she considered all that she'd just been told. Her right eyebrow slowly arched upward, while her muttered, "Hmm, again I say: curiouser and curiouser," was barely audible.

Sylvester shook himself once, settled back down into a sitting position, and advised, "If Valledai has captured Catie, soon he will come after the amulet again. With it and her, he means to become the master of time and move freely between worlds. He could easily bring back any number of monstrosities to destroy Medregai. 'Tis devilish to even think, but he would be able to wreak havoc wherever he goes with impunity. Therefore, Donemere, he must never be allowed to possess the amulet." The cat stared long at Donnie before intoning loudly, over the boombox's repeated volume increase of the song's chorus, "You, as the most powerful Codlebærn ever, must stop him before he obtains it."

Donnie returned her familiar's stare and pointed out, "A bit heavy on the melodrama, don't ya think? Personally, I'm for all of us stopping him, instead of trying to make it a one-woman show. So how about it; are you in, little kitty? Are you willing to risk life and limb to stop this lunatic megalomaniac of yours?" Something was nagging at her, somewhere in the back of her mind, something to do with the boombox. What was it?...Oh.

The cat, poised to respond to Donnie's inquiry, was stopped by her altered expression and by the wrenching of the front door as it exploded open. Donnie was looking at the boombox, her head cocked to the side, with a seriously puzzled brow. "You want me to what?" she gulped disbelievingly.

At practically the same moment, Rex barreled into the room, yelling excitedly, "He's here, he's here! The bad guy you're looking for is here!"

Chapter 8
Take a Little Trip with Me

"What?" Donnie yowled at the dog, frantically leaping to her feet. "He's here already? At the house?"

"Well, no," Rex admitted in a worried voice, "but he's on our lands and he'll be here really, really soon!" The German Shepherd Dog was running wildly around and between the chairs, panting loudly, bouncing up and down from end to end, and otherwise presenting a perfectly frenzied picture of panic until Warren caught hold of his collar to still his movements.

"Oh, hell's hounds, puppy dog, you had me terrified for a minute!" cried Donnie as her heart rate skipped again and finally began to slow. "Okay, honey," she breathed, "calm down and tell me exactly where he is. How far away?"

The dog whipped around and strained against Warren's restraint, but the Wolf King held him tight. Rex relented and finally sat down. He looked over at his mama to explain, "The guy's only about four miles to the north and he's riding hard, just like he knows where he's goin'. He'll be here in a few minutes, so you'd better hurry up!" He broke free from the werewolf's suddenly relaxed grip and trotted up behind Donnie, pushed his way between her legs and sat down. "Whatcha gonna do with him, Mama? You gonna turn him into a toad?" Looking straight up at her from between her thighs and trembling all over, he added timidly, "Are there gonna be any loud noises?" Rex had always hated loud noises, even when he was a little bitty puppy.

Donnie gazed down at him and put a tender hand under his greying snout. "No, I don't think so, baby dog," she reassured him.

"Promise? That's okay then." He scooted backward from between her legs and shook himself hard. "Man, I flew here just as soon as I got the message from the skunks. So, whatcha gonna do, Mama? Do you know?"

Donnie reflected on this question, then shrugged and said, "I'm going to go outside and meet him. And, if he wants to, I'm going to let him search the farm. What else can I do?"

Sylvester and Warren both began to speak at once, the gist of which was that they felt this would be a bad idea unless she did a little judicious magic first. Together, they quickly worked out their plan.

Warren would have to leave the farm proper, as his presence would most surely alarm the man, especially if the man *was* the Black Rider who had attacked Catie before. But the wolf would stay within sight of the cottage, in case he was needed.

Sylvester was to hide on the roof and keep watch. If Donnie needed Warren, Sylvester would wave his tail furiously. If she really needed Warren, the cat was to let out an ear-splitting screech—Donnie's words, not Sylvester's.

Sylvester suggested that she disguise herself as a crone and that she materialize the injured man to different places whenever the bad guy got too close to him. Donnie agreed to the former, but not the latter. There was still that little issue she had with dematerializing living matter, she reminded him. When he began to protest, she interrupted him flatly with, "Don't worry, Sylvester, I will think of something. Just leave it alone, okay?"

"Well, you must be quick about it," her familiar exclaimed, "the man approaches!"

"Too true that!" she agreed heartily. "You guys had better split now. I'll go outside and meet him there. But first," she picked up the amulet from the arm of the chair and stepped in front of Rex, "you take this because the safest place for it right now is around your neck." Warren and Sylvester nodded, and then both dashed out of the room.

Donnie knelt down and made her pup look her squarely in the eyes. "Sweetheart, you need to get it away from here, so run west. Go at least five miles out and keep moving. I'll call for you once it's safe to bring that thing back here. Whatever you do, don't lose it, okay? And Rex?"

The dog, about to take off running, stopped and turned his head back toward her. "Yes, Mama?"

Donnie hesitated a moment. Should she alarm him unduly by impressing upon him the need to be extremely careful and stay out of sight of anyone he might encounter? He had a tendency to hide rather effectively when frightened or upset, and she hadn't yet been able to determine where he went during these frequent disappearances. On the other hand, she didn't want him taking dangerous chances. She decided to compromise and told him, "Make sure you stay on my lands, okay? Don't go off them at all because I want to be able to call you back quickly."

The dog blinked disappointedly at his mama a couple of times and lowered his head as he slunk out the door of her workroom, Donnie right behind him. "Okay, I got it. I'll stay here," he mumbled. And with that ambiguous reply, he trotted out the front door.

The others were already in place, or at least they were nowhere in sight when Donnie went outside. She did catch a glimpse of Rex's tail as he disappeared into the forest above her, on the western edge of the valley. She registered vaguely that he seemed to have gotten there much sooner than she would have expected, but her mind was on other things and she let the thought pass out of her head almost as soon as it entered. She hurriedly jogged to the stables and stood in front of her friends' stalls. Turning around frequently to look outside, she explained to Diana and Otis what was going on and asked Diana to stand in front of the injured man to hide as much of him as she possibly could.

Out of sight, the boombox came to life with "Take a Little Trip with Me" by Fuego de Guerre. Donnie leaned backward so she could see the boombox sitting on the ledge of the well. She could just barely hear the words of the song. "Oh, boy, what great timing that thing has," she muttered distractedly, straightening to stand tall again.

She put her hands over her face and, hoping for the best, she concentrated on transmogrifying her face, skin and hair to that of an old woman. She felt her features transform beneath her hands. She took out the elastic band she had in her hair and shook her long locks free. Good, her hair was white and her hands had developed age spots. She snapped her fingers and an old, faded, tan cotton sundress of hers and one of Catie's thick blouses, a deep purple one with overly long sleeves, appeared across her arm. Hurrying, Donnie got out of her sweats and sent them back to the wardrobe, put the blouse and sundress on, then took off her shoes, going barefoot. As an afterthought, she materialized her witch's hat and jammed it onto her head, figuring that most women of this time would probably wear some sort of head covering to protect themselves from the sun.

"How do I look?" she asked Diana when she finished her transformation. She was shivering slightly from the coolness of the earth on her bare feet. The boombox drew her attention once more when it cranked up its volume for just the first part of the next verse where the singer informs his audience that *Pablo sabe todas las calles de la ciudad.* The volume then dropped back down to its previous level.

Diana had watched Donnie change her appearance with wonder and now admired her friend's profile, telling her, "Hoo-girl, you are so good at that! I wouldn't recognize you if I didn't know it was you. Seriously, you genuinely look like an old woman. But, you'd better disguise your voice too."

Donnie turned back toward Diana and nodded her head in assent. Thoughtfully, she walked out of the stables and stood over the boombox for a minute, staring at it intently when its volume increased yet again and she was warned that it apparently would be prudent to take a trip with this unknown Pablo—just what she was supposed to discover on this trip or where it should be to, she had no idea.

"Go away!" she finally hissed at the boombox, thoroughly annoyed. "You can't be here right now!"

It abruptly stopped playing, making the sound of a needle screeching off the end of a record. Its lights flashed once sulkily, then it disappeared.

Donnie "hmmphed!" at the spot it had been a second before, hunched herself over and began slowly crab-walking to the other side of the well. Once there, she let the bucket slide to the water. When it filled, she started to crank the handle to bring the bucket upward, keeping her movements deliberate and slow, doing her best to emulate those of a person almost twice her age. She faintly heard the sounds of approaching hooves from the trail to the north.

When the rider arrived at the farm, Donnie turned toward him, the sun in her face. She put her hand to her hat brim and called out, making her voice shaky, "Who is there? Who is it that has come to visit my old bones?"

An impressive black figure sat mounted on a proud, skittish black stallion. The horse's eyes rolled and he appeared to want to bolt. He bucked and turned, neighing loudly. A battle of wills ensued between horse and rider, but the iron hand of the rider soon won out. The man dismounted lightly and spoke soothingly into the horse's ear, then he left the animal to take a couple of unhurried steps toward Donnie.

The newcomer was dressed in a dusty cape, shirt, muddy tight pants, high boots, and dirty gloves, all of which were of some black material. His black gaucho hat was lavishly embroidered with swirls and curls in silver thread. This same intricate pattern was copied around the neck and edges of his cape, in the cape's solid silver and turquoise clasp, and upon the horse's colorful tack. The handle of his ornate silver rapier gleamed prettily in the sunlight. It had obviously been kept cleaner than the rest of the man and his equipment. The bottom half of the stranger's face was covered by a black mask, which was tied tightly at the nape of his neck. After he removed both the hat and the mask, the man flashed Donnie a toothsome smile and bowed low.

She gave a visible start upon seeing his face. "Holy anachronisms, he doesn't belong here!" she whispered under her breath, afterward adding silently to herself, *Aw c'mon, it can't be him, can it? He's not even real!*

"Pardon me, *vieja mujer*?" the man in black asked politely and with a heavy Spanish accent as he straightened to stand in a relaxed attitude just in front of his horse. His smoldering black eyes took in every inch of Donnie, then swept around the clearing, noting the various buildings, missing nothing. His gaze lingered on the addition at the back of the house, an entire wall of which could be seen from their position near the well.

Mentally, Donnie apologized to the boombox. She just hadn't been quick enough to realize that it was giving her information on the man who stood before her, proud, arrogant and exuding more animal magnetism than any other man she'd ever known. He made her blood stir and her loins tingle for the third time today. She now understood how Catie could have fallen under his spell so easily. He was gorgeous. And without being told or having any corroborating information, Donnie knew without doubt that here was the Black Rider who'd tried to steal the amulet and kill Catie. What she didn't know was why he'd done that.

"I said, dearie, it appears your horse does not want to be here," she croaked in her best old-charwoman's voice.

With a wave of his hand, the man dismissed her remark. "He will remain where he is." Once again, the Black Rider flashed his brilliant, sultry smile at her. "May I trouble you for some water? We have traveled far and are in need of refreshment."

"Certainly, young man. You may help yourself."

The man strode over to Donnie, taking the well's crank lever out of her hand. For a moment, his hand covered hers and, even through the leather of his glove, she felt the shock of his rakish heat. Donnie pulled her hand away, stepping back quickly—too quickly for an old woman. She hoped he hadn't noticed and cursed her foolish, errant body silently.

The man turned to stare deeply into her eyes. Donnie dropped her gaze immediately and backed off more slowly, saying, "Take as much as you need. There is plenty for you both." She walked stiffly to the other side of the well and sat down on the long bench that stood partly under the shade of Sisnos, the apple tree nearest to the stables.

The stranger thanked her cordially and remained silent while he pulled up the well bucket the last few feet, setting it on the ledge. He reached over and took down the tin cup that hung on a nail there, filled it from the bucket, and drank its liquid in one long, parched draw. When he finished, he let the bucket slide back down to the water, then walked over to his horse. He led the horse to the animals' watering trough, where it noisily slurped down a gallon or two of the cold, clear water.

While neither Donnie nor the man had spoken for almost two minutes, both had been acutely aware of the other's movements, each watching the other surreptitiously. The Black Rider was obviously certain he could handle Donnie, but she was not so sure she could say the same of herself.

Which is more about you than him, she admonished herself in her head. *Okay, so your libido is getting quite a workout today after being dormant for months. Surely you can handle that, can't you? You're not that much out of practice. Just keep control of your hormones and everything will be fine.*

Keep control of her hormones? Her? Well...that could happen, she supposed.

She decided to take the bull by the horns. Squinting her eyes, she turned her face toward the man and asked, "You say you are travelers, eh? Where are you traveling to, if I may be so bold as to ask?" There, it made her feel a whole lot better to assume an offensive stance!

The stranger walked slowly and sensually toward Donnie, his thick, black, curly hair glinting in the sunlight, as he began to explain his presence. "A *compadre* and I have been journeying together for some time now, seeking adventure, but we were parted in the storm of yesterday. I searched for him all night and all day. Alas, I fear he was injured when his horse slipped down a hillside into a quarry and they were both lost to the fog. I followed his horse's trail, faint though it was, as best I could. Early this afternoon, I found where he spent the night."

The man sat down close to Donnie, letting his right arm and leg rest firmly against her. She willed her body to be still and behave like a lady against his oh-so hard muscles.

He continued with his story. "As I say, I fear my friend is injured because I found much blood there. I continued to follow his trail, but when I caught sight of his horse an hour ago, it was without rider. I retraced my steps and found that another horse's tracks veered away from my friend's trail. I followed this new trail here, to your cottage. Possibly you have seen my friend? He is tall and fair," the Black Rider said, then he smiled again at Donnie and gestured toward himself ruefully, "and clothed in much more suitable attire than I. I am hopeful that you have rescued him and attended his wounds. Please tell me you have him here and that he is well. That is the way of it; *sí?*"

Donnie hoped her face wasn't as flushed as it felt. Those eyes of his were beguiling, especially this close-up. She completely forgot what she'd been going to tell him about the horse tracks and managed only to squeak, "No, dearie. I have not seen another soul since I came here. I am afraid your journey to my niece's little cottage has been for nothing."

The man moved his head closer to hers and he again flashed his winning smile. "Oh, I do not think it was *por nada, buena madre*; do you? Tell me...where is Catie?" he asked seductively.

At this, Donnie forced herself to regain control of her hyperactive hormones, keeping her expression deliberately innocent when she met his eyes. "So, you know my Catie?" she asked, smiling widely so that the skin around her eyes crinkled, making her look quite merry. "I too have been wondering where she could be. Allow me to introduce myself. I am her auntie; Mathilda's my name. Yes, yes, Auntie Mat she calls me. Ha ha! Says no one will ever make a doormat out of me. Get it? Ha ha! That girl! Yes, yes, she is quite admirable, do you not agree? She never sits still long though, does she? Always off on some new adventure, with such tales to tell when she returns!" Donnie smiled broadly at the man, then abruptly inquired, "How do you know my niece?"

The stranger's eyes narrowed at Donnie's sudden, direct question and his back stiffened. He made his reply slow in coming. "We had...an encounter some time ago," he said. "Did she not tell you of it?"

"Ach no, I have not seen my sweet little Catie for some time. I only drop in every year or so, you know." Donnie smiled archly at him, laying it on thick. "Tell me, m'lad, would you be wantin' some victuals? You must be fair famished if you have searched for this friend of yours since yesterday. Hie, sit you there and I shall bring out a bit o' bread and cheese, and mebbe some beer for us both. There be plenty to spare and you can provide an old woman some respite from her loneliness by sharin' your company with her throughout a meal. What say you?"

The Black Rider visibly relaxed and smiled again. He bowed his head to her respectfully and replied, "That is most gracious of you, *buena madre*. Food would be much welcomed."

"Then you best take your horse into the stables and give him some oats for his dinner." Donnie thought she heard a gasp come from the vicinity of the roof of the cottage and silently willed Sylvester to remain calm.

Doing her best to make her movements as natural and welcoming as possible, Donnie gestured toward the stables with her arm. The man turned around to look behind him. She hoped he hadn't done so in time to notice the barn shimmer from her spell. Additionally, she dematerialized all of the injured man's belongings, the unused poultices and their accompanying medical paraphernalia into her wardrobe. Oh, well, an endless supply of the man's armor and lethal weapons, combined with her poultices and bandages, though admittedly dissonant, might not be such a bad thing one day, she supposed wryly.

She said aloud, "Be careful of the second cow, dearie, the older one. She will be birthing soon and she must stay still. I cannot believe Catie left her in this state, without waitin' for the birth. I am a midwife myself and should have no problem helpin' the poor calf along, though another pair of hands would be much welcomed. It shall be a difficult birth, I fear, for the cow is almost too old to have another calf. So give her a wide berth—ha ha!—so to speak, if you would be so kind, m'lad. But, otherwise, feel free to make friends of the animals. The horse especially loves carrots, as do both the cows. You will find carrots in the box to the left of the door. Your own horse might also enjoy them."

Donnie turned around unsteadily and crab-walked her way to the house. She resisted the urge to throw off the mantle of her disguise once inside and slowly went about gathering food and drink for their dinner. Ten minutes should give the Black Rider plenty of time to search the stables and Catie's workshop shouldn't it? Heck, she'd give him fifteen so he could be really thorough, she decided.

The Black Rider led his dark steed into the stables, poured a few oats into a feed bag and put it on the horse. He began a methodical search of the building. He led the huge, white horse out of its stall and checked the walls and floor carefully. He looked not just for the man or his blood, but for any sign of a trap door or hidden room. There was nothing in the stall except hay and horse droppings, so he quickly returned the horse to it.

He stepped into the cows' stall. The nearest cow was chewing some hay and looked lazily at him when he entered. The other cow was asleep and breathing deeply. It lay on its belly, with its front legs underneath its nose and its back legs sprawled to the side. He had never seen a cow sleep like that before, but then, this was a witch's cow. While he had not been in this land all that long, he was familiar enough with it to know that its magical creatures were capable of almost anything.

He walked around the cows, again searching for any sign of a trap door or hidden room which could hide the man from him. And again he found nothing. He got out two carrots and gave them to the horse and the cow that was awake.

He looked outside and saw that the old woman had not yet returned. If that was really what she was, which he doubted. There was something odd about her eyes.

He slipped around the front of the stables to the workshop in the back. He started on the left and worked his way around the room, even going so far as to peer into the largest of the many iron cauldrons stored there. No sign of blood, of the man, or of a trap door in this room either. He climbed the stairs up to the hayloft. Curiously, it contained a number of black trunks, all of which were locked and stacked tightly against each other in the back. But there was no wounded man, not even within the hay at the front.

The Black Rider smiled grimly to himself. He knew the old woman was lying about not seeing the man he was after. Any novice tracker could tell that her horse's prints had been much deeper on their return trip back to the cottage, while his foe's horse had just as obviously been unburdened when it ran from the place they had spent the night. The woman's horse had carried something heavy to the little farm, which certainly meant his foe was here somewhere. He'd find him, no matter what. He now needed to think of an excuse to get into the house to search it.

By the time Donnie came outside with a small platter of bread and cheese and two tankards of beer, the Black Rider was sitting where she'd left him, looking as though he'd been nonchalantly sunning himself on the end of the bench the entire time she'd been in the house. But she noticed the fresh mud on his boots. The only spot that stayed muddy after a rain was in front of Catie's workshop because the forest overshadowed the doorway. She allowed herself a self-satisfied smile.

"Here you go, dearie, have some beer," said Donnie, offering one of the tankards to the man. "Not sure where Catie gets it, but I can attest to its admirable flavor. Drink ye down, my boy."

The Black Rider waited until she'd taken a sip before even tasting his own.

" 'Tis good, is it not, *señor*?" Oh, shoot! What was she thinking, calling him that? Donnie hoped against hope that he wouldn't take notice of her blunder. She wanted to play along with him for a while more before getting rid of him.

The Black Rider did notice the slip of her tongue and his suspicions about her true identity were strengthened. Was this the other witch he'd overheard Catie and the man talking about that night around their campfire; was she the one from the future? Or was she someone else? Whoever she was, he would play along with her for a while more before getting rid of her.

Donnie slid the platter of food closer to the man and said, "Have some of this cheese. It too comes from Catie's stock. Alas, the bread is my own poor concoction and does not stand up to the quality of the cheese and beer. 'Tis edible, though barely. Come, my friend, and join me."

The Black Rider looked somewhat dubiously at the square bread offered, wondering if it was drugged or magicked or both. He had never seen a loaf shaped such as this. The old woman began to eat it, so he tried some. She had lied about the bread. It may have been her own concoction, but it was light and flavorful, redolent with rosemary, and he ate it hungrily.

"Tell me of this friend of yours. How did you meet him? Oh, and who would he be?" Donnie asked, trying to keep her tone conversational.

The Black Rider looked up at the old woman and asked himself why she had not questioned him for his own name yet. Did she know it already? Could this perhaps be Catie in disguise? The ridiculous hat perched on this woman's head was the sort Catie would undoubtedly wear. But no, he dismissed the notion emphatically, he would know if it was her. He knew Catie's smell and this woman's was different, very different.

He paused only momentarily before responding to Donnie's questions. "My friend and I met traveling north of here nearly a fortnight past," he explained. "While we were enjoying the warmth of our fire that night, he told me he had journeyed far and wide for more than a year after the death of his wife and child. Ever since that time, he has searched for something he has been unable to define or grasp. Alas, I fear his life will be forfeit if I cannot find him soon, for I know he was greatly injured by his fall. I pray that I am able to pick up his trail again when I leave here. I will look for his horse first, I think. It is just possible the horse may lead me to my friend, Lord Falwaïn."

"Lord Falwaïn?" Donnie squeaked disbelievingly. She turned her head away, her mind racing frantically. So, that's why he looked familiar to her, because he looked just like Noah Taylor, who'd played the role of Falwaïn's counterpart, Bæltan, in Martin Drake's movies—or rather Noah Taylor looked just the man, this Lord Falwaïn, who, right now, was tucked safely away in Diana's stall!

Oh, hysterical histories, what had she been dragged into? Here she is, breaking bread with an Andreo Feráme look-alike who, so far, seemed to be a very real Galto or someone akin to him, while Taylor's look-alike, a.k.a. the fictional Bæltan, a.k.a. the very real Lord Falwaïn, was hidden in her stables as a cow? And don't forget Warren, or rather, Chase Egan, who in his role as Lucius the great wolf hunter went after werewolves who looked very much like Warren—well, except that *his* body hair and razor sharp claws are real. She felt like Frannie at the end of her adventures telling Mike, Bob and Dan, "And you were there, and you, and you."

The Black Rider finished his beer and contemplated Donnie's profile. "Yes, Lord Falwaïn. Do you know him?" he asked, his voice soft and careful.

"No-no. No. No," Donnie repeated firmly, turning back toward her strange visitor at last, shaking her head. "Well, I have heard of him, of course, but who amongst us has not? Ha ha! He and King Belnesem are quite well known in these parts. Yes, most certainly. Quite, quite well known." She was babbling and she knew it, but this was too much for her. *Kitty's got a whole lot more explaining to do*, she thought to herself grimly. She shook her head to clear it and looked the Black Rider straight in the eye with an unflinching gaze.

He returned her look just as determinedly, deciding the time had come to end this farce. "Where is he? I know you have him here somewhere." The sultry foreigner's low voice had become steely and hostile. "If you give me that which Catie stole, I will leave you in peace without harm to you or to your magical cat who hides so poorly in plain sight."

Donnie stood up, playing the part of outraged host. "I do not know what you are thinking, young man. Your friend, as I have already told you—"

She got no further than that because, in the blink of an eye, the Black Rider's left hand was on her throat, while his right had unsheathed his sword and brought it to her neck. Donnie willed Sylvester to stay calm.

The dark stranger was furious. He demanded, "Who are you? You are not who you seem, of that I am certain. Show yourself, witch! Or are you really a feeble old woman who will die easily by my blade, as Catie nearly did?"

Donnie stiffened in his grip and let her appearance go back to its natural form. The Black Rider gave a sharp intake of breath and thrust her from him, his eyes searing over every inch of her.

"I bet you have a pretty fair idea of who I am," she replied sharply, breathing fast. That had been close, but she'd had to test him to see how cold-blooded he was. If provoked a second time, she had no doubt that whoever this man really was, he would do more than try to frighten her. She hadn't missed the desperation in his eyes.

She took a few steps backward and leant on Sisnos for support. Passing her hands over her face and hair, she looked beyond the stranger toward the roof of the house, where she could just make out the blue-black of Sylvester's tail wagging crazily. She again willed him to stop freaking out.

"Where is Catie?" The Black Rider's face had taken on a hard, resolute look when he asked this.

Donnie gasped and refocused her gaze onto him, her right eyebrow raised high. "I thought you were kidding when you asked that before. Don't you guys have her?"

A momentary flicker of surprise crossed the man's face. He looked at Donnie warily and said, "Do not play games with me, m'lady, or I will cut your pretty throat."

Donnie straightened from the tree and retorted with spirit, "Oh, no, you won't! If you try, you might be dead in less than one second. Do you really not know who I am or what I can do? Did your *master* not warn you to beware of me?"

"I have no master!" the Black Rider all but screamed at her, working hard to control his rage. Donnie could see his Adam's apple bobbing furiously and his left hand clenching and unclenching into a tight fist, while his right held his sword in a death grip. With monumental effort, he finally overcame his anger, literally shaking it off. "I am my own master," he informed her in ominous, quiet tones.

"Then why are you doing his bidding, this Valley Gu—Valledai character?" demanded Donnie querulously, her own anger beginning to rise. "Why have you come back to Catie's?"

The Black Rider stared at her arrogantly. "Lord Falwaïn carries with him the amulet that will send me back to my time, so I followed him here. He has given it to you now; has he not?" The dark stranger's voice dropped to a throaty growl. "You will relinquish it to me, witch, or you will die! Do you hear me? You will die!"

Donnie waved her hands impatiently and informed him, "It's not here right now." She drifted away to stand in front of Fûltíne (the elder of the apple trees situated near the well), putting her back to the house so that she could see if Warren had moved into place yet behind the stables.

The Black Rider nodded, following Donnie, watching her every move. "No, I can feel that it is not here at the farm. But you know where it is, do you not? If you do not give it to me, I shall kill all who are here, beginning with your cows—both of them. One of them is Lord Falwaïn, is he not?"

Impressed, Donnie look upon him with admiration. She crossed her arms in front of her and declared, "Well, I'll be darned! When'd ya figure that out?" she asked curiously.

The Black Rider was taken aback by both her question and her increasingly casual demeanor. He lowered his rapier a few inches, although maintaining a firm grasp upon it, and admitted, "Only a few moments ago, unfortunately. I recalled that Catie had only one cow, not two, nor would there be any reason for her to obtain a second. If I had realized this earlier, I would have killed him when I searched the stables." He sighed resolutely, then stared hard at her again. "I must have the amulet and take it back to Valledai," he said quietly. "He has promised to send me back to my time with it."

But you're not real, Donnie thought to herself, *so how can you have a time to go back to?* Suddenly assailed by doubt, she asked aloud, "Tell me two things first. Are you really Galto and, if so, how did you get to *this* time?"

The man's black eyes narrowed suspiciously. "You know who I am? That is not surprising, I think, since it was your friend Catie who brought me back from one of her expeditions through the time portal," he explained bitterly. "She took me away from all that I have ever known and sent me to the village of Banaff Dír. If Valledai had not found me and helped me to escape from its murderous citizens, I would have been killed by them. They looked upon me as if I were a terrible monster who must be immediately exterminated. He saved my life, while she took my world from me. I will do the same to you as I did to her—"

"Yeah, yeah, hold your horses," muttered Donnie, waving her hands irritably at him. "I get it, okay? I get it. That's why you wanted to kill her the first time you were here. I've heard all about it, so *puhleeze* spare me the details." She stopped speaking and leaned back against Fûltíne, staring at her visitor critically, crossing her arms again in front of her, although her palms were pressed to her shoulders now. She began to glow with just a hint of blue. "I don't suppose anything I say will convince you that Catie wasn't the one who brought you here and that it was most likely this Valley Guy who did? No-o-o, I didn't think so. Look, I think you should understand a few things. Firstly, I'm not Catie and I don't have her guilt trips. You see, I had nothing to do with you being brought here. Secondly, I was also yanked out of my own time and I'm just as angry about that as you are. And thirdly, I'm a mighty powerful witch and can kick your ass easily if provoked. I guess you gotta ask yourself, *How lucky do I feel today?* So, go on, push me. Or, you can ride away right now and we'll forget any of this ever even happened."

Of course Galto lunged at Donnie, his sword coming up and around to slice her neck. Warren, not waiting for Sylvester's screech, had crept up to the back of the stables after the Black Rider had searched the building and, almost before Galto had even begun to move the four steps toward Donnie, he bounded out to attack the foreigner from behind. Sylvester, caterwauling for all he was worth, leapt from the roof and hit the ground running, also intent upon attacking Galto. Even Fûltíne began to dip his boughs.

Donnie waved her arms and froze them all where and as they were, then ducked around Galto's blade, ignoring the small wave of power that emanated from her midsection. She saw that everyone's eyes were still aware and could move, then she realized that she'd only wanted to freeze their bodies, not their minds too. Noting the distinction for future reference, she unfroze her friends and gave them a moment to grasp the situation more fully and for Warren to pick himself up from where he'd dropped in suspended mid-gait.

Donnie stood tall before them, with Galto still frozen solid behind her, informing them of what they were going to do with their captive. "Okay," she said firmly, "we put him on his horse and one of us has to lead the horse off my lands. It'll have to be either you, Warren, or Rex or Otis, as Sylvester and I aren't really good for twenty-five miles there and twenty-five miles back. Get this, though—nobody harms him. Nobody even so much as touches a hair on his head. I'm really not up to letting anyone hurt Andreo Feráme right now, so we're just gonna let him leave peacefully. And then we'll see if Valley Guy can figure out how to unfreeze him. C'mon, Warren, let's do our best to get him onto his horse without breaking his legs."

"No, don't argue with me, Sylvester," Donnie commanded as the cat opened his mouth to speak. She was just too peeved with him to listen to anything he might have to say right now. "This guy has had the same thing done to him that was done to me," she pointed out angrily, "only the really sucky part for him is that he wasn't made the most powerful witch of all time. Look, he's not bad, he's just been conned into thinking that we're the bad guys in this tale. He's expecting me to kill him, or else he'll kill me. Well, neither of those is going to happen, which may, just may, go a long way toward convincing him that maybe he's on the wrong side, not us. Therefore, we're just going to let him go, right?" She leaned menacingly toward the cat. "Right?" she insisted.

Sylvester sat down and wrapped his tail around his front paws, acquiescing meekly with a murmured, "Very well, Donemere. But I do not see how can you be so certain he is not evil."

Donnie glared meaningfully at the cat and said, "Okay, first, we'll pretend that I don't know who he is. Well then, I know he's not evil because the boombox wanted me to let him come onto the farm and search for his quote-unquote friend. No way would the boombox have put us in jeopardy if he was really as bad as all that. And it also would've played a different song to identify him. Maybe something like "Gone Bad," something along those lines. But it didn't, it played "Take a Little Trip with Me," which is about one totally cool dude, if you get what I mean. And it did not escape my notice that the line which played the loudest was the one where it said something about him being the one to travel with because he knows all the streets of the city. Which means that before this is over, I'm going to need Galto's help in finding my way to something. And in case that's not enough, all you have to do is read the stories written about him to know that he always fights for what he believes to be the side of good, not evil. So, I say he leaves here unharmed!"

Warren and Donnie managed to get the Black Rider onto his horse without too much trouble. Thankfully, he'd been in mid-lunge when he was frozen, so his knees were already bent. Donnie levitated him onto the horse while Warren steadied him and guided his feet into the stirrups as best he could.

Donnie floated up the few feet necessary to take the sword out of Galto's stiff hand and then slid the blade into its sheath. She looked into the man's frantic, darting eyes with compassion and said, "Don't worry, if your master can't unfreeze you, the next time I see you, I will. And believe me, I will see you again. Until then, you're just gonna have to keep like that because, well, to be quite honest, I don't trust you. Nothing personal, you see, but you're working for the wrong side right now and I need to make sure you're out of commission for a while. I promise it's not permanent—Girl Guide's honor." And naturally, she raised her hand, three fingers straight, while she swore her solemn oath to Galto because that's what Girl Guides do. Okay, okay, so she'd never actually been a Girl Guide, but why bother him with that detail?

By the time she drifted back to the ground, Donnie felt distinctly queasy. The few times she'd levitated herself over the past few months, even just lifting herself a few inches off the ground had always produced this very same response within seconds. She'd hoped that particular side effect would pass on its own once she got used to the sensation of being airborne, but alas, it had not. She doubted that it ever would, since she couldn't play high-action video games for the same reason; that is, because of motion sickness. But, hey, what good was being the most powerful witch in history if she couldn't come up with a potion or spell that would keep her from getting sick when flying? And after all, her sassy sassafras broom might actually behave now that the binding spell had been broken. She found she was excited at the very real probability that she would get to experience something that, to her, defined classic witchdom—the very singular skill of broomstick flying. She was certainly going to attempt that soon, she vowed to herself now, as her feet hit the ground and she was once again on terra firma.

They used a rope to tie the Black Rider securely to his horse, looping it around his legs and waist and over the horse several times. When they were finished, Galto was tied up tight. He wasn't going anywhere without the horse.

Unfortunately, there wasn't much Donnie could do about the position of his arms or the expression on his face without unfreezing him. Oh, well, she supposed he'd just have to take his chances when he passed through any villages or near other people. After all, he had tried to kill her and that still rankled a bit.

She immediately chided herself for sheer wickedness. She'd better charm his journey back to Valley Guy. That would be the fair thing to do and it really would make her feel better to know that Galto would get there in one piece, looking the way he did and all. Donnie thought for a moment, then quickly canted:

"This man on his horse shall be safe to pass,
To Valledai he'll ride,

Through all the lands between here and there,
Trussed up and hog-tied.
   While along the way,
No harm shall come to him or his, er, to his ass."

It was by no means her best bit of doggerel, but it had a certain verisimilitude about it that Donnie felt was endearing. She slapped Galto's horse on the rump and willed it to follow Warren until he abandoned them, and then to take his master the rest of the way back to Valledai by himself. She watched as they disappeared into the forest, with Warren leading the way far enough in front so that he stayed in wolf form.

Rex had not been called back yet, but at least Donnie knew he was safe because she could feel him with her mind. She sent this message to him telepathically, "You can come home now, you big scaredy-cat. The bad guy's gone."

Sylvester had sat quietly off to the side since Donnie had rebuked him. He was amazed at the sudden change that had come over this trying and tempestuous pupil of his. She strode purposefully now and used her magic with confidence and imagination. She appeared to be accepting her powers fully and was nearly fit to fight Valledai, he thought with triumph. Even her aura had strengthened in larger bursts than usual with each passing hour today. She now seemed almost ready to become Fægre.

He began to preen himself. Yes, he had undeniably performed extremely well at instructing Donemere on the finer points of Wiccecræft, and he congratulated himself heartily on a job well done. Teaching her craft to her had been a thankless task, but he had been up to it. The proof of this was now standing in front of him waving her arms wide, joyfully shouting something to him about his exceptional character.

"Hey! Earth to Sylvester, are you in there?" Donnie demanded loudly. "I said, how did a completely fictional character end up in our sorry little story? What's up with bringing Galto to life? And too, the man lying in the stables, this Lord Falwaïn? He reminds me just a little too closely of a very similar character in the book from my time that I was telling you about earlier; you know, the one that's a near-facsimile of Medregai's history. Only, the guy in that story was named Bæltan. Now, both he and Galto are supposedly figments of two very imaginative authors, and both of them are almost dead-ringers for the actors who portrayed them in the movie versions of their stories. You, kitty-kitty, have got more explaining to do. Just how the heck did Catie, or Valley Guy, whichever it was, manage to make this mess?"

Sylvester blinked hard, taken aback at Donnie's frontal assault, just when he was about to compliment her on maturing into a wise and powerful witch. He searched his mind frantically for the answers to her questions. Catie must have told him, had she not? Vaguely, he recalled a conversation he had had with his former mistress that, at the time had made no sense whatsoever to him, which might now provide the illumination Donemere sought.

He huffed uncertainly before saying, "Catie told me once, after one of her many sojourns to the future, that she had been having a bit of fun with some authors and some other people called directors, whatever they are. Something to do with these actors you reference, that much I recall. She said she had visited many time periods and she liked to study someone who was brave but rather obscure from one, then leap ahead to a different time. There she would find an author and appear to them in their dreams, telling them the story of the person from this other period. That way, even though their history should have been lost to oblivion, it was now recorded in a different century. Ofttimes as fiction, but at least they were recorded, she said."

Sylvester licked his lips nervously and began rushing his explanation because of the thunderous look that had gradually overtaken Donnie's features. "As for these men having similar appearances to actors from your time, she said she would also appear to these people called directors and some others I cannot recall the names of—oh, yes, you are correct, producers—ah, er, ahem, and she would appear to them in their dreams then, imprinting upon their minds an image of the person the story was about and urging them to find someone who closely resembled the, oh, what was it, what did she call them, the proto something. Yes, protagonist. My thanks to you, Donemere," the cat thanked her earnestly, regarding her with an uneasy smile.

Donnie, who was staring at him in great alarm, shouted incredulously, "Are you telling me that Catie was not only playing muse to the authors, she was also the casting agent for the movies?" Donnie paced around excitedly, all the while windmilling her arms as she ranted at her familiar. "I'll bet Martin Drake would be more than a little shocked to learn that! Hell, for that matter, Pareto Rodriguez would positively turn in his grave, as would Erik Mueler—once he gets there, that is—if they knew that the wonderful, fantastical stories they'd imagined they imagined, were not so darned fantastical or imaginary, or even theirs! And, good heavens, Sylvester, whatever was Catie thinking by bringing Galto back here?"

"Oh, Catie would never have brought that man here," Sylvester assured Donnie confidently. "She held to very strict principles whenever traveling through time. For instance, she never went to the past for fear of meeting herself and she never transported anything or anyone from one time to another—er, not to stay, that is," he hastily amended this declaration.

Donnie eyed him with disbelief, her right eyebrow slowly arching ever higher toward her hairline. "Never, huh? Well, you'll forgive me if I have a spot of trouble swallowing that one whole, given my circumstances," she pointed out, her voice dripping with sarcasm. She again paced back and forth in front of the cat. "Criminy, didn't she even think about the space/time continuum problem? I wonder just how much she changed the future by insisting that history be recorded, come hell or high water. Oh, no," groaned Donnie suddenly, stopping in her tracks and rolling her eyes toward the heavens, "how many other times did she do it? Who else is going to show up here? Heeeyyy, I just thought of something, if Valley Guy really is the one who brought Galto back here, why isn't he mad at Valley Guy? Why does he think Valley Guy's the good, Catie's the bad, and I'm the ugly? Is it possible that Galto truly doesn't know who brought him here? Now, how did Valley Guy get around that one?"

Sylvester responded with a series of helpless shrugs throughout this litany of rhetorical queries. Donnie ignored him. At the end, she expelled a heavy breath that underscored her immense irritation and hissed, "Questions, questions, and so *few* answers!"

Rex came slinking into the yard just then, looking about him anxiously. "Is he really gone?" the dog asked. "Is he? What happened? Did ya turn him into a toad? What did you do to him, Mama? Huh?" He laid down, promptly started retching and hacking, and finally threw up twice. He'd obviously been eating grass again to soothe an upset tummy.

Donnie, as soon as her dog began retching, went and stood over him, rubbing his sides to calm him, telling him that everything was okay, there was no need to be afraid now, she'd taken care of Galto without turning him into anything but a statue and that was only temporary, and that he, Rex, was a good boy, such a good boy, and it was okay to throw up because he'd feel so much better once he did. She also threw in a motherly warning about eating grass whenever he was nervous, knowing full well it fell on deaf ears. Rex always threw up when he was upset and if there was even one blade of grass remotely within reach, he would find it and scarf it down. Which just facilitated his reaction to stress.

And, as usual, once he'd emptied his tummy of its acid and grass, the dog was perfectly fine. He got up now and ran around, telling Donnie proudly, "Look Mama, I still have the necklace thingy you put around my neck. It almost came off a couple of times when I was jumpin'. You know, as I hit the ground, I mean. And one time it got caught on a branch, but I got away from that nasty old tree and didn't even break the chain part of it, although that old branch was hanging on pretty tight. Don't be mad at me, but I went a little farther than you wanted me to, well, 'cause I was going so fast and it just kinda happened that way. But this thing makes me feel really sick, Mama, like it's got a lot of magical power, and it keeps making my head ache and my heart beat in time with it. Can I take it off now?" he finished abruptly, cocking his head sideways to look up expectantly at his mama, his tail wagging hopefully along the ground.

Donnie went over to the dog and knelt down, taking the amulet from around his neck. She cupped it in her hands and felt the pulsations emanating from it. Rex was right, it *was* throbbing like a heartbeat. She fingered the snakeheads again, but they remained unmovable. "I seem to keep saying this today, but I'll say it again: curiouser and curiouser," she mused aloud. "Will the mysteries never end?" She dropped the amulet into the pocket of her sundress thoughtfully. There hadn't been any pulses coming from it an hour ago. She wondered what, or who, had set it off in the interim.

She turned around and noticed that Sylvester had slipped away while she'd been distracted with Rex. She guessed that he was probably greatly affronted by her tirade about Catie. "Well, he's just going to have to stay that way for a while!" Donnie declared angrily. She had other things to worry about right now.

She went into the stables to check on her patient because she wanted to try something she'd been thinking about. She was going to see if she could heal him with her magic. Her sight charm was still running, so she waved her hand in front of her and the image of the second cow dissolved. She stood back and studied the man's face. She supposed she ought to start thinking of him as Falwaïn, or would that be *Lord* Falwaïn? Donnie didn't know what they should call him when he regained consciousness. But, yep, he really did look almost exactly like the guy who'd portrayed Bæltan in Martin Drake's first great epic.

She explained to Diana and Otis what all had occurred in the last hour or so. They expressed a suitable degree of surprise at their injured visitor's identity, explaining that, naturally, they both had heard of him and were quite honored by his presence in their humble abode. They then both wondered aloud regarding the reason *for* his presence.

Donnie nodded her head. "Yeah, I'm kinda curious about that myself. And about Galto too." She knelt down, unpacked Falwaïn's wounds, and inspected them closely. Although her experience with this sort of thing was limited—well, okay, pretty much nonexistent—all of the cuts seemed much better already. At least blood was no longer seeping out of any of them.

She sat down beside her patient cross-legged and folded her hands together in her lap. Closing her eyes and making her breaths long and even, she focused her mind's eye on the larger of the cuts, the ones that made up the slightly embellished "X" shape on his abdomen. Donnie concentrated on the outer edge of one of the cuts and funneled her mind into it, down deeper and deeper, until she was almost at the cellular level. She was focusing her mind's sight so hard, she could see the myriad blood vessels in the tissue. Taking a deep breath, she forced herself to see the tissue on either side of the cut begin to repair itself, healing from the inside out, while low, whispered words tumbled rhythmically from between her lips.

Mending the wound was a slow process and, before she was even a fourth done, she had to stop from exhaustion. She opened her eyes to look at the wound. She'd done it! The soft tissue within the wound had knitted together quite noticeably.

Falwaïn's eyelids open suddenly, just for a moment, his eyes glazed, but blue as the morning sky; although, perhaps that was somewhat due to the wave of cerulean that had emanated from Donnie as soon as she'd finished her healing chant. It dissipated about the same time the man's eyelids stilled.

Even with the power increase she'd just experienced, Donnie didn't think she had enough energy to heal the big wound totally, so she decided to give the other, smaller but deeper cut on her patient's leg a running start with its healing process. Again, after staring at it for a minute, Donnie closed her eyes and slowed her breathing, focusing her mind's eye on the cut. She was only able to maintain her healing trance for about a minute, but it was enough to mend the wound almost halfway.

This was fantastic. She would try some more tomorrow morning and, possibly by nightfall or definitely the day after tomorrow, she'd have the major wounds gone. Her patient's lesser cuts should be relatively easy to heal, although there were so many, it was going to take a while to get to all of them.

Donnie left the wounds uncovered to air out a bit while she returned to the cottage and went to the wardrobe to ask for fresh poultices. She made up another solution with the Klein Liniment and sent everything to the stables, walking back out there herself a moment later. Carefully, she bathed Falwaïn again and packed and bandaged his wounds for the night. It was almost dark now, so she fed the animals, then went inside the cottage to take a shower, preparing a spare supper for herself afterwards. She wasn't much hungry, but she was certainly very tired.

It occurred to her during dinner that Warren had not come back yet. But she could feel him if she reached out with her mind, as she had earlier with Rex.

With a strong measure of surprise, the Wolf King felt her mind touch his. He was safe and was still leading Galto to make sure he was well away from Donemere's lands before abandoning him. He knew her question had come through as pure thought, although it seemed to him that he actually heard it with his keen ears and that it was asked in Donemere's own voice. Bewildered by this paradox, he nonetheless remained composed and replied to her calmly, unconsciously speaking aloud, telling her that he would return to the farm with the dawn; they had much to discuss and plan.

This was the first time Donnie had been successful at establishing this method of contact with another magical being whom she didn't know all that well. And previously she could only do it within the confines of the valley. She'd tried several times with Mickey T after she'd watch him fly over the rim of the little valley and off into the endless, darkening sky, but to no avail. While she'd been able to feel the old bat's mind, something had always denied her entry into it or any contact with it once he'd passed over the boundary of the valley; no doubt because of the binding spell, as she now knew.

Thinking about it, she realized that, until today, the only power she had successfully extended beyond the valley was her materialization skills, and that only when she was able to visualize what she wanted or the place where it could be found. How many other parlor tricks could she use anywhere now, she wondered wryly. And just how far would her range go?

Might she now be able to listen with her mind to the Earth farther than a mile away from where her body stood? While that was certainly possible, she'd undoubtedly still have difficulty separating and identifying sounds, which would mean she'd be unlikely to find her way around all that accurately, let alone get back to her body with ease. Not surprisingly, Donnie really didn't want her mind literally wandering the Earth for months or years before one day finding its way back to her emaciated body by pure dumb luck alone. No, this was a power that needed more finesse than what she'd been able to show it so far. Before she could call it a learned skill, one that she could count on to work whenever she used it, she'd have to become a great deal better at it.

But how could she do that? This was something she'd asked herself a thousand times before, but had not thought of an answer to yet; not one that worked anyway. Unfortunately, because Catie hadn't talked much about the skill to Sylvester, he didn't have any tips for Donnie other than what he'd already provided.

When Donnie went into the bedroom a few hours later, she saw the cat curled up on the foot of her bed, ostensibly sound asleep. Rex, as usual, was nowhere to be seen, but she could hear him softly snoring, so she knew he was in the room somewhere, probably by her bed with his nose underneath. When she stumbled over him and fell onto the bed, Donnie found her assumption had been correct. She was too tired to yell at him for the umpteenth time about lying right in her path, so she called the dog to her, kissed him right between the eyes in the mama spot, then mumbled a goodnight to both animals through a wide yawn. Rex, annoyed at having been woken, grudgingly jumped up onto the straw mattress and laid down with his back to his mama. She turned her own back to him and snuggled up against his long, warm length, their favorite position whenever sleeping together.

Donnie's head hit the pillow hard after she pulled the covers up over the dog and herself, with Rex already fast asleep again and snoring. Sylvester moved up to burrow down in the curve of her hip and sighed contentedly. The dog's slow, rhythmic breathing lulled Donnie to sleep almost immediately, where she dreamed of a blue-eyed, handsome man with long, fair hair.

Chapter 9
Find My Girl

Falwaïn's eyes fluttered open and shut. Disoriented, and dragging himself up from the deep well of unconsciousness, he heard voices outside; loud, angry voices. Or was it one voice? He could not distinguish that because his head was reeling and his ears buzzing. It sounded like a woman's voice, he thought, then he passed into oblivion once more.

He came to again a little while later, hearing the woman's voice nearby. She was chanting something low in a language foreign to him. He listened for a while, wondering where he was and who she could be. He felt the throbbing in his leg and his side, and from that he knew he was injured. He had the impression the woman was trying to heal him. After a few moments, he felt it might be safe to look through his eyelids at her. He thought she must be very close to him because he could smell her scent, that of a flower he had encountered only twice before in his life, in Ro'Ighaglæd. It was called gardenia and he considered it a pleasing fragrance.

He opened his eyelids to slits, just to get a glimpse of either her or his surroundings, which should be enough for him to tell whether she was friend or foe, he thought to himself. She was sitting on the floor beside him, leaning slightly forward. A sparkling halo of long, straight amber hair, gleaming rich in color as the most fertile of lavender honey will do in bright sunlight, hung around her face so that he could not see much of her features, but they too seemed pleasing.

Suddenly, he had the oddest sensation somewhere above his right hip, on his abdomen. The pain there lessened considerably for a few moments, while, as he would later swear, he actually felt his skin knitting itself back together again. *Impossible*, he thought, *flesh cannot do that.* He wanted to speak to her, but before he could even make a sound or movement, he found himself getting sucked back into the black pool of insensibility. His last conscious thought ran something like: Was that truly a cow standing behind her?

Falwaïn slept deeply and dreamt of the honey woman. He struggled to consciousness when she came to his side again and repeated her chant. His injuries were healing nicely, he heard her say when she stopped chanting, but to whom he could not tell. There was still only the cow in the background.

Half awake, half asleep, another woman's face floated into his waking dream, the young, golden one who called herself Catie. She had been insistent he go somewhere. Where was it? And why did she want him to go there? Ah, yes; that was it. She had wanted to warn him about the Black Rider. And she had given Falwaïn something, something important she needed him to take south.

He saw the amulet in his dream and again felt the pulsations of its rising power and the movement of the snake heads on the stone as she placed it around his neck. Catie had told him to ignore its movement and its vibration. Her fear was running high at the moment, she said, but the amulet would be still soon.

There, that was what she needed from him—she wanted him to take the amulet to someone in particular. In Falwaïn's half-dream state, Catie once again sat before his fire, deep within the Brumal Mountains, her pale face gleaming in the flickering light. She had wrapped her blanket around herself tightly, informing him of the ominous deeds recently committed by legions of dark creatures throughout the Annûar Province, some of which he already knew—except, of course, for her part in battling them.

She was a witch of the highest order, descended from the gods themselves, she said, and she had been traveling through time with the aid of this amulet. Unawares, in her travels to here or there, she had picked up a dark, powerful being named Valledai, who kept following her through time as a shadow, but who always returned with her to Medregai. Not yet a year erst, this Valledai had grown to be even more powerful; indeed, too much so for her to handle alone. And he had a man helping him, a Black Rider, who wanted this time portal very badly.

Yes, that was what she had called the amulet, Falwaïn now recollected; it was a time portal. She said that she had been running from the Black Rider for more than six moons now and she had to rest or die. The Black Rider was not far behind, possibly a half day at most, and when he caught up with her next, it was likely he would capture her, then take both her and the amulet back to Valledai. She had not the will to resist Valledai's magic for much longer, she said. She then passionately declared herself in quite a pickle, the phrasing of which had amused Falwaïn.

Catie went on to say that certain death was everywhere for her, except through the time portal. She needed to go through the portal to hide, but she could not take it with her or Valledai would go along too, and then no one would be safe from him, least of all her. The amulet must remain here and, thereby, this Valledai too; while she herself must go, she asserted firmly, adding wistfully that, without the amulet, she would be unable to return to Medregai and could be of no more service to this beautiful land.

The little witch had begged Falwaïn to take the amulet to the one she had called to this venerable world, the most powerful witch in any land or age ever, she said. She listed which roads and paths he must travel to find her cottage, where this, this Donnie—yes, that was her name—where this Donnie would be waiting. Catie had seemed very sure that her Donnie would know what to do with the amulet.

Almost as an afterthought, Catie had asked Falwaïn if he was free to help her, or was he perhaps already bound to another mission for the king? He gave a succinct recounting of his life for the past two years, ending by maintaining that he was his own master and would be quite happy to help if he could.

Just as Catie was telling him what to say to this Donnie, Falwaïn heard a noise outside their encampment. He put a finger to his lips and motioned for the young witch to step back against a boulder, out of the firelight. A black figure appeared on the far edge of light, his eyes masked, but his lower face gleamed palely. In his hand he held a sword such as Falwaïn had never seen before. It was oddly thin and made a lethal, wicking sound while its owner deftly brandished it.

Falwaïn unsheathed his own broadsword, standing at the ready between Catie and the newcomer.

"I see you have acquired a champion, *querida*." The words came in a whisper, the exotic tones of the speaker carried on a light breeze.

Falwaïn turned to see Catie step out from behind him, her blue eyes shining black in the light of the small fire.

"I 'ave more than one, dear Don Diego, as ye shall soon discover. This one ye may 'ave a chance against, but the other..." her voice trailed off, her smile secret. "The other is not for ye, dearie. She is 'ere ta defeat yer master, as ye shall one day see. Ye 'ave not the power even ta touch 'er unless she allows it, though ye shall try to kill her. Ye shall try," she repeated quietly, "and ye shall fail. But fear not, she be fair minded, and so ye shall not lose yer life, only yer breath."

The figure in black came closer as Catie spoke, his eyes burning, the flames of the fire reflected in their dark depths. Falwaïn matched his breathing to that of the stranger. Slow and deliberate, they circled each other in a crouch, preparing to advance.

But before they had opportunity to match swords, Catie mumbled something under her breath and the newcomer disappeared—just simply vanished as though he were no more. Falwaïn whirled toward Catie in shock.

"I sent 'im as far away as I am able," Catie answered the question in Falwaïn's eyes. "But I swear ta ye, 'e 'as come ta no 'arm. We Codlebærn are strictly forbidden ta kill unless commanded by the gods ta do so. Be sure ta tell Donnie that, in case Tanny forgets. If she kills any knowin' soul, 'er powers shall be forfeited ta the next strongest in our line. That might very well be me and I canna say I want 'em!"

The funny little woman cocked her head to the side and considered this, before murmuring with finality, "No, 'tis already been proved that be not *my* destiny."

She then scurried to Falwaïn and spread her hands upon his chest, speaking now in despair. "I beg of ye again, ye must take this trinket ta my Donnie. Ye must guard it with yer very life, for 'tis imperative it reach 'er safely. Once ye are near 'er lands, she shall find ye. But beware o' the Black Rider, for 'e may mean death ta both of us. Ye shall best 'im yet, but not ere 'e brands ye with 'is mark. Be assured, m'lord, 'e shall be on yer 'eels well within the hour, so ye must be away quick."

Catie took the amulet from her neck and put it around Falwaïn's. " 'Ere, take it," she said. "Be not concerned about its movement; it only dances like that when me fear is runnin' 'igh, as 'tis now. The dratted thing feeds offa me fear and I am ready to admit that I shall not be sorry to part with that bit!" She sighed dramatically and then confessed, "I am near dead from tryin' ta keep ahead of our lovely Don Diego and 'is master. Alas, I dunna 'ave much power left in me and 'tis gettin' used up so quick ennymore, I must go through the portal before the Don catches up ta me again. The amulet shall be still once I am gone." She looked up at Falwaïn, her eyes shining, but with tears of regret or relief, he could not discern. "I am sorry, m'lord, ta be leavin' ye like this, but I must go now or I shan't be able ta summon enuff magic ta open the portal. Only when I am safely away can I rest and restore me powers. Remember what I 'ave told ye and all ye 'ave seen here. Ye must relay it faithfully ta my Donnie."

Catie gave Falwaïn no time to reply to this. Turning on her heel, she took up her leather sack, stuffed her blanket into it, and slung the sack over her shoulder. She moved back toward him and stood for a moment with her eyes closed. Her lips moved in a whisper as she raised her hands high. The amulet, dangling from its chain around his neck, began to pulsate even more strongly and glowed a deep red against his breast. To Falwaïn's surprise, a beam of light shot out of it and lit up a circle on the ground a few feet away, with a column of red light rising from it to the heavens. Catie stepped into the column and was gone, her exit sounding a low *thwump*. The red light also vanished and, all at once, the amulet was still.

In his dream, Falwaïn saw himself packing up his belongings and dousing the fire. After that, he had ridden his horse hard for two days, sometimes catching sight of his pursuer in the far distance. He had urged Arthewyll on through the deep snow of the mountains, ever harder and faster, until both horse and rider were exhausted. He was less than two days' ride from his destination, south of Marn Dím, and thankfully in familiar and warmer territory, when the Black Rider caught up to him.

Falwaïn had stopped for a short time only to give himself and his horse food and water. They were just finishing when Falwaïn heard the other man coming up from the left. Falwaïn grabbed his sword and whirled in time to parry the Black Rider's first arcing stroke of his strange blade. They traded blows for some time, dancing around the encampment, over the boulders and under the trees. Falwaïn had time to admire the other man's agility and grace. They would have been fairly matched if not for the difference in their weapons.

Don Diego's cape swirled around him, and too many times Falwaïn's broadsword caught nothing but the soft cloth. Because the Black Rider's sword was so light, his parries were quicker and sharper, and many more of them hit home than did Falwaïn's. He would pirouette just out of reach of Falwaïn's heavy blade, his own slimmer one finding Falwaïn's flesh increasingly often, its thin cuts stinging sharply. Falwaïn did his best to protect himself, but he was growing tired, his thrusts becoming more and more sluggish. Both men knew he would soon die.

The Black Rider, having sliced deeply into Falwaïn's leg, backed off a moment to let Falwaïn recover his balance. He then stepped in quickly and made two deep cuts on Falwaïn's side, dancing backwards with a satisfied grunt. He thrust suddenly forward again for yet another bold cut, which Falwaïn nearly blocked but could not return in kind.

Falwaïn had to do something quickly. He was not going to allow himself to be killed by this strange man in mysterious costume with his needle-like blade. He maneuvered himself and the Black Rider so that they were near some trees, next to a massive rock formation. He scrambled up the side of this, with the Black Rider close behind, and made his way up three, four levels of boulders and solid rock, pushing down after him as much as he could of the loose rock and pebbles along his path to delay his foe. He darted around the side of a particularly large outcropping of rock, on the other side of which stood the upper lengths of a young, spindly pine tree. Breathlessly, he stopped and reached over to the tree top, pulling it toward him, and held the main bough in front of his chest. Falwaïn's muscles strained at the weight of the bent tree; he prayed they would hold it long enough. The Black Rider suddenly careened around the side of the rock wall and at the same moment

Falwaïn let go of the tree. It whipped up into the Black Rider, catching him in the chest and face on its rebounding arc.

Don Diego was thrown outwardly to land on the hard dirt below, where he lay still. Falwaïn made his way down the rocks quickly. His descent ended a few feet from the prone man. He gathered up his gear, had the presence of mind to dig out his armored breastplate and slip it over his chest, and carefully mounted his horse. He could not take the time to see if the other man were dead or only had the breath knocked out of him; he needed to get away fast. He wheeled his horse to the south and kicked his heels into its flesh. Arthewyll took off with a mighty leap, running hard. Falwaïn looked back after a minute and saw the Black Rider was where he had left him, still not moving.

In Falwaïn's dream, he watched all this as though he were a player outside the drama, viewing it mostly from above. He saw himself riding hard, growing weaker with every stride of his mount. Once he reached the moors south of Banaff Dír, he had to give the horse its head because he was straining just to keep himself upright. When or where he finally lost consciousness, he did not know. That was the last thing he remembered, until finding himself here with the honey woman.

His dream shifted to a time nearly three years earlier, when his wife, Sémere, was still alive and with child. The day she began her childing had started out as a happy morning, filled with the anticipation an imminent birth instills. But when, a few hours after arising, the birthing pains came, with Sémere bleeding heavily, the day turned into the most terrible, heart-wrenching one of Falwaïn's life. He watched his strong, brave wife writhing in agony, her cries of pain echoing throughout the halls of the keep. Mercifully, her death had come swiftly, with the birth of their stillborn son.

He could see, again as an observer from afar, his friends proffering their comfort, attempting to ease his sorrow as best they could, themselves grieving for the friend they had lost. He stayed on at his home in Hörthanc for months, becoming a shadow of his former self. For life without Sémere was no life. Their first son, Malwé, was twelve, nearly thirteen by that time, and already in service as page to the king in Anûmanétus. Falwaïn seemed to have little with which to occupy himself, since the affairs of Faen Eárna were so well ordered by now, the region almost ran itself. And nothing could still the torment within his heart, the ache that would not heal.

The following spring, when his friends were all preparing to return to their own homes, Falwaïn had requested leave from his friend and king, Belnesem, to travel unaccompanied to the wild northern lands. The Annûar region was in dire need of king's emissaries, Falwaïn reminded his friend, and *he* was in need of industry. He jested lightheartedly that he had become bored and wished to go in search of adventure because his life as the Prince of Faen Eárna had made him soft. But they both knew that what Falwaïn was truly seeking was death. The king reluctantly agreed to his friend's request and officially installed a steward in Falwaïn's place. Within the fortnight, Falwaïn had started on his way north.

Adventures he had certainly had over the last two years, but none that had placed him in real danger of losing his life, until the night he met the witch, Catie. She had charged him with a mission, giving him no opportunity of refusal after the arrival of the Black Rider.

But through her actions and because of her need, Falwaïn had found new purpose and, with it, he realized that he had acquired somewhere within the long road of his travels the desire to live. Sémere's face, once so sharply defined in both his sleeping and waking dreams, had become almost obscured and resided now mainly in shadows, showing itself to him less and less clearly.

He thought of her as he dreamed, tried now to see her beloved features. But it was not her countenance that came to him; it was the honey woman's, mostly hidden by the silky, flaming hair that framed her face and which he could not help but compare to the deep color of the sweet amber nectar of the beehive.

Falwaïn woke slowly many hours later, bewildered and wary. He could hear the honey woman's voice, talking this time, not chanting. She was bathing him. Her hands were soft, yet, in their way, quite hard—lean hard, not calloused hard, though. She finished rinsing his hair and wrapped a soft cloth of some sort around his head, then patted his face dry. She had apparently been bathing him for some time already.

With a warm, wet cloth that smelled of heather, she washed his arms, running her hands down their length afterward with a dry cloth. He would swear that he was floating in mid-air, if he did not know better. He could feel a draft on his back, and she even brought the washing cloth down and around his shoulder, to his back. But that would be impossible, as he was lying face up, was he not? His disorientation must be worse than he thought—or perhaps this was yet a new dream?

The woman washed his back, making him ever more drowsy with her slow rhythmic strokes, then again took the soft cloth and gently toweled him dry. She moved her ministrations to his chest and seemed to linger here. He could feel her hot breath on his skin and felt the kindling of desire in his loins. *This is no dream, of that I am certain*, he thought to himself. *I must be crazed to feel this way when I have not had even a proper look at her. I know not who or what she is.*

Nonetheless, she was stimulating an eager response in him. The honey woman finished with his chest and moved down to his legs. She washed and dried each one separately, taking great care not to disturb the wound in the left one, which still throbbed, but only slightly.

Falwaïn felt that he could safely sneak another peek at her. Today, her red-blonde hair was pulled back loosely and caught up by some sort of round comb-like thing with interlocking fingers. She somehow seemed closer to him than before, as if he were on a low table. But, if so, he could not feel its surface beneath him.

He noted her graceful neck and the curve of her cheek when she pushed an errant strand of silky hair behind her ear. Her earlobe bore three small, silver rings that glinted with light. Her strong fingers were reddened from the hot water.

She turned her face suddenly toward him and glanced down at something beside her. He closed his eyes quickly so that she would not notice his stare, but not before he got a chance to see that her cat-like green eyes were serious as she concentrated on her task.

At last she came to his middle. Falwaïn wondered how she would deal with this part of him, and smiled secretly to himself. With growing astonishment, he felt her lift the cloth covering him and continue on to clean every bit of him. He heard her murmured surprise at the response she had generated in his body, but she kept her touch impersonal. She handled him as if this were an everyday occurrence to her, until at last he was clean all over.

Furthering his bewilderment, Falwaïn again felt as though he were floating through the air until his backside finally touched a cool cloth lying beneath him. The honey woman covered him with another cloth, tucking it tightly around him. He could tell that she did this last part as an excuse to keep touching him because, this time, her hands lingered for too long, the light caress of her fingers on his bare arms and chest holding a message of desire for him.

Throughout most of his bath she had spoken nary a word, but now she whispered low, "My, my, you certainly are the bees' knees, aren't you?" She groaned audibly and said, "Leave him alone, Donnie. You promised Sylvester and Warren that you wouldn't touch him while he's like this."

Falwaïn felt her move away, then place something heavy over his legs. It was a heated blanket, which the honey woman pulled up to his chin and also tucked closely around him. He was feeling very drowsy again and was not quite sure if he truly heard her say, "Hey, Diana, wanna get some exercise before or after I milk you? C'mon, let's go outside so we can leave our patient here in peace."

Still dozy, Falwaïn watched her and the cow leave the stall. He nestled down into the luxuriant softness of the pillow beneath his head and wondered fleetingly about the brightness and the strange material of the red blanket covering him. It occurred to him that if the honey woman, whose green eyes and strong features even now were again intruding into his dreams, was indeed the Donnie that Catie had spoken of, then he had somehow managed to reach his destination and he could sleep peacefully now. He allowed himself to sink back into slumber.

He awoke later feeling much restored. The honey woman had obviously been back, for he now had a blue blanket covering him and his wounds felt almost healed. Whatever she had been doing to him, it had been effective. He raised up on his elbow and took a proper look at his surroundings. He was indeed in a stable, but there were no animals present, except for two or three chickens. The cow must be outside.

Tying the strangely soft blanket around his naked body, Falwaïn rolled over to the nearest of the stall's rails and got to his knees, his head heavy and cloudy. He was very thirsty. Slowly, he pulled himself to his feet, then clung to the rail as a redness filled his eyes, his heart pumping furiously. He stayed there, eyes closed, until his vision cleared. He stumbled along the side of the stall to its open gate.

"Better," he encouraged himself grimly, biting the words out through the pain and dizziness he was feeling, "with each step, I am becoming stronger." Holding his leg where the deepest wound still ached, he kept the other hand on something, anything, a rail, a post, as he shuffled across the stables to the door.

The sunlight blinded and hurt his eyes. Falwaïn raised his hand to shade them, giving them time to adjust to the sudden brightness, and he withdrew back into the stables. He felt for the doorway with his other hand and pressed himself to the wall there.

What was that clamor? Music of some sort, obviously, but nothing such as he had ever heard before. It was not just the notes or the instruments on which the music was played that were foreign to him, but the sound itself was odd, as though it were somehow not real. The music was not at all unpleasant, he decided after listening to it for a few moments. He took his hand from his eyes and peered around the doorframe, expecting to see a troupe of minstrels.

His eyes widened in confusion. There were only two humans and some animals standing just beyond a well in the yard, and none of them were playing instruments; and yet, he distinctly heard music!

The honey woman, this Donnie, who Catie had said was from the future, was there with her back to Falwaïn, crouching in front of something. She stood and moved away from it and he saw that it was a dog, one unlike any he had seen before, with black and brown markings. Next to it was a cat, a horse and the cow he had seen earlier. He spied his own horse, Arthewyll, grazing on the hillside across the valley. Sitting on a bench to the right, also facing away, was a dark-haired man in a cloak. The man was speaking to Donnie, but because of the music and the distance between him and they, Falwaïn could not hear what was being discussed. The man arose, then he and the dog ran off to the left, moving out of view.

The cat went through the open door of the cottage and disappeared. Donnie turned and said something to the two remaining figures. Falwaïn swore the horse replied first, then the cow. He could hear their voices and see their lips move, but again, he was not close enough to catch their words. He rubbed his eyes at the sight. He had seen many strange things in his time, but this was different. This was magic in its most consummate form, he realized, for he had never heard of any farm animals who could talk, not even in the days of the Álvar, the ancient wise ones. The wonder of it made his blood course and his heart beat fast. This pure and strong of a magic was something Falwaïn had thought he would never see again after Déagmun had made the exodus to Canavar.

Donnie bent down and touched a small blue-black box at her feet. By that movement, Falwaïn apprehended that the music was emanating from it because, upon her touch, the music changed and a different melody began. The honey woman from the future danced to the music, moving her body in the sort of gyrations Falwaïn had seen only amongst the heathen women of the Mehen'Adríum. The cow and the horse also swayed and stepped in time with the rhythms of the music, the three of them making for quite an unusual spectacle. Falwaïn looked around him and noticed a stool in the corner. Carefully, he walked over to it, placed his hand on a post to balance himself, picked up the stool and slowly carried it to the door, his thirst forgotten for the moment. He watched with interest as one melody ended and another started, the three figures still dancing, completely unaware of their observer. The cat came back out after a while and leapt up onto the well, from which vantage point he also watched the three cavorting to the music. He did not appear to want to join them.

A new song began, which set the honey woman to crowing with delight. It went on for a while, the sound from the box growing until it was loud enough for Falwaïn to recognize that it was the tale of a man traveling the world looking for his girl, asserting that he would not rest until he had found her. Falwaïn let a melancholy smile touch his lips; he understood only too well how the unfortunate leôthe felt.

Donnie held out one arm to the side and slowly raised the other over her head to grasp her wrist, then slid that hand up the length of her bare arm, bringing it in front of her body and stretching both arms wide. All the while, her entire body shook in time with the underlying drum beat of the music. Falwaïn was enchanted, both by this music of the future and by the honey woman.

The next verse of the song began as he leaned his shoulder against the doorframe, his vision becoming hazy again. He heard the woman shout something that sounded like, "Watch this!" Her hands reached toward the heavens and, in perfect unison with the song, from her fingertips shot a breathtaking and intricate webbing of blue light that surrounded the valley with its beauty, filling the skies above with her magic.

Falwaïn's eyelids flew wide and he straightened, gasping with awe, marveling at the magical energy electrifying the very air he was breathing. But it was with deepening shock that he turned his attention back to the words of the lay, believing that within them he recognized the names of a place and a creature of much evil to him.

Sémere's face rose up instantly in Falwaïn's memory and his head began to spin. He must have cried out, for his presence was suddenly noticed by the cow, who had just swung around to face the stables.

Chapter 10
Look What's Goin' Down

"Hey, look; the man's awake!" exclaimed Diana and the boombox shut itself off. Everyone turned to stare at Falwaïn. In return, he gave them a feeble smile, looking as though he was ready to pass out at any second.

Donnie sprinted the fifty or so feet to the stables, the animals close behind her. She stopped in front of her patient, her face set in an expression of deep concern. "So you're the reason that song played," she said. "Are you all right? You don't look so good," she told him bluntly.

Falwaïn mumbled something about thirst, then slumped off the stool and onto the ground. The animals began babbling at the same time.

"You must get him back to Diana's stall. He is not well enough to be out of bed!" Sylvester admonished.

"Whoa, that can't be good. He still looks really sick, don'tcha think?" Otis asked.

"Hey, he's not bad looking, and did you see that smile of his? *Sex-y!*" Diana observed tartly.

Donnie turned to face them, an amused grin on her lips. "Okay, can you all stop stating the obvious? No, he doesn't look well; no, he shouldn't be up; and yes, he *does* have a gorgeous smile, doesn't he?" Her own smile widened. "I think he just may have that 'it' I've been looking for all my life. Who'd've thunk I'd have to come thousands of years in the past to find it? Hey, Sylvester, can I do a charm or spell to guarantee he falls in love with me? Can I?"

Her advanced years of experience caught up with her suddenly and she added, more reservedly, "Well, I guess before I do that, I better make sure I'd want him to fall in love with me. He might turn out to be a real drip and then I wouldn't like him at all!"

Sylvester shook his head silently and stalked into the stables.

Donnie shrugged at the receding end of the cat, playfully mugging at the other two (both of whom were laughing in great guffaws), then she levitated Falwaïn from where he lay and carefully floated him back to Diana's stall. Once there, Donnie gently laid him on the sheet that was still spread over the bed of hay. Using her telekinesis power, she had the drinking cup sail down into the well, fill itself, then fly back up and out of the well to the stables and into her hand.

Falwaïn was stirring again. Donnie held his head up and put the cup to his mouth, dribbling a little water through his parted lips. His hands covered hers and he took the cup from her, drinking deeply. After he'd drained the liquid, he pushed his head back down to the pillow.

He opened his eyes and Donnie could see their blueness and their clarity. Honest as the day is long, she mused privately. At least, that's how he looked. And according to both Mueler and the unknown author of the Medregai history book, absolutely pure of heart and never even tempted by evil darkness or its obsessive power. She didn't think she'd need to test him.

She smiled at him while these thoughts ran through her mind. "Feel better?" she asked aloud.

Falwaïn nodded and discreetly cleared his throat, letting his head nestle into the pillow. He took his time looking her over. Her honey-tinted red hair, on further inspection, had some few strands of grey in it. Her wide, green eyes were intelligent and filled with humor at the moment. Her nose was straight, not too long, and her mouth was full and nicely shaped; suitable for kissing, if one should desire to do so. He let his gaze fall down her graceful neck to what he could discern of her body through her strange attire. It was lean, yet all the usual curves were exactly where they should be. He returned his gaze to Donnie's and she met it with a devilish glint in her eyes. She seemed to be telling him to go ahead and look all he wanted. He gave her a tired but roguish smile and said, "Yes, I am feeling much better and I am indebted to you for your ministrations to my wounds."

"Oh, think nothing of it," she replied airily. "Really. It was all in a day's work and, er, it gave me a chance to apply what I've learned about healing in a practical setting." Donnie admitted ruefully, "Okay, I could've done without all the blood and gore; but, hey, there you go, the first time you experience something horrible is always the most traumatic. I'll bet the next time I have to nurse someone back to health, I won't even have nightmares about it. At least I hope I don't. Believe me, they were more than a little disturbing," she said with a shudder.

She took a deep breath and sent the cup, which had been residing in Falwaïn's loose grasp, flying back to the well to be refilled. "I suppose we should probably leave you to rest a bit more," she suggested. "I'll tell you what, I'll refill the cup and leave it right here next to you so you can have it when you wake up again." The cup had returned, filled with water, by the time she finished speaking. Donnie caught it deftly with her right hand.

Falwaïn's eyes widened in wonder. "That is a very neat trick," he said solemnly. "I gather you too are a witch of the highest order, descended from the gods themselves?"

Sylvester gasped, jumped onto Donnie's lap and whispered to her chin, "He has certainly been talking to Catie, for that is how she *always* describes herself." He sat back on his haunches and blinked soberly up at Donnie.

Donnie nodded and pointed out in a low voice that she made sure was clearly audible to the others, "We kinda knew that much already, didn't we, since he had Catie's amulet on him when we found him?"

The cat nodded his head in assent and turned around in her lap, settling down with his tail curled around his front paws. His demeanor showed that he had decided to let Donemere handle things from here on.

Donnie, hiding a smile at the cat's behavior, asked Falwaïn if he did indeed wish to sleep or if he wouldn't mind answering a few questions. He picked up the cup, quaffed its contents once more, then propped himself up on one elbow. Donnie immediately sent the cup to be refilled.

"I think it best I explain to you what part I have played in this adventure," Falwaïn said, watching the filled cup zoom back into her hand, whereupon he accepted it from her without further comment. "But first, Catie's amulet, is it safe?" Donnie reassured him it was and that he could see it presently. Falwaïn wet his parched throat again and proceeded to tell of his meeting with Catie, faithfully relaying her warnings to Donnie and of his subsequent encounters with the Black Rider, whom Catie had called Don Diego.

When he finished, he wanted to ask questions of his own, starting with the last lay the box from the future had played. It was unlike any he had heard before and he thought it strange that it sang of Baleraime and the evil creature Daux. He wanted to know how this was possible, if their legend had survived so long through time.

Donnie leaned back against the wall of Diana's stall and thought about how much she should hold back. Should she at least explain about Mueler's books and that the song was about that tale, which, granted, was a near facsimile to the story of Medregai? That would certainly open up a whole new can of worms, wouldn't it? And if she explained even just a little bit more than that to him, what kind of damage would occur to the historical timeline, once she sent him back to his own lands?

She looked at Falwaïn appraisingly, still unsure of just what to tell him, and said, "That's a really hard question to answer right now without giving you more information than what's good for you to know. The long and short of that is, I'm not prepared to answer that particular question at this time. Ask another."

Falwaïn stuck his jaw out stubbornly, then gauged it would be wise to wait. Donnie did not strike him as someone who would prevaricate without good reason. He had so many questions to ask, so much to learn about this strange honey woman and her even stranger friends, he must give her time to get to know him. He switched tactics and asked who was this Don Diego with the exotic accent and the strange sword?

Donnie grimaced. "Um, well, I guess you have a right to know something about the guy who attacked you," she began, carefully picking her way through the verbal land mines set before her. "He's, ah, he's from another time too. One of them, either Catie or Valley Guy—that's Valledai to you—brought him back here to this time. It's not really clear how he got here or why he was brought back. As for his sword and his accent, well, that's because he's not from this land, not even in his time. Obviously, he knows English—er, well, I guess you call it *Mannish* here, don't you? Anyway, because of the phonetics—oh, do you even know that word? No? Well, okay then, because of the sounds and rhythm of his native language, he has this exotic accent, as you call it."

"Is he from your time?" Falwaïn asked, nodding his comprehension.

"Ah, no. No, not my time," Donnie replied uncomfortably.

"How far in the future is your time?" A smile tugged at the corner of Falwaïn's mouth. He had finally caught on that she was not willing to readily impart information about the future and he'd decided to have some fun with her dilemma.

"Oh, long, long time," she replied hastily, "and so's Galto—er, Don Diego. Galto's his pseudonym, or nickname rather, if that helps any." Seeing that Falwaïn still looked at her with curiosity, Donnie decided to disclose a general outline of Galto's story. To that end, she added, "He and six friends swore one day that they would take up masked personas in order to right the wrongs committed on the poor by the rich; sort of a war against wealth and injustice, if you will. They wore the masks so no one in the community could identify them. They were referred to as the acérokȟolá, which I think means steel brothers or steel friends, one of the two. This particular member, the one you know as the Black Rider, called himself Galto. But his real name, when he wasn't wearing the mask I mean, was Diego Gaél Anzio Lituñius Tórando Ortiz. Whew, that's a mouthful, innit? I'm pretty sure I didn't leave any names out in that little recitation, but don't hold me to it. I only know his full name because I looked him up in a book—oh, shoot, I wasn't gonna tell you that part!" she exclaimed, faltering momentarily before pushing on. "Anyway, because of the social position he held in his time, he's called a Don, sort of like you're called Lord or Prince, oh, whatever it is you're called—your title, I mean." Donnie stopped and breathed heavily, realizing with dismay that she was literally sweating this, so she mopped her glistening brow with her sleeve and flashed her princely patient a self-conscious grin.

Falwaïn studied her, considering what she had just told him with her words and with her expressions. "Then he must be from a time before you, seeing as you have a book about him in your library and know so much of his background," he observed cautiously, making it more of a question than a statement by raising an enquiring eyebrow.

Donnie smiled her surprise and let out a nervous laugh. "That's a good guess!" she exclaimed appreciatively. "Yes, as a matter of fact, he is from before me. I read the books about his exploits when I was really young and watched the—ah—well, let's just keep it at that. He's, in truth, a pretty good guy—I know that's hard to believe right now," she interposed quickly when Falwaïn looked as though he'd argue the point, "but you have to realize that he's been brought back here against his will, probably told a pack of lies, and now he thinks we're the enemy. The trick will be to get him to see the truth. Once we do that, I guarantee he'll be on our side." She prayed that had come out as confidently as she'd intended. "And we could use him," she added, "he's very handy with that sword of his."

"As I found to my peril," Falwaïn admitted resentfully.

"Yes, well, you'll have quite a scar to go along with the harrowing tale, won't you?" Donnie noted.

Falwaïn eyed her with mild astonishment. "What do you mean by that?" he demanded.

Donnie's lips formed a silent "O," and then, more than a shade diffidently, she replied, "I thought that, well, that you would have realized already, I mean, because of what Catie predicted about him branding you. Er, well...okay, see, if he gets the chance, he slashes an 'X' on his foes with the tip of his sword to declare war against them."

The muscles around Falwaïn's jaw tightened perceptibly. "And I have this same mark on me?" he asked, holding her gaze intently for several silent and uncomfortable seconds.

Rueful now, Donnie replied, "Yes, on your side. But at least he added the arrowhead on the lower left terminus," she said, hastily explaining further when Falwaïn sent her a horrified glare, "which meant that he thought you were worthy of his respect, even if he was declaring war on you. The symbology comes from the language of his mother's tribe, by the way, the Iquakawi." Donnie sighed and smiled weakly. "Yes, well, I, er...if we hadn't rescued you yesterday, you might be dead by now, you know," she pointed out, hoping to change the subject.

Falwaïn acknowledged the truth of this statement with a small nod. "It would not be the first occasion death has settled upon my shoulder, poised to usher me into the next life," he announced gravely, looking down at one of the old, healed scars on his right side, the tip of which was visible above the line of the blanket.

"Yeah, that was a nasty one, and so unnecessary." It was out before she thought about what she was saying. Falwaïn's head snapped up immediately, catching her momentary moue of chagrin. Donnie pursed her lips, then quoted, "Und to him, at the last, Unthgor drew his Falwaïn, his true arrow."

Falwaïn studied her for some time with an expression of thoughtful curiosity before remarking slowly, "You know my father's lament, it seems, though we have just met. Have you also read of me in your library—am I too in a book somewhere?" he inquired. "Is that why a melody from your time refers to Baleraime and the evil creature Daux?"

Donnie was hopelessly trapped. She asked herself the question again of just how much she should impart to him. She wished mightily that Rex or Warren would come back and cause a much-welcomed interruption, but that did not occur.

She waited another moment and looked around at her friends. Each of them was staring at her with complete absorption. She realized that the fascination they had for anything from her time was immense by now. Oh, good heavens, how much harm had she herself already committed? She needed a plan, something along the lines of erasing their memories when this was all over, or taking them with her when she went back to her time if she could, something like that. Some way to ensure that their knowledge of the future did not in any way affect the peoples of the present time.

Donnie again scanned her friends' faces and then came to a decision. "Actually, there are two versions of your story in my library," she informed Falwaïn, "but they are uncannily similar. You see, Catie has a book detailing the history of Írtha, which was retold in another tale from my time, although the main noakie in that version was called Pully and the man who would later become the king was known as Aniselm. You know them as Dreena and Belnesem. The story from my time is about how they matured into their very pivotal roles in the saga of the destruction of the *Book of the Var*, along with you, your brother Mílwaïn, and your whacked out father, Unthgor," Donnie explained, again unthinkingly blunt with her words. "The tale from my time is comprised of a series of three books called *The Songs of the Earth*, which was written by a guy named Erik Mueler. Obviously, he added a lot more detail than what is included in Catie's book about the happenings here in Írtha. Anyway, Catie apparently traveled through time and told him the story in his dreams, and he then wrote the books from those dreams. All the names of those involved are different, though. Like your name was changed to Bæltan, your brother's to Lælter, and your father to Fenridth. As for the song you heard that mentioned Baleraime and Daux, well, that exists just because of how popular the books have always been. Mueler wrote them when I was just a little girl and the song was produced about a decade after the first book was published."

Donnie licked her lips nervously, waiting for him to say something in response, but when he remained silent, she offered, "If you want to read the books to either story or see the lyrics to the song, I have a copy of each in the house. So, yes, you are in my library."

She leaned forward with a somewhat lopsided grin, adding, "Oh, there's something you should probably know about the library before you use it. If you go up to any shelf with a particular book or subject in mind, the exact book or books you're looking for will be on the shelf you're searching. It gives you precisely what you want, with all the information you'll need. The books also open to the correct pages and will flip when you're ready to go on to the next page or subject. And the text you're looking for will be highlighted on the page. It's a little charm I worked up because I hate searching for things, only to have them be in the last possible place they could be. So see, now they're always in the *first* possible place they could be! Actually, the entire house, well, this whole area is charmed in one way or another to make my life easier. I've made certain the charms will work for you too. If you have any questions regarding how one or more of them work, feel free to ask. I thought I'd better warn you about them so that you don't freak out since most of them work automatically. Er...they work by themselves, how's that?"

Falwaïn's suddenly quizzical expression cleared upon her last explanation. "Perhaps it is good that I am not more deeply involved in your adventure," he allowed slowly. "It would take some time for me to become acquainted with your manner of speech. 'Tis...more than a little foreign to this land."

"Yeah, about that," Donnie began, admitting apologetically, "I think I do need your help, so I really hope you're a quick study 'cause we seem to be running out of time. Warren and Rex should be returning pretty soon and they'll be bringing back news of Valley Guy and your friend Galto and also of some rather strange happenings up north. Now, whatever I have to do to get you to help us, I'll agree to, okay? Er, that is, whatever you want that's within reason and within my power to give, of course. I can handle Valley Guy, or at least I hope I can. But you're gonna have to take care of Galto. Oh, and you're going to have to do it without killing him, okay? I know it's a lot to ask, and you were most likely looking forward to going back home, but if you cou—"

Falwaïn interrupted her at this point, holding up a hand for silence, then declared, "I accept your request for assistance, though I may not be well enough to ride for several days." He glanced down at his side and his leg and their respective wounds.

"Oh, those will be healed in the next few minutes," Donnie assured him. "And once that's done, you should feel better almost immediately. I've been healing you with magic, you know. It's getting easier for me and I'm pretty sure I only need to do one more session before you'll be right as rain. Well, okay, there's not much I can do magically for the surrounding tissue and the trauma it's experienced, but I'll give you some medication for that, which should take care of most of the pain. So, lie down, will you, and I'll do the final healing."

Falwaïn found himself immediately complying. He laid back and put his hands behind his head, resting it upon them. Their fates, his and this honey woman from the future, were entwined now, he thought with satisfaction, though why this gave him such pleasure, he was uncertain. He watched with interest as Donnie unbandaged his wounds, first rearranging the blanket he'd wrapped around him so that it covered only his mid-section. While she was doing this, a bowl of steaming water, a bar of soap and some folded hand towels appeared suddenly by his side. He gave a consternated start.

Donnie murmured, "Multitasking," and continued unwrapping the bandages. She removed the used poultices and, for the first time, Falwaïn got to see his wounds. When he saw the shape of the cuts on his abdomen, once again, his jaw tightened noticeably.

"Can you do any magic to conceal the scar?" he inquired.

Donnie turned around to look at the others assembled around them. "I can't think of anything, can you guys?"

"There is no spell or charm I know of which erases scars," Sylvester answered promptly, although he was, by now, deep in the throes of battling one of those elusive noseeums in a corner of the stall.

"Rub some of my milk on the scar every day and in a matter of weeks it'll disappear," Diana offered, munching on some hay beside Otis in the doorway to the stall, who was doing the same.

"I remember being told when I was just a colt that if you rub hard against tree bark, scars will disappear," Otis added as he chewed his mouthful of hay.

Donnie looked at the horse with indignantly raised eyebrows. "Owwwwwch!" she cried. "Yeah, sure it'll disappear if you mutilate all the surrounding skin with the bark! I think we should try something a little less visceral first, don't you? Like maybe aloe vera. I've got some of that and it'd be worth a try. It can't hurt, that's for sure. Not like rubbing yourself against tree bark would, anyway."

"It need not necessarily erase it," Falwaïn interjected, "as long as it makes the scar less visible. Moreover, I am not one for rubbing against trees." With a slight grin curving the corners of his mouth, he looked directly at Diana and demurred politely, "As for the milk, I thank you for your kind offer, gentle lady, but I do not believe that will succeed."

All of them stopped what they were doing and stared open-mouthed at Falwaïn.

"You understood what they said?" Donnie finally eked out.

"Yes," Falwaïn replied, gazing at her steadily, "I presumed that was normal here."

"Have you ever been able to understand animal speech before now?" Donnie asked.

Falwaïn shook his head and conceded thoughtfully, "Not since just after the Battle of the Var when most magical creatures disappeared, no, and never any domesticated ones. Why can I now? Is it not because they are magical and are able to make themselves understood to men?"

Donnie swung her head back and forth. She pressed her palms to her temples and groaned, "Aw jeez, this can't be good! We've got to get you off these lands, and I mean quick! The last thing I need on my hands is a schizophrenic psychopath who's armed with a very sharp broadsword." She looked over at the cat and inquired, "How long do we have before he goes nuts, Sylvester?"

The cat shook his head, shocked by this unwelcome turn of events. "One, possibly two days more. He would not be trustworthy beyond that, I fear," he warned.

"What does he mean, not trustworthy? I do not understand your concern over my ability to hear your magical creatures speak." Falwaïn stated this firmly and then stared at Donnie, tight-lipped.

She gave him an unhappy wince and explained, "Oh, it's this really odd conundrum-type thing. Since magic is supposedly dying out now, if you're not magical and you spend too much time on magical lands, you become a stark, raving idiot. After, of course, first absorbing a little bit of magic yourself."

"You are certain that I will be mad within two days if I do not leave these lands?" Falwaïn asked, his own alarm beginning to show.

"Yeah, well, fairly certain," Donnie admitted. "But don't worry; I'm also fairly certain that we're supposed to go on a trip, so we'll leave tomorrow and, *voilà*, the problem will no longer exist. Everything's going to be hunky dory, just you wait and see. No-no, nobody's going to argue with me for the moment, okay? I'm going to do the final healing and then we'll start planning what we have to do next. No, seriously," she held up her hand authoritatively when everyone began to babel at her in protest, "no more for now!" she added in a sharp voice. "I need time to think."

They all went silent, although Donnie noticed that Falwaïn in particular was giving her a distinctly mutinous glare. While she understood his frustration, right now she couldn't take the time to appease him. So she ignored his ire.

Sylvester, also clearly peeved at Donnie's high-handedness, stalked out of the stables without another word.

Donnie forced all thoughts from her mind except those directed toward healing the wound on Falwaïn's leg. Studying the gash carefully, she closed her eyes and focused her will upon it. Her mind's eye slipped past the edges of the wound and down into the remaining gap created by Galto's blade. She saw the cut healing, knitting the tissue and repairing the severed capillaries, arteries and veins of the corium, and finally the layers of epidermis. The wound sealed quickly from within in seconds. When Donnie opened her eyes, only a red scar remained to mark the cut. Her time spent with some medical books and then practicing what she'd learned from them on Falwaïn's smaller cuts early this morning had paid off. She'd really gotten into a groove doing the healing and was much, much better at it today than she had been only yesterday, when she'd first tried it.

Donnie then concentrated on Falwaïn's abdominal wound and resumed her healing trance, starting at the center or apex of the 'X' and moving outward toward each terminus in turn, leaving the left lower one for the last. All the while she was unaware that, as she healed her patient, she once again chanted an old healing charm in a language she had never consciously learned. She began with the full charm, *"Pâduar néthamon, o' mada víss, luqarí el set amon, aht trílan eld hura amai kélam han élidamon,"* believing herself to be saying, "Hear my plea, o' wise mother, the cry that is mine, and remove this hurt I see with my mind." She soon shortened it to, *"Pâduar néthamon, o' mada víss, aht trílan eld hura,"* still completely oblivious to the strange words rolling off her tongue.

This wound, because it was much more extensive, took her far longer than the other to repair. Nonetheless, when she opened her eyes, she saw that it too was completely mended and only angry red welts remained. She took up the soap bar, dipped it into the water and washed the healed wounds, then dried them gently with a towel. Not that she had to do this; it just made her feel better. Falwaïn obviously wasn't going to need sponge baths from her any longer and she was really going to miss that part of nursing him back to health.

"How do you feel?" she asked him anxiously, silently berating herself for her lechery.

He gave her a knowing smile, which made her flush in response. "Remarkably, much better," he replied. "The pain has nearly vanished and is quite bearable. I would like to get up and move around now, possibly take some sustenance, but I seem to have lost my vestments and armor. Do you suppose you could return them to me?"

"Um, sure thing," Donnie nodded, keeping her tone bright, "but I think you oughta take a shower first, don't you? I mean, sponge baths are okay in a pinch, but they're nowhere near as good as the real thing. Tell you what, why don't you wrap that blanket around you again and we'll go into the house so I can show you how to work the shower in the bathroom."

She snapped her fingers and the water bowl, soap and towels disappeared, then she rose to her feet and turned her back on Falwaïn. He got up slowly, wrapping the blanket around his waist tightly, and told her that he was ready for this "shower," whatever that would entail. She twisted around and flashed him a quick smile. "Never had an indoor shower, eh? Well, you're in for quite an experience then."

Donnie led the way to the house, with Falwaïn following behind, his measured footsteps becoming more sure once he realized his injuries truly were healed. Donnie went through the open door of the cottage and stood to the side. A moment later, Falwaïn stepped in beside her and stopped on the threshold, allowing his eyes to adjust to the much dimmer light in the house. He let his wondering gaze travel over the room slowly, taking in every detail wordlessly and lingering for some time on Donnie's various kitchen appliances. Eventually, his eyes came round to her. He inclined his head and held out his hand as if to say, *After you.*

She led him into her bedroom and stood in the doorway to the bathroom. "Here we are," she announced. "It might be easier if I just explain what each thing is." She started with the sink, then the shower. Falwaïn looked at her as if she were crazy, but once Donnie demonstrated how to turn the water on, he became delighted. Lastly, she explained the use of the toilet. He shook his head slowly and asked where it was flushed to, so she explained the sewage system to him. He asked intelligent, thoughtful questions and finally pronounced it a true marvel. Thanking him, Donnie showed him where the clean towels were kept, sent a few zaps to the cistern in order to heat the water for his shower, then turned to close the door behind her.

"Your new clothes'll be in the bedroom ready for you to put on," she said. "Oh, two things before I go: Firstly, please put both the seat and the lid down, especially the seat, whenever you finish using the toilet. It's a pet peeve of almost every woman I've ever known, me included. I would charm it to do that automatically, but a few months ago the others banned me from placing any new charms on household items and I gave them my word that I would contain myself until the summer solstice. Seems they think I'm addicted to laying charms. And they might be right about that. Anyway, the second thing I wanted to say was, be prepared for a good chat. Feel free to tell them to go away!"

She politely shut the door on Falwaïn's suddenly confused expression. Twenty minutes later, he emerged from the bedroom in perfectly replicated and intact copies of his own clothing, which had been duplicated by her wardrobe. His hair was wet and he looked gorgeous. A lump rose in Donnie's throat. There had to be something wrong with him, didn't there?

He strode over to the kitchen table and laid a hand on the back of the chair that stood directly across from Donnie, then snatched it away when the chair slid out from under the table, all on its own volition. Eyeing the chair dubiously, Falwaïn slowly sank down onto its seat.

"You could have given me fairer warning about the walls, you know." He smiled broadly so as to soften his reproach.

Donnie grinned back at him. "I firmly believe that, since the creation of my bathroom is due to an unwitting set of circumstances unlike any other throughout history, it should be experienced to its fullest measure without prescience," she explained pompously. "Don't you agree?" Again grinning at him, this time over her cup of linden tea, she added, "And besides, where's the fun in warning you? So...how long were you in there before the trees talked to you?"

Falwaïn's amused smile widened further. "Not long. We then proceeded to have an interesting discussion about you, which was most helpful in explaining some of your more obvious peculiarities. You have apparently spent *some* time in there."

Donnie felt her face grow pink, and she retorted defensively, "Not really, no. You see, the same trees make up the walls of my workshop and my library. And I do spend a lot of time in those rooms." She thought about this for a moment and decided she didn't want to know what the trees had told him about her, so she changed the subject hastily. "I've been waiting for Rex and Warren to get back. Rex is on his way and should be here in a few minutes. Warren will be a little while yet."

Falwaïn shot her a quizzical glance. "Who are this Rex and Warren of whom you have spoken repeatedly? Your captains of war?" he inquired.

Donnie pulled on her lip uncertainly before replying, "Captains of war? No, I don't think I'd call Rex that. Warren, maybe yes, but definitely not Rex. You'll meet them soon enough and then you'll understand. In the meantime, while we're waiting for their return, I thought I'd show you where you're going to sleep. I took the liberty this morning of clearing out Catie's workshop at the back of the stables. I've outfitted it with a bed and bedclothes, and whatever else I thought you might find useful. If you'd like to check it out now, that'd be great. Then you can tell me if I've missed anything you need."

They went to the workshop together to see the renovations Donnie had made. The first thing she'd done was to empty the room of Catie's furniture and tools, then cleaned and organized it all, using her magic to speed the process considerably. After that, she'd moved Catie's bed frame back into the room and stuffed an extra mattress for Falwaïn, covering it with some of her own sheets and blankets. Donnie had also left him Catie's small chest of drawers, in which resided five newly duplicated sets of his clothing. Catie's table and chairs were placed near the center of the room. All furniture had been sanded smooth and washed down. Catie's tools and molds had been neatly organized and stacked near the forge. The barrels of salt had been moved to the front of the hayloft, along with all of the iron cauldrons—except for those few being used by Donnie in the house. Catie's pentacle still adorned the center of the workshop, stalwartly resisting Donnie's scrubbing of the rough flooring.

While the room was dark because of the lack of windows, it looked wholesome and cheery in the light of the candles Donnie lit with a wave of her hand. She'd even built a stone hearth for a small open fire for whenever the temperature dropped. The smoke from the fire should rise to the hayloft above and drift out the small door up there, so she hadn't needed to rig a ventilation system for it like she had for the fireplaces in the house.

Seeing the room once again, Donnie was relieved that she'd resisted the absurd impulse to decorate it with touches of gingham. "It's all yours for as long as you need it," she said as Falwaïn walked through the open door and moved to stand just in front of her.

He looked around the room, studying the furnishings curiously, then turned to give her a lazy smile, thanking her warmly.

She smiled back and said, "You're welcome. And just so you know, I'm still trying to work out a way to stop you from going insane from my magic. I haven't come up with anything yet, other than leaving the magical lands, but I feel confident that I'll find something. Especially since some of its effects might very well follow me wherever I go, you know?" she confessed ruefully, then added, "Oh, we should go outside now because Rex is back."

Falwaïn caught her by the arm as she was turning to leave and pulled her close to him. Donnie could feel the heat of his body through the cotton material of her warm-up. His eyes searched her face and lingered on her mouth. "The walls in your bath told me the story of how you came to be caught up in all this," he informed her quietly. "I see now why you feel an affinity for this Galto man, if, indeed it is true that the same thing was done to him. I beseech you to be wary of him or it may mean peril to us all. We are both aware that he fully intended to kill me and would have succeeded had I not been familiar with the terrain. You have powerful enemies in him and his master, but you also have me as your champion. My people, if called, will come to your aid. Please know that you will not face Valledai and his evil creatures alone."

Donnie's breaths were coming shorter and faster, as Falwaïn's lips hovered above hers. His hand was still on her arm, keeping her close. She cleared her throat and shook her head a little to dissipate the fog inside it when she heard her dog calling to her. "Yeah, I-I know I'm not alone," she muttered. "And how about you come meet my other champion? He may not be as fierce or as brave as you, but he certainly has some unusual talents."

They broke apart and went outside. Donnie snapped her fingers and all of the candles in the room were extinguished.

***

Strains of their conversation had wafted up to the biggest beast in the hayloft but, although it had considered making its presence known, it had judged against doing so for now. It felt this was not the proper time for discovery, as it was not strong enough yet. Instead, it would continue to concentrate on its own sweet, internal music a while, it decided. Almost immediately it went back to sleep and, in the meantime, continued to absorb more and more of Donnie's magic.

***

Rex was waiting nervously, wondering where his mama could be. Just then, Donnie came around the corner of the building, followed by Falwaïn, and Rex shouted, "Mama, Mama, I've got some news—hey, he's awake!" The dog began barking furiously at the tall newcomer. It took a minute or two for his barks to lose their intensity. As usual, each time Donnie told him, "No bark!" he'd bark once immediately, until, again as usual, she was the first to give up.

She turned to Falwaïn. "Sorry about that," she apologized. "He's always had to have the last word, even when he was just a pup. I mean before we were brought here and became magical." Donnie bit her lip and said, "Man, it's so weird to hear me say that! You'd think I'd have adjusted to it by now, wouldn't you? I guess I haven't, not completely. Anyway, Falwaïn, meet Rex The Wonder Dog. Rex, honey, this is Falwaïn. We like him, all right? And we're going to be nice to him, yes? No biting him, got that?" she admonished the dog sternly.

Rex settled his long bulk on the ground with his huge front paws extended before him, his nose resting on top of them. He gave Donnie a dolorous look and replied petulantly, "Okay, okay," then heaved a long, displeased sigh. He would never have bitten the guy all that hard, which his mama ought to know by now. Rex never broke the skin of humans—bruises, big ugly ones were more his style. He liked people to know that while he *could* do major damage if he really wanted to, he was consciously choosing not to. This usually kept them in line around his mama and, after all, her protection was the most important duty he had. He wasn't really sure what his other duties were, but this one he always tried to perform to his utmost.

Donnie walked over to the bench and sat down, smiling affectionately at her dog. "Wonderful," she said. "Come on over here, you big goof, and tell me your news."

Rex jumped up and trotted over to sit in front of her, cocking his head to the side and staring at his shadow on the ground as though it were about to attack him and he'd have to dash away from it fast before it could nab him. Donnie grabbed her dog's snout and made him look at her, breaking his train of thought away from the shadow. "Oh, okay, let me think what all happened..." he began, casting his memory backward.

Donnie leaned back and waited patiently for his brain to click, silently urging it to be soon. Falwaïn sat down on the bench beside her, while Sylvester came up to them and jumped onto Donnie's lap. He sat there with his tail curled tightly around his front paws, his locket jingling just a little on its chain around his neck.

"The birds," Donnie supplied helpfully after a few more moments of silence.

"Oh, yeah, the birds!" Rex exclaimed, his somewhat confounded expression clearing. "It was easy to find out about them. A bunch more of 'em went missing only yesterday, so the others aren't flying much. It's just like Mickey T said it was. Seems there's some machine thingy goin' around turning whoever it can find into stone, even nonmagical birds. It's been doing that for a couple of months now."

Donnie heard Falwaïn give a startled gasp and realized he wasn't up on current events. She turned to him and explained, "Sylvester noticed that the skies were unusually empty the past couple of days and that the few birds who were around would only fly in really low, short hops. Rex went out earlier this morning to find out what's going on." She turned again to face the dog. "Okay, tell me about this machine thingy."

"Weeeeellllll..." Rex drew the word out long and cocked his head the other way, looking up at the sky. Donnie wanted to scratch his head for him to complete the picture, but consoled herself with an impatient hiss. It was enough to recall Rex back to his purpose once again. "The skunks heard about it from the deer, who heard about it from the rabbits, who heard about it from a Peregrine Falcon named Téo who almost got caught by it two weeks ago. It's some machine that flies around and shoots out these streams of light at the birds. It mostly hunts at night, but lately it's been coming out sometimes during the day too, and if it catches someone in its beams, they turn to stone and fall to the ground. Then they get pulverized see, 'cause they're usually really high up and when they fall, well, what with gravity, their faster rate of descent due to their increased weight and all, they hit the ground pretty hard and break into millions of pieces. I saw some piles of 'em that Téo showed me. You could still see the heads and claws and stuff. It was way cool, Mama. Tough way to go though—y'know what I mean?" The dog snapped at a fly that was buzzing around his snout, then blinked expectantly at his mama.

She was regarding him with a mixture of alarm and disbelief. "Yeah, I know what you mean," she replied. "And how, may I ask, do you know about gravity and faster rates of descent because of increased weight? Since when did you become Physics Dog?"

Rex confessed a little sheepishly, "You used to have the TV tuned to the Science and Engineering Channel a lot back home and I watched the shows. Here and there, between naps. Only now, I get what they were talking about."

Donnie grunted with dismay, then cried, "Oh, really? And I would've sworn you never paid attention to anything unless there was food associated with it! Huh! Just goes to show how wrong a gal can be." She sighed, shook her head, and asked, "Do you know where this machine hangs out?"

Rex gave a careless shrug, snapping at another fly that shot past his nose. "North of here somewhere," he supplied, not at all helpfully. "Not sure where, though. It just appears out of nowhere and boom, you're as good as dust! Or you're a statue, 'cause it's not just goin' after flying animals anymore. It runs down pretty much anything that moves, even tree branches swaying in the wind. Since, like I said, the machine mostly comes out at night, it probably uses infrared sensors to watch for heat and movement."

Donnie just stared at the dog, utter stupefaction making her eyes glaze over.

Falwaïn took advantage of the lull in their conversation to inquire, "What do you mean by a machine and what is gravity? And what were the other things—infrared sensors?"

Donnie finally drew her bemused gaze from the dog to Falwaïn. After doing her best to answer each of his questions succinctly, she returned her attention to Rex and observed with a tight smile, "By the end of this, I'm gonna have to rename you Phyton, aren't I?"

The dog grinned at her happily.

"How would we destroy this machine?" Falwaïn interjected.

"Well...there probably isn't anything *you* can do about it. I think this one is mine," Donnie replied distractedly, still thoroughly flummoxed by Rex's revelations about himself. "Warren'll be back soon to report what he's found out. Something else weird has been occurring up north with the humans; we heard some very odd rumors from the animals and trees, and Warren's gone off to reconnoiter. You know, to see if it has anything to do with Valley Guy or Galto or the flying machine. Anyway, he should be here any minute."

"You sound quite certain of that," Falwaïn noted matter-of-factly.

Donnie nodded, looking out at the fields below and across from the house, absentmindedly stroking the cat's fur on his back. "Yep. I've found that I can hear every blade of grass, every tree, every insect, and every animal on my lands nowadays; when I tune my mind to it, that is. Warren's less than a quarter of a mile north of the valley, on a dead run. He'll come through those trees up there in a few seconds." She inclined her head toward the forest at the top of the valley.

As predicted, the great blue-black wolf soon sprang from between two trees and sprinted down into the valley, disappearing from view in seconds. Falwaïn, taken aback by the appearance of the wolf, gasped in an awe-filled voice, "Mynydd Uchaf!"

Donnie whirled toward him in surprise, disturbing the cat so much that he leapt to the ground. "You know him?" she exclaimed. "Really? 'Cause he doesn't know you."

Falwaïn shook his head and corrected her, "We have never met, but the Wolf King is well known throughout the land."

By this time, Warren had reached the top of the rise where the cottage was situated and he, as usual, transformed into his werewolf form once he got near the humans. Falwaïn sprang to his feet, looking around for a weapon, until Donnie put her hand on his forearm and pulled him back onto the bench.

"Whoa, big boy," she cautioned, "it's only Warren, er, what you called him." Under her breath, she went on to explain, "He's under some spell of Valley Guy's where he changes shape whenever he gets around humans. That's another problem I'm working on. It drives him nuts to keep transforming into one or the other every time he turns around. But I don't think he's going to like what I have to tell him about that."

On his way up the hill, Warren had picked up his cloak, which he still wrapped around himself whenever he was in Donnie's company, at her unyielding insistence. When he'd changed form, he'd stopped, turning around so that he could shrug into the garment, then had stridden purposefully up to the group assembled by the bench. Donnie made the introductions between the two strangers, who discovered they had a mutual acquaintance in Déagmun, the Meurdane.

Donnie's eyes glazed over again, but only momentarily, then she briefly relayed Falwaïn's and Rex's information to Warren. Next, she urged him to tell what he'd found out about the peculiar happenings he'd been investigating.

Warren looked down at her intently for some time before replying quietly, "Hard times have fallen on Mâlendian."

"Um, okay, what's a Mâlendian?" Donnie asked uncomfortably, her brow furrowed with concern.

" 'Tis the largest village within range of here, more than twenty leagues away," Warren informed her. "A strange sickness, more of a derangement, has beset its citizens. The tales were so fantastic, we—I went there myself to see it." He hesitated and gave Donnie another discerning stare. "When I entered the town, I found its streets deserted. I heard noises and followed them to the town square, where the people had gathered. They were all there, standing in lines…" again Warren paused, finally adding with more than a little perplexity, "and they were dancing."

"What?" Donnie squeaked in disbelief. "Every man, jack, and one of 'em were dancing?"

The werewolf nodded, his expression grim. "Anyone able to stand and walk, yes, while those who could not, sat to the sides of the square and sang along with the dancers. All of them are caught up in this predicament," he explained. "From what they were singing, I gather it is a dance called the *Boogie Oogie*."

"*Boogie Oogie?*" Donnie repeated, then she jumped up and growled to the air, "Get back here, right now!" adding angry shouts of, "Do! You! Hear me!"

Rex, about to bound down the hillside so he could go play, now slunk back over to Donnie and head-butted her knees, saying in a muffled voice, "I'm right here, Mama."

She took a short but deep breath, then reached down to give his ears and muzzle a few soft, loving pats, afterward stepping away from him. She knew how much he hated it when she got upset. "Sweetie, this one has nothing to do with you, I promise," she said brightly, "so you're not the one who's in trouble. Tell you what, why don't you go play with the skunks?" She waited until Rex was gone before she put her hands on her hips and began tapping her toe. "I'm waiting!" she bit out between clenched teeth, looking up at the sky. "But I won't wait much longer! If you don't come here right now, I will turn you off for good. Got that?"

The boombox suddenly materialized on the ground in front of Donnie. It was silent.

She looked down at it exasperatedly and yelled, "Of all the line dances you could have taught the good people of Mâlendian, you chose *Boogie Oogie*? I don't even have that in my collection, so how do you know it?"

Falwaïn, his face exhibiting a mixed expression of amusement and consternation, inquired, "Is this box possessed by a demon?"

Donnie gave one sharp, negative shake of her head and glared at the boombox. "No," she said, "it just has an overdeveloped sense of humor. And how odd that it's very much like mine. And even odder that it's apparently controlling those people just to get a laugh."

The boombox came to life then, beeped furiously a number of times, and was silent again for a moment before it softly began to play "Look What's Goin' Down" by Bare Times.

Donnie grunted at it in frustration. "Okay, Funky Robot, let me guess," she snapped, "you used the power of suggestion and they did the rest by themselves, seeing as they're goin' a little loco on magic, is that it? And otherwise you are perfectly innocent, I presume. Yeah, well, I've heard that when you're schizophrenic, those voices in your head can be mighty potent." She whirled back toward Warren and asked desperately, "You say this Mâlendian is more than twenty leagues away? That's what, like seventy miles or so? What were the humans like in-between here and there? What were they doing, Warren?"

He studied her without answering, looking more than a little reluctant, but finally replied, "They were all in Mâlendian dancing this *Boogie*

Oogie dance. And Donnie? They not only appear unable to stop dancing, they are completely unaware of what goes on around them."

"All of them are like that?" Donnie cried, her voice cracking a little. Her eyes were wide and had started to fill with scared tears. " For how long? How long have they been like this?" she whispered, stepping forward to clutch at Warren's arm.

He caught her hand in his and held it. "A little more than a day," he said gently. "My sources tell me that they began gathering in Mâlendian yesterday morning, after we rescued Lord Falwaïn."

"Omigod, are they in danger?" she asked, worriedly searching his eyes for the answer.

He looked at her kindly and said, "Not at the present time, no. I have set a falcon scout to watch over them, so we shall know quickly if any threats to their safety appear." Warren squeezed Donnie's hand reassuringly, then advised, "But something must be done for them soon."

"You realize what this means, don't you?" Donnie exclaimed, biting her lip to stem the tears already spilling from her eyes. The boombox loudly remonstrated her to look at what was going down.

But she was too upset to heed it. She dashed her tears away with the back of her hand and began pacing back and forth in front of the bench, her body glowing blue, as did the path she took while pacing.

"But this can't happen!" she protested, more to herself than the others. "It's supposed to be the Age of Men. Magic's supposed to be dying out now, not growing stronger! It's me, isn't it? It is me; I know it is, and so does the boombox! Yesterday morning I finally began to truly embrace my powers, and almost immediately my magical lands more than double in size? Oh, this is not good; this is *really* not good. I'm all for letting Precept Prime fall to the wayside within our little group, but this? This is different! I'm affecting all these people, not from what I know of the future, but because of my magic, something that's supposed to be in the past? Good God, how do you turn me off?"

Sylvester jumped onto the rim of the well and also began pacing swiftly back and forth. "It may not be you, Donemere!" he chastised her sharply. "It may be Valledai. It may be someone or something else entirely. I do not believe you should distress yourself like this when we do not yet know if what you fear is true."

Donnie moved her shoulders jerkily, by now thoroughly agitated by Warren's news such that arcs of her magical power were escaping her fingertips, shooting outward several inches and greatly alarming the others. "I can't explain how I know it's me, but trust me, I'm the one causing this!" she declared with certainty. "Just look at that stupid boombox, and the fridge, and now every other electronic gadget I own is springing to life, becoming practically sentient beings all by themselves, and that is clearly happening solely because of *my* magic!"

The volume on the boombox suddenly rose, belting out the verse regarding the effects of paranoia and once again entreating her to look at what's going down.

Donnie stood stock still, listening to the song's warning, glanced downward, then shouted at the music box, "Oh, shut up! This is *not* funny! And yeah, okay, I get it! You were merely trying to show me that my power is seeping into the ground. And what clearer way of doing that than by turning our neighbors into dancing queens, especially when their discotheque is over sixty miles away from me? I'm sure you thought it a very clever idea. Well, I don't; I think it's awful of you! And heaven help you if you took my mirror ball there too!"

She turned toward the others, who were watching her mounting anxiety with varying degrees of concern on their faces. "Holy hags, it looks like I've turned out to be one big magical power station; haven't I just? I know I'm supposed to be *the most powerful witch that ever was*," she mimicked in falsetto, almost spitting it at the cat, "but I can't believe that this is supposed to happen! How the hell did Catie make me so damned powerful? Oh, I said shut up, boombox, and go away! But don't you dare go back to that town, do you hear me?"

She shook a stern finger at it, then whirled around again, obviously hysterical at this point. "Oh! My! God! All we're missing here is Avery Stein screaming, *It's alive! It's alive!* at the top of his lungs! Hell's bells, I guess you'd better start calling me Monster! You might as well, seeing as we've already got the Wolfman here. What's next, Drakul the Vampire? I swear, if someone looking like Garreth Brown shows up anytime soon, that's it, I'm quitting! I am so done with this shit—"

Falwaïn stepped up to Donnie at this point, took her by the shoulders and shook her once, very hard, then had to let go of her when her magic gave him a strong electric shock.

Donnie gasped and bit her lip, then counted to ten audibly. By fifty, she had calmed down enough to speak again. Even her fingers had stopped sparking. She peered out at him through the hair that had been shaken in front of her face and stated, "That was gutsy of you." Her tone was forebodingly quiet.

"You were babbling nonsense and it had to be stopped," Falwaïn pointed out, dismissing Donnie's histrionics. He was shaking his hands, which were still tingling from the shock they'd received.

"Yeah, well, thanks for not slapping me!" she snapped peevishly, a fierce scowl marring her brow.

Falwaïn sent her a confounded look and assured her, "I would never do that to any woman—ah, of course. It was another of your jests, wasn't it?"

"It's my way of dealing with stress, you know?" Donnie ran her hands over her hair to smooth it back, then made a big show of arranging her clothing. When finished, she straightened her shoulders, looked at the others, and asked with forced calm, "What now?" The blue of her power had dimmed to a faint glow that merely tinged the color of her skin, making it seem slightly more white than normal.

Warren leaned against the well to the right of Sylvester and shrugged his shoulders. "We might be able to use this to our advantage. Your magic may well safeguard the forest and field creatures from attack by Valledai's forces. If so, perhaps they can aid us in defending your lands."

Donnie snorted skeptically at this. "Oh, let's not kid ourselves about that. My magic isn't *safeguarding* anyone from that flying machine, so it's unlikely it'll protect either the forest or the field creatures from something like okûn, which I'm presuming really do exist, right? Yeah, I figured as much. Oh, boy, I so can't wait to meet them!" She rolled her eyes at that undesirable prospect, then reminded Warren, "Wasn't it you who said that Valley Guy and his okûn hordes are going to run right over every animal in their path and literally have them for lunch? Well, you have to understand, if that happens, there's not a dang thing I can do to help, unless, of course, the gods let me interfere, which, since it's kind of a natural occurrence—death in battle, I mean—it's probably something they'll never allow! And that will spell absolute slaughter for the magical animals. So, nope, no way; they simply cannot be involved in this fight. They need to stay home and stay safe. I mean, really, for heaven's sake, just what're the rabbits going to do to help, anyway? Build a huge wall around my lands by stacking themselves up, gazillions thick, then have that flying machine turn them to stone? Even they can't reproduce fast enough for that plan to work!"

"Do not discount the animal world so lightly," Sylvester huffed.

Donnie shook her head at him, her tone increasingly disparaging against his protest. "Well, I suppose a thousand bee stings could be very effective, even on the kinds of creatures Mueler and the other guy described in their books." She shook her head again and took a deep breath. "No," she repeated firmly. "What we really need is for the good people of Mâlendian and the other villages to be freed up from doing the *Boogie Oogie* day and night, and they have to be willing to fight Valledai's forces, if it truly comes to that. Otherwise, I think we're toast, and burnt toast at that."

"There are always my people, the armies of my king," Falwaïn suggested. "Their numbers are in the thousands. And they, at least, are trained warriors."

Gaping at him incredulously, Donnie replied, "Oh, c'mon, I was kinda kidding about the battling and the death and destruction parts, so how about we not go that route unless we absolutely have to? Sheesh, haven't you guys ever heard of diplomatic negotiations? Honestly, I'd much prefer to get through this without bloodshed, if we can."

"Then what do you suggest we do?" Falwaïn retorted sharply. It was his turn to be skeptical.

As a matter of fact, he was not the only one viewing her in such a manner. Warren had snapped his head up in shocked disbelief at her last words. Sylvester was, perhaps, the only one of the three who realized that, to Donemere, killing was something nice people just did not do to each other.

"Oh, I don't know what to do," Donnie groaned miserably, "I wish I did! I'm completely useless at this. Heavens, I can't even control, let alone *contain* my own powers, so how am I ever going to defeat this Valley Guy of yours?"

"First, you must refrain from feeling sorry for yourself," Warren rebuked her callously. "You will be of much more use to us then."

Donnie blinked at him, hurt and astonishment showing on her face. But, to be perfectly truthful, he was absolutely, positively correct: she *was* feeling sorry for herself once again. And that would do no one any good.

Warren sighed before continuing, but refused to be apologetic. He knew only too well that they needed Donemere to be sharp-witted or else they would all die by Valledai's hand. "Whatever we decide to do, we will have to set it in motion soon. I believe one of our first tasks must be to find out who Valledai has imprisoned. For all we know, he may very well have Catie. We know she was fatigued, but otherwise well, when she disappeared in front of Lord Falwaïn. What we do not know is whether she went through the portal to another time or merely to another place in Írtha, one that is far from here. Which means we cannot be certain she is safe. If Valledai does have her, she will not be able to withstand his tortures for much longer. If he learns how to use the amulet, it may not matter if he has it in his possession, he may be able to use it while it is in ours. Therefore, we must stop him before he learns how to go through the portal to bring back something from another time, some creature or another machine which we might not be at all equipped to defeat. 'Tis certain he holds someone prisoner, but my people have been unable to ascertain who that is."

"True, true," Sylvester murmured sagely, nodding his head. "We must discover who he holds captive."

"Do you at least know where this prisoner is being held?" Falwaïn asked.

Warren shook his head, looking aggrieved. "We do not know even that much," he confessed quietly.

Donnie stood tall and squared her shoulders before speaking. "Which means we have to go to Valley Guy and see if he'll let slip who he's holding, or at least where they're being held," she suggested. "Always go to the horse's mouth when you want to know what's really going on. I think we should start by following Galto's trail; that will lead us directly to Valley Guy. Remember? I charmed him to go to wherever Valley Guy is. Given Galto's condition when he left here, he's gotta be pretty easy to follow."

She nodded once sharply, as if having come to a decision. "I think it's probably time I met this Valley Guy of yours anyway," she pointed out. "Hopefully, there'll be some signs to mark his lair's whereabouts. I don't suppose we'll be lucky enough to see any huge billboards proclaiming 'Valley Guy's Hideout, Next Exit, Three Miles,' or anything quite so useful. Who knows, maybe we'll just be able to *smell* the evil all the way in. And while we're at it, I mean to do something about freeing the good people of Mâlendian from their dance craze. We'll leave in the morning, just like I told you we would, Falwaïn."

Warren smiled and nodded approvingly at Donnie. The shrewdness and resolve she had exhibited while dealing with the Black Rider had returned to her eyes.

Chapter 11
Soul's Solace

Sylvester, Warren and Falwaïn followed Donnie into the house, ostensibly to lay plans for the journey north the next day, but once Falwaïn and Warren sat at the kitchen table, they began reminiscing about times of old. Donnie used her magic to lay the table with various cheeses, breads and fruits since it was well past two o'clock and neither she nor Falwaïn had eaten lunch.

The talk at first was grave, at times even heated, as the men passionately aired their views on the treachery of Orgos and Kaledar. Warren, it seemed, had been captured by Orgos's forces and given to Kaledar as a prize for the wizard's service to Orgos. He then became Kaledar's wern sire at Íarnweald, where he watched his wolven body be transformed into the larger form of a wern through the combined efforts of the two dark sorcerers. Warren ground his teeth as he told of the evil that had infiltrated his soul, bending it foremost to Orgos's, then Kaledar's, black will. He and the other captured wolves, who like him had been transformed into werns and were not born to that state, were prized as prime breeders because of their innate wolven cunning and also because they were magical. Unfortunately, Warren said, they were all Ísolé and therefore helpless to fight the wizards, although their magic did help them to survive their battles as werns.

When the Zal'Dorek vinca, Fírrin elves and Sarn armies, all sworn enemies of the Var, marched heedlessly on Íarnweald and drove Kaledar and his troll and goblin forces back to their forest dwellings, the breeding werns witnessed the devastation of the trolls' stone dam from above the wizard's new tower, which stood almost directly in the path of the freed River Gâlgwin. Many of the werns were swept away when the river waters were released by the explosive arrows of the enemy combatants, the raging torrent drowning all wern pups and adolescents, along with many of the adult werns chained within the breeding pens. The terrific force of the flood swept away bodies, chains and posts in seconds.

Only a small group of fifteen changeling breeder werns were left alive. Hatred for all free creatures filled their hearts as they watched their progeny tumble into the torrential waters. The survivors remained where they were chained until four days later when the defeat of Orgos occurred, at which time his evil influence over the wolves was forever broken. Each wolf transformed back into their natural state and were then able to slip from their collars and chains to freedom.

But instead of going their separate ways, Warren convinced his brethren that they should travel the short distance to Íarnméath Wéard to defend that fortress and its adjacent mountain pass along with the elves, vinca, men and other free creatures there, whom the wolves had long called enemy, from the bands of marauding okûn that were pouring north to Annûar. This was wolf-kind's chance to finally and truly be free of the darkness that too frequently had enslaved them throughout millennia, he argued passionately. The other wolves reluctantly agreed to the new plan, their enkindled desire for freedom overcoming ancient enmities.

It was then that an alliance, uneasy at first, was forged between the Free Wolves and the peoples of Medregai. The bonds of this alliance eventually turned to friendship, which continued to solidify and strengthen in the ensuing years, until the arrival of Valledai, when once again werns and werewolves roamed the Earth. But still, many Free Wolves remained, so far unsullied by Valledai's evil. Together with myriad other fair creatures, they fought the increasing number of okûn who were once again appearing throughout the Annûar Province, and the Free Wolves spied on Valledai and his followers, sharing any information they could glean regarding Valledai's dark plans.

None of the others, so deeply engaged in their discussion were they, appeared to notice that Donnie had gone very quiet as more and more details about the War of Unity and its aftermath came to light. She was grateful when they finally moved on to more recent times. Even Sylvester was able to add some startling revelations then regarding the extent of Valledai's perfidy. Donnie remained silent and listened to their discourse for as long as she could, eating so slowly that the others were finished long before she was. She found she was having trouble accepting that all of this was actually real, and talk of the time period of which Mueler and the unknown historian had written about made her head swim and her heart palpitate, once again reminding her of her first few months here. She forced herself to calm down and breathe naturally, hoping her anxiety would slide away from her. *No sense in getting het up over a done deal*, she reprimanded herself severely, *you're here and this is all true!*

The men and the cat were still noisily gliding down memory lane by the time Donnie finished her meal. With a flick of her hand, the used plates levitated to the sink and the leftovers floated into containers, which then zoomed into the fridge. Wordlessly, Donnie got up and went over to the sink to wash her hands. The others remembered her presence only when she rose from her chair, at which point they apologized profusely for not including her in their conversation.

Her back to them by now, Donnie rinsed the soap bubbles from her fingers, then waved a deliberately careless hand. Her voice, though, when she replied was a bit tight and her face was set in a distressed scowl. "It's no matter, really. But I think I'll go outside for a while and leave you guys to it." After thinking about this, she decided that it was just the ticket and nodded her head vigorously, all the while drying her hands on a towel as she turned, her expression inscrutable now that she was facing the others. "If you need maps, paper, all that stuff, you can go to my office to get them. The writing materials are in my desk and you can get any maps you require from the library."

Warren and Falwaïn nodded their heads and immediately resumed their discussion, once again forgetting that Donnie was there. Sylvester turned to watch her go and then he too rejoined the conversation.

And so, Donnie was able to slip away quietly to the stables, intent on finishing her saddle. This she took from the wall where it hung and slid it onto a section of railing. She dearly hoped that completing this mundane task would foster the return of a sense of normalcy to her unsettled mind. Too many events were happening way too quickly; she couldn't take them all in fast enough. She needed time to digest things, parse through the mountains of information that had been thrust at her so she could analyze it all effectively. To do that, though, she first needed to find peace within herself. She thought about this for a minute and then decided to do what she always did at times like this; she would meditate.

She sat on the ground, arranged herself in her usual meditative position, and focused on her breathing, slowly filtering out the sounds of spring all around her: the buzzing of flies, the drone of a bee, the chirping of the few birds who had ventured from their nests today, even the sounds of the cow and horses as they lazily ate some hay and periodically moved their heavy feet on the hard-packed dirt floor behind her.

When Donnie opened her eyes some twenty minutes later, she was completely calm and felt much better prepared to carry on with her day. Pleased, she set to work on the saddle. Nearly a week before, she'd fashioned new stirrups from a piece of the wood left over from her home improvement projects. The wood came from Brindle, with whom she had developed a special relationship, possibly because he was the only one of the house trees used for something in all of the rooms, be it a wall, floor, cistern or door, so she spent the most time around him.

Donnie reached up and took the stirrups off the shelf just inside the doorway of the stables. She ran her hands over them to dust them off, rubbing the moist warmth of the living wood with her fingertips. She also grabbed her sewing kit and some heavy fishing line from the shelf and placed these on the rail near the saddle. She sat down on the stool below where the saddle hung and threaded the fishing line through the large needle. Then she wrapped a thick strap of linen around one of the stirrups and began sewing the loop shut, using magic to force the needle through the dense material. As she began the process of attaching the stirrups, she informed Brindle firmly, "Well, dear friend, it's time to attach you to the new saddle. We've got some riding to do tonight."

"What is our destination, Donnie?" the old wood's gravelly voice rumbled the question at her.

"Oh, no particular place," she answered him absentmindedly. "We're just gonna ride around for a while, looking for a flying machine thingy that's turning our forest friends to stone. I want to get a close look at it, so we'll have to be quick once we locate it."

From his open stall, Otis volunteered, "I'll be ready whenever you say, Donnie."

She looked up, not for the first time wishing heartily that she'd paid more attention to the sewing classes in her high school Home Economics class, and replied to the horse, "No need, Otis. We won't be riding you."

His face took on a hurt expression as he tossed his head toward the stall where Gallantry had established residence the day before. "I suppose you'll be taking him?"

"Nope."

Somewhat mollified, Otis looked at her curiously. "Then who are you taking?"

Donnie grimaced facetiously. "It's not a who, it's a what. At least I hope it's a what and not a who...but, then again, the way previously inanimate objects are reacting to my powers lately, it may very well be a who by now." She emitted a low groan of exasperation. "Oh, well, the fun is only starting, it seems. Hey, Otis, how about giving me a lesson in Medregai geography? Where exactly are we located?"

The white stallion finished another mouthful of hay before responding. "We are in the southern part of what was once the realm of the Red Warlock of Fal'Adîn, in the northern section of Medregai," he began. "It's a region called Annûar and its capital is Marn Dím, which lies north of here two to three days' ride with good weather. More than a millennia ago, the Red Warlock's realm was destroyed by the Gossalyn forces in the War of Sorrow. In recent years, Marn Dím has been rebuilt through an alliance of Mountain Men and the Sarn and is now a thriving city, worthy of King Belnesem's allegiance. Between here and Marn Dím is the village of Mâlendian, almost due north by approximately twenty leagues. On the road to Mâlendian lies the fortress of Banaff Dír. There are also several smaller settlements along the way.

"South of us a good ten leagues are the Ettin Moors, so named for the giants who long ago wandered its cliffs and bogs, where the moors are even more treacherous than those surrounding us. To the east are the Brumal Mountains, and to the west is a region called Sedarau, and beyond that Gainál, where, it's only fitting, the King of Men has once again made his capital at Anûmanétus. That is the central city of the ancient Aldera, the old name for the west of Medregai." Donnie made Otis repeat this a few times so she could get her bearings when she studied some maps later. She didn't want to get lost tonight.

Sylvester, Warren and Falwaïn walked into the stables as she was charming the finished saddle, just in time to hear her cant:

"I deem this saddle,
Made from cotton,
Sound and whole,
And padded well.
  It shall keep me astride,
All in one piece,
And when I ride,
Be kind to my bottom.
  If we're anywhere on Earth,
In the heavens,
And especially in hell!

"If we ever go to hell, that is, or anywhere like it," Donnie amended quickly, "which I'm really, really, really hoping won't ever happen." A small wave of cerulean light shimmered over the saddle, then settled into its depths, lending the white of the cotton a distinct bluish cast.

Falwaïn came over to inspect the saddle, studying it for a minute before grinning at Donnie. "It is most certainly unlike any other saddle, is it not?" he observed.

"Yes, and I'll thank you not to make fun of it. It's going to be just fine for me," she retorted.

"Are you set to ride it somewhere in particular, I wonder?" he inquired. "And who shall you ride with it? I suspect no self-respecting horse would allow themselves to be fitted with a saddle such as that." He smiled teasingly at her to soften his words.

"Oh," interjected Otis, "she said she's not taking a who but a whaaa—ouch, that hurt!" the horse cried when Donnie stepped backward to his stall and shoved him hard with her shoulder.

"It did not, you loudmouth. Ixnay on the atwhay uffstay, illysay," Donnie griped, giving him a dark look.

The horse took a half-second to translate this, nodded agreeably, and chirped, "Kay-o." He then went back to eating hay.

Donnie gave the others a recalcitrant glare and told them, "Don't ask." She put the saddle back on the fence and remarked somewhat sharply, "So, we're all set for tomorrow, right? Know where we're going and all that, I suppose?"

Falwaïn moved to within her line of sight and peered at her curiously. Donnie studiously avoided his gaze.

Warren looked at them both with a glint of amusement in his crystal-blue eyes before replying, "Yes, Donemere, we have finished laying our plans for the morrow. We shall follow the Annûar Path to Mâlendian, where we will stay the night while you do what you can to free the people of their...affliction. Then it is on to Marn Dím. The last I saw of him, Galto was headed north, toward the Bitterbend Marshes. We can discuss the journey further later." He held Donnie's gaze for a long moment, finally asking, "Have you an answer for me?"

She nodded her head and pursed her lips, then looked down at the ground and began doodling with the toe of her sneaker in the dirt and hay. "Yeah," she replied, "but you're probably not going to like what I have to say because I can't do what you asked of me. It's just that—oh, come on, let's go into the library, shall we? We can get comfortable and talk about it there." She did not look at Warren's disappointed face, but rather strode purposefully toward the house.

Once again, the other three followed her through the front door of the cottage and then on into the library. Warren and Falwaïn each sat in one of the sateen armchairs, while Sylvester curled up close beside Donnie on the sofa and immediately began purring.

When everyone was settled, Donnie looked at Falwaïn and explained, "As you've seen for yourself, Warren's got a particularly annoying habit of changing forms against his will, often at the most inopportune moments for him. It's from a Valley Guy spell that was halted by Catie and some mysterious friends of hers before it could completely transform him and consume his soul with evil. I've been rereading Catie's journals to see if there's something in them which might tell me how to change him back to his original form and make him stay that way."

She turned to Warren as she absently stroked the cat's fur. "To put it bluntly, that's not possible. Only the one who put the spell on you in the first place can reverse it, and I think we can safely assume Valley Guy's not going to do that." She sent the werewolf a sympathetic look. "Catie's journal says she was working on this same problem the week or so before she disappeared. Now, according to her notes, the best I can do is give you the freedom of choice of what form you take and when you take it. I can give you control over it, but I can't reverse it. I'm truly sorry, Warren, but it appears even I can't do more than that."

Through his reverberations, Sylvester pointed out, "That is morrre than most witches and wizarrrrds could do. 'Tis extrrrremely difficult to modify anotherrrr's transmogrrrrifying spell." After saying this, the cat crept even closer to Donnie.

"Well, actually, I think I'll be able to modify it pretty easily now," she declared, somewhat insouciantly. "Maybe later, as my powers continue to get stronger, I might even be able to break it and change you back to the way you were seeing as I'm supposedly the most powerful witch that ever was, or so Catie apparently hoped. Theoretically, if Catie is right about that part, I guess I may also be the most powerful witch that will *ever* be. Which probably means my powers will keep growing until I die or until the very last witch ever born dies, and who knows when that might be—something I realized only yesterday."

Sylvester gave a start of surprise and looked up at Donnie quickly, watching her closely as she continued speaking.

"Guess I just avoided thinking about issues like those until now because they kinda creep me out," admitted Donnie. "I don't mind telling you, having that much power is a very scary thought for me." She stared at the far wall for a few, awkward seconds, her expression pained. When Sylvester climbed onto her lap and laid a paw on her forearm, she shook herself out of her reverie, leaned forward over him and put her elbows on her knees. "I feel I should warn you though, Warren, I've never done this type of spell before. I've never cast a protected circle. Which means I don't know if I can control it. Honestly, I don't even know what all's going to happen in it. Maybe nothing, if the spell is rejected by the gods. If it's accepted, things may get pretty wild in there. You and I might never step out of it again if something goes wrong and I can't stop it. On the other hand, if all goes well and the gods decide to grant the spell and mix their magic with mine, the spell will definitely give you control over which shape you take and when.

"But—and this is the kicker—if you want to wait to see if my powers do get to the point where I can effectively break Valley Guy's spell, presupposing you live that long, then I can't do anything at all for you now. Once I cast my spell to modify his, I will never be able to reverse both spells."

She paused, looking at Warren gravely. "In other words," she warned, "you'll pretty much have to stay forever the way my spell makes you. That's just the way magic works, especially when it's a hefty spell of the sort we're talking about, you know? Once my spell takes effect, the two will become so intertwined they can never be separated again and, therefore, can never be reversed. At least not with Witch-magic, nor, according to Catie's journal, with Wizard-magic. Maybe one day we'll run across a magic which is powerful enough to break the combined spells, but I think the chances of that happening are pretty slim, especially since the magic would also have to be wielded by someone who believes it would be right to help you. From what I've studied about immensely powerful magical entities, most of them just aren't that philanthropic—um, kind, I mean."

Warren, his eyes dark and expressionless, nodded once curtly at her, then looked off into space, lost for the time-being inside himself.

"What about Diana?" Sylvester asked, looking up at Donnie.

"It's really the only choice I can offer her too. She's thinking it over."

In response to Falwaïn's unspoken inquiry, Donnie replied, "Diana's the cow whose stall you were sharing. She wasn't born a cow, you know. Well, I don't suppose anyone's ever born a cow, are they? What I mean is, to be a cow, you're either born a bovine calf or you're born a little girl who, for whatever reason, grows up to behave like a right pain in the ass. I'm sure we've all known a few of those in our time. I invariably find them at clothing shops working as sales clerks, and I use the term 'working' very loosely there. Did you ever notice how they always seem to be on the phone with their friends right when you need their help? Okay, I suppose that's not something either of you can relate to…anyway, Diana was born a slave girl of the Mehen'Adríum and was given to Kaledar as a gift. When she steadfastly refused his advances because he totally grossed her out, he called her a cow, and the next thing she knew, she literally was a cow! Thank all the louts in this world that he didn't call her a silly cow, 'cause I don't think I could fix that."

Falwaïn chuckled merrily at her joke, which made Donnie feel warm and happy all over, and then asked her, "Am I therefore to understand that Diana desires to become human again?"

Donnie shook her head. "Well, no, not exactly; but she is beginning to think that she may want to take human form sometimes. Oddly enough, she's generally rather happy being a cow, although it's a bit restricting at times, you know? Right now she's upset because I won't let her go with us when we leave tomorrow, but I really think a cow is a bit too conspicuous, don't you? Nor is she exactly fleet of foot, which could prove fatal if we have to run away from something. I'm just planning for contingencies, so don't glare at me like that, Sylvester. You never know, if I can't handle Valley Guy, we might have to beat a hasty retreat. What if he's not a witch? He could be more powerful than I am then. And besides, wouldn't running that hard turn Diana's milk sour? Do you know if it would?" Donnie gave Falwaïn a very curious look when she asked him this question. "I suppose, what with being a prince or steward or, well, whatever you are, you don't do much hands-on farming, do you? You'd kinda leave things like milking cows to the farmers, I imagine."

"Do you always meander so in your conversation?" Falwaïn asked, his dark blue eyes twinkling with amusement.

Donnie stared at him, nonplussed. "I, er, I...probably," she admitted ruefully, laughing. "I never really noticed it before, but yeah, I guess my conversations do tend to wander nowadays. I don't remember that happening before I came here, so it must be a side-effect of either becoming a witch or having had no human contact for six months until you. I mean, it's helped to have the animals and the trees, of course, but I also spend a lot of time alone, so I rather think the latter is most likely since I may have talked to myself just a little too much here. And, you know, when you do that kind of stream-of-consciousness monologue, it comes out sounding like you have ADD. Oops, there I go again!" she groaned.

Falwaïn said nothing in reply, but got up and walked over to the nearest bookshelf. The books on it shifted suddenly, with different ones appearing to replace those that vanished. He reached over and picked out a large volume, opening the front cover. The pages of the book turned by themselves to the first of those he wanted. When Donnie started to speak again, he held up a finger for silence. He appeared to glance at three sets of facing pages, their recto pages turning immediately, one after the other, and then a large group of pages riffled to the left by themselves to open the book to a page nearer the back. And again, Falwaïn seemed to only glance, although at several sets of pages this time, completely unaware that a cursory glimpse was all that was necessary. Yet, if asked, he could've recited the text on each of the pages he'd read, nearly verbatim.

And so, only a few seconds after opening it, Falwaïn put the book back on the shelf, then returned to the armchair to sit down facing Donnie again. "I now understand what you said," he announced, "and I agree with you. Stream of consciousness, almost by definition, does tend to wander and could easily be mistaken for Attention Deficit Disorder."

"Wow, that was quick," gasped Donnie, grinning disbelievingly at him. "You got all that just by skimming that book for what, maybe fifteen seconds total? You grasped the definitions for both of those *that* quickly?"

He gave a surprised frown and said, "Hmm, I had not marked that particular feat until this moment, but, yes, I got all that and more by skimming the book for perhaps fifteen of your seconds. It seems that I am indeed the fast study you said would be required if I were to help you in your quest. That being said, after my literary lesson in afflictions of the human brain and their neurotransmitters, I feel it only proper to point out that I do not believe ADD is the precise diagnosis of your problem, Donemere." He bantered coyly with her now, glancing over at the desk when the boombox materialized upon it and began playing Birmingham's "Soul's Solace."

"Oh? And just what do you think is my problem?" Donnie responded, smiling back at him coquettishly.

"I will do it now!"

Warren blurted out the statement defiantly and leaned forward in his seat, effectively ending Donnie and Falwaïn's palaver. The werewolf's eyes refocused as he shifted his gaze to Donnie and stared at her. She and the others were startled by the vigor of his outburst, but kept silent and waited for him to continue. "I...cannot go through the oncoming battle never knowing when I shall change form," he explained slowly. "That would be foolhardy, and very likely fatal. You may put your spell on me as soon as you are prepared, Donemere."

Donnie studied him for a few moments, then asked firmly, "You're absolutely certain this is what you want?"

Very determined and almost regal in manner, Warren straightened his shoulders and nodded, replying with a forceful, "Yes!"

Donnie picked up Sylvester and deposited him on the cushion beside her, encompassing him and Falwaïn in her look. "Okey dokey then, let's get crackin'," she said. "I'm going to ask you two to stay back while I do the spell. I don't want either of you being affected by it. Remember this, no matter what happens, or appears to be happening, do not step into the circle. Don't even attempt to do that—bad, *bad* things will result if you do."

To give them something to do, she asked Falwaïn and Warren to move the furniture back to clear some space for her to work in. She watched while they did this and, when Warren began to roll up the huge rug that lay underfoot, she took some chalk from her desk. It was a big chunk of the stuff, thick and white with small silvery flecks throughout its mass. She'd found it in Catie's workshop while setting the room up for Falwaïn. Although every resource she'd checked this morning had averred that she did not need to draw a physical sacred circle or pentacle, when Donnie had touched the chalk, she'd somehow known that was exactly what she must do with it. When asked about it, Sylvester had shrugged and replied that Catie too had felt that same need when she'd happened upon the chalk in her travels.

Donnie stepped over the rug, then got down on her haunches in the middle of the cleared space. Using the chalk, she began to draw a large, glittering pentacle around her on the wooden floor in an unbroken line.

After drawing the protective circle around its outer edge, she would consecrate the sacred space during her ceremonial invocation of the gods.

Suddenly, the boombox's volume increased when the song's second chorus began and exhorted its listeners to work toward achieving inner peace. Everyone turned toward it in surprise.

Donnie, her mind constantly abuzz at the abruptness with which her life had once again been changed by outside forces, snickered. Just what would constitute soul's solace for her, she wondered. It truly had been only in the last day or so—since leaving the valley to rescue Falwaïn, to be precise—that she had finally felt emotionally ready to analyze exactly what had been done to her. For months, she'd mostly focused on learning her craft and had done her best to avoid thinking too deeply about the long-term ramifications of her predicament. But now that she had begun to air out those consequences, Donnie was finding them more than a little distressing.

She'd been thrust into magic with no chance of refusal and, from what she'd been told so far, it looked as though she was going to have to risk everything, including both her life and her soul (an extremely unreal concept for a modern, average Jane like herself to face), in this forced fight with Valley Guy. If she didn't find a way to beat him—well, that just wasn't an option, was it? She had to beat him, if she wanted to get home anytime soon. The fight of her life was fast approaching, and she felt like she was being hurled into it headlong and almost completely blind.

And all for what? Simply because it was the right thing to do? You see a bad guy and you have the power to stop him, aren't you obligated to do just that? No, there was more to it than that. Something much bigger was happening here than what either Sylvester or Warren knew. Somehow Donnie was certain, far down within her, that they had both told her almost everything they knew of her situation. At least the whats of it.

But there was so much more they couldn't explain. For instance, who had engineered this whole sordid little scenario? And why? Was there even a good reason for any of it? It couldn't be just about Valley Guy. No, it was somehow about her, Donnie. Otherwise, why not take another of Catie's progeny? Sylvester insisted that she was the only one Catie had been able to call to, so it had to be something specific about Donnie herself that made her be the one to have her life uprooted and altered so drastically forever.

Deeply engaged in sifting through what she knew about her situation, Donnie nevertheless continued preparing the room for the ritual. As she finished drawing the pentacle and began marking the outside circle with her right hand, she moved her left hand in a come-hither motion and five candles levitated smoothly over toward her from a shelf on the wall behind the couch, each one settling just inside the points of the star she'd drawn. After snapping her fingers, all candles in the room except the five in her circle ignited. Moments later, the scents of cedar and lavender pervaded the room, combining for an almost heady, penetrating fragrance. With a wave of Donnie's hand, the heavy drapes on the window drew together and the room darkened, lit dreamily by the flickering candlelight.

Falwaïn, sitting behind the desk, which had been moved back toward the wall, watched Donnie closely. He realized that he had never witnessed a witch practice her craft until now. Although he had beheld the results of magic many times before, in only a few more minutes, he would see the ritualistic invocation of it and the inception of one of its most powerful spells for the first time in his life. Even Déagmun had never let his young apprentice bear witness to the wizard's most sacred ceremonies in the years they had spent together.

A brief, somewhat sad smile flitted across Falwaïn's features. More so than his real father, Unthgor, who had spent his days alternately ignoring and berating his youngest son, Déagmun had been the benevolent father figure the young Falwaïn had needed. Perhaps if he had been allowed to be Déagmun's apprentice for longer, many things would have ended differently…Falwaïn let that thought trail away as Sylvester began to speak.

The cat sat on the desk, his tail curled around his front paws, and indicated that he would explain the ritual in detail to Warren and Falwaïn. He cleared his throat importantly and said, "As you can see, Donemere begins by drawing the pentacle in an unbroken line. She will tell you, Mynydd Uchaf, when you may step into its center, at which time she will seal the protected circle. Then she will call the Quarters, who represent the four sacred elements of Air, Fire, Water and Earth, and who are the Guardians of the Lord and Lady. Next, she will invite the Lord and Lady to appear, according them the honor that is rightfully theirs. She will most likely call upon Cernunnos and Ceridwen for this particular spell, who will act as the Great Father and Mother Earth in the ritual. Ceridwen is a goddess of regeneration and transformation, while Cernunnos is a lord of the animals. He is half-man, half-beast, or, as Donemere informed me during our studies, he is what is called a therianthropic god." The cat rolled his eyes and murmured something unintelligible about Donnie's fetish for denotations. He stole a quick glance at her, but could tell she had not registered his complaint. No, she was absorbed by something else entirely.

"When she feels their presence," he continued, his eyes narrowing as he now openly watched Donnie's crouched form, "she will welcome them, request their aid, and recite her spell. The gods will join their powers with hers to cast the spell only if they feel 'tis worthy and that her heart is true. As I have informed you already, altering another's transmogrifying spell is one of the most difficult spells to cast." He paused to look at the men directly, then turned back toward the center of the room to study his pupil. Something was happening inside her, but he did not yet know what it was.

He resumed speaking. "It will take great skill," he said, "and only witches who have achieved a deep communion of power with the gods have ever been successful in casting a spell of this magnitude. Once the spell has been cast, Donemere will thank the venerable Lady and Lord for their assistance and guidance, inviting them to return back to their own realm. The same will occur with the Quarters. And finally, Donemere will open the circle, then she and Mynydd Uchaf can step safely out of the pentacle. 'Tis an ancient ritual of magic which must be performed with holy reverence."

Still lost in her own thoughts, Donnie only half-listened to Sylvester's commentary. She knew she needed help in figuring out what was really going on here in this strange, magical world she'd been brought to, but who was there to help her, truly? The only real magical assistance she'd received so far was from a maniacal boombox that thought it perfectly appropriate to have entire towns dancing to disco music just to get a message to her! A bit over the top, she'd say. Should she even trust that kind of help?

And, by the way, who was controlling the damn thing? Who was it that was constantly trying to provide clues to Donnie? Were they, this mysterious force behind the music, genuinely trying to help her, or were they leading her down a specific path for some even more mysterious purpose of their own, or were they just screwing with her for the heck of it and everything the boombox suggested she do was the one wrong thing she could do at that particular moment?

No, the last one certainly didn't feel right. Actually, so far the boombox had been pretty accurate. She'd almost come to rely on it, although it would be quite foolish to trust a deranged boombox at the best of times, and these were hardly that. She glanced over toward it as it again urged her to look ahead.

"Look ahead to what?" she muttered bitterly under her breath. Forfeiting her soul and becoming some evil creature if she did lose the fight with Valley Guy? Or was she supposed to look ahead to battling who knows what kinds of strange beasts throughout eternity if she were to win against him? Bad enough being ripped away from her world and all the people she loved, not to mention becoming a real, magical witch, but Donnie realized now that she was literally being led down the garden path by converging forces, to begin a life which could well be long and lonely, and most certainly would be fraught with unimaginable perils. It might even be an endless journey, for all she knew. And as far as she could tell, there was not a damn thing she could do to prevent any of it. Not realistically, that is.

So again, she wondered, who was doing this to her? She was pretty certain there was more than one mystical force at play here. Whoever had put the binding spell on them all was probably not the same force behind the boombox. The methodologies were too dissimilar; one serious, the other playful. Which begged the question of exactly how many players were involved. Well, whoever they all were, they appeared to be much more powerful than Catie, probably even Donnie. "But who?" she breathed to herself. "And why? And, as I've already asked a million times, *why me?*" she seethed quietly, drawing the last few inches of her circle.

She realized with mounting frustration that she was indeed left with no real choices. If she wanted to go home, and heavens knows she wanted nothing more than that, then she had to play out the hand that had been dealt her. Because, even if she found out how to make the amulet work and could send herself, Rex and Galto back to their proper times, she couldn't leave the people here in Medregai to battle Valley Guy by themselves. No, she had to help them defeat the nasty villain Catie had helped create. It was in Donnie's nature to do the right thing, something which she felt had been counted on by at least one of the shadowy forces controlling her destiny. Which meant, whoever had put this whole fiasco together probably knew Donnie pretty well already. Either that, or they were even more of a gambler than she was and had betted that, once she knew what was at stake, she wouldn't let an entire civilization or the time continuum be destroyed when she had the power within her to stop either of those catastrophes from occurring.

Donnie thought about all of this and decided that she'd never, ever liked being manipulated. As a matter of fact, it really pissed her off.

Getting up, she walked over to the desk, tossed the chalk onto its wooden surface, and smiled stiffly at first the men and then the cat, who had just finished his explanations. "It's mostly show, really. Oh, don't look so miffed, Sylvester," she rebuked tightly, all the while vigorously ruffling the fur on his head. "I'll grant that it certainly doesn't hurt to appease the gods, which is why I'm taking the scenic route. As kitty-cat here knows darn well, I don't need anyone's help with this, not even the gods'. It's a tough spell to cast, to be sure. One that most other witches wouldn't be able to do at all. But then, I am the Monster, after all. Yep, that's me, Monster Magic Woman. I'll just keep getting stronger and stronger, no matter what—isn't that right, Sylvester? Whether I want to or not." Donnie stepped back and stared nastily at the cat, who held himself very still and watched his pupil closely, his eyes widening with apprehension.

"You didn't think I'd one day realize what all that implies, did you? Tschaw, silly cat!" she said, an unpleasant grimace on her face. "You mean to tell me, you honestly didn't think I'd figure out that once a witch acquires enough power to come close to mine, my own powers will likely expand in response? Or that every witch with a dark heart will come gunning for me from now until, what, the end of time? And probably not just witches; it's highly likely that every dark magical being who's strong enough to challenge me will show up on my doorstep eventually. I'll bet a number of fair ones will too, seeking pearls of wisdom, no doubt. Which is absolutely, positively going to kindle such warm and fuzzy feelings in me—oh yeah, we can all see that happening, can't we?" she added sardonically.

"Did you honestly believe I wouldn't realize that this is never going to stop until one of us, be it magic or me, dies out?" she asked, only this time she looked upward, not at the cat. "You know what? I'm not even sure I *can* die as long as magic lives because that would break the whole, most-powerful-witch-that-ever-was line of Catie's spell. Why, we can't have me die, can we, then forty centuries later have a witch come along who's more powerful than I was! Nope, no way. I'll have to stick around to become even more powerful than they are." She turned her gaze back to the cat and snarled, "Who knows, I just might live long enough to meet my newborn self in 1982—now that should be a real treat! And, oh yeah, it's going to be heartrendingly hilarious watching my friends and my entire family die while I continue living, fighting my way through bad guy after bad guy over the coming millennia. So tell me, did I ask for this special treatment? Well, did I, Sylvester?" Donnie leaned down to within a couple inches of the cat's face, her expression fierce and mutinous. His green eyes blinked rapidly back at hers, the locket at his throat gleaming in the candlelight.

Falwaïn and Warren watched intently from behind the desk, unsure of how to stop Donnie, if that were to become necessary. The two of them shivered, not only because there was a noticeable drop in temperature within the room, but also because the air had darkened and a thick black cloud had begun to billow violently around Donnie.

"You should know, my little feline friend," she ground out between clenched teeth, her anger fulminating now, "I am only *just* managing to keep myself from getting completely, totally furious at both you and Catie because, no, I did not ask for any of this to happen! You two forced me into it, along with whoever it is you're taking orders from, and oh, let me guess, you can't tell me who that is, can you? What is it this time? I'm not ready to know that part yet, or are you still under the effects of the binding spell?"

She straightened, crossed her arms in front of her, and leaned back on her hips, her eyes glittering and razor sharp. "You have to understand, Sylvester, until coming here, my life didn't include magic in any form. Hell, I don't even know if my kind of magic was still alive in my time! I do know that my time's Witchcraft was much more peaceful, more benevolent—maybe it was just plain old weaker than what I've got in my fingertips. Like I said, I don't know if my kind of magic had died out or just mellowed by then, but our witches weren't going around literally turning people into toads—most likely because they *couldn't* turn people into toads!"

Her voice now positively dripped with sarcasm and her features contorted into a scathing expression of derision. "Oh, excuse me," she scoffed, "that's right, you said it was a *tortoise* in that ridiculous story about Catie acquiring the amulet. I don't know how she actually got hold of the damn thing, but common sense tells me that she told you a crock of lies about it. No way was that how it really happened."

Sylvester and Warren both gasped at this allegation.

"Oh, don't look so affronted, either of you," Donnie remonstrated them. "Of course she lied about it! Why, her story's got more holes in it than a mile-long chain-link fence! Like any Codlebærn would go to such extremes over a friggin' necklace! And when she supposedly didn't even know what it really did? No, no Codlebærn would ever transform someone into a tortoise over something as piddling as a pretty trinket— not and expect to keep her powers, that is. Heck, even I know we can't abuse them like that!

"I mean really, has that girl told any of you the truth about what's going on here? Apparently not! Think about it, she not only lied about how she acquired the amulet, she lied about not going to the past with it, and then she lied about how many times she used it after she knew about Valledai. How do I know those too are lies, you ask? Trust me, it wasn't hard to find the truth because the answers are right there in her journals;

that is, if you can stomach wading through her tortuous spelling *and* you're up for a long and exhausting exercise in deduction.

"Her very first journal says that she left home to travel back through the ages so she could complete some big, scary duty she really would've preferred to avoid, if that were at all possible. Information on whether she completed it, what it was, or even where or when she went to wasn't provided, of course. But she went there at least three times, according to that first book, so who knows how many other times she went to the past? Ha! You truly are surprised she lied to you, aren't you, Sylvester?" Donnie didn't even pause for a breath after asking the astonished cat this question. "Well, I'm not," she declared tightly, "not after mucking through her thoughts for the last six months. You think she only screwed with what's to come? I reckon she did as much damage to the past as you say she has to the future!"

Donnie's movements were becoming more natural and animated as her anger began to dissipate, as though ranting it all through was helping to assuage her deeply held frustrations. "As to Catie's last lie," continued Donnie, "the goods on that story are in her latest journal. She used the amulet at least twice, maybe even three or four times, after finding out about Valley Guy. And I'm not counting the last two times she used it, which I'm pretty sure are just when she came to get me and then when she gave the thing to Falwaïn. See, a good six weeks or more before she ruined my life, she went to the future to check on the family bloodline. And before that, she made at least one other trip to the future, but I'm not sure why, other than perhaps to begin her search of the family witches for someone to take her place. That part's unclear in her journal. And personally, no matter what you say, Sylvester, I think she brought Galto back here, but why she would do that still remains a mystery. Catie's really not one for recording all that many details of her traveling itineraries, blithely leaving out names of people and places, dates—you know, anything really useful in figuring out what's actually going on, especially here in Medregai. Now, why is that, I wonder? Could it be because she caused this mess?" Donnie glared at the cat and growled, "Well? *Is* this all her fault, Sylvester, or don't you know even that much about your former mistress?"

Sylvester swallowed uncomfortably, fearing another rise in Donemere's temper if he informed her that he had no idea who was to blame for the current troubles of Medregai. He knew she would be unlikely to believe him, regardless of how earnestly he protested his ignorance. He therefore remained silent.

Donnie looked up at Warren and then down again at Sylvester, informing them didactically, "Oh, by the way, when Catie went to her workshop and left all you magical animals alone at your big, Valley Guy pow-wow—and there's you, wondering where she's wandered off to while there are still important matters to discuss—well, that was when she made at least one trip ahead to check on the bloodline. And I'll bet you dollars to doughnuts, Valley Guy went with her that night and brought back something from the future, because I gather things here in Medregai got a whole lot worse and in a hurry right after that trip. And whatever it was he picked up there made him much stronger magically because, after that, Catie was mighty afraid of him."

Grunting with exasperation, Donnie exclaimed, "Aberrant ancestors, Catie's not even a good liar! She tells you guys a twisted tale, writes the straight dope in her journals, then leaves those lying around for anyone to decipher, as long as they have the intestinal fortitude to plow through them all. How pathetic is that? I can't believe we're truly related! Sheesh, even my mother lies better than Catie does!

"And one thing more, Sylvester," Donnie huffed, pointing a finger at the cat, "I would suggest that you stop trying to protect Catie and *start* protecting me. I'm already extremely tired of slogging my way, all by my little lonesome, through this mire that Catie created, and I've only been at it a couple of days so far! If there's anything more you can tell me about what's really going on here, then you'd better come clean about it soon; time's a wastin' and it seems I've got some mighty big fish to fry. If you're not going to help me, tell me now and I'll talk to the gods when I call 'em about finding a replacement familiar."

At this point, Donnie straightened up with a blustery shake, swept her hair back behind her ears, and let out a sharp, deep sigh. She felt much better, soothed even, as evidenced by her anger fizzling out near the end of her tirade. After all, Sylvester seemed to be as much of a pawn in this game as she herself was. She now gave the cat a wry, half-grin and admitted, "Just had to get that off my chest, Sylvester. I'm okay now, feel a bunch better and all that, but don't for a moment think I didn't mean any of it. That would be a big mistake on your part, O' Master Cat. I'm really not likin' what's being done to me, but I don't have the luxury of saying no to it, do I?" She frowned at him and turned to walk away.

The cat had settled his length onto the desk at the beginning of her onslaught, his ears laid flat against his head, trembling with fear while she let loose upon him verbally. They both knew that she had every right to be angry. From what little Catie *had* told him before disappearing, all that Donemere had predicted might well come true. Her immortal life was likely to be filled with one battle after another, each one increasing her magic until she was powerful enough to meet her destiny. After spending only a few weeks in Donemere's company, he had come to the conclusion that she was not going to like what that destiny was. Magic was a lark to her, and until the last couple of days, he had doubted that she would ever be strong enough to warrant any part of the binding spell being released. Yet that day had finally come, as Catie had prophesied. Which meant that sometime in the next few days, the second part of the prophesy would also come to fruition and Donemere would be forced to meet the next step in her destiny, whether she was ready for it or no.

But Sylvester was still unable to tell her this; she was also right about the binding spell not being lifted in total. Because she was not ready to hear it, he could not warn her about what was intended for her. Reflecting upon how upset Donemere had been a few moments ago, the cat wondered if it was possible that she already knew the answer to what lay ahead in that regard. Clearly, if she had indeed somehow discerned what the future held for her, she did not like it. Although, he staunchly reassured himself, she was most definitely beginning to accept it. At least, he hoped so.

He had to admit that he was now a great deal impressed with Donemere, her powers and her inner resolve. She had allowed her anger at him and Catie to rise within her until it had become almost palpable, filling the very air of the room with an alternating mantle of hot rage and a bone-chilling cold dread that they could all see and feel—they had even been able to smell the dankness and the noisome odor of consummate evil all around. Donemere had a naturally clear blue aura that Sylvester had been able to detect around her always, even if only faintly, ever since she had accepted her powers six months ago. But just now, for a few minutes, it had turned so thick and dark, it was almost terrifyingly black, darkening her eyes and her hair, creating a stark contrast between her preternaturally pale skin and the shadows created by her rage.

And yet, somehow, she had found the strength to pull herself back from the edge of a darkness that would have easily drawn more experienced witches to their black doom, caught in a state of being where only evil flourishes. The desire for retribution is often too enticing for many to forego, especially when the slight is as great as that done to Donemere. But, already, her aura registered as a deep blue, which was growing clearer and lighter in color with each passing second. And the soft scent of the burning candles once again reigned over the room.

Sylvester let his fear slide away from him. The moment had passed and would not return; Donemere truly was mastering her powers now. Yet, although this oft-irritating charge of his had finally and wholly become his mistress, he had one more lesson to impart to her now.

"Donemere," he said quietly, "we both know you have every right to be angry. I shall not quibble with you over that. But you have slighted the gods in the swells of your anger. You must now appease them or they will not appear when you call. None of them will appear."

Donnie turned back to Sylvester and sighed, knowing full well he was right. She shouldn't have deliberately offended them just to spite the cat if she truly wanted their help. And instinct told her that she actually needed something from them anyway, if only to ensure that she really did pull off this particular spell effectively. With a resigned air, she nodded, then asked, "And just how do I do that?"

"You must offer them an orisoun, renouncing your wickedness."

Donnie raised an eyebrow at him. "*All* of my wickedness, or just that of today?"

The cat blinked back at her, replying carefully, "You must forswear the insult you paid them a few moments ago by respectfully petitioning their favor."

"Oh...that's what an orisoun is then? A respectful petition?"

"If it is given to a god, yes. And Donemere?"

"Yes, Sylvester?"

"Please try to take this seriously."

"I will, Sylvester, I promise."

No one else moved or spoke when Donnie hung her head and crossed her arms in front of her, pressing her hands to her shoulders while sending out this entreaty to the universe: "Hear my plea, most loving Mother and Father, Sisters and Brothers. In your infinite wisdom and compassion, I ask that you remain patient with me. I am merely a novice, and sometimes a fool, and am only now learning to wear the cloak of my destiny. I respectfully request your pardon of my insult to your Divine Power, and dare to hope that you will bestow your presence on me within my protected circle this day. I ask this in the name of all that is holy and in the most sacred gift any of us possess—the beneficence of life."

She lifted her head, squared her shoulders, then strode over to the burled oak cabinet that stood in the corner behind the doorway to the kitchen and opened its upper double doors, not needing to look backward at Sylvester to know that he was nodding his head in approval. A flutter of her hand brought two small candles from the desk floating to her sides so she could see better into the dimness of the recesses opened to her. Inside this part of the cabinet was revealed three shelves on which numerous objects glittered, their metal, glass, and jeweled components reflecting myriad, multi-colored beams of shimmering light.

The bottom shelf housed an antique alabaster mantle clock with fittings of bronze and a face of sunstone, Catie's mirror and brush set still safely ensconced in their velvet bag, and a small ebony chest inlaid with cedar and sycamore carved in the shapes of lotus flowers. The chest's drawers were opened to reveal several cherished trinkets, such as the heavy, gold pocket watch, the meerschaum pipe hand-carved with a dragon's claw holding the bowl, and the blue onyx cabochon ring belonging to Donnie's grandfather. In the next drawer down nestled her grandmother's Victorian three-strand natural pearl necklace and its matching brooch, along with several loose gemstones. The final drawer held assorted treasures from Donnie's childhood: there were steel pins and obsidian arrowheads, glass and metal beads, and little crystal balls and baubles galore, each with its own special memory.

Above that shelf sat the twisted pot Donnie had blown up and kept because of its riveting form of splayed cast iron reaching toward the heavens. In front of this was an old cast-iron lock she had bought in London before coming to Wales, having fallen in love with the strangely delicate, flowing filigree that grew outwardly from the lock proper.

To the right of the pot floated the knife that had attacked Donnie a month before, whirling endlessly in confined suspension. It emitted a lambent blue illumination that glinted off the razor-sharp blade as it slowly gyrated within its orbed prison.

Even when she'd stopped the knife that day in mid-air, only a few inches from her neck, it had strained increasingly to drive itself downward. She'd searched through the library for a possible explanation of its behavior or even a counter spell, finding nothing to help her. After leaving the knife suspended for some time, with it still slowly creeping toward the floor, she'd finally dematerialized it outside and allowed it to finish its course, where it had instantly rammed itself deep into the earth. She'd left it there overnight, leery of touching it, even with magic. The incident had created quite a stir at the farm, with everyone disavowing any knowledge of the knife's presence in the house or its mission.

The knife had then attacked Donnie a second time, as if the demented blade were determined to accomplish its objective come hell or high water, as she'd discovered when she went running the next morning and, within moments, felt it winging its way toward her neck. She'd stopped it well before it hit its target, side-stepped out of its way, and then let it drive itself into the ground at her feet, where it immediately tried to dislodge itself again from the earth. After that, setting aside her misgivings about touching it and telling absolutely no one of her second encounter with it, she'd encased the knife in its magical prison and stored it here in the cabinet, surrounded by a thick, perpetual and tightly tensioned sphere of her power.

On either side of this glowing cage stood two bronze statuettes. To the left was an odd-looking bird, with wickedly hooked beak and ruby eyes, that was hunkered down as if it were about to take flight; and on the right was a fox, sitting docilely, a very pleased and secretive smile curving its lips upward. Its bright, lively eyes of emerald shone with an empyrean radiance from the combined illumination of the orb and the floating candles.

And finally, on the topmost shelf of the cupboard resided an ornately carved hazelwood stand. Upon this rested a straight, double-edged knife, bearing a black pearl handle inlaid with an intricate, curling design of iridescent mother-of-pearl. The handle was studded down its length on either side with small, refulgent pearls in varied, lustrous colors. A row of highly polished, gleaming black pearls was embedded within the mirror-like blade itself, running from the hilt to its sharply pointed tip. It had been given to Donnie by her parents after they'd purchased it in Istanbul's Spice Market while on vacation in Turkey, back in the spring of 2009. Sylvester had taken one look at it when Donnie had unpacked its display case six months ago and pedantically informed her that it would serve quite admirably as her athame. To which Donnie had replied, "There you go, done deal." Then, of course, Sylvester had had to explain to her what an athame was. But since she'd never cast a circle before or called upon the gods, she'd not had occasion to use the ceremonial knife until today.

Donnie closed her eyes and stretched her arms out in front of her, palms facing in and fingertips touching. She focused her energy inwardly, willing her power to begin building inside her body. She brought her palms in to touch her forehead, then stretched her arms outward again, always keeping the palms facing in. She repeated this part of the ritual two times more, once touching her heart, and the other kneeling down to touch her feet. A soft blue light began to radiate from within her midsection, building in intensity until it outlined her entire form. Unlike the turbulent blackness that had engulfed her during her tirade, this field of power was controlled and translucent. Donnie gently took her athame from its stand and raised it above her head, its glimmering blade inverted toward the floor, then brought the knife down slowly, holding it close-in to her chest.

Turning to face the room, she nodded at Warren, inviting him to join her in the center of the drawn pentacle. The other two remained silent, held still where they were, marveling at the certain feel of unseen electricity in the room now and how it both stimulated and refreshed their minds and bodies. Warren too felt it alternately resisting and drawing him in as he moved into place in the circle.

Ruefully, Donnie realized that she must redraw her pentacle because of her angry outburst at Sylvester, which, if left undone, would taint the sanctity of her circle. She held the athame pointing toward the floor and carefully traced the outline of her pentacle in the air. The chalked pentacle responded by glowing brightly and the silvery flecks within its protozoan shells twinkled, sending out small beams of multicolored lights that were just short of dazzling. Donnie stretched her arms out straight in front of her again, athame held in both hands, facing outward this time. She walked the circle three times sunwise, reciting a chant that forbade any evil from entering once she'd closed the circle:

"A sacred space I call,
A place between where worlds may meet.
A shield I raise,
A place where all within are safe, our triunes protected, our energies contained.
Thrice do I conjure this circle,
Thrice do I protect all within.
Where the spirit and matter are one in perfect love and perfect trust,
May the Divine reside.
So must it be!"

Falwaïn and Sylvester gazed with growing wonder at the field of blue light around Donnie; it expanded to the edges of the pentacle as she progressed around the circle, creating a sphere of magical energy. This barrier enclosed her and Warren, its protective layer of light strengthening noticeably with each pass she made. After the first turn was completed, the floor within the circle seemed to drop away, leaving only the glowing pentacle and an invisible plane upon which Donnie and Warren stood. As Donnie made the final turn and closed the circle, the electrical charge in the room withdrew totally to the pentacle and, suddenly bereft, the two watchers both felt inexplicably forlorn in its absence.

Donnie brought her athame back in to her chest, her body glowing a vivid blue, except for the iridescent green of her eyes. In a rich, exultant voice, she canted a circle prayer from one of her favorite modern witches:

"By the earth that is Her body,
By the air that is Her breath,
By the fire of Her bright spirit,
By the waters of Her living womb,
Throughout and about, around and round,
This circle is drawn, this circle is bound."

Donnie suddenly flicked the knife upward, and then downward, adding, "Above and below, the circle is sealed." The five candles within the pentacle ignited simultaneously.

Donnie took a deep, cleansing breath and called the Quarters to her. She began by turning east, pointing with the knife around the circle and facing each direction while invoking its element. Donnie herself comprised the fifth point of the star, taking her part in the ritual as the ruling metaphysical element of Spirit.

"I call upon the element of Air, ministering spirit from the east; meet your powers with mine in this rite. Bring to me your intuition and communication, and your protection for all who stand within my circle. I ask this of you. Hail, and be welcome!

"I call upon the element of Fire, ministering spirit from the south; meet your powers with mine in this rite. Bring to me your creativity and passion, and your protection for all who stand within my circle. I ask this of you. Hail, and be welcome!

"I call upon the element of Water, ministering spirit from the west; meet your powers with mine in this rite. Bring to me your love and cleansing, and your protection for all who stand within my circle. I ask this of you. Hail, and be welcome!

"I call upon the element of Earth, ministering spirit from the north; meet your powers with mine in this rite. Bring to me your stability and growth, and your protection for all who stand within my circle. I ask this of you. Hail, and be welcome!"

As Donnie completed the invocation, there came an almost instantaneous surge of the elemental Guardians, each swirling around the circumference of the magical sphere, blending with Donnie's own power to create a semi-transparent wall of churning colors that streaked and curled and rolled into fantastical patterns which occasionally occluded the view of those outside it.

Still holding the knife in both hands, Donnie moved to stand in front of Warren, bidding him to take hold of the athame, to become part of her power while in her circle. The Wolf King clasped his hands around hers a little unsteadily, for each of his nerves, muscles and bones were sharply stimulated by her concentrated magic. The deep nothingness and, conversely, the fullness that surrounded him were also disturbing, for everywhere he looked, other than at Donnie or the lit candles on the points of the pentacle (as if they somehow grounded him in reality), all he could see was forever in the ages of the Earth. He caught a glimpse of its birth over there, and then everything shifted. Out of the corner of his eye, he saw tall spires adorning the Earth's surface, with what looked like flies buzzing around countless graceful towers against the backdrop of a waning Sun. Suddenly, the shift repeated and he watched huge, lumbering beasts make their way across a plain, the Sun now brilliant and red in the distance; and then a darkness engulfed the Earth after something very large flew at it from the heavens. Yet none of these snatched visions stayed put or could be looked at directly; rather, they swirled all around him dizzyingly, and between them was the taste of true freedom and a sense of immense power.

Feeling as though this must surely be a waking dream, as soon as he touched Donnie's skin, he was startled by the extreme clarity of his eyesight and his ability to focus on his greatest desire of becoming his own master once again. With her power (which he knew instinctively was being tempered so as not to cause him harm) now coursing through his body, he took a moment to consider what it must be like for her to have this much magic within her, to feel it running through every bone, every sinew always, relentlessly injecting her with its energy, just as it now was doing to him. He thought it must be truly frightening at times.

Once Warren's hands were wrapped around hers, Donnie lifted her head high and invited the Goddess and God of her craft, crying out in a warm, clear voice, "O' merciful Mother Earth, I call upon you from my circle of power. You, who bear the fruit of all life; we are your beloved children and guileless students of your teachings. We are blessed to be born unto you at the beginning of this life's journey and graced to return to your folds when that journey changes to the next. Great Father, I call upon you from my circle of power. You, who bring grace and movement to all who wander our Mother's beautiful lands and waters, and who bestows upon us the gifts of smell, sight, and sound as your endowment to our future. The racing of our hearts, the coursing of our blood is our tribute to you. Your strength fills our dreams with truth, for which we are forever thankful. Dearest Mother and Father, I beseech you to come to me now. Your aid is needed in rectifying a most egregious wrong. I ask this of you. Hail, and be welcome!"

Two forms of pure energy, both robed in flowing gowns of blazing light, emerged slowly to stand on either side of Donnie, facing her. The Lord appeared first, a magnificent set of antlers set atop his stag's head, and the Lady arrived but a second later, her long robes billowing with color. Delicate, rolling tendrils of argent energy silently emanated here and there from their regal bodies. Their beauty was breathtaking and their light infused the room with its Divine radiance.

Despite the sudden rush of low roars that were intrinsic to each of the elements, Falwaïn distinctly heard Sylvester utter an imprecation. He looked down at the cat enquiringly, then had to lean close-in to hear the reply.

"I have never seen the Goddess, the God, nor the Guardians manifested so strongly," explained Sylvester. "Verily, I have heard of such a manifestation only once before, in all my more than four hundred years as a familiar. 'Tis truly a wondrous sight; one that few who may walk the Earth shall ever be allowed to witness." The cat spoke solemnly, obviously awestruck.

Falwaïn straightened in the desk chair, his own expression thoughtful.

Donnie asked the Lord and Lady to clasp the athame. More tendrils of their power filled the circle as the ghostly entities closed their hands over Donnie's and Warren's, these lashes of pure magical energy clouding the watchers' view of the circle even further. Donnie was silent for a moment, then made her request of the Divinities surrounding her. Falwaïn and Sylvester were just able to make out her words over the growing din of the Guardians.

"Within this circle stands a man who is not a man, and who once was a wolf but is no more. He seeks to gain his balance in the alternating mantle that was thrust upon him by evil. Light his path for him, my elemental Sisters and Brothers. Join your power with mine, most honorable Ceridwen and Cernunnos, and stand beside me while I gift to him control over his destiny, that for which he asks. Will you grant his request and answer my plea?"

Through the diffuse, whorling screen of the elements, the watchers could just make out the Mother and Father nodding affirmatively to Donnie's request. Four androgynous faces, their eyes shining with blinding energy, appeared out of the storm of colors encircling Donnie and Warren and also gave their answer by a gentle, approving nod from each. Donnie canted the spell once by herself and twice with the wispy echoes of the Gods joining her:

"Our powers joined,
To make Warren whole.
The choice is his,
He alone has control."

The scene before the watchers shifted instantly at the end of the spell. It appeared as though all figures within the pentacle were sucked into the spirit wall encircling them, drawing them into its churning mass, Donnie and Warren included. The cacophony of the elements continued to rise as this roiling chromatic tempest expanded inwardly to fill the entire circle. Falwaïn gasped with alarm and stood suddenly, as did Sylvester. But when Falwaïn made as though to come around the desk, Sylvester checked him loudly. "No, Lord Falwaïn!" the cat remonstrated. "Donemere forbade us to enter the circle. We must trust that she is powerful enough to control the force of her own magic combined with that of the Gods."

"What if she is not?" Falwaïn shouted back, frantically searching the jumbled refractions of light for any sign of Donnie. He realized with an unsettling jolt that he had already begun to think of this honey woman as his own, almost as though she were predestined to belong to him. Sylvester had to call his name three times before he managed to tear his eyes from the circle and stare at the cat. Their gazes locked for a long moment and finally Falwaïn felt calm returning to his troubled soul.

"We must trust in her and do as she asked," Sylvester repeated firmly. "We shall wait here, in this spot, until the spell is complete. That is *all* we can do, Lord Falwaïn."

Falwaïn gave a short nod of agreement and slowly sank back down into the chair. His eyes were fixed upon the circle once more. He could see the hues of the elemental Quarters, combined with the silvery white light of the Gods, the pure blue of Donnie, and a blue-black streak which he presumed was Mynydd Uchaf. The wail of the Guardians soon became almost deafening, each element's inherent clamor alternating haphazardly with the others: here the crackle of Fire, there the whistling and moaning of the Wind, then the rumble of the Earth, followed by the thunder of Water. Yet still, the five candles within the circle burned quietly, their flames flickering only occasionally, perfectly undisturbed by the spiritual maelstrom raging around them.

After what seemed an eternity, the blue light separated from the others and Donnie's form slowly emerged until she was once again flesh and bone. Her eyes were closed and her hands still gripped the athame. She spoke some words which Falwaïn couldn't hear through the din, then the blue-black light separated from the circling bands of magical energy and Mynydd Uchaf appeared. He had no real substance though. Donnie opened her eyes and raised the athame to a point above his head. With one swift cut, she split him down the middle: wolf on one side, werewolf on the other. Her lips moved again, and suddenly Mynydd Uchaf's two forms were reunited. His body began to coalesce now, but all the while rapidly changing from one form to the other until they were alternating so quickly, it was impossible to tell the difference between them.

Donnie waited patiently, allowing Warren the time to gain mastery over his shifting shape. When he did so, he too became flesh and bone once more. He stood before her proudly, slightly changed in appearance so that he was more man-like, and raised his head with a smile. The God and Goddess slowly separated from the Quarters, then stood silently beside Donnie and Warren. The Guardians receded to the perimeter of the circle, and the four figures in the center again faced each other as the room quietened.

Donnie smiled lovingly at the Goddess and God before bowing her head to them in veneration. "Mother and Father, I am beholden to you, as any child should be," she acknowledged reverently. "Your wisdom has shown me that I should no longer fear my own powers. Your love has taught me how to be at peace with my new life. These are two most precious gifts to receive. I take with me that part of you which you have given freely and which I shall hold sacred for eternity. I will use it when I must, when I am ready. And I shall do the other as bidden." She lifted her head and gave them both a somewhat secretive smile. The God nodded back at her and the Goddess reached up to caress her cheek, both deities tenderly returning Donnie's smile.

Donnie took a deep breath, amazed at how light her spirit felt, and the sheer joy of it bubbled up inside her and could be heard in her tone when she said, "My Lord and Lady, you have my enduring esteem and praise as we depart this circle. May you always find it worthy to aid me in what I do. We thank you for your blessings this day and for honoring us with your presence. Hail, and farewell, dearest Ceridwen and Cernunnos."

The Lord and Lady bowed their heads to her this time, straightened to beam approvingly upon both Donnie and Warren and then, the Lady going first, they dissipated into nothingness.

Stepping back from the center, Donnie raised her hands toward the ceiling and cried in a throaty, elated voice to the Guardians, "Spirits of the Air, Fire, Water, and Earth, you also have my enduring esteem and praise as we depart this circle! May you always find it worthy to aid me in what I do. We thank you for your blessings this day and for honoring us with your presence. Hail, and farewell, my watchful Sisters and Brothers." The Quarters smiled benevolently upon Donnie and Warren, then they too slowly dissipated until all were gone, taking with them their symphony of elemental music.

Holding the athame stretched out in front of her, palms facing in, Donnie walked around the protected pentacle widdershins three times while reciting a chant to open her circle:

"In perfect love, in perfect trust,
The circle is open, but never broken.
Residing in our triunes forever shall be,
The foundations of freedom the Lord and Lady have granted us this day.
This circle is open, but never broken."

As she traveled the circle's circumference, her steps quick and buoyant, more and more of the blue light fell away and flowed back to outline her form, strengthening around her with each pass she made, until the circle was no more. At the very moment the circle opened, the five candles on the points of the star extinguished.

Donnie nodded at Warren and gave him leave to quit her pentacle, then she walked over to the cabinet and slowly placed the athame back on its stand. She crossed her forearms and held them tightly to her chest, palms pressed to her shoulders, and allowed her light to diminish until it was within her. Exhaling with relief, she turned around to face Warren, who had followed her to the cupboard, and gave him an expectant, "Well?"

He bowed his head at once and replied, "My undying gratitude to you, Donemere of the Codlebærn. I am at peace for the first time in many months. I no longer feel the conflict within from my two selves. We are one, and only I can choose which form to take. I am indebted to your service and pray that you will grant me the privilege of calling you friend."

Donnie reached up to touch his cheek. "Okay, friend," she said happily. "You've also given me a great gift. Never again shall I take magic or my powers lightly. Nor do they fill me with such grief as they did only moments before we began the ritual. You've helped me make another huge step forward in accepting who I must be. I am the better for your need, and I'm thankful that we both have received numinous gifts from the Gods today." She smiled again, but kept her eyes averted from his naked body, which was noticeably less hirsute now. Curiously, the Quarters had asked for his cloak, and Warren, as she'd thought he would, had relinquished it unhesitatingly. What the Guardians wanted with it, though, Donnie had no clue.

She turned back toward the cabinet and stooped down, sliding the heavy German Shepherd Dog brass doorstopper to the left a few inches so she could open one of the cabinet's lower drawers. From its capacious depths, she pulled out some clothes and handed them to Warren. "Here, put these on. I copied them from Falwaïn's and I've charmed them so that when you're in wolf form, they'll disappear, but when you're in human—er, werewolf—oh, whatever form you choose—you know what I mean, right? Anyhoo, they'll reappear whenever you're not in wolf form. That way I won't have to see so much of you every time you change into a man. Not that you aren't one fine man to look at, believe you me! Because you are—ah, fine looking, that is."

Donnie laughed, wholeheartedly embarrassed. She moved away while Warren dressed and, with a wave of her hand, levitated the five candles within the pentacle back to their shelf. With another wave, she opened the curtains and snuffed out about half of the other candles. She gave a low whistle when she turned back toward Warren, who stood almost beside her now, lacing up his shirtfront, and declared to him, "You do look very nice, my friend, very nice indeed. Oh, your boots are in the corner by the cabinet. Okay, now you can discuss the plans for tomorrow with me more fully. Oh, can you guys move the furniture back into place, please?" she asked, encompassing both Warren and Falwaïn in her questioning look.

Falwaïn and Sylvester, who up to this point had remained motionless, held fast by the magnitude of what they had witnessed over the past hour, now sprang to life. Falwaïn hurried around the desk and clapped Warren on the back, congratulating him heartily. Sylvester sat with his tail curled around his feet on the edge of the desk and added his own pleased and somewhat long-winded salutations, periodically gazing proudly upon Donnie, a faint blue glow emanating from the locket around his neck.

Warren grinned, his toothsome smile noticeably more human than before. He sat down and pulled on his boots, shoving his pant legs into them. His raiment gave off little sparkles of blue light that floated around him until he was finished dressing, particles which then suddenly settled back into the clothing, making the fabric glimmer in the reflected sunlight radiating through the window.

The two men set to righting the disarranged furniture, while Donnie scooped Sylvester into her arms and held him close. "I'm glad I did the spell that way, Sylvester," she told him. "Warren's not the only one at peace now. I can even forgive you and Catie for what you did to me by bringing me here. I think I just might be ready to accept this new life you've given me, although I'll probably always miss my old one. I'm going to need you as my familiar now more than ever, you know."

The cat looked into his mistress's face and nodded. "Yes," was all he could manage. She'd swear that his eyes teared up as he stretched over to nuzzle her neck, purring contentedly.

Warren outlined the route for their journey next morning, ending by saying he would patrol the areas north and east of the valley tonight and that he would contact his forest friends to learn if there were any new developments. He would meet Donnie and the others before first light back here at the cottage, in preparation for an early departure. It had already been decided that Falwaïn and Donnie would pack the provisions to be carried on Otis and Gallantry. Falwaïn informed Donnie that, at some point this evening, he wished to practice with his sword to see how well he'd healed. Warren bestowed upon them another huge grin and, standing right next to Donnie, changed into his wolf form, his black fur glistening with a distinct hint of blue, and bade them good day. He was gone from the room in one spirited bound.

Donnie and Falwaïn went into the kitchen to lay out what they'd need on the dining table. She got a green backpack out for her to wear the next day and some canvas bags that they could hang on their saddles. Into them she would cram bread, fruit, cheese and eggs.

At Donnie's behest, Falwaïn went out to the stables and retrieved his saddle bags. When he returned, she informed him that Catie had quite a prodigious supply of bottled ales and beers down in the buttery, which Donnie had barely touched over the last six months. The two of them descended to the cellar, where Donnie grabbed six bottles of ale and slid them into the two sides of the saddle bags, adding a half dozen small, plastic bottles of water that she had stored in the buttery to keep them cold. Falwaïn took up a bottle and stared at it with fascination, running his hands over the smooth plastic. With an amused grin, Donnie reached over and twisted off its top, then told him to drink the contents. He did so in one long pull, smacking his lips with satisfaction at the end, declaring the cold, pure, spring water most delicious, although he could not see the point to storing it in this manner. These bottles, he said, were too small to do much good on a journey of any length, were they not? Was that because the future did not possess enough wells and springs to allow everyone to drink freely of them or was water, perhaps, rationed for some other reason? Donnie explained to him that, except between friends, very little food or drink was ever free in her world because almost everything had its price and money ruled. They both considered this silently for a few moments, then Donnie agreed with him that, yes, it was a rather sad way of life.

She had him follow her to the back part of her workshop, where she bustled around the shelves, choosing just what they'd take with them on their trip. Together they pulled out her folding camp chairs, tent, camp stove, cooler, sleeping mat and bag, and camp pillow. Donnie duplicated a mat, sleeping bag and pillow for Falwaïn, much against his wishes. She playfully bet him all the cooking chores for the trip that he would thank her after only one night on them. He merely shook his head and grinned at her.

Donnie dug out a supply of paper plates and napkins and plastic forks and knives, along with a lightweight pot and pan, her camp coffee pot, and her old coffee strainer just in case they didn't have time to percolate coffee in the mornings. She poured some fresh ground coffee into a container, charmed it so it would not empty while they were away, then took another container and filled it with teabags, charming it in the same manner. These she packed in one of the canvas bags, along with eggs and fruit. The rest of the food would go into either the other canvas bag or the cooler. She really wasn't sure how they were going to haul the cooler and the cooking equipment, but since they'd always proved essential on her previous camping trips, she was determined to see if they could figure out a way to take them. Again, Falwaïn shook his head, doing his utmost to refrain from commenting on the apparent habits of travelers in the future.

Into her backpack, Donnie crammed a few rolls of toilet paper, some tissues, a toothbrush for both of them, plus a new tube of toothpaste, along with a new bar of soap, and two travel bottles of shampoo and hair conditioner that she took from the cupboards in the bathroom. She also got out her creams and facial cleanser and packed them too. Falwaïn looked at all of this skeptically, but kept silent, although his ever-growing amusement was becoming more and more difficult to contain. Caught up in the moment, Donnie duplicated another backpack for him and stuffed it with three sets of clean clothes for them both, including an extra pair of shoes.

This finally sent Falwaïn into fits. He sat down on the bed and bent over, laughing hard. "We *will* be coming back, you know!" he teased her, his sky-blue eyes flashing with devilish humor. "I do not believe that we need carry the cottage and its entire contents with us; do we truly? And besides, that bag will not fit easily over my cloak and will most likely bind my shoulders, which makes it impractical for me to wear. It, and dare I say, most everything else you have packed, should remain here." He peered up at her, biting back another laugh at the look on her face, and observed, "You are not exactly versed in the art of traveling light, are you?"

She stuck her tongue out at him, but nevertheless unpacked two sets of clothing, leaving only the one set for each to take with them, along with those they'd be wearing when they left in the morning. She'd just have to wash one set daily, she decided. As for shoes, the pair they rode out with would have to suffice. By lightening the load so drastically, Donnie managed to stuff all their clothing and toiletries into the one backpack that she would wear.

Falwaïn continued to chortle so much at her, it wasn't long before she reminded him that he had a very sharp sword to play with and wasn't it time he did so? And while he was out there, noble lord though he be, he could still make himself useful by feeding the animals and cleaning the tack, couldn't he?

Her "noble lord" sobered as much as he was able, managing to reply with only a slight smirk, "My lady, what you say holds verity. I am at your service and shall do as you command." His sides shaking, he rose from the bed and strode purposefully across the room and on into the kitchen, exiting the cottage a moment later.

Even from the bedroom, Donnie could hear the hearty peals of laughter he let out as he made his way to the stables. She also had to smile at herself; after all, she was going way overboard with the packing, as had always been her habit. And at least Falwaïn had had the grace to (mostly) hold it together until he got outside before he again collapsed in complete hysterics.

Ironically, she realized the cause of her problem. Not only was this her first time being away from the cottage overnight since she'd arrived here, but this was also their first camping trip together and she wanted it to be perfect.

"Which is just plain silly, given the circumstances dictating the necessity for the trip in the first place," Donnie admonished her overactive imagination. "You are not a couple, you idiot, and this is no pleasure trip you're taking here. Get real, will you?"

Nonetheless, she was very much looking forward to spending the next few days in Falwaïn's company.

Chapter 12
Lone Tree Requiem

After Falwaïn left, Donnie set various kitchen utensils and appliances to work making dinner with a flick of her hand. Cutlery, bowls and bread mixer all could be heard snipping, clinking and whirring busily while Donnie carried on with the packing, or perhaps that should be the *un*packing, of various items for their journey. And before repairing to her bedroom to take a shower, she spent an hour in the library.

By the time she reappeared in the kitchen, the bread was baked and nicely browned, as were the Gruyère scalloped potatoes. The loaf of French bread was already cooling on the cutting board and the potatoes were steaming in their covered casserole dish on the table. As soon as Donnie entered the room, the bread knife automatically sliced the new loaf uniformly; a feat which Donnie had been unable to perform well (to be honest, more like disastrously) before magic entered her fingertips. She took two slices of the still-warm bread and placed some shredded Fontina cheese between them, buttered the outsides of the sandwich with her homemade rosemary, garlic and olive butter, then set the sandwich in the frying pan. She began to make another for herself while reading the book that hovered in front of her face, its movements matching hers perfectly, as though it were somehow held fast by her line of sight.

The front door swung open and Falwaïn stepped through it a moment later, regarding the door warily.

Realizing that so far he must've gone through it only when it was already open, and that she'd obviously forgotten to inform him about the charm placed on all the outside doors and windows of the cottage, Donnie shot him an amused smile. She returned her attention to cooking, sent the book zooming back to the library, and carefully positioned the second sandwich in the pan, waiting for the burner to turn itself on to medium heat before explaining blithely to Falwaïn, "The door does that. Remember when I told you that many things around here are charmed to work by themselves? Well, the outer doors let only certain souls in and out of the house—whoever I designate to have access, I mean. It's a great charm, you know. I've modified it several times, just to see if I could do it, like limiting the number of times someone's allowed to come in through a specific door, or citing the specific day or days they're welcome through *any* of the doors in the house. Each time I modified it, I tested it on everybody here and on a few of our forest friends and, I must say, it's always worked like a—well, I was going to say it works like a charm, but that's redundant, innit?" She giggled. "A charm that works like a charm?"

Falwaïn eyed her dubiously as he walked away from the door, apparently not seeing the humor in what she'd said. Donnie thought about this a moment and decided she had to agree with him on that count.

"I see...tell me, how long am I to be granted entry?" he inquired, a hint of mischief flitting across his face.

She smiled sweetly at him, her tone matching his jesting mood when she replied, "Well, for the time being, there's no limit to your access. But, you never know, that could change at a moment's notice."

He grinned appreciatively. When he came far enough into the light to where Donnie could get a closer look at him, she told him pertly that he had to clean up before she was going to eat dinner with him. "Nobody sits at my table with dirty hands," she told him.

Falwaïn raised an eyebrow while he inspected the offending appendages, but otherwise did as asked without comment. After washing his hands, he sat at the kitchen table, comfortably making small talk with Donnie until she was ready to serve the meal, closely watching her magical antics with fascination.

She levitated the sandwiches to flip them when needed, then floated them onto plates once they were done cooking. The lid on the scalloped potatoes lifted and the spoon scooped a sizeable portion onto each plate. Donnie opened a bottle of white zinfandel and filled two wine glasses. She also placed a bowl of steaming green beans on the table.

She had decided to keep over half of the sliced potatoes back so she could fry them up as potato chips, which they would take with them on the trip north tomorrow. While they were eating, Donnie materialized these chips into some hot olive oil and let them cook for a couple of minutes before rematerializing them onto paper towels and lightly salting them. Falwaïn was watching this magical process with great interest and did not notice when Donnie asked him how he was feeling after his practice session. She got his attention by throwing a piece of bread at him, which hit him on the hand.

He turned and looked at her with a lopsided grin stuck on his face. "More multitasking?" he joked, jerking his head in the direction of the stovetop.

"Yes, magic's really quite useful for that," she replied, her cheeks growing warm because of his deliciously wonderful smile. "Um, I guess you didn't hear me a moment ago when I asked how you're feeling after your practice session with your sword."

"Quite well," he assured her, his expression turning serious, then he sat back and wiped his mouth with his napkin. "There was some pain earlier, but I took two more of those pills you gave me and they eased the ache. I am almost completely well now, and shall be fit to travel and fight by the morrow," he ended with satisfaction. "What progress have you made on packing supplies for our journey? Have you managed to leave anything behind?"

Donnie immediately turned several shades of brilliant red and nodded her head, using her fork to play with the remaining potatoes on her plate. "Yes, I packed just enough food for lunch tomorrow into the canvas bags and, of course, the overnight bag with our clothes. Oh, and the ale and water in your saddle bags. I finally realized that I should be able to materialize anything we need from here anyway, so what's the point of burdening ourselves unnecessarily with too much stuff? I know, I was a bit slow about that, wasn't I?" She glanced suspiciously at him as he hastily took another bite of food so that she could not see the laughter in his eyes and on his lips. "How do you like it?" she asked, indicating the sandwich by brandishing her own.

Falwaïn nodded his head animatedly and declared, "I like it very much! What did you call it—a toasted cheese sandwich? But it is the bread which is toasted, not the cheese, I believe is how you explained it. Rather unusual, this 'sandwich' concept, and very tidy. And these potatoes are superior to any others I have tasted. They would make a noakie swoon, believe me. And noakies are very particular about their potatoes. Here, why do you look like that? What have I said wrong?" he cried with alarm when Donnie's face took on a scrunched-up look of pain.

She clasped her hands together under her chin, keeping her eyes downcast, and sighed. It was time to tell him. "Well, you see," she began, "when I admitted that you were in my library, I meant that, until I came here, I thought your story was pure fiction. You know, something that isn't true, as in 'made up out of someone's imagination.' Y'see, for my world, you're not real, as is nothing that happened here in Medregai—or as the author from my time called it, Erde—and therefore there are no such things as vinca, or elves, or goblins, or okûn, or trolls, or noakies; there's no Déagmun or Kaledar or Orgos—okay, okay, I know, you get it. So, it's really hard for me to switch tracks suddenly and get smacked in the face with the realization that something like noakies actually *do* exist. Does that make sense? Do you see what I'm getting at?" she asked somewhat desperately. She was afraid she'd freaked Falwaïn out now too, judging by the look on his face.

He finished chewing the last bite of his sandwich mechanically and pushed his plate away from him. He got up, carried his dishes to the sink, then strode across the room to walk through the darkened doorway of Donnie's library, never uttering a word. A moment later, he came back for a candle, which he took from the table. He continued to move silently, his expression inscrutable.

Sitting back in her chair, Donnie watched him with misery. He was clearly upset and that was her fault. Otherwise, why hadn't he taken some light with him the first time he went into the office, she wondered extraneously, a slight frown marring her features. She decided that it would be most prudent to cast a charm on some of the room candles throughout the property so that they'd light and extinguish themselves automatically whenever one of her friends entered or exited a darkened room, charming ban or no. With a wave of her hand, the charm was set.

Afterward, Donnie bit her lip, wondering if she should not have told Falwaïn that, for the people of her world, he was supposed to be nothing more than a fictional character. Not a very pleasant thing to hear, especially when you know darned well that you exist. But what if he'd found out on his own, she asked herself, would that have been any better?

She got up and put her dishes in the sink too. A moment later the pot scrubber began furiously scrubbing them. Donnie watched it clean a couple of dishes, then quietly joined Falwaïn in the office. His single candle was sitting on the middle of her desk, while the few others that had been lit by her new charm lent the room a ghostly feel. Falwaïn was standing in front of the nearest bookshelf, his hand on a book. For a full minute after Donnie entered the room, he continued to contemplate whether or not to pull the book from the shelf. Finally, steeling himself, he slid the book out and carried it to the desk, where he sat down and opened its pages.

It was a beautifully illustrated, hard-bound copy of *Songs of the Earth, Book One: The Journey of the Dead*. Still berating herself for having told him so callously that he wasn't supposed to be real, Donnie went over to the shelf and got the two remaining *Songs of the Earth* books and also Catie's hefty tome on Medregai, and placed them all on the desk to the side. She lit most of the candles in the room and the wood in the fireplace with a snap of her fingers so that there was now more than adequate light to read by. She left the room and closed the door softly. This was one journey Falwaïn would have to take by himself.

Donnie finished clearing the dinner dishes and putting away the leftovers. Then she packed the last odds and ends for their trip the next day, making sure everything was ready for an early start in the morning, the whole time chatting with Brindle and Parry. She glanced at the clock on the wall; it was shortly before eight o'clock. A few minutes later, she went back into her bedroom after brushing her teeth in the bathroom and sat down on the edge of the bed to dry her still slightly damp hair by running her hairbrush through it for a while.

Okay, she was now ready for bed. Which meant it was time to open the hidey-hole. When she'd cast the spell for Warren and had communed with the gods, Donnie had also asked for help in unraveling what was going on here in Medregai. She'd figured it was worth a shot; after all, what did she have to lose? Ceridwen and Cernunnos had promised that she would receive a written response tonight just before she retired. The hidey-hole was the only place she could think of where such a message could be physically relayed in secret.

Slowly, she walked up to the fireplace and reached to the back of the mantelpiece to unlock the spring door on the hidden cavity. The little door swung open to reveal a scroll of parchment curled up inside the recess.

Donnie breathed a deep breath, took the scroll out gingerly and carried it over to the bed with her, where she stood, gazing thoughtfully at the stirring cat. After considering the ramifications of what she was about to do, she willed Sylvester to remain asleep until just before dawn, then sat down again on the bed beside his still form.

Donnie moistened her lips with her nervous tongue, gave a long and resolute look at the loosely rolled parchment in her hand, then nodded her head decisively before untying the white silk ribbon wrapped around the scroll. The curling paper fell open to reveal its contents. Its text was written in English with a beautiful, flowing hand in rich, black ink. It began:

> Ye petitioned the Gods for guidance. Thy plea has been granted. Know this, Donemere of the Codlebœrn, by reading these words Thy Path Begins. 'Tis of wide span and unknown length, pocked throughout with hazards.
>
> Be aware Thy Choices Matter.
>
> What ye seek is concealed, tho' its secret may be unmasked by meeting the following trials as only a Treue Witch is able. Ye may be certain there shall be others. Heed Well These Words, and read them often. Ere five days have passed, ye shall.

Below this were listed what could best be described as five "trials" spread out over the top half of the page. There were large spaces between each line, as though a line or two were still missing from each. Donnie read on.

Reach for the heavens to meet thy treue self.
Demand death, tho' ye must accept the life that is gifted.
Lay bare the fruit of thy heart. If it be of bold valor, ye may reap its harvest.
Breathe the still waters to mark thy journey to enlightenment.
Be pressed beyond what thy heart may endure.

Near the bottom of the page was this warning, *Ye must Prove Thy Worth ere ye may proceed.*

Donnie studied the list, going over each trial carefully. "Okay, the first one I mostly get. But the others?" She rolled her eyes at the ceiling and muttered with resignation, "Those're pretty much clear as mud."

She read through the writing once more, taking her time with it, her mind beginning to race. "So, it's a test, is it? Okay then, I'm up for that, I s'pose. But hmm...I wonder..." A series of expressions flitted across her face as she pondered this new development, her thoughts still whizzing around in her head. What would happen if she refused to meet these trials set by the gods; would she be sent home immediately? Could that be her way back to her world? No, she reminded herself testily, what about Galto and the people of Medregai? Who would help them? Yet, perhaps, if she did refuse to go on with the test, whoever brought her here might send for another of Catie's progeny in her stead. No again; they'd already invested six months in Donnie, so they couldn't afford to waste more time with someone else. And since no other descendent had answered Catie's call, that meant she, Donnie, must go on because she couldn't abandon her responsibility toward the people here, even though it had been forced upon her.

"But what, I wonder," she said aloud, a somewhat reluctant, but nonetheless determined set to her features as she studied the list of trials, "will happen if I flat-out fail on one or more of these?"

Below the last line of writing a new one appeared, with a second line following a moment later. They were written in a noticeably different hand, almost more of a hurried scrawl, and read:

There is no turning back now, Donnie, my girl.
And failure is not an option!

Donnie grimaced and blew a heavy breath, exclaiming, "Hoo! Well, *that*, at least, is clear enough...innit? Dang!" She folded the scroll until it was about the size of a big bookmark, got up from the bed and stepped over to the wardrobe. Reaching inside its door, she felt for her waterproof money belt and pulled that out. She slid the paper into it and then put the belt on under the waistband of her sweat pants. Going back over to the bed, she stretched out on it and mentally willed herself to go to sleep immediately, but to wake up in a little over three hours.

When her eyes opened later, the house was quiet and still. She heard the soft, gentle breathing of the cat, who was now lying in the curve of her hip. She rolled away from him and slid her feet out from under the covers and onto the floor, moving noiselessly. She grabbed her boots and socks, after pulling her old leather motorcycle pants over her sweats, and went to the outer room.

There was still light coming from under the door to the office. Donnie dared not go in there in case Falwaïn was awake. As quietly as possible, she sat down on a chair and donned her footwear. She tiptoed to the front door, where she put on a sweatshirt and her black goose-down jacket. Before going outside, she jammed on her witch's hat and grabbed the sassafras broom she'd placed in the corner earlier in the evening.

Once outside by the well, she flipped the broom level and gently pushed it away, sending it floating into the air. It did not disappear this time. The stick dipped and wobbled a little, then stabilized. Donnie nodded her head sharply and grinned at the acquiescent broomstick with smug satisfaction.

Her boots crunched a little on the hard, cold mud as she made her way toward the stables by the light of a floating, blue light-ball she'd conjured to light her path. The bright globe hovered beside her all the way into the stables, where Otis and Diana greeted this disturbance with long yawns. Donnie softly bade them, "Go back to sleep, my friends. No reason we should all be up in the middle of the night."

Rex was snoring to her right, where she could just make out the vague imprint of his body in a pile of hay near the far wall. He must have his nose under some of the hay since he was otherwise invisible. Donnie lifted her saddle off the railing and carried it outside to where she had the broom levitating. The broomstick was still floating horizontally in the air near the well, about four feet off the ground. Eddies of wind were again making it sway as Donnie approached it and flipped the saddle onto its length.

The boombox suddenly appeared near the front end of the stick. Donnie gave it an appraising look, then agreed to its intentions. "All right," she said. "But you're going to have to hang on by yourself. Do not slide down the stick and mangle my hands. If you do, you'll never fly with me again." The handle of the boombox instantly appeared to meld into the broomstick's wood, firmly securing itself as Donnie jammed the light-ball onto the front end of the broom.

Grabbing the strap underneath the saddle, Donnie threaded it through the cinch. The saddle immediately molded itself onto the broom handle, becoming one with it. Donnie heard Brindle's voice when he was wakened by the sudden surge of magic. "Donemere," he rumbled, "is that you? Are we ready to ride?"

"Yes, Brindle, we are ready. Well, almost. I just need a minute to do something important." Donnie put her foot in the stirrup and hoisted herself into the saddle, making the broomstick angle upward a few degrees. The saddle grew around her, encasing her legs and hips, and expanded beneath her to give a soft, cushiony seat. It felt great on her bottom. She wiggled around in it a bit, an exuberant smile on her face. The saddle was perfect, plushly comfortable and obviously not going to let go of her until she was good and ready to be let go of! Still smiling, Donnie crossed her forearms in front of her, palms pressed to her shoulders, and focused on allowing her powers to rise within her before canting quickly:

"When I am flying,
I will not be sick,
I *will* not be sick,
I will *not* be sick,
I will not *be* sick,
I will not be *sick*.
When I am flying,
I—will—not—be—sick!"

She grabbed the horn on the saddle. Okay, what should she do now? Was she supposed to cackle horribly and recite something in Latin? Was that even necessary?

"Er, Brindle?"

"Yes, Donnie?"

"Got any idea what I should do next? You know, to make this thing go?"

The boombox began to play China Back's "Runnin' into Disaster." Donnie flashed a wry grimace in its general direction, murmuring under her breath, "Very funny."

"Does not one typically dig in their heels to urge their steed forward?" suggested Brindle. "Possibly that would work?"

It worked.

The broomstick took off like a shot, nearly making Donnie lose her hat. She willed the darn thing to stay on until she wanted it off. Her next thought was that if she didn't do something immediately to change direction, she was going to fly straight into a huge oak tree on the perimeter of the valley that was fast looming large, and which lay dead ahead. She had one, maybe two seconds before she'd slam into its trunk and prove the boombox right.

Yanking up hard on the broom handle, Donnie changed course abruptly, grazing the outer twigs of the oak tree. But this, she found, was little better because now she was flying vertically, deep into the night sky, and almost instantly she became frantic. She could see nothing in front of her except the moon, a few clouds and a lot of stars. And her peripheral vision told her that the Earth was receding behind her much too quickly for her liking. She was racing upward blindly, hurtling toward outer space and, truth be told, this scared the bejeezus out of her. It took at least ten seconds or so for her to calm down (that is, to finish the increasingly bloodcurdling scream she'd begun almost immediately at take-off) long enough to think of pushing downward on the broomstick.

She bore down on the stick with both hands, unwittingly putting her full weight into her thrust because she so desperately wanted to halt her ascent. This sudden pitch forward made her spin end-over-end (and let loose on yet another shrill scream while she tumbled helplessly through the air), all the while still gaining altitude. But, of course, as soon as she took her hands off the broomstick to cover her face in terror, convinced that she was about to die of apoplexy, the broomstick quit spinning. Slowly, Donnie pulled her hands away and opened her eyes to find she was once again on an even keel and that, at last, the broomstick had stopped climbing. Emitting a huge groan of relief, she sagged down in the saddle and took a long moment just to breathe.

Determined to overcome her fears, she forced her head up and looked around nervously. The features of the land more than two miles below her were only dimly outlined by the light of the full moon. Two miles is a very long way to be when you're up in the air on nothing but a broomstick, especially when you're traveling at a speed of almost forty miles per hour. So much for that age-old, exhilarating flying dream that everyone and their mother experiences at one time or another, that dream where you spread your arms out wide and take off gracefully into the air, a warm, gentle wind rustling through your hair. You soar above your home, your neighbors' homes, all the places you know so well, completely in control and thoroughly comfortable with the whole concept of flying like a bird. Only, isn't it wonderful that you don't have to flap anything? When you're done, you float gently to the ground in a slow, lazy kind of controlled landing, still moving gracefully.

You come away from the dream with the sense that flying is serenely beautiful, riveting, breathtaking, fulfilling—in fact, all those wonderfully inspiring superlatives and many more besides. It's one of the finest and safest experiences you'll ever have, and one you're likely never to forget. And also one you kid yourself you'd love to have for real one day. Why not, when it seems it would be just like when Felix sprinkled fairy dust on the Woodbine brothers and suddenly they could all fly. Who wouldn't want to have a wondrous adventure such as that of the Woodbine brothers of old?

Ah, but what Donnie had experienced so far tonight during her amateurish and blundering aeronautical attempts…well…this was completely unlike any of the recurring flying dreams she'd had in her youth. Nope, this was the real thing and, obviously, both grace and control had left the building.

She now found herself shooting wildly through the air, utterly terrified. She was a hair's breadth away from screaming her lungs out yet again (simply because she'd found it made her feel much better to vocalize her fears the two times she'd done it previously), with absolutely no confidence in her ability to maneuver the broomstick and with a distinctly uncomfortable crush of cold air slamming into her face, making breathing nigh-on impossible. Adding to the unshakeable belief that she was still careening through the air, completely out of control, was the absence of any sound reaching her ears other than the faint strains of the boombox floating backward. She could barely even hear her own screams when she let loose on them. All of which were details of flying for real that Donnie just had not bargained on.

As if all that wasn't bad enough, she also felt weightless and wobbly at the same time. This feeling was further encouraged when she stoically leaned over in the saddle (apparently too far) to study the landscape below her, trying to determine her position relative to the farm, and the next moment found herself, Brindle and the boombox zooming along upside down, just as the song went into its last chorus.

"What's that you say about dragging a big load behind you, boombox?" grumbled Donnie angrily, now thoroughly vexed with herself. "Dangling dilettantes, how the heck do I get back up?" she cried. "I can't fly around upside down like this all bloody, friggin' night! I won't be able to find my way anywhere if I have to do that. Oh, no," she groaned, "I just thought of something else. How am I supposed to land if I'm upside down? Besides painfully, I mean. Well, Donnie, my girl, you'd better put that in your pipe and smoke it for a while because you're not allowed to fail at this, remember?" She leaned toward her saddle and shouted, "Got any ideas for this one, Brindle?"

He called back that he was quite sorry, but he did not know the answer to even one of her questions. Just for a moment, Donnie suspected that he was laughing at her. She shook her head to clear it, chewed her bottom lip for a while, and wondered what would happen if she gave a little push on only the right stirrup. Tapping it lightly once with her foot got her part-way righted. She tapped it a few more times and, suddenly, there she was, sitting tall and upright in the saddle.

Greatly relieved, she leaned over (only a little ways, this time) to again examine the land below her. It was unfamiliar to her eyes, yet when she looked closely, she'd swear she could just make out the light from the window in the library of her house and the rim of the forest at the top of her valley. But how could that possibly be the farm? What if the "light" was only the reflection of the moon on a pond? She'd been flying for some time already and had no clue how far she'd gone or, as she now realized grimly, in what direction.

"Ye gads, Brindle, what the hell was I thinkin', flying for the first time in the black of night?" she complained miserably to the tree. "What if I can't find the way back home?"

Not knowing the answer to these questions either, or how to soothe her frazzled nerves, Brindle thought it best to maintain a confident silence. Donnie would figure something out, that much he did know.

Taking a few deep, calming breaths and telling herself firmly to get a grip, Donnie peered around her through the night air, searching for any landmarks that might help in getting her bearings. Nothing. Everything looked distorted beyond recognition and completely foreign to her. She couldn't even tell if those really were the Brumal Mountains behind her or just dark clouds in the distance. The panic within her breast was rising again, about to bubble over. Okay, who knew her heart could beat this loudly? Or this fast? Forget apoplexy, she should be more worried about her heart exploding.

As a last-ditch effort to check her mounting fear, she closed her eyes and tried seeing with her mind's eye, focusing her mind downward, listening to the Earth and hoping desperately that it would provide a means of orientating herself with the landscape below. At the very least, it should calm her nerves—*Please, gods, let it calm my nerves*, she prayed fervently.

Keeping her eyes closed tightly, Donnie concentrated on what was going on directly below her. Used as she was to looking underground this way, to her surprise, tonight it was like looking through night-vision goggles—as long as she kept her mind's eye aboveground, that is. With it, she could see everything as though it were daylight, but almost like what you'd view in a film negative. Not only that, but she could now hear the sounds of the surface night creatures all around, like the scrabbling and chittering of a raccoon up a tree, or the hoot of an owl and then the scratch of its claws and flap-flap of its wings as it took flight. She could also feel the souls of these animals. This gave her the "eureka" idea she'd been looking for—she focused on Rex's soul, since his was the one she knew best. Her mind's eye swiveled back behind her and to the left. It rushed to the barn, where, astonishingly, she could now see her pup clearly, even though his nose was still buried and he was invisible to the naked eye.

Crowing with delight, Donnie gave the broomstick a steady, soft push to the left with her right hand, flying a wide arc until she was headed back toward the farm. Homing in on Rex's soul would be the perfect way for her to find her way back! It wasn't quite like listening to the Earth, which was perfectly fine, since she couldn't go too far with that anyway because of all the noise and the resulting confusion it still generated in her mind. But, she figured the connection between her and Rex was so strong, she'd be able to find him anywhere.

She looked at him again with her mind's eye and thought about what a wonderful soul he had—sweet, loving and faithful. He was full of joy and fun, and ofttimes pure mischief, combined with a deep love for living every moment as if it were his best and his last. Admittedly never the brightest bulb in the package, he was no dimwit either, especially lately. Okay, common sense he sometimes lacked, but his book learnin' seemed to have come a long way now that he was magical. His familiar, warm, genuinely loving soul filled her with the fortitude she needed way up here, so high in the sky where she was precariously perched and unprotected.

Unprotected. Donnie suddenly realized that her teeth were chattering. It was freezing up here. She really was unprotected—from absolutely everything. Until now, her almost continuous rushes of adrenaline had kept her from feeling the cold anywhere but on her face, namely her nose. She hadn't planned for this very irritating and, what could soon become quite debilitating, new drawback. On the bright side though, she thought to herself, trying her best to stay positive, her flying charm had worked beautifully and, throughout the crazy gyrations she'd been experiencing, she hadn't felt any motion sickness or vertigo. Sure, she'd had the scare of her life, and her heart still resided firmly in her throat at the moment, but at least she hadn't been dizzy or nauseous. It was a small victory, yes; yet she took comfort from it.

But what to do about the cold? She ruminated over this for a while and eventually murmured to herself, "It worked on the septic tank. But this one will have to stop pretty much everything from reaching me…while still supporting a breathable atmosphere. Oh, and it'll have to protect me from as much of the cold air as possible, of course, and from whatever else I might need protection from without me having to even think about that kind of stuff. And it'll have to fit like a glove so I can fly through tight spaces, instead of just being a big block shield like the one

I used for the septic tank. Plus, it's gonna take a *lot* of power, judging from past experience. Nevertheless, it should work; after all, it always does in the movies. Well, that is, until someone figures out the frequency they're using for the shield, and then the darn things don't work so well at all, do they?...Um, yeah, well, I'll just have to alternate frequencies periodically then, won't I?" She stopped talking abruptly and banged herself on the forehead with a closed fist. "Fer chrissakes, what am I saying, alternating frequencies? What for? Like anyone's got a gizmo here to find the *one* frequency I'll be using? I mean, seriously, you idiot, get a grip and at least try it out!"

Having convinced herself of its potential viability, Donnie conjured a protective shield around herself, willing it to encase her in a bubble of her own energy that closely followed the contours of both her and the broomstick, like an integument covering a vital organ. Because she'd created a breathable shield like this one before, she knew just which gases to fill it with and at what ratios, and also how to filtrate the expelled carbon dioxide. She made minute adjustments to the gas proportions and then blew a warming breath into the protective membrane. Then another one, and another. Now that was much better. She felt almost human again; so much so that she took off her gloves and stuffed them into her pockets, the faintly blue shield matching her every movement perfectly.

When she'd created the shield, she had also willed it to cushion her from being whipped and buffeted by branches and the like while she was flying, so at least she shouldn't get hurt tonight. The only drawback was that the shield really did sap a lot of her power to generate and maintain; but, what the hay, Donnie figured it was worth it if it kept her safe and unharmed, although it also meant her reserve power might very well be depleted tonight, which could make for a real problem.

But she would just have to worry about that tomorrow. She and Brindle had a job to do tonight and, just like that demented knife in her cupboard, they were going to do it! Steeling herself, Donnie informed her erratically beating heart that it was time to get serious about this flying stuff. She mentally reviewed what she'd learned so far regarding the maneuverability of her magical steed. One good thing had certainly come of her wild ride—she'd learned exactly what *not* to do on the broomstick.

The next song the boombox let loose on was "Flyin' High Above It All" by Shiloh. Donnie chided it for being so obvious. It ignored her and played the song anyway.

Donnie increased the power of the blue light-ball on the end of the broomstick, narrowing its field so that it became a powerful headlight illuminating her skyway, and proceeded to put herself through her paces, practicing every possible maneuver she could think up for the broomstick, using mostly the pressure of her hands on the broomstick for steering and altitude (yaw and pitch, for those into aeronautical terms) and her feet as the accelerator and brakes and, of course, to spin (a.k.a., thrust and roll). As her flight prowess improved, she began to use weight ratios to spin and curve more efficiently, learning quickly just how much she should lean or how fast she should whip her body around to facilitate the turn or spin, depending on her speed. To see if she could improve her aerodynamics, she tried stretching her body out nearly flat on the broomstick, her protective shield following her movements so that she looked like a long, blue bullet racing across the sky. While Donnie could see where this might get her a few more miles per hour, especially when flying close to the ground, it was extremely uncomfortable and, as one should do with any failed experiment, she abandoned the idea and sat up tall in the saddle.

Within half an hour, she'd quite gotten the hang of flying the broomstick and was zooming into narrow spaces between tree tops. Then, becoming braver, she threaded her way around tree trunks and under low branches, skimmed over mountain-tops and down their sides, plowed into the still waters of lakes with her boots making trails on their surface, and flipped through narrow ravines as if she'd been born to flying a broomstick. Only once did she almost crash and burn, and that simply because she'd gotten reckless. She flew a little too close to a huge oak and just barely brushed her right side against the tree's trunk, a mistake that sent her spinning and bouncing uncontrollably off other trees. After she smacked into the seventh tree in as many seconds, Donnie ricocheted into a clearing where a small stream bubbled merrily and she was able to right herself.

Hallelujah, hallelujah, hallelujah! Her shield and saddle had both worked wonders during the crash and she felt no worse for wear than if she'd been losing at bumper cars. She grinned beatifically and lowered her shield momentarily to dip a shaky, relieved hand into the stream so she could splash her face with it, finding herself unable to resist drinking a couple handfuls of the cold, oddly invigorating water, and was more than a little disconcerted a moment later when she received a strong sense of déjà vu from these actions. Shaking the odd feeling off, she sped on once more, coming around to attempt the same route as before, only this time she missed the oak by at least an inch.

Nearing the end of her training run, she came to a stop and hovered above a thick, fluffy cloud that was moving slowly over her little cottage and its valley. The boombox began playing "Spend the Day Your Way" by Blind Moment. Okay, this was it, Donnie told herself sternly, she only had to do one more test of her aeronautical nerve and she'd be ready to begin her hunt. It was time to test rocket mode.

She pointed the broom straight up once again and zoomed higher and higher. Several seconds later she looked back over her shoulder to see the Earth receding quickly. Not high enough yet. She kicked the stirrups harder. The broomstick responded by leaping ahead at almost double its previous speed.

When Donnie felt that she was finally high enough for her test, she came to a stop, pushed down slowly on the broomstick so that she was parallel to the Earth, and floated in mid-air. Since she was getting cold again, she blew another warming breath into her protective shield. She looked down and could just make out the outlines of the lands and seas below her. She could see all the way to the ends of the Earth, or at least to where its horizons curved round. The moon gleamed large and white, straight ahead as it made its latest pass around the Earth, and a few more grey, puffy clouds floated serenely far beneath Donnie. She lifted her gaze toward the heavens above and finally saw almost every one of those billions and billions of stars that Carlton Averworthy had forever alluded to in his *Universe* specials. He'd been right, their scope *is* breathtaking.

"So, this is the middle atmosphere, huh? It's very pretty up here, innit? A bit cold, though. Hey, Brindle, you there?" Donnie asked.

"Yes, Donemere," the tree responded.

"You okay?"

"Yes."

"Are you having fun?"

"Fun?" Brindle was obviously perplexed by her question.

"Yeah, you know, amusement, pleasure, that kind of thing."

The old tree thought hard, then replied, "It is exhilarating to move so nimbly and, of course, it's quite pleasurable to travel. But then, I have always been one to journey far afield whenever I explored the world. In my youth, I wandered the lands from Annûar to Aldera and on to the farthest reaches of the Cordain Mountains, just beyond the Brumals. I watched the doings of vinca and men and elves and wizards, of okûn and trolls and other beings, some magical, some not. Many times I envied their ability to move freely, while I was forced to root myself for very long periods. It now appears that you have given me the capacity to move freely without being tethered to one place. If that is fun, then yes, Donemere, I am having it."

The boombox was playing the softer section of the song now, which was Donnie's favorite part. While it was perfect for way up here in the mesosphere, it was also time to get a move on. Donnie took one last look up at the stars and then said to her saddle, "I'm glad of that, my friend. Hopefully, you'll still think so positively of it a few minutes from now. Um, you can't actually see where we're going, can you, Brindle?"

"In my fashion, yes. Would you prefer I not do that?"

"No, it's okay. I just don't want you to freak out because of what I'm about to have us do. But you trust me, right?"

"Implicitly."

"That's good. At least one of us does," she joked. "Well, here goes nuthin'."

Because she was never one for half-measures, Donnie flipped them around so that they were facing straight down, leaned back in the saddle and kicked her feet hard several times, all in one smooth movement. The song ratcheted back up to its driving tempo just as the broom shot toward the ground, the stick building up speed quickly until it broke the sound barrier less than two miles later. The loud, continuous *BOOM!* and the accompanying sudden flash of brilliant blue as Donnie's powers tripled awoke all sleeping creatures within earshot of its report and scared the daylights out of those who were already awake.

Meanwhile, the broomstick was still in its breakneck nose-dive. With the ground approaching at nearly eight hundred miles per hour, Donnie, a self-satisfied smile playing upon her lips, was preoccupied with congratulating herself heartily for not only having the forethought to re-strengthen her shield to protect them from the G-forces she knew they'd experience in the dive, but for thinking of it *before* they took off in rocket mode. Looking straight ahead of her, or to be more precise, straight down toward the ground, she could make out the cottage now, with the forest circled around it. "Yep, that's home all right," she muttered bemusedly, watching the valley become more recognizable in but a few seconds.

It suddenly occurred to her that she was fast running out of time. She'd calculated that she'd have about three minutes to fly in rocket mode safely from her starting point in the mesosphere. That time was almost up and if she didn't do something soon, either turn out of the nose dive or come to a stop, she was going to crash into the ground at somewhere a bit over the speed of sound. Which would probably hurt, and pretty badly at that. Could her saddle and shield protect her well enough from a crash like that? What if she was wrong and she wasn't immortal, or rather, wasn't immortal *yet*? What if becoming immortal was the somewhat questionable "prize" for passing the tests the gods had set for her? She thought about all of this in the instant before she squeezed her eyes shut and stomped on the stirrups, holding on for dear life as she abruptly came to a jerking halt.

There was no resulting crash, but she *was* suddenly engulfed by a blindingly bright light. Donnie opened her eyes and found herself staring at the roof of the stables, the nose of the broomstick hovering no more than two inches from it. The glare was coming from the reflection of the light-ball off the bright yellow thatch covering the stables' roof. Donnie gulped down some air and pulled the broomstick up so that it was horizontal once more, the blazing light now focused in front of her at the deep black of the night air.

Boudreau's "Free" came on the boombox, perfectly echoing the overwhelming sentiment Donnie held in her heart. She sat there listening to it for a minute as a slow smile spread across her face. She hadn't given up; frightened out of her wits as she'd been, she hadn't given up! Never had she felt so free, and now she could actually fly!

She heard Falwaïn's voice calling to her as he bounded off the back porch and ran toward the stables. "Donemere, is that you? Do you need help? I heard a long, loud explosion of some sort—" and then, "Donnie! What are you doing up there?" he shouted incredulously when he reached the far side of the stables and could now see Donnie floating above it on the broomstick. She let out a peal of confident laughter and shouted back to him that she was fine, just fine. He repeated his question, wanting to know what she was doing. Then he wanted to know whatever could she be flying on? He told her to come down, but Donnie said no, she couldn't do that. She had something very important to do first. Her voice edged with ecstasy, she explained to him that she'd just passed her first test and now needed to get on with her other ones so that she could be a witch in good standing.

Good standing with who, Falwaïn wanted to know, but Donnie was already hurtling upward when she heard his question. She flew a wide loop around the farm and then a tight vertical one above it, whooping with joy mainly because, well, who wouldn't in these circumstances? Now that she'd gotten the hang of it, flying on the broomstick made her feel almost reborn because, right now, in this very moment, she was so completely in tune with herself and her powers. She just knew that she could do anything she set her mind or heart to, as if both were entwined and firmly encased by the very depths of her soul. She was right where she was supposed to be and she was strong within herself, stronger than she'd ever been before, with or without magic in her fingertips. And, man, was she ever relieved to finally begin her quest for home in earnest. She was more than ready to meet her challenges—heck, she was actually looking forward to them!

As she once again zoomed away from the farm, she shouted down an answer to Falwaïn's question, but he was certain he could not have heard her correctly. Whatever could the gods have to do with her flying about in the heavens upon what appeared to be a kitchen broom?

Setting a course toward the northeast, Donnie extinguished the lightball for the present, guiding herself by ambient light or, as she liked to think of it, by the light of the silvery moon. She could see the Brumal Mountains looming ever larger as she rapidly approached their towering peaks. She stayed west of them and flew a jagged line north, searching the skies in front of her for any sign of the flying machine that was turning her forest friends to stone, all the while swaying and bouncing crazily in the saddle to song after song. Brindle kept watch behind them and they both checked to the sides. They'd been searching for almost an hour when suddenly the boombox began going crazy, playing bits of Debra Mait's "Turned Your Heart to Stone" and then "Camera" by Golden Lion.

Donnie turned eastwardly and spotted their prey, right as it was releasing several beams of light toward the ground, near the foot of the mountains. The beams swept the area for a few seconds, then suddenly disappeared. But Donnie was almost upon the machine by this time and she could just see the faint running lights around its middle. She zoomed all the way up to what she discovered was some sort of rondure and stopped a couple of feet away, relighting the light-ball on the end of the broomstick so that the hovering sphere, as it turned out to be, was now bathed in a brilliant blue glow. The boombox continued alternating songs until Donnie hissed at it in exasperation, "Yeah, okay, okay, enough! I get it now, so hush while I think." The boombox fell silent with a flash of its red LED lights.

The mechanical globe was about three feet in diameter and made of smooth metal plates, with what appeared to be extendible glass lenses every six inches or so dotted around its exterior. Donnie could just make out a weirdly shimmering logo imprinted near the running lights.

One of the sphere's lenses whirred and clicked as it focused on Donnie. She looked directly into it and cheerfully baited it with, "Got your heart set on playing *Fun with Field Mice*? Or are you up for a game of *Whack the Witch*? What's it gonna be, my feckless little artificial foe?"

As if in answer, the machine darted to within a couple inches of her and shot out some grappling hooks from flaps hidden within its metal plating. They flailed vainly in Donnie's wake as she zoomed up and over the sphere. She spun around quickly, floating in the air about twenty feet distant.

She focused her mind's eye upon the sphere, probing its inner workings. Ah, yes, it was most definitely run by computer code comprised of a set of extremely complex algorithms that were flashing white across her mind at unreadable speeds. "So, it can think for itself, can it?" Donnie mused. Rats, she'd hoped it was controlled remotely, which would've meant a time delay and a bit of an edge for her, while the controller programmed instructions to it. "Is nothing ever easy?" she complained with a heavy, dramatic sigh, cocking her head sideways. "Am I doomed to always having to do things the hard way?"

The sphere powered up four of the lenses facing her and released a beam of light from each. Donnie swore she could feel the very air below her solidify and drop to the ground as she once again shot over the top of the metallic beast, the light-beams missing her by a millionth of a second. Brindle called out that the machine was approaching fast on their hindquarters.

"Game on!" Donnie challenged the mechanical monster pursuing them.

George Thurl's "Midnight Flight" came on the boombox. Donnie shot an amused grin at the thing, then sang along with the song at the top of her lungs. With the music of the future echoing over the land, she led the sphere on a merry chase, first high in the skies and then down below the tree tops in the hopes that the thing would make even the tiniest of mistakes and end up smashing itself on a rock or a tree trunk. She once again re-strengthened her shield to protect herself from being whipped by the branches of the trees as she passed by them, often perilously close. Zigzagging her way through the forest, she could hear the beams of light from the zooming globe petrifying parts of the trees along its path. Donnie continued to flip and twirl the broomstick through seemingly impossible holes in the intricate weave of the forest ceiling, the maniacal machine always close on her tail. She sent a searing lightning bolt of magic at it, hoping to blow it up, but it dodged to the right and she only succeeded in damaging a tree, blasting off half the branches on one side. She vowed not to try that twice.

Still berating herself for her blunder, she skyrocketed up and out of the trees, ascending to the heavens once more. The sphere followed. Donnie dove to the ground, pulling out of the dive at the last moment to glide inches above the earth. No more than a second later, she heard the loud crack of the ground beneath her as it was transformed into stone. Swinging around some boulders, she zoomed to the forest again, when suddenly the boombox changed songs, popping from "Wailin' Back to Biloxi" by Little Jimmy Smith into Tension's otherworldly lament, "Lone Tree Requiem."

With trees and rocks flying by so quickly they were almost unrecognizable, Donnie concentrated on the broomstick's speed more than movement, and managed to put a little distance between herself and her pursuer. Calamitous cameras, she *really* needed to do something fast before that aberrant shutterfly turned the entire area to stone! Could she write an error line to its code, a bug of some sort that would cause a glitch in its programming? Donnie tried to insert a line of nonsense, just to see if she could. Immediately, the algorithm changed and she was locked out, blocked from even being able to view the code. Then she realized what song the boombox was playing.

"Brindle!" Donnie shouted through the rush of oncoming air.

"Yes?" the tree called back.

"Are there any magical forests around here?"

"The closest is yours."

Oh, great, that was too far away. "Are you sure there aren't any magical trees around here? There's got to be at least one, and I know you know him!"

Brindle thought hard and finally said, "There was one I knew who was traveling this way many, many years ago. His name was Cyllwyn Mérd."

Donnie sent a call out to the tree with her mind and waited for a response. Getting none, she shot upward again and flew higher, sending out another, more powerful call. To the northeast she heard a faint rumbling noise, then a groggy, "Who calls me from slumber?"

Donnie spun to her right and flew in a straight, fast line toward the voice. She touched the weeping willow tree's mind with her own, opening herself up so that he could see inside her and know that what she had to tell him was true. She explained what she and Brindle were doing by sending him a series of mental pictures. Then she relayed her plan to the tree in the same manner. Cyllwyn Mérd regretfully informed her that he no longer had the power to do as she asked because he was dying and his magic had ebbed to the shores of Canavar.

"You needn't worry about that because I can give you a shot of mine," replied Donnie. "I ask only if you're willing to go along with my plan. I can't force you to do it, nor will I try to talk you into it. This has to be your choice, pure and simple. You know what it's likely to do to you, right? And that it would happen tonight—well, actually right now..." she trailed off, her voice tentative and full of apology.

Cyllwyn Mérd's reply took a while to come, but when he answered, it was with conviction. "I am willing, though it means my farewell to this fair and glorious land this sad night. But then, perhaps 'tis time for me to leave this life and begin a new journey, as I truly cannot last much more on this one. I am old and weak, and have traveled too many lands that no longer bear the Wonder of the Wise to believe that I shall have enough of that sweet power within me ever again to journey elsewhere in Medregai. Yes, I will aid you most eagerly, Donemere of the Codlebærn, for I am grateful to be provided an opportunity to leave my life the way I have lived it; amongst my friends and fighting for what is good in this world."

By this time the sphere had caught up to Donnie and was riding her tail hard, forcing her to resort once more to evasive maneuvers. Donnie, holding tightly to the broomstick, looked miserable. "Please accept my deepest apology, Cyllwyn Mérd," she cried to the tree, "but I honestly cannot think of another way to rid Medregai of this anachronistic monster tonight. Your sacrifice will not go unnoticed by the gods; I'll see to that." She squared her jaw determinedly and repeated her vow, "I'll see to that myself. Farewell to you, Cyllwyn Mérd, and may you enjoy safe passage through your next three lives. Blessed be, my friend. I shall carry you with me always." As she blessed the tree, Donnie pushed on the broomstick and rode it downward, skimming along the Earth's surface and through the forest where Cyllwyn Mérd stood atop a small hill in the center of a bog, the boombox mysteriously assuring her that she would see him again one day.

Donnie slowed her speed to make sure the sphere was right behind her and would have no chance for recovery. She broke out of the forest and headed straight up the hillside toward the great willow's trunk. Before she veered at the last micro-second, Donnie shot a bolt of blue light from her right hand into the trunk, imbuing the gigantic tree with just enough of her magical power to put her plan into action. Instantly, the tree's outer branches closed up like a many-fingered fist. It allowed Donnie to slip through mostly untouched, while at the same time it maintained a firm grasp on the sphere.

When Donnie was about to clear the last branch, it swayed in front of her. A twig broke off as she passed by and she instinctively reached beyond her shield to catch it in her hand, wanting to keep a part of the living tree with her.

The moment the twig touched her skin, she felt a jolt of power, her own power, reintegrate itself into her body. Along with it came a panoply of images that flashed through her mind as the weeping willow's massive life essence poured into her. Its memories tumbled into Donnie all at once and, in that instant, she gained Cyllwyn Mérd's entire life history. With great tenderness, Donnie felt the soul he had nurtured within himself, that of a kind and wise friend to all fair creatures. He, like Brindle and Sophie, had been alive a very, very long time and had recorded much of Medregai's history within his growth rings.

Vastly humbled and more than a little bewildered by the overpowering experience, Donnie realized, as she brought the broomstick to a halt, that her last statement to the ancient tree had come true. Cyllwyn Mérd had somehow gifted his soul to her so that it could live on forever within her. Donnie's heart ached at the beauty and the sheer sadness of that deed. She let loose of the twig, no longer needing a keepsake with which to remember the valiant tree. A long series of loud cracks resounded as the metal sphere radiated beams from each of its lenses until Cyllwyn Mérd and the surrounding earth and bushes were all completely petrified. While all this devastation was being wrought, Donnie hovered nearby, sorrowfully listening to the tree's tightly curved limbs being changed into stone, just barely keeping her tears at bay.

The boombox fell silent when the last, mournful strains of the song faded. Donnie stayed where she was for a very long time, listening to the rattling of the sphere against its self-made cage as it tried to break itself free. But the stone willow's many branches held it fast. Donnie kept calling out to Cyllwyn Mérd with her mind, hoping against all odds that she'd been wrong about his demise and that she was merely holding his essence for temporary safekeeping, that perhaps the time to see him again was now. But no response came.

A deepening anguish overtook her and she told Brindle in a small voice, her breath hitching, "Let's go home." She slowly wheeled the broomstick around and they zoomed south, flying in a straight line back toward the cottage.

She took out the folded scroll, wanting to reread what it had said about demanding a life. She redirected the light from the light-ball on the front of the broomstick so that she could see properly. When she unfolded the parchment, she saw through tear-blurred eyes that new lines of text had been added under the first trial, and only the first one. It now read:

Reach for the heavens to meet thy treue self.
Thy noble triune of mind, heart, and soul shall be made whole and one with Time.
Allow it to be thy inmost guide.

She had not passed the second trial then, at least not yet. But how, she agonized, was she ever supposed to accept that the beautiful, wise old tree was no more, solely because of her own actions?

Donnie forced the broomstick to its, as of yet, fastest speed because of an urgent need to seek comfort from her friends. Within a quarter hour, she saw light coming from behind the curtains of the office, faintly illuminating the steps of the back porch. The boombox disappeared as soon as Donnie's feet hit the ground. Numb from the emotional drain of her roller-coaster experiences during the past few hours, Donnie's movements were purely mechanical as she floated the saddle back onto the rail in the stables and said goodnight to Brindle. She stood the broomstick on end, placed her witch's hat on top of its handle, then dematerialized both to the kitchen.

When the outside door of the library opened to admit her a minute later, the candlelight spilled into the night, reflecting off her pale and drawn face. Falwaïn jumped up from the desk and spun to face her. Donnie stood there with tears finally beginning to roll freely down her cheeks. Falwaïn quickly crossed the distance between them and placed his arm around her shoulders, drawing her inside the room. The door closed solidly behind them.

He led Donnie to the couch, where she sat, looking small and tired, her breaths coming in hiccups of despair. After pouring her some brandy from the sideboard, he knelt before her, placed the glass in her hands and lifted it to her mouth, bidding her to drink. She took a small sip, but shook her head and pushed the glass away. Falwaïn put it on the side table and sat next to her on the couch, gathering her to his breast.

And then he let her cry, soothing her with soft caresses and calming words until her tears eventually ran dry. They sat quietly for some time, his arms wrapped tightly around her and her face buried in his chest. They parted only when she stirred. He handed her the glass of brandy once more, along with a box of tissues from the table, and asked what had occurred. After drying her cheeks and blowing her nose, Donnie stood up and began shedding her outer wear while, as succinctly as possible, she told him what she'd done.

Taking hold of her hand when she finished her tale, Falwaïn drew her back down onto the couch with him. "Tell me, little one, why does besting this machine fill you with such sadness?" His concerned look deepened as his eyes searched her desolated ones.

Donnie shook her head, wiping her mouth with the back of her hand. "That part doesn't. Oh, see, it's like this—since I came to Witchcraft, I've become the kind of person who, whenever I find a spider or some other bug in the house, instead of squashing it, I pick it up and put it outside because I can feel its soul, simple though it be. The rare times I do kill one by accident, I always beg its forgiveness and wish it well on its next life's journey, grieving for its loss.

"But tonight, I deliberately killed someone with a knowing soul. I understood exactly what I was asking Cyllwyn Mérd to do and so did he. And yet he still agreed to do it. I only knew him for a few minutes, but he gave himself to me, let me see inside his rings of memory so that I could know him, *really* know him. He desperately wanted to live on within me...and then a moment later, I killed him." She stared at Falwaïn, wide-eyed with self-loathing.

He brushed the hair from around her face tenderly before replying, his tone solemn. "But you did not kill him, Donemere. Even the gods must believe that because you still have your powers. No, he made his choice freely. If he'd chosen not to do as you asked, you would've found another way to defeat that machine. Perhaps not tonight, but you would've prevailed on another night. And remember, Cyllwyn Mérd himself told you that he was near death anyway. You said his voice had faded and he admitted that his magic was no more. Possibly you have set him on a far better path, to begin his next journey through an act of love and self-sacrifice. That is a happier end than most of us will receive when our time has come."

Donnie looked at Falwaïn gratefully and whispered her thanks. His words gave her peace because he was right. Cyllwyn Mérd had given his life willingly in order to save his friends of the forest, and because of his sacrifice, Donnie had therefore been allowed to bless his next three lives in accordance with the Law of Return. There was nothing more she could have done. She must accept his death and her part in it.

Furthermore, the camera would now stay where it was until its power source ran down and it was eventually disintegrated by the elements. Donnie thought she could probably help those processes along some. Together, she and Cyllwyn Mérd had ensured that thousands of creatures could live their lives, from this night onward, without fear of being turned to stone every time they ventured away from the safety of their nest or den.

As she thought all this and felt its acceptance in her heart, she realized that the second trial had just been passed because a small blue wave of magical energy flew outwardly from her mid-section, startling Falwaïn. Closing her eyes, she concentrated her mind's eye on the scroll lying flat along her belly. Yes, the lines below the second trial had been filled in. They read:

> *Demand death, tho' ye must accept the life that is gifted.*
> *Revere death as ye do life, for neither is the end of the journey.*
> *Be mindful that the dead, not solely the living, may provide wise counsel.*

Unsure what the last line meant, Donnie snuggled into Falwaïn's shoulder and molded herself to his warmth. For the first time since arriving back at the cottage, she glanced at the desk and saw that it was covered with several tall stacks of books and magazines. Arching an eyebrow, she observed dryly, "Looks like you've been very busy yourself tonight. Some of that's pretty heavy reading. And some of it's not, I see."

She felt his nod over the top of her head. "I've been learning about your world," he said slowly, his voice contemplative and serious." It must be a strange and wondrous place. Yet for all its advances and wonders, it doesn't appear to be a place of contentment. Nonetheless, I hope to visit it one day with you. It's quite possible you might make sense of it for me where I see none now."

"Mmm," said Donnie noncommittally. "Did you read any of the Mueler books?" she asked, then yawned widely.

Falwaïn laid his cheek against her hair. "Yes, and several other books and articles about various versions of Medregai, or Midgard or Middle Earth as it is called in your time. What I read in the Mueler books was fairly accurate, although there are a few embellishments and a number of small errors in both renditions. And, of course, the names are all quite different in the one from your time."

"To protect the innocent, apparently." She sighed in response to his quizzical expression. "Yeah, that didn't work the other day with Warren and Sylvester either. Well, all I can say is, welcome to recorded history. It's always like that, you know—subjective, I mean. Ten people see the same event, and when you ask them about it an hour later, you get ten different stories." She yawned again.

Falwaïn smiled and lightly kissed her forehead. "You're in need of sleep, my lady. Off to bed with you."

"What about you? Don't you need sleep?"

"I'm long accustomed to having no sleep for many days at a time. And besides, I've slept so much of late, I might not need more for an entire cycle of the moon. I'm enjoying my—my research, I believe is what you'd call it, and so I shall remain here until it's light. Come, I'll see you to your bed." He grinned down at her once again. "But no more than that...for now, at least."

He was true to his word, tucking the bedclothes around Donnie and pressing a lingering kiss on her temple before leaving. She passed into dreams almost immediately, taking only a moment to pinpoint something that was bothering her. As her mind tumbled toward sleep, she realized that Falwaïn's speech pattern had changed after reading about her world tonight; he'd used several modern contractions in their late-night conversation.

Soon, she would need to decide just what she was going to do with him when this was all over.

Chapter 13
Love Prayer

The next morning, for the first time in months, Donnie did not awaken because of the rising sun, nor was there accompanying music. In fact, what roused her from slumber was the sudden pressure of a body sitting on the bed next to her, and all she could hear was light breathing.

She opened her eyes and saw Falwaïn's clear blue ones twinkling down at her.

"Good morn, my lady," he said pleasantly. "I was beginning to wonder if you'd ever awaken. It's been daylight for some time now. Warren has arrived, and we've saddled and packed your bags on the horses. We await your presence so that we may break our fast and be on our way." He shook Donnie lightly when her eyelids closed again. "Ah-ah, none of that; you must arise!" he told her in a stern voice.

She grinned sleepily and put her hand on his arm where it lay against her stomach, sending its warmth coursing through her. "Had a busy night, you know, so I'm a sleepy gal." Her eyes opened wide as she realized what he'd just said. "Heeeyyy, wait a minute, you called him Warren and not his real name!"

Falwaïn shrugged his shoulders. "He's decided he prefers that name, now that *he* is master of his destiny, that is."

"Huh, really? Well, I'm glad I could help him out. You know, new destiny, new name. All in a day's work!" Donnie gave a huge yawn behind her hand and then smiled sweetly. "Tell you what, give me six minutes and I'll be out, ready to eat. You can even time me, if you'd like."

She'd given him her grandfather's old wristwatch the day before and shown him how to use it. Falwaïn checked it now and asked if she wanted to put a wager on the time she'd need.

Donnie's right eyebrow rose as she sat up and beamed back at him. "Oh, sure, you're on! The loser makes breakfast." Although Falwaïn was not to know this, her morning ablutions never took longer than six minutes. She, on the other hand, knew this quite well, simply because she'd timed herself on many, many occasions, she had been *that* bored here. Even when she did shower, it would add only another six minutes. So, did she feel bad about making this bet with him now, knowing full well that she'd win it? Are you kidding?

When she opened the bedroom door and walked into the outer room a few minutes later, fully clothed, hair and teeth brushed, and still with thirty seconds to spare, she crowed smugly, "I win and I'm starving! What're you gonna make for breakfast?" She blinked innocently at Falwaïn, who was standing in front of the stove.

She could see him shake with mirth. "The trees told me yesterday that you never spend more than six minutes getting ready in the morning, so I knew I would lose our wager," he conceded as he backed away from the stove and gestured toward a large pan with a number of eggs frying in it. "As you can see, breakfast is nearly ready." He turned back to the heat complacently.

A little deflated, Donnie glanced about the kitchen. The table was set for four and the loaf of bread from last night was sitting beside a plate that had some pats of plain butter laid out on it. She went to the fridge, grabbed the strawberry jam jar and placed it on the table. Then she retrieved the four-slice toaster from its cupboard and, on the off-chance it would work, cut four slices of bread and slid them into the slots. When she pushed down on the handle, the heating elements began to glow.

She shook her head wonderingly and declared, "At least I have the satisfaction of knowing that I'll never again have to write a check for an exorbitant and insanely inflated utility bill. Thank heavens the oil industry doesn't control the flow of magic. Have you seen the prices of oil and gasoline these days—they're outrageous!" she complained, looking at Falwaïn with a cynical expression on her face. "You must know what I'm talkin' about, since I noticed last night that you'd been reading several newspapers and magazines from my world."

Falwaïn turned around again, excitement on his features now, with the metal turner in his hand bobbing and weaving as he admitted fervently, "Yes, I did read about that in several of the periodicals from the last few months. And there was another story about it in this morning's *SFTimes*. I see that California has one of the highest gasoline prices in your country because of the stricter emission rates the gas suppliers must meet. I gather that's because of pollution, correct? I must admit, though, I'm not exactly certain for what those particular types of fuel are used, especially the crude oil, other than to make gasoline for these machines called cars that are pictured repeatedly throughout your magazines and newspapers; which tells me that they are obviously quite popular in your world. Nor am I sure I understand your world's money system. There are so many, many types of currency, I can't imagine how everyone keeps them all straight, and why you must use one currency in one place, but an entirely different one right next door, instead of just using gold coin everywhere. As I'm sure you can tell, I didn't spend a lot of time studying those subjects.

"What I did read about rather extensively last night, though, was *electricity*." Falwaïn's eyes fairly gleamed with electricity as he went on about this subject. "And I learned that practically all the machines in your kitchen need it to work. I also learned how electricity is generated—the turbine concept is fascinating, by the way. I would never have thought to harness elements such as wind and water to produce an energy source that can be used the way your civilization does. And the solar technology is stunning, truly quite impressive." His expression showed just how impressive he thought this was. "Yes, well, my point is that now I understand why you were so upset by Warren's news of Mâlendian yesterday. The human body's electrical pulse is normally so small, it could never be used to power the machines of your world. Yet you appear to be generating a plentiful supply of magical power that is being picked up, not only by the good people of Mâlendian, as you call them, but also by your appliances." Falwaïn turned back to the eggs and moved them around in the butter, going on to remark shyly, "It's quite possible that more of your machines will also work now. If so, at some point, I'd like to view this television box I read about during the night. I realize it'll only work here with a DVD, but I'm rather hoping you'll agree to show it to me. It's both a video and an audio experience I should very much like to have."

By the time he finished speaking, Donnie had been staring open-mouthed at him for at least a full minute. "Ah, yeah," she gulped. "What else did you read about last night?"

Falwaïn's head shook slowly from side to side when he replied, "Many, many things. Man has made great strides in knowledge by your time. So many of the concepts are difficult for me to accept, some even to understand. But perhaps we can fill time today by going over some of it—would you be amenable to that?" He flipped the eggs over and looked at her, jerking his head toward the pan, "Are these acceptable this way? Over-easy, I mean."

Donnie shut her gaping mouth once again and nodded without even glancing at the pan. "Sure, they're fine." She continued to stare at Falwaïn. She hadn't figured on him having such an insatiable curiosity, or being driven enough to attempt satisfying it by apparently reading almost everything in her library in one night. "Did you get *any* sleep?" she asked him.

"An hour, no more, before Warren returned."

"And you read all that in one night?" she squeaked, awestruck. "Wow, you make Martha Farell look like a beginner!"

"Oh, not quite!" Falwaïn protested, chuckling proudly. "Her speeds were truly admirable. As for my own paltry abilities, it helps that you charmed the books to turn to the precise page that contains the desired information. I'm afraid, though, that something I did made your library grow."

Donnie snickered. "Oh, that's nothing you did, trust me," she laughingly reassured him. She inserted four more slices of bread into the toaster and then set the butter knife to buttering the finished toast. "See, when I charmed the library," she explained, turning back to him, "without really thinking about it, I put in a line about always being able to find any book or information I might ever need. What I didn't realize at the time was that the charm would somehow reproduce absolutely any book—even though it's never been in my library! It crosses time to find what it's looking for and, *pffft*, suddenly there it is, large as life, right on the bookshelf in front of me. But the sweetest part, as you found out, is that I can still get a copy of the latest *SFTimes* whenever I want it. Oh, by the way, a bunch more of the back issues are stacked up on one of the bookshelves in the last row, in case you want to leaf through them later."

"I might do that," said Falwaïn, glancing at her over his shoulder as he turned his attention to the eggs again. "Perhaps they will help me to understand more about your world. It really is a wonderfully extensive library you have here; there is so much information contained in it. Before this, I never imagined anything like it could exist anywhere. I walked around its shelves for a while last night just to read the book titles and was amazed at the range and depth of the subject matter," he admitted, cracking another four eggs into the frying pan after off-loading the cooked ones onto a couple of plates.

Donnie looked pleased and informed him, "Do you know, I started out with less than a tenth of the books I have now! Thankfully, the walls extend automatically whenever more bookcases get added." She paused dramatically before adding, "Yet another example of why you should be very careful about what you ask for—especially with magic. Now watch, with you also using it, I'll bet the library's going to grow exponentially, so that we'll probably end up with more books than the Library of Congress!"

"Wouldn't that be marvelous?" Falwaïn mused dreamily and Donnie, taken aback by the abject joy this prospect seemed to generate in him, agreed with a silent nod, wondering just what she had kindled within him. He gave her a quick grin, said he'd call the others in to eat, and strode out the front door.

While he was gone, Donnie toasted and buttered another round of bread, afterward stacking the toast on a plate in the middle of the table. She flipped the eggs over with a quick wave, had the pan dump them onto the waiting plates, and then cracked four more into the pan, returning it to the burner's heat. She also got out her coffee maker and proceeded to brew some coffee for the meal.

The dog and cat came in together, followed by the men, who first washed their hands at the kitchen sink, then sat down at the table, while Donnie retrieved coffee mugs from the cupboard. It appeared that each of them had built up quite an appetite overnight, for every morsel of food was gone in under ten minutes, and conversation was kept to the minimum of "Pass the toast, please," or "Might I have more of that delicious strawberry jam?"

Sylvester sat on the end of the table and delicately ate his eggs, his defiant back turned toward Donnie, pointedly ignoring her after having first glared balefully at her when he'd darted through the front door. He was obviously quite upset with her, presumably about last night.

Rex, on the other hand, plowed gleefully through the eggs and the three cups of kibble in his food bowl, as always eating as though it were his last meal. He then let out a huge belch.

"Good out, honey! You haven't burped like that in a while," praised Donnie as she leaned back and smiled at her pup.

"I feel real good, Mama. Happy, you know?" Rex wagged his tail furiously at her. "It's about time you left here. It'll be kinda like a vacation. You're gonna like it out there, it's a very pretty land. I should know, 'cause I've gotten to explore it lots of times over the last few months."

Donnie became very still, staring at him in surprise. "Oh?" she said. "And just how did you do that?"

Rex stopped, blinked once, then blinked again nervously, saying in a rush, "Well, I just kinda went out and toured around a bit. Here and there, I mean. Well, most days, I guess. Y'see, I can run for a really long while now and, er, you know, I'm super-fast, so I can cover a lot of ground!"

Warren grinned at Donnie and bade her, "Don't brace his cups, Donemere, he's honest and true. And a good dog. Leave him be."

She smiled faintly in response to this. "I would, except for one thing. Up until a few days ago, this whole valley and all the lands around here were under the binding spell, remember? Nobody could get in or out, except for Mickey T and the few other animals who were allowed through to pass messages between you and Sylvester." Donnie abruptly turned back toward the dog. "And—I'm guessin'—you. Is that right? *Have* you been able to leave, while the rest of us have been stuck here, O' doggie dog mine?"

Her dog looked at her sheepishly. "Why, Mama, all this time I didn't even know there was a binding spell put on the valley. Well, to be honest, I'm not sure I know 'zactly what a binding spell is. Sylvester tried to explain a few times 'bout one, but I didn't understand what little he could actually manage to eke out about it."

Donnie studied her pup for a few moments, then raised an eyebrow, looking at him disbelievingly. "Who are you tryin' to kid, Science Boy?"

Rex glanced guiltily at first her, and then the cat. "Sorry, Sylvester. I told you she'd find out somehow—she always knows when I'm lyin'."

Sylvester rolled his eyes at the dog and muttered exasperatedly under his breath, "Possibly because you do it so badly!" as Donnie turned on the cat with, "You knew he's been leaving and you didn't feel it necessary to tell me that, Sylvester? A fine familiar you've turned out to be!"

"I could not tell you until the spell was released!" the cat retorted, clearly flustered. "And there simply has not been an appropriate time between then and now to inform you of it. Might I point out that last night, while you were off capturing the flying machine, may have been the perfect opportunity for us to discuss it! But that would have meant you had taken me with you and not charmed me to sleep the night through; would it not? And before you ask further, I do not know why Rex was allowed to leave when we were not. The most likely explanation is that whoever cast the spell was unaware of his presence when they bound us." The baleful glare was back.

Only somewhat mollified, Donnie continued to eye the cat suspiciously. "Okay, I'll let it go for now," she said at last. "I don't guess it matters all that much anyway...hopefully. As to last night, knowing you, you would've tried to stop me, telling me I wasn't ready for it yet or some such nonsense as that. And I couldn't take you with me the first time I flew. There's a lot more to it than you think, so let's just say I had to work out the kinks before I was going to let anyone ride with me. So, end of argument!"

Sylvester looked at her with a stony gaze, not yet ready to forgive her, although he knew as well as she did that her rebuttal had merit.

Donnie turned to the Wolf King and said, "Tell me something, Warren. Before dinner yesterday, I did a little research on Medregai and, according to what I read, wolves have always been on the dark side before now. I get why you're here helping us, but what about your brethren? How can we trust them not to go over to the other side? And not only them, but also creatures such as the bats, like Mickey T?"

Warren waited until he'd swallowed his last bite of toast and egg to reply. "A fair question, that," he agreed, nodding. "As we were discussing yesterday, dark forces have held sway over my people, along with other magical animal nations like the bats, since before the beginning of recorded history in Írtha. But when the dark power's hold on us was destroyed at the end of the Battle of the Var, at last we became the fair creatures we were originally intended to be. As you know already, those of my kind who had become werns or werewolves were changed back into our natural form and we've roamed the lands ever since as Free Wolves.

"Most of us still are, except for those who have been caught under Valledai's powers. You have an ally in us, Donemere, not a foe," he assured her confidently." We have sampled freedom for many long years now, and it has become engrained in our nature. My people will fight to the death to defeat this new darkness, in that you can rely. As will many other creatures who were taken over by dark magic in previous times—again, such as the bats. At the end of the last war, most of us vowed then that we would never again give up our freedom without a fight, even if it means our deaths." After calmly proclaiming this, he rose from the table to put his plate in the sink.

"Many fell creatures reverted to their fair forms after the Battle of the Var," Falwaïn added, gamely picking up the threads of Warren's explanation of events after the famed conflict in order to expand the account even more. "The Free Wolves have aided in reclaiming land from the okûn, trolls and goblins, fighting fiercely beside the Sarn and other groups of Free Peoples in their efforts to establish a more fruitful existence for all creatures of Medregai.

"This area, the north, is the last to be reclaimed by the Free Peoples. The settlements we've established are no older than ten years, with a few exceptions such as Banaff Dír and Marn Dím. Marn Dím was one of the first cities to be rebuilt after the Sire Lord, Orgos, was defeated. King Belnesem felt that Annûar, even more than many other regions in Medregai, needed to be cleared of its foulness. Regrettably, it now appears that we've failed in our efforts to rid the land of the evil that resided for centuries deep within the Brumal Mountains." With this dire pronouncement, Falwaïn also rose from the table, his plate and silverware in his hands. He carried them to the sink and laid them on top of Warren's, adding, "Once again, an evil force arises to threaten the lives of those who would be free. Only this time, it is a darkness from the future."

"What makes you say that?" Donnie asked him as she too stood up and put her own and the animals' dishes in the sink.

Falwaïn shrugged. "It only makes sense that Valledai must be from the future. At the end of the War of Unity, the Var King, Thaundré, was betrayed and his throat cut by Orgos. Orgos was then utterly defeated by Belnesem shattering the would-be god's magical staff to break its bond over the thousands of creatures caught in its power. No trace of him has been known since then, but it is presumed he too was destroyed when the staff was splintered by Belnesem's mighty blow. Orgos's second in command, a virulent little toad named Ashtak, had his heart pierced when he took a misstep and ran into *my* sword." Falwaïn's eyes gleamed with remembrance. "Kaledar's attack was thwarted by Déagmun, and Kaledar himself was killed by one of his own bootlicking servants. These were the most powerful dark forces here. Therefore, this new sorcerer can't have originated in Medregai. Since, from my research last night, it appears that ours is the first advanced civilization to inhabit the Earth, Valledai must have joined Catie during one of her sojourns to the future."

Donnie nodded silently, contemplating this. "Yeah, I guess that makes sense," she allowed hesitantly. "I know that flying camera I trapped last night was definitely from the future. Oh, sorry, I didn't tell you it was a camera, did I?" she apologized in reply to the visible start Falwaïn gave at her words. "But I'm bettin' you know just what a camera is, don't you? From your reading last night, right?"

He replied "Yes," while Warren and Sylvester both pointed out that they did not know what a camera was.

So Donnie explained to them, "It's a machine that takes a picture, almost like an instantaneous painting or image, of something. It's captured on this thing called a negative, and then usually printed out on paper. Unless it's a digital camera and, well, you don't even want me to start on that explanation, 'cause then we'll be here all day. I'll dig mine out later and show you. But anyway, this thing last night started out as a regular film camera, albeit a lot more advanced than those of my time, and it utilized both film and digital technologies. It was built to fly by itself and contained its own brain, if you can call it that, so it was able to think for itself. To my knowledge, nobody had even thought about making a camera that would do that in my time, except maybe in Hollywood as a special effect."

"But then it wouldn't be a real, working camera, would it?" Falwaïn interjected.

Donnie studied him steadily for a long moment. "My, my, you *were* busy last night, weren't you?" she drawled facetiously. "You're right, though. It wouldn't have been a working camera if it was just a special effect, while this thing last night was definitely real. I looked inside it with my mind and saw both the film and the computer code—er, its brain. But the thing had been changed, hexed I would hazard, so that when it took a picture of something, it turned the subject matter into an image made of stone; basically reversing the process, see? Anyway, like

I said, it was definitely from the future, from way beyond even my time. But I feel I should point out that just because it's from the future, it doesn't necessarily follow that Valley Guy is too. Catie visited any number of time periods before she noticed that she had a hitchhiker tagging along with her, and I've already proven that just because she said she only went to the future, doesn't make it so. For all we know, our villainous Valley Guy may well be from here."

Sylvester shook his head widely from side to side, summarily dismissing her conjecture. "But Lord Falwaïn just told you, Donemere, all dark forces powerful enough to accomplish what Valledai has were destroyed either during or immediately after the Battle of the Var! Magic is dying out now. Or it was before Valledai appeared and began his pernicious stratagems, precipitating Catie bringing you here to fight in her stead."

By this time, Falwaïn had turned around and absentmindedly reached for the pot scrubber, apparently intending to wash the dishes. The scrubber flew up and rapped the back of his hand hard a couple of times and then zoomed back to its usual position on the side of the sink. Falwaïn yowled and Donnie laughed.

"Sorry," she apologized, still giggling, "I probably should've warned you yesterday—the pot scrubber washes the dishes automatically. It takes its job very seriously and is thoroughly offended if anyone tries to use it manually. Actually, it takes its job so seriously, that many's the time I've come in to find it scrubbing dishes just for the fun of it, and if I try to stop it, it goes all sulky for days and chases me around the room if I step within two feet of the sink. The only way I can mollify it is by dirtying half my kitchen."

Still shaking his hand, which was continuing to throb where the wooden handle had connected with a knuckle, Falwaïn agreed circumspectly, "It does get rather testy, doesn't it? Well, it needn't worry, I promise to never try that again." He looked up from his injury, turning toward Donnie. "Its behavior must be the result of another of your charms, I presume."

"Absolutely!" she beamed, adding hastily, "Well, not the assault part, no, just the rest of it." She then turned back toward the cat and said, "You know what, Sylvester? I'm not willing to throw out the possibility that Valley Guy's from here just yet. Maybe he's some baddie from Medregai's past, like around the First Age or something, and somehow Catie brought him forward in time. Who was the guy who tried to destroy everything back then—he apparently had Orgos for an apprentice, something like that? What was that guy's name; Milker, Melder?"

Falwaïn gave her an amused smile before supplying, "His name was Malkôr, the Red Warlock. He became known as Nírgoth, after he'd stolen the Five Jewels of Light. He is considered to be the manifestation of all that is evil in the world."

"Whoa, now that's a hefty role," Donnie joked, deadpanning. "But see, Valley Guy could be him! Do we know what happened to this Goth guy?"

Falwaïn inclined his head slightly and replied, "Legend has it that the Red Warlock of Fal'Adîn was banished from this world forever by the Venár after the War of Sorrow."

Donnie's face wore a pained look at this news. "Okay," she conceded, "maybe it's not him. But I bet between him and Orgos and the Var King—oh, let's not forget Kaledar and the toad guy—I bet they all had plenty of bad guys allied to them, and probably every one of them was magical. Y'see, it's just that I can't think of any other reason why Valley Guy has stayed in this time period. Why not remain in one of the others that he and Catie visited? He could have done a lot of damage unhindered in any one of them, but he always chose to come back here with her instead, where she could keep him somewhat in check. So, why would he take the hard road instead of the easy one? Is it just because of the amulet? Or is there something else he's looking for? No, we still have way too many questions for us to rule out anything yet. For now, I think we should just consider this trip to be a fact-finding mission. Reconnaissance, if you will, and leave all possibilities on the table until we know more about what we're up against."

The others grudgingly nodded their agreement with her and everyone made moves toward assembling outside.

Donnie took a few minutes to freshen up in the bathroom after her meal and made her goodbyes to the trees. They wished her farewell, with Fine Fellow informing her that he would really miss her new friend, as Falwaïn had been kind enough to read to him from the encyclopedia last night. They'd gotten the rest of the way through the Qs, Fine Fellow said, so when Donnie got back, she should be prepared to start the Rs with him.

She smiled and touched one of his boards, telling him, "Sure thing, my friend. I'll miss our reading hour too."

Parry and Carly wished her a safe journey, while Sophie—well, Sophie was asleep again, they told her.

Mournful Jack was the last to respond to Donnie's goodbyes. He whispered to her, somewhat enigmatically, "Take great care on your journey, Donemere, not to forget the kind of world in which you are living now. Stark contrasts and fantastical beings will meet your gaze wherever you direct your eyes not only to look, but to see. It is not such a world as you are accustomed, nor shall it ever be. But there," he intoned abruptly, "I have said enough for now. I wish you well on your travels, my dear. You will learn much of Medregai and I shall be eager to discuss it with you when you return." And then he sighed.

Donnie nodded thoughtfully, stepped into her workshop and, a moment later, came back out to the kitchen. She poured some hot tea for herself into a thermos and some coffee into a larger one for the others, then hastily threw Catie's long grey cloak around her shoulders before carrying the thermoses outside.

Her black down parka was strapped to her saddle, as were the two canvas bags and the backpack she'd packed last night. Donnie handed the larger thermos to Falwaïn, which he slid into his saddlebag, while she stowed the smaller one in a bag attached to her own saddle.

She ran into the stables to say farewell to Diana, and the chickens too, of course. When Donnie entered the cow's stall, she was stopped cold by the sight of her friend. Diana was sitting down in the middle of the stall, looking thoroughly miserable.

Donnie bit her lip and announced as cheerfully as possible, "Hey, you, we're ready to leave now, but I wanted to say goodbye before we go."

"I can't believe you're gonna leave me here all alone with just the chickens for company!" wailed Diana, the ghost of a tear forming in her eye. "Oh, c'mon Donnie, take me with you! I can help, I know I can!"

"Diana, we've been through this already—"

"I know, but I don't think you appreciate my position here. What if someone comes along and steals me?" Diana asked querulously.

Donnie shook her head. "Nobody will step foot anywhere near here, you know that. Most people are all way too scared of the magical lands," she reassured her friend. "But if, by chance, someone does come along, just go into the house, both you and the chickens; you'll be completely safe in there. Besides, Mickey T and his friends have agreed to keep an eye out for any strangers. So, if someone does wander onto my lands, you'll know about it long before said intruder can possibly make it to the cottage. You're going to be all right, really."

"But I'll get heavy with milk and it'll be painful to walk and—"

Donnie interrupted Diana's complaints, saying soothingly, "I promise to milk you magically every morning and to collect the chickens' eggs the same way, so none of you has anything to worry about. You'll be taken care of just as well as if I were really here, I promise. It'll just be a whole lot quieter. I'll tell you what, I'll have the boombox come back and keep you company whenever it's not doing its level best to annoy the hell out of me, okay? And I'll tell it to play as much Jet Black as you can stand."

"With some Billie thrown in too," Diana demanded mock-petulantly, her normal good humor already beginning to return.

"Oh, absolutely!" exclaimed Donnie, grinning. "A little 'Funky River' oughta get you shakin' your booty all over the yard! And you'll have the library all to yourself, so you can practice your reading skills, which, may I say, are coming along rather nicely. Hey, just think of it, you can devour as many romance novels as you want to over the next few days without any of us around to razz you about it. So see, there are *some* pluses to this arrangement."

Diana eyed her witchy friend sardonically. "When did you turn into Cheerful Cherry?"

Laughing, Donnie walked over to put her arms around the cow's neck and gave Diana a huge hug. "Just taking a page from your book for once, my dear, that's all. Now, I really do have to go. Have some fun while we're gone, okay? There's plenty of alfalfa in the fridge if you want it. I've charmed everything in the house so that it works automatically for you while we're gone—oh, don't look at me like that! The charm will go away once we're back, so you needn't worry that I've gone on a charming binge again."

Diana nodded and stood up. "Goodbye then," she said with resignation. "I guess I'll just tell ya the usual stuff you're supposed to say when someone's going away for a while: Be very careful, take lots of pictures, buy me a souvenir or something, and send me a postcard if you get time!" She stopped and looked at Donnie guiltily, then allowed, "Seriously, Donnie, I really am sorry I've been so rotten about this. I just didn't expect that all of you would have to go away, ya know? Or so darned soon!"

"I know, sweetie." Donnie caressed her friend's shoulder. "Hey, while we're gone," she suggested seriously, "why don't you try real hard to decide whether you want to become human again? You know I'll be happy to do whatever you want. You just say the word, sister, and we'll have you bipeddin' it in no time!"

Donnie hugged the cow one more time, then turned around and left the stall. The chickens crowded around her feet, bawking and squawking their farewells, so she squatted down to pet them. From underneath some of the hens ran several new little chicks. The six who'd been born the other day were already almost mature now and towered above the fresh arrivals.

"Ah, so we're expecting more company, are we?" Donnie asked, giving one of the chicks a gentle tickling. "I wonder who it'll be? Well, thanks for the heads up, and I'll see you guys in a few days too, okay? I'd try to give you an idea of how many eggs we're going to need while we're away and when we'll need them, but you seem to be much better at gauging that sort of thing than I could ever be. How do you do it, I wonder, you affectionate little prognosticators?" She gave them a tender smile before rising to leave.

When she walked up to the waiting men, Donnie went straight to Falwaïn and took hold of his hand. His expression was one of curiosity. From the pocket of the sweatshirt she wore underneath Catie's cloak, she pulled out the amulet and placed it in his palm.

"I thought about this for a long time," she said quietly, "Catie entrusted you to safeguard this thing and I can't think of anyone more suited to that job. Would you mind wearing it and continuing to guard it until we can figure out how to use it?"

Falwaïn accepted the amulet without saying anything, put it around his neck, and tucked it under his clothing. He then smiled warmly and complimented her on her saddle, adding that he was genuinely impressed by it. It had molded itself to Otis the moment he'd cinched it.

Donnie felt a light-hearted pleasure at his praise and hoisted herself up in the saddle after donning her backpack. The saddle did the same thing it had done the night before; it instantly expanded to encase her legs and hips and give her a comfortable seat. Falwaïn and Warren exchanged surprised glances. Otis declared that it even felt great on his back, like no saddle he'd ever known before. It was almost like getting a massage, the horse added happily.

Sylvester jumped up onto Donnie's sleeping bag tied to the saddle behind her and settled into its soft folds. Warren changed into his wolven form and stood beside Rex, a good two inches taller and several inches longer than the big dog. Together, they all headed north.

They journeyed for several hours through Donnie's lands, picking their way carefully around the rough moors. She was thoroughly disconcerted by how many of the magical animals obviously knew Rex and their plans quite well, calling out to hail him hearty farewells all along the trail. Rex, always a most polite dog, even when hunting, introduced every one of them to his mama, which slowed the travelers' progress significantly.

Perhaps the most startling of these introductions was to Bronadulach, the Cave Bear King. Warren informed Donnie that he was the mightiest of all living Great Bears and was the Kaerdír, or Master of the magical lands. The enormous black bear got up and walked away from the tree where he'd been resting, then hefted his great bulk up on two legs when their little troupe came near. He stood a little over twenty feet on his hind legs and, as Donnie gauged him, weighed in at well over three tons. He towered over them. His voice was gruff, but his affection for Rex was plain to see, although he mistakenly hailed Rex as King. Rex amiably corrected him, saying that he was going by his real name today, and the Great Bear's reception became even warmer. As much as Donnie wished to stay and get to know Bronadulach because she was so fascinated by him, Warren and Sylvester both reminded her that their journey north had purpose, one which should be delayed no more than necessary. They moved on, with Donnie becoming acquainted with more and more of the thousands of magical animals who dwelt on her lands.

In between these introductions, which became less frequent the farther away from the valley the group went, Falwaïn and Warren asked Donnie questions about her world, her answers to which kept them all enthralled until they reached the Annûar Path. This was a wide track, with deep ruts from the carts that passed along it frequently. Falwaïn explained that it was the only road in these reaches. He went on to warn that it was dangerous to leave the path because of the many bogs on the moorland. Which meant all manner of travelers might be encountered upon the way and they should therefore be on their guard.

The boombox appeared at this moment and attached itself to Donnie's saddle. They listened silently to Gregory Shore's sad lament, "On the Road Alone." After a minute or so, Donnie reached down and hit the "Next" button, telling the music box, "That's a truly lovely song, boombox, but it's just a bit too sad right now, don'tcha think? How about playing something more upbeat?"

Frank-n-Sense's ribald "Sausage Boogie" came on immediately. Donnie hung her head and whispered, "Okay, okay, I'll keep my mouth shut from now on about your choice of songs. But, whenever we get near other people, you have to stop playing because you're just gonna freak them out. Get it?"

The boombox flashed its lights and turned down the volume a little as a concession to Donnie's remonstrances.

An hour later, Warren and Rex were out in front of the others when they came within sight of Banaff Dír. Although they had passed several smaller settlements on their journey, all of which were set some ways distant from the Annûar Path (many with nothing more to show they existed than a faint cart path leading off into the distance, much the same as the path to Donnie's lands), the gates of Banaff Dír sat directly adjacent to the road. The town was a large, enclosed, stone and wooden fortress built on a high bluff that stood near the foot of the Brumal Mountains. Its oaken turrets looked deserted to Donnie from this distance. The travelers quickened their pace and reached the unmanned gates in only a few minutes more. Warren changed from wolf into werewolf form and turned to look at Falwaïn, who nodded and murmured, "We'll stay here."

Warren took hold of Rex's collar and together they walked through the gates of the village.

Donnie looking puzzled, finally ventured, "I don't know why he took Rex with him. I mean, he's not exactly the bravest dog in the world."

Falwaïn turned toward her when she spoke and smiled. "You might be surprised at the various talents your dog has acquired. He's most unlike any other I've encountered. He'll be fierce enough when called upon. Warren and I decided it would be best if they go in first, as they'll be able to discern quickly if anyone is about. You never know, the townspeople may not all be in Mâlendian. If any are left here, they might not take kindly to our presence."

"Plus, you're worried what their reaction will be to coming in such close proximity to the center of my magic," Donnie stated matter-of-factly. And when Falwaïn gave her an appraising look, she added, "I'm just as worried about that as you guys are. It's a good idea, them going in to check out the scene before I get any closer. So, tell me…" she paused, glancing archly at him, "how are you feeling, being as you're in such close proximity to me?"

His amusement evident, he replied, "Disturbed. But not, I think, from your magical powers."

Sylvester coughed loudly, feeling that this was truly not the proper time or setting for romance. Besides, he was still reeling over the kittens who had crowded around his Meludya the other day, when he'd finally been able to visit her after the long winter months spent in the valley. He recalled the sight of their orange fur and his jealousy reared up once again, making him fretful. He was afraid that he must face the undeniable and distasteful fact that his Mela had been unfaithful to him while he had been bound to the farm.

It was some time before Warren and Rex came through the gates. When they did, Warren strode up to Donnie and Falwaïn, while Rex waited at the town entrance. "There are none here," he said, "but it appears to have been looted recently by okûn. Their stench is unmistakable. They too have gone, but only a short time ago and may still be near. We must keep a sharp lookout for them. Rex will stay at the gate to keep watch while we go inside and water the horses." He turned and walked back inside the gate, the others following close behind.

The town looked like some of the renaissance fairs Donnie had attended in the States, and of just about any of the medieval towns of England, if you disregard the imposing wall encircling it. The great timbers of the houses already looked ancient and worn, though the stone work was immaculate and precise. They walked through the silent streets, the horses' hooves echoing loudly in the stillness.

At the center of town, they found a small meeting square with a huge well and a high, stone platform set in its midst. Here, Donnie and Falwaïn dismounted to let the horses drink their fill of the fresh water flowing through the sluice provided for this purpose. Donnie unpacked some of the potato chips and handed them around. Sylvester was particularly delighted by them and ate his allotment, plus half of Donnie's.

They stayed less than a quarter of an hour, the eeriness of the town finally overwhelming Donnie, who hurriedly packed up and remounted Otis, saying almost frantically, "I need to get out of here now. This place gives me the creeps." The others acquiesced without argument and, in just a few moments, they returned to the Annûar Path.

Donnie did not breathe easily again until they were more than two miles away from the town. When they'd exited the gates, she'd set a fast pace, which the others matched or surpassed wordlessly. Finally slowing down, Donnie smiled for the first time since entering Banaff Dír.

Falwaïn smiled back and asked if she felt better.

"Yes," she replied, grateful to be in the open air once more, "much better. Something was wrong back there. I couldn't figure out what it was, but it wasn't just the fact that it was deserted."

"Possibly you are sensitive to the malignancy left by the presence of okûn," he suggested. "It is not an uncommon feeling."

"Tell me about them, the okûn, I mean."

Falwaïn reflected on her question, then explained, "Okûn means *of the shadows*. They are called this because they are so far removed from the real world and can only interact with its edges. You see, they were born from rogue vinca who renounced all bonds to the fair, free world many millennia ago. These vinca were allied with Malkôr, the Red Warlock, sickeningly bound to him even as he tortured them, experimenting on them until he had created a race of creatures he named the *kûn*, or the shadows. And those accursed creatures were fated to spell the warlock's downfall when he—" Falwaïn stopped short and stared up the road toward the hill before them and the dark clouds gathering beyond it.

Warren, who'd earlier changed into his wolf form and gone ahead, had suddenly come into view, racing toward them headlong, Rex loping alongside him. When they got close enough, Warren transformed back into werewolf and a moment later took hold of the horses' reins to stop them. "We must hurry. The okûn are on their way to Mâlendian and they have begun to move quickly."

Donnie stared at him in horror. "But the people there," she gasped, "they won't be able to defend themselves. And I—I don't know what to do yet about the effects of my magic on them. I've been waiting for an epiphany, but so far, no luck. I could try a spell, right now, I guess, but I think I have to be closer; don't I, Sylvester?"

The cat leapt around her to sit on Otis's shoulders and looked up at her sternly. "It is most likely," he replied sternly. " 'Tis also most likely that your spell will fail regardless. If, as we fear, you are the cause of their affliction, then the problem lies not with them, but with you. Any spell you cast upon them will not break the hold your magic has over them. It may, in fact, serve to heighten their response to it. No, you must learn to control your power more efficiently. Indeed, if it is your magic causing their malignancy, then it is obviously seeping out of you in some manner, which must be stopped. Also, may I point out that unless you find a way to stem this leakage, you will not have enough power within you to defeat Valledai?"

Donnie cast her eyes heavenward before crying out almost hysterically, "I didn't ask for all of that! I merely asked if I could cast a spell from here and the short version would've been enough, you know!"

"Very well!" the cat huffed. "No, a spell from here is not the correct answer. Satisfied?"

"Regardless, we must hasten to Mâlendian," Warren interrupted them to urge. "You will not have much time to determine what you are going to do, Donnie. You must fasten on your plan quickly."

Sylvester cleared his throat loudly, gave Donnie the fifth or sixth baleful glare of the morning, then dared her with, "You know what you could do, if you would overcome this nonsensical aversion you have to it. It would mean we could be there before the okûn themselves arrive."

"No!" Donnie retorted, "I can't materialize us there. I won't! All along you've tried to pound into me that I have to embrace my powers, to settle into them and become one with them. Well, that's the one power I still can't get accustomed to, not as far as working it on living, sentient beings. I just know one of us will die if I try it. You can ask me to do almost anything else, but not that—I'm not ready for it yet, so we'll have to ride the horses there." She looked over at Falwaïn to ask desperately, "Do you think we can catch up to the okûn if we ride really fast? How far do we have to go?"

He looked up the road, toward the direction of the town, before turning back to respond to her. "It's just short of eight leagues from here, which will take us at least an hour at a hard gallop. We're fortunate the wind blows from the north, so the okûn shouldn't be aware of our presence behind them for quite some time, especially if they too are moving fast." He searched her eyes, looking beyond her tears to the fear that shone from their depths. "My lady," he assured her gently, "we'll ride as hard as we can. We will make it there in time because we must. But I warn you, okûn are no bugs to be picked up and put outside to live another day. They are the kind of bugs we must squash. If you wish to bless their next life, that is your business. But we must be willing to send them on that journey."

Donnie looked at him dolefully before lowering her head. Truthfully, all through Banaff Dír, she'd been having trouble accepting that okûn actually do exist and that she was probably going to run into one someday. She hadn't expected it to be today. She needed more time to steel herself for that particular experience, but it seemed she wasn't going to be given that luxury.

Warren took off without another word, changing back into his wolf form on a dead run. Gallantry and Otis charged after him, galloping full tilt, with Rex bounding alongside easily.

They met no one on the road to Mâlendian, nor did they speak to each other. Otis gamely kept pace with the younger horse, while Rex would occasionally catch up with Warren for a while far ahead, then drop back to run with the horses for a few miles. They galloped hard all the way, making good time, and arrived at the gates to the town five minutes over an hour. The sky was darkest here and no sunlight penetrated the black clouds hovering above the fortress, their dark depths threatening an imminent downpour.

Warren and Rex were waiting for them just inside the gates. Both he and the dog were barely winded, although the horses' flesh was steaming and a light foam could be seen around their mouths. They trotted through the gates and into the town, Warren and Rex leading the way again. As they neared the center of town, they could hear voices singing. And laughter—hideous yips of it.

Warren transformed into his werewolf shape and observed quietly, "We are in time then."

Falwaïn nodded, his lips set in a grim line.

They hurried along the town's main thoroughfare until they came upon the huge town square, where they stopped and stood on its edge. Donnie and Falwaïn dismounted and let the horses go to a nearby watering trough. Donnie surveyed the scene playing out before them with growing dismay.

Hundreds of townspeople, glowing faintly blue in color, were separated into more than ten long lines and stood arm-in-arm, humming the melody of Ken Allen's instrumental dance song. Each row was turned back-to-back with the one behind, with only a foot of so separating them; whereas, the aisle in front was quite wide to accommodate the swinging movements of more than a thousand legs. The people kicked and stepped in unison, their eyes glazed over, shouting encouragement to all to do the *Boogie Oogie*. Sitting around the edges of the square were another couple hundred people, including babies and the elderly and infirm, all of whom were swaying and clapping in time with the dancers.

Out of the corner of her eye, Donnie caught the red glow of the LED light on the boombox. "Don't even think it, do you hear me?" she hissed at the box. "No more *Boogie Oogie* or I really will turn you off for good, you know!" she threatened it, not at all certain she could actually make good on that promise. Nevertheless, the box came to life, playing Melanie Murphy's "Love Prayer." Inspiration flashed and Donnie now gave the boombox a dumbstruck gape, before shooting it a grin of pleased surprise.

The others had been scanning the perimeter of the square, including Sylvester, who sat atop Donnie's shoulder. Warren turned to Falwaïn and murmured, "They are here."

Falwaïn nodded.

Donnie, recalled to the impending showdown by Warren's words, looked from one man to the other and squeaked, "Where?"

Rex leaned against her leg and directed her to, "Look in the shadows, Mama. Look there."

Donnie strained to see, but could discern nothing more than darkness in the shadowy recesses between the town's buildings and in the open doorways of the stores, taverns and homes that lined the streets. She took a deep breath and closed her eyes, using her mind's eye instead.

Her vision tunneled to one shadow after another, displaying what could only be described as savage, almost feral beasts either waiting in the buildings or positioning themselves for attack. Spine-chilling yips of laughter were coming from several of the darkened doorways. There were both big and small okûn, most of whom were wearing long, dark, thickly netted cloaks with full hoods that covered even the face. As the clouds overhead were growing ever darker, many of the okûn were now in the process of pulling off and tossing their cloaks behind them, revealing mostly tattered, filthy clothing underneath.

Donnie noted that about one in twenty or so wore a more typical cloak, one that was not comprised of the weird netting and full hood. She wondered why this was, but could not devise an answer from what she knew about the creatures—they were purportedly afflicted with a high sensitivity to the sun's rays, which could cause lasting damage to their skin and eyes, she had gathered from the reading she had done on them. But what did it mean that some few apparently did not have that same extreme sensitivity to sunlight?

She slowed her virtual gaze to scrutinize the okûn in more detail. They had muscular arms covered with skin of a sickly yellow, unnatural color. The smaller okûn were hunched over, standing only about four feet in height, and their movements seemed almost preternaturally quick once they had shed their cloaks and she could get a better look at them. The larger ones, who moved more slowly (but were by no means *slow*), were as tall as Falwaïn and Warren, and every one of them looked strong enough to pull a small bus. Each of the okûn had protuberant black-rimmed yellow eyes, with big black irises, which stood out horribly in their blotchy and malformed faces. Their heads were somewhat elongated at the top, with what looked like large, pointed scales tightly covering their skullcaps, beginning at the ears, which were oversized and pointed slightly upward—a throwback to the vinca, Donnie assumed. Their faces looked frozen into expressions of hatred, deep gashes of enmity furrowing their brows, their cheeks, even their lips, many of which were permanently drawn back in ferocious snarls. This bared their greyish teeth, which looked as though they could probably bite through tough leather on the first try. Actually, their incisors reminded Donnie of short ice picks that appeared to have been sharpened with some sort of tool; how recently, she couldn't tell. The okûn were, without a doubt, the most frightening and, in their way, sad creatures she'd ever seen. It seemed to her their hatred for others had twisted and deformed them much more than the experiments of any wizard would account for.

"Hideous hides, there's hundreds of them!" she gasped, withdrawing her attention from the okûn and back to her companions, unable to stop the visible shudder that rippled through her.

"There are one hundred and eighty-seven of 'em, to be exact," Rex corrected her matter-of-factly. "I counted their tracks on the way here." He looked up, saw her increasingly dazed expression, then blinked anxiously. "You okay, Mama?"

Donnie moved her shoulders, clearly much agitated, and exclaimed, "Well, other than the fact that I have a counting dog and my magic is making these people participate in a dance marathon totally against their will, which means they're all about to be butchered by a marauding horde of okûn—oh, excuse me, make that one hundred and eighty-seven marauding okûn—yeah, I'd say I'm doin' just dandy."

Melanie Murphy complacently reminded her that all she needed was love, whereas Sylvester advised her harshly, "Donemere, you must focus your power inwardly. You *must* control it, somehow draw it out of the land and the people, so that they may be freed from it. Otherwise, they will all surely die. They have only Warren and Falwaïn to protect them now. Which means the good people of Mâlendian are not the only ones who shall die today."

"No added pressure there, eh, Sylvester?" Donnie retorted acerbically, watching the cat jump to the ground. "But you know what? I think I know exactly what to do, and it seems I have Melanie Murphy to thank for the idea. See, she became a very famous proponent of meditation. I myself practice Vipassana meditation on an almost daily basis. You know, it's the technique I use to find peace that you think is stupid, Sylvester. Anyway, there are different…er, *levels* to it, shall we say, which are all designed to center your power within yourself. Now that I know there's so much of my own power out there, it should be a simple matter for me to pull it all back into the ground and store what I need of it within me. But first, according to Lady Melanie, a bit of Metta meditation is what's needed most!"

The two men looked at her uncertainly, but she waved them on their way. "You go do what you have to do. I'll do my stuff right there in the middle of the square, up on that dais."

Falwaïn stepped up to her, withdrew his knife from its sheath and placed its handle in her palm. "Take this," he said. "Defend yourself with it. Remember what I told you about them at Banaff Dír—they are weakest at the neck. Rex, you go with your mistress and guard her. Sylvester, you must also go with her and do your utmost to protect her. Warren and I will try to hold off the okûn until you have freed the townspeople." After saying this, he pulled Donnie close and pressed his lips to her forehead, looking deeply into her eyes with reassurance in his own. Then he was gone.

Donnie grabbed the boombox off her saddle and carried it with her. She weaved her way to the center of the square, carefully avoiding the enthusiastic kicks of the vacant-eyed dancers, and climbed the six steps to the dais positioned there. She set the boombox and knife down next to each other, handling the knife with distaste. No way was she ever going to use that on a living being. A bit stiffly, she sat on the wooden flooring and crossed her legs, bending them into the lotus position. Then she closed her eyes, sat up straight, and folded her hands loosely in her lap, with her thumbs lightly pressed against each other, end to end.

She tried to clear her mind of everything except her breathing, but all she could concentrate on was the darned song, which, at this point, was totally rocking out. She opened her eyes and glowered fiercely down at the little music machine. "Yeah, yeah, yeah, that's enough. Thanks very much for the tip, but you'll really have to leave now. Why don't you go keep Diana company for a while?" she suggested irritably, confident the boombox had no more wisdom to impart to her today and could therefore be anywhere but with her. It stopped playing, beeped encouragingly at her, and then disappeared.

Donnie tried again, focusing her mind, her energy, and her heart inwardly, listening to her breaths and concentrating on their effortless rhythm. Errant thoughts drifted into her head here and there, but after each one, she slowly herded her mind back to her breathing.

She was vaguely aware that Falwaïn and Warren were attempting to shake some of the men out of their stupor; apparently to no avail. As her mind was emptying, she heard the two of them discussing their chosen plan and its preparation. The next thing she heard was them gathering up the weapons that had been left carelessly by the townspeople on some abandoned carts that stood at either entryway to the square.

She let these sounds and thoughts flow freely through her mind until the frequency of their intrusion lessened. Once her mind quit racing, she found that she could focus on the sensations emanating within her body. Deeper and deeper she went into her mind, reaching into its core, allowing herself to feel her emotions freely. She thought of what she wanted to do next, permitting her plans to drift unhindered through her mind.

Sylvester heard her slowly begin mumbling in English and then, suddenly, she shifted to an entirely different language, one he recognized almost immediately. He stared at her in astonishment. But how could this be? Donemere speaking in Elanéra, the shared language of the gods?

"*Telec'hu tí, raegunumon set laha,*" she chanted. "*Amai see raegunumon, aht raegunumon setimai.*" To Donnie, she knew it as, "Deep within me, my power is whole. I am my power, and my power is me."

The cat's expression changed to a mixture of respect and consternation. As close as he'd come to the gods during his four centuries as Catie's familiar, he himself knew no more than twenty words of Elanéra. It had taken Catie over eight years to learn it, and she'd been tutored by Gwydion himself! Where then, and how, had Donemere learned the language, and in less than six months?

Donnie continued her chant, stumbling over the words at first, then repeating them more clearly so that she was almost singing them. Her hands moved to her shoulders, her arms crossed in front of her. As her power began filtering through the Earth, back into her and making her glow bright blue, she unconsciously shortened her chant to "*Amai see raegunumon, aht raegunumon setimai.*"

After they'd dispersed as many weapons as they could amongst the townspeople, placing them in front of all able-bodied men, Falwaïn and Warren had taken up a stance at each end of the square, where the lines of dancers and those sitting on the ground ended. Here were the only true entry points to the meeting square, as most of the carts and wagons were crowded tightly together along the square's lengths, essentially surrounding the townspeople. The two men waited patiently for the okûn attack. The okûn either hadn't seen what they'd been doing with the weaponry or didn't care, as their assault was slow in coming.

Falwaïn stood to the left of the square with his sword at the ready. He gazed around him into the deepening shadows of the open storefronts and homes, and those between the buildings. The okûn lieutenants had finished directing their troops some time before, who were all also waiting silently. Out of the corner of his eye, to the right, he caught movement. The biggest, ugliest okûn he'd ever seen stepped from one of the local taverns on the north side of the square and belched. After first looking up at the skies with satisfaction (for they were now nearly black as night), this monster pushed and shoved his way to the fore through the ranks of okûn who were suddenly pouring from their hiding places and lining up along the streets.

Donnie was deeply into her trance by the time the okûn rushed from their hiding places, and so did not hear the okûn captain's cry of "Attack!" Warren and Falwaïn were ready for it though, and ran toward the oncoming okûn, fiercely shouting their own war cries. Falwaïn struck down three okûn with the first swinging arc of his sword.

Warren too had noticed the arrival of the okûn captain from the tavern, and had rightly guessed that this was the cause of the delayed invasion. Praying Donemere's efforts would take hold and release at least a few of the men before long, he ran toward an approaching group of okûn. With his razor-sharp claws extended, he ripped open the necks of the first two who reached him.

Both men held the initial rush of okûn on their corners of the square at bay, but the other corners were left exposed. The okûn flooded the square, wanting to make their victory quick in order to minimize any possible exposure to the sun's light, although the sun, in truth, was nowhere to be seen. It began to rain softly, then built to a torrent within the space of a minute.

Donnie was completely unaware any of this was happening. She'd channeled part of her mind to see her power as a big blue ball in the midst of her soul, and was concentrating her will on withdrawing all the magical power that had seeped from her into the people through the land, pulling it back into the ground and up into her power ball. At first, she focused on draining her power from only the men so that they could aid in the battle with the okûn. With each passing second, she could see the ball burning brighter and brighter, the energy crackling inside her and making her glow an ever more vivid blue with its increasing intensity.

Only moments after the okûn attacked, several of the men were released from their trance. These men, warriors and farmers alike, took up the weapons left by Warren and Falwaïn and rounded on their attackers. It was not long before all the men were freed of Donnie's power and had joined in the muddy offensive.

Donnie was focusing another compartment of her mind on the Metta meditation. This was a new form of meditation to her, and it became a welcomed method of discovery. She felt the love and compassion inside her heart grow, encompassing first herself, as who she was now and who she'd been throughout her life, starting as a child. She saw again her struggles and tribulations, and knew that others had also labored long and hard, and had experienced their own misfortunes. For no one passes through life completely unscathed by pain and suffering. There is great comfort in numbers, in knowing that you are not alone on the darkened paths that life can set before you.

Loving-kindness filled Donnie's heart and she let it grow, sending it outward, first to the two animals guarding her. They felt it pour into their hearts and knew that Donnie was protecting them with it. She expanded its reach to include her other friends here in Medregai. As the seconds ticked by, she sent more and more of her compassion and love outwardly, letting it flow around and into the elderly and the women and children caught by her magic. Their movements stilled as her magical power slowly began to drain from their bodies, while her love cocooned them in its glow. She sent this goodwill out toward all creatures in the town, imbuing them with her love. To her great sorrow, she found that she could not penetrate the souls or hearts of the enemy, as though a great, impervious wall of evil surrounded them.

All who were held still by both Donnie's power and her love suddenly disappeared, leaving only faint blue outlines of themselves that glistened in the half-light of the violently stormy day. These "ghosts" could be neither touched nor smelled, and their presence would have gone undetected were it not for the glimmering of their souls. Mouths hanging open, Rex and Sylvester contemplated the coruscating town square with obvious wonder.

A smallish okûn suddenly jumped onto the dais and stood looking down with fiendish curiosity at the strange trio seated there. He smiled a nasty smile, his uneven teeth snapping together with undisguised relish when he registered the scents of human, cat and another wilder, fain fragrance. He thrust his face at Rex and asked, "What manner of wolf are you?"

His confoundment when Rex answered his question was evident. The dog calmly looked up at him and replied, "Oh, I'm not a wolf. But he is," and inclined his head to where Warren had just leapt from the right, behind the okûn. The okûn turned in time to see Warren's claws tear across his throat, then he fell dead where he stood. Rex carefully used his snout as leverage to push its carcass off the dais after Warren jumped back into the fray.

As the battle wore on, Warren would suddenly change into wolf form to leap twenty feet across the square, then just as suddenly change back into his werewolf form, sharp claws exposed. Or, as he found to his surprise, he could take on a purely human form and use the weapons of his foes against their numbers without fear of his claws making his grip loosen. He would grab their swords and swing them with both hands, fighting and cutting his way through the crush of their attack. The warrior moves Falwaïn had shown him that morning, while they were waiting for Donemere to arise, were proving to be most effective.

Falwaïn also was enjoying great success with them. He'd mixed several moves from the two martial arts books he'd studied the night before, creating what he thought of as his own style of fighting which utilized leaps, kicks and chops from a couple of martial arts forms, and which deftly incorporated the huge broadsword into the regimen of moves. He'd also taught himself to pirouette and dance around in a manner similar to that of his nemesis, Galto. All of which improved his already formidable fighting skills, making them more economical as far as motion and energy expended were concerned—and considerably more deadly.

Earlier, he'd seen an okûn reach the dais and had shouted Donnie's name to get Warren's attention, since the Wolf King was far closer to her than he himself was. To Falwaïn's great relief, Warren had dispatched the okûn within moments. Falwaïn now saw that another okûn, much bigger and obviously a seasoned fighter, was standing directly behind Donnie, already poised to swing his sword at her neck. Neither he nor Warren were near enough to stop the okûn's blade.

Falwaïn caught his breath, his heart stopping as the metal edge entered the blue of Donnie's intense power field. The okûn's face assumed an expression of sheer dumbfoundedness as his sword was caught and held by the field. The last glimpse Falwaïn had of this scene, as he spun into a high roundhouse kick that dropped the two okûn attempting to double-team him from behind, was of several lashes of brilliant, cobalt-colored energy emanating from Donnie.

In fact, more than two score of these fingers of blue light shot out and encompassed the okûn's body in an intricate webbing that held him fast. In a blinding flash, his form changed to that of his race's ancestor, the vinca. After a few moments, the blue light retreated from around him, then ran back down his blade and into Donnie. The newly transformed vinca, who was now a smooth light-grey in color, with the standard exquisitely classical features of his race, spun around and attacked his former brethren, stabbing and chopping his way through their midst, intent only on making it out of there as quickly as possible so that he could get to Anûmanétus and inform the Sarn King of Valledai's plans. By the time Falwaïn could look around again, the vinca was already halfway through the crowd of okûn on the back side of the square and so, passed through the battle unseen by either Falwaïn or Warren.

Falwaïn's heart stopped racing only when he had an opportunity to see Donemere still sitting calmly upon the dais, her eyes closed and arms crossed, with both the dog and cat settled safely in front of her, their backs to him as they stared at their mistress.

The battle raged on for some time before all of the okûn were dead. Donnie still sat in the middle of it, mostly oblivious to what was happening around her, not even registering the abrupt waning of the storm above her. Her focus now was on keeping a few, rather annoying tendrils of blue energy from escaping her internal ball. Eventually, she succeeded in gathering all of her errant energy and was able to contain it within herself. She pushed it farther and farther down inside, willing it to remain whole.

Part of her mind registered that the battle was over; that part which had sent her loving-kindness out to protect those still held by her magic. When it was safe to do so, Donnie withdrew her goodwill and the remainder of her power from the townspeople, freeing them all at the same moment.

By the time she came out of her trance, recovery was underway and the sun was shining brightly. The most badly wounded had already been moved inside to receive immediate medical attention, while those less injured and able to walk remained outside to await the ministrations of their healers. The dog and cat had guarded Donnie faithfully all the while, not allowing any of the townspeople near her, snarling or hissing at those who tried to approach.

With a slight moan, Donnie slumped forward and covered her face with her hands. She was afraid of what she would see when she lowered them because she could smell the stench of blood and death all around her, and could hear the groans of the wounded. "How bad is it? Did we win?" she asked mournfully.

Sylvester harrumphed at her, adding, "Do not be so cowardly that you cannot view the results for yourself. The battle is over and we are victorious. The okûn are all dead."

Donnie let out a loud sigh and raised her head. Her breath caught again as she looked at the gruesome sights surrounding them, and her eyes filled with tears. "So many fallen? Oh, sweet Goddesses, how many of the townspeople are dead?"

Falwaïn had joined them now and knelt in front of her, his hands clasping tightly to one of Donnie's. "None so far, my lady," he replied. " 'Tis a good day; one in which to rejoice and be thankful we have survived. It looks worse than it is, I promise. It seems that okûn prefer to maim instead of killing outright. Keeps their supper fresh longer, or at least that's what one of their lieutenants shouted as encouragement to his troops during the battle."

"Eeeeuuuuwwww!" wailed Donnie. "I didn't need to know that! Tell you what, you can leave little insights like that out of our future conversations, 'kay?" She scowled, avoiding Falwaïn's gaze. "Are you sure no one's dead?" she insisted desperately, not waiting for a response before burying her face in her hands again. "Oh, you stupid shite!" she cursed at herself. "This is all my fault!"

Falwaïn pulled her hands away from her face and hauled her to her feet. "I am told that everyone lives, so far," he assured her firmly. "But there are at least a score who may not survive the day without your aid." He cupped her chin in his hand and told her, "Look around you at the hundreds who are unharmed. We were well met today, Donemere. Be thankful that all were not slaughtered before our arrival. And though some of the men may die today, we shall rejoice in their victory. The lives of the dead are not forsaken here in Medregai because we don't fear death, as those in your time do.

"Yes, I read about that too last night." He let go of her before continuing, correctly reading the surprise in her eyes. "Death for us is a release, a gift of sorts, which sets us on the path to our next journey. Most often, it's a comfort when it arrives. Those who may die here today will soon be on their way to the Chamber of Reckoning, where Mændís will send them on further—possibly even to Canavar. Do not grieve for them, but rather, give them a blessing. That is something they can use, especially from you."

"Is that how you felt when your wife and son died, Falwaïn?" Donnie asked. She ignored his sudden, harsh intake of breath, stumbling on with, "That they were merely continuing their journey to the next life? Did that thought give you comfort?"

He stared down at the ground, stone-faced. When he looked up at her a few moments later, he reluctantly admitted, "No, that is not how I felt."

She nodded in compassion. "I thought not. There is no comfort in death, except maybe for those in great pain or sickness. And there is only loss for those who are left behind. That much even I've learned."

Nevertheless, Falwaïn wiped the tears from her cheeks and chided her gently for crying. "Save your tears, Donnie, and come with me to meet some of the good people we saved today, while we make our way to those who need you most." He drew her to the closest group of townspeople, who were all tired and somewhat disoriented, but very happy to be alive. They thanked Donnie profusely and with quiet dignity for the blessings she gave them as she passed by. Every face she looked into she blessed either silently or with a heartfelt, "Blessed be."

The thirsty ground had absorbed most of the rainwater and the mud was already hardening as they made their way across the square. Inside the town's largest tavern was where the most badly wounded had been laid out on tables and benches. Donnie visited those who were near death, moving from one to the next as soon as she could, beginning the healing process of those she could save. By the end of the day, eight men had died from the wounds they'd received in the battle. Five of them were just too far gone for Donnie to heal. Three others had died only moments before she'd awoken from her trance.

Donnie grieved immeasurably for them, trying to draw as much strength as possible from within to help her face this new ordeal, and focused her heart on the tenets of Witchcraft. She reminded herself that all creatures die; this is a necessary part of life. And she must understand that these men had not had their lives *taken* from them; but rather, they had given them freely so that others might live. Because of that great gift, they had earned the right to have the Rule of Three invoked on their behalf, and so she had accordingly blessed their next three lives.

The five she could not heal because they were so near death when she was brought to them, she watched meet their fate with unflinching courage, their loved ones pressing close for these final, precious moments. Donnie closed her eyes and focused her power on opening the hearts of those crowded around the mortally wounded men. The love from their families poured into the dying, who then embraced it and returned it a thousand-fold before drawing their last breath. This, at least, was something Donnie could do for them, even if she was unable to give them their lives back.

It was all somewhat blurred and unreal to her because she'd never been forced to watch a person die before this. The experience left her stunned and silent at first, deeply saddened and furious with herself as she struggled to keep hold of her beliefs. She eventually sought a quiet corner for herself and sat down, her heart heavy. Taking the parchment from the belt around her waist, she surreptitiously unfolded the top part and once again read its words regarding death.

> ...ye must accept the life that is gifted. Revere death as ye do life, for neither is the end of the journey.

Donnie closed her eyes and tried to make her peace with death. Suddenly, the paper in her hands fluttered. Opening her eyes, she could see no one around who would account for the movement. She looked down at the paper, undid all its folds, and realized that the third trial was filled in now. It read:

> Lay bare the fruit of thy heart. If it be of bold valor, ye may reap its harvest.
>
> Know that love for all beings is the Great Unifier of the universe. Welcome its release from within, and be glad it lives on forever all around ye.

The gods were right; death is only one of the many stages of existence. Loving is another, obviously the most important one. Donnie now knew from opening wide the hearts of the dying and their families that love is a form of pure energy, a form she herself had clearly witnessed with her mind's eye as it flowed from the men and into their loved ones. Love is real, perhaps the one true gift we give, both in life and in death, for all else is transient and destructible. But love can never die. Though it be shunned, thwarted, stolen, turned, even shattered, once it is given, its energy exists forever and surrounds us all with its harvest. Regardless of whether we open our hearts to it, it is still there in the world with us.

Closing her eyes and looking around the makeshift emergency room with her mind's eye, Donnie could once more see love's soft, white glow flowing freely amongst and into all the people in the room, including herself. Love was something that not even death could take from these people. She smiled faintly before opening her eyes and rejoining the others, wondering at these truths the gods were teaching her.

She visited each of the wounded once again to make sure they were well on the road to recovery, carefully healing all injuries by at least half, even though it left her exhausted and shaking. The okûn bodies had been taken to a place a couple of miles east of town and were burned just before sunset. Donnie and her friends followed the long line of funereal carts to the gigantic pyre, where Donnie surreptitiously murmured a blessing for the okûns' souls as she watched their bodies burn. After a few minutes, she turned away, greatly saddened again, and rode Otis back the way they'd come, with her friends flanking her all around. The three humans in their little group worked tirelessly at setting the town to rights until well after the night sky appeared.

Deep into the evening, the denizens of Mâlendian opened their houses and pooled their food and libations, leading this day of death and fear into a night of celebration for life and friendship. A feast was laid out in the town square, of roasted bird and pig, with huge platters of potatoes and other root vegetables placed on every table. Breads and pastries were plentiful, as was the seemingly endless supply of ale.

Warren noted quietly to his friends that no one had remarked upon his shape-shifting abilities, for which he was thankful. The townspeople seemed to accept him as he was since he had been heavily instrumental in the defeat of the okûn, and were quite willing to include him in their victorious festivities as repayment for this debt.

Donnie could sympathize with his fears. She herself was very grateful indeed that discussion of the peoples' affliction of the last couple of days was studiously avoided by all. Only she and her friends realized that most had not eaten for more than two days, ensuring their appetites were voracious, and not just for food.

The townspeople's merrymaking looked to go on until the wee hours of the morning, but Donnie cried off around eleven o'clock, pleading exhaustion. Earlier in the revelry, the innkeeper had informed the weary travelers that they were to be given the best rooms in the Four Bells Inn. Her friends now followed Donnie back to the inn, glad to have an excuse to leave the party, and joined together in her room.

Warren wasted no time in small talk. As soon as the door was closed behind them, he said, "The okûn who attacked Mâlendian today were allied with Valledai."

"How can you be certain?"

Falwaïn sat down on the bed next to Donnie as he asked this, after having first looked out the thickly paned window and down into the street below. Sylvester jumped onto the foot of the bed beside Donnie, while Rex curled up on the floor at her feet.

"Before I tore his throat out," Warren answered, his lustrous blue eyes glinting with satisfaction at the memory, "the okûn captain told me that we would never defeat Valledai, even *with* a Madra Witch. He boasted that no wizard could do it, and dared me to try calling Déagmun back. But it's too late for that; Déagmun is gone."

"Yeah, well, if I can't defeat Valley Guy, I don't think Déagmun could've either," said Donnie. "So let's hope your nasty little informer was wrong." She leaned back and rested her weight on her hands. "Do you think they came to Mâlendian because Valley Guy told them to?" Through the blanket and bed linens, she could feel the soft down of the mattress beneath. Instantly, she craved sleep more than anything else in the whole wide world.

Warren shook his head uncertainly at her question. "I would think not," he replied carefully. "How could he know the townspeople were in such a vulnerable state? No, I believe the okûn were merely taking advantage of the townspeople's inability to defend themselves. I think that is why they sacked Banaff Dír also, happenstance only. And hunger, of course."

Falwaïn nodded in agreement and said, "They were most likely traveling north anyway to join Valledai's forces that the North Wolves reported were assembling in the mountains near Marn Dím. It's lucky we came; else there would've been slaughter done here, affliction or no," he asserted, his voice thick with emotion. He looked at Donnie meaningfully and murmured softly, "We really did do a lot of good today, Donemere."

He was propped up on his elbow and, as Donnie realized with astonishment, Sylvester had jumped between them to allow both Donnie and Falwaïn to stroke him. The cat was now nearly asleep, his eyes closed tightly in ecstasy as Falwaïn's hand ran gently down his length, while Donnie scratched under his chin. She marveled, as always when confronted with it, at the unqualified acceptance of others within the hearts of her animal friends.

Rex, noticing for the first time that the cat was having lavish attention paid to it, rolled over onto his back and hooked his leg behind Donnie's ankle, giving her a subtle reminder where her primary loyalties were supposed to lie. *So much for unqualified acceptance*, she chuckled to herself ruefully. She rubbed Rex's belly with her bare foot and nodded her head, finally responding to Falwaïn's comment.

"Yeah, I know. I've pretty much made my peace with everything that happened today. For the time being, at least. Tomorrow may be another story. Up-down, up-down, that's me. Gee, I wonder if my depression's turning manic?" She gave a tired smile before continuing. "Well, if the okûn were going north anyway, then we're probably on the right track," she noted. "Valley Guy's current lair must be up that way. I guess we should just continue to Marn Dím and see what we find there."

The men nodded their agreement with this loose plan.

Donnie laid back onto the bed and stretched, mumbling, "Oh, feeble foibles, what a day it's been. I am so very tired, and so very sorry about the eight men who died. But at least their love lives on in their families and in all of us. Which is more than I can say for the one hundred and eighty-seven dead okûn. I'm not sure my blessing'll help them one bit in their next lives; they truly are evil—"

"One hundred and eighty-*six* okûn are dead, Donemere," interrupted Sylvester, sitting up and shaking off Falwaïn's hand to regard her with great seriousness. "Are you not aware of the one you changed?"

"The one I changed? What do you mean by changed?" Donnie sat back up, giving him a puzzled look.

"He tried to kill you, Mama, but he couldn't," Rex replied sleepily. "He turned all blue for a little bit when his sword hit you and then, suddenly, he wasn't a nasty, butt-ugly okûn anymore." The dog raised his head, looking straight up at her. "He was all silvery and clean once you were done with him, even his clothes, although they were still those god-awful okûn ones. His eyes even sparkled like rainbows. The whole thing was way cool, wasn't it, Sylvester? How d'ya do it, Mama?"

Donnie shook her head, thoroughly nonplussed by this news. "Since I don't know what you're talking about, I can't answer that. And besides, I thought you were just a tad color-blind? No? Or just not anymore? Is seeing things in Technicolor yet another power that's been granted to you, Dog Wonder?"

The dog grinned at her unabashedly, replied that nope, he still had trouble with reds and greens, then laid his head down and promptly went to sleep. It was left to Sylvester to explain about the okûn whom Donnie had unknowingly transformed into a vinca. The cat couldn't remember seeing him for long, though. The vinca appeared to have vanished quickly, leaving at least a score of dead okûn in his wake.

"Wow, who knew I could do that?" Donnie acknowledged with a wide yawn. "I'll have to ponder that one awhile. Turning fell creatures to fair...hmm, that just might come in handy, don't you think? Maybe I can repeat it sometime, only this time actually be conscious I'm doing it. In a flash of blue, you say? Just like that, he was changed from okûn to vinca? I wonder if it had anything to do with the Metta meditation?" she mumbled, then yawned again, her craving for bed growing stronger with each passing second.

"Were you aware of what was happening to those still afflicted by your power?" Sylvester asked her curiously.

Donnie nodded. "You mean the whole, mostly invisible thing? Yeah, that *was* a side effect of my Metta meditation. Metta's all about sending loving-kindness from deep within you out into the world. Well, because those particular townspeople were still held by my magical power at the same time as when I sent that loving-kindness toward them, and because I had willed them to be completely protected from danger, the combination of my magic and my goodwill sort of took them out of the world so that they couldn't be harmed by anything *in* it.

"I guess that was because it was only here that they could be harmed. I'm not sure where they went, but, boy-oh-boy, I gather it was someplace pretty darn delightful since they were all happy as pigs in you-know-what when I released them. You must've felt it too—I mean, most of them were positively giddy all afternoon long! Even in my trance, I was nearly bowled over by all the peace, love and understanding that was emanating back to me. Granted, it's faded somewhat by now, but I'll bet they're all gonna have one heck of a love hangover tomorrow, even the men, because they were affected by it too. I imagine that's why we were accepted so readily, considering that Warren's a shape-shifter and I'm quite obviously magical too. I don't think they figured out that anyone else is, though."

Falwaïn suddenly sat up, disturbing Sylvester's balance, and looked at Warren before enquiring abruptly, "How many people did you tell that Donnie is a Madra Witch?"

"Only the healers," replied the Wolf King, "and that was because they were present when she healed the most seriously wounded. To the others, I called her a holy woman and told them her prayers would bring blessings upon their houses."

Falwaïn nodded. "As did I."

"Why? What's it really matter?" Donnie stifled yet another yawn behind her hand. Something was niggling at the back of her mind, but she couldn't raise it yet. Something about this whole mess was wrong. Very wrong.

"Well, for one thing, witches are not always welcomed in Medregai," Falwaïn explained somberly.

"Aw jeez, you're not gonna let me sleep in this wonderful, soft bed, are you?" Donnie cried. "Dang it, I've been sleepin' on straw for months! Please don't do this to me, not tonight. Tell me we can get at least a few hours of sleep before the good people of Mâlendian come to burn me at the stake!"

Warren and Falwaïn looked at each other and reached an agreement wordlessly. Falwaïn spoke their plan. "We'll all stay in this room. It's positioned most advantageously, with the stables just around the corner. If we must, we'll leave by the window. At most, it's a small drop to the street. I'll take first watch and awaken you later, Warren. But we must be on the road long before first light. Pray that the healers do not inform the others until the morrow."

Donnie expelled a low, grateful sigh and scooted up the bed to lie on its length, pulling the covers over her. She remained dressed in case they had to make a hasty exit. When she called him, Rex jumped onto the bed, received his goodnight kiss, and laid down behind her, his back snugly fitted to hers, while Sylvester curled up in the bend of her knees. All three were fast asleep within moments.

Warren changed into his wolf form and laid in front of the door. He too was asleep quickly. Falwaïn doused all the candles after a few minutes and sat watch in a chair in the corner, listening closely to the carousing that was still going on in the streets below.

He woke Warren at the appointed time, then shooed Rex from the bed. Lifting the covers, he joined his warmth with Donnie's. Instinctively, she rolled over to lay her head in the crook of his shoulder and snuggled closer, her body molding to his. He held his breath as his desire for her caught flame. His arms tightened around her and his mouth brushed her forehead and temple. With an effort, he stilled his wanton desire and let his hold on her loosen. He smiled in the dark and rested his cheek on her forehead, finally drifting into a light and only fitful sleep.

They left through the window a couple hours later because there were still revelers in the bar downstairs. Quietly, they slipped down the street and into the stables. Falwaïn and Donnie saddled the horses and packed their gear, while Rex and Warren kept watch. Their belongings had clearly been searched. A few things were missing, like Donnie's parka and the potato chips. Donnie waited until they were a couple miles away before she materialized everything back to their rightful owners; all except the potato chips, that is, which nobody had any desire to reclaim now anyways.

When the good people of Mâlendian stormed their rooms at dawn, shouting cries of, "Burn the witch, behead the werewolf!" the travelers were already more than fifteen miles north of town.

Chapter 14
Stay and Talk with Me a While

"So, what's wrong with witches?" Donnie wanted to know once they were well away from Mâlendian. "I get why werewolves aren't all that popular with the general public; but witches? What's up with that?" She was munching on a slice of bread she'd toasted and buttered, then materialized from home.

"Hmm?" murmured Falwaïn, who'd been keeping a watchful eye on their surroundings, looking for possible threats. He turned to her with a questioning expression on his handsome features.

They were alone. Rex and Warren had gone ahead and were nowhere in sight. Sylvester had jumped off the horse a couple minutes before to run down his breakfast; preferably a big juicy rat, he'd informed them hungrily. Even Otis, being a talented horse, wasn't really there as he'd long ago mastered the ability to doze off to sleep while still being perfectly capable of walking on a path. Gallantry, being nonmagical, didn't count since he couldn't understand their conversation anyway, or so Donnie hoped. There already seemed to be a plethora of magical animals surrounding her, and she still didn't think she needed yet another. That left only Brindle, but his attention was usually focused on things at the cottage.

"You know, what do people here have against witches?" Donnie restated her question.

Falwaïn gave her a brief smile before responding. "There have been few witches in these lands and they were pretty much either Yfel or Déadl, with only a handful being Madra, and *those* witches were loyal to Orgos through Kaledar. It's believed they were never trustworthy and are still feared by many. You would likely be categorized the same as they, with or without cause, by nearly everyone in Medregai. Fægre Witches, by the way, have been even scarcer throughout our history. As a matter of fact, I've heard of only two, and they lived some centuries ago."

Something in his answer struck a discordant note in Donnie's mind, way back there where that vague something was still niggling. Falwaïn noticed the puzzled expression on her face and asked why she gave it.

"Oh, it's just that there's something wrong here," she told him. "Something I'm missing. Something I know or I've heard that doesn't fit with everything else. But I can't grasp what it is yet. You ever have that happen?"

He nodded his head. "If you stop attempting to recall it, you may enjoy more success," he suggested.

"Funny, we use a similar expression in my time," noted Donnie. "So, how do you know about the different levels of Witchcraft? Through Déagmun?"

Falwaïn shook his head, letting his eyes drift across the landscape, all the while searching the darkest places for movement. "They're quite well-known throughout Medregai actually," he said, "and have long been a part of our lore. You know, Donnie, it's not just witches who are feared now, so do not take offense. All magic is distrusted. Man's memory is short and many forget that not so long ago our world was threatened by black magic and saved by white. They've convinced themselves that Déagmun and the other magical creatures who were allied to men were not needed to bring about the defeat of Orgos." Falwaïn looked at her once again and she saw the flash of his sardonic smile. "I wonder how they will react to the resurgence of the okûn under Valledai's command."

"Who knows, maybe I'll become quite popular in Medregai society, asked to dine at the finest tables and all that?" Donnie ventured saucily. "Well, once they know I'm on their side, that is."

He chuckled merrily.

"You don't think so, huh? Well, you're probably right," Donnie conceded. "I did get a distinctly unfriendly vibe from some of the good people of Mâlendian. The healers mostly, but even some of the others didn't buy that story about me being a holy woman. And they really didn't like me blessing the souls of the okûn."

"No, that they did not understand," agreed Falwaïn. "And it's likely some few were able to remember what had happened to them over the past few days. Your power, when you drew it from the land and into yourself, was visible for all to see. They would have resented anyone with that sort of influence over them."

"I can't say as I blame them for that. But," she began, her eyes glinting impishly at him, "more to the point, and I want you to be completely honest about this, by the way. When we first got to the town square, you wanted to get up there and join in the dance, didn't you?" She tried, unsuccessfully, to keep a straight face.

Falwaïn laughed outright at this, but shook his head a moment later, swearing gravely, "No, I did not."

"No? Then maybe you are immune to my magic," she observed coyly.

He allowed his eyes to drift up and down her, his gaze lingering on her lips. "Possibly to your magic," he murmured softly.

A wave of hot desire flooded over her and she found herself breathing hard. A whimpered, "Hoo," was all she could manage in reply.

They continued at a slow pace until the morning sun had risen. The far-off majestic Brumal Mountains were silhouetted in its rays on the horizon. Sylvester rejoined Donnie and Falwaïn first, then, only a minute later, Warren and Rex came racing back together along the road, matching strides. The horses pulled up and waited for them to approach.

Warren changed into his human form as soon as he stopped running and informed his friends crisply, "We've found several okûn trails ahead, mostly moving northward. They appear to be joining the Annûar Path from the Brumal Mountains. We must be on our guard and watch for more of the beasts. Unfortunately, if we continue at our current rate, we shall not reach Bitterbend by midday, so we must make haste regardless of the okûn."

"Why? What are you not saying about these Bitterbend Marshes that I should know?" Donnie asked him suspiciously.

"Fell creatures dwell in and around the murky depths of Bitterbend," warned the Wolf King. He laid his hand on Rex's head and began scratching behind the dog's ears, both of them seeming to enjoy the fond gesture.

"What, like more okûn?" asked Donnie, trying to stay positive about this new development. At least she was semi-prepared for okûn.

"No, much worse," Warren replied, giving her a level stare.

"Trolls?" she ventured brightly.

"No."

"Um, needy spirits like Dreena and Fred met in the Cursed Wood?"

"I don't believe so." Warren responded uncertainly to this, being unfamiliar with exactly the sorts of spirits the famed noakies had encountered.

"Okay, I give up. What are these *fell creatures* then?" Donnie inquired, bracing herself for the worst, whatever that might be.

"They are Great Serpents," Warren answered her grimly.

"Snakes?" cried Donnie, exuberance in her voice and on her face. "Oh, kewl, I love snakes! They're always getting a bad rap, you know, which is such a shame, 'cause what most people don't realize is that they often serve a really useful purpose."

Warren raised an eyebrow, drawling, "If these have a useful purpose, it is not an obvious one. It is best we make it through the marshes by mid-afternoon because the serpents are at their least active during the midday sun. Believe me, Donemere, when I tell you that the Bitterbend Marshes have long claimed thousands of souls unfortunate enough to travel the road beside them at any other time of the day. Now, come, we must hurry."

"Agreed." Falwaïn turned toward Donnie, who had her chin stuck out and an obstinate look in her eyes, to warn her sternly, "These are not your common, garden variety of snake, Donnie."

She shot him an appalled look, retorting, "My gawd, you did get an awful lot of reading in the other night, didn't you? Okay, okay, I'll be good, I promise. Let's go already," she griped, sending a mutinous, sideways glare at his amused expression.

They rode at a brisk, extended canter until a little past ten o'clock, when the road curved noticeably to the west. Here, they slowed to a walk; Donnie wanted to know why, covering her mouth with her hand to filter out some of the stench blowing into their faces from the northeasterly wind.

"Because the least disturbance we make, the better off we'll be." Falwaïn gave a little shake of his head and chuckled. "I know you believe that you want to see the Great Serpents, but you'll have to take my word for it that you don't, not really. It truly is for the best, Donnie."

Donnie let out a disbelieving grunt, but otherwise remained silent. She materialized a bandana from home and tied it around her face. It helped only a little with the smell. They turned the bend and when the forest ended abruptly they could see the marshes of Bitterbend extending to the north and east for as far as the eye could see. A few solitary trees, watery and dripping from the wispy, receding fog that still hugged the surface of the water, sprang up here and there along the marsh edges, where thick reeds choked out most other plant life. The road continued to the west, running along the southern border of the marshland.

"Was that bend we just passed Bitterbend?" Donnie nearly whispered her question, a little unnerved by the eerie silence of the marshes.

Falwaïn's voice was also low when he replied, "No, that is yet to come."

"You say that like it's a bad thing."

He bestowed upon her his best lopsided grin and enjoined, "Pray that it is not. Our timing has been fortunate. This is the safest hour of the day to begin traversing Bitterbend's marshes. We should have passed the most dangerous section by two o'clock at the very latest. The Great Serpents will begin to stir around that time."

"You mean, unless something else wakens them, I gather."

He flashed her another grin. "Yes, but we shall not make enough noise to disturb their slumber. And that is a good thing, Donemere Saunders."

Donnie gave him a quick smile in return, surprised at how nice it was to hear her real name spoken aloud again. She'd almost begun to think of herself as Donemere of the Codlebærn.

They traveled quietly through the cool of the late morning and into the noonday warmth. The marshes went on solidly, relentlessly boring from this viewpoint. When they'd started riding by them, Donnie couldn't resist thinking about all the life that must be teeming underneath the surface of the waters and within the mud. Since becoming a witch, she'd developed an avid interest in biology and therefore itched to get down off Otis to check out the creatures of the marshes up-close and personal. But a promise was a promise and so she remained in her saddle.

Which didn't mean she couldn't look with her mind's eye. Ever mindful of Mournful Jack's advice that she *see* the sights of Medregai and not just look at them, Donnie focused her attention fully upon the denizens of Bitterbend. For the next few hours, she observed the daily lives of the millions of aquatic bugs, mammals, amphibians, reptiles and various types of fish that thrived within the extensive marsh waters and the deep lake that lay in their center.

One fish species, which Donnie dubbed "Glitterfish," repeatedly swam downward through the lake in large groups. Along their protracted bodies, their mirror-like silver scales glowed brighter and brighter with a shimmering rainbow of colors as they dived deeper and faster. Then, suddenly, they would stop, their light would go dark and, as one, they would turn quickly and attack the schools of smaller fish that had been attracted to them by the artificial glow of their scales. The Glitterfish were fascinating and quite ruthless, although also extraordinarily beautiful. Donnie was mesmerized by them and, in fact, by many of the creatures of Bitterbend, all somehow seemingly either larger or more dangerous than what she was accustomed to. Some were so industrious in their relentless search for food, they made her tired just watching them.

Perhaps the most fascinating aspect of her journey through the marshes occurred whenever Donnie probed into the hearts, minds and souls of the more advances organisms. Most of them had normal, ordinary triunes, engaged mainly in the business of survival. But Donnie could also feel more complex, darker creatures suspended far, far down in the deepest regions of the lake, much farther down than she wanted to go. She could feel them lying in wait, intending to sleep the afternoon away, and knew that what Falwaïn had said was absolutely true; these were not your common, garden variety of snake. They had highly developed brains and were the undisputed rulers of this underwater world. And every other soul in the marshes, whether it was a knowing soul or a simpler one, was deathly afraid of these sleeping giants.

A little before one o'clock, the travelers came upon a sharp right-hand bend in the road, which headed them almost due north. Everyone walked very quietly, the only sound being the soft clip-clop of the horses' hooves on the dirt and the buzzing of some flies and other insects in the air. Donnie was gazing off to the west, having finally satiated her curiosity for the marsh depths. The sun shone warmly down onto her bare face, lulling her into a kind of languishing stupor that had lasted for some long while, which she now struggled to shake off. The bandana she'd sent back to the wardrobe earlier since it hadn't done much good anyway, and by then she'd gotten used to the foul smell of Bitterbend's brackish waters.

She noticed that the land over to the west appeared to consist of gently rolling moors. Puzzled, she asked Falwaïn, "Why doesn't the road go over there? I mean, these moors aren't anywhere near as bad as the ones around my house, so wouldn't it make more sense to have the road there, to get it away from the marshes and its fell creatures?"

The boombox suddenly came to life at a very low volume, and began to play Black Adder's country rock classic "Stay and Talk with Me a While." Falwaïn frowned at it, then looked to his left at where Donnie had indicated, replying quietly, "It has fell creatures of its own. There are caves throughout that part of the land which used to be filled with trolls. Many still are."

"Oooohhhhh," Donnie whispered. She was silent a moment, then added, "I don't think I want to meet any trolls."

Falwaïn smiled faintly and inclined his head in agreement with her. "Allow me to echo that sentiment," he said. "I too have no desire to encounter a troll on our journey."

"But you've run into them before, right?"

"Yes, and they are not to be trifled with," he informed her. "There is no reasoning with them, no bartering, no politicking, or any such rational interaction as that. Everyone they come upon, they fully intend to kill and eat, and not necessarily in that order. Which, as I said, makes them extremely dangerous, leaving one with the only recourse of kill or be killed. And trolls are very hard to kill."

After digesting this information for a few seconds, Donnie again whispered, "Oooohhhhh." She chewed her lip with worry, then asked, "What about Gâ'Duk? Wasn't he friends with you all during the Battle of the Var?"

"Yes," admitted Falwaïn, "but he went adventuring to other lands several years back and has not been heard from since. I doubt even King

Belnesem knows his whereabouts. If you are thinking that perhaps some of his troll kin might help us through their country, I don't believe we could count on that happening. No, I am certain we are on the best course we can take."

"Okay…I guess you're right," Donnie conceded.

"By the way, *that*," Falwaïn continued, as he turned around and pointed at the curve behind them, "was Bitterbend. We are well over halfway through the marshes now."

Donnie looked at him curiously. "You know this area pretty well, don't you? The north, that is, not just Bitterbend."

He shrugged his assent. "I suppose you could say that. I've traveled these lands for two years now."

"Why? I mean, why did you come to this area when you had your own lands and all that? Was it just because your wife and child died and you wanted to get away for a while?"

His manner thoughtful, he admitted, "That is what I told everyone, yes. Honestly though, I found that I had lost my desire to live without my wife, so I went in search of a warrior's death. But it has not found me yet…and I find I'm beginning to be glad of that." He stared at Donnie intently, then reached for the boombox when its volume increased and John During described what could only be classified as a very, very dangerous situation.

"Not too loud, you know; we don't want to waken anything scary," Donnie hissed at the thing unthinkingly, also reaching for the volume dial, when suddenly her hand stilled. Her shoulders slumped and she groaned, "Oh, please God no, don't tell me that! Falwaïn, I really think we should—uh-oh, what's that?"

Falwaïn had already brought his hand back and steered his horse into Otis, moving them both to the left, while Warren and Rex loped back to stand in front of them. The boombox volume increased as the source of the noise came into view.

Around Bitterbend careened six riders, hollering and whooping loudly, their horses' hooves thundering on the dry, packed dirt of the Annûar Path. They raced past the little group assembled to the side of the road, the Mountain Men laughing devilishly and their steeds galloping hell-bent for leather. A long cloud of yellow dust trailed in their wake.

The boombox cranked up its volume as they sped by, wailing out the chorus of the song, with During now telling how the lawman in the story coerced them all into sitting down for a little chat, convincing them it would be in their best interests to hear him out.

Donnie, distracted by the song, realized she could no longer see her hands in front of her and used her magical breath to blow the thick haze of dirt swirling around her and her friends back down toward the ground. Once the air was clear again, she indignantly shouted the same thing she always did when a particularly arrogant and self-entitled driver cut in front of her back home. "Oh, sure, it's all about you, isn't it!" she cried to the riders' receding backsides.

Her friends gaped at her, then turned to watch in horror as the water in front of them began to bubble and foam. Donnie cringed and apologized in a tight voice, "Let me just say right now, I am extremely sorry for my part in whatever is about to happen."

Warren turned back toward her when she spoke, then shouted, "Behind you!" great alarm distorting his wolven features.

They all swung around and saw three very large black snakes, each easily fifty feet long, come round the bend, slithering up the road toward them and advancing fast. The travelers heard the water behind them erupt to an ear-splitting, raucous chorus of some curlews who apparently were resting in one of the nearby trees. As a group, Donnie and the others whirled toward the direction of the birds' calls. A gigantic snake, no more than a hundred feet from them, roiled out of the water with a stentorian bellow and swayed its dark head thirty feet in the air. The curlews, only a stone's throw from its massive snapping jaws, swung away to the south, flying as hard and fast as they could.

This reptilian behemoth, much larger than his three brethren coming up the road, struck at the raucous devil-makers in the blink of an eye and caught the last of the riders with its mouth. It nimbly tossed both him and his horse a short distance into the air, snatching at the huge man and devouring him in one gulp. His horse dropped toward the ground and would have slammed helplessly into it if Donnie hadn't caught him with her magic and set him on his feet. Utterly terrified, the horse sped away, following his friends. The Great Serpent turned to stare at the little group huddled to the side of the road. Donnie could almost feel its cold stare zero in on her as the boombox now exhorted them to get moving.

"This way, to the moors!" Falwaïn wheeled Gallantry around. "Come!" he shouted. Both horses sprang from the road and hit the grassland with hooves flying. Rex disappeared. Warren raced ahead of Donnie and Falwaïn in wolf form. They'd gone less than thirty yards when Donnie saw the tail of the largest Great Serpent reach in front of her and coil around her, lifting her off Otis to snatch her backward. Her shrieks of goodbye were drowned in the pounding of the horses' hooves.

The snake pulled his captive down under the water, steadily plunging them deeper and deeper. At first, Donnie got a lung-full of the putrid water up her nose before she finally had the presence of mind to conjure an impenetrable bubble of atmosphere around her face so that she could breath, along with a screen-type shield (just to see if she could create one of this kind) to protect her head, shoulders and legs from being slammed every other second by the various flotsam and jetsam floating in the marsh water. The rest of her body was still getting wet, but at least with the breathing bubble in place, the water was no longer rushing up her nose and into her lungs.

After coughing up the swallowed water and loudly cursing first the snake and then the gods, she muttered angrily, "You didn't have to be so freaking literal about the still waters thing, did you?"

It took less than thirty seconds for the snake to grab her and get them about half a mile away and under more than a hundred feet of water, where it slowed and wrapped itself tightly around Donnie's length. She let her screen shield dissipate while the serpent turned her around three times in its coils, leaving only her head and feet visible. She looked up at the receding light of day, which, by now, was no more than a soft glow. A quick glance downward told her that way brought only blackness; naturally, the snake sped on in that direction.

Donnie made sure to keep a tiny part of her mind focused on a very large snail she'd caught a glimpse of on the edge of the marsh as they flew over him and hit the water. His uncomplicated soul rang out strong and determined, providing an unwavering, mostly stationary point of reference for her, as though it were a thread of silk for her to latch onto which she could use to track her way back to relative safety, if need be.

She was also keeping another part of her mind focused on Otis, using him to watch over those she'd left behind. "The guys can handle those three itty bitty snakes—if it really comes to that, I mean," she told herself confidently. She'd hoped they would run instead of fight, but she already knew the two men well enough to know that another fight was just what they were itching for.

***

Otis, now unburdened, surged ahead of Gallantry and Warren to shout, "Stop! Donnie's gone!"

They all wheeled around and looked back at the marshes just in time to see her head disappear under the water's surface. The other three snakes had veered off the road and were almost upon the men and horses. Falwaïn jumped off Gallantry, his sword unsheathed and at the ready the moment he touched ground. Warren transformed into his werewolf form, with razor-sharp claws extended. He let out a loud, angry howl that ended in a snarl, challenging the snakes to keep on coming.

In seconds, the Great Serpents reached them. The two men each met a snake head-on, attacking it at full throttle. The third snake tried to wrap itself around Otis when he and Gallantry stepped into its path, instinctively recognizing Otis as the older and, what the Great Serpent had assumed to be, the weaker of the two horses. Otis was having none of that though. He reared back and kicked his sharp hooves at the snake, landing a couple of slicing blows that sent its reptilian head reeling backward drunkenly. Gallantry, once again taking his cue from his friend, began to stomp on the snake's middle.

Just a couple minutes later, Falwaïn made the final decisive cut on his serpent from his position astride it. He'd hung on tightly with his legs for a wild ride as he'd swung his blade rhythmically, first cutting the snake's neck on the left side, then flipping the sword over to slash on the right. This way, he weakened the Great Serpent enough to pierce and chop through its thick scales so that he was finally able to cut it in two. He leapt from its flailing carcass and saw the third snake attempt to slam its tail against Otis's legs. The horse, by a hair's breadth, and with a flash of blue, only just managed to escape the snake's reach.

Falwaïn ran straight at the snake. It hissed and thrust its head toward the right, aiming to come around and grab him from behind. Falwaïn whirled just as the snake's head neared, his sword singing through the air until it was buried to the hilt under the Great Serpent's jaw. He shoved the handle from side to side quickly, then withdrew the dripping blade. The snake dropped heavily to the ground, lifeless.

Falwaïn turned to see Warren standing over the shredded body of the final serpent. A composed smile spread across Warren's features as his claws receded, the blood forced from their lengths when he took on his human form.

All three snakes were oozing a noisome, blackish blood from their wounds, which immediately sent the men and horses upwind of the carcasses to ascertain if any injuries had been sustained to anyone in their party. None had.

Falwaïn strode purposefully to the water's edge and began shedding his armaments. Warren ran to him quickly and placed a hand on his arm to stop him. "No, my friend, we cannot follow."

Falwaïn looked at Warren in agony. "I can't leave her to die. I will find her and free her. I must!"

Warren took hold of the other man by the shoulders and shook him. "You cannot swim where that thing has taken her! She is leagues from here by now. If it had wanted Donnie dead, it would not have taken her like that; she would *be* dead now, the same as that Mountain Man. Or she would still be here with us and the Great Serpent would be very sorry indeed that it had ever trifled with her. No, Falwaïn, we should trust in her. She must have gone with him willingly and, if so, then she will find a way to free herself."

"Yes, she is nothing if not resourceful, our Donemere," Sylvester offered confidently from his perch on Otis. He'd already begun smoothing his ruffled fur from the earlier fracas. "She will not be bested by a mere reptile. I believe we should continue on to Marn Dím, though I hesitate to do so without Rex. But he too is most likely many leagues from here by now. Donemere will find him when she frees herself, so we must not waste time waiting for him. No, on to the city it is for us. If Donemere is to find us, it will be there," he directed the two men sharply.

"No! I cannot leave her here, do you not see that?" Falwaïn exploded, shoving Warren away to begin unbuckling his knife belt.

Warren stepped forward again and thrust his face into Falwaïn's. "I see a man who is not thinking clearly!" he shouted back. "I see a man who is in love with a witch who has just been stolen away from him to the depths of Medregai. I see a man who is in love with not just any witch, but with the most powerful witch of all time! And I see that you, my friend, must learn to believe in Donnie and her powers. If you cannot do that, your feelings for her are doomed because she will never accept the love of a man who does not believe in her. That is what I see." The waters behind Falwaïn began to bubble ominously again. "I also see that it is time to go. Come, we must fly!"

Falwaïn turned to give one last, longing look at the roiling water and then jumped onto Gallantry, who followed the others down the Annûar Path at full gallop.

***

An hour later, Donnie was trying to figure out if she was angry or bored or both. Both, she finally decided. She knew it had been an hour because she'd managed to push her left hand between the snake's coils just enough so that she could see the lighted dial of her wristwatch.

Feeling her way along the tendril connecting her mind with that of the snail back at the marsh's edge and realizing just how far the snake had gone, Donnie groused irritably, "Where is this thing taking me? Eastward, definitely, by at least fifty—no, it's closer to sixty miles now, if my internal sonar is still working correctly, and I have the utmost faith that it is. Which means, according to the maps I studied yesterday, we must be nearing the eastern border of the marshes, at the foot of the northern part of the Brumal Mountains, and I suppose we're in some underground mountain river that feeds into Bitterbend." She grunted in discomfort, watching more blurry objects fly by with no clues as to what they were, and reached out farther with another part of her mind to search for Falwaïn's triune.

***

"She's alive!" Falwaïn suddenly yelled to the others. Their group had slowed to a trot a short time before, having passed quickly and safely through the remainder of the marshes.

Warren, still in his human shape and sitting astride Otis, was bemusedly encased by Donnie's saddle. To the best of his recollection, he had never felt anything so comfortable before in his life.

Sylvester, on the other hand, had his claws dug desperately into Donnie's sleeping bag to keep from being bounced off it by the jerking motion of the horse. He demanded querulously of Falwaïn, "Are you certain? How do you know?"

"I can hear her—no, feel her. In my head."

"She is touching your mind?" Warren grinned at him in appreciation. "Startling, is it not?"

"Yes, you could say that," Falwaïn replied dryly. "She is fine and says that she's...mad as a wet hen...uncomfortable as all get-out...and bored out of her skull...but otherwise just peachy keen." His smile was broad. This was so much in keeping with what he knew of Donnie already. While other women, and men alike too, he must allow, would be violently terrified in the snake's grasp, she was angry, uncomfortable and bored. Was this because of her modern sensibilities or was it just her way now that she was magical, he wondered to himself.

He caught the expectant look on Warren's face and hastily continued relaying Donnie's message. "She apparently took quite a dousing when they first went underwater and is still coiled tightly in the serpent's tail. She says she decided to let the thing take her because she wants to do some sleuthing, as she calls it. That's why her saddle let go of her."

"I could have told you that, if only you had asked," interjected Brindle, his voice making all except the horses jump in surprise.

"Brindle? You're here? But where are you?" Warren inquired incredulously.

"The stirrups on Donnie's saddle are made from me," the tree replied.

"Donnie's gone now," Falwaïn informed the others. Not knowing where else to look, he gazed at the stirrup facing him and asked, "Tell us, Brindle, did she really want to go with that thing?"

"At first, no," said Brindle, "but then she thought it wise to see what it wanted of her. She deduced it must want something because it caught her with its tail. When I let go of her, she then said something strange about it beginning her journey to enlightenment."

Falwaïn glanced appraisingly at both Warren and Sylvester. "That must be what she meant by her sleuthing. She said that she will meet us at Marn Dím later tonight and that we are to get a room for her at the inn of our choice." He then conceded, somewhat shamefaced, "You were right, Warren, I should never have doubted her; I should've believed in her. From this point forward, I always shall. But that is something she must find out for herself."

***

The Great Serpent, holding Donnie tightly in its grip, entered a wide tunnel that curved upward rather sharply. It swam to a point where there was no longer any water, erupting out of its surface with a violent spray of briny brew, then slithered along the floor of the tunnel without losing one iota of speed. Even though they were now on comparatively dry land, Donnie decided to keep her protective bubble around her head just in case they were submerged again anytime soon.

A little farther on, the tunnel curved downward and then dove ever deeper into the Earth's crust until some while later it finally evened out. This part of the tunnel was long and straight, and wet with dripping water and steam from the almost stifling heat. A ghostly phosphorescent-like glow lit the tunnel walls well enough so that Donnie could see their length stretching out in front of her to what looked like infinity. The tunnel reeked of dampness and decay.

They had traveled for a long while more when, suddenly, another snake joined them from one of the side tunnels that Donnie now realized were appearing regularly. She could see that there were several of these adjuncts along their route. The snakes began to hiss at each other in their own language. Donnie willed herself to understand their whispery conversation and was more than a little astounded when that actually worked.

"—will await masssster'ssss command there. Go now and return quickly, little brother." This was said by the snake holding Donnie in its grasp.

The other snake shot ahead of them into a new tunnel to the left and disappeared.

Not long afterward, Donnie's snake slowed when the tunnel they were traveling in suddenly widened to a cavern. It was even hotter and more humid in here than it had been in the tunnel. Jets of natural gas had been lit and were burning eerily, providing a dim sort of half-light.

The snake slithered to the middle of the cavern where an extensive pool of water lay and submerged most of his two hundred foot length in it, except for his head and for his tail, where Donnie remained completely straitjacketed by his coils. He delicately—for him, that is—coughed up something on the far shore. Judging from the existing piles of bones nearby, Donnie could make an educated guess as to what it was.

She waited a minute or so and when nothing more happened, she called out to it, "Hey, Nidhogg? How about setting me down for a while? I presume this is as far we go, right? Hellooooo?...Are you listening, Nidhogg? Seriously, can I get down now or do I have to wait until your brother returns from visiting your *masssster*?"

The snake slowly turned his head to look at her, eyeing her suspiciously. "You undersssstand Sssserpent Tongue?" it hissed at her.

"Could be..." Donnie replied, giving this due consideration as she studied the ceiling. Just how had she managed to make herself understand their language? She honestly didn't know, or for that matter, what had made her even think of trying it. It was almost as though she'd known beforehand that it would work and so had simply flipped a switch inside her head to make it happen. She brought her gaze back to the snake and declared, "Maybe I've just developed a good ear for languages, who knows?"

The snake turned away and laid its head in the shoals of the little lake.

Donnie tried again. "Um, yoo-hoo, Nidhogg? I answered your question, but you didn't answer mine. How about setting me down for a while? I mean, it's not like I'll go anywhere...I swear I won't...Girl Guide's honor...really, I mean it."

Donnie waited in silence between each sentence, but nothing generated a response from the snake.

"It's really hot in here, you know that?" she complained. "And it stinks. And I've got this one hair that's stuck to my eyelid. Tell you what, if you let loose on me a little, let me get the hair thing taken care of, I promise I'll put my arm right back in and let you squeeze me again. Honest I will. And trust me, I'll be a much happier camper then. Otherwise...well, I've got a feeling you'll like me a whole lot better if you literally cut me some slack here."

The snake slid its tail a little farther down into the water. Donnie could feel the heat of it on her legs. Well...at least she'd finally gotten a response of sorts.

She pursed her lips and looked around her as best she could. The cavern was easily as high as a six-story building and at least two football fields long. The pool of slightly steaming water covered more than half of it, with its pebbled shore extending out of the water for maybe fifty feet or so. Beyond that were mainly boulders of varying sizes and shapes piled high along the walls, some of which were smoothed over until they shone like glass. And all around the ceiling were what her friend Liz, a life-long avid spelunker, had once informed Donnie were called "pretties," or mineralized cave formations.

Donnie also studied the various piles of bones strewn on the embankment, all of which looked to have come from bipeds. Most were way too small, many others far too large, to be human. There were a number of horse carcasses decaying on the far bank to her right, which appeared to be the cause of the distinctly nidorous smell filling her nostrils. She adjusted her bubble of atmosphere to filter out the unbelievably awful aroma of rotting animal flesh.

With each passing second, she grew ever more uncomfortable, bored and irritable. Waiting only about another minute, she again tried with the snake, deciding to use flattery this time. "Hey, Nidhogg? You've got quite a nice place here, you know that? It's certainly secluded, I'll say that for it. With a little ingenuity and some tasteful furnishings, maybe clean it up a bit—you know, get rid of the bones and the smelly carcasses—you could turn this into a real showplace. If you let me down on the bank over there, I'd be happy to demonstrate what I mean. Um, are you there, Nidhogg?"

The snake suddenly snapped his head toward her, stopping just before he reached her so that no more than a foot separated their faces. Donnie blinked at him in surprise. Those huge, yellow eyes of his…she let the thought trail away.

"My name issss not Nidhogg. It issss Ungôl," he informed her angrily.

"*Uncle*? Honestly?" Donnie grinned mischievously at this, recovering her equanimity quickly. "Aw shucks, what a shame! As luck would have it, I've already got an uncle—Uncle Bob. Well, okay, most people probably have an Uncle Bob somewhere in their family tree. They seem like they're pretty much ubiquitous, you know what I mean?" she asked the snake earnestly. "As they say, Bob's your uncle, only in my case that's true! So…what's next, Uncle? I gather we're just gonna sit here for a while and wait for orders from this *masssster* of yours—am I right? But what do we do in the meantime, eh?" She continued to meet his penetrating gaze, her own steady and clear. "Hmm," she murmured. "I suppose we could play a riddle game while we're waiting. I hear those are extremely popular in situations like this."

The snake glared at her as several silent seconds ticked by.

"Oh, please, let's; shall we?" Donnie mimicked in high falsetto, then nodded her head and lowered her voice to its natural tone. "Sure thing,

Uncle, if you really want to. Okay then, why don't I go first? Um, let me see...oh, I know! What's a big strong Great Serpent like Uncle want with a puny little witch like Donnie?" she asked as blithely as she could, working to cover her growing nervousness at his proximity and the oh-so obvious fact that he could swallow her whole right now, with very little effort on his part. Which would be one extremely horrid experience she'd really rather avoid, thank you very much.

Ungôl did not acknowledge in any visible manner that she'd spoken.

"D'you mean to tell me, you're not even going to guess at the answer?" Donnie feigned astonishment. "Gee, what a shame! Here I sit, waiting desperately for you to enlighten me since, obviously, I don't know the answer myself. Yeah, I agree it wasn't much of a riddle—okay, so it was totally lame as a riddle, but c'mon, Uncle, you of all people—er, forgive me—you of all Great Serpents must know the answer!" She continued to stare at his mouth, mesmerized by the pointed tips of his teeth, which showed menacingly between his open lips. Had she mentioned yet that they were wickedly sharp teeth? She shuddered at them for about the tenth time.

Brushing aside her revulsion, Donnie decided to prod the snake a bit more. "I'm still waiting for you to loosen up your coils a bit, Uncle dear," she told him, "so I can brush that hair out of my eyes. Just thought you'd like to know that I haven't given up on that request yet. I'm a stubborn beggar, aren't I? Just ask my cat, he'll be quite happy to go on and on about exactly how stubborn I can be...Nuthin' doin', eh?...Okay then, it appears riddles aren't your thing. Tell ya what, we can play a word game if you like, and I'll let you go first this time. Why, I'll even let you choose the category! Let me see, what are our favorites back home? Oh, how about something from, say, 'Words Never Used Outside the Physical Sciences' or 'Epithets Only My Aunt Bea Thinks Are Appropriate for Polite Society'? That last one'll give you lots of latitude, 'cause there's not much that's off-limits to my Aunt Bea! Oh, heck, that reminds me, Uncle, one day you should meet my aunt. She's a—oh well, let's just say she's quite a character. Nobody, and I mean nobody, ever forgets my Aunt Bea once they've met her."

Donnie chuckled and gave the snake a wide grin. "I'll warn you though, while my aunt's really quite hilarious, she's also just as often an embarrassing handful too. She does things like abruptly shouting at young women she passes on the street, 'That skirt with those knees?' even when the knees in question are really quite lovely. It's not that Aunt Bea's mean-spirited, don't get me wrong. No, she's just a rather erratic, holy terror and, personally, I think she revels in that *rôle*, if you know what I mean. So many things seem to send her off on another tirade or mission of mischief, usually at the oddest of times, and often with absolutely no apparent provocation, that there's just no telling how she'll behave from one minute to the next." Donnie suddenly cocked her head and inquired, "You got anybody like that in your family tree?"

Ungôl stared at her and moved his snout an inch or two closer to her face. He was just about touching her protective bubble of filtered air now, so Donnie made it smaller. She grimaced when she felt the shield close upon her skin.

"Yeah, okay, I get it, enough about my Aunt Bea." Donnie rolled her eyes and then asked briskly, "Well, what d'ya think then, shall we play the word game? Oh, you needn't worry about not knowing which words to ask about because, when you choose the category, I'll also give you a listing and their definitions. Then you can make up the clues yourself. My dog just loves this game, I tell ya. Whenever he and his favorite tree get started on it, they can go for hours and hours. So, what do you think; are you ready to give it a try? Er, ahem, forgive me for asking this, but you *can* read, can't you, Uncle? If not, you shouldn't be ashamed, 'cause I've found there's a deplorable lack of literacy amongst magical creatures here in Medregai. Kinda makes me wonder if that's to keep the masses quiet; but for the life of me I can't figure out who would want to do that to them. Could it be your masssster who's responsible, whoever he is? Hmm?...Anyway, whaddya say? Ready to play, Uncle?"

The snake hissed at her again, the overpowering rush of his breath nearly sending her unconscious until she readjusted her protective shield. "My name issss Ungôl! And I have no wishhhh to play your gamessss."

Then he smiled at her, or at least Donnie presumed that's what it was intended to be. "My massssster will be pleasssssed I have caught you. He hassss promissssed a bounty for the one who capturessss you."

Donnie leaned her head back as far as possible from the set of eight-inch long spikes that constituted his upper and lower teeth. "Bounty? What kind of bounty?" she inquired, eyeing him warily.

Just for a second, so quickly did it pass that Donnie wasn't sure if she'd imagined it, his eyes seemed dull and glazed. Then they cleared and he sibilated, "For me, it will mean I sssshall reign over Bitterbend assss itssss Sssserpent King. My gratitude to you, Donemere of the Codlebærnsss, for sssshowing yoursssself to me on the Annûar Path. I knew you would passss by today, but I did not know when. You made it eassssy for me." His lips widened once again in a terrifying smile.

"Um, yeah sure, always happy to help a friend in need," said Donnie, trying to smile back at him but finding that she could only manage a half-hearted smirk because her mouth simply refused to contort into an actual smile with those spikes so near her tender flesh. "By the way, how'd you know it was me? I mean, is your master passing out 'Most Wanted' posters of me or something?"

The serpent pulled his head back a foot or two, his expression still malevolent, then hissed arrogantly, "No other witchhhh in Medregai would have dared to interfere with my attack on the Mountain Men."

Donnie let out a nervous little laugh. "They all know better, huh?" she joked. "Serves me right for coming to the meeting late and missin' that key piece of information! Well, at least that explains why you grabbed me. I really couldn't believe one less dead horse meant that much to you. But how, I wonder, did you hear that I'd be passing by today? From the okûn?"

"Okûn?" Ungôl's voice was filled with ridicule. "They are good for one purposssse only."

"Oh?" said Donnie, eyeing him questioningly. "And that would be...?"

"Assss a meal," he replied with relish, his tongue flicking out a couple of times.

Donnie nodded her head knowingly, observing with more than a little trepidation, "Ah, yours is not a discerning palate then, is it? I'm guessin' you'd eat anyone or anything that interferes with your, um, meals, huh? Now, please understand, this is merely to assuage my curiosity and is not to be construed as a suggestion but, pray tell, is that what you're about to do with me? You know, make a meal of me?"

Ungôl's eyes narrowed. "That sssshall not be my pleassssure. The massssster wantsss you alive, witchhhh."

"Darn the luck, eh?" commiserated Donnie. She wriggled in the snake's grasp, her back aching miserably. More than anything, she just wanted this to be over so she could move freely again. "I'll tell you what, if you let one of my arms loose, I can knock off that ugly bug that's attached itself to your cheek. And really, I'd be quite happy to do it for you. I was serious when I said I like helping others. So, how about it?" She glanced at the red, pulsating, four-inch long insect that was, even now, attempting to burrow its curved mandibles deeper into the snake's scales and scowled distastefully. "Unless it's like some symbiotic thing you got goin' with it."

The Great Serpent edged a few inches closer again, looking down his black, glistening nose at her with his menacing, yellow eyes and said, "No."

"D'ya like having your chin scratched? I could do that for you, probably put you right to sleep," Donnie offered brightly. "And you look like you could use some sleep. Honestly, you're lookin' a bit peaked, you know?"

Ungôl breathed hard once, his displeasure at his captive's apparent lack of fear evident.

Donnie grinned sillily at her motionless captor. She was pretty sure she was going to go bonkers if she didn't get to move one or all of her limbs soon. It really was unbelievably maddening to have your body forced to remain in one position for such an extended period of time. Really, it was just awful—uh-oh, here it came; her conscience, speeding straight at her and slamming her squarely between the eyes. It informed her darkly that she was getting no worse than she deserved; wasn't she just? Did she not think that perhaps she should have unfrozen Galto before sending him on his way—hmm? Surely there must have been some other method of securing his cooperation than turning him into a statue, of all things? Especially a conscious one, at that! Had she completely forgotten the Rule of Three and what it would mean for her?

"Oh, pernicious paybacks!" she hissed, her expression turning to one of exasperation as these thoughts whizzed through her head.

Ungôl backed away and stared at her as if she were just this moment going completely nuts.

Donnie ignored him and continued to argue with herself. "Okay, what I did to him *was* mean, I'll give you that. But he kinda pissed me off, you know, when he tried to kill me. Yeah, yeah, I know, he wouldn't have been able to succeed at that anyway, but it's the principle of the thing. He shouldn't go around trying to kill every witch he happens on here in Medregai—after all, he is two for two on attempted murder. So, all right already, I'll unfreeze him," she grumbled to that reproving voice in her head, hoping she could right this particular wrong immediately.

She searched the land for Galto's soul, sending out call after call, but was unsuccessful in receiving a reply or even an echo of him anywhere. She figured that meant Valley Guy had him and was shielding him from her. Well, at least she must've already done enough good with her magic to have somewhat mitigated her punishment for her misdeed, judging from the fact that her own forced paralysis would be over well within the day; or, to be more precise, so Donnie was determined it would be. Therefore, she'd just have to lump her situation until it came to its natural conclusion, otherwise there'd be more hell to pay and she'd still be the one owing!

She thought about her options, which were clearly limited, then set a part of her mind to meditating, hoping to overcome the constant stream of urgent and overwhelming impulses to scratch her nose, brush that darned (okay, it was actually fictitious) hair out of her eyes, move her foot, bend her knee, stir anything more than just her one hand and her head.

Maybe she should try a little Metta meditation while she was at it and see if she could work her magic with Uncle just like she had with that okûn at Mâlendian? "That's just the ticket!" she encouraged herself enthusiastically under her breath. But she should probably keep the Great Serpent's attention otherwise engaged until his brother returned, however long that might take, so he didn't realize what she was trying to do. After all, it might not sit well with him.

Ungôl watched the various emotions flit across the witch's face, all the while giving her his most imposing stare. He was, in fact, quite consternated by her behavior and completely bewildered by her incoherent ramblings. Was this merely an obvious ploy to get him to relax his grip on her or was she indeed unfazed by her predicament? Whichever was the truth, she *was* beginning to irritate him. And all these questions she asked were giving him a headache.

Taking a deep breath, Donnie opened her mouth, and soon surprised even herself with her subconsciously chosen tactics. "Well then, tell me, Uncle, how are we going to pass the time until your brother gets back? Lemme see…you say you don't like riddles or games…oh, I know! How about we simply get to know one another? You know, just chat idly for a while, see if we can't really open up to each other. I'm quite a good listener—really, I am. My boombox let me know earlier that this would be a very good idea for both of us and my boombox is never wrong."

The snake's eyes narrowed in suspicion.

Donnie waited a few extra moments before continuing, surprising herself even more with what came out of her mouth next. "Tell me, Uncle, are you happy in your job? 'Cause if you're not happy there, you won't be happy anywhere. I mean, considering how much time we all spend at our jobs on a daily basis. I'm kinda thinkin' you're not; after all, there's that king quest you got goin'. You've obviously got some illusions of grandeur and whatnot; but then hey, it's good to dream big." She gave a hesitant laugh at this and waited to see if Uncle would respond.

He did not.

Growing more and more bothered by her extreme physical discomfort and the fact that, so far, her attempts at meditation were failing miserably, Donnie realized that there was more of her Aunt Bea in her than she would've thought possible, as she exclaimed crossly, "Oh, look here, you moping servile serpent, I am merely trying to be sociable, pass the time for both of us with a little small talk, the pleasantries, that kind of stuff, because who knows how long it's going to take your brother to get back? Unless, of course, you feel like just telling me exactly who your master is, why he wants me, and what he intends to do with me, then release me so I can go on my merry way? No? Well, let's try it my way for a little while then, 'kay? Would you like me to go first? Tell you what, you can ask me any question you want. Go on, seriously, ask me anything you've always wanted to know about humans."

Ungôl hissed slowly in response to her increasingly peevish manner. She was seeking information about the master, was she?

Upon again receiving no verbal reply, Donnie sighed dramatically and rolled her head back onto the topmost of his coils. "Yep, you're a real serpentine charmer, aren't you? You unceremoniously kidnap me off my horse, drag me through miles and miles of marsh water down into this stinking sauna you call home, and then don't even have the decency to engage in real conversation, let alone offer refreshments! When I get back to my library, I think I'm gonna have to check what Millicent Manners would say about your behavior—frightful dearth of etiquette is probably how she'd describe it!"

This, at least, got Ungôl to respond, albeit negatively. "You are an exxxsssstremely annoying human," he informed Donnie icily.

"Oh, now that just tells me you haven't been around us humans much," she replied, her own tone acerbic because she really was offended. "I don't think I'm any more annoying than the next person, and it was very rude of you to say so. You try experiencing what I've been through since you grabbed me off my divinely cushy saddle, without even so much as a by-your-leave, and let's see how cheerful you are an hour and a half later! Especially when you're wrapped up so tightly you can barely breathe!" She then opined to the cavern at large, "The nerve of this rude reptile, calling *me* annoying!"

Then she looked at the serpent again, her eyebrow arched high as she inquired ever so sweetly, "It's only a guess, but you probably don't spend a whole lot of time with the people you meet, do ya? Betcha barely even give 'em time to get a word in edgewise before you pop 'em right down your throat, just like you did that guy back on the path! So you really have no idea how many possibly stimulating, possibly annoying conversations you've missed out on in the past, have you?"

Ungôl smiled with remembrance, inching closer until this time his snout was nearly touching her nose. "Usssually, my prey are sssscreaming," he said with enjoyment. "That issss, until I crushhhh their bodiesssss in my coilsssss. Ssssometimessss they even live long enough to feel me feed upon them."

Donnie swallowed with difficulty and gave him a disgusted look. "Well, that's certainly gruesome, I'll give you that. And even though you say you're not allowed, I'll bet you're just dyin' to do that same thing to me, aren't ya?" she dared him.

His tongue darted out between his teeth and slipped along Donnie's cheek with its roughened edge. She only just managed to turn off her protective shield in time.

"I can tasssste your fear and it whetssss my hunger." Saliva actually began leaking from the corners of his mouth and his tongue shot across her cheek again.

"Eeeuuuwwww, you're creepy." Donnie twisted her head away, then she turned back to glare at him, reinstating her bubble so she could breathe again. "If I really am so damned annoying, why don't you just kill me and be done with it? You could tell your master that you slipped on the slimy bottom of the pool and the next thing you knew, boom, I was dead! Then you had to eat me. I mean, there's no sense in letting a perfectly fresh corpse go to waste, is there? And who's to know it was deliberate? Besides, what's the worst that could happen to you, huh?"

Ungôl pulled his head away from her, a flicker of unease passing over his features. "It issss tempting, but I musssst do assss the massssster wantssss."

It was Donnie's turn to narrow her eyes at him. "Talking of fear, I do believe you're deeply afraid of this master of yours! Come on, you can't fool me, unctuous Uncle. I saw those shadows of abject terror in your avuncular eyes. He must be some bully to frighten the likes of you! See, I was right, you are unhappy in your job, aren't you? You poor slithering sneak," she intoned mock-sympathetically. "Tell me, Uncle dear, what's his name, where's his hideout and what, specifically, are his plans for me? You give me that info and I'll take care of him for ya, I promise. You won't have to worry about a thing; I swear, he'll never know you snitched on him."

Ungôl's mouth closed tightly. He should not have responded to her goading again, he berated himself sternly. He was becoming confused, and sincerely hoped the master would forgive him his mistakes today. If only the witch had been unable to understand Serpent Tongue, he could easily have pretended that he did not understand her Mannish, and no conversation would have passed between them. As it was, he felt that he had already provided too much information to her, much more than the master would like.

Donnie cocked her head and stared at the stubbornly unresponsive serpent, her mood growing ever more fractious because her attempts at meditation were still going nowhere. She couldn't even do her usual form, she was so stiff and tired of the pressure the snake was exerting on her bones. So much for that method of relieving her stress, at least in this particular setting. Should she—no, she reminded herself firmly, she would just have to endure the situation as best she could. A debt's a debt, and this one she wanted paid in full by the time she was finally freed of the snake's grasp.

But that didn't mean she had to be the only one who was miserable throughout the entire wait, did it? After all, Uncle had already said that he found her quite annoying, and she hadn't even been trying all that hard. He really had no idea just how irritating she could be, but he was about to find out. Yep, there was definitely more of her Aunt Bea in her than she'd ever realized.

"You know what, my umbrageous and unholy Uncle? I hired a life coach once—awesome woman, the best thing I could've done for myself. She gave me all kinds of self-help tricks I could use to make me feel better and more in control of where I was headed in life, like with my job, my personal and professional relationships—well, heck, with just about every aspect of my life. Tell you what, I'll pass some of her pearls of wisdom along to you. Paying it forward, so to speak. Then you can pass them on to someone else you think might need them."

Donnie wet her lips as she warmed to her subject. "I suggest you keep a life journal to write down your thoughts and feelings. It'll help you track your progress, so to speak. And, if you have trouble with depression, as most of us do—well, thinking about it, in your case it might be more of a Missed Opportunity Syndrome, huh? But we'll just call it depression for now. Which means we'll have to look at both the positive and negative reinforcements you're receiving from those around you.

"Now, before going to bed each night, you need to write in this journal at least three good things that happened to you that day, even if one of them's simply that you got out of bed in the morning. No, seriously, that really can count as one of the three! Kinda funny, innit? And see, then you only need two more to meet your quota. Hey, Uncle, you never did tell me whether or not you can read and write. Has your master allowed you and your kind to learn anything really useful like reading or math or science? No? Well, we can't have you broadening your minds, can we? Tell you what, out of the goodness of my soul, I will make you the same offer I do to all my animal friends: feel free to come by the house anytime and I'll teach you how to read and write, do math, all that stuff."

She looked down momentarily at the nearest of Uncle's coils and added, "I'm pretty sure you'd have no trouble holding a big pencil or piece of chalk in this oh-so prehensile tail of yours. But I have to warn you though, I have one restriction, which is that you are not allowed to have lunch while you're on the premises; if you get my drift. To put it plainly, there will be no eating your classmates, 'cause then I'd have to hurt ya. Trust me, my friend, emetics are no fun at all for the one taking them, and I know right where to get as much ipecac as I'd need, even for someone as big as you! Now, let's get back to life coaching."

Donnie droned on and on, using every bit of psychobabble she could recall, all the while expounding various theories on areas such as self-esteem, compassion, bonding and transference, doing her best to keep her mind active, when all she really wanted was to give in to the pressure of the snake's coils on her body and slip into unconsciousness for a while, maybe a long while. After a few minutes, Ungôl laid his head down on the embankment again, eventually sliding it deeper into the water as Donnie relentlessly continued her painfully long-winded and obnoxious lecture (Sylvester would've been proud). She only talked louder then, figuring that it wouldn't be fair for her captor to go to sleep while she was having such trouble forcing herself to remain conscious.

As she talked, she let her head rest upon the coil wrapped around her shoulders and cast her mind's eye all about the cavern, searching carefully for any other egress besides the main entrance. After a while, she opened her eyes and studied the roof, where thousands of very large stalactites hung, having formed there over the millennia from the dripping steam that filled the top of the cavern.

Nearly two hours later, she was burning hot and covered in sweat, barely able to keep awake, and still waiting impatiently for the brother snake's return. She'd just checked the lighted dial of her watch for the umpteenth time when he slithered into the cavern and slipped under the water to the other side to join his brethren, hefting his great bulk around so that the two serpents were facing each other.

Donnie's heart lifted with relief and, so that she could listen to the siblings' whispered conversation, she immediately stopped her incessant lecturing (she'd moved on to the importance of eating properly, a subject which she'd felt strangely compelled to address with her captor).

Ungôl said in a low hiss, "Quietly, little brother, ssshhhe can undersssstand Sssserpent Tongue. What doessss masssster want done with her?"

"When Valledai—aaarrr! Why did you do that?" the brother cried, his voice filled with outrage after Ungôl brutally nipped him in the neck.

"Use no names!" Ungôl ordered angrily.

"Too late, my dears, I heard that!" Donnie murmured to herself triumphantly. "So, Valley Guy must be the one who put the bounty on me. Hmm, that might make our journey north even more troublesome, mightn't it?"

The brother snake looked as though he'd protest further his sibling's treatment of him, but after a moment's reflection, he merely shot a sulky glance at Ungôl and continued to relay his message. "He conssssulted the book when I said you had capttttured the witcccchhh." He looked over at Donnie, his stare menacing.

What's this about a book? she wondered, greatly intrigued by its mention. A sense of foreboding came over her—Medregai did not have a good track record with books.

The brother snake turned back around and leaned closer to Ungôl, so that Donnie could barely hear him speak. "It ssssaid sshhhe would turn ussss into sssomething unssssspeakable, mosssst likely a toad, or ssshe might blow ussss into many piecesssss with boltssss of fire, or possibly ssshe will turn usss to ssstone, jussst assss ssshe did that man from the future! Ssshe issss not to be underesssstimated, brother. He wantssss ussss to keep her bound, taking sssspeccccial care to keep her handssss ssssstill. We mussst take her to Moên Grím quickly, where the masssster himsssself will deal with her. He ssssaid to make hasssste."

"Then we mussst leave now," Ungôl commanded decisively.

"Yessss, brother."

Both snakes lifted their heads and began turning around to move toward the cavern's entrance, the brother in the lead.

Donnie closed her eyes, calling out to Brindle with her mind. "Where are you? Are you still with the saddle?" she asked him.

"Yes, in the stables at Marn Dím."

"Is there anyone about?"

"No, I am quite alone," the old tree replied.

"Good. Look, I need you and the broomstick here, but you're going to have to do your thing really quickly to both of us, got that?"

"You may rely on it, Donemere."

"Great. Give me just a minute."

"Yoo-hoo, Uncle!" Donnie shouted out loud to the snakes. "Where we goin'? I thought maybe we could have a group session here, see what insights your brother has to share about you."

The brother snake halted and turned toward her curiously, causing Ungôl too to stop and look back at her.

She continued with, "I truly believe I could help you guys get in touch with your inner selves, you know? I'm really quite a powerful witch, in case your master didn't tell you that. I may be in the minority on this, but I happen to think you're worth saving. So, whaddya say? Cast down this master of yours, tell him to go to blazes, and let's explore the deepest depths of our souls. I'll make the chai tea."

The serpents looked at each other with unspoken agreement, then turned their heads back to the front and resumed moving their massive bodies toward the entryway. Several long and thick stalactites hanging over the arched opening suddenly broke from the roof and shot downward, lodging solidly into the floor. They blocked the entrance to the cavern, which, according to Donnie's prior and extended scrutiny of the place with her mind's eye, was also the only exit.

Ungôl turned to Donnie and thrust his face at hers again. "You did thisssss!" he hissed at her.

"Oh, sure, it was easy," she admitted cheerfully. "This book your *masssster* consulted was way wrong about me. What kind of book is it, anyway? Something like a Book of Shadows? Wonder what it says about me?" She cocked her head to the side, her brow furrowed in curiosity, and posited in a dramatic voice, " 'Beware! The Donnie witch likes to turn dark creatures into toads, shoot lightning bolts from her fingertips at them, or, most terrifying of all, make statues out of them!' " She scoffed at this and then declared, "Believe me, guys, there is so much more to me than that!"

Ungôl inched ever closer to her face, threateningly. "Releasssse usss," he demanded. He knew he must get her to the master as quickly as possible or the bounty would be lost forever if she escaped. He thought quickly about what he must do next. While he'd been ordered not to kill her, he could certainly take her to the very edge of death if need be. After all, the master had said nothing about not injuring her.

Ignoring the angry waves of danger emanating from the two serpents, Donnie smiled agreeably and told them, "Well, I would let you go, but I just don't think it's time for us to leave yet. Tell you what, I'll give you another chance. Let me down over there on the embankment and I'll see what I can do for you. I really think I could change those black hearts of yours and make them fair and free. Honestly, I did it just yesterday to an okûn. I bet I could do it to you too and tea needn't even be involved. I was only kidding about that part, anyway 'cause I'm not a real big chai fan myself; jasmine or Earl Grey are more my cuppa.

"But seriously, guys, consider what I'm offering you—no more master, you can do whatever you like, survival of the fittest kind of stuff, without interference. You could be fat and happy down here and never have to leave the farm, so to speak. Unless, of course, you wanted to leave, say…maybe to help us defeat your former master? No? Well, then just think of it, the freedom you'd have being your own masters! Okay, sure, things would mostly be just like they are now, I'll grant ya that, but actually it'll be better because you won't ever have the likes of me huntin' you down. Otherwise, I have the feeling that one of us is going to be pursuing the other real soon. And let me just say here and now, I don't intend to lose when that happens. So, how about it? How about changing sides?"

Ungôl ordered his brother to clear the entrance.

The younger snake turned around and began bashing his heavy tail on the stalactites. When this netted no appreciable results, he started beating his whipcord-like neck against the columns of rock. A few of them crashed over, but most held firm. There was now possibly enough space for the snakes to slip free, one at a time, but their lengths would have to be uncoiled.

Ungôl turned back to her again and demanded, "Releasssse meeeeee!"

Donnie's eyes grew round as she shot back wryly at him, "Got that a little backwards, don't ya, pal, since you're the one who's got hold of me! Oh, silly me, of course I see what you mean."

Her manner suddenly became solemn. "Like I said before," she intoned gravely, "I don't intend to lose this game, Uncle, be it here and now or somewhere else later. I've a rather competitive nature, see? Now, you can slither on through to freedom—after all, it's right there in front of you—but, oh darn…you'll have to leave me behind. Or, you can keep me here until someone comes looking for you, probably your master. Then again, when he arrives he's likely to be more than a little miffed at having to come so far out of his way because of little ol' me."

She let her tone get flippant once more. "Or, hey, you can always eat me—but, oops, there again, we already discussed that one and you told me that your master would be mighty upset if you don't leave the pleasure of killing me to him. Huh, looks like your choices are limited, aren't they? So, tell me, what's it gonna be, boys?" She crooked a mock-disapproving eyebrow at Ungôl and added, "Yes…or…no?"

As one, the infuriated snakes began whipping their necks at the fallen stalactites, attempting in vain to dislodge more of them. Finally, when it was clear that no more of the rock could be smashed aside, Ungôl, by now wholly vexed, turned his face back toward Donnie. He raised his tail up high with the obvious intention of slamming it, and her, into the water and screamed, "I *will* kill you, Witchhhh!"

Donnie could feel just how much he meant it; she could feel his hatred of her as though it were actually tangible. Regrettably, she accepted that she couldn't reach him, let alone turn him fair, even though she'd been projecting love and lovingkindness at him for hours. Closing her eyes, she pushed her power outside her body, enveloping herself fully in its protective blue halo. The coils around her stretched wide and before they hit the water, she levitated herself clear of Ungôl's tail, while at the same moment materializing both the broom and the saddle underneath her.

Brindle, true to his word, encased both her and the broomstick instantly. They rocketed past the heads of the two surprised snakes and hurtled through the opening in the columns. Donnie sent three more huge stalactites shooting down right behind her to block the hole as she fled into the outer tunnel, the beginnings of the Great Serpents' enraged screeches already echoing throughout the tunneled chambers of Bitterbend's snake city.

Chapter 15
Little Mysteries

Donnie slowed the broomstick using levitation to press her drenched feet forward in the stirrups, and then expanded the bubble of atmosphere around her face so that she didn't feel so claustrophobic. She took a moment just to breathe.

The vengeful shrieks of the two Great Serpents in the cavern behind her were positively deafening. She figured she'd better get the heck out of the marsh tunnels before their brethren heard their call and came rushing to the rescue. The stalactites would hold forever, if Donnie wanted, but she now settled a charm on them that would dissolve the rock later, giving herself three hours to find her way out of the tunnels. But she had a more immediate problem to consider—and a significant one at that. Her limbs were completely numb and essentially useless from having been immobilized for so long with the hard, constant pressure that had been placed upon them by the snake's thick coils. Another quarter hour in there and she probably wouldn't have been able to move even one muscle in her arms and legs. As it was, she'd spent the last of her waning physical strength on kicking her heels hard in the stirrups to get out of the cavern.

Sharp needles of pain were slowly beginning to emerge in various parts of her body. Voicing a long stream of agonized ow's under her breath, Donnie drifted through the endless warren of tunnels around her, until she finally had to admit that she was well and truly lost. The main tunnel was just not to be found and the fleeting dark shadows that darted away from her wherever she turned were really creeping her out.

"Damn, Brindle, sorry about this," she apologized to the old tree, "but I would've sworn Uncle—oh, that's the snake who grabbed me, by the way. Anyway, I really thought he ran a straight line from the marshes here to the caverns, but I am obviously wrong!" She bemoaned their predicament fervently and rubbed clumsy hands over her arms, trying to slap life back into them. She looked around her in disgust. What was Uncle screaming now—something about a promise?

"You are certain none of these around us is the correct tunnel?" Brindle asked, interrupting Donnie's thoughts.

"Oh, yeah," she assured him. "Seriously, you can't miss the one I'm talkin' about; it goes on forever and you can see straight down it for miles. I guess we must've turned off it somewhere, maybe even more than once, and I didn't realize it 'cause we were goin' so fast. I mean, look at all the passages leading off that junction down there to the left—this place is crazy with tunnels, innit? Bless my grey hairs, how does anyone ever find their way around? Even with this funny light coming from the walls, it's impossible to make sense of this oversized maze. Well, screw it, we'll never get out this way and, besides, something's making the hairs on the back of my neck stand up straight. I get the distinct feeling that we're being hunted; although why our lovely predators haven't struck yet is beyond me."

From somewhere not too far behind her, Donnie heard another caustic bellow that matched those of Uncle and his brother, but their latest affronted bleats were still echoing from the tunnel to her right. Uh-oh, reinforcements were definitely on the way, which meant she was officially out of time.

Concentrating hard on a spot in the roof about a hundred feet ahead, she began levitating out the earth above her, creating her own small tunnel that shot straight up. As she flew up the tunnel, displaced rock and earth bounced off her protective shield and fell downward, eventually cutting off access behind her to even the smallest of Great Serpents. After nearly a mile of tunneling, she broke through the bedrock into the deep, stygian waters of the Bitterbend Marshes.

***

Falwaïn waited in his room at the inn, carefully sharpening the blades of his weapons. The boombox had joined him two hours earlier and had played one love song after another; each one reminding him more and more of Donemere and the fact that no word had been received from her yet. The one time he'd heard someone in the room next door, which was to be Donnie's, he'd raced over there, only to find it was a maid changing the bed clothing and, red-faced, he'd hurriedly excused himself for bursting in on her.

He realized that he was now sharpening his knives for the third time, which meant he had to get out of this room, do something to keep his mind occupied as well as his hands. A new song came on, its haunting melody eventually stilling his movements. The singer's lament was of living with an aching heart, all the while searching for that elusive woman of his.

Falwaïn shook his head impatiently. Truly, he could no longer wait here for Donnie's return; he would search for Warren and find out if he'd learned where the Black Rider had gone. Hurriedly, Falwaïn began putting things away, packing what wasn't needed and strapping on his weapon belts.

The song was cut in mid-note when the boombox abruptly disappeared into thin air. Falwaïn whirled to stare at the empty space it had been occupying. His smile was wide as he slid his sword into its scabbard.

***

Donnie zoomed through almost a mile of the marsh water, exploding from its surface on the huge wave created by her momentum. She let out a "Whoopee" of pure joy, gladder than glad to be in the sunshine once more, and did her best to slough off most of the mud and water from her agonizing sojourn through the marshes. She stretched her shoulders and back, immensely grateful that normal feeling had, at long last, returned to her limbs, although they were still inordinately tired.

The boombox appeared on the end of the broomstick and began playing "Little Mysteries" by Torn Pages. Donnie hailed it and laughed, grabbing tightly to the broomstick, and zoomed straight up toward the heavens. There she floated, the late afternoon sun's rays warming her while she did more stretching to make sure movement of all her appendages was now normal. She bounced happily in the saddle with the song, singing the chorus and some of the verses, wondering why this particular tune was playing. Was the boombox trying to give her another message and, if so, what exactly was it hoping to impart? Its volume suddenly increased and the song told of a dog who had just up and vanished.

With that clue, Donnie exclaimed happily, "I see what you're trying to tell me about mysteries. Man, I'm gettin' good at this! So, yeah, you're right. Not only has my kitty been less than forthcoming, it appears my puppy has also been hiding something from me. Something pretty important, by the looks of it. And not only that, but I've got a feeling that I just learned something else pretty important while I was down in the marshes. Maybe it's something about the book Valley Guy's got. Now, *that* was a surprise!" She chewed her lip for a moment, contemplating the book's existence and its purpose.

Pushing this tantalizing bit of information away for the time being, she took the folded scroll of paper from the belt around her waist and opened it flat. Yes, her instincts were correct; the fourth trial had been filled in. It now read:

Breathe the still waters to mark thy journey to enlightenment.
Ye must forever pursue treue knowledge.
Patience may reveal that which lies below the surface, when naught else can.

Patience? Well, she wasn't sure that was exactly what she'd exhibited with Uncle, unless you called it *forced* patience. Donnie put the paper away thoughtfully. Pretty soon she was going to need some time just to think for a good long while about what she'd learned so far. Looking down at the filth covering her, she decided the perfect opportunity for that would come at bath time. She kicked her heels in the stirrups and the broom slowly moved over the marshes. With her mind, she called out to her dog.

"Yes, Mama?" Rex responded, giving a surprised start. He'd been sniffing the ground closely, following a very interesting smell; another rabbit, if his nose was not deceiving him.

"Where are you?" Donnie asked him.

"Um, I don't really know."

"Well, let me see if I can find you." She concentrated on her dog and felt his presence to her left, in the southern-most part of the moors that lay west of the marshes. She opened her eyes and told him, "Stay where you are." She took off, quickly reaching, and then maintaining a speed of just over two hundred and fifty miles per hour.

When she touched down and dismounted almost fifteen minutes later, her blue-colored protective shields dissipated. Rex came bounding over, his tail wagging and body wiggling joyously. He completely forgot about his quarry with the return of his mama. The boombox disappeared from the broomstick and the dusk air was silent until the dog began talking in a rush from where he now sat between Donnie's legs, gazing up at her with adoration.

"Gee, Mama, I wasn't sure what to do," the dog gushed, "whether I should go home, or whether I should follow you guys, or if I should just wait around for you to find me. Did those big terrible snakes get anybody? Is everyone okay? What happened, Mama, what happened?" he ended urgently, then twisted his head to one side before asking curiously, "Hey, why are you all wet and muddy?"

Donnie shook her head. "Uh-uh, you'll have to wait until we get to the others to find that out because I am not explaining myself twice." Mindful of the boombox's point, she moved in front of him and squatted, taking hold of his snout to make him look at her. "I have a question for you, though, my love. How did you disappear like that? You've got another secret, haven't you?"

Rex eyed her guiltily. "Well...um, yeah, I guess so," he mumbled. "I didn't tell you about it before because you get all funny about that kind of thing."

She raised an apprehensive eyebrow and asked, "What kind of thing?"

Her puppy dog now refused to meet her gaze. "Oh, you know. The magical stuff I can do."

"Oh, that kind of thing." Donnie sighed, rolling her eyes reflexively, and finally ventured, "What's this one?"

Rex turned his gaze back to her with glee and said, "Well, I can run really fast now. I mean really, really, really fast—way faster than the wind even!" He suddenly checked himself and looked abashed. "Oh, see, Mama? There's that funny look you always get when I tell you about my magical powers, 'specially when they expand."

She *was* staring at her dog completely aghast. "What? Do you fly now, too?" she spluttered. "Aw jeez, don't tell me—you can leap tall buildings in a single bound, can't you, Dog Wonder? Oh, great joy, it seems I'm mothering a budding super hero and I had absolutely no clue! We really should talk more often, you know that?"

The dog sat there grinning at her. Donnie took a deep breath and grinned tenderly back at him. "Okay," she said in a serious tone, "I don't want you to be afraid anymore to tell me about your new abilities. And I promise I won't get funny about them ever again. But you have to promise to never disappear on me like that again unless I tell you to, okay? Okay. Now look, if I hold onto your collar and sit on your back, can you get us both to Marn Dím like that? It's at least a couple hundred miles north, and east just a little. Or am I too heavy for you to carry?"

Rex shook his head carelessly, replying, "Nope, I'm really strong now too. I've carried Warren that way a few times, so it should be easier carrying you. But you're gonna slow me down, 'cause any extra weight tends to do that, you know?"

"That's okay," Donnie acknowledged this wryly. "I think that even if you run at a tenth of the speed you went back at the marshes, we'll still get there in good time. And I certainly can't go on my broomstick. I'd bet the townspeople would find that just a tad alarming, don't you?"

"Yeah, prob'ly," Rex agreed, his eyes getting big.

Donnie chuckled at him, giving him a quick hug. "Well, at least now I understand how Warren got all the way to Mâlendian and back to the cottage in just a few hours the other day." She suddenly went silent, turning her head to listen to something. She could swear that she heard what sounded like a babbling brook over to her right. "Honey, wait here a minute, all right?" she instructed her pup.

She climbed around a large outcropping of granite and found that she was correct. Good heavens, was she ever thirsty! Kneeling down on the stream's bank, she splashed her hands around in the freezing fresh water to rinse them, then cupped them and took a few much-needed gulps of the invigorating elixir. She scooped up more of the water and splashed her face and hair, wanting to rinse the stench of the marshes from the immediate area around her nose and its sensitive olfactory capabilities. She ended up just plunging her head into the cold water for a few seconds, but soon almost threw herself backward from the stream after a strange vision suddenly flashed through her mind.

In the unbidden illusion, she saw a clearing, somewhere deep within a forest, dappled by sunlight and still as death. Nothing moved in it and there was no sound other than her own breathing, which was impossible since her head was completely underwater in the stream. Her gaze roamed the clearing for a few seconds, and she had just caught the unmistakable and strong whiff of blood when the entire image vanished from her mind. That was because she had instinctively whipped her head up and out of the water and sat back on her haunches.

Dripping with water, she wiped her face with her hands and shook her head, looking around her with astonishment. "What the hell was that?" she whispered aloud, disturbed by the startling vision. She was almost certain there had been dead bodies scattered around the clearing, but the hallucination had lasted such a short time that she could not be absolutely positive of that, or really of anything other than the overwhelming smell of blood that had wafted to her just before the vision had ended. Puzzled, she leaned forward and drank more of the stream's refreshing waters, half hoping to catch more of the vision, but that was not to be.

When her thirst was finally satiated and she was feeling more herself, she returned to where she'd left the dog, who had, by now, resumed his investigation of the rabbit trail. Donnie recalled him and he obligingly loped back to her. She asked him if he'd drunk the water from the stream she'd just visited, but he shook his head and said, "I didn't even know there was a stream around here."

Donnie looked at him in surprise, then shrugged the strange experience off with a decided sense of relief, and turned toward the floating broomstick and saddle. "Hey, Brindle?" she said.

"Yes, Donnie?" the old tree replied.

"I need you to go back to Marn Dím. If you see any of the others—well, besides Otis and Gallantry—tell them Rex and I are on our way and I, for one, am famished. Would you mind doing that for me, please?" she asked. "Tell them we should be there in less than an hour and not to worry, we'll find the stables by ourselves, wherever they are. And Brindle? Thanks for being so quick back there. I couldn't have escaped without you." The saddle disappeared a moment later, as did the broomstick.

Donnie straddled the dog and took hold of his collar, admonishing him, "Seriously, Rex, you don't have to go at top speed, you know. In other words, please do not snap my neck when we take off, okay?"

The dog grinned, extraordinarily pleased that he could finally show her what he could do. He started off with a big leap that only slightly jarred his mama's spine, then picked up speed with each subsequent bound, until they were going so fast, Donnie could barely see anything outside the tunnel her vision had created.

They crested the hill a mile south of the gates of Marn Dím exactly six minutes later, with Rex not even slightly winded, which made Donnie shake her head in amazement, though she made no comment. When he came to a halt, she unwrapped her legs from around his rib cage unsteadily and stood up, feeling a bit dizzy from the ride. She surveyed the distant city in the deepening dusk light until her equilibrium returned to normal, trying to ignore the fact that her dog had somehow grown a good ten inches in height and almost twice that in length when he'd taken off with her on his back, while he'd just now shrunk back to his normal size when they'd stopped. No matter what she'd said about not freaking out over his magical powers, she found that right now she just didn't have the nerve to ask him about his newfound elasticity.

Marn Dím nestled far up into the mountainside and had a high, black stone wall surrounding its lower levels on three sides. The fourth side was the mountain itself, its sheer face behind the city running straight up toward the sky. The city was huge, with a strange beauty all its own. It looked quite ancient, even from this distance, with many breaks and scars on the obsidian surfaces of its towering buildings. Carved stone turrets hunched on top of several of the rooftops and along the outer wall, but only the ones on the wall appeared to be manned, as Donnie realized when they were about a quarter mile away.

The streets were mostly obscured by the barrier surrounding the city, except for those on the upper levels. But a ghostly yellow glow reflected off the black stone buildings within the outer wall's perimeter, hinting at a bustling community. As she walked through its gates, Donnie saw that the city was indeed teeming with sound and light, as night had begun to fall in earnest. She told her dog to follow the scents of their friends, but also to stay near her. "And don't do anything, you know, magical. The last thing we need is to cause a disturbance."

Rex nodded agreeably and said, "Yeah, I know, you don't want to get burned at the stake."

Donnie glanced down at the dog and said, "Not tonight, no."

He walked slightly in front of his mama, nose to the ground. She kept her hand resting on his back so she wouldn't lose him in the crush of the streets. People were everywhere—unhealthy, staring people. She began to feel quite nervous.

What was it the men had talked about the other day around her kitchen table? Something regarding not only the resurgence of dark magical creatures, but also the growing hostilities in the Annûar Province between the Sarn and the Mountain Men, who were long-time adversaries in Medregai.

Marn Dím certainly looked to be the Mountain Men's capital city, as it was filled to the brim with thousands of these frowning, unkempt, rough-looking, and obviously hardy and hardened peoples, pretty much all of whom seemed in dire need of both a bath and a bit of joy in their lives. At first Donnie thought this was just because they were desperately poor, until she saw several transactions of large stacks of silver coins change hands, and then she realized that many of these people actually *chose* to live their lives this way.

Which made her wonder why anyone would want to deliberately lead such a dismal, squalid existence. Was it because this was all they knew and, as she herself had found only a few days ago, there is real comfort in the familiar, that breaking away from established routine is ofttimes too daunting to even contemplate? Or had the king's efforts to integrate this region and its peoples fallen short of Marn Dím for some reason? She couldn't remember exactly what the men had said about it, but that explanation didn't fit in with her concept of what Aniselm, née Belnesem, would have become as king. He'd seemed pretty fair and trustworthy in both the book on Medregai and in Mueler's epic.

Besides, she did remember Falwaïn saying that Belnesem had attempted to make this region a priority in the reclamation and outreach efforts to build a unified west. Seeing them now, Donnie couldn't help but question just how hard the king and his emissaries had tried to win over the Mountain People. It seemed to her that Marn Dím was ripe for the picking by Valley Guy, and there had to be some reason for this. She could feel the hostility growing within the heart of the city, in her noisy streets and her sullen denizens. The city would not be safe much longer for anyone Valley Guy considered to be an enemy.

Donnie urged Rex to go faster and they broke into a trot, weaving in and out of the restless crowds. She kept her eyes on the dog, not wanting to see the hard stares directed at them both. She finally had to concede that maybe, just maybe, Sylvester had been right about her attire. She hissed at Rex to go into an empty, darkened alleyway and, once there, she materialized an old cotton dress of Catie's from home and changed her clothes quickly. The dress was too short and showed more of her legs than was customary here, but it was otherwise reprehensible enough to allow her to blend in with the other people in the streets, especially with Catie's grey cloak wrapped around her, which she also materialized. Her boots could pass as they were, muddied and soaked. Donnie bundled up her sweats and sent them to the wardrobe at home to be cleaned.

They emerged from the alleyway and Rex took up the scent again. Passersby were still obviously curious about the dog, but not her so much since she looked very similar to the other ragamuffin derelicts wandering the streets. Well, other than the periodic, clean ones with long, fair hair, who surveilled her and the dog from darkened doorways. But then, Donnie didn't notice their presence.

***

When the boombox had disappeared, Falwaïn went first to the stables to check on an idea of his. It was as he thought; Brindle was indeed gone.

Warren walked in a moment later and asked, "Have you received word from Donemere?"

Falwaïn explained about the boombox and Brindle, ending with, "I believe Donnie has freed herself."

"Yes, it appears so." Warren nodded his head appreciatively.

Falwaïn lounged against a post, inquiring laconically, "What have you learned of Galto's whereabouts?"

"I followed three men into the Black Pony Tavern who were laughing about him. They had seen him on the road near Marn Dím and watched as he passed the gates, headed north. He was just as we'd left him, trussed up and hog-tied, as Donnie decreed he should be." Warren smiled. "They were quite drunk and soon started an argument with three other men at the table next to them, who were equally as drunk. I'm afraid a brawl ensued and I was unable to learn more. They were the only people I've heard discussing him this day. But I've also learnt that okûn appear to be on the uprise, attacking settlements all over the area in the last few days. Hordes of not only them, but other dark creatures too, are reportedly still gathering in Moên Gjendeben. For what purpose, I have not yet been able to determine fully."

"That's interesting. I wonder exactly what it is they're planning and when they're planning on doing it." Falwaïn contemplated the possibilities this presented, then looked at his friend and asked, "Where is Sylvester? Have you seen him?"

Warren shrugged. "No, not since he disappeared when we left the rooms at the inn. I suggest we visit the Black Pony together now. It caters to the sort of Mountain Folk we're seeking. Possibly we can find out where Galto went, or at least, what it is that lies north of here that may be his intended destination. If we're still unable to learn more at the tavern, then I shall leave the city after sundown and find my people. By now, they may have been able to gather information that will help us locate both Galto and Valledai."

When the two men walked into the long, timbered main room of the dilapidated, but nonetheless crowded tavern, the din subsided for at least a minute as many resentful eyes turned toward them. The proprietor of the Black Pony found Warren and Falwaïn a table in a corner and went back to the bar, returning promptly with a copper ewer of ale and two stone mugs. The crowd had forgotten about the newcomers by then and had gone back to their own drinks and conversation. The two men sat for nearly an hour, eating what passed for supper at the tavern: a roasted bird of indeterminate breed, soggy potatoes, and even soggier bread. All the while, they listened carefully to the talk going on around them.

Three particularly rough-looking creatures were arguing loudly amongst themselves at the bar and, after some time had passed, they moved to a table near Falwaïn and Warren as soon as the opportunity arose.

The largest, a mountain of a man with wild black hair and wilder black eyes, looked over at Falwaïn and began a new discussion once he and his friends were settled. "Gaw, that king o' ourn is wastin' his time cummin' up here and makin' the north fit fer all Free Peepols," he said, almost chewing on the words as they struggled to escape his mouth. "Didchu see that minster o' his? Queer sort o' fella ta send us. 'Tis good we sent him packin'. I wud jestassoon quarter me an elf, as sit down ta supper wi' one!" He spit soundly on the floor after saying this.

"Weeeeellllll, whatcha expeck from a king wot was raised by 'em?" The eldest of the trio by a good twenty years glanced over at Falwaïn and Warren and then back to his compatriots, nodding his head. " 'E nowt be wurrayed abowt makin' frenns wi' the likes o' us. No sir, 'e be wantin' to make feeble 'and pressers owt o' us. And barrin' that, 'im and his forces will run us as far narth as we be willin' ta go, jest ye wait 'n see. Har, har! Gorn, ain't that the 'orse's tail? Grab on, I says, and we shall see whar we take 'im! We can give 'im a wild ride through the Brumal Mountuns, one 'e will niver forget, that be fair certain! Thar be 'ole armies o' ohkoons 'idin' up there, jest waitin' fer our *fair* king ta set foot in Marn Dim. They be everywhere, and 'e will be in Gjendeben before 'e even knows wots 'appened ta 'im and 'is prittee elfs and those vile, trait'rous vinca!"

"Which is right where thay shud be, ta my way o' thinkin'. Free Peepols, he says, but he dunna mean *us*. He took our wimmen and dun what he likes widdem. Yassir, he shorely did! An' I hear he liked ol'

Fet's dotter the best. Hee, hee, hee!" The third man, a wiry, scrappy looking individual, laughed lasciviously at this thought.

"Weeeeellllll, she be a fine lookin' lass, at that," the elder man informed the tavern at large. "An' she be a 'andful, in more ways 'an one—an' ye both know what I be spickin' of. No wonder our *fair* king lusted arfter 'er and finally took 'er ta 'is bed. That icy elf queen o' 'is canna 'old 'alf a flame ta Fet's dotter."

Falwaïn, greatly repulsed by this talk, made a move to get up and said, "Let's go. We're not going to learn anything here." Warren nodded and followed him from the table.

As they passed by the obnoxious trio, the eldest stood and blocked their way. "Yews nowt be leavin', are ye? We didna mean ta offend. No sir, that we didna mean ta du. Naow, you be frenns o' the king, if yer costumes be enythin' ta go by. Izzat right?"

Falwaïn stood tall and pulled his head back from the other's mean breath. "What of it?" He could feel movement behind him and his peripheral vision told him that the tables around them were hastily being vacated.

"Weeeeellllll, 'tis jest that we was thinkin' the king ahrt to be tole by one o' 'is kinsman that we dunna want 'im 'ere in these parts. Mebbe yourn jest the one ta tell 'im that. Whaddya think, lads? Shall we send a message by way o' dese two?"

The biggest one suddenly wrapped his thick arm around Warren's throat, also trapping his victim's right arm behind his back. Just as quickly, the youngest man slammed his fist into Warren's gut. Sensing this happening behind him, Falwaïn gave the man in front of him a blow to the chin that sent the old codger reeling backward into the next table.

***

Donnie and Rex arrived at the stables to find Sylvester waiting for them. He jumped down off Brindle and weaved around his mistress's legs, meowing until she picked him up and put him on her shoulder.

"Why, Sylvester, I do believe you were worried about me," she teased him reproachfully.

"You could have let me know your plan, instead of relaying it only to Brindle," he snapped peevishly into her ear.

Donnie chuckled. "In the two microseconds I had to formulate it? Gee, sweetie, I'm flattered you think I'm that good, but I'm not, not really. Since I sometimes let Brindle and myself be connected mentally while I'm in the saddle, he pretty much knows what I'm thinking as soon as I think it, which cuts down on the amount of explaining I have to do, and you know how much I love using magic to save time. Now, tell me, where are the others?"

The cat shook his head. "I have not seen them since soon after we arrived here. When I returned to the stables a little while ago, Brindle gave me your message and Otis said that the others were here earlier and left together. Warren spoke of a place called the Black Pony."

"I can find 'em, Mama," Rex volunteered.

Donnie nodded. "Okay, then let's go. I want to get to the hotel and take a bath. They do have facilities for such a thing, don't they, Sylvester?"

"If so, *I* am unaware of their existence." The cat looked at her as though he thought her a loon for even asking him such a question.

She grunted in agreement with his opinion of her, then chirped brightly, "Well, a girl can have hope, can't she? C'mon, let's go get the guys." She followed Rex outside. The three of them trooped up the side of the city's steep, main thoroughfare, which eventually led to some low stairs that were carved into the black rock of the mountain, bringing them to the next level of town. This neighborhood was even rougher than what Donnie had seen in the lower reaches of the city. Very few women were about, so she stood out conspicuously. She felt like every eye was closely watching her movements and she purposely ignored several leering grins aimed at her. A wave of antipathy washed over her; these men were filthy, in pretty much every sense of the word!

They rounded a corner and saw the sign for the Black Pony Tavern. It looked like an old establishment and was obviously popular, judging from the roars emanating from it. Donnie stood outside the entrance, eyeing its door dubiously, uncertain just what she should do; should she go in herself or send in one of the others? Well, considering that both she and Rex would undoubtedly garner way too much attention, the cat would probably be the best choice.

"Sylvester?"

The cat remained silent, hunched down on her shoulder, acting for all the world as though she'd not just spoken to him.

"Sylvester!" she repeated insistently.

"I am not going in there, Donemere."

She glanced at him, her right eyebrow raised. "Well, someone has to. Rex causes too much of a stir wherever he goes and I'm a woman. I don't think women are exactly safe in a place like this, do you?"

"You are a Madra Witch," the cat reminded her, his tone more than a touch sarcastic. "You would be safe almost anywhere."

"Yeah, but still…it'll cause a mighty big disturbance if I go in there," Donnie pointed out.

At this moment, the door to the tavern opened and a body was thrown out, which landed at her feet. It coughed and shook itself as the door opened again and another body was thrown out after the first.

Falwaïn and Warren stood and brushed themselves off, staring at Donnie with astonishment. She had her arms crossed in front of her and was tapping the toe of her boot on the cobbled street.

"Guess I don't have to ask if you were winning," was all she said to them.

The two men grinned at her sheepishly, then clapped each other around the shoulders, laughing uproariously. "We held our own for quite some time," Falwaïn informed her proudly.

Warren nodded and laughed again, gazing earnestly at Donnie. "You should see the three who attacked us by the time we were done with them. They've learned a thing or two about the quality of the king's men today. After that, it took four of their largest to subdue each of us and throw us out."

Donnie gave him a reproving sigh and pointed out, "You're probably very lucky they didn't kill you."

Falwaïn sobered a little and walked up to caress her cheek. "We are not so easy to kill," he said softly, "and neither are you, it seems. My heart is gladdened to see that you have returned to us in one piece."

She turned on her heel and began walking back down the way she'd come, refusing to acknowledge the flip her own heart did at both his touch and his words. The others followed hastily, with Warren soon leading the way and Rex prancing happily beside him. He really liked Warren.

It took a few moments before Donnie responded grouchily to Falwaïn's greeting because she didn't like her heart doing somersaults over anyone right now. "Yeah, well, I'm a bit cranky because my blood sugar's low. To put it bluntly, I need food. Don't suppose we can go back in that place, so how about if we go to the hotel, er, inn, whatever it's called here, and get me some supper? But first a bath. Then, and only then, will I sit down and tell you guys anything. By the way, what the heck were you two doing in there? It doesn't seem like your kind of place, if you know what I mean."

"Seeking information on your friend Galto," Falwaïn answered.

"Well, did you find out anything about him?" she asked after waiting, apparently in vain, for him to continue.

Warren called over his shoulder, "Only that he passed by here and continued north."

Sylvester, from beside Donnie's ear, whispered, "I have news of his whereabouts. We must take great care. There are many who hide in darkness here and they are watching for us."

"Well, we're a little hard to miss, don't you think?" she carped back to the cat. "I mean, one woman, two men, two horses, a cat and a dog? Just how many groups of travelers fit that generalized description? Hmm, let me think...I'm guessin' we're probably the only ones."

"Nonetheless, we must be on our guard," the cat stated flatly.

"When aren't we?" Donnie growled.

Falwaïn turned toward her, his teeth flashing white in the near darkness. "You truly do need food, don't you?"

She looked around Sylvester at him and conceded resentfully, "Yes. Now leave me alone and don't you dare laugh at me. I know this dress is ugly and too short for me, but hey, at least I don't look out of place here. Other than the bruises you just sustained, you guys look like Wall Street suits compared to everyone else around here."

Falwaïn took hold of her arm and guided her toward a large inn with a sign hanging above its door that proclaimed it to be the Maidenfair Arms. "I gather you're referring to the quality of our clothing. May I remind you that you are the one who gave them to us?"

"Well, they're only copies of what you already had," Donnie retorted.

Falwaïn protested, "Yes, but they are newly cut and not as worn as mine were."

"Well, they're a bit worn now, wouldn't you say?" Donnie glared at him in the dim light emanating from the lamp over the door, where they'd paused before entering the inn. Falwaïn glared back at her, his own temper beginning to rise.

"Whatcha arguing about, Mama?" Rex came up behind her and stood between the two tense figures, thrusting his snout into Donnie's right hand.

Warren, turning to hide his smile, said, "Leave them be, boy. True love always takes a tortuous course."

With that, he disappeared into the inn, Falwaïn and Rex right behind him. Donnie just stood there, nonplussed. Was it that obvious she was in danger of falling in love with Falwaïn?

Sylvester nipped her ear and remonstrated, "Do not merely stand here on the doorstep of the inn after all the complaining you have just subjected us to!"

She crooked an eyebrow, sent the cat a withering stare, then, without another word, stepped through the door of the inn.

Their rooms turned out to be small and spare, but at least they were clean. To Donnie's relief, there apparently was a tub in a room downstairs for bathing, but when she got a look at it, she muttered, "No way," under her breath.

The amply (and overtly) buxom proprietress, whose thick and abundant black hair was swept off her pink face and piled high on the top of her head in a huge, wide bun that had greasy, harried tendrils flying from it in all directions, had led Donnie into the bathing room and then primly instructed her on the rules of the house. There weren't many. When she'd ticked those off two fingers, she asked where it was that Donnie and her friends were headed. Donnie didn't even bother to respond.

The woman then commented lewdly on how fair Donnie's two traveling companions were, and how much she wished her husband, poor old frog-faced Mittelin, were half as fair as either of Donnie's friends. The garrulous proprietress (whose name, as she relayed to Donnie between hurried, in-drawn breaths, was Gladria) made reference to some sexual proclivities she obviously thought Donnie shared with her, and then went on to inform Donnie that old frog-face just could no longer manage.

But then again, Gladria had to admit, she lived very well compared to some in Marn Dím. Her dresses were mostly new and richly appointed—that was, for their station in life, Gladria amended hastily. After all, they were only innkeepers. (Donnie looked over the sample of wardrobe the chatty proprietress currently wore and managed a small smile and nod, as if in complete agreement. The dress was actually some horrid affair of blue and brown heavy material that left most of the woman's huge bosom exposed and did nothing to conceal her rather substantial waistline.) Gladria jabbered on. He was a good provider, her frog-face, she said, for there were far worse men in the city, that was fair certain!

Donnie again remained mute, but pointedly turned away, hoping the awful woman would take the hint and leave very, very soon. But an unfortunate, final question was already forming on Gladria's lips. The salacious, inquisitive woman asked archly whether anyone would be joining Donnie in her bath.

Donnie whirled around and stared hard at the proprietress before snarling, "They sure as hell hadn't better, if they know what's good for them. Now, don't you have other guests to attend who actually *want* your company?"

Gladria pursed her lips and scurried off in a huff. Donnie firmly closed the door the moment she was alone, sighing with immense relief as she sank back upon its boards. The next thing she did was to surreptitiously charm the door so that it wouldn't open until she was ready to leave, and then she magically closed the knothole on the far wall, which obviously opened to a darkened room beyond. With a barely noticeable wave of her hand, Donnie made the wood stretch until the knothole was no more.

As far as she could tell, it was the only way of seeing into the room from the outside, so she could now safely use her magic and bathe completely unobserved. She looked around her. Besides the big copper tub sitting in the middle of the room, against the walls were a couple of benches that looked as though they needed a good scrubbing before anyone should ever sit on them again. Next to the benches, some wooden pegs were attached to the walls at about shoulder height, which Donnie presumed were for hanging clothing. These were all the furnishings in the room, making it a bit dismal and barren, although at least it had a fireplace with a big, beautiful stone hearth and roaring fire.

She walked over to the tub and eyed it with extreme distaste. It would have to be thoroughly cleaned before she'd place one toe into it. But first she'd have to empty it of the scummy, murky remains from the inn's previous bathers.

She decided to use her breath to blow the water out of the tub. Donnie recalled with a smile how she'd come up with this particular skill months ago, after building the addition onto the cottage and moving her things inside. She'd been confronted with the problem of keeping her food fresh and cold, or frozen if need be. This was not a problem for long; within a day or so, she'd come up with the idea of simply filling her big ice chest with water from the well, then freezing it with one big frozen puff of breath. Once she had the water in the ice chest frozen solid, she levitated the ice block into her largest roasting pan and set it on the bottom of the refrigerator cavity. It kept food quite cold and fresh for a long time. Anything that needed to be frozen, Donnie merely placed upon the ice itself. (The system had worked quite well until she'd realized, about four months after her arrival in Medregai, that it had become superfluous because the fridge was actually working on its own.)

Blowing freezing breaths had been the first of her own rather innovative magical powers. She'd gotten the idea from comic books she'd read in her youth. She found that if she made a very small "O" of her mouth and drew in a long, light breath, then slowly expelled it, her breath remained cool. It took a while to master, but she eventually became so proficient at it, she could reliably get within a hundredth degree of her target temperature.

After that, Donnie practiced other types of breaths; one for warming and another for clearing out smoke or mist. For warming breaths, she took in a huge gulp of air and then blew it out from her diaphragm, with her mouth opened much wider than for cooling breaths.

For the clearing breath, she puffed out her cheeks like a horn player in a school band and blew hard. Within a month, she was so adept with it, she could open a path ten feet wide and just as high for at least fifty feet in front of her, even in the densest fog. And on the few occasions when the cottage became too smoke-filled because of inadvertently burning green or wet wood in one of the fireplaces, she could effortlessly direct the errant smoke up into the chimney, clearing the entire enclosed space in seconds with only one breath.

Donnie's latest breath trick, which was by no means perfected, was to blow whole bucketfuls of water in waves through the air by blowing into the bucket with what she called "dancing" breaths; so named because they made the water appear to dance. This trick she came up with because she'd found that dematerializing water from one receptacle and rematerializing it into another was relatively easy, but usually messy, often ending with a great deal of splash-over, especially when the two receptacles were shaped differently. The problem was that the dematerialized water held its form when rematerialized, so Donnie had been looking for a way to transfer and suspend the water above its destination, then release it in controlled streams, when she'd stumbled upon the concept of dancing the water.

Her initial goal was to send the waves of water flying through the air into an empty bucket a few yards away without losing a drop, but it didn't take long before she was leaving them suspended in the air to undulate in rolling curls around her head. Which gave her fits of giggles, much like those of a three-year old when blowing bubbles, as she weaved and bobbed around and between the waves, poking her fingers into them and swirling the water around and around so that a small vortex was created, which would inevitably collapse right onto her head. Or she'd unfurl the hovering waves into lengthy trails, drawing all sorts of intricate, shimmering pictures or writing her own and her friends' names in the air with the water. One auspicious day, much to Sylvester's disdain (which he'd aired quite vocally), she'd thought of animating her pictures, creating some rather hilarious water movies that had her, Rex, Diana and Otis convulsing with laughter. Admittedly, this was not exactly what you'd call a practical magical power, but it was certainly entertaining.

Donnie learned to keep lots of dry towels stacked nearby whenever practicing this particular skill, which was a small price to pay considering the amount of enjoyment it provided her and the others. She was beginning to master it by now, but only on a small scale.

Recently, she'd begun mixing the two methods of conveying liquid, dematerializing the top six inches or so of water from the well into the air, then immediately blowing it in waves to keep it suspended as soon as it rematerialized. These waves she would then direct in a large, slow stream, one after the other, down to their intended receptacles. One day, she hoped to be able to move large quantities of liquids with it, although that day was still probably a long way off.

With a shake of her head, she recalled herself to the task at hand and got busy blowing. Her dancing breath soon lifted every drop of the filthy water from the inn's tub into airborne, gently rolling waves. Peering down into the dry tub with revulsion, Donnie dematerialized the remaining dirt particles and other gunk from the metal sides of the tub, sending it all to the floating water. While she bathed, she would leave the rippling waves suspended high in the corner behind her, so she wouldn't have to view them or the filth they carried.

By the time she was finished magically scrubbing the tub, its newly burnished copper gleamed brightly in the light of the torches on the walls. She materialized some lemony disinfectant wipes and had them wash down the inside of the tub, then floated the germ-infested sheets into the fire. Only when she was positive that the tub was as clean as she could possibly get it did she materialize bucketfuls of water from the well back at the cottage, dumping each one into the tub magically and then sending the bucket back for more. When the tub was full, she shot two big zaps into the water's depths to make it the perfect temperature for her bath. She also materialized the small, three-tiered tile and iron table and its matching chair from her bathroom. On the table, she placed her soap, washcloth, shampoo, conditioner, a big fluffy towel and her favorite body spray. Her bath was finally ready for her.

With the door securely locked, the spy hole plugged, the copper tub both cleaned and disinfected, and gallons of steaming water beckoning to her, Donnie gratefully climbed into the tub and submerged herself in its velvety warmth, spending the next thirty minutes basking in the healing properties of her bath and becoming human once more.

Once she had slowly and thoroughly washed her hair, face and body, she leaned back in the tub and mulled over what she'd learned so far. Nothing new about the amulet, unfortunately. She still had no clue how to open the time portal or how to make sure you got sent to the specified time and place, let alone how to make sure you came back to the right ones. It wasn't just a question of willing it to be so—no, she was pretty sure there was an incantation of some sort.

Was that what the inscription was? She must remember to check the back of the amulet again, see if she could figure out what was etched there, Donnie told herself drowsily, submerging into the water again to rinse off her hair conditioner. Realistically though, she'd found out nothing new about the amulet, right?

But then again...there was something, something almost familiar about it, she realized with a jolt, suddenly thrusting her head out of the water to sit upright. When she'd first held it, the amulet had felt warm to her touch and that had stirred the beginnings of a memory in her. What the memory was, she really didn't know. Not yet anyway, but it would come to her. Things like that always did, eventually.

She leaned back again and relaxed. Okay, so what exactly had she learned in the marshes of Bitterbend? Well, first, there was the oddity of Uncle. She thought about her recurring dreams of the tunnel and the cavern—could he be the one haunting her? No, it was not his eyes that pulled at her heartstrings so, although he'd undoubtedly shown up in her dreams more than once; Donnie was certain of it. But why, she mused, and how? How could she possibly know about him before even meeting him? She'd always failed miserably whenever Sylvester had tested her at prognostication, an obvious hole in her skill-set that neither she nor the cat had ever been able to fathom. She shook her head. Her encounter with the Great Serpent had been bewildering—what was it that made him so desperate to be king of the marshes? It wasn't just greed or the desire to rule over others, Donnie knew. She'd been able to look far enough into his soul to see that much. No, he wanted it for some other reason, that had been clear, something to do with a promise he had given someone.

There was something else quite strange about him—why were he and his brother so gigantic, whereas the three Great Serpents the guys had battled on the Annûar Path, along with those who had studiously avoided her when she'd tried to find her way through the underground passages of Bitterbend, had all been less than half their size? That was really quite perplexing, in its way. Had Valley Guy given Uncle and his sibling some sort of serum to make them grow? Or was it because of something else entirely? Could they be a different species perhaps, she wondered, or just freaks of nature? Other than size, all of the serpents had seemed nearly identical, although she had not gotten that close of a look at the smaller ones. But if they were different species, then who, exactly, were the Great Serpents: Uncle and his brother or the others who'd hidden from her? Donnie sighed with frustration because her travels, or should that be *travails*, in the marshes seemed to have given her more questions than answers.

The one really useful piece of information she'd learned from Uncle was that she'd been written about in Valley Guy's Book of Shadows, or in this case, she supposed it would be called the Book of Light. But why was this important to the gods; so much so, they made finding out about it one of her trials?

"Well, I wonder what it takes to 'vanquish' me? And who else is in the book?" Donnie murmured curiously. Was it maybe a book about fair magical creatures that crossed time? If so, it might give her an idea of who could be an ally in the future. She'd love to get a look at it, even if only to see what it said her weaknesses were. Yawning widely, she moved on in her ruminations.

Okay, it was clear that merely sending out love energy wasn't enough to turn dark creatures fair. Maybe some of them simply couldn't be turned from the dark side? Or, which was highly more likely, she'd just done it wrong. She wished she knew how she'd done it to the okûn at Mâlendian. Exhaling a long, deeply contented sigh, Donnie once again let her thoughts flow, moving on to what happened after leaving the marshes.

Why had she had that vision in the stream? What was its purpose, she wondered, and whatever had triggered it? She gave up pretty quickly on this subject because she just didn't have enough information about it yet. She considered the possibility that she might never understand the fantastical illusion, but her gut told her differently. Well then, she would have to wait for events to catch up with her gut, apparently. She dismissed this subject from her mind and went to the next.

What the heck was the deal with Rex? Why hadn't he been bound to the farm with the rest of its inhabitants? And his magical powers were nothing short of amazing. He appeared to have practiced them extensively without her even being aware he had them because he was very comfortable with them. As a matter of fact, they didn't seem to faze him in the least.

She thought back to the ride here. It had been like riding a bullet (albeit, one that made microsecond adjustments for obstacles), only way faster. And Rex had taken his time, he said, because he didn't want to really freak her out. He hadn't even needed a protective shield, while she always did when she went that fast. So how could he withstand the G-forces when she couldn't? Donnie suspected that he might even be able to run quite a bit faster, when he was unburdened and really trying that is, than she could fly on her broomstick. Since she'd managed to just barely break Mach five the other night (she'd had to top off at that speed because she'd had too much difficulty maintaining her protective shields when she tried going any faster), Rex's running abilities were indeed impressive.

"They might come in rather handy one day," Donnie noted. "And that growing thing he can do is pretty darned astounding too and, well, kind of alarming, now that I think about it. I'll have to have a serious talk with him soon about what else he can do." Heaving another tired, but relaxed sigh, she again smoothed the soap bar over her legs and feet, nearly finished both with her bath and her musings.

So Valley Guy had placed a bounty on her head, eh? Interesting, though not particularly surprising; it was, undoubtedly, the done thing around here. But now he knew that Donnie and her friends were on the move, which meant they probably weren't safe here in Marn Dím, at least not for long. Hopefully, nothing would happen to them tonight because she'd really like to get in a nice, long sleep without being bushwhacked by Valley Guy's henchmen.

Who was this Valley Guy anyway, and what did he want with Medregai? Or with her, for that matter? Was he a witch? Donnie hoped so, for the obvious implications that would have for her and her odds of defeating him with magic. He was apparently quite powerful, given that both Catie and Uncle had been scared to death of him. What kind of abilities did he have—she wondered if there were any he'd cultivated specially. If so, he was sure to be very, very good at them. She was going to have to be extremely wary of him until she'd gotten an idea of what all he could do.

When she felt that she was wrinkly enough, Donnie got out of her bath and dried herself off with the towel. She dressed in a long, white cotton sleeveless nightdress she'd materialized from the end of her bed at home. She sent Catie's clothing and her own boots back to her wardrobe at home and materialized a clean set of clothes for her to use tomorrow.

She dematerialized the tub's contents to the back yard of the cottage, then blew the inn's suspended filthy water and dirt particles back down to refill the copper receptacle. She glanced with revulsion at the oily water in the still-gleaming, clean tub before leaving the bathing room. Let the nosy proprietress wonder about that little mystery, along with the closed knothole, which Donnie refused to reopen.

When Donnie went back to her room, she found that her supper had been delivered and placed on the small table beside the bed. She walked in to find Falwaïn lying there, staring at her food. He too had been busy freshening up, by the looks of him. He said the others were waiting with Warren downstairs in the bar and that he would get them when she was ready to discuss their plans for the morrow.

Donnie shoved her clothes into her backpack, glad it had been hitched to her saddle when Uncle had grabbed her and had therefore come through the day unscathed, then she sat down on the side of the bed by the table to eat. Turning, she said quietly, "Um, I just wanted to say that

I'm sorry about earlier. You know, when I was cranky with you. It was rude of me and I apologize."

Falwaïn considered this, pausing before responding. "I accept your apology," he said graciously. "It's clear, though, that in the future, we shall have to make certain you are well fed at all times." He grinned after saying this, looking first at her plate and then at her, meaningfully.

The food certainly did look surprisingly appetizing. Her tummy suddenly, and very loudly, reminded Donnie that she was ravenous. They both feigned fear at the noise it made, with Falwaïn joking that it was the most intimidating thing he'd ever heard in his life, which set them to laughing even harder.

Still smiling to herself, Donnie picked up a piece of the chicken with her fingers and practically devoured it and the other two pieces. Falwaïn sat up next to her and kept eyeing her plate hungrily. So much so, she finally raised an enquiring eyebrow at him.

Unabashed, he reminded her, "Well, you were very rude to me earlier."

Donnie gave a small chuckle and told him to dig in if he wanted. His reply was to instantly take up some bread and mop it in the sauce from the chicken. Apparently, it tasted like heaven to him.

He leaned closer to Donnie each time he soaked the bread with more sauce. The scent of her was wonderful. She smelled of the light sandalwood soap she'd used, along with that of the gardenia spray, the special fragrance he now thought of as hers. His cheek brushed the bare skin of her shoulder and he felt her shiver.

Donnie laid the last of her chicken bones on her plate and put her hands on the linen towel in her lap. Falwaïn took hold of her right hand and brought it to his mouth, sensually licking the juices from her fingers. Her eyes closed and she breathed deeply, her face suffused with color. When he'd licked each of her fingers clean, Falwaïn let his lips brush the back of her hand and then placed it back in her lap, whispering that he'd return in a few minutes with the others.

Donnie heard the door close and let out the breath she'd been holding. She shivered again and opened her eyes, mentally rousing herself out of a daydream. In her fool's paradise, she and Falwaïn had been in bed together, making love. She was hot all over and had to use the towel to wipe the sweat off her brow and the back of her neck. There was definitely something special about that man.

Shaking her head ruefully, Donnie got up and washed her hands and face in the basin, then cleared the tray from the table, setting it outside the door. She sat down on the bed with her knees to her chest, her back scooted all the way up against the wall, and waited for the arrival of the others.

Her mind was still half-occupied with thoughts of Falwaïn when a knock sounded on the door and she heard Warren's voice. She called out for her friends to come in. As soon as the door opened, Rex bounded through it, followed closely by Sylvester. Falwaïn came in last, looking somewhat bemused himself, and had to sit on the end of the bed when Warren took the only chair in the room. Rex laid between Donnie and Falwaïn, almost jumping on top of Donnie in pure joy at seeing his mama again. He nudged her repeatedly with his snout until she straightened her legs out in front of her so he could snuggle up to her properly. Sylvester hopped onto the small table beside the bed.

"We should get an early start," Warren began, "it'll be a long, hard journey. From what Sylvester's told me, we must travel at least twenty-five to thirty leagues to the north to find where Galto has gone. Snow still covers the ground there."

"Yes," the cat seconded absentmindedly. He'd been studying Donemere carefully since he'd entered the room. There was something different about her now, a quality which became more pronounced hour by hour. He'd noticed it for the first time after she'd cast the circle spell. She was enigmatic now, clearly hiding something from him and the others.

Did that have to do with her magic...or with Lord Falwaïn? Their eyes sought each other's almost constantly and their shared smiles were secretive. It seemed as though Warren was correct and they *were* falling in love with each other. This prospect had worried Sylvester greatly for the past hour in the bar downstairs. Unfortunately, he could not prevent it from happening, though he prayed dearly that Donemere would not be diverted from her purpose by such a foolish obstacle as love. She would bear close watching on his part, and if she were indeed swayed by her heart, Lord Falwaïn would have to be prevailed upon to aid in shepherding her back onto her path. While he himself was not privy to what Donemere's ultimate task was to be, Sylvester knew that she must first save Medregai; for if she were to fail here, the future, as she knew it, would be no more.

This all flashed through the cat's mind in the moment before he recalled himself and relayed his information to the others. "I agree," he said in response to Warren's suggestion, "we must be away no later than dawn or we shall not escape Valledai's forces. I will explain my actions of this afternoon. When we arrived, I scouted the city and soon discovered a tunnel leading into the mountain upon which Marn Dím is built. I saw an oddly cloaked figure that moved suspiciously like an okûn enter this passage. I followed him through it, at a safe distance, of course, until I came upon a group of five of the beasts sitting around a fire. The fiend I was tracking was amongst them. I presume they were charged with guarding the tunnel; but, if so, I must say they were not doing it well. Quite obviously, they were profoundly lazy and stupid creatures," the cat sniffed superiorly.

"I listened to them for more than an hour from my vantage point in a recess carved into the wall, only a few feet from where they were gathered. Eventually, they spoke of a mountain, Moên Flírbann, which lies north of here. Valledai has made it a temporary base and 'tis to this mountain that Galto has ridden. His condition, when he passed by the city two days ago, has been the source of much amusement for the population of Marn Dím. Both Valledai and Galto appear to be at Flírbann now. The okûn I followed told of how he had only just returned from there. It should be a simple matter to follow their trail northward."

Sylvester leaned in conspiratorially, staring intently at each of his friends in turn. "But more importantly," he intoned in a grave voice, "I have learned that the okûn are intending to rise up quite soon, with Valledai as their new master. It appears they are poised to take Marn Dím tomorrow at sunrise. And 'tis ripe for the taking by Valledai and his armies. Most of its inhabitants are Mountain People, Donemere, and they have never been content to be subjects of the king. They will openly welcome Valledai, whom they are already calling the next Var King of Annûar. No, Valledai's forces will encounter virtually no resistance when they march on the city tomorrow. We must be away long before it is taken."

"Okay," agreed Donnie, "but I really don't understand why your king doesn't protect this city better. I mean, even in my time in San Francisco we still have a fully manned presidio." She yawned sleepily behind her hand, looking at Falwaïn when she asked the question, unaware of the confused looks her remark caused from Warren and Sylvester.

Falwaïn smiled understandingly, knowing that her mistake came from sheer weariness. He turned to the others and supplied, "She means a garrison of guards." He looked back at a confounded Donnie and explained, "The Mountain People are rather tricky to negotiate such things with, that's why. Several years ago, a treaty was signed by King Belnescm and the Mountain leaders, wherein it was agreed that, in return for their avoidance of the settlements south of the Bitterbend Marshes, the Mountain People, most especially those here in Marn Dím, would have almost complete autonomy. You see, before that, when Marn Dím was first reestablished, the Mountain Men regularly raided both Mâlendian and Banaff Dír, along with their surrounding settlements, all of which are inhabited by Free Peoples. It was not long before the hostilities between the north and south of the Annûar Province were escalating alarmingly. The king felt it prudent to give the Mountain Folk their own realm, but managed to obtain their oath of allegiance to the government of the west. This oath was sworn reluctantly and has, at best, provided for an unstable, but nonetheless lasting peace in the region."

Sylvester stepped forward on the table and interjected dramatically, "A peace which is about to be shattered by Valledai's forces." He sat back down and curled his tail around his front paws. "After listening to the okûn a while longer, they confirmed that Moên Gjendeben is indeed filled with their kind, all awaiting Valledai's orders to march west. More come every day. And 'tis not just okûn who are gathering there. Every dark creature left alive after the Battle of the Var is migrating to Gjendeben. As we feared, when they are ready, they intend to march on the southern settlements of the province, and Medregai shall be at war with itself once again. What is most dire to us is that, not only are they all aware of our existence, many are actively hunting us because Valledai has placed a bounty on our heads—or more precisely, on Donemere's."

"Yeah, I know about that part," Donnie nodded. She went on to relay most of what she'd learned from Uncle and his brother, then asked the others her question about the identity of the Great Serpents.

Falwaïn twisted around to look at her, a hint of amusement in his voice as he commented on one of the more humorous proclivities of the human race. "Few survive an attack by the Great Serpents and, of those who do, their tales of escape naturally get more embellished and the serpents themselves seem to grow larger with each and every retelling. Having never seen one myself before today, I cannot answer your question."

Sylvester and Warren both admitted that they too had never seen one before and so were unable to explain the difference in size of the Great Serpents.

Falwaïn asked Donnie, "Do you truly believe that they're different species?"

She shrugged and thought about this for a moment. "No, not really. It could just be that Uncle and his brother are the next step in the Great Serpent evolution or, conversely, maybe the others are, since that's the way many species evolve—by getting smaller, I mean. Or, perhaps those two are just a lot older than the others and in another fifty or, who knows, maybe a thousand years, depending on how long they normally live—anyway, maybe one day all of the Great Serpents will be the same size. But then, if that were true, one would think that Uncle would already be King of the Marshes just based on sheer size alone, huh?" She lifted her shoulders again and let them fall, conceding regretfully, "Frankly, I have no clue; I just know it's odd in some way. Well, I suppose we'll figure it out one day; preferably long before it causes more trouble for us. But, getting back to our previous discussion, tell me exactly where this Mount Genda Benda place is situated."

Sitting back in his chair and crossing his arms, Warren replied, "It lies slightly northeast of the cottage, but on the far eastern edge of the Brumal Mountains."

"Are you sure it's not directly east of the marshes?"

He inclined his head with a faint smile. "I'm quite certain, Donemere."

"Then what is east of Bitterbend?"

The Wolf King shrugged. "More of the Brumal Mountains."

"Have you ever heard of a place called Moên Grím?" she enquired.

All except the snoring Rex drew their breaths in sharply and exclaimed, "Moên Grím!"

"That mountain has never been found by any fair creature," Falwaïn informed her, being the first to recover from their collective surprise. "It's located somewhere amongst the Brumal Mountains and is the closely secreted capital of the okûn," he elaborated. "It was rumored, after the war, that the okûn tribal kings escaped to Moên Grím in order to rebuild their armies. That is why King Belnesem has fought so hard to establish his presence in these lands. He hopes to make them safe for all peoples to live in and to bring the Mountain Folk more fully into our alliance of freedom. But, tell us, what did you hear of Moên Grím from the Great Serpents?"

"Well, apparently, Valley Guy was also there earlier today, in addition to this Flea-Bound Mountain place." Donnie waved a hand, then added, murmuring almost to herself, "Which means that he was at both, very distant places within, what, one day, at the most? Now, that's got to be rather unusual for around here. Hmm, I wonder if he too can fly?"

"Might these two mountains not be one and the same?" Sylvester interrupted her abruptly. "You could have become confused and made a mistake in the direction taken by the brother snake. He may very well have gone to Moên Flírbann."

Donnie shook her head, certain she was right. "No, I checked on him occasionally by focusing on his soul and, I'm telling you, he was definitely going east. Besides, he only went a little over seventy-five miles to his destination in an almost due eastwardly direction, hung out there for a quarter of an hour, then turned around and came back. I know I'm right about the distance because he was absent roughly three hours and he generally maintained an approximate speed of sixty in the tunnel he was taking, so that means he had to have gone less than one hundred and eighty miles round-trip. I'm no math genius, but even I can figure that one out. Now, I reckon this place we're going to tomorrow must be at least a couple hundred miles north of the snake caverns, right? Even allowing, say, only two minutes for the brother to make his report to Valley Guy, that still wouldn't leave him enough time to have gotten all the way up there and then back to the cavern in only three hours. So his destination had to've been closer."

"But you may not have seen their fastest speed and therefore your calculations may still be incorrect," Sylvester cautioned. "After all, may I remind you, you did have great difficulty finding your way out of the marsh tunnels."

"No, he went east, not north; I'm positive about that," Donnie maintained staunchly. "Okay, so I did get lost when I was escaping, but that's kinda understandable since I was a little busy making sure I didn't run into any more snakes and, well, there are a lot of tunnels down there, you know? I really had no idea when, or even if, the Great Serpents prowling all around me were going to attack. But I am absolutely certain about the direction Uncle's brother took and about his speed. And you guys will just have to trust me on this one!" she added, an obstinate set to her jaw.

"I, for one, can do that quite easily," Falwaïn smiled at her, his blue eyes glinting. "I've learned already that you are exceptionally talented and if you say something is so, then it is so." His expression changed, becoming more thoughtful. "I think I may know how Valledai could be in two such distant locations in one day. I recall Déagmun speaking on a few occasions of deep, subterranean tunnels that run throughout these mountains, passageways which were birthed by creatures such as the Ghérôntog, or possibly even the legendary Brumal Ettins, who, besides a Munus or higher Wizard or a Fægre Witch, were the Ghérôntog's only true enemy. If there is such a tunnel from the marshes to Moên Grím, and it was through this that the brother serpent traveled, then there are certain to be more tunnels between their other lairs; perhaps even one that connects Moên Grím to Flírbann."

Warren nodded. "That makes sense. It would reduce the distance to be traveled to a minimum and would provide sufficient terrain on which to make good time. A strong horse, for instance, might be able to span such a tunnel in half a day."

Donnie, who'd just yawned yet again, decided it would not be prudent to point out that there were modern machines that could cover the distance much faster than any horse could, and it was likely that Valley Guy would also be aware of this and had probably brought some of these back here with him, since he undoubtedly had no qualms about doing such a thing. Instead, she scooted to the edge of the bed and stood up, telling the others, "Okay, so we're all agreed; we're up before dawn to blow this popstand before it becomes Okûn City. I hope everybody brought their woolies, 'cause I think it's gonna be mighty cold where we're going."

She shooed the two men out of her room, insisting that she needed her beauty rest, and slid the bolt to lock the door behind them. Then she sank back against the wood and said, "He's dreamy."

"Who?" Sylvester eyes widened with surprise.

"Who do you think? Falwaïn, you idiot. He makes my heart flip, even though I don't want it to," Donnie admitted honestly. "I know, conventional wisdom says it's unwise to start an office romance, but then I've always been one to live dangerously. And he's not only gorgeous, but smart and kind and sexy. And brave and built like a brick house and, did I mention sexy? And he likes me right back. I can tell." She wrapped her arms around her, her smile wide and sunny, and danced around the room.

Rex, disturbed from his slumber, lifted his head to glare at his mama and huff his annoyance, then put his head back down and immediately resumed snoring. Sylvester watched Donnie for a minute or so with mounting irritation, until he snippily pointed out that they had an early day tomorrow and she really should come to bed.

Reluctantly, Donnie slipped under the covers, gave Rex his kiss, and waved her hand to snuff out the candles, shoving the dog over toward the wall a little more. The cat settled in the crook of her knees and fell asleep. Donnie couldn't keep her mind from racing at first with very naughty, though extremely satisfying daydreams of her and Falwaïn. At ten o'clock, she finally *willed* herself to go to sleep. Right before she fell into dreamland, a sudden reminder intruded on her thoughts. "I haven't asked Falwaïn about the inscription on the back of the amulet yet," she muttered to herself drowsily. "Maybe he can read it. Ah well, tomorrow then."

The three of them awoke later at the same moment, their internal clocks in sync. Rex stretched and yawned, then stepped over Donnie to jump onto the floor. He turned and gave her a small kiss, which effectively stopped her from falling back to sleep. Donnie looked at her watch through one eye. It read four-thirty three. With a disgruntled sigh, she snapped her fingers to light one candle and scrambled up off the bed. Sleepily, she dressed in clean sweats and boots, then quickly finished packing her knapsack. Three minutes after she arose, she heard a gentle tap on her door. Rex said it was Warren and Falwaïn. Once Donnie was ready to go, they all filed quietly down the staircase.

Someone was awake and moving around in the bar. They crept past the bar's entrance to the outside door, which was locked. Withdrawing the heavy bolts on the locks with a wave of her hand, Donnie opened the creaky door and they left the inn. She and Rex went first, almost running in their haste, with Sylvester riding on her shoulder.

They were barely across the street when the door reopened and a figure emerged, dimly outlined by the light of the bar. It was the proprietor, old frog-face himself. Falwaïn and Warren turned to look back at him, but continued walking. The other three were already around the corner by this time. Falwaïn called out that they were getting an early start and expressed his thanks for the hospitality shown to them. Frog-face waved his hand and closed the door of the inn, unsure which guests they were. A moment later, they heard the bolts being shot home.

Donnie, Sylvester and Rex waited in the darkness of the alley that was situated to the side of the stables while the men saddled the horses and brought them out. Donnie put her parka on under Catie's cloak, glad she'd brought both, and she and Falwaïn mounted their horses. Sylvester had already jumped onto her sleeping bag and was snuggled down into its folds. Warren stepped into the shadows as the others trotted off down the street, hurrying after them a moment later in his wolven form.

At the gate to the city, Donnie stayed a little behind Falwaïn so the gatekeeper wouldn't get a proper look at her face or her clothing. When the heavy door within the huge gate swung open, Otis surged through it and darted to the right, followed by Gallantry, with what appeared to the gatekeeper to be two fierce-looking wolves running alongside them. Donnie and her friends were on the road again.

Chapter 16
We're All Guilty of Something

As Donnie had predicted the night before in Marn Dím, it became much colder the farther north they traveled, with the temperature soon dropping to near freezing point, although the sun burned brightly in a cloudless sky. The elevation increased noticeably and intermittent patches of snow began to appear.

Just after eleven o'clock, the Annûar Path came to an abrupt end, but by keeping to a fast pace all morning, Donnie and her friends managed to get more than two-thirds of the way to their destination. Both Falwaïn and Warren knew the way to Moên Flírbann from the terminus of the main path and began to debate the different routes to take. At Donnie's urging, they finally chose the most direct, which appeared to be a trail blazed long ago but which also bore clear signs of recent passage by others.

"Okay, so what creepy creatures inhabit this area?" she asked after the issue had been settled.

"Snow Trolls." That lazy, lopsided grin of Falwaïn's once again set Donnie's heart beating faster.

"Oh, yay, something new!" Donnie joked before taking and expelling a deep breath. She grimaced humorously and added, "I can hardly wait. Really. See the anticipation on my face? Look harder and you'll find it." After she took another deep breath and had released it in a long groan, she asked a little deliriously, "Tell me, will we get to see hordes of them or will they be in small packs, hunched around a fire? And can we feed them or do we have to remain in the car with the windows rolled up?"

Falwaïn turned and flashed a quick, reassuring grin at her. "They'll most likely leave us alone," he said, "because normally they only come out at night, when it's coldest. And if we are unlucky enough to encounter one, it'll be nothing we can't handle between us."

Donnie nodded silently at him and put on a fake smile that turned into a scowl.

Falwaïn moved Gallantry closer and took hold of her hand. "Tired of all this, aren't you?"

"At the moment, yes," Donnie replied seriously. "I kinda go in waves, you know? One minute, I'm riding the crest and everything's just jake; I can accept where I am and what I'm doing. The next, I'm way down in the trough between waves and wondering what the hell am I going to do if I see something like a troll or another okûn or Great Serpent or something even worse, heaven forbid."

"You will behave with the same ingenuity and cleverness that you exhibited with the Great Serpents, the camera and with Galto. Of this, I am certain," Falwaïn proclaimed firmly, looking deep into her eyes.

Donnie forced herself to smile and quipped, "Oh, yeah, that's me all right, little Miss Ingenious Slash Clever. Otherwise known as a total smartass. A wiseacre. Or, as my high school principal put it, another one of those yo-yos and yardbirds. But, honestly, I don't know if I have the intestinal fortitude to see this thing through. It's just so darned overwhelming and, well, plain old odd. It is so far removed from my reality, I can't even begin to express how inordinately strange all of this is to me. You've grown up around it, so a troll's a troll, an okûn's an okûn, an elf's an—hey, wait a minute, will I get to see any elves, d'ya think? I'd love to meet, er, what's his name – er, Galæron. Is he still around?" Her eyes sparkled with anticipation. "He was played by this really cute guy in the mov—um, well, he sounded really wonderful in the books from my time," she finished lamely, cursing herself for yet another near-blunder of the time continuum.

"I am well aware that a movie was made of your world's version of our history," Falwaïn said unconcernedly. "More of my reading material the other night. Why do you think I want to see this television of yours? I presume you have the DVD and, therefore, I can see how your century depicts my century."

"I am not at all surprised that you already know about movies and DVDs." Donnie beamed at him affably after making this comment. "Actually though," she explained, "the story's split into three films, just like the books, although the fourth book was due out right around the time I was brought here, so I'm sure another movie can't be far behind. I think you'll like the movies they've done so far. I mean, there are some obvious differences between what they imagined and what's truly here; but, all in all, Martin Drake and crew are doing an exceptionally fine job with the story. Might be a little freaky for you to see the actors who are portraying you and your friends though."

"Why do you think that?" Falwaïn asked curiously.

Donnie pursed her lips and frowned before responding. "Well, for you, at least, let's just say there's a remarkable resemblance between you and the actor playing your counterpart in the movie, especially the way they've made him up; you know, how they've dressed him, cut his hair, all that stuff. I don't know if that's true for any of the others, but…"

"It is, to some degree," Falwaïn assured her, admitting apologetically, "I've already seen a few of the still photographs from the movies. And, yes, one of those was a picture of my doppelganger."

"Doppelganger?" Donnie laughed in disbelief. "Dazzling dictionaries, what'd you do, memorize the entire unabridged Taylor's the other night? Or, knowing you, you probably went for all twenty volumes of the KED, didn't you?" He grinned roguishly at her, making her heart flip again—darn the thing! "How about the others then?" she asked. "Your friends, I mean. Which ones of them also have doppelgangers in the movies?"

"Only some are very similar in appearance to those here in Medregai, while many others are not," he replied. "If you remain here long enough, you just may have the opportunity to meet most of them and then you can find out for yourself."

"Now see, that's exactly the kind of thing that freaks me out!" exclaimed Donnie. "If I just go about this naturally, viewing it simply as this is the way my life is right now, I'm okay. But every time I get smacked in the face with something from my culture's version of your world, that's when things start to get all haywired for me. The two cultures clash and intertwine, and it makes me dizzy." She let out a frustrated groan, then smiled at Falwaïn. "I'll be okay. But thanks for caring."

He smiled back and kept hold of her hand for a while. Surprisingly, she was very much comforted by his touch and soon felt her spirits rising once more.

By late afternoon, heavy, wet snow blanketed the moors. To their advantage, several fresh okûn and horse trails not only gave the travelers a path to follow, but also made their ascent much easier than it would have been in uncut snow. Nonetheless, the journey was wearying for the horses and their hot breath steamed from their nostrils at a brisk rate whenever the group traversed the steeper moors. While it was well into spring, and elsewhere flowers were blooming, they were now heading to the icy north and the far expanses of the Brumal Mountains, toward Flírgai; which translated simply to North Land, as Falwaïn explained to Donnie. There, the snow never fully melted. Which meant it was going to get even colder before they reached their destination.

Sylvester eventually crawled into Donnie's parka and their respective body heat kept each other a little warmer. When it became almost unbearably cold, Donnie conjured up a shield around herself and the cat, and then blew some warming breaths into it; but not long afterward, Otis asked her to quit doing this as it made him sweat terribly on his back. Donnie obligingly made mini-shields for her feet, hands and torso, which was just enough to keep her and the cat from turning into icicles.

Falwaïn didn't seem to notice the cold and Rex and Warren playfully chased each other through the drifts whenever the mood suited them. The horses somehow managed to maintain a steady, but hurried pace throughout the day, even with the moors becoming steeper and harder to mount, making the trail more difficult to follow, let alone travel. When the sun was ready to set, Donnie conjured up some light-balls to light their way.

A little after nine o'clock that evening, they reached a huge plateau that Warren and Falwaïn agreed should be relatively near the foot of Moên Flírbann. They made camp there, close to the forest they'd been skirting for the past twenty minutes, its tall firs swaying and rustling in the gusting wind that had sprung up an hour before. Donnie cleared an extensive camp area in the snow for them, then materialized her largest tent, having it set itself up in mere seconds. Because it wasn't big enough for everyone to move around in comfortably, nor was she about to leave the horses out in the extreme cold, she quadrupled the tent's size and that of its tarp. Still not happy, she doubled their size again, and settled a charm on the gigantic tent to re-strengthen its supports. She then blew into its interior to warm it and their entire group hurried inside.

They looked through their packs and discovered that most of their ready food stores were depleted. Donnie materialized a cold dinner for them, along with the kitchen table and chairs from the cottage. Two tubs appeared in the corner where the horses stood, one filled with oats and the other with water. They all ate hungrily and when dinner was over Donnie cleared the table with another wave of her hand. She again blew into the air of the tent, warming it by a few more degrees.

They agreed to get an early start in the morning and arose from the table. Donnie sent the table back to the cottage to clear out some space in the tent, but left the chairs. They unpacked their sleeping bags and laid them out in the middle of the tent. Donnie duplicated one for Warren, spreading it beside the others. Hers was flanked by those of the two men. Donnie laid down first and was asleep within minutes, Rex at her feet and Sylvester curled up on the pillow beside her head. The two men stayed up talking for some while.

Falwaïn again took first watch. When it was over, he awoke Warren and laid down in his sleeping bag, marveling at the warmth and cushioning it provided. He rolled onto his side and could just make out the faint outline of Donnie's sleeping face, which was turned toward him. This honey woman was taking over his heart, he realized. Her strange ways and stranger vocabulary intrigued him. He wanted to know her and her world, to be able to meet her on her terms. He wondered sleepily if he'd be given the chance to do that.

In the morning, they breakfasted quickly. As was her habit when roughing it, Donnie griped about having to go potty outdoors, but was otherwise cheerful. Rex and Warren ran off early to investigate the mountain, while Falwaïn tended the horses and Donnie packed her knapsack, filling it with bottled water and egg sandwiches. Sylvester was outside chasing down his own meal.

Warren and Rex were back in half an hour, with the cat following them into the tent almost immediately, still licking his whiskers. Warren changed into his human form and joined Donnie and Falwaïn at the table. "There is an entrance to the mountain almost halfway up its southern face," he announced. "You can see the open entryway from the north edge of this plateau and from there the mountain is little more than a league distant. The tunnel looks to be too small for the horses, so they will have to remain here."

Rex sat down primly next to Warren's chair and added, "That guy's scent is really strong close to the mountain, Mama—you know, that Galto character, I mean. And his trail leads right to the tunnel entrance."

Donnie was eyeing both Warren and the dog skeptically, her tongue pushing on her cheek for a moment. "You say this tunnel entrance is just there, completely open to any Tom, Dick or Harry who happens by? Nothing blocking it, no doors with a secret code in Elvish or Dwarvish, or whatever?"

Warren nodded in response, a slow smile beginning to spread across his features.

"Innat a bit peculiar?" Donnie observed. "Mueler's books especially made it sound like there's nary a cave or tunnel entrance anywhere here that would just stand wide open, practically inviting whoever to come on in and make themselves to home. Well, unless there's a good reason for it to be like that."

"I believe we are expected," Warren pontificated sardonically, then leaned back in his chair and grinned even more widely at her and Falwaïn.

Falwaïn chuckled with agreement. "Which is as we thought." He added mischievously, "It appears that we shall soon see what new fun awaits us in the depths of this Flea-Bound Mountain, as Donnie would most likely express it."

She laughed and added jokingly, "Yeah, and we'll have to be on our guard, won't we?"

They finished preparing for the trip into the mountain. Donnie pulled on her parka, gloves and knit hat, jammed her witch's hat on top of that, slipped on her backpack, and declared herself ready to go. Rex led the way across the plateau, then up the first moor and over the next, until they came to the foot of Moên Flírbann and hiked up its side path, arriving at the tunnel entrance nearly two hours after setting out from their camp. On the way, Falwaïn and Warren, still in his human form, flanked Donnie from the front and from behind, respectively, while Sylvester wormed his way down into Donnie's parka again.

Donnie had not been at all thrilled at the prospect of slushing her way through the knee-deep, heavy snow on the steep moors between the plateau and the mountain. Somewhere last night, they'd drifted from the trail blazed by Valledai's henchmen and had wound up forging their own way to their campsite. Less than five minutes after setting out this morning, Donnie had begun to magically clear a path for them to follow through the hard-packed, uncut snow that blanketed the land all around them. In fact, the snow, for as far as the eye could see, was marred only by the recurring, widespread sets of footprints left by Rex on the reconnaissance trip to the tunnel entrance.

Even with Donnie's aid, the trek was a hard one. Warren and Falwaïn, fortunately, laughed away Donnie's complaints and did their best to keep her mind occupied so that she wouldn't dwell on her bodily discomfort along the way. Question after question about her world streamed from both of them until Donnie thought her head would spin. But it worked perfectly as a diversion for her and before she knew it they were already scaling the footpath that had been carved into the mountainside. After a minute or two on this trail, which was covered by only a light coating of snow and a thin layer of ice, she remarked on the steepness and slipperiness of its grade, saying that she now wished she'd brought along some climbing gear.

The men, exaggeratedly solicitous in their manner, offered to carry her.

Feeling her face flame with embarrassment, Donnie retorted, "No, I shall pull my own weight, thank you very much, no matter how many times I slip to my poor, knobby knees, nor how mottled my miserable mug becomes from the exertion of mounting this maleficent massif!" She held her head high when alliterating this declaration, nearly falling a second later on yet another patch of ice. She gave the snickering men an outraged glare each and dared them to best her when it came to twisting words. They raised their hands in mock-surrender and silence, then Falwaïn took pity and laced his arm with hers to steady her climb.

When their arduous haul was finally over and they had reached the tunnel's entrance, everyone accordingly cheered their relief. Here, the carved path they'd been following stopped just a few feet beyond the darkened passageway they sought. They stood grouped closely together and surveyed the mountain towering over them, its right side still bathed in mid-morning sunlight. Sylvester even crawled out of Donnie's coat to perch upon her shoulder and gaze upward. It was a couple minutes before anyone said anything.

"Is it just me, or is that an awful lot of rubble to be sittin' on top of that tunnel entrance?" Donnie eventually asked.

Everybody either nodded solemnly or murmured their agreement. Each of them was studying the top of the tunnel suspiciously. An archway had been built into the mountainside, into which a small, rather narrow doorway had been set. All around this doorway, within its stone facing, were carved weathered outlines of, exactly what, it was impossible to tell any longer. The archway itself was easily ten feet wide and fifteen tall, and atop it sat three very large mounds of snow-covered boulders, piled precariously on a base of loose dirt and small rocks.

"It looks like rather fresh rubble," Falwaïn noted.

"I was just going to say that." Warren turned his head toward Falwaïn and nodded, adding speculatively, "It also looks…unnaturally placed."

"As though some particular personage piled it there purposely, in three perfectly proportioned pyramids," Falwaïn suggested, returning Warren's glancing nod.

"Agreed. 'Tis very neatly done, though a bit obvious."

"Oh, yes, I'd call it sophomoric even."

"*Sophomoric*, eh?" Warren commented, obviously impressed. "You certainly appear to be much better at learning Donnie's language than I am, I see. And your alliteration was quite prettily done, much better than Donnie's a few minutes ago."

Falwaïn bowed his head slightly and acknowledged this praise with a pleased, "Why, thank you, my friend."

"Think nothing of it," said Warren, directing his gaze back to the top of the entrance. He grinned slyly before positing, "I would wager that Flat-Finger is the architect of this treacherous triad, which I believe is meant to trap our little troupe inside this towering tumulus and twist it into a tomb."

"Treacherous triad? Towering tumulus? Some rather sweet bits of alliteration there yourself, you know," Falwaïn complimented Warren, whose turn it was to bow low and murmur his appreciation for the euphonic recognition.

Warren then proffered like a shot, "And do your own conjectures concur with my conclusion?"

"Oh, yes, quite clearly there is consensus concerning said conclusion," Falwaïn reassured the Wolf King immediately.

Throughout this rapid exchange, Donnie merely stared at the two men with increasing amusement etched on her mobile features. She now asked dryly, "Just when did I end up with Kennedy and Taylor as my traveling companions?"

The two men mugged at her in response, both reminding her that it *had* been her challenge to them, with Warren noting that they had finally found something they could definitely best her in! He then looked down at Rex and winked. The dog had a big, happy smile plastered to his face; he was very proud of his pupil's vocabulary progress.

Sylvester, though, cleared his throat loudly and impatiently. Would they please get on with it, his manner said. This was producing no viable results and he was becoming quite cold.

Warren and Falwaïn exchanged devilish glances again.

"Right then, now that we've agreed upon the perpetrator of this dastardly deed, we must revisit the problem of the trap itself. We should not leave it like this," Warren said decisively.

Falwaïn nodded. "I'll grant you that, certainly. It shall have to be removed before we go inside. No sense in asking for that sort of trouble, is there?"

"I suppose one of us could climb up and shove the whole mess down there." Warren pointed toward the lower regions of the mountainside.

But Falwaïn shook his head. "No. Too much work for either of us, I think."

They both turned to Donnie at the same time with identical, droll expressions on their faces. "This one is most definitely yours," Warren informed her soberly.

Laughter bubbled from her throat once more. "Okay, of course I'll take care of it," she readily consented. "But, first, who is Flat-Finger? Or do I not want to know that?"

Falwaïn clasped his hands behind his back and rocked on his toes, replying, "Oh, I am certain you'll be most pleased to learn that he is a Stone Giant."

"A giant!" Donnie squeaked, almost choking on the word. "Are you serious?"

"Oh, quite, quite," Falwaïn assured her. "And not just any giant, but a Stone Giant of the Brumal Ettins, no less. Flat-Finger is enormously famous all around Annûar, by the way. You can always tell where he's been by the shape of the boulders he invariably stacks in exceedingly neat piles. Rumor has it, he was imprisoned somewhere for centuries, but was released, oh, let me see, by your calendar it would be approximately seven months ago. Since then, there have been several sightings of him."

Falwaïn continued rocking back and forth from heel to toe as he expounded on the giant's nervous proclivity for tidiness. "As I'm sure you'll remember from the books on our world, Ettins, and Stone Giants in particular, love to—let's say, *bowl* during violent storms. Well, once again, rumor has it that Flat-Finger tends to become a bit fussy when it's not his turn. You see, he apparently frets and fidgets when he has nothing to occupy his fingers, and while he is busy with this fretting and fidgeting, he unconsciously picks up small boulders and worries them with the aforementioned digits until they have that distinctive, flattened shape. He then apparently feels the unrelenting need to arrange them in perfectly geometric patterns—a need, by the way, that long ago became an obsession, such that he can no longer help but perform this rather curious activity wherever he goes. Why do you look at me that way, Donemere? Although I didn't read his books all the way through, I'm fairly certain that Master Mueler must've written something about our giants. I know the Medregai history book discussed them at some length."

Warren turned to Falwaïn and declared, "I really must read these books you keep mentioning by this man, this Master Mueler; they sound fascinating! On the other hand, I have read Catie's book on our world, and I too recall it explaining much of what is known of the giants' history."

Falwaïn regarded him with a small measure of surprise. "Pardon me, I don't mean to offend, but I was unaware that you could actually read."

"Oh, yes, my friend. Been able to since I can remember," said Warren. "And, of late, Rex has generously shared his knowledge of some rather arcane words, including explanation of their spellings and definitions. Thankfully, he's also been quite useful in defining Donnie's more esoteric epithets."

Rex shot his mama a sheepish grin in response to her raised eyebrow.

Sylvester piped up from inside Donnie's parka, which he'd crawled back into a few moments before (seeing as no one appeared to be doing anything about the trap other than talking about it), "You must avail yourself of Donemere's library, Warren," his muffled voice called out. " 'Tis most informative and entertaining; much better than Catie's was."

And Rex added, "Oh, yeah, you gotta check it out. Mama's got some really great stories there, full of all kinds of adventures. Most of 'em are about humans, though, which is kind of a drag. But there's one, *The Wilderness*—oh man, what a story! Gets ya right in the gut, you know?"

Donnie gaped at her dog incredulously. "Since when do you read novels?" she demanded to know. "And no, I'm not freaking out, I just hardly ever see you reading anything other than the dictionary or encyclopedia!"

"But, Mama, I've always loved to read all kinds of stuff!" the dog protested. "Don't you remember? After you put one of my beds next to the bookshelf—oh, what was it, a couple, maybe three years ago, I think. And you'd come home to find books scattered on the floor? You thought it was funny to joke, 'Hey, honey, did you enjoy the Barfield plays?' or 'How was Kipenger today? Was Michael still Michael?' But what you didn't know was that I *was* actually reading them, I just didn't know how to tell you that 'cause I couldn't talk back then."

"Omigod, you were magical back in our time too?" gulped Donnie.

Rex went from gazing at her innocently to gaping at her in surprise. "You know what, Mama, I guess I was!" he exclaimed. "But since you weren't, you never noticed that I was. And I didn't even know what that meant then—to be magical, I mean. Honestly, I just assumed that every other dog could read and understand English too. But now I know better."

Warren got down on his haunches and looked the dog in the face, choosing his words carefully. "Are you telling us that you could do *all* the things there that you can do here?"

"Nope, just a few," the dog replied matter-of-factly. "Soon after we got here though, I realized I could do a whole lot more things now. Don't know why."

"Could that be the reason he wasn't affected by the binding spell? Is it possible, Sylvester?" inquired Falwaïn, turning to look at the cat, who was now peering out the "V" of Donnie's parka zipper, staring at the dog.

Sylvester gave a thoughtful nod to this question. "It very well might be and 'tis certainly something that warrants further investigation—at a later date, of course. May I remind you all that today we must meet whatever awaits us inside this mountain, be it fun or no," he prompted them dourly.

Donnie grunted her agreement, and turned back to study the trap and the mountainside around it. After a moment, she concentrated on lifting the boulders and heavier rocks into the air and sent them rolling down the long slope of the mountain to their far right. The remainder of the loose gravel and smaller rocks she shoved to their left with a wave of her hand, sending it down the winding pathway carved into the mountainside, the couple tons or so of dirt and pebbles settling into one long, smooth layer of rubble.

"There, that's better," she said. "All it needs is a touch more resurfacing, and then even I wouldn't be afraid to go down that trail, at least the upper part of it." She bowed to the others and gestured with a grand flourish toward the entryway. "After you, my lords."

Inside, the tunnel started out little more wide enough than for two people to walk abreast of each other. They had gone about a hundred feet in when Falwaïn placed his full weight upon the first in a long set of steps. Behind them, they heard the rumbling of moving rock. Everyone wheeled around and watched as a thin cloud of dust fell in front of the entryway when the overhanging roof of the tunnel entrance retracted into the façade wall. They gave each other knowing smiles and turned back toward the stairway.

Falwaïn led the way for some time, while Warren brought up the rear behind Donnie. Sylvester climbed back onto Donnie's shoulder as soon as they left the influence of the icy winds howling outside. Rex heeled quietly at either Donnie's or Warren's side until the passageway eventually widened to about fifteen feet across and they could all walk abreast for a while.

Donnie conjured a blue light-ball as soon as they were away from the illumination provided by the tunnel entrance and blew on the magical sphere, breaking it into several more light-balls that took a moment to grow to full size. These she floated high in the air in front and in back of their little group, giving them plenty of light to see the rough-hewn walls of the tunnel glisten and become smoother as they went farther into the mountain.

Their journey through the tunnel was quite tiring at first, ascending sharply over three long series of winding steps, then descending even more sharply until the grade finally leveled out. Deeper and deeper into the mountain they went, hampered only a little by the sometimes copious amounts of debris in their path. After she'd recognized that these piles were mainly bones and clothing, Donnie refused to look down again and just kept waving her hand so that their path was cleared through these sadly forsaken remains.

***

Valledai was sitting in a brightly lit room at the back of Olganôgwéard, the great cavern that lay underneath Moên Flírbann. The room he was in had originally served the dwarves as a ceremonial chamber of greeting, while the cavern itself had been a regional assembly place for the peoples and gods of Írtha during religious celebrations of old. This underground fortress had later doubled as a stronghold in case of attack from Írtha's southern nations, who, until that fool, King Belnesem, rose to power, had been lasting enemies of the northern races from ancient to modern times because of a divisive event that pre-dated even the War of Sorrow and that had torn the north and south asunder ever since it had occurred. Recent diplomatic forays by the king's emissaries had been successful in the signing of various treaties with the

Mehen'Adríum and Zi'ahn Lo'ba, although several other southern peoples remained staunch adversaries of Medregai despite Belnesem's traitorous efforts to win their favor.

Back when the fortress of Olganôg was freshly excavated, there had been a reception chamber for each of Írtha's governing races of extant magical beings, but most of these had by now fallen into unusable disrepair. Olganôg and its appurtenant chambers were but one of three strongholds in Medregai built in the name of the ancient gods to protect their penitents in time of battle. Olganôgwéard had originally had three entry points, but only two remained passable, with the third having been cut off by the dwarves after the fall of Olganôg during the War of Sorrow, when the much lamented massacre within the fortress claimed the war's largest number of civilian casualties.

Approximately twenty-two hundred years ago, the cavern and its side chambers were carved by the dwarves into the belly of the mountain, then adorned with furnishings and prayers by committees of other races, and were lastly graced in ritual by the gods. While these divine blessings had served admirably to shield the location of Olganôg from Medregai's enemies, they had not been enough to keep out the Red Warlock's brave armies during the War of Sorrow, as evidenced throughout the mountain, where broken axes, hammers, spears, swords, knives and all manner of shattered weaponry lay tarnished and forgotten and where the carved walls and floors were pocked with heavy blows from ferocious and frenzied creatures from both sides of the fray. Numerous maces, hefty in weight, were buried deeply within the rock in several locations, their exposed sharpened points covered by centuries of cobwebs and dust, and therefore hidden from easy view. But Valledai knew they were there, silent witnesses to the cries of torture the fanciful among the living swear can still be heard echoing around the mountain whenever the moon is full. The many thousands of dead resulting from the sacking of the fortress had been piled high along the outer perimeter of the great cavern by the army sent too late to rescue them and left there undisturbed since, their flesh and viscera gone eons ago, and now with not much more than settled mounds of dried bones and bone dust to mark their passing.

Perhaps their souls did, even now, scream out on a moonlit night…who could say with absolute surety that they did not?

Valledai shook himself out of his reverie, turning his thoughts away from his surroundings and his bittersweet memories. For much of that morning, he had been obsessed with reading the book in front of him whenever new text appeared upon its magical pages. The book was nearly finished and, considering how well his plans had gone so far, Valledai was confident this meant his victory was approaching and

Donemere's tale would soon come to an end. He was seated in the Ha'del of Graunther Goghodder, who had been the dwarves' ambassador to the other races at the time of the War of Sorrow. Valledai now stood from the rune-covered stone chair, placed the open book on the commodious seat and barked peremptory orders at the okûn captain in the hallway.

The harassed officer again assured his master that, yes, all was well with their plan. He was then summarily dismissed with an irritated wave. After the creature's exit from the room, Valledai gazed unseeingly for some time at both the scurrying okûn racing past the archway and at the dilapidated dwarve furnishings and relics that surrounded him, once again drawn by his own vivid recollections to a past that still haunted his dreams. It was with great effort that he forced himself back to the present and the new threat he faced.

Flat-Finger would be most aggrieved by the failure of his trap at the entryway, as he was indeed the one who had set it. Valledai had not appreciated the humor behind the silly exchange at the tunnel entrance and was disappointed that the plan for entombing Donemere and her followers in the mountain had been thwarted, though he had never been convinced it would succeed because it was too obvious, as he had informed both his benefactors and the giant when they had insisted upon it being laid.

Valledai shook his head wearily. There was still so much to do, so much to be coordinated. Perhaps it would be best if Flat-Finger were to go immediately to Moên Gjendeben to guard the women, since there would be no point in his returning here. Valledai decided that later, when he himself arrived back at Moên Grím, after dealing with this witch-woman and her friends, he would send for Flat-Finger. The giant would surely have completed his task in the forest by then. When he left for the journey south two days ago, Flat-Finger had confidently assured Valledai that he could free the flying camera from its self-made prison, although, in truth, Valledai was not so certain this was possible. Nor was he willing to trust in the Stone Giant's pledges. After all, Flat-Finger had also sworn that his plan to trap the witch and her party within the mountain could not fail, and yet *fail* it had.

Yes, he would attend to the giant tomorrow. For now, his interest was caught by something else entirely. He too wondered what it could mean that the witch's dog had been magical long before coming to Medregai with his mistress. Was this somehow part of his benefactors' plan? If so, they would undoubtedly not explain its purpose. They would assert, as they had this very morning, and as had been their consuetude since this particular witch had been brought to Medregai, "All in good time," they would say, "all shall be made clear to you once you have defeated the witch. Remember this, the woman is to be tested whenever possible. The range and extent of her powers must be fully explored so that you will know what to expect when the proper time comes to mount a final assault upon her and your other enemies."

Well, Valledai thought to himself, he would have the opportunity to test her himself soon, and also her companions. Perhaps he might be able to bend one or more of them to his will. That should please his benefactors and would make the defeat of the witch and her friends a much simpler and sweeter task were he to acquire a servant in their midst.

Who would be the weakest, but would also be the one Donemere would never believe would betray her? The cat? No, the dog…yes, it would have to be the dog. The dog's powers were exciting to Valledai, an added benefit in choosing him to turn away from his mistress. If he could control that animal, force it to do his bidding, he could—

"You could what?" that other voice snarled in his head, the voice belonging to the witch-man, Franklin Vale. "What makes you think I'll let you harm her or control her dog? You can't even control me yet, can you?' it reminded him angrily.

Valledai tightened his grip on the imprisoned triune residing in the same body as he, forcing the other man's consciousness back into submission. He could feel the witch-man's renewed pain as he once again twisted the man's mind to horrible, nightmarish images of mutilation and death for those he loved, starting with the ravagement of his wife and her ensuing, viciously brutal murder by Valledai's army of killing monsters. He ended with the promise of torture for the man's children, sleeping unsuspectingly in their beds. It would all be perfectly simple to effectuate, Valledai gravely reminded Franklin, as little trouble to murder the man's family as it had been for him to abscond with the body they now shared. Then he projected an image of the dægírus of old suckling the blood through the severed fingertips of the boy and girl until every ounce of their life elixir had been drained from their tiny forms.

That final image could be relied upon to crush any objection his host raised, as Valledai knew with long confidence, and so he shoved it savagely at the already sniveling wretch, sending the witch-man's consciousness spiraling into the deepest recesses of his broken and foolish heart. While Franklin still denied him access to that last bit of his triune, Valledai had found effective measures such as these to counteract the man's resistance and now controlled almost all of the witch-man's magic.

When that other voice was stilled, even its whimpering silenced, and Franklin's triune dismissed, Valledai smiled triumphantly. He took a few calming breaths and glanced down at the book, realizing impatiently that the words detailing his actions and thoughts were emerging onto its thin sheaves of paper. So...it appeared that now he too had a place in its pages. He must be more guarded with his deliberations in the future, for if he somehow lost the book to the witch, he did not want her discovering anything about himself that might be of aid to her. He thought about ripping out the offending pages, but remembered that his benefactors had warned him to never deface the book. Of course they had not explained why, Valledai thought with malice. They told him only what they wished him to know, and only when they wanted him to know it. Yet on occasion, even they were wrong, he reminded himself.

If only he had not needed their assistance in order to taste freedom again...if only he had not wanted their machines, their knowledge of the future, their prowess with all things biological...if only he could have this witch-woman's power—a power he could feel simmering within her even from here—ah, then he would need no one. He would already be the master of Medregai and from there it would take only one step more before all people throughout time would bow to him in fear.

But these suppositions were useless to him. Events were what they were and he had not the power to change the past, only a compelling determination to control the future. Grimly, Valledai cleared his mind of all speculation and forced himself to wait serenely for more text regarding his approaching quarry.

***

For more than two hours, Donnie and her friends made the grueling descent through the mountain's winding tunnel, a sense of depression weighing heavier and heavier upon their minds, although several tries were made by each in turn to combat this otherworldly oppression. These attempts had achieved only small success, but it was enough to keep their group moving at a good pace. The air had grown warmer shortly after they'd begun their initial ascent inside the mountain and, after they'd reached the pinnacle of that incline, the heat had continued to build the farther down they went. While it was still a little chilly because the tunnel was quite drafty, Donnie had unzipped her parka, sent her witch's hat home, taken off the knit cap, and stuffed it and her gloves into the pockets of her coat.

At present, she and the others were waiting for Warren to come back through the latest archway in the tunnel, where he'd gone ahead momentarily to reconnoiter what lay in the darkness beyond. Donnie touched a wall with her bare hand and used her mind's eye to see that they were now nearly five hundred feet below ground level. Her mind registered this fact and then her hand came away involuntarily when she was hit by what she could only describe as a screaming, almost shrieking wave of pain and fear, which threatened to shatter her to the core. The overpowering feeling vanished as soon as her hand left the stone wall, as if the rock itself held the agony of thousands, which she had heard and experienced inside her mind for only a couple of seconds, mercifully. Instinctively, her heart responded with a blast of love, a blessing to the tortured souls she had felt crying out to her. She shimmered with blue light until this glow fell away from her like rain, dropping into the floor and then soaking into the parched rock.

To hide her sudden and extreme discomfiture with what had just occurred, she strode blindly to the doorway Warren had disappeared through a half-minute earlier. Before she could go through it, the Wolf King materialized in the gloom and stopped short, just managing not to run her over. He looked at her curiously, but she sent him a bright, forced smile that told him nothing. He turned around in silence and led them into what appeared to be a vast chamber, its walls hidden in blackness that was deepened by Donnie's blue light-balls as these bright spheres moved forward into the cavern ahead of the wary travelers.

Donnie increased the lumens of the light-balls and sent them outward and upward until they lit the roof of what turned out to be an enormous cavern, towering at least a hundred feet above. All around, thick columns, countless in number, rose from the stone floor to arch gracefully into the roof above. These were engraved with what Sylvester, Falwaïn and Warren all recognized as mostly ancient Dwarvish runes, with what looked to be Elvish, Vincan and Sarnian runes thrown in here and there, they said. They did not know the meanings of these runes though, nor if any other languages were included in the engravings.

By silent agreement, the group moved toward a faint light that could be seen far in the distance. This movement brought them near the central corridor of the cavern, where colossal statues of granite, some well over eighty feet tall, were placed facing inward. Upon their approach to the closest of these silent giants, Falwaïn informed them that he had seen something similar long ago and he wondered if these figures represented the Council of Arathnilôk, who had banded together during the ancient War of Sorrow to bring about the defeat of Nírgoth, the Red Warlock. If he was correct in his surmise of the statues' identities, then those on the left were the Venár, the greater gods and protectors of Írtha, who were comprised of representatives from various Írthian races. The first and largest of the statues was of Baclan the Blacksmith, he said, who was one of the eight greatest Venár, called the Ethtár.

Falwaïn went on to explain that Baclan was the Venár who had most concerned himself with rock and metal, the great loves of the dwarves. He was the builder and inventor within the Venár and, as his legend ran, was the Everlasting God, or Ér Ainíl, of the dwarve races. His sculpted face was quite similar to those of the dwarve statues opposite him, only much more idealized.

Intrigued, Donnie asked about the statues on the right and Falwaïn said that he assumed the largest of these statues represented the Sacred Nine, the leaders of the nine dwarve tribes who would go on to sacrifice themselves in their mad, feverish defeat of the Red Warlock's forces at the Vincan fortress of Canta'Lem in Aldera, in what is now Gainál. To subsequent avid inquiries from Donnie, Falwaïn explained that Nírgoth's army, the Malacham An, had been composed mostly of his deformed kûn, along with many other similarly fiendish monsters and beasts. The Gossalyn forces, or those allied against the Red Warlock such as the dwarves, men, elves and vinca, had suffered devastating losses under the many barbaric attacks of the Malacham An. Sadly, this was the extent of Falwaïn's knowledge of the dwarves' history of that time, so he could only speculate as to the importance and purpose of the cavern here. The dwarves, he said, were very secretive folk and the history of this particular cavern had clearly been lost in the ages seeing as he had never even heard of its existence before today.

Donnie, fascinated by the statues, which gave her her first glimpse at some of the other races here that she had yet to meet, shot Falwaïn a puzzled look. "But it is unusual for the different races to have statues in the same place, right?" she asked. "From what I've read about the dwarves, I wouldn't think they'd ever allow a statue of a human, an elf or a vinca or any of these other beings depicted here to be placed within one of their halls, even if they were there to honor the gods."

Falwaïn shrugged. "I do not know how the ancient dwarves would have felt about that when this cavern was constructed," he admitted apologetically. "Today, yes, you would be unlikely to find such representations of any other races within a dwarve dwelling. Perhaps this place was considered neutral ground to the races and existed as a meeting place for them. I have heard rumor of a major dwarve city in these parts, which reportedly lies much deeper in the earth than this place does. Maybe this was once the main approach to it, although I really have no idea where that city is or what its name is—nor even if it still thrives with the living. As I say, the dwarves are very secretive folk."

Donnie looked around, nodding pensively. "Huh," she grunted, considering what Falwaïn had told them. She looked at Warren questioningly to see what he could possibly add, but he shook his head.

"I know nothing of this place," he conceded regretfully.

"Nor I," replied Sylvester, when Donnie looked over at him where he sat upon a small ledge carved into the base of one of the statues.

Donnie smiled sadly. "What a shame," she said, "and we'll probably never know much about this place since it seems to have been forgotten a very, very long time ago. I mean, just look at this dust on the floor, it has to be at least an inch thick, and those cobwebs look older than, well, than dirt. Are we sure we're in the right place, that we didn't miss a turn-off somewhere?" she suggested, suddenly worried. "I mean, don't you think we should have met a reception party by now?"

"We are most definitely in the correct place," Warren attested firmly, going on to note, "Galto's trail is still strong through here and I found several of his horse's hoofprints over there, mixed with others." Warren pointed to a wide trail of footprints that led away from the tunnel and into the darkened cavern, where this trail then split off several times in various directions, although the main trail appeared to run parallel to the avenue of statues that Donnie and the others were currently wandering.

Donnie again nodded thoughtfully, then handed out the sandwiches she'd packed for lunch. Speaking in hushed tones, they studied the nearest statues, discussing just who each of them was most likely to represent. Donnie thought the one of a human woman looked a lot like her mother and wondered aloud if the woman was a Codlebærn. Sylvester posited that perhaps it was Margawse, since it was certainly not Catie.

When they'd finished eating and Donnie had stowed their trash into her backpack, the group once more headed down the colonnade. They walked another ten minutes before they could just make out that the light they were walking toward was a platform, still a good half mile away at the other end of the cavern.

"Wow, this is some elaborate trap they're setting for us, don't you think?" Donnie murmured to the others.

"Yes," Warren whispered back, "and we are being watched. Can you feel it?"

Falwaïn nodded. "Okûn, by the smell of them. But only a few."

"Perhaps twenty," Warren agreed, "but no more than that. They're moving to either side of us, keeping pace with our progress."

"Oh, great," Donnie hissed, "how come I'm the last to know that? Man, I need to work on my olfactory capabilities! Then again, I don't think I want to memorize what an okûn smells like, do I? Which is probably just as well because the merest mention of them scares the heck out of me as it is. They're such...*ugly* creatures."

Falwaïn lightly touched her shoulder. "This from the woman who looked one of the Great Serpents in the eye and lived to tell about it?" he teased. "I should think little would frighten you after that."

"Yeah, well, that's because you're not a woman. We are sometimes unfathomable, my good man!" Donnie informed him spiritedly and then flashed an impudent smile at him.

Falwaïn grinned back, nodding with affected sagacity. They calmly continued walking into the trap Valledai had so carefully prepared for them.

Once they were closer to the brightly lit platform, they could see that at its back edge stood a chair carved from stone and in that chair sat a very strange figure. Warren was the first to recognize it as Galto. The poor man was frozen in the same position as when Donnie had sent him away on his horse.

Donnie and her friends tramped up the steps, moving into the light that flickered from several burning braziers placed around the edges of the platform. Donnie let her light-balls disappear when their little assembly reached the top step. The platform was very large, easily a hundred feet long and fifty wide and, other than the chair and braziers, was bereft of adornment.

Galto glared at Donnie with hatred.

"Valley Guy couldn't free you, huh?" she observed sympathetically. "I'll bet he didn't even really try." With a small wave of her hand, Donnie unfroze the man. He collapsed in a heap to the floor, then slowly pulled himself to a sitting position in the chair.

Donnie took a deep breath and decided she should eat a little crow. Apologizing profusely for her total-body confinement of him, she told Galto that she'd tried to unfreeze him yesterday but couldn't find him to do so, and she now saw that what she'd done to him was very, very wrong. Galto looked as though he didn't believe her. Figuring that was to be expected, Donnie told him to rub his atrophied muscles vigorously. At first he ignored her, but when she insisted, he began doing it, albeit only half-heartedly.

"Where's your master?" she asked him after a minute had gone by with no sign of Valledai.

"I told you before, *bruja fatuo*, I have no master," Galto reminded her resentfully.

Donnie gave him an ill-tempered smile in return. "Yeah, whatever. I gotta tell you though, I'll only put up with just so much of that kind of attitude. And whether or not you have a *master* is purely a matter of semantics. You say pah-tah-to and I say pah-tay-to. But it still doesn't tell me where he is."

She stepped to the middle of the platform and turned about as she called, "Where are you, Valley Guy? I've come all this way to meet you; don't tell me you're going to disappoint me! Yoo-hoo! Anybody home? Oh, Valley Guuuyyyy...come out, come out, wherever you are! Hey, guys, you know what? This would have made a great stage for a Black Adder concert back in their heyday. Can't you just see all the fans going wild? I'll bet this place could hold several hundred thousand hard-core rockers, easy peasy."

The boombox appeared on the stone floor in front of Galto and began playing Black Adder's "That Ain't No Way to Have Fun." Donnie laughed, pointing at the music box. "See, even the boombox agrees with me!" she exclaimed.

A sudden explosion behind Galto got everyone's attention. Donnie swung back around and waited for the air to clear. A masked figure with billowing red robes stalked out of the swirling smoke and stood beside Galto.

Donnie gave an appreciative whistle and noted, "Wow, that was impressive. You're an illusionist fan, I see."

Behind the ornately carved wooden mask, Valledai's eyes turned with annoyance to the boombox. Though he tried to turn the thing off, to silence it somehow, he found he had no power over it. He stared fixedly at it for a few moments more, then focused his gaze on the dog.

Donnie waited for Valledai to respond, agreeing wholeheartedly with the sentiments expressed in the song, especially when a chorus of voices yipped horribly from the outer edges of the lighted platform. Their cries made her skin crawl. Like the guy in the song, she hoped nobody would turn up the lights because she had absolutely no desire to see the okûn surrounding them.

She felt the others draw near, their backs turned toward her. Falwaïn unsheathed his broadsword and held it at the ready, while Warren bared and fully extended his claws. Even Rex and Sylvester growled and crouched down, ears flattened to their heads. They all realized, given the nature of the song the boombox had chosen to play, that only bad things were likely to come of this encounter with Valledai.

And all Donnie could think of at the moment was the fifth challenge from the gods. It was still looming on the horizon, she knew, and she had not liked the sound of that one at all. Was the boombox now trying to warn her about its imminence, telling her to steel herself for the worst? That no matter what Valley Guy did here in this mountain, she must remember that she was a treue witch now, whatever that meant, and she had some very strict laws to guide her? As the song went into the next verse, she nervously reminded herself of the tenets of Witchcraft, which she sincerely believed in, and just what they meant to her. And with that reminder, she fortified herself, made more secure in the knowledge that she was a Codlebærn, descended from the gods themselves. Her shoulders squared and her back straightened. She could almost hear the ghostly cries of support from generations of her ancestors and knew that she had to be ready for whatever was about to happen.

"You were foolish to come here, Donemere." Valledai's deep, sneering voice filled the cavern, setting it to rumbling. "Look at you, with your *pets* and your Sarn lord, trembling and greatly outnumbered." Donnie felt Warren's back stiffen at the implied insult.

A jolt of surprise coursed through Valledai. There was something almost frightening about the dog. His was a soul unlike any Valledai had ever encountered. It was true and pure, and around it lay an impenetrable mantle of—what was it exactly? After a moment's more investigation, Valledai shuddered with revulsion. Love! That was what it was. Instantly, he withdrew his mind from the dog's, already feeling the irresistible draw it was exacting on his soul. Shaken, he swore to himself that he must never try that again, or his own triune would be lost in the labyrinth of light and fidelity which marked the true nature of this particular beast.

Angered by his failure to reach the dog, Valledai turned derisively upon the werewolf. "And just how is the discarded *Ulf* in you faring, Mynydd Uchaf? Does it not still define who you truly are, deep within? Tell me, what is behind this newfound desire of yours to become a man when you were once a strong, proud Wolf King? Have you turned so far from your own flesh and blood? Do they mean so little to you that you wish to denounce their very existence?"

Valledai sensed that his foul insinuations were hitting home. He smiled behind his mask. "Your pack will be greatly disappointed when I tell them of your new way of life," he said, his voice barely above a whisper. "Bauffæla in particular will be most aggrieved. Shall I send your mate to you so that you may reunite with her? Perhaps she can make you see reason where I cannot. After all, she is so very forceful, as well you know." He had begun pacing the back of the platform, but he now stopped and turned to look directly at Warren before landing his most cutting blow. "Ah yes, your dear wife, Bauffæla. She is quite an insatiable—and ferocious—killer. Unfortunately, not one of your children survived her ravenous appetite the night I claimed her for mine."

Warren was breathing hard and his arms hung listlessly at his sides. He felt his raw pain exposed for all to see, and he was at full mercy of the shame and guilt he'd carried so long within for having been unable to protect his family from Valledai's darkness. Without looking at him, Donnie could sense his utter distress and, after an agonized moment of silence, she said to him, her voice husky and ringing with the conviction of truth, "Don't let him do this to you, Warren. You've known for some time that your family was lost to you. And you have grieved for that loss."

Warren's downcast eyes began to clear at the sound of his friend's voice. Donnie stepped around to face him, her own heart aching in reflection of the despair she recognized in the tortured depths of his darkened eyes as their gazes met. Searching her mind frantically for the right words to bring him strength, Donnie's voice shook with even more emotion when she found them. "It is a pain that can no longer touch you, for you have looked its evil full in the face and you have mastered it. His dark words hold no magic for you now. You are free from his embrace forever, my friend. Remember that, you are free! And so are your children, for a mother's love will surmount any evil threatening her young, even when its poison comes from within."

Warren looked deeply into Donnie's shining eyes and felt the dishonor, and along with it the guilt, drain from his heart. A moment later, he snapped his head back toward Valledai and furiously challenged this evil lord who had stolen so much from him. "Send Bauffæla to me whenever you choose, Valledai. I will gladly end her torment and reclaim her soul! It shall then be hers, and hers alone, for all eternity."

Valledai straightened haughtily. The wolf had indeed grown strong under this witch-woman's influence. It would be pointless to continue needling him when she was quite correct, Valledai's magic could no longer touch the wolf unless he allowed it. How had the witch managed that, Valledai wondered.

He shifted his attention to the cat. On the surface, its triune seemed nearly as pure and true as the dog's, only without the accompanying mantle of love. But Valledai persevered and was rewarded when he found a dark glimmer in a corner of the cat's mind. He targeted his will upon that. Ah, yes, he might have more luck with this one, for here the cat's soul was clouded. Almost instantly, he was forced away when the cat perceived his presence there.

Valledai again smiled behind his mask. Though he had failed to connect with the cat's triune, he had felt its real base and had recognized its resemblance to his own benefactors. Obviously, the cat had more than one secret it was keeping from Donemere. Was there, in fact, already a dark servant amongst the witch's friends?

Made cognizant of the waiting okûn surrounding them by their restless titters, Valledai spread his arms and motioned for these soldiers to come closer. The twenty okûn scrambled up onto the platform into the light and Valledai was delighted to see their effect upon his foe.

Donnie, who had been trying to understand Valledai's soul (which was puzzling her greatly because something about it was not quite right), stopped upon seeing this company of monsters appear and backed up closer to her friends, hoping her knees wouldn't buckle if any of the okûn came closer.

Ignoring the malicious, deformed faces of the horrifying creatures who were positively salivating with blood-lust, and who now almost completely encircled her and her friends, jeering and laughing, snarling with hunger, Donnie stared through their line at Galto. When the boombox remonstrated once again that this was no way to have fun, Donnie called out, "The boombox is right, Don Diego. Seems you picked some fine friends to hang with, didn't you?"

Galto's expression told her that he was even more alarmed at the appearance of these unfortunate souls than she was. Maybe there was hope for him yet.

"Do they frighten you?" Valledai inquired silkily. "Then as a show of good faith that our meeting here today is not intended to be lethal to anyone, I shall send them away." And with a benevolent wave of his hand, the okûn retreated, reluctantly melting into the shadows behind their master.

Donnie could hear the rustle of their shuffling footsteps and their disappointed whispers fade as they receded farther into the mountain. Warren and Falwaïn stepped up to flank Donnie on either side, facing Valledai and Galto.

"Got an escape tunnel there, I see. Where's it lead, I wonder?" asked Donnie. "That Genda Benda Mountain everybody's talkin' about?"

"What do you know of Gjendeben?" the voice behind the mask bit out, its tone dripping with condescension. Valledai eyed the witch with hatred, every sinew in his body tense with anticipation of possessing the time portal. Was she correct about this mystifying inscription on the back of the amulet—could it be the spell to open the portal? Or was it something more? He would soon know because he fully intended to be wearing the amulet when he left the mountain today, regardless of who he had to kill to acquire it. Possibly this arrogant lord with whom Donemere has fallen in love? Or this fool of a man from the future, who believes anything told to him because he so desperately wishes to return home?

Either man's death would further Valledai's cause: that of keeping Donemere off-balance, the one and only way he could do this, by harming those around her. His benefactors had assured him that he would be unable to touch her physically because her magic was far too strong, but they'd insisted that others' pain, and their subsequent deaths, would move her to where he needed her to be emotionally. She would make mistakes then.

Yes, one of these men would die today; of this he, Valledai, must make certain. Secretly, while he kept the witch preoccupied, he would nurture the men's hatred for each other until it consumed them both. As he knew well, hate made murder such a bountiful fruit to cultivate.

And, he reminded himself with relish, he had a very special treat for Donemere; one that would land a blow such as she had never imagined. The gods' lessons and her witchly laws would be all but forgotten and she would retaliate, perhaps wickedly enough to warrant forfeiting her powers. Or, with any luck, she might be unable to recover quickly enough from the shock to save herself and her friends—oh, with every fiber of his being, Valledai wanted them all to die in this mountain today! His triune thrilled at this thought and his breath came fast and quick until he forced himself to refocus his efforts on increasing the enmity between the two men.

Donnie debated Valledai's question regarding Gjendeben, trying to decide just how much to let on of what they knew of Valledai's plans. The least said, the better. To this end, she replied, "Oh, I don't know much about that mountain, when it comes right down to it. Heck, I'm not even sure where it is, to tell you the truth."

The song ended at this point and the boombox went silent. Donnie again waited for a response to her remarks from Valledai, but none came. He seemed to be concerned solely with his own thoughts. What was he attempting to do? Was he trying to feel her soul? If so, then he was very stealthy about it because she didn't feel anything like that happening. If only she could see his face, maybe then she'd be able to tell what he was doing.

"Hey, don'tcha think it's time to take off the mask? Or are you too frightened of me?" she asked him coyly, her mocking smile making Valledai's fingers long to test her magical abilities to see if, in fact, his benefactors were in error and his magic could not only reach her, but also harm her.

With great effort, he quashed the desire. This was not the moment for confrontation; soon enough that time would come. He instead considered her jeer. Yes, he could take the risk, it was impossible that she would know who Franklin Vale was. He bowed his head to take off the mask.

"Oh, my gawd, Lew Plante's a Valley guy!" Donnie roared, staring disbelievingly at the man standing before her. "Heeeyyy...wait a minute, wait one cotton-pickin' minute!" She glanced around and grinned humorously, enjoying the affect her shout had had on the others. "Okay, so it's just your hair that makes you look like that particular character," she admitted, shrugging and rolling her eyes. "Guess I just thought I should go with the recurrent theme we seem to have going here in my little part of Medregai. Besides, there's no way that character was a Valley guy. Nope, Lew was definitely from Hollyweird." She suddenly stared frozenly at a spot on the floor in front of her for a second, her features screwed into a painful grimace. She then glanced around at her companions once more to ask under her breath, "Does no one here find it particularly sad that I even know that?"

"You have something I need," Valledai said ominously.

"What's that?" Donnie swung her gaze over to him again. "My CD collection? My cat? It better not be my bathroom fixtures, 'cause there's no way in hell you're gettin' those!"

Valledai's face became suffused with red. "You dare to taunt me?"

And Sylvester, once he could speak, spluttered with horror, "Your cat! You would give me to him?"

Donnie spared her familiar a quick glance only, since she really wasn't sure what Valley Guy was capable of doing next. "Of course not, silly," she replied in feigned exasperation, "didn't you hear him say it was a taunt? Jeez, Sylvester, I've only just met him and he already understands me well enough to know I was kidding. Crabby kittens, is this your first day on the tour or what?"

Somewhat mollified, Sylvester leapt to her shoulder and sat there with his tail tucked tightly around his front feet.

"You will give me what I need, Donemere, one way or another...of that you may be certain," Valledai informed her softly, ignoring her interaction with the cat.

"Oh, I don't think you can make me do that or anything else, for that matter. I think that, unlike Catie, I can keep you in check pretty easily."

This earned Donnie a sneer. "Catie is a fool," observed Valledai.

"I'll concede that point only because I happen to agree with you," Donnie said, her expression set obstinately. "Although, I don't think she's the kind of fool you think she is."

"No?" Valledai almost whispered the word.

"No."

"What kind of fool do I think she is?" Valledai smiled again, but there was no humor in his eyes.

Donnie looked at him knowingly and replied just as softly as he had a moment before. "You think she's stupid. Whereas, I think she's thoughtless, probably even reckless, but not stupid. Definitely not stupid."

Valledai raised a disbelieving eyebrow. "Why? Merely because she was successful in bringing you back here and bestowing upon you a few...meager powers? That does not require intelligence, so much as good fortune. She took a desperate gamble her spell would work with you. And she got lucky, no more." Valledai's eyes glittered as he composed his face into a contrived facsimile of concern. "How are you feeling about that now? Better, I hope. But have you truly accepted your powers and the fact that you will surely outlive all your loved ones, if what you fear is true? Are you even certain that you are the most powerful witch there shall ever be? You may have a long wait before that is proven, you know."

Donnie shrugged. "Maybe, maybe not. Maybe it'll be proven right here, right now, if you're willing. I can feel your magic, you know. It's Witch-magic, isn't it? Mixed with something else, but whatever that is, it's not strong enough to defeat me. Well, heck, even your Witch-magic isn't strong enough to fight me properly. But I have to wonder how you acquired the Witch-magic because that's not your own, is it...or is it? Huh, how funny! I can't tell which is really yours! Now, didn't Catie say something about other witches—oh, hey, so you're finally ready for a little magical combat, huh?" said Donnie when Valledai took a few strides to his left, his magic suddenly crackling red from his fingertips. "Okay, I can go along with that."

After suggesting quietly to Sylvester that it might be best if he were not on her shoulder at this particular moment, Donnie also stepped to her left, so that she and Valledai were circling each other. The cat leapt lightly to the ground, and he and the others moved with Donnie.

Valledai suddenly shot a crimson lightning bolt at the group, targeting Falwaïn. As the bolt crossed the distance between them, Donnie shouted, "Golf umbrella!" and a fully opened, red and white golf umbrella appeared in her outstretched hand. The lightning bolt changed course to the metal pole in the center of the umbrella. The rubber handle sizzled and smoked, but the umbrella held the charge.

"As every good golfer knows, it pays to buy quality equipment," Donnie announced pedantically, obviously much pleased with herself. The burned and smoking umbrella disappeared from her hand.

Valledai shouted a curse at her. "We shall see what you do with this!" He cupped his hand in front of him and in it appeared a flaming ball of fire, which he hurled straight at Sylvester.

Donnie sidestepped in front of the cat and yelled, "Batter up!" with a baseball bat in her hands. She swung low at the fireball, ricocheting it off the meaty part of the bat and into right field, far beyond the perimeter of the braziers. "Rats! I think I pulled it. Did you see, did it go foul?" she turned to ask Falwaïn.

He gave her that glorious smile, the one that really drove her crazy. It said to her, *You are doing just fine!*

"I could kill you, here and now," snarled Valledai, his tone low and menacing.

"No, you can't," Donnie disagreed insolently. "And even if you could, you wouldn't. You just said I have something you want. I'm guessing it's the amulet."

"The amulet?" Valledai laughed, his expression contemptuous. "Why should I ask that of you when I could take it from your lord here anytime I wish?" he sneered. "No, Donemere, you have something else I desire. I believe we can strike a bargain, considering that I am in possession of something I am more than confident you will want most dearly once you have seen it."

"Oh, yeah?" Donnie sneered back. "I don't believe you. You don't have anything I'd ever want, nor can you take the amulet away from Falwaïn!"

Valledai's eyes narrowed, and with a wave of his hand he set Galto onto his feet. Galto flicked his rapier so that it made a wicking sound and raised its gleaming blade in front of his face.

"Well, apparently his muscles weren't that atrophied, were they?" Donnie muttered under her breath.

Using only his expressive, dark eyes, Galto dared Falwaïn to step forward and fight. Before Donnie could say anything to defuse the situation, Falwaïn sprang to the center of the platform in answer to the unspoken challenge. The men's swords clashed within seconds.

Donnie, Sylvester and Warren nervously waited beside each other near one end of the platform, helplessly watching the two figures fight, all of them using body English as encouragement to their friend. Rex stood behind Donnie, leaning against her legs and panting loudly while he searched the shadows for more of those "butt-ugly creatures that scare the bejeezus out of me and Mama." Valledai moved casually to the far end of the platform.

This time, Falwaïn held the upper hand in the contest between himself and his greatest enemy, even though he still fought with his heavier broadsword. As a result, his thrusts were hitting home far more often than Galto's. The two men danced and pirouetted around each other for some time, thrusting and dodging, dodging and thrusting, one sending the other off-balance seemingly every few seconds. They would then recover and begin their fight anew.

Finally, Falwaïn drove Galto to the front edge of the platform and down a couple of steps. Galto lost his footing again, but just as Falwaïn was getting himself set to deliver a particularly crushing blow, Galto's blade swept upward and its tip caught on the chain of the amulet, which had somehow loosed itself from under Falwaïn's clothing. The chain broke in a flash of red and Galto flicked it hard in Valledai's direction, with some obvious help from Valledai.

Since Falwaïn's back was to her, Donnie didn't realize what was happening until she caught just a glint of red as the amulet flew over Valledai's head and disappeared. Unable to see the thing, Donnie couldn't get a bead on it quickly enough to dematerialize it back to safety before Valledai dove down the stairs. And then, unexpectedly, she could no longer even feel the amulet's presence.

The boombox came to life and began playing the long intro to Jaro's "We're All Guilty of Something." Falwaïn ran toward Valledai. He stopped when, a moment later, Valledai floated up from the shadows to the platform, the amulet dangling from his fingers. Donnie did try to dematerialize it this time, but nothing happened; the amulet merely gleamed in the suddenly fluttering firelight, its heavy chain wrapped firmly around Valledai's hand.

Falwaïn whirled back toward Galto, hate and anger contorting his handsome features. He renewed his attack on his foe and swung his sword with blinding speed. Galto managed to parry a couple of the initial thrusts, backing away slowly toward the center of the platform, but others found their way to fragile skin and bone and at last he fell in a heap at Falwaïn's feet. The volume on the boombox increased as the listeners were sardonically invited to punish and even to kill.

Donnie rushed to where Falwaïn stood over Galto, the others close on her heels. She screamed, "No!" at him as he was about to skewer the fallen man. "No, Falwaïn, you mustn't kill him!"

Falwaïn stopped, the tip of his sword pushing against Galto's chest, and drew himself back, shouting, "Ahhh!" in frustration. He let his sword clatter to the stone floor. With monumental control, he stood tall and breathed deeply to release the pent-up tension of his hatred.

Relieved, Donnie turned to face Valledai, with the others doing the same.

He shimmered in the dim light, laughing derisively. "You are no match for me, Donemere!" he crowed. "I have powers you will never comprehend."

He reveled in his triumph. Although it was unfortunate that he had been unsuccessful at bending his dark will upon Donemere's pets and in breaking her lord's honor, nonetheless, he had won the amulet as planned. And Donemere and her friends must still make their way out of the mountain; a contingency for which he had already arranged. He was almost certain none of them would survive his deadfall spell. And their deaths, if they were to indeed occur here and now, he would read about in the book with the greatest satisfaction. But, in case she lived this day through, it was now time to destroy Donemere's heart.

"Allow me to illuminate my offering to our arrangement." Valledai gestured toward the wall behind him at the picture that had begun evolving on its pocked surface.

The two objects portrayed were soon clear enough for Donnie to recognize them. Her eyes darted to Valley Guy. "You're holding my mattress and couch hostage?" she exclaimed in bemused disbelief. "Well, sure, I miss 'em, but not that much."

Valledai's laugh was cruel. "That humor of yours will be your undoing. Look closer, Donemere Saunders, if you dare see what lies upon the articles I stole from your home."

She looked back to the now rapidly developing picture. It zoomed in suddenly, revealing two prone women, one on the couch and the other on the mattress.

This was who he was holding prisoner?

Donnie gulped breathlessly, unable to form coherent words for several seconds, all the while struggling to rein in her exponentially exploding grief and anger. "If you harm them, I swear to every god throughout time, *I will kill you!*" she ground out harshly at last, giving voice to the anguish welling up inside her.

Falwaïn and Warren looked at her in confusion, whereas Rex and Sylvester both emitted long, low growls, the hair on their backs standing straight with fury as they too stared at the faces on the wall.

Donnie felt sure she'd never breathe again. She croaked through parched lips, "They have nothing to do with this. Let. Them. Go." Profound rage carved her features and her eyes blackened. "You have the amulet now, so send them back to their time. Leave me here forever—I don't care, but send them back now!"

Valledai's voice was ever so velvety and smooth, taunting Donemere to defy him. But she would not, for he had her right where he wanted her. She would do whatever he asked of her now. "I shall send them back only after you have provided your part of our bargain. If you do not willingly give to me that which I require, I will take it from you by force.

But then, ah, yes..." he gave a short laugh, "then you and your friends will all die."

Donnie couldn't tear her eyes away from the projection on the wall. Liz and Julia looked scared, dirty, and thin—so very thin and frightened after six months in Valledai's sadistic captivity. The picture had been moved in close enough now so that it could be viewed with excruciatingly vivid detail, the haunted expressions in her friends' dark eyes dominating their fatigued faces. Donnie's anger threatened to consume her, but grief suddenly won over and shoved aside the rage to envelope her instead. "Six long months. Six...long...months," she said in a broken voice, her eyes fixed on the wall and her heart overflowing with shattering misery. She managed to wrench her gaze from the women's gaunt faces only when Falwaïn shouted that Valledai had escaped, though no one had seen him go. They'd been too preoccupied with Donnie's reaction to the images on the wall and had not noticed when he'd vanished.

"Donnie, who are they; who are these women?" Falwaïn asked for the third time, watching her intently, grave concern etched deeply upon his face. He took a couple of steps toward her, intending to pull her into the comfort of his arms.

But she spun away blindly before he could reach her, the images on the wall forever seared into her mind. She staggered to the front edge of the platform, and there she fell to her knees. She leaned forward as though in great physical pain, her hands curled tightly into fists that she held rigidly crossed in front of her, and screamed out her despair before crumpling to the floor, convulsing uncontrollably. Rex ran to his mama's side and burrowed his head in her neck, his lacrimal glands so overwhelmed that real tears spilled down his face.

The wild, hurt-animal sounds of Donnie's agony bounced off the walls and roof of the cavern, echoing down its entire length for what seemed an eternity. Quietly, Sylvester explained to the men who the prisoners were as the final strains of Donnie's cries faded and the song came to its end.

Chapter 17
Magic Carpet

The image on the wall changed, with Valledai's face and shoulders filling the picture now. When he spoke, his voice resonated from somewhere above the platform and echoed throughout the great cavern. Donnie sat up straight and whirled around, though she remained on her knees because she didn't trust her legs at the moment. Rex also turned to stare at Valledai's hated visage, another angry growl forming deep in his throat.

"You have five days before I take everything from you by force, Donemere," said Valledai in a ruthless, cruel tone. "By that time, my armies will be fully assembled at Moên Gjendeben. We shall march on your cottage and destroy it first. We shall then take Banaff Dír and Mâlendian. Marn Dím presented no resistance; it fell quite easily when we took it before first light yesterday. Alas, to my great disappointment, you had only just fled the city by the time we were ready to make it ours."

He smiled and gave an arrogant lift to his head, while his eyes seemed to gleam red. "Once the Sarn King's realm in Annûar Varán has been destroyed, we shall march on Sedarau, and from there Gainál. It will provide me the greatest pleasure to bring the insolent Sarn and their allies to their knees," he said scornfully. "My armies will take Medregai, piece by piece, and I shall then make a new future of my choosing for all its peoples."

He waved his hand in a regal gesture, his smile changing to one of feigned benevolent generosity. "Surrender to me what I want ere five days have passed, and I shall return you and your friends back to your time. Take longer, and you will never see them again." His eyes turned hard and black now when he vowed, "Their deaths will be most painful, seeing as the okûn do so love the taste of human flesh."

Weirdly, Valledai's gaze was aimed at Donnie as though he could see her still as he added, "I have faith in you, Witch, you will puzzle out what it is I require. You are almost there now, I think. Give me that freely, and I shall see to it that you are returned in time to make your goodbyes to your family before I destroy all timelines forever. Remember, you have but five days to meet my demands."

The picture dissolved, but a roaring thunder grew within the cavern. A moment later, the boombox vanished, reappearing about two hundred feet down the cavern, blasting out "How Fast Can You Run?" by Stealing Home.

Donnie looked around at her friends with alarm as the rumbling got louder and the platform began to shake. The boombox blared that it was time to get out, but before she could do more than rise uncertainly to her feet, the entire face of the cavern's back wall crashed forward and a huge creature burst through the opening, roaring its ire. Its leathery, yellow-grey hide was covered with wispy, dirty white hair, its dark eyes looked sunken and mean, and it bore a set of imposing horns upon its head that ended in wickedly sharp tips that faced forward. It stood at least three times as tall as either of the men and was commensurately wide and thick, making it monstrously enormous.

"What the hell is that?" Donnie screeched, staring up at the thing wildly, mesmerized by its great, dark eyes, which pierced through her with bone-chilling malevolence.

Over the din that both it and the music box were making, Falwaïn shouted, "*That* is a Snow Troll!"

The troll let out another great, bellowing cry and smashed its immense fist down on the back of the platform, producing a huge crack at the point of impact that quickly traveled the width of the platform, leaving a gap of about an inch at the front where Donnie stood gazing down at it in horror. She had stared helplessly at the crack as it hurtled straight toward her, unable to step away from it. Now, dimly, she felt Falwaïn spin her around and then yank her down the stairs. They hit the bottom step moments later on a dead run.

Donnie noted as they flew by him that Galto had already managed to pull himself to the bottom and was half crawling, half staggering back the way she and her friends were headed. She wondered why he hadn't taken the same route Valledai had—did this mean he really was not a follower of the false wizard? She slowed and twisted to look behind her.

The Snow Troll had stomped to the center of the platform, still shouting its bleating cry, its clawed hands spread wide to its sides as it shook its chest with anger. The light from the braziers lit its ugly face with a dancing, yellow glow that deepened the sickly color of the creature's hide. Its cry finally complete, it relaxed its posture and Donnie saw that there were sharp horns protruding along its shoulders and down the entire lengths of its arms.

The floor of the cavern began to shake in rhythm with what sounded like thunderous footsteps. Donnie stumbled and nearly fell when she saw two more Snow Trolls come thumping into view from behind the first. They would be through the hole and into the great cavern in seconds.

Donnie came to a full stop, paralyzed with fear. "Sweet bloody murder," she swore in disbelief, "there's three of them!" She gulped, her eyes widening as full realization hit her as to what their fate was meant to be.

Rex had stopped too and now stood beside her, howling in response to the trolls' cries. He was determined not to get far from his mama this time, even though these huge, hairy, roaring things scared him even more than the giant snakes had. They also scared his mama, which meant Rex had to stick around to protect her, no matter what.

Warren, hearing Rex's howl, darted back to them, shouting to Donnie, "We have to run!" He grabbed her by the shoulders, shaking her out of her shock. "Now, Donnie! We must leave now!" he insisted fiercely.

Again, they raced toward the other end of the cavern, but the trolls were catching up quickly. Once more, Donnie stopped and watched as the first one kicked Galto ahead of him thirty feet. She winced and willed the unfortunate man to tuck and roll, as one accident-prone friend had advised her long ago was the only way to prevent injury in all types of accidents.

Galto's body immediately curled up in mid-air. He landed hard on his back, rolling several times, but got to his feet instantly and staggered painfully toward Donnie once more. The first troll began stalking him, slowly, tauntingly. Galto looked behind him with a mixture of terror and rage, evidently deciding that if he could but help it, today was not the day he would die. He turned forward and resolutely resumed lurching in Donnie's direction.

As soon as Falwaïn saw that Donnie was no longer running beside him, he shouted for the others to come back and everyone returned to her side.

"Donnie, this is madness, we must leave now," Falwaïn urged.

She shook her head, staring intently at the three trolls. "No, I have to stop them here. We can't outrun them all the way back to the tunnel." Sylvester hopped onto her shoulder while the others stepped in close to her, waiting to see what she was going to do.

The second and third trolls had paused when they saw Donnie standing still and had begun slamming themselves into two of the columns, working their tempers into a frenzied fury. Donnie now looked up at the top of the columns they were hitting and saw that were beginning to come away from their moorings at the roof, tumbling down section by section. Since they were coming down anyway, Donnie waved her hand and helped a few chunks along, using her magic to direct their paths. The sections crashed on top of the two unsuspecting trolls, knocking them out cold and burying them in rubble. But now, the ceiling around the platform began to crack and shake and glow red. Donnie looked up at it with a sense of foreboding. If that should come down...

The first troll screamed loud and long at the mounds of stone covering his brethren, a cry which nearly deafened Donnie and her friends. He glared at Donnie with hatred and let out another stentorian bleat as he came barreling straight toward her and the others, heedless of the pieces of crumbling columns that filled the air. Several piercing replies came from somewhere far behind the platform.

Donnie's eyes narrowed with determination and she shouted back, "No, you don't! You're not calling any more of your Yeti buddies here to die with you!" With another flick of her hand, she directed one of the descending sections so that it arced around and careened straight at the creature, sending him ricocheting all the way back to the steps of the platform, the huge chunk of column nestled firmly into his belly. His dull eyes were still wide with surprise when he hit the steps, where his eyelids suddenly snapped shut into unconsciousness. She sent the rest of the falling debris flying backward to fill up the hole in the wall he had created upon his entrance.

More columns began to break away from their roof moorings. They groaned and creaked, and came down with a deafening roar. The ceiling right above the platform caved in with a flash of deep red, its malevolent glow now spreading outward. Donnie shook her head and expelled a worried breath. The entire back of the cavern would be history soon, plus she was pretty sure the Snow Trolls would start coming around any moment now, even with being buried under tons of rock debris. No matter which came first, she and her friends had to get out of there fast.

Donnie turned to Rex and squatted down, holding his snout loosely in her hands to make him look at her, and asked, "Can you make it out of here with all of us sitting on you? You know, if you do that growing thing you did when I rode you the other night?"

The dog turned and peered down the long, dark cavern in the direction of the tunnel entrance, then looked back at her. "I think so, Mama. Maybe. Well, no, probably not, not like we did it when it was just you and me. I don't think I have enough power yet to go as fast as we need to with that much weight on me. And besides, if I make myself big enough to carry everyone, I won't fit through the entrance to the cavern, not to mention the tunnel out of here."

The boombox suddenly switched to the beginning notes of Wasteland's "Magic Carpet." Donnie spared it a glance and crowed excitedly, "Yes, that's it! Thank you, boombox!" She stood up and materialized the big rug from her office so that it was now under her feet.

She also brought along Rex's skijoring harness, the belt for around her own waist, and the tow line to run between them, all of which materialized snapped firmly into place.

"Donnie, whatever you intend to do, you'd better be quick about it. Those Snow Trolls are beginning to stir, and more of the roof is coming down fast!" Falwaïn warned.

She nodded and yelled back loudly to her friends, "Listen to me, everyone line up on the carpet right behind each other and hold on tight. I mean it, hold tightly to each other or the rug. But whatever you do, don't let go, because we won't be able to come back for you!"

They scrambled onto the rug one behind the other, the boombox disappearing and then reappearing a moment later to a spot just in front of Donnie, down at her feet. The rug levitated off the ground about six inches.

"Wait for my command, Rex," Donnie told the dog calmly, turning away from the others so that he could hear her, but they couldn't. She looked back and waited, seemingly oblivious to her friends' anxious faces.

Sylvester, from his position behind Falwaïn's feet, ordered, "Now, Donemere! We must leave now!"

She shook her head. Just as Warren, the last in line on the rug but seated a good five feet from its back edge, started to turn around to see what Donnie was looking at, she called out, "Haul ass, Rex!" At the same moment, Warren roared in surprise, "What are you doing—?" But from then onward, it was all any of them could do to hang on and his protest was drowned by the roar in their ears as they were suddenly jerked forward.

The front edge of the rug flapped up against the back of the boombox as Rex made his first huge leap. He was so very frightened and all he could think about was how much he wanted to get out of there, right now!

To balance herself, Donnie stood with her knees bent and her hands pressed against the semi-permeable shield she'd conjured in front of the flying carpet. The shield deflected the brunt of the sudden rush of G-forces and eased the drag on the tow line connected to her waist belt, while still allowing the polyethylene rope to get through, which she had strengthened with her magic. Falwaïn held tightly to her waist. Behind him, both Sylvester and Warren had their claws dug deeply into the carpet. They all rocked backward with every leap the dog made, as each push from his powerful hind legs brought an exponential increase in his acceleration rate.

Once Rex had built up enough speed, several long bounds got them nearly a tenth of the way down the cavern. Behind them, the huge columns swayed and tumbled with increasing thunder as more of the roof came crashing to the floor, crushing the Snow Trolls just when they were all surging to their feet. A domino effect of falling columns and statues began, chasing the dog and carpet down the length of the long cavern, building up speed and advancing fast from behind. Valledai's deadfall spell had been set in motion.

Rex not only could feel the ground beneath his paws convulse with each falling stone, but because of the statues' massive weights, as they crashed into columns and into each other before collapsing onto the floor, they sent wave after wave of concussive tremors through the bedrock, which the dog could actually see shimmer past him, spurring him on ever faster.

The perimeter of Valledai's sickening magic had surpassed them several moments before, so that now they were bathed fully within the evil spell's crimson light. Ahead, they could tell that it too was hurtling toward the other end of the cavern. All but Donnie and Rex felt its dark power pressing heavily into their hearts. Just when it felt as though the best thing would be to let go and allow the red inside, a new power, weak but determined, held firm against the deadfall spell and slowed it, the bloody color of Valledai's hatred and the faintly glowing blue of Donnie's blessing for the mountain's dead warring visibly in a thick curtain of magic, lending renewed hope to the desperate beings clutching the carpet as they flew through this wild maelstrom.

With little more than an hour's respite from their torment of ages, the supernal souls of Olganôg made one last stand so as to repay the witchwoman who had freed them from their conjoined misery. They had delayed their journey to Canavar specifically for this purpose, to do what they could against the dark, familiar power that long ago had trapped their souls here in this chamber of death.

It seemed an eternity passed before Rex approached the tunnel. Falwaïn could see the roof in front of them already falling downward, a heavy coating of dust and rubble raining down upon their heads and shoulders with the approaching avalanche of rock from both above and behind. He shouted a warning to the dog, which Warren and Sylvester seconded. Donnie had her eyes closed and was mumbling something that only she and, apparently, the boombox could hear because it was now exhorting her to let the music guide her.

Rex dug deeper inside himself to ratchet up the speed even higher. Two more bounds was all he needed to get them out of the cavern. The boombox wailed out the hard-driving instrumental part of the song as they shot through the entryway and into the tunnel beyond. They cleared the cavern entrance a split-second before it was blocked forever by the roof's wreckage, the deafening roar of the imploding cavern following them through the mountain. Behind them, the tunnel held valiantly for a few moments, but then it too succumbed to Valledai's spell.

Rex began the long ascent out of the mountain. He leaped again and again up the tunnel stairs, allowing himself to grow to almost four times his normal size so that his enlarged back legs could aid their flight upward as much as possible; yet he was mindful not to become so huge that he couldn't fit through the narrower portions of the passageway. With each leap, he was gaining on the leading edge of Valledai's spell. Halfway through the tunnel, with the top steps just barely in sight, another monumental bound from Rex pulled them just slightly ahead of the crimson magic that had been released from its demonic wielder for one purpose alone—to bring this mountain crashing down upon Donnie and her friends today, no matter who or what else got caught in its path of annihilation.

Rex, panting hard and tiring fast from the amount of weight he'd been pulling so long uphill, had felt his mama's mind touching his throughout their escape, both soothing and energizing him, making him feel invincible, like he could do anything as long as he was with her. But now, right when his strength appeared to be nearly expended, and the only thing he wanted to do was to stop, to lie down and rest, he felt Donnie's power surging all around him. It was as though she were not only behind him and inside his mind, but also in front of him, to the sides, above and below, completely surrounding him, injecting his muscles with energy, and engulfing him entirely in her magic. He'd never experienced anything like this before. It was so intense, and somehow it seemed to him that he could actually see with her eyes and could think with her mind, so that he knew just exactly where to touch ground with each stride.

And suddenly, only moments after a wave of bright blue light shot outwardly above his head, Rex could see every color of the spectrum! He wanted to shout, to turn and tell his mama, he was so excited; yet no sooner had he completed the thought but did he feel her voice in his head, and his heart was warmed by the loving smile he could tell she wore. "It's my gift to you, my love, for being the bravest dog ever. Knowing you, you will appreciate it anew every day for the rest of your life. Enjoy it, honey."

His newly changed eyes reflecting the blue of Donnie's heightened power within their depths, Rex steeled his will and flexed his lean muscles, lengthening his strides to match his mama's directions. They reached the top of the tunnel and began the steep decline to the tunnel's entrance. With an enduring sense of peace and satisfaction, Rex allowed himself to return to normal size so that he could fit through the upcoming narrow passages, and reached ever deeper inside himself, into heretofore unknown reserves to maintain his hurtling pace, which kept them just inches ahead of the collapsing ceiling and the malevolent red glow of evil that chased them faster and faster through the tunnel. Inches their lead might be, but it was enough; they would survive this mountain. Rex would see to that.

When they rocketed from the tunnel entrance in a brilliant flash of blue that lit the sky for miles around, the red haze following right behind them disintegrated into millions of scattering particles as soon as it hit the fresh, clean air. The souls of Olganôg's dead, releasing their small but helpful stranglehold on Valledai's evil, gathered above the crumbling mountain and bowed their heads for their liberator and her friends, a last prayer before the bells of Canavar called them home.

Rex bounded once onto the ledge in front of him and then leapt into the air with blind faith that they would not plummet to their deaths. His unwavering belief in his mama and her magic was well placed, for they soared high over the base of the rumbling mountain, the carpet acting much like a glider until they sailed safely to the ground almost half a mile away. Once there, the dog landed on a dead run and quickly regained his speed atop the snow, refusing to slow down until they were all the way back to their camp.

"No sudden stops, sweetheart. Make it a nice easy approach, okay?" Donnie called to Rex softly. The dog reduced his speed gradually, making wide circles around the tent until he was only trotting. The rich blue of Donnie's expanded power slipped slowly away from his body and back up the tow line to her. As soon as Rex came to a halt, he collapsed where he stood, completely exhausted. Donnie let the carpet float gently down to the ground, which was still shaking from the cave-in deep within the mountain miles away.

Warren jumped up and around, snarling at the figure seated behind him who was still holding onto the rug with both hands in a death grip. Diego forced himself to let go of the carpet's folds and scrambled to his feet too. He stood ready to fight, his rapier wicking slowly and clumsily through the air. He was bleeding heavily from a cut on his left arm and another on his midsection, and therefore had to hunch over some because of the hot pain from his wounds, but he nonetheless looked as though he would defend himself to the death, if need be.

Falwaïn brushed past Warren to stand within an inch of the Black Rider. "What are you doing here?" he asked angrily, knocking the sword out of the other man's weakened grip.

Diego looked at the faces of his two adversaries and took a step backward.

Donnie, who was cradling Rex in her arms and telling him how much she loved him and what a wonderful boy he was, turned around from where she knelt and called out sharply, "Okay, guys, cut it out. We're all on the same side here."

Warren whirled toward her and asked, obviously incensed, "Did you intend for him to escape with us?"

Donnie replied to his glare and his query with a simple, but calm, "Yes."

He, Falwaïn and Sylvester were staring hard at her, but she ignored them as she stood, crossed her arms in front of her and placed her hands on her shoulders, concentrating on pulling her power into an internal ball such that her body no longer glowed blue with it. When she was satisfied with her efforts, she walked over to Diego and laid a comforting hand on his shoulder. "You didn't know he had my friends captive, did you?" she asked him.

Mutely, he shook his head.

Donnie lowered her hand. "It seems you have a decision to make, *mi amigo*. You can help us out, or you can ride off and try to make a new life for yourself somewhere here in Medregai until I find a way of sending you back to your proper time. Or, you can always go back to Valley Guy, although I really wouldn't recommend that since he just tried to kill you too.

"You see that, don't you? He left you in there to stall us in order to give himself plenty of time to get out safely. I'm pretty sure he was already gone when we saw him with the amulet." She suddenly slapped herself on the forehead with the palm of her hand and cried, "Well, hell's hags, Donnie, of course he was! I thought he felt far away when he spoke to us after that, but I was too distracted to fully comprehend why." She raised her hands about shoulder height and clenched her fists for a second in frustration. "Bah! But I just couldn't get a good read on his soul, you know? And that's the first time that's ever happened." She looked over at Sylvester questioningly.

Before the cat could respond, Donnie groaned and said, "Now I get why he was all shimmery after he came back up the stairs with the amulet! Or rather, that's what we were supposed to believe was happening, when actually, he was already long gone. And that's why I couldn't dematerialize the amulet away from him, simply because it wasn't there anymore! Well, I'll be whipped red and black with licorice sticks! The sheer ingenuity of it—you do realize, don't ya, that that whole scene he played on the steps with the amulet dangling so seductively from his hand would be easy enough to set up back in his escape tunnel with a hologram projector."

She paused before adding, more to herself than the others, "My, my, he was certainly prepared, our Valley Guy; wasn't he just? Almost as if he already knew what was coming. Perhaps prognostication is one of his métiers, which, much to my chagrin, is not one of mine. But, then again, he doesn't have my chickens or the boombox, does he?" she reminded herself, her lips curving into a brief, satisfied smile. "Anyway," she continued, mentally shaking herself out of her reverie, "I think he got himself to safety long before any of us even realized he was already gone—well, besides the boombox, that is. Yep, all in all, I think it's pretty clear that Valley Guy intended that cavern to be our collective sepulcher, er, burial chamber, I mean. You included, Don Diego. Which means, my friend, you need to face the fact that he never intended to send you back to your time. But if you stick with me, we still have a good chance of doing just that."

Falwaïn stepped forward angrily. "Donnie, you can't be serious," he said. "We can't take this traitor with us; he is not to be trusted!"

Warren also spoke up. "I agree, he must not be allowed to travel with us. What if he reports our plans to his master?"

Diego looked as though he would protest this, but Donnie forestalled him by holding up her hand and noting, "Yeah, I know; you have no master." She turned to the other two and studied them silently. She then asked, "Can't you just trust me on this for a little while? At least until we get back to the cottage and then I can prove to you that he's really not one of Valley Guy's minions? Please?" Okay, sure, she was wheedling to get her way and would grovel next if she had to, but she wanted Diego with them. Not only had the boombox indicated that he knew the way to someplace she must go, her own instincts also told her they needed him. "Trust me?" she asked, bestowing a forced smile upon the others.

The men maintained their resolute stances for a moment, then both of them sighed, nodding their heads slowly. When Donnie shot Sylvester an enquiring look, the cat also nodded once, although he too was loathe to agree. While he was proud that she had finally made the transition to the next level of Wiccecræft, rightfully earning herself the rank of Fægre in their escape from the mountain, he realized that he must now trust in her no matter what, even with an alarming decision such as this.

Diego had been studying Donnie with puzzlement for some while, and he now enquired, "Because of me, Valledai has the amulet, yet still you saved my life. Why? I do not understand."

Donnie stared right back and chided, "Oh, mystified mages, you didn't really think I was going to let you die in there, did you? Let me ask you this, how many times have you been married?"

Clearly bewildered by the question, Diego shook his head and replied, "Once. My wife died five years ago."

Donnie mugged at him. "Well, if I remember correctly, you've got like two or three more marriages still to come. Can't let you miss those other wedding dates, can we? All I ask is that you save me a piece of cake from each. I love cake," she explained to him airily, almost hysterically so.

Her mind was racing and she got lost in the quagmire of her emotions again. It had taken every ounce of control she had not to lash out lethally at either Valley Guy or the Snow Trolls back there in the mountain. Even the desperate scream she'd let out had released only some of the deep rage, grief and guilt she felt when her brain had finally comprehended that Liz and Julia were Valley Guy's prisoners. She knew that this was the fifth trial the gods had set her, and she was worried that this one was going to be too much for her. Forcing her roiling thoughts back below the surface once more, Donnie presented what was now a stony gaze to Diego's face and asked the practical question of, "Do you know where your horse is?"

Diego's eyes widened in further confusion, but his wounds were bothering him greatly and he winced with the pain of them before answering. "I—I am uncertain," he said, saying nothing of the extreme change in her manner. "Valledai ordered some of his men to take me down from Ampago when I arrived here, still in the condition in which you placed me," he added reproachfully. "I do not know what they did with him after that. Hopefully, they set him free." He put two fingers to his mouth and turned his head before letting out an ear-piercing whistle. A few moments later, his black horse came running from the forest they'd camped near, still bridled and saddled.

Donnie nodded her approval and said with a deliberate, firm manner, "Well, thank heaven he's still around. C'mon, let's go into the tent so I can heal your wounds, and then maybe we can eat a little something." She expanded the tent by another six feet in length and they all went inside, the men moving warily around each other and around her because her tension was making her features strained and white, so much so that she looked quite ill, to be honest. Unaware of how badly she was hiding her true feelings, she absentmindedly heated the tent enclosure with a small warming breath.

Otis hailed them when they came in and Donnie walked over to feed him a carrot, leaning on him a long moment. When she pulled back from pressing her face to his neck, he looked at her questioningly, but she just shook her head.

She could not say the words out loud yet. She could not tell him that Liz, her dearest friend ever, and Liz's sister Julia were being held by Valledai and had been there the entire time that she, Donnie, had been "learning her magic." She could not yet confess that she had mostly played at learning it, had bucked and argued merrily with Sylvester against learning it, and that she had undoubtedly prolonged the period of her friends' horrific and sadistic suffering at Valledai's hands through her childishness.

No, she could not yet say those honest words aloud to anyone.

She moved on, giving the other two horses a carrot each, then asked the wounded men to lie on their sleeping bags, after she'd duplicated one for Diego with a small wave of her hand.

Now that she was a Fægre Witch, Donnie found that her power was sufficient to completely heal the men in no time at all. Being more than a little familiar with human nature, she understood that if she wanted to nurture a truce between them, there had to be a hierarchy about this, so Falwaïn came first. She had his wounds neatly healed in seconds, and then she worked on Diego's more plentiful, though mostly shallow wounds.

Falwaïn had obviously not wanted to really hurt Diego throughout the main portion of their fight, just make it clear who was truly the better swordsman. But the damage done in the last round had produced two deep lacerations. Nonetheless, it took only the time for her to visualize each cut healing before they were all reduced to red welts that merely itched a bit and were slightly tender for another minute or so. Her prowess at healing had certainly increased substantially, as neither man complained later of residual muscle trauma.

When she'd finished with their wounds, Donnie materialized the kitchen table and chairs from the cottage and covered the middle of the table with a bottle of wine, a carafe of water, some breads and cheeses, a bowl of left-over tabbouleh, some nuts, fresh fruit and vegetables, along with mustard and mayonnaise. The four chairs backed away from the table, awaiting their expected occupants.

Diego looked stunned at the sudden arrival of this feast, sinking slowly onto his chair once the others had sat on theirs. He carefully reached over to take up some bread and cheese after a few more moments of uncertainty. The others had dug in greedily as soon as they'd gotten within a foot of the table, the stress and fear they'd experienced during their trip into the mountain and their subsequent hair-raising escape having produced a distinct edge to their appetites.

The cat and dog were handed several pieces of cheese before, by mutual agreement, they left the tent to do some hunting together. When everyone was finished eating, Donnie cleared the table with a wave of her hand and burped daintily.

Over the top of her napkin, she said, "Oh, man, did I need that! Food or sex, whichever, to hit the spot after that adrenaline rush."

Diego raised his eyes in shock, nearly choking down the water he'd been drinking, while Warren smiled, shaking his head at the realization that not only was he becoming used to Donnie's flippant outrageousness, he was also beginning to enjoy it.

Falwaïn looked sideways at Donnie and grinned. "Either would have been fine with me," he murmured.

She cocked her head and grinned back wearily, saying, "It's a stress reaction, I guess," then put her head down on her arms and began to weep.

Warren and Diego looked surprised and uncomfortable, but Falwaïn only shook his head and motioned for them all to leave, including the horses. They went outside and stopped the cat and dog from running back into the tent when they returned from their hunt. Diego busied himself with his horse, while the others built a small fire in the center of a large outcropping of rocks with some of the wood Donnie had materialized for their use the night before and then they sat around the crackling flames to wait.

Donnie came out after a while, her face tear-stained and red, but when she walked up to the others, her manner was that of hardened resolve. "We have to free them—Liz and Julia, I mean. I can't let them stay with Valley Guy a minute longer than necessary."

Everyone nodded.

"He will not harm them as long as you have what he wants," Warren reminded her. "Do you know what that is?"

Donnie sat down next to Falwaïn and replied, "I have no clue, even though he thinks I do. Something about the amulet, I suppose. Maybe he can't see the inscription and wants to know if I know what it says." Rex moved from beside Warren to lie on her feet and promptly began snoring again, while the cat jumped to her lap. Diego slowly came to stand at the edge of their group.

"What inscription?" Falwaïn asked. "I saw no inscription on it, even though I inspected it quite thoroughly."

"Not you too?" cried Donnie." Honestly, I don't understand why I'm the only one who can see it. Believe me, there really is an inscription on the back, but I couldn't read it, it was too blurry. Sylvester and Warren couldn't see it either, but they could at least feel it. I meant to ask you about it yesterday, but I forgot." She smiled apologetically at Falwaïn, then shot Warren a perplexed look and posited, "Like I said, maybe Valley Guy knows about the inscription, saw it somehow when Catie used the amulet, but he can't read it either and thinks I can. That's if it's the spell to open the portal. Otherwise...maybe it's just that he doesn't know how to work the amulet and thinks I do, that Catie left me instructions. But if I knew how to work it, I would've gone home already." She scoffed at herself suddenly and exclaimed, "What am I saying—no, I would not have done that! Valley Guy was probably counting on my wanting to return Diego to his time too, so I'd have to stick around and find him in order to do that. And Valley Guy had him pretty well shielded up here. Oh, I don't know, you guys. I really don't know what that bully boyd wants, but he sure seemed convinced that I'd figure it out, didn't he? I *am* certain of one thing, though; you have to have the amulet in your possession to make it work, or at the very least, be within a few feet of it."

Warren looked at her curiously. "Why do you believe that?"

She shrugged before replying, "Sometimes I know things without knowing *how* I know them, almost like it's a real memory stored deep down inside me of things that haven't occurred yet, or of events that happen without me being around when they occur. I call it my foresight usually. I've had it all my life, so I don't think it's anything magical, like having the ability to foretell the future. I don't get visions of what's to come or anything like that, and I can't do it on demand. It's just that sometimes I know things. F'r instance, I don't really know about the amulet, but there's something decidedly familiar about it, way down in the back of my mind, like I've seen the amulet being used before...something like that. Which is ridiculous because I know I'd never seen the darn thing before Falwaïn brought it to me. I don't get it either, so don't snort at me like I'm nuts, Sylvester. I'm just absolutely positive that you have to be close to it to use it."

"I wish now that Catie had never entrusted it to me." Falwaïn scowled at Diego. "It appears I am unable to safeguard it properly."

The object of his disfavor turned away and walked back to his horse, tightening the saddle strap through the cinch.

Warren asked a question that had been on his mind since the subject had arisen in the cavern. "Donnie, back there in the mountain, you said something about Valledai possessing two types of magic. What did you mean by that? And how would that even be possible?"

Diego broke into their conversation, quietly informing them, "It is as if he is of two minds, one within the other, that man you call Valley Guy." He deliberately talked solely to Donnie, even though all eyes now swung toward him. "On occasion, I could feel the other one struggling inside the one who is dominant. I do not understand why, but Valledai is greatly conflicted from within."

Ignoring the disdain of the others, he continued to speak only to the witch, wishing to aid this amazing woman who had saved him from certain death twice in the cavern. He had felt her power protecting him, urging him to safety both when that monster had sent him careening through the air, and also when she had insisted on waiting until he too had climbed onto the carpet, her magic providing him the strength to outrun a falling column so that he could reach the relative safety of the carpet in time for their escape. For that, he owed her. If she were to ask anything, anything at all of him, he would give it gladly. But her friends would not allow this, he knew. When he finally did look at them, he saw the mistrust in their eyes and he stood a little taller. He would not bend to their contempt.

Donnie studied Diego's proud expression curiously. "Hmm, that's interesting," she said. "Thanks for the info." She shot him a quick smile, which he answered with a curt nod.

"There's something definitely not right about Valley Guy's soul, that's for sure," she said, looking over at Warren. "But I don't quite get what it is because he's very good at masking it. To answer your question...well, okay, not to get too in-depth about it, but as I'm sure you must be aware, there are different kinds of magical beings, each with their own sets of constraints or limitations, depending on exactly where they draw their magic from. To suffice for now," she paused and wet her lips, "let's just say that Valley Guy has whatever is his native magic, while the other one he possesses is foreign to him. How he has managed to obtain that foreign magic, I don't know. But I don't think he's able to wield both completely, or at least they're not working all that well together—although, I must say, his deadfall spell was masterly. I've got a feeling he's practiced that one a bunch, or maybe it was just that he put so much of his real self into the spell, it worked perfectly and very nearly trapped us in that mountain. Anyway, I'm not sure which of his magics is native because he distracted me pretty effectively by suddenly attacking us when he felt me rummaging around in his mind. And like I said, he's really good at masking what he's thinking and feeling. But the next time we meet, you can bet I'll be working on that angle some more. Maybe then I'll understand it—hey, wait a minute, does anyone remember what I was saying to him when he suddenly made it clear the time had come for a magic fight? I think I must've been on the right track then to figuring out his dual magic conundrum."

Warren shook his head slowly. "You talked about the two types of magic you could feel in him. That is all I recall. Perhaps it has something to do with what he wants from you?"

None of the others, it appeared, could remember her exact words either. Donnie let it pass, murmuring that it would come to her sooner or later.

By this time, Diego had successfully convinced himself that it was time to leave. He had relayed what he felt was the most important information he had about Valledai, so there was really no reason to stay any longer where he was obviously not welcomed by any but the witch-woman. If she wanted something more from him, he was certain she would have no trouble finding him, especially as he intended to remain just out of sight of her friends from this point forward so that, in case she did need him, he would always be close by. He would lay down his life for her, if necessary, for she was the first true friend he had encountered in this strange world. Silently, he prepared to mount his horse.

Donnie watched him haul himself into the saddle and give his horse a light kick with his heels before calling out, "If you really want to leave, you can, Don Diego, but I wish you'd think about staying. Your best chance of getting home lies here, with us. Besides, I think you know where they're keeping my friends!"

Her last, almost shouted words finally got a rise from him and he wheeled his horse around to protest, "*No*, I swear I do not know where they are being held! If I did, I would tell you now, before I leave; you have my word on that," he assured her, his dark eyes flashing.

Donnie stared back at him intently, finally allowing, "Okay, maybe you're not aware that you know it, but I'll bet you know it anyway. The boombox hasn't been wrong so far." She suddenly gave him a weak smile and, out of habit, added, "Seriously, y'wanna bet me?"

Diego gaped at her in consternation, letting his horse take a few steps back toward the group assembled around the fire. "How could I know where your friends are when I have never seen them before today? I was unaware even of their existence until Valledai showed them to us in there." He jerked his head in the direction of Moên Flírbann.

Donnie sat back and crossed her arms in front of her. "Have you ever been to a place called Moên Grím? No? Then what about the other mountain we mentioned in the cavern, the one called Gjendeben? Ah, that's the one you know! And that's probably why Valley Guy wanted you dead, 'cause you know how to get to my friends, and as long as he can keep them hidden, he's got us by the short hairs. When were you there?"

Forgetting all else but her question, Diego dismounted his horse and approached the fire. "It was soon after I was brought here. I had been caught by some men who took me to the village of Banaff Dír. There, they brought me before their magistrate, who decreed that I should be stoned to death as a wicked blasphemer of their gods, calling me some sort of evil dream. The townspeople were unreasonable and gave me no chance to explain myself. They took me outside after only a few minutes and tied me to a post in the center of their town, while they gathered stones to aid in my murder."

"Wow, that was quick." Donnie leaned forward over Sylvester, placed her elbows on her raised knees, and peered into the bonfire's flames. "It's just a guess, but I wouldn't be surprised if Valley Guy didn't have a hand in their homicidal urgency. Makes good cover for him, you know?" She turned her head back toward Diego and arched an enquiring eyebrow. "What happened next?"

Diego dusted the snow off another rock outcropping and sat down before resuming his tale. "They kept me there and began hurling their rocks at me. Because I was restrained to the post, I could do nothing to avoid being hit. Suddenly, a great storm began to build very quickly, with much lightning and rain. All there were soaked within moments. Soon after the storm began, a stone hit me on the side of my head and I knew no more. When I awoke, I was already on my horse, being led though the mountains by Valledai. We rode several days' passage to this mountain, this Moên Gjendeben, of which you spoke. He took me inside through many tunnels and had his servants, these wild men and women whom he called the Mountain People, tend to my wounds and care for my every need.

"Later, when I was recovered, he told me that he had called up the storm to free me. A lightning strike had set some buildings ablaze and all the townspeople rushed to douse the fire, leaving me unattended. While they were otherwise engaged, Valledai freed me and we made good our escape. That was when he told me of Catie, that she was a powerful witch who had brought me here because she liked to see sport of this kind. He said that she had offered me to the people of Banaff Dír as a sacrifice to their gods since my dark skin would lead them to believe I was one of their long-time sworn enemies. He told me he had heard rumor the day before that the witch had brought back yet another victim with her through the time portal, and so he had come in search of me, to rescue me, he said, but he did not find me until I was already in the custody of the townspeople of Banaff Dír."

Donnie looked at Diego with disbelief. "And that made sense to you?"

He spread his hands before him, shaking his head. "I did not know what to believe. He told me that this Catie possessed an amulet, which she always wore on a chain around her neck. The amulet would send me home, he said. He asked me, as repayment for the debt on my life, to find Catie and take the amulet from her. He swore that if I brought it to him, he could send me back to my time with it."

"And you wanted to go home so badly, you were willing to believe just about anything." Donnie nodded sympathetically. "I understand that only too well."

"How long did you spend inside the mountain?" Warren asked, setting aside his hostility toward the Black Rider for the moment. "Did you come to know it well?"

"*Sí*, I spent some few weeks there. My wounds healed slowly—Valledai has no such healing powers as yours, Donemere, or if he does, he chooses not to employ them. He allowed me to wander the tunnels of Gjendeben freely while I recovered and I came to know them well."

"Could you not tell by the okûn there that this Valledai was not to be trusted?" Falwaïn inquired harshly, his expression and his tone both condemning.

Diego looked puzzled by the question. "I do not know what an okûn is. Perhaps if you describe it, I can tell you if I have ever seen one."

Falwaïn gave an impatient hiss at this, informing the other man heatedly, "Moên Gjendeben is their capital city; you could hardly have wandered its corridors freely and not have seen them! They are the short, ugly creatures who move with spider-like agility and speed that we encountered today within the mountain."

"*Lo juro por Dios*, I saw no such creatures before this day, I swear it!" Diego assured them earnestly, his eyes filled with revulsion. "If I had, then as you say, I would have known my false savior was lying to me."

"Which, I'm sure, is exactly why he didn't let you see them," Donnie interposed. "But I'll bet they were there and that they saw you." She leaned back against Falwaïn's shoulder and felt him relax a little. "And after that was when you went in search of Catie and found her at the cottage? Is that right?"

Diego turned to look at her again. "*Sí*. I was so incensed by her refusal to hand over the amulet, I nearly killed her."

"Luckily, I stopped you before you could do that," Warren interjected, his eyes boring into Diego's and his jaw noticeably hardened with anger.

Diego inclined his head in agreement, his gaze meeting and never wavering from Warren's. "*Sí*, and now it appears I owe you a debt of gratitude for that. I have no desire to take a life unless I know it is truly warranted. I admit that I was wrong to fear Catie, just as I was wrong about you and about Valledai." He turned to Donnie as he said this, adding expressively, "You cannot possibly want my assistance after the harm I have caused. I see in your soldiers' hearts no room for forgiveness. But if you allow me to help you, I pledge to give my life in freeing your friends and helping you defeat Valledai in exchange for your promise to send me back to my home when you have taken the amulet from him."

Donnie shook her head indignantly. "Oh, quit being silly!" she said stoutly, surprising the others. "I am not making a deal with you or anybody else. All bets are off here, for everyone. Either you help me or you don't. You all must make your own choices, plain and simple. I mean that. None of you, well, except for Sylvester and Rex, need feel as though you have to help me. But no matter what, once I get that amulet back and figure out how to use it, rest assured, I will send all of us time travelers back to our proper worlds. You don't belong here anymore than Rex and I do, or my two friends, and I can't let any of us stay. We'd throw things too far out of whack and who knows what kind of future we'd end up with then! I'll do what I have to to keep the time continuum constant. And if any of you die here before I can regain the amulet, then, when I do get it from Valley Guy, I'll go back in time before your deaths to send us all back home, alive and well, and long before we can influence what's to come. Well, I will if the gods allow me to, that is. Nevertheless, as far as I'm concerned, the future's the most important thing right now, besides freeing Liz and Julia. Therefore, each of you should think long and hard about what may happen to us and make your own decision regarding whether you are in or out."

"I am in, of course." Diego spread his hands, again expressive in his demeanor. "What else can I do? I must atone for my part in Valledai's intrigues. It is a matter of honor to me," he declared proudly.

Donnie nodded at him. Falwaïn gave a small, disgusted snort at hearing the Black Rider's oath, but otherwise refrained from comment.

Warren glanced down at the fire and then met Donnie's gaze, saying crisply, "I too am in. But we must summon aid from elsewhere, for we can't face Valledai and his host with just us in the fray. And with you being a Codlebærn, Donnie, your involvement will probably be limited by the gods, especially now that you are Fægre."

Donnie gaped at him silently for a few long seconds.

He smiled back at her, pride reflected in his eyes, before explaining quietly, "Yes, I felt your transition. It was as though a piece of the universe that had gone askew long ago somehow snapped into place. And it was fine." He nodded his head and smiled again at her. "And it was right."

Donnie's eyes shone with sudden tears, but before she could say anything, Warren continued. "As I say, you will probably not be allowed to interfere with anyone but Valledai, which means it will likely require a great host of our own to defeat his forces and free your friends, and the townspeople of Banaff Dír and Mâlendian are too few to effect a victory against his battalions of okûn. What have you to suggest, Falwaïn?" he asked, turning to his friend.

Falwaïn had watched their interaction with interest and he now bent his head slowly and respectfully toward Donnie. When he looked up at her again, he said, "I've already pledged my allegiance to you, my lady, and that will not waiver, no matter what comes. I shall stand by your side until this is finished. In the meantime, we should send word to my friends at Anûmanétus. There are a great many warriors there," he offered, explaining further when he saw the questioning look on Donnie's face. "The king maintains an army of over ten thousand troops within the city. He has long feared another uprising such as this and wanted to be prepared in case one formed."

"How long before they could be at the cottage?" Donnie asked, the blush his intense regard had caused thankfully starting to fade from her cheeks.

He considered her question seriously before responding. "Most of them could be there in perhaps five days," he said. "That would be in time to meet Valledai's forces."

Warren pointed out, "Only if we get word to them immediately. And we would have to ensure that Valledai does indeed come to the cottage first, which could be arranged, I suppose, given that we have the proper bait. But how would we get a message to Anûmanétus that quickly?" He looked over at Donnie. "Unless you have a way to do that? Can you call out to the king as you did to us before?"

"No, not really," Donnie informed him regretfully. "I have to know the soul of the person, at least a little bit, otherwise I can't really be sure about who I'm getting through to. Which means I need to have met them or been close enough to them to know that the soul I'm feeling is truly theirs. Sorta like putting a face to a name. Well, I mean like when you know a name really well, but you've never seen that person's face. They could walk right up to you and you'd never know it was them unless they introduced themselves. It's like that with me and souls, you know?"

Warren nodded his understanding. "Then do we have another method of quickly sending a message to the king?"

"Funny you should ask that," Donnie replied. "I believe we do have a way of accomplishing that very task in the morning." She looked down tenderly at her sleeping dog. "But, first, I think our messenger deserves a good night's rest, don't you?"

Warren smiled his agreement.

Donnie continued, determination returning to her voice, "We can't let Liz and Julia stay with Valley Guy for another five days, though. I definitely won't let that happen. Which means we'll have to free them ourselves. As we've already figured, they must be in this Genda Benda Mountain, so the best place to start on that crazy adventure is from home. Is there any other route we can take from here that's more direct to the cottage?"

Warren and Falwaïn both shook their heads.

"There are only the moors, which are guarded by Valledai's trolls," Falwaïn replied, "and that way might well prove to be more perilous than the Annûar Path. Perhaps we should take our chances and return the way we came," he suggested, looking at Donnie and Warren in turn.

But Donnie rejected this immediately. "Uh-uh, that route's not gonna work. Valley Guy's henchmen will be out looking for us, and I have absolutely no desire to go near the Bitterbend Marshes ever again in my natural born life or even in this unnatural life. Therefore, the moors it's got to be. If we can manage a pretty direct line, we might shave off a full day from traveling, right?"

The men argued with her for some time, but she was obstinate. She repeated that she was not going near the Great Serpents again and besides, she believed that the Annûar Path would be even more dangerous for them, especially since they most certainly could not go by way of Marn Dím now that Valley Guy controlled it. In the end, they reluctantly agreed with her plan.

Night had fallen. They doused the fire with snow and went inside the tent. Donnie laid down in her sleeping bag, with the cat and dog in the same positions as the previous night, and soon all was quiet within the tent. Falwaïn took first watch, then Warren. They both steadfastly refused to allow Diego to help.

It was some time before Donnie's breathing became regular and deep, signaling that she had finally managed to fall into slumber. There would be much to do in the next few days, not the least of which was to settle into the new powers granted to her now that she was Fægre. As was typical with such a transition, her skin felt über-alive and tingly and small blue arcs of magical power were escaping her fingertips again, so she made sure to tuck them into the sleeping bag in order not to alarm the others. In each stage of her development she'd found that, until she had matured into her new witchly powers, she could control these arcs only when she consciously dampened them, but in unconscious moments they would flash erratically, usually causing much consternation in those around her.

Snuggling down further into her pillow, she contemplated for some time what it would mean to be Fægre, the weight of that decision resting as heavily on her as her grief over her friends did. For it had been Donnie's choice to become Fægre, which, she supposed, was part of what it meant to *be* Fægre, to knowingly take that step, to choose to wield that much power with the clear understanding of what terrible things could be done with it and the even more terrible price it could exact on all involved if she did not wield it wisely. But she had made the step with her eyes and heart wide open, knowing that she would do anything now to be able to rescue her friends and get everyone home safely, while also protecting all knowing souls living in Medregai from the threat posed by Valledai and his army. It no longer mattered to her that her life had been irrevocably changed six months ago, undoubtedly because she had accepted that she was on a new path, one that would never look back to what she was, but rather look forward to what she could be. That was what it meant to be Fægre for her; to choose to be counted as a Codlebærn for the rest of her life.

And Warren had described her transition perfectly—it *had* been as though something that had long been out of place was suddenly exactly where it belonged.

She felt the rightness of her choice settle into her soul and the feverish magic within her skin quietened, settling into her bones and muscles for the moment to meld with all that she was until it became a soothing fullness of spirit. As she drifted to sleep, the radiant blue aura that had begun to glow around her once she had lain down and relaxed now fell back to her skin, leaving only a faint hue that looked just slightly otherworldly. Both the cat and the dog hitched themselves a bit closer to her in their sleep, the three of them ready to face together whatever might come on the morrow.

Epilogue I

Alone in his chamber, Ungôl brooded. His head ached and his pride remained greatly wounded. It was only yesterday that he had held the witch within his grasp and his inability to keep her bound by his coils for more than a few hours still stung. He had remained in his cavern, restlessly wearing the rough edges of the lakeside rubble, including the bones and other detritus of past meals, down to mirror quality with his ceaseless prowling—until earlier tonight, that is, when he had ignored the entreaties of the others that he join them in reporting back to the master, and had settled his bulk into the steamy waters of his private lake.

He could not keep his mind on anything but the witch and his miserable, infuriating debacle with her. To be left caged like that, both he and Palat, trapped in their den, with only Sonau and Felin free to search for her. Of course, by the time his youngest brothers had found her escape route amongst the endless passages of the Great Serpent City of Bitterbend, the sharp, mineralized spears trapping him and Palat were all but dissolved.

And yet, even though she had humiliated him, he could not help but admire her tenacity, nor to wonder why, if she was able to free herself with such ease, she had not effected that escape much sooner than she had done. Perhaps even more astounding was her leaving both himself and Palat unharmed. When telling of the bounty upon the witch's head, the master had impressed upon him and his brothers that she was cruel and dangerous in her magical arts—two commanding qualities, to be sure, although they were also qualities which she certainly had not exhibited in her dealings here. Why should she be so merciful—what did she hope to gain? These were but some of the questions he had savagely ruminated over until the sharp pains in his head had grown to where they could no longer be ignored and he had stilled his actions.

A noise outside the cavern distracted him from his thoughts and his ache lessened. He lifted his head from the waters of his bed, watching silently as Palat's form slid through the crushed wreckage of the deteriorated stalactites with which the witch had imprisoned them, a mortifying, powdery reminder of their failure to hold her that Ungôl had avoided touching, refusing even to leave the chamber when Felin came to report how the witch had made good her escape, instead sending Palat to investigate and verify that she truly was gone.

Palat maneuvered his long body around so that he and his brother were facing each other. "Valledai directssss ussss to leave here. We are to report immediately to the Withering Hillssss. He ssssaid there issss a ssssurprisssse awaiting ussss there. We are to enjoy it, but we are alsssso to be prepared at a moment'ssss noticcccce to join him at Moên Grím to fulfill our dutiessss regarding the demisssse of the witcccch. The otherssss have gone on ahead of ussss already."

Ungôl grunted with displeasure. What *surprise* was it that waited for them at the old dragon rookery? He felt a distinct uneasiness creep over him. Should he refuse the order? While Valledai was too unpredictable to trust the fate that surely lay before Ungôl and his brothers, he was also far too powerful for them to disobey. And there was Murlain and the twins to be considered. Reluctantly, Ungôl nodded his head and slithered toward the chamber's entrance, sliding heavily through its opening.

Palat followed him into the tunnel. Both were glad to be leaving the Great Serpent City behind, having never accustomed themselves to its closeness or to the brackish waters of the Bitterbend Marshes. They reached the main passage and were about to head east when their way was suddenly blocked by the Great Serpents' leaders, Cebara and Sissalu.

The male, Cebara, hissed scornfully, "You are leaving ussss? I assssume it issss for good thissss time. Whicccch makessss thissss a joyoussss day for all Great Sssserpentssss." Glancing down the tunnel, he clicked his teeth in wordless command and, quietly, from all around, in every side tunnel, slithered yet more snakes. They lined up just inside the entryways, staring hatefully toward Ungôl and at Palat behind him.

"You will not be returning," Cebara went on to state matter-of-factly. "Your welcome hassss been tenuoussss at bessssst and issss now worn thin."

Ungôl lifted his head and neck arrogantly to declare with undisguised defiance, "If we wissssh to return to thissss ssssstinkhole, we ssssshall do sssso." He purposely towered over the others, drawing himself up to the fullest height allowed by the tunnel roof, his powerful muscles rippling with each of his graceful movements, no matter how slight. Here was the king he was meant to be shining through the bonds of servitude tying him to his master.

Doing her best to appear unmoved by this impressive display, Sissalu threatened, "Then we will have no recoursssse but to kill you." Her voice was higher by several octaves than her mate's, but no less raw, no less hostile. "And your massssster will be at war with ussss. Be warned, we are many, and we are formidable foessss." She dipped her head, her yellow eyes flashing with anger. "Perhapssss the witccccch would welcome our aid," she added cunningly.

"You wissssh to turn traitor?" Ungôl sneered in contempt. "That issss not ssssuprissssing, consssssidering your inferior bloodline. Vírat dessssscendantssss you may be, but clearly there issss more ignoble reptile in you than venerable vírat." He slitted his eyes and drew back his lips menacingly. "Let ussss passss."

"With pleassssure, my liege." Cebara mocked, though neither he nor Sissalu moved aside. "But firssst, there issss the matter of my wound." He curved his neck to the right, revealing a jagged, gaping hole in his scaly hide that was seeping fresh blood.

Disdain dripping in his voice, Ungôl retorted, "Your *wound* issss no matter of mine."

Cebara and Sissalu pressed their bodies together even more tightly, their expressions outraged. "I have kept true to our agreement," Cebara reminded Ungôl. "The promisssse I made to you hasss been fulfilled. My wound musssst be allowed to heal."

Every sinew in Ungôl's body was tightened to breaking point and his ire was, by now, quite high and still rising. How dare these worms make demands of him! He was sick of them, of their city, of their marshes, but most of all, he was sick of their lies.

He jeered with relish, "Do you know what your own brethren call you, Cebara? They refer to you assss dassssstard, a whimpering, sssssniveling dolt!" Furious and just barely in control, Ungôl leaned forward to enquire in an ominously quiet tone, "Tell me, when the witccccch esssscaped, why did you do nothing to sssstop her?"

Cebara looked up at the greater beast with intensified loathing. "I ssssswore we would aid you in capttttturing her and we did sssso!" he shouted, his angry echoes resounding throughout the city. He stared unflinchingly at these arrogant intruders of his domain, these unwanted and distant cousins who had no fealty to any but their master, then he hissed and spit on the ground in front of him. "Three of my own kin died sssso that you could pluck the witccccch from above and bring her here," he reminded the other. "It wassss not for ussss to enssssure that you kept her! Our duty hassss been met and I call upon you to honor your part in our accord!" he demanded righteously.

But Ungôl shrieked back at him, "I will honor no bargain made with one who ussssessss decccceit to massssk cowardicccce!" He slammed his rigid body violently from side to side, forcing the snakes nearby to withdraw into their respective tunnels. The ground shook with the force of his anger. He moved toward the eastbound tunnel, fully prepared, if need be, to run over the two Great Serpents still huddled closely together there.

They parted reluctantly.

When he was about to sweep past them, he stopped, his eyes somehow growing even colder as he snarled, "I informed you when we came here that I am a Badûran Vírat. The priccce you pay for breaking your oath to one succch assss I issss death. I assssure you, Cebara, your oath-wound *will* conssssume you, no matter how many of your brethren you ssssend to die in your sssstead." Ungôl paused, thrusting his face into the serpent king's. "You ssssee, fool, your kin did not make the promisssse to me; you did! And it issss only your death that can ssssatissssfy the badûr now!"

Epilogue II

The library seemed intensely quiet to Sophie tonight, with only the nocturnal sounds from outside infiltrating Donemere's expanding repository of literary works. Sophie, who had her attention split between this room and the kitchen, was lulled to a sense of focused watchfulness by the softly rhythmic chirping of crickets in the bushes and trees surrounding the house and found herself oddly reassured by the occasional clicking of bats as they flew overhead and the ghostly hooting of owls in the trees as they too stood their nightly guard over the house. It was a lonely night, the wise old tree thought to herself fancifully, a sense of frigid, almost paralyzing isolation stealing into the deep silence filling the cottage. But then, underlying everything these days was a tenseness that emanated from the other souls within the magical lands, she noted abstractly, recognizing that it came from fear of what was to come.

Believing there was great strength in numbers, Sophie herself was glad she was now one of many in Donemere's army, a small cog only, which meant that uncertainty of the future was not hers to worry about. She took solace in that and urged others to also, since every creature big and small within the borders of Donnie's lands (between themselves known as the *Ganlonds*) had been assigned specific tasks to keep them from dwelling too long on the possibilities of failure in the conflict threatening on the horizon and because there was widespread desire to be prepared for either battle or retreat, as events may require. Some were set to watching, others to protecting, while others still were awakening old magical memories, dredging up the details of pacts made centuries ago between the animal and weald nations to keep the Ganlonds safe.

Yes, Sophie was one of the few who were unconcerned about the future, for she had put her faith in Donemere months ago when she had agreed to be put to use in the sylvan addition to the little stone cottage, and there her faith remained. She was nevertheless diligent in her duties and, whenever it was her turn to monitor the house, she was uncharacteristically alert for any change or unusual occurrence inside it and also in its external surroundings for as far she was able to see using the starlight radiating from the heavens.

The house itself seemed cold and empty without even the cat to stalk around all night constantly checking doors and windows or Donnie to build a cheery fire. Sophie decided she liked the house much better when it was alive with these bright souls and wished that Diana had not decided to spend the night in the stables. While Sophie did not know what it was about Diana that she did not trust, she did like the cow's company. She was sure that Diana was hiding something of significance from the others and Sophie was intrigued by this. She hoped one day to get Diana to open up to her, although her long years told her that was unlikely to happen. She accepted this with the same patience and peace with which she accepted everything else. Nevertheless, she would try again with the cow and would keep on trying until the secret was revealed, very subtly encouraging Diana to share it. Sophie did not doubt that Diana would one day confide in Donemere, at the very least, and that is what Sophie really wanted anyway.

It was very near to four in the morning when Fine Fellow's voice sounded from his boards within the library's walls to inform her that all was still quiet in the bedroom, bathroom and workshop. Sophie acknowledged this and then reported the same to him for her part of the house. He withdrew his consciousness from the library and presumably went back to the office.

It was a little over an hour later that Sophie's attention was caught by a low rustling noise on one of the shelves in the back of the library. She, like all the house trees, had come to know every single item that was kept in the cottage, including every book in the library, and she noticed now in the beginning light of the soon-to-be rising sun that a new book had been added to the shelf in question. Its spine was dark blue and bore silver gilded lettering for a title that Sophie could just make out in the early morning gloom.

The tree was surprised by the sudden appearance of the book and by its title. These were indeed uncommon circumstances for any book to be added to the library, and this book seemed to her a very curious tome, for it would presumably provide details of events to this point in Donemere's journey. Sophie thought on this awhile, wondering who should be informed of its appearance, finally coming to the conclusion that she would not tell Donnie because Sophie was sure that the powerful witch must discover the book's existence on her own. Brindle had warned Sophie that to interfere too much in Donemere's path might cause her to fail and that was the one thing no one could afford. No, she should keep this to herself and Brindle for now. Brindle would know just when Donemere should be told.

Sophie trusted in this simply because she believed that Cyllwyn Mérd had fully prepared his oaken friend, Bryn Ddu, many centuries ago for Donemere's arrival in their world. While Sophie had never met the venerable old tree, Cyllwyn Mérd was legendary amongst the weald for being always in the right place at the right time and for having the ability to foretell the future with unerring accuracy; almost as if he were recalling it from memory, was how Brindle described Cyllwyn Mérd's uncanniness. Sophie thought back to the day Donemere had asked the trees to become part of her magical house. Unbeknownst to Donnie, and even to Sylvester, Brindle had strongly urged each of the volunteer trees to respond in the affirmative. He later explained that, according to Cyllwyn Mérd's instructions, they each had important roles to play in the events to come.

Sophie now toyed with telling the other house trees of her discovery but could see no goodly reason to do so because the only one she trusted, truly, was Brindle. In her estimation, Carly was too young to understand the ramifications of the situation, Fine Fellow was too talkative to keep any secret, while Mournful Jack was not talkative enough and Sophie, if she were honest, was unsure of his loyalties. That just left Parry, who was too wary of the long friendship between Sophie and Brindle and in a fit of jealousy might say something unwise in Donnie's hearing—not that Parry had ever actually done that before, but still…

No, it would have to be hers and Brindle's secret. But instinct told Sophie that she must hide the book from the others for now.

She allowed her consciousness to pool in front of a bookshelf deep within the darkest regions of the library at a place where she felt no other tree's presence. She then wished for the book and was pleased when it appeared on the shelf in front of her. Using her considerable will, she focused on the tome and it began to move smoothly out of the bookcase, finally hovering over the floorboard where Sophie's triune was currently emplaced. The book lowered slowly into the wood, which changed to an almost gelatinous state as Sophie concentrated. Hiding the book within her would also give her time to absorb its contents before Brindle returned and she must of course relinquish it to him. With any luck, something within the book might be helpful in defeating Valledai and his armies. She would read it carefully and commit as much as possible of it to her long memory.

Satisfied she had accomplished her objective of safeguarding the book without disturbing any of the other house trees, Sophie again spread her consciousness to encompass all battery limits of her watch and went back to looking and listening for anything out of the ordinary, perhaps not fully comprehending just how extraordinary were her own actions of the night, nor how important they would be in the coming days.

About the Author:

Beginning when she was a very young girl in Wellsboro, Pennsylvania, Ms. Gross wrote fictional stories, sharing them with family and friends but never having quite enough confidence to attempt publishing them. By default, she fell into a career of technical writing, earning herself a niche in the technical editing market of mining study reports. She currently resides in the Santa Cruz, California area, although she has lived and traveled to various places throughout the world. Several years ago, she decided to take a hiatus from her professional work and focused on writing novels. The idea for **Donemere's Music** was born then and *Thy Path Begins* is the first of the books she wrote during this period. After some reworking, it is finally ready to take flight. The second book in the series will also be published soon, so be on the lookout for *The Cunning Sister Arises*.

Other titles by Cheryl A. Gross:
The Cunning Sister Arises (2017)

Connect with Ms. Gross on Facebook:
https://www.facebook.com/DonemeresMusic1/

Made in the USA
San Bernardino, CA
14 December 2016